El Primo

The Black Hand of the Sinaloa Cartel

Donald Thompkins

Neith Publishing

ISBN: 979-8-9888629-1-8

Contents

Title 1

Foreword 2

1. 12739 HAMBURG 5

2. BLACK BOTTOM EASTSIDE OF DETROIT 17

3. NO BODY, BUT WAYNE 49

4. "I DON'T HAVE ANY MONEY, BUT.......... 65

5. MY BROTHER'S KEEPER 75

6. ARIZONA BABY DOLL 84

7. MEXICALI 95

8. TIJUANA CARTEL 111

9. TIJUANA CARTEL 2 127

10. SHE HAS A VERY VERY BAD ATTITUDE......... 129

11. ROCKY POINT MEXICO 142

12. BUENO ESTRATEGA 157

13. THE RIDE 164

14. NEVER SAY, NEVER 170

15. THE END, THAT BEGINS 186

16. THE END THAT BEGINS PART 2 198

17. CIUDAD JUÁREZ 224

18. BALTIMORE 243

19. UN AMIGO DE MI AMIGO DE MI OTRO AMIGO (A FRIEND OF A FRIEND OF A FRIEND). 251

20. NORMA JEANS 264

21. JUAREZ CARTEL 282

22. BALD HEAD 292

23. VINCENTE CARRILLO FUENTES 342

24. CULIACAN, SINALOA 386

25. THE CHIEF IS VERY SICK 427

26. THE WAR 474

27. DETROIT 2 542

28. EVEN THE DOGS, WILL DANCE 566

Foreword

Something intended to wake one up. 2.: something startling, surprising, or enlightening.

THAT IS THE DEFINITION of an Eye-opener and that is exactly what the author has produced with *El Primo,* a genuine eye opener. In this 100 percent factual account Mr. Thompkins A.K.A *"El Primo"* himself details his rise from the gritty streets of Detroit's east side, through the vast Marijuana fields of Sinaloa Mexico, to the glitzy music scene of Atlanta. The author's immersive writing style captures the reader's attention and one is transported into the dangerous world of international drug trafficking. Very few are capable of explaining this complex and secretive world, even fewer are qualified to, and even fewer still are willing to. Luckily for the reader Mr. Thompkins is all three. He chronicles how he grew from local hustler to negotiating directly with the Sinaloa Cartel boss "El Chapo" Guzman. Striking deals in which a mistake didn't just cost you money, it cost you your life.

We watch as Mr. Thompkins describes how he simultaneously navigated the chaos and pitfalls of high level business both legal and illegal. He vividly recounts his brushes with death, including multiple close calls with law enforcement and rival cartels. But through it all, *El Primo* emerges as a shrewd and cunning businessman, with a remarkable ability to make deals and turn profits.

El Primo is more than just a thrilling tale of one man's journey through the drug trade.

It is a cautionary tale, a warning to those who might be tempted by the allure of easy money and fast living. Mr. Thompkins does not glamorize the world he inhabited; he exposes it for the dangerous and destructive force that it is. He writes with a raw honesty that is rare in any genre, let alone in a book about organized crime.

But this book is not just a warning or a confession. It is also a celebration of resilience, of the human spirit's ability to overcome incredible odds. Mr. Thompkins is a survivor, and he tells his story with a sense of pride and defiance that is both inspiring and humbling. He is a man who has seen the worst that life has to offer and has emerged from it with a deep appreciation for the value of hard work and perseverance.

El Primo is a remarkable achievement, not just for its gripping narrative and immersive writing style, but for its broader cultural significance. This book sheds light on a world that is often ignored or sensationalized by the media, and it does so with a rare combination of insight and empathy. It is a book that demands to be read, not just for its entertainment value, but for the important truths it reveals about our society.

As a reader, you will be taken on a wild and unforgettable ride through the underworld of drug trafficking. But you will also come away from this book with a deeper understanding of the human cost of this illicit industry. You will see the devastating impact it has on individuals and communities alike, and you will be reminded of the importance of standing up against such destructive forces.

In short, *El Primo* is a book that will stay with you long after you have finished reading it. It is a book that will challenge your assumptions, broaden your horizons, and make you think deeply about the choices we make and the consequences they have. It is a book that is intended to wake you up, to startle and surprise you, and to enlighten you. And in that sense, it is a genuine Eye-opener.

CHAPTER 1

12739 HAMBURG

HAMBURG RAISED ME AND provided a platform for several other personalities to play distinct roles in my challenging path. The house on Hamburg Street became the center of many people's universe, and I became the professor there.

I moved to Hamburg at the age of nineteen. I was asked to move in by my aunt Ernestine. I was attending WC3 Community College then, and my major was psychology. I would use public transportation to go back and forth to school. Dennis Horn Trucking and Rubbish Company employed me. The Nimrod family stayed right down the street from the house my aunt was renting from a wonderful gentleman, Dave. The Nimrod family was a wonderful family but unique. The family was excellent with a split personality of the Addams family type. A set of twins headed the matriarchal family. These two beautiful women had several children with interesting nicknames. My aunt Earnestine had five children of her own. Between the Nimrod sisters and my aunts' kids, Hamburg had nearly twenty kids on the street, ranging from bad to unbelievably bad and hazardous. I ended up befriending McGee, who was fourteen then, which surprised me because the kid had a thick full beard. When I met McGee whom I would soon call Gee, he was talking with my aunt in the dining room. What made me take note was his extremely high feminine voice. I also saw that he had on a bulletproof vest. I later noticed that he could only lay it over his chest and back because he was so big and couldn't connect it on the sides. Gee also carried a 38-caliber revolver and a 25-caliber pistol. My aunt introduced him to me and told him he needed to get with me and stop doing what he was doing. He ran with a group of young men headed by a young man named Hand. He had a young brother named Mal and a little sister. They also stayed on Hamburg, as did a few other young guys; this group wreaked havoc up and down east Six Mile. Over time we became close friends with a big brother significant-little brother connection.

As we got closer, so did our families. I got to meet more of the Nimrod family, like the other siblings of the twin sisters. I learned that this family believed in love. They did not have a particular type of love either: man, woman, man, man, woman, woman. It did not matter as long as there was love, and it was never in short supply. I would often go down to Gee's house after classes at WC3. The twins were traditional women who believed in cooking noticeably big meals.

The twins had a brother that they called Beau. Mr. Beau Dine was a same-sex gentleman with a very colorful personality. Beau Dine was flamboyant and wore a half-blonde and black high-top haircut. I would come down to Gee's house and guess who would always come across the street, Mr. Beau Dine. He would walk back and forth by the table I would be studying at and would say things like, "You're studying, huh? I bet you are getting all the good grades too. How many girlfriends have you got? After this went on for some time, I stopped paying any attention.

Gee would pick at me sometimes about it too. Gee's mom would always say, "That damn boy is crazy about you, boy." "You better keep an eye out for him!" One day I came down to the house as always, and they were bringing groceries in. Naturally, I started to help. After everything was in place, Gee's mom told him to take some things across the street to his aunt's house. We had to help her carry the meat to the basement to place in the big deep freezer. She went across the street momentarily and told me to continue taking the stuff to the basement. I am carrying my second load of meat into the basement now. I am placing the meat into the deep freezer at the time, and I hear the upstairs door to the basement close softly.

I hear a few footsteps coming down the stairs, then the light on the stairs goes out. I started to wonder what's up, and then I looked, and I saw Beau Dine, wide-eyed and bushy-tailed with his blond high-top haircut, coming toward me. Then I hear the upstairs door swing open, the light on the stairs come on, and rapid footsteps coming down the steps. A very high-pitched voice said, "Man, I'm coming down here and helping you because you are taking too long!"

Beau Dine stopped in his tracks as Gee hurried past him. He said, "Oh, Beau Dine, my mom wants you to come to help her put those ribs on the grill across the street." Beau Dine looks at me, then slowly turns and heads up the stairs. Gee started to help me put the meat in the freezer.

Then he looked at me and said, "NIGGA YO ASS, was in big trouble!" As he started to laugh loudly we went upstairs, and his mom walked back into the house, saying, "I told you to keep an eye on his sneaky ass! As I am walking into my sister's house, he shoots out the door and runs across the street to my house! That is why I told McGee to hurry over there with you in the basement, so you don't kill my little brother, Because he was coming over there to try you."

As time passed, things started to become increasingly challenging financially. The owner of the house my aunt rented wanted to get rid of the house and get out of homeownership at that time. This gentleman was a Detroit police officer. Dave was an exceptionally good man with a divine heart; who put me in a position to become a first-time homeowner just because he took an enormous liking to me. This was an Irish gentleman.

Dave was a Caucasian male who cared about single black mothers in the city. Over that time of renting to my aunt, every time Dave came over to fix things, we would have conversations about politics and some of everything. Over this time, Dave and I built a close relationship. He shared several things with me, allowing me to see the inside of his heart and, I guess, get a good look at mine at the same time. He had been a Detroit police officer for about twenty or so years and was immensely proud. This was during the time when the Detroit police department was majority white and had a very strained relationship with the black community in which the police have the charge to protect and serve. Out of all these challenging times between my city and the Detroit police department, there were many good men on the police force, including Dave.

Dave had an agreement with my aunt on the property she was renting from him; however she decided that she wanted to move on from that particular property into a better neighborhood. So Dave came to me and made me an offer by asking me, "Have you ever thought about home ownership, Wayne?" I told Dave that it had never crossed my mind even to consider something like that. It is essential to understand that these are the conversations that Dave and I would always have.

I did not think he was making me an offer to become the homeowner of that property. Dave sprung it on me, and I was lost for words. I was very insecure about the idea, but he encouraged me, telling me I could do it. He then asked me how much money I had in my pocket. I may have had about $300, if that.

Dave told me to give him that money, and he would draw up an agreement for me to make payments to him for the property over the next year and that he would switch the property into my name after that. I waited a couple of weeks for Dave to come back to finalize our agreement. Dave never returned, and I received a deed to the property in the mail in my name for what was equivalent to around $300. Dave just disappeared into the sunset without collecting the rest of his money. Dave disappeared for like three years and popped back up out of nowhere. His father owned a few houses on that block.

Dave stopped by to see all the improvements I had made to the house. After looking at the improvements Dave ended up convincing his father to provide me with another home on that block. This house had sentimental value for Dave's father because his father was born and raised in it. People were trying to buy this house from his father, but he had his father give it to me for nothing, or should I say to help me get a leg up, just because he saw promise in a kind heart. I remember the day his father came down and had me walk from my place with him down into his childhood home. He walked me through the house, pointing out different areas and rooms and giving me the story behind every square inch of that house.

After touring it all, he just stopped to release a sigh of emotion and state, "Well, my son is just like you, kid." He says I am too old now to manage these houses, and he wants you to have this house. Do you know he stopped talking to me because I refused? I know he is right and I am getting old; I can't afford to lose my son over this God-damn house. So, kid, you have made a good impression on my son and a wonderful one on me. "He said as he signed the paperwork over to me and said, "It is all yours now, kid, but I am just asking you for one favor."

"Could you call my son and tell him that the house is yours now... because I want my son back?"

This moved my soul. I don't know why Mr. Dave did this for me; I am clueless. I was so profoundly thankful but emotional over the fact I never got a chance to thank him, and I do not know if he would have even allowed it. In Detroit, where whites have always had a very tumultuous relationship with black people, this man was a shining example of everything right about this country. Not enough stories are being told of these good men and women who do things like this and others because... it is the right thing to do.

As I stated things were getting challenging financially, Gee and I were spending a lot more time together in my room playing video games. We had to wear boots in the summertime with shorts. I felt good because I got him to stop running around those guys terrorizing East 6 Mile. I had just had a son, and I was not the man my grandfather had taught me to be. I had sold drugs as a young teen and was homeless, living in vacant houses with no water or heat. Being homeless appeared to become my reality again, and I knew the feeling all too well.

The Hand was coming back around and trying to get Gee to start back with his old ways. After a couple of years of playing Tecmo Bowl video games in the backroom of my aunt's house, things were not getting much better. Gee was about to turn 16 years old at this point. I swear, over those two years. He had almost 20 or 30 get-rich ideas. The only issue for me was that every single one of those ideas ended with him and me being big-time drug dealers.

The only thing different about this time was that I was starting to listen. His uncle had just gotten a big lawsuit and purchased me a blue four-door Chevy Caprice. I just had to pay him back in payments, but things kept getting worse for me. I had a cousin I grew up with named Sean, whom I often went to see. Sean and I were close and even wore the same clothes growing up. He was staying with his grandmother at the time. He had an aunt and uncle named Jan and Joe, with whom I was in diapers as I was growing up.

Jan was always an unbelievably beautiful girl, a true showstopper as a young adult. Jan's eyes would change colors daily; her eyes would be assorted colors from each other. I never look at her other than family. Our whole families were remarkably close to where their mother would drop Jan and Joe over to my granny's house with me while she went to work. I would often fight with Joe. But Jan was the one who would be the cause of me coming up on the short end of a number of these fights. My win-loss record with Joe took a hell of a beating because of her. I wish I had known about cups then; she was hard on the family jewels. These fights had us super close as young adults.

For the record, I only lost the fights to Joe because Jan cheated, and my grandpa taught me never to hit a lady. If that caused me to throw a few fights, so be it. Otherwise, what would Big Red think? That would devastate the man, HONESTLY!

Jan had a boyfriend named Dee after we came of age. Dee was that guy and had bricks for days, and "I was family" to him as well. I would always go over to see my cousin Sean and often see Dee over the years. One day, I was going over to see Sean, but he was not there. Dee answered the door and invited me inside to wait for Sean to return. He expressed to me that he heard I was having some financial issues. I told him what was going on at the time with me. He tossed me something, and I caught it—it was powder cocaine.

"Jan told me to help you out," Dee said. Before I could say anything, he said, "We are good; Just get back on your feet Cuz." He walked away and went upstairs, leaving me sitting in the living room. Gee was with me; his eyes were the size of silver dollar coins.

This was just the beginning of what started me back to hustling. I'll say it like my super-huge aunt would always say when she sent me to get her a bowl of ice cream: "Oh my God, you know this is way too much ice cream for me... You know I do not eat that much.... but don't worry about it, THIS TIME. Just don't bring me so much next time."

Based on her size, I don't think it necessary to tell you what would happen to you if you bring anything less. I set out to catch up on everything. Gee was right there and loving every minute of it. Also, at this time, I had two additions to my family. I had three kids, one boy, and two girls now. I am doing exceptionally well for myself and providing much better for my kids financially now. I paid off Gee's uncle and other loose ends, and my plans were to be done with hustling after I got caught up on everything. I even saved a little extra money.

Even though I felt I was on top of the world, I wasn't doing anything significant. My aunt was married at the time, and her husband was over at the house; his name was Calvin. He had an older brother named Benny. Benny was always over, talking with Calvin and my aunt Earnestine. Benny was terribly upset and complaining about my aunt, Big Al. Big Al met Benny about two months earlier at a little get-together my aunt Ernestine had at her house. My aunt Al lived directly across the street from us.

Well, Benny had a thing for ridiculously cheap liquor then, too. Benny is telling Calvin he can't stay in the house with Big Al anymore. Well, Calvin asked Benny what was wrong with a genuine concerned look on his face. Benny dropped his head and said, "Man, that God-damned woman fucks way too much!"

Calvin laughed, saying, "Man, I was thinking somebody was trying to kill you or something."

Benny looked at him, laughing, and started yelling, "somebody is trying to kill me."

Now understand Benny was a man in the late nineties wearing a button-up shirt, jeans with white tube socks, dress shoes, and an incredibly old sports jacket. Benny always loves to talk while using his hands and pointing with his fingers to accent his words. The finger accent was colorful because Benny had noticeably short fingers, like little people's.

Calvin said, “How is Big Al trying to kill you?” while laughing at how Benny was acting.

Benny jumped to his feet, pointed one of his little fingers at Calvin, and said, “OK. Mutha Fucka, you think this is SHIT funny! Calvin, she is a good woman, and I do not want anything to do with her over there. But all she wants to do is fuck! Man, I can’t even put on any clothes,” said Benny. “I can tell her I want to get a drink of water, and she will tell me, ‘No, I will get it. Calvin, when I told her I wanted to walk to the store to get liquor and cigarettes, she told me, ‘Don’t worry about it; I will get it.’ By the time she returned to the house, I had put some underwear on, Calvin. The damn woman got highly upset and came to me and said, ‘What the hell do you think you are doing?!’”

Calvin said, “Well, what did you do to make her say that?”

“Nigga, are you listening to anything I am saying to you? I just put my underwear back on, man! She doesn’t want me out of bed, and I must stay naked!” Benny said, “Haven’t you noticed that you haven’t seen me in about two or three weeks, Calvin?”

“Well, yeah, but I thought you were good, Benny.”

“Hell, no, I wasn’t good!’ Benny exclaimed. “She got me locked in the house over there when she leaves to go to work; she put the deadbolt lock on the doors and then take the key with her.”

“Why don’t you try the windows?”

“How do you think I got over here now? I had to climb out the kitchen window!”

Calvin asked, “Why didn’t you just use the windows leading to the front porch?"

“Every window in the house is nailed down, and I had to pull the air conditioner out of the kitchen window to escape!” Benny exclaimed.

"I can't believe you are acting like this when you've got a good woman waiting on you hand and foot and giving you all that good love," Calvin said while laughing.

Benny just looked at Calvin for a moment and then started to speak firmly before returning to a yell. "Well, Calvin," pointing one of his little fingers at Calvin as his voice boomed, "How about you go over there and let me stay here then?" After that, Benny walked out of the house and headed up the street. Before Benny left, he made it clear that what he was doing was not leaving; the appropriate description was that he escaped!

As time moved forward with all these memories of the past, I took over the responsibilities of the house as my aunt elected to move to a better neighborhood. Gee had moved in with me by this time.

Gee's friend Hand was shipped off to a state prison. Hand's little brother lived down the street with Ms. Marilyn after his mother moved south. Snoop also had a little friend that was always over.

Snoop's friend was called Tez. Tez was one of the little bad ass kids on Hamburg but they moved off the street. Snoop and Tez remained the best of friends. They would always come down to the house and visit with me. Around that time, I had all the latest CDs and tapes of R&B, hip-hop, pop, and some rock. I had boxes of music. Snoop always came down to borrow music and make copies. Tez would always be with him. I don't recall speaking to Tez, which didn't seem to bother him. I think he may have come down to the house two or three times to borrow or return CDs and tapes. Tez started showing up without Snoop trying to borrow music, and I would tell him no. I swear if he saw me twenty times in one day, Tez would have spoken to me twenty-one times. He complimented everything I did or purchased.

He would drive me crazy because he would always catch me and start talking. Half the time, I wouldn't know what he was talking about. The reason is that he always had to give everything a name when it already had one. Like he called my Caprice classic, the heavy Chevy, naming people after Transformers, and named my very frisky aunt, Big Al. The boy even started calling his mouth-dropping beautiful mama "Murph," which is short for Charlie Murphy. I was not exempt; he would call me "Ol Waynee Pants. Which, in time, became "Da Pants' ' for short.

Time passes, and I start to fix everything in the house. My house became the only house on Hamburg with central air; I put in new Windows, a roof, a kitchen, etc. Ms. Marilyn, who lived down the street with Snoop, had to relocate because of her job; Snoop didn't want to move with her and leave the high school he was at. He went to Gee and asked him to talk to me to see if he could move in so he wouldn't have to leave with Ms. Marilyn. I was initially reluctant because I didn't care too much about his big brother and how he lived. Yet, he was a terrific kid, so I agreed; Hamburg was our Lil Village, which was reflective of how we viewed each other on that block. The hustle was getting much better, and my brother was coming around me increasingly, getting money with us.

My brother Vito was a pure crook too. I mean, he always had some slick shit up. I swear he was just one of those people who just couldn't do shit right. He was not even a good crook; he had just pulled one of those stunts recently, and I had not spoken with him in a few weeks. One night, kind of late, I heard a loud knock at my door. "Who the fuck is coming to my house this late?" I said as I got out of bed.

Grabbed that 9-millimeter Ruger and went to the door. "Who is it?" I yell through the door.

I hear a whisper, "Vito." I said who?"

"Man, it's Vito." A little louder.

"I do not know no Fucking Vito." I said with an angry tone.

"Come on and stop playing, man! Vito, the broke Italian" he said much louder. "Ooooooh, VITO!!!"

CHAPTER 2

BLACK BOTTOM EASTSIDE OF DETROIT

IS WHERE I WAS born. I was born on Pierce Street to Shirley Ann Thompkins and Donald Wayne Mac. I lost my mother at the age of three years old. My father was a shining example of a waste of air placed in a human being. Black Bottom could not be a more fitting description for my start in life. The name Black Bottom is said to have been given to the Detroit Eastside neighborhood by the French settlers in 1701. The French settlers gave the name based on the rich souls in the area. This area became home to Irish, Italians, Romanians, Germans, and European Jews. 1840 was the first year of significant migration of Black people from the South. Between 1840 and 1850, the population grew from 193 to 587 (Wikipedia 2023).

During the Great Depression, Detroit's population grew to 993,578 people, including 120,000 Black people. Black Bottom, Eastside Detroit, was the major end of those 120,000 Black people. Millions of Black people headed north based on the auto industry's hiring of Black people. This migration ended up giving birth to a housing shortage. Property owners refused to rent to two migrating black people; this resulted in black bottom Detroit becoming one of the very few places that could be called home. Besides the many obvious challenges, black people did very well.

Black-owned businesses, including hospitals, social institutions, barber shops, pharmacies, and nightclubs, were remarkably successful.

Black Bottom became nationally famous for the entertainment of big bands, jazz artists, and numerous legends regularly performed. The struggle for equality was still present and caused racial tension. This dark presence expressed itself in the historical race riots of 1943 and 1967. The riots of the sixties sent the communities into a death spiral that they could not recover from, but one thing did not die: a very close-knit feeling of family, regardless of the considerable number of families.

Johnny and Mildred Thompkins relocated from the South as part of the great migration north. My grandfather got a job with the city water board as a World War II vet. He stood about 6 '4, or so it appeared to me at the time. My grandfather was a biracial man with a white father and a very fair-skinned African American mother. According to what he described to me, his mother was able to pass for a Caucasian woman, and most people in the town thought she was a Caucasian woman. He would tell me that his father left his mother once his little brother was born, Wallace Thompkins. My uncle Wallace was visibly a darker child than my grandfather and older brother, Archie Thompkins. I don't think he ever got past his parents' splitting up either. He spoke often of his older brother, who lost his life while on active duty in World War II.

My grandfather was often called "Big Red" because he was tall with very red hair, like an Irishman's hair. My grandfather lost his license for some reason, he never talked about it, but I think it may have been because of his inability to read. He often explained to me how he hated the South and the racial tension that was in his town. And how he would often be kicked in the rear end by whites in town and called racial names after the townspeople found out his mother was a black woman. He also spoke about the educational system, segregation, and limited access to any form of education.

However, he did incredibly well on what he could do. He owned several cars, but he would not drive. He would often express, "I am not going to break the law," as he would often say. He would also continue to talk about the day when everything was made in America. How the older cars were better quality than these new cars made of plastic because these cars were made from American steel. Then he would go on to give you an example of the quality of the older cars versus the cars that were plastic. "Like this", as he turned to hit the front fender of his Rambler that he would wash and wax often), now watch this right here, popping the dent back out. "Now let me do that to one of these plastic cars today."

One day, a white journalist was riding up the street, and this did not happen in Black Bottom. The man stopped and had a long talk with my grandfather. The gentleman took a picture of my grandfather sitting on the hood of his Rambler. Next day, that picture was on the front page of the newspaper. Johnny was not going to break the law, so he pulled out his bike.

My grandfather's bike was very tall, similar to him. He sits on this damn bike that appeared to be even taller; the handlebars were set straight up off the frame, and the seat was at his highest point. He had a basket on the front and back of his bike that he placed on himself. He always wore a gentleman's hat and, at times, a sports jacket. My aunts and uncles would complain to my grandmother about him riding his bike throughout Black Bottom. They will often say that he looked like "*The Wicked Witch Of The West*" from The Wizard of Oz when riding that bike.

They would go on to add that I looked like Toto from The Wizard of Oz as I rode along with my fat legs hanging over the buggy just dangling as my grandfather rode along, as my aunt Alice would describe. We would return home, and my grandfather would eat after my grandmother made our plates, and then go wind up his radio and jam. After this, he would pull out his harmonica, and it will be his turn to jam now; and I am part of the band too. He would tell me, "Listen, you've got to keep the beat for me now, Waynee. You gotta smack your hand back and forth like this." as he gave me as an example.

I mean, he would blow that damn thing like never before. We would jam for hours, and he would make it feel like it was just a few minutes. I would be sitting on his legs, and we would get down. I would barely be able to walk the next day because my thigh would be black and blue from the night before. My grandmother would get really upset with my grandfather and blame him for my thighs being in that condition, but I did not care; I was part of the band. These are just some of the things he did for me to help ease me a little from the void that he knew I would revisit as I got older: the death of my mother.

My mother was 15 years old when she had me, and I lost her by age 3. I ended up growing up with my uncle Mark and aunt Ernestine. They often refer to me as their brother. Besides our sibling bond with my older aunts and uncles, I always felt like the odd one out of the family. I guess one could only wonder how you felt like an outcast at such an early age, but outside of my grandfather, my auntie Liz, and my aunt Alice, this is how I felt as a kid.

At the age of five or six years old, I weighed about one hundred pounds. I was having issues remembering how to spell my last name. I felt personally, why did I have to have a name that had so many letters? With that in mind and feeling that it was unnecessarily long, I had a problem spelling it. I also didn't know my birthday. The teachers didn't really push me because they were also the same ones who instructed my mother and all my aunts and uncles. Black Bottom was a small and close community where everybody was family, so I believe deep down inside the teachers understood my struggle.

I had a lot of problems in school. All the kids would pick on me based on that. Jan and Joe would always come to my defense. I did a lot of fighting and became particularly good at it, except when it came to Joe. Janet and Joe have identical twins that were born just a few months after me. We would all be in the same class and even walk home to my grandmother's house. their mother, who was just like a mother to me as well, would get them from my grandmother's house after school. She was an actual teacher at the school and took a lot of time helping me learn. We were noticeably young to be walking home alone at that age for those days. Well, that was not the issue in Black Bottom because the whole neighborhood was out, and they knew you were traveling in the right direction. There were adults out on the corners, keeping you moving. My uncle Donald was always around and was like the one who kept order in the family. My grandparents had twelve children, and when you did bad, you had to see Uncle Don.

You did not want to see Big Red at all. My uncle Donald was a street fighter, and a good one too. I recall things not going so well for him in his street fight in front of my grandparents' house one day. It was common for parents to come down to the parents of another neighbor's family to work out issues, and sometimes the issues would be settled with a fight only among the boys. Both sets of parents would stand and watch the two boys fight, win, lose, or draw. It would be settled afterward, and both boys would have to shake hands and hug afterwards.

However, tonight my uncle Donald's winning streak came to a rude end. This was going so badly to the point he decided to head for the hills in flight by foot. From the excruciating scream that my cousin Sean released at the sight of his hero, my uncle Donald, taking off running, you would have thought someone lost their life. My cousin screamed for my uncle, but my uncle did not stop, nor did he show that he heard, and from the speed at which he would run, I do not think he cared. He was getting the hell out of dodge.

My grandfather said to the parents standing with him, "Well, I guess the boy then had enough." My aunt Alice was the only one my grandfather really depended on. Any official business, he called her. She was the only one who made sure I had a Christmas and birthday cake and my aunt Liz made sure my hair was combed with hygiene attended to. My grandparents were extremely poor, and with so many kids, there was not much time or extra anything. I have always loved my aunt Alice as my mother. My aunt had three girls, and I was the son she never had.

I would get up early in the morning on Saturdays, sometimes with Jan, Joe, and a few other kids in the neighborhood. We will go down and sit on these big steps, and at some point, an elderly Jewish man will come out and give us candy. This is something that I learned from my aunts and uncles that had been going on for who knows how long. Every Sunday this Jewish man would come out and give us candy at this candy factory. Until one day, no one came out anymore.

This candy factory had closed among countless businesses that were owned by the different ethnic groups that I described earlier. They all started to move out of the area. As a child, I didn't understand why? All I knew was that the Jewish man never came out anymore. I went on for weeks sitting on the big stairs on Saturday before Super Friends came on, waiting for the excessively big brown door that seemed larger than life to me to open, but it never did again.

Once I figured out that it was the end for that source of candy, which I like so much, I knew I would have to figure out a way to have some. There was absolutely no money, and there really was no way to earn money as an adult or a child at that time. Everything was closing; there were really no businesses left. The city had decided to destroy Black

Bottom, splitting it by bringing a major freeway right through the heart of it and forcing a mass exodus of all the businesses out of the city.

What I would discover is that I was blessed with the ability to always be able to encounter money at an early age. One of the most unfortunate side effects of this blessed ability was that I was often robbed by my older aunts, uncles, and even grandmother at times.

I caught pure hell getting that spandex-tight T-shirt off my head since my arms were straight up in the air. I also could never figure out why all my pants had holes worn in between the thighs. I would go straight to the pool hall and buy all flavors of Now and Later with my money. Then I will remove all of them from the wrappers too. This way, they would not be able to return them either. I was no longer going to get my ass kicked, robbed, and be without candy too. I would take the former to eliminate the latitude.

Shortly, I figured out how to have them beholden to me by using the power of Big Red. I was noticeably young, but I always knew everything about them. All their likes and dislikes, then coming in between them, forcing them to barter with me. They would often say, "You've got to watch that fat Mutha Fucka! That little son of a bitch is evil." I think back on how ironic it was that they said that when I was the one being robbed by them, as well as being verbally assaulted while getting my ass kicked.

"Vito, why the fuck you are coming by so late?" I'm saying as I locked the door behind him. We sat down, and I looked at him as if I were saying, OK, what?

Vito said, "OK, I know I messed up" Again! "I fucked the money up, man. I didn't come back right away because I was hustling back up."

I cut him off with a "NIGGA. I know you didn't get me out of the damn bed for this chicken shit story. Vito, get your ass out of here before I hurt you" though my tone was forgiving.

"Okay, I am about to go, but, you know, our brother is about to get out," he said.

"Now, I do, and I thank you for telling me, Vito." as I am pushing him out the door.

I locked the door, while he went to the window and yelled through the window. "So, we are good Then, right?"

I went back to bed....

The next morning, I went downtown to this nice restaurant named Franklin. This was a nice soul-food restaurant with an upscale touch. Majority of the city officials would eat at Franklin. I had taken a very nice-looking young lady to lunch with me there. This young lady was Asian and Black. She had a major future for herself. I was a regular at Franklin's, and I had my favorite server also. While me and my friend enjoyed our meal, I noticed a few older gentlemen looking our way. Which did not bother me, because she was a very stunningly beautiful young lady. After some time had passed, one of the gentlemen got my attention. "Excuse me, sir, are those Coogi socks you are wearing?"

I turned to him and said, "Yes, sir, they most certainly are." He apologized to me and my friend for being rude.

He then handed me a card and said, "You appear to be a young man that can appreciate the finer things in life, based on your style of dress. I can see that this is expressed in the most important parts of your life as well."

As he nodded to my friend, "My name is Bayon; give me a call. I am in town for a few days, and I have some nice pieces in men's wear that may interest you. Bayon and his two friends got up and left. They were well-dressed older men with an East Coast-type speaking accent. I was questioning myself at this point. I am doing OK financially, and I just met her. To be honest, I was just as stunned by her as they were. I dropped my friend off at her car and went to my mother's house. Once

I got to my mom's, I saw my brother Willie, who had just been released from the state prison. My brother Willie was a big person, and I do not mean from years of weight training either.

Everyone called my brother Big Dawg since we were little. I ended up living with my brothers Vito and Willie and three sisters when I was like 13 years old. I was homeless at the time, and Jean, who was their mother, became my mother too.

Big Dawg was always producing hustle. But his problem was that he was not that good at building and executing ideas. Also, Vito was always ripping him off too. Vito was not a bad hustler. He was just a damn crook, and he done such crook shit that you could not find the logic in it. In one case, Big Dawg had a safe and gave himself and Vito access to it in case of emergency. Suddenly Vito went missing, and no one knew where to find him. I said to my brother, "Big Dawg, You better check your safe." Big Dawg went, checked the safe, and came back, walking slowly. "What's up, man?" I spoke.

He sat down and said, "See for yourself. I left it open." I ran upstairs and saw the safe sitting wide open with several small pieces of paper in it but no money. I looked at the paper and said they were all I.O.U. notes with dollar amounts on them. That coming from Vito, you knew that you were never going to be paid, and you have been had. I could never blame Big Dawg because I really believed he was the ugliest man alive.

This was a natural ugly, not from any kind of misgiving or accident either. He put you in the mind, body, and soul of a Black uncle from the Addams family. Vito would always do things to Big Dawg because he knew it was always next to impossible to get him to react violently. I was always the one to start fighting for him or on his behalf.

Whenever Big Dawg had an idea and ran into issues with his planning, he would always call me so we could go upstairs and talk. He would throw a lot of situational issues at me, and I would tell him what I thought or poke holes in his plan while introducing other ideas. I would look up, and it would be his plan. And he never split any of the lion's share of my brainstorming with me either. However, I assume my portion would still be received because Vito was always there to accept it for me, I guess. I was much too young to know it then. I had a wealth of knowledge that I didn't know the value of at that time from being raised and taught by one of the experts in the game, Larry Chambers, of the Chambers brothers.

Big Dawg would fight with me when we were younger. One day he pushed me so hard that I got stuck in the drywall; another time he pushed me through the window from the front porch.

I guess I should be happy he didn't give me a good one. I was in my early to mid-teens, and he was in his late teens or early twenties. There was always a sibling-type rivalry with him toward me. I never saw it then, though. I walked into the house, and I gave my brother a big hug. We had some small talk, and I asked him about the struggle of being away for 10 years. We then got to the reason Vito had stopped by so late to tell me about. My brother wanted to get back on his feet. I blessed him with a little something, and he pulled out this old ass triple beam scale to weigh what I just gave him.

He looked at me with a crazy look, and said, "Who in the hell do you think I am? I ain't no fool."

Then he threw the damn drugs at me! I was like, "What the fuck is wrong with this nigga?" He yelled and said, "The weight on that shit is off. You got me fucked up!" I just took my stuff and didn't even say anything else to him, got in my car and left my mother's home. Vito came by later that day to check on me.

I ask Vito, "What in the hell is wrong with your brother?"

He said, "he is fucking crazy. I asked this nigga what that shit weighted when he pulled it off the scale. Man, once he told me, I called him all kinds of stupid Mutha Fuckas." Vito said that he didn't understand how much the game has changed since he was last out. We both just laughed about it. I told Vito about the older gentleman I met at Franklin earlier that day. I was invited down to their room at the Renaissance hotel off the Detroit River. I told him I wanted him to go with me down there. He agreed, and we headed downtown. We arrived at the hotel, and I called Bayon on my cell phone and asked him to greet us in the lobby of the hotel. Bayon greeted us and took Vito and I up to his room. We walked in and were seated. There were boxes of shoes for every damn person. A gentleman named Smoochie came over to me and introduced himself to me and Vito. He asked what my shoe size was and brought a few pairs of Maury Gators skin shoes over to me to try on.

Detroit is known for its Gator shoes. Countless entertainers have even recounted this fact. One of the biggest is the Notorious BIG of Bad Boy Entertainment. His lyrics, "Stink Pink Gators," are about my Detroit players. I was shocked to see so many huge boxes with Maury Gators on them. I had only found one store in downtown Detroit to carry them. The name of this place is synonymous with Detroit's underworld history; the store was called City Slickers. The guy that all the big hustlers in this city would name was George at City Slickers. Vito and I just sat around waiting for Smoochie to finish clearing the store with buyers.

Then Smoochie and Bayon started to tell me more about themselves. Smoochie told me that he was exceptionally good friends with the owner of the Italian shoe company. And Bayon was good friends with Smoochie. But Bayon had a particularly good relationship with someone close to the king of Thailand. The king was a ridiculously huge fan of American boxing. Bayon was charged with the task of putting on a boxing exhibition for a surprise birthday gathering for the king around the summer and Bayon promised to keep me updated so I could come over and enjoy myself. I set eyes on some loud rainbow-pimp colored Gator shoes.

Smoochie told me that he wanted $1,000 for the shoes, but I only had $500 in my pocket at that time. I was out of my comfort zone going down to that hotel to meet these guys. I didn't know what to expect, but I know one thing: whatever the cost, I wouldn't lose more than five hundred dollars. I told Smoochie that I only had five hundred on me. Bayon said to Smoochie, and I got him covered. meaning he would ensure the other's $500. Smoochie gave me his information and phone number so I could mail it to him when I got it. I noticed that he was from Baltimore, MD.

Vito and I left, and I gave those ugly ass pimp shoes to Vito. He did not understand why I would spend that much on some shoes I didn't even like. I told him that's how business is done in certain circles. To me that was a small investment into a relationship that may yield a respectable return one day. The next day I sent the $500 to Smoochie via mail. I recall much later asking him why he trusted me or trusted that I was sending the remainder of the balance to him. He responded in a very Smoochie-type way: "If $500 is going to keep me from knowing you, then I don't need to know you!" which just tickled me because that statement says it all. It was one of the best investments I ever made in my life, not having anything to do with anything financial but everything to do with gaining a father that I desperately needed in my life. God found mercy in my life and blessed me with just that, my pops Smoochie.

Every day that passed brought more success in my hustle. this started to be realized by others around me at the time. My cousin Sean came to me concerning investments in his own male group named Today. I heard the guys singing and fell in love with their talent level vocally.

Even though at that time I didn't move forward with investing in them at the time. I was called back to the possibility by my fraternity brother, Big New, whose mother fell in love with them and brought me in as an investor with her for the group.

She found one of the top producers in Detroit at the time, named Marcus Divine. When I first met Marcus at his studio, we instantly clicked. I was a superfan of his artistry and what he did for the group. In time, we became extremely close brothers, and he was a brother I could lean on from that point forward, as well as someone he could call on whenever needed and without question. He cut several records for the guys.

I ended up meeting another gentleman by the name of Ray through the local music scene in the city. Ray had a female group by the name of Sai that he took over and started to manage. This group was a little different because the girls' ages ranged from 11 to 13 years old. He had four girls in his group, and I had four guys in my young male adult group, which Ray was a fan of as well. Ray was having issues with the financial aspect of the girl group, and he leaned on me for assistance financially. I leaned on him for assistance with his connections and being able to get into doors without much effort. People loved him, which created opportunities that exposed my guys. Ray was incredibly good at politics, and he kept his word. Under our agreement, Ray went to work, and things started to really move with his girls as well as my guys. Ray had put me in contact with a young lady out of Atlanta who was holding auditions for a movie. She had a talent agency down in Atlanta, and this is where Ray made the arrangements for me to travel with my guys down to audition. I invited the guys over to tell them the exciting news. They arrived and came in, and I told them the great news. Then I heard someone at the door, and I asked Tez to see who it was. Well, I should have been able to guess easily because I have a house full of very handsome young men: Big Al. My aunt, Al, lived directly across the street, and she's always in the market for a young, handsome, viral man. The guys are super excited about the news. I heard a loud noise of a door slamming open. Then I hear, "Wayne, Wayne, Oh shit! God damn this woman strong." Tez yelled!

"I TOLD YO, LITTLE BLACK CHOCOLATE SEXY ASS!! I was gone, get Cha! YOU GONE STOP TEASING ME." Big AL yelled! My guys are freaking out at this point. I had to run and split them.

Tez yelled, "Woman, you are crazy!"

"I told your sexy black ass." Big Al, yells.

"I know! But you just want me to spank that big old flat ass of yours, like this couch." Tez started to slap my black leather couch in a spanking type of motion.

"Ima, get Yo black ass, watch," Big Al shouts as she charges in Tez's direction!

This Nigga ran and left me to wrestle with her and her passion. I finally calmed her down. Then she had the nerve to say, "OK, I am OK now. I'm ready for you to introduce me to your fine acapella group!"

"Oh no, you have grabbed and groped enough fine asses for one night. "I said as I led her to the door. I return to explain to the guys that I will be making the arrangements for us to go down to Atlanta.

I also had to go over to the studio and pay for two 10-hour blocks of recording time for my guys and Ray's group as well. For so many things to be going so well at that time, I received a call extremely late that night, which crushed me to my soul.

Dee and Jan had been murdered that night. I swear that was one of the worst days of my life, even to this day. Jan was one of the sweetest and most pure souls on this planet. Dee had a lot of people very jealous of him. That man was really getting that money. Detroit is a town where the wolves will come lurking to steal. Any hustler of any importance knows that to get robbed is a death sentence. I guess we accept that risk at the end of the day. They killed Jan, only leaving the baby alive. I understand all sides of this business of the streets and hustling and have seen a lot of it over my lifetime. I would never understand COWARD FUCK SHIT like that though. You just don't do nefarious shit and touch a man's family just to fucking steal!

From that day forward, any niggas that like jacking and robbing folks trying to earn a living doesn't deserve life. It is always only a matter of time before it's your turn one day. I was mentally and emotionally destroyed for some time after that date. Everything that had developed had to come to a complete stop. I was doing well for myself based on the opportunity Jan created for me with Dee.

I was really getting a nice piece of money, which was financing everything that was going on and creating another lane to do other things. Then to lose some lives that were so precious—this is still something from which I have never recovered. Throughout my whole childhood, I never had anyone really stand up for me. Jan and Joe never allowed people to just pick on me, not just because of something I may have had because I did not have anything as a child. Then, as a young adult, she still created an opportunity for me with nothing, and just because I was her brother, this shit still hurts.

I still took the guys down to Atlanta, and they got the part in the movie that was being directed by David Lassiter called "Pay the Price." We filmed the parts for the movie on the Clark, Spellman, and Morehouse universities' campuses. This movie, after being shopped, ended up being renamed and is now commonly known as Drumline after some questionable business dealings that lead to Mr. Lassiter being paid allegedly for his silence.

We also traveled to Tennessee and a few other states to do pilots for another series called Off the Hook, which was a spinoff of a European show that Michael Pennington had come up with and ended up becoming America's Got Talent from my understanding. He also had another idea called "Black Napoleon," which would feature conversations like the ones that ARE had in Black barber shops. According to him, this was shown to a gentleman formerly of a rap group out of California. Just like the Pay the Price movie that my guys participated in it was supposedly shopped to THE top Black music of that time. None of those opportunities, regardless of our participation in them, panned out for us.

Things really started to dry up for me, just like the desert, but I was living it, so it was worse. A lot of things that I was doing and investing in had really dried up for me and were stagnant.

This is around the time that Gee caught a break when he ended up meeting this older dude from the Brewster projects. This older gentleman really took a liking to Gee and based on this relationship that he had developed; things were starting to look up for us again.

Gee didn't know how to manage or move the product. He turned to me at this time, and I started to structure a crew to start. I already had a good friend of mine named Big New. Big New was already making some major moves on the other side of Gratiot Ave. He would talk with me from time to time about how to increase his already good turnover of products. I worked with Big New in the past and showed him a prominent level of understanding of the business. Big New looked out for me in a major way. He introduced me to some guys that had the Cocaine on the east side at that point.

This was a crew that we connected with through The Winning Team slogan, which was directly related to Big New's crew, which dealt mostly in heroin. My guy's Devan and D Rock got me together; now I have my hustling drug of choice back and am not dealing just with heroin.

After arranging things for a moment, he really started to grow. Gee was moving about 15,000 to 20,000 dollars' worth of product a day. I went down to Black Bottom, Detroit and set up. Black Bottom is a ghost town at this time with nothing left but junkies. There were two serious old school heavyweights on the heroin scene that had been known in Black Bottom since the late seventies. The name of the two blow products at that time was called Homicide, and Monster. The names of the brands were not particularly important, no different than your food franchises or even athleticwear, to name a few. The principles are the same because it is all commerce at the end of the day.

When dealing with heroin for street consumption, branding was imperative, which I guess to an extent is the same thing as stamps on the bricks of cocaine. It's all branding and street level marketing at the grassroots for the blow or heroin. The name "Homicide" was for the sole purpose of stating that it was such a good product that it could kill you. It may sound backwards, but if the streets ever said a package of blow killed someone, all the consumers would start asking what the name of the blow was and start looking for it, and I mean everyone too.

I moved into that area and started to work. I put together a strategy that locked the Homicide brand in a ridiculously small corner of the neighborhood. But the whole thing was to do it without them knowing it. Within time, they would most certainly say no, but it would be too late. Now Gee is doing very well, and his guys are pleased with him. When Gee first started with this guy, I would always go over there with him. Whenever his guy would have any questions about the business of things, he always wanted me to answer and address his concerns. It wasn't long before that changed for some reason. Gee didn't want me going over there with him anymore when things started rolling very well.

His guy called me “NAILS” because my nails always grow long. Gee told me that his dude didn’t care for me. I felt that was interesting. There was plenty of money being made, and I started on my house again now. I was caught off guard, to say the least, by this new revelation. I always thought that when major money and growth were being shown to buy new talent, which was Gee for him. Why wouldn’t you like the team that helps create the magic? It wasn’t for him to like, so it didn’t matter as long as the work kept flowing, and my philosophy was that as long as my guy was winning, so was I.

I had a friend over, and Gee had his little lady over too. We are in the front room, joking and laughing. Then Gee says, “Yo Wayne, it looks like your uncle is coming up the street.”

"I wonder who in the hell this could be because I don’t really fuck with them like that." I said to Gee.

“What does he look like?”

“An old ass man with a walking cane,” Gee said.

I’m thinking, “*Damn, he must have just gotten out of the state jail.*” There is a knock at the door. Sure, as hard as it hit, it was my uncle Donald. I told Gee to let him in the house.

When he steps in, he says, “Hey, nephew, it looks like life is good around here! Man, you have really turned this house around. Nephew, is it OK for me to look at some of the improvements you made?”

I said, “Stop that; we are family now!” We both laughed as he went toward the dining room and kitchen. I went into the kitchen and said, “Let me get you a little something to drink.”

He responded, “Naw, I’m good, Nephew... Man, you really brought this house back, baby!”

“Unc, sit down and let me get you something to drink now!” His voice switched from an excited happiness for me to a serious tone. “Naw, Naw, nephew... this isn’t a social visit.”

I look at him and say, "You are trippin'; take a load off, nah!"

"Naaaaaw, Nephew, this ain't a social visit. With a calm voice, he said, "I'm here to kick your ass.

I said, "What the fuck did you say??..."

"Your aunt told me how you took her house. And, you have been really disrespectful too. So, I'm here to straighten you out," he said. not yelling but in a very calm tone.

"Y'all move out of the way because I'm about to fuck his old ass up!"

"Naw, you have a nice house here now. I'm not going to disrespect your place. I will meet you outside."

He turned and walked out the door. He walked to Gee's lady car and leaned his cane up against her car. Then he unbuttoned his shirt, folded it up nicely, and placed it on the trunk of her car. He then pulled his glasses off, with the elastic holding them on to his head, and placed them on the top of his shirt. I went to the back of the house to change into some attire fitting for the moment.

I hear Gee yelling out to me, "Wayne, your uncle is in the middle of the damn Street. shadowboxing! Man, his ass is moving damn good too. He doesn't need a damn cane." I came from out the back with one of my 9-millimeter black and silver Ruger pistols. As I get ready to exit the house, Gee jumps in front of the door. "Man, I don't think you should do this," he said, with a genuinely concerned look on his face.

"Gee, I've got to go out there; the girls are out there waiting!"

"FUCK THEM BITCHES!" Then he slammed the door and locked it. Locking the girls out there with my uncle.

"Watch out, man," as I slightly pushed him to the side. I went out on the porch and said there was a nice little crowd gathered outside my house. Apparently, everybody knew there was going to be a fight before I did. I showed my uncle the pistol just before I set it down and said, "Yo, don't pull any shanks or dirty shit or this dude here is going to shoot the shit out of you."

"Nephew, we are going to do this the old-fashioned way, as men." Not looking up at me but still getting loose. My old ass auntie was in attendance for this bout that she surely arranged. I walked off the porch as I entered the middle of the street, and with not one word stated, he engaged me fast. Throwing jabs extremely fast at my head. I'm backpedaling with rapid steps while leaning back, and the punches were not even inches from connecting with my face. I was thinking, *"Oh, shit, I should have locked the freaking door too!"*

I knew I had to do something quick to slow this **SHIT** down. I could not let him make quick work out of me. He was taller and had a serious reach advantage over me. I side stepped his super-aggressive advance on me, and I countered with a straight right cross that connected to the side of his head. I stunned him with that punch, and he stumbled just a bit. I will admit that the whole move was pure desperation, which worked out to my advantage, that time! I could not hope for that luck to strike twice.

I could see much more respect for me in his eyes now. One thing was clear: his boxing skills were something special. He engaged me again, but working one hand and trying to move me too is right. Then he threw his right, and I moved up under it, hitting him with two haymaker-type punches. At this point, Unc was having issues with the power of my punches. I stayed inside at this point, and he dropped his head. I started throwing short, Mike Tyson-style haymaker punches toward his head. I swear, I couldn't land anything from his bobbing and weaving like a pro boxer. I was trying to knock his head off his shoulders but couldn't connect.

I finally connected slightly again, and now, stumbling, he started throwing those damn jabs to push me back out. I knew I was going to knock him out shortly. I get back in on him and connect twice, and then out of the corner of my eye, I see someone moving fast toward me from the side, and I move toward it. As I was getting ready to swing, I saw it was no good ass auntie. I stopped myself from swinging, "She is a woman even if she doesn't think so herself at times."

She was coming to assist her hit man since she saw he was about to go down. I told her, "You step any closer to me..." She backed off fast. I turned back to my uncle, saying, "Where the fuck are you going, NIGGA!"

"I'm done! I have had enough." I still wanted my undisputed victory over him, but he had conducted himself as a gentleman throughout. and went out of his way to be respectful of my newfound man hood, even while challenging it. He grabbed his cane and put his shirt back on, then turned to me and said some old eighties action movie type stuff like, "You won the battle, but you won't win the war!"

I just shook my head and let him have that moment. Gee, I, and the ladies went back inside. I was the tough guy, but I understood that women like to see men doing manly stuff. They started getting ready to feed the champion. Gee leaned into me and whispered, "Man, if your uncle had been about 10 or 15 years younger. You would have been in big trouble today."

I looked at him in agreement and said, "You saw that SHIT too, huh?!"

The following days, my buddy named Face came by, as he generally always did. Face was a top guy with the crew down in Black Bottom named Homicide. One of our guys was having legal issues at the time. He was telling myself and Gee that hustlers make a huge misstep by retaining a lawyer when they get in trouble. "The attorney doesn't know you, and you're nothing more than a paying client." He said, "The only way he is going to use personal relationships for you is if there is history between you and him or her. Gee had a brother in the state joint serving life for murder."

He told him about an attorney whose name was going around the prison system for his very high rate of success. The name of this attorney was Gerald M. Lorence. His brother had to tell him about the exceptional work that he does as a trial attorney and then as an appeals attorney. Gee, called and set an appointment for us to go down and meet with him. We traveled to downtown Detroit and arrived at the Penobscot Building. Attorney Lorence's office was at the very top of this exceptionally large historical building in downtown Detroit.

Once we get to the top and exit the elevator, it's a short haul. The left end of the hall was an attorney's office, and attorney Lorence's office was to the right. When Gee and I went to have our meeting with him, I noticed that in the meeting at one point all his questions were to me. Nevertheless, we left his office pleased. When I was leaving downtown, my brother Big Dawg called me on my cell. He told me that he needed to use my Internet for a second. I pulled up to the house, and there he was with his short but well-dressed buddy. Big Dawg introduced his gentleman to me by the name of Frank, from Arizona. He told me Frank needed to use the Internet.

Frank said, "So this is your brother that you have been telling me so much about, Big Dawg?"

Big Dawg replied: "Yeah, this is his funny acting ass brother."

This was to address my withdrawn attitude towards Frank. Big Dawg knows I have serious issues with being drawn into a setting without being aware of any additional persons. Plus, I know my brother. His ass was up to something! After my brother and his friend left my house, I was left thinking,

"How often is it that you meet a Hispanic person with a given name, Frank?"

******

I received a call from Ray, telling me that he had another opportunity for my R&B group with the same talent agency down in Atlanta. It was an opportunity where a movie was being shot, and my guy's bio was shown to the director. There was major interest from my guys to be a part of the project. I called my boys and told them to pack up. We hit the road to Atlanta for this casting. I didn't know if you ever traveled with a young singing group. These guys sing, sing, and sing some more. I just so happened to switch out with one of the guys on driving duty. I totally crashed in the back of the van.

I woke up and didn't know where the hell I was, but the van was packed and parked. I think we had to be between the bottom part of Ohio and Kentucky, with Michigan plates on the van. I didn't see anything but a bunch of pickup trucks, and everything had a Confederate flag on it. These niggas was up in this damn diner.

"I swear if I had had an extra set of keys... them Niggas would have gotten left".

I walked into the diner, and I think every set of eyes in the place looked me over. I sat down with the guys, who were nervous as hell. Everybody that looked over at the table saw me nod my head to speak, with a country accent or as best as I could.

I told the boys, "Hey, hurry and eat up." I already had it in my mind that if shit got out of hand, I'm running! The guys noticed I was nervous. Then I heard a noticeably light humming, followed by additional hums building around the melody note. I started saying "no, no, no," exceptionally light but aggressive, and my eyes were big. They came to the harmony and went directly to the Boys II Men acapella version of John Lennon's **Yesterday**. Strong harmony, and then, "yesterday... do do do."

I just dropped my head saying to myself, "*That ain't country music!!*" I'm sitting here trying to sound country, like we're from around those parts. The guys are going to start singing R&B songs in the middle of the fucking Rust Belt, with "***No Niggers allowed after dark!***" signs along the highway! We are about to die, but to their credit, this song was a huge hit in the 60s or 70s. There was a calm that came over that whole diner. The people's eyes started to light up, and there were huge smiles on everyone's face. The cooks came out of the back to listen. Everyone in the diner sang, and they circled around us as they sang. I mean, we couldn't get back on the road on time because people in the diner kept asking them to sing different songs. They were even calling friends and family to come up to the diner.

Well, I finally got the guys out of there, and we didn't die. But the power of good music isn't subject to race or human hatred and division. We headed on up the highway, and I found out that this was Tez's idea to stop at this diner. And the reason I was left in the car there was because there wasn't any room in this place for me. Tez was moonlighting as the manager of the guys and a whole roster of talent.

As Tez told the guys, these are white people who think all Black people look the same! We are going in here and singing Boys II Men songs, and they are going to think you all are them!

We arrived in Atlanta, and things went fast. We went to the casting call, and the director loved my guys. He wanted them just for one or two scenes, singing parts in the movie. but ended up casting them for a few other roles too. One of my guys was a serious heartbreaker. He likes to call himself "Japan," which is an acronym for "JUST ANOTHER PRETTY ASS NIGGA." He ended up with much more work on the set than everyone else.

Come to find out why the assistant casting director fell in love with him on site. She was an unbelievably beautiful woman too. She would come to the house I was renting through relationships the talent agent had with a real estate company. After we left the set, she would come by late and pick him up. Tez had an issue with this for some reason. I said to him, “Why are you hating on that man?”

“I ain’t hating on him man! You just don’t know him like I do.” Tez replied. “What up, kick it with me!” Tez continues; "you remember when we were down in Memphis filming the Off-The-Hook pilot?”

“Yeah, OK, I’m listening.” I told him.

“That dirty NIGGA One of the reporters at the news station was feeling him. She agreed to come by his room late that night. He told me I could hide in the bathroom and sneak out to watch once they got going. I was hiding out in that damn bathroom all that time, waiting; just for him to come knock on the fucking door and put me out. He was calling me all kinds of freaky Mutha Fuckas. Like he didn’t know I was in there!”

What Tez didn’t know is that I knew about it and that I knew he was watching the man’s room and tried to slip in there and hide in the bathroom in hopes of watching. Dave Lassiter got the idea for this movie from his college days in a black marching band. He told me that this movie would be the first of its kind. The movie was shot on Clark, Morehouse, and Spelman university campuses. The movie was called ***Pay the Price***. I stayed in touch with Dave as he went on to Cannes in France.

He later told me the idea was stolen by a well-known Atlanta producer and that he shopped the complete idea too. He told me the name of the movie was going to be called ***Drumline***. Dave said he was suing, and I watched him on BET address the issue in an interview. I spoke with him once more after this, and he told me he was going to settle over his idea being stolen. He also made me aware that he would no longer be able to discuss it after that period.

I never spoke with Dave again after that date, but while in Atlanta, I got a chance to meet a hot female producer named LJ. She cut a few records for my guys. I ended up meeting her brother, named Woo. Woo had been a late-round draft pick by the Atlanta Falcons, but he ran into a few legal issues with the government that hampered that for him. It was nothing to have current NFL players stop by to see him. He took a serious interest in my group at that time too. Woo And I started to develop a relationship outside of my group. There is a saying, "Game recognizes game," and he looked familiar.

We returned to Detroit, and just as I entered town on I-94, I got a call: D. Rock was killed last night. I had called D Rock as soon as we jumped down on the freeway to return to the city, just as I told him I would do. The plan was for us to get together as soon as I got back to town. D. Rock and I were remarkably close at this point. The same thing that takes so many: jackers and robbers

SHIT!

It took me a few days to become functional again. I put a call in to my attorney, who will be known from this point forward as "Atty Lorence." I needed to develop a record label with contracts to sign my artists. Lawrence started to work on this for me. The death of D Rock was still heavy on my mind, and the way it happened was the problem for me. D Rock had just told me a few weeks ago that several dudes were plotting to rob Gee. He told me to be careful and try to slow Gee down from flashing so much. He warned me, and I ended up going down the path he warned me about.

Soon after getting back in the city, my dude Big New reached out to me, saying he wanted to run into me to talk about a few issues. I was not surprised by his wanting to sit down. He was really moving things on his side of the town, but things were starting to slow down for him.

The man showed me major love when I needed it, so I had to go hear what he had to say. I went over to his hood and met up with him. He started to walk and talk. He told me that he fell out with his line and supplier, and things were getting bad for him. He said that he decided to go out and went to the Right Goal Post on the east side. One of the bouncers at the door knew him. Big New was telling the guy how things were a little slow for him. The bouncer had just come home from the Feds and had met a man from the West Side while he was in. The dude on the Westside had bricks of that dog food: heroin. Big News had his friend arrange a meeting with his friend for him. Big New told me that he just left that meeting.

I am thinking to myself, "*OK*." He said, "The reason I called you over here was to warn you."

"Warn me about what?" I said.

"Did you find somebody else to get work from?" I laughed at him.

Big New looked at me with a dead serious face. I slowly stopped laughing. "The guy I met today is the guy who gives some of your people work. Did Gee tell you that this guy calls you Nails?"

I responded to Big New. "Yeah, Gee, he told me that his guy called me Nails before."

Then Big New started to tell me some things that I didn't know, like the reason he called me Nails, which wasn't because my nails grew long either. Big New told me that he called me "*Nails for; fingers that steal*."

I was really shocked to hear that by stating, "What the FUCK?!"

He went on to tell me that this guy was trying to pay him for information to find another dude from our side of town named DD. DD was a guy that Big New and I knew fairly well from southwest Detroit. From my understanding, DD owed this man like seventy racks. He wanted to contact DD to tell him that he knew it was not his fault. He just needed DD to give him info on where he could send hitters for me! Now that he is telling me this, it explains why DD was going around buying drugs from other people and not dealing with his Guy. He also wasn't around in the hood lately either.

DD's cousins know this man; they kept calling looking for him. His cousin just wasn't saying why. He also told me that once he left the meeting with the supplier, He told the bouncer guy the truth, and he turned the car around and went back to the house.

Big New went back in and told the guy the truth. That nigga was gambling a lot and doing a lot of tricking and just being super flashy with jewelry and everything else suddenly. I was the one that helped advise on the machine that was moving everything. He also told him that we had a huge falling out and I haven't dealt with DD in some time concerning business. That is how his customer base started to disappear. He also made him aware that Gee was the reason I was still working and that he could confirm I had nothing to do with DD's debt.

Big New told me that DD's supplier made sense out of what he told him. But he still wanted me to be careful. I never said anything about what I found out from Big New. I was just lost for words once again after everything I did to help this dude come up. He was telling his guy that I was stealing that man's money and running off with it. I had a unique skill level in knowing how to build a crew of hustlers as well as how to arrange a system through houses to distribute enormous quantities of drugs. This is a skill set that I learned from Larry Chambers, who used the Chambers Brothers' formula from the mid-eighties in the introduction of the crack cocaine era in our city.

He taught me the economics of it, from cooking the product to managing a crew to making sure there were laws that the crew followed up on administering punishment to the crew for breaking laws. Having foresight to circumvent issues by knowing the signs of issues that were starting to bug his head, etc. I was under the impression that this guy believes Big New. Starting to hear the calls from this guy to DD has become less aggressive. Allowed me to relax a little. That, coupled with hearing that DD had gotten a hold of some more drugs, made plans to see the guy to make good on what he owed.

This calls for a celebration, or so I felt at the time. That night we decided to go to the strip club right off Seven Mile and Conant. It was called Chocolate City. There were a lot of us that night going to the club. We had a wonderful time and got back to the house about 3:00 a.m. the next morning.

About 4:00 AM in the morning, I hear some very loud boom, boom, boom on the front door. I woke up like, *"Oh yeah!" YOU MUTHA FUCKERS trying to pull off some robbery?"*

I grabbed my two black and silver 9-mm Ruger and ran toward the dining room. I'm running toward the front door to unleash hell on the niggas before they get all the way up in the house. I knew once they got up in the house, you were dead! I got to the dining room, and Gee is running through the house, with only his draws on, yelling to me as he ran past in the opposite direction,

"I'm about to get my shit!" his eyes, like a deer in headlights, as he went into his room. I stood in the back of the dining room with my back against the wall and both pistols pointed at the corner that they would have to turn around after rushing through the front door and running through the living room to enter the dining room. I wanted to make sure everyone got in.

I'm standing there thinking "you are the same NIGGAS that killed Dee and Jan, and D rock! I'm about to kill all you fuck niggas tonight" I firmly whispered to Gee's father to come back toward me and stay on the floor, and I yell to Gee, who was coming back out of the room, to stay back and just be ready. I was going to let loose a barrage of bullets with bad intentions, and I didn't need any friendly fire.

The door opens, and I can see the flashlights in the living room. I have both pistols steady with one in the hole on each. Then I hear Detroit police: "Detroit police!" , "Oh shit!" I had two pistols in my hands, both hot (one in the chamber). I got back, put the pistols up, and jumped under the covers. all with my hands up.

Don't ask me how I did it because I don't know. I was called from the back room and told to lay on the floor in the dining room. I left out the fact that I slept naked too. Gee and I were placed against the wall. Detroit police went straight into Gee's room with the dog and found a whole lot of things they were not supposed to even be in the house. I looked at him, and he just dropped his head. He knew we had strict rules for no drugs in the house. Early that morning, they hit my house, his house down the street, as well as his aunt's house simultaneously. and Tez had to go through that shit as well. That really hurt me the most because these were young guys just out of high school and was not about that life. We were all taken to Gratiot and Hoover. Everyone called it the "Glass House" because there were no bars, and the slabs of glass and cement were too thick for you to sit or lay on.

I called Lorence, and he came down to get me out. Gee's attorney got him out on a writ and was the reason for both of us getting a writ. There was a period of several months that went by without any formal charges. I found out that the state was sending the caseload over to the feds, and the feds kept sending it back until finally Atty Lorence called me and told me to call him from a payphone. I went to a payphone and called him as he requested, and he told me that the city had just filed charges and my name was not on them. I was shocked, wondering how this could happen?

He told me that he went to law school with the DA, and the DA knew that if he tried to file charges against me with what he had, he would kick his ass all over and around that courtroom. Gee was charged and took a cop to what was found in his room as well as whatever they found in the raid on his mom's and aunt's house. which was stand-up shit that could only be respected. He wasn't about to let his mom and aunt get charged with some bullshit. However, after accepting the plea, he went on the run, but in time they caught up with him, and he went and laid down (: means jail time).

After that whole exchange, I stopped hustling. The latter part of that summer just got worse and worse. I lost my other guy, Devan, who was like a brother to me. I got a call that Devan had been killed on the west side. I rushed over to the west side and arrived to see him still laying in the middle of the parking lot. His wife, Kia, called me to join her at the hospital. She was there to identify his body. When I got there, I was just sitting in the waiting area with a few of her friends. That was a difficult moment for me. I had just spoken with Devan a couple of days prior, and he had the word that someone was trying to catch him up. At that time, I had just started being a loan officer, and I had just refinanced one of his houses for him. He came up to the office, got the check, and told me he was heading out of town and taking things slow. My guy Kevin had advised him of that, and that was what he was going to do. I didn't know until I got that call about him that night that he didn't go. I know one thing: he couldn't have found himself a better wife than Kia: real rider or die!

I know this wasn't the right venue for this, but one of her friends there was smoking. I didn't really try to say anything to her. Too many people did not know me. I had never been a major player on the hustle scene. I made enough money to qualify. My strong point was vision and creating ideas for making large sums. Selling drugs never interests me at all. I didn't want to be known for that. To be a great hustler, you need to be known and friendly. I wasn't good at that either. I asked the smoking young lady her name. She told me her name was Lay Lay; And you are?... before I could answer, a voice said, That ain't nobody but Wayne girl.

CHAPTER 3

NO BODY, BUT WAYNE

NOBODY BUT WAYNE... PRETTY much sums up the story of my life. I just never fit the ideal image of a dope boy. I never really liked the need for attention of most that embrace the culture. I just didn't like to be seen or make a scene. I hated the club scene and the recycling of women within those circles. That was a running joke among the guys, concerning my not trying to screw every woman I talked to.

They will say things like, "Girl, you need to talk to him and take his money!" because he would never try to hurt you.

I was just not normal for that culture on the street. I was often looked past by women. I was nobody but Wayne to the few that knew me. I never really talked much and enjoyed being by myself. For the most part, no one even knew who I was.

Kia put me in contact with her friend named Lay Lay. After the funeral of my very good friend Ivan I could recall that tattoo of Betty Boo on her calf. Lay Lay came to visit me a few times. We made plans to go out on a second date after she stood me up on the first one. Needless to say, I got stood up on that second date. I wish I could say that this was a misunderstanding in the planning; I got stood up two more times by her. I got the point and swore it wouldn't happen to me again.

After a few weeks have passed with me not being receptive to Lay Lay's advancements, Kia called me and asked what was wrong. I told Kia what her friend had done repeatedly to me. Kia was aware of the first time but was shocked to hear of the additional two times. She opened up and told me what the issue was. Kia told me that Lay's best friend told her that I wouldn't be worth her time.

I was not a serious money-getting dude, and I was a freaking hermit and a serious lame. She believed we were best friends since every time she came to see me, I was at home in my room on the computer. She was starting to think I was a weirdo. Kia got on her, telling her not to be a fool listening to her friend who didn't know shit about how to pick a good man with a great upside. Kia knew every nigga in the city and the surrounding cities. Any dope boy that was about anything, she knew them. I wasn't anything major, but she knew I didn't have a bunch of mileage or drama associated with me. I started to just talk with Lay Lay on the phone every night then. She missed many more calls than I took from her.

I received a call from Atlanta concerning my R&B group. LJ wanted me to bring my boys down so she could cut a few records with them. I loaded the boys and Tez up, and we got on the road.

We arrived in Atlanta, and LJ invited us into the home that she shared with her brother Woo. I started to get a look at the inside of how music is handled in the music industry. I didn't understand what it meant to "cut records down" in Atlanta. My guys were used to getting a track of music and taking it home to practice. Then return later to cut the record. We learned on a music industry level: You hear the music and you are feeling it. You write the record right there if it's not a completed idea already; you cut the record on the spot. My guys had to adjust fast and understand that this is a business, and you are dealing with professionals.

My guys were cutting music every day. We ended up meeting a songwriter named Wish from Georgia. He was being managed by a gentleman named G-Boi, also from Atlanta. G-Boi worked with Slip

Launch Slide records at the time from my understanding. He managed a number of southern rap artists like JT Money, the Poison Clan, Gucci Mane, and a host of others. G-Boi was particularly good friends with Woo.

G-Boi was in the studio as Wish was producing one of the records he was cutting for my guys. Woo was trying to get me to sign my R&B group to his label, Infrared. But this night took a big turn for my group. G-boi was a huge fan of my R&B group. He brought an executive from the Red Zone named Liz Gardner.

Red Zone was like the hottest product producer in the game at that time period, and Liz Gardner worked directly for Tricky and Shakespeare at Red Zone. Tricky was fresh off one of the biggest hits by TLC, "No Scrubs." Ms. Gardner fell in love with my group, Sadie. G-Boi showed her the bio of my group, and she wanted to see them and meet me. She stood in the studio and listened to the guys record. She stepped out of the studio and talked with G-Boi. G-Boi turned and called me out of the studio to talk. Ms. Gardner started to ask me a number of questions about the guys. She then told me if you leave with me right now. Shakespeare and Tricky will be doing a production for your group at the Red Zone tomorrow!

Woo emerged from the studio to hear her make her extremely aggressive offer to me. Big E started frantically calling me as he stood near Woo. Liz looked at me with a stern I and restated it: "Your group will be recording at the red zone tomorrow morning! being produced by the number one producer in the country."

Being clueless of the names of the producers and the production label "Red Zone," I turned and walked away from Ms. Gardner. Returning to the studio, Woo said "Man, what are you doing?" That white woman runs the business for Red Zone and can make your group! You've got to go back out there and at least accept her card, man."

Not understanding the night and day etiquette between a dope boy and business. I told Wish that I gave him my word concerning his label "Infrared" and my guys. Big E came to me and thanked me for being a man of my word. Woo was happy about the decision I had just made. I turn to Wish and say, "My word and loyalty are more important to me."

That word, "loyalty," is one of the most dangerous words in street indoctrination, causing critical harm. To most people's surprise, it's also used out of content: "loyalty" and its original context from the 1500s refers to a sovereign or sovereign government in relation to its subjects.

Wish met up with me to cut a few more records on my group and told me, "Man, you know Liz just signed a male R&B group over at Red Zone. Man, they had the same look and image as your group too. They are calling them B2K too. Their project is basically open, meaning they're accepting songs for their project or album."

After that whole opportunity that I mishandled, Big E and I developed a rather good relationship. I found out the Big E was from New York and was a prison guard at one point, and this is how he met Woo. Big E left his job at some point to come to Atlanta with Woo. Big E was a very die-hard loyal person.

The time came for me to return with my group back to Detroit. I recall Big E packing to go to Japan. Things were getting financially challenging for Woo, and it's labeled Infrared. Big E brought up the idea of him taking a chance with packing marijuana and taking it to Japan. I tried hard to talk Big E out of this idea. He felt he needed to take the risk or take one for the team to help fund the label. Within a week of me and the guys returning to Detroit, Wish told me that Big E had been caught in Japan at the airport with marijuana.

Big Dawg gave me a call, saying he wants to stop by and talk with me for a second. I told him that I was at the house and would swing by.

Then I hear doors closing outside the house. I looked out the window and said, "This mutha fucker always has an angle!" Big Dawg has Frank with him again. I let my brother in with his friend. Big Dawg asked me if his friend could use my computer to access the Internet? Plus, according to him, he wanted to speak with me off to the side.

We walked away from his friend, who was not on the computer. Big Dawg tells me how things are increasing for him and that we need to get together. I told him again that I had no interest in hustling anymore. Then he told me that he wanted my advice on some issues he was having with a few things concerning the loads of marijuana that were starting to come into him. I told him that I needed to address a few of his issues and thought that first I would mix him up a formula to address his remaining concern. Big Dawg was happy with the ideas I gave him and was looking forward to my special formula for the bigger issues. He collected Frank and went on his way.

“Where is my fucking high school cap and gown?”

“Wayne, and you already know where your shit is when it goes missing.”

I think to myself, "Oh my God, this Mutha Fucka. Tez done you got me again! I proceed upstairs to his room. His ass knocked out sleep, and I smacked his forehead, waking him up.

He wakes up yelling in shock, "Oh shit Oh shit"

I started yelling, "Where is my fucking high school cap and gown?"

Tez responded "It's over there man!" as he points in the direction of it. I turn to go and grab it, while Tez yells out: “Hold On Wayne.” I turned and looked back at him with a puzzling look on my face. Tez starts to speak in a hesitant manner, “you may want to allow me to get it cleaned for you first. .... THOUGH!”

“And why are you such a cheap ass that you are so willing to get it clean, Tez?”

“Do you remember the girl I went to my high school prom with? Well, you know I haven't talked to her in a while, right?” He continues, "I just so happened to run back into her, and she came by to visit. She was really upset because she registered for school late.”

“Tez, She is a sweet young lady, but what does this have to do with my cap and gown?” I asked.

“Well, she was nervous about having to see the dean of admissions, and I offered to help her.”

Getting more upset with him, I said, "So who are you and how was my cap and gown going to help, Tez?"

“Well, I became the dean of admissions, and I needed a gown. I felt that she needed to have alternative means of persuasion at her disposal! Just in case the meeting do not go in her favor. Education is very important now!”

I looked at him with a look of disgust and said, "You sick fuck!" Get my shit clean today, you fucking freak and stop needing my stuff when you decide to play dress up!

Hamburg has changed at this point. Gee, he's serving his seven-year sentence in the state prison. I wasn't hustling anymore either. We pretty much kept drug groups off the block. A group moved in on the block now, selling drugs. I wasn't in the business anymore. Gee’s family had a lot of females in their family. They have grown to be some very good-looking young ladies. The group down the street was a group of young men or young people coming into their own, and I'm an old head to them. I was already expecting some issues from these young cats anyway.

An older street hustler from the late 1960s and early 1970s named Con Man came to warn me of hearing these young guys talk about trying me. Con Man was a huge man and was a strong man in his day for the top hustlers of his day. Con Man told me that he told these young guys: Wayne ain't nothing to be fucking with. Don't let his quiet and laid-back appearance fool you. Con Man had been with me in a number of very challenging engagements. He has seen me. In game time, when you hear the whistling that passes your ears. The song of hollow-point bullets when they're flying past your head Con man knew that I even knew his secret... when it got too thick for him, and he chose life, leaving me to defend mine.

The young guys didn't heed the con man's warning. Maybe because he was a much older man at this point in his life, but he came to warn an old friend out of respect.

This is a holiday, and I head down the street on Hamburg, walking to Gee's aunt's house. She always cooked big meals on every holiday. The girls see me coming, so they come to hug me and say hi. These are the same girls I would buy ice cream off the ice cream truck for as little girls. They're all my little nieces, but old enough. The younger guys got upset because Gee Mane's little cousins all came over to me.

The tough guy of the group named Cheese had walked up on me and said, "Yo man! Don't save them, man!" Meaning, don't give them any money or call me a "sugar daddy." Now he had already shot a couple of guys in the neighborhood. Even one day chasing a car full of guys up the street in their car shooting at them, while, kids were out on the block, playing. But I'm no longer hustling, so I stay out of it all.

I gently tried to create some space between myself and him. I'm really not thinking much about it. Cheese then smacks my full arm and says, "FUCK NIGGA." Get your hands off me! Then he knocks my glasses off my face. Then say, "with those old ASS GLASSES!" which kind of hurt my feelings because I had been hearing from my friends that my glasses were getting old and no longer fashionable either. This is what I was thinking to myself at that moment.

I turned to a couple of guys I knew and said, "Man, you all need to talk to him," as they were pulling him back.

The guys in return tell me, "You should not have put your hands on him!"

I knew now that this is what the con man had warned me about. But, the two guys I was talking to, I had been taking care of for years until I stopped hustling. Proof of these being relationships based in commerce or business, I just shut my mouth and picked my glasses up calmly, then walked back to my house. I'm listening to my nieces get upset, saying, "Wayne is our family. While you do that?"

I was in a no-win situation and had to get out of it. I knew this was what they were looking to do. They were living in my shadow but felt they were free of it now. I know from experience that shit would get unbelievably bad on the block now. And it would not be long before they started breaking into my house and robbing me personally, looking to run me off the block. I was without my two black and silver 9-millimeter Ruger pistols. They had been taken in the raid on my house. I jumped in my car and went to see my dude, L. Dog.

L DOG And we had been friends since my late teens. I arrived at his house and told him what had just happened to me. On Hamburg, there were a lot of houses missing from the block around that time. L DOG He told me that he and his cousin were going to follow me back to my hood and set up on the next block over. I was to go on my block and bust off a few shots at those guys for forcing them through the field. L DOG And his cousin had two Russian-style AK-47s. Those would mow them down as they came through the field on the opposite block. I looked at L DOG; I'm thinking, maybe I should leave you out of this! I don't know exactly what I was thinking since we both came from the Reagan era of hustle. These kids weren't built like that.

I said, "Hell yeah!! That will take care of that SHIT period! But, for right now, let me hold your 40-caliber Glock. I will just hit you yourself if I need you."

I was just telling him what had happened to me. I didn't want to come murder the whole freakin' block! I hadn't even asked him to come anyway. I just wanted a pistol or two to defend myself. At that point, I just wanted to get out of there, but make sure he stayed home!

Being a seasoned vet of the crack epidemic in a wild, wild West, I understand the basis of a new drug era filled with violence on the street. I knew that if these kids didn't have that 100-yard stare, that empty stare in their eyes, there wasn't the truth because, after years of being in a war zone, you never forget what that looks like, making it clear to identify the impostor.

I made it back to the block, and all those guys were gone. I walked down the street to Gee Mane's aunts' house. Everyone was asking me if I was OK. I asked the girls what the whole thing was about. Everyone was outside—kids were playing and people were sitting on their porches. The weather was nice outside. But out of nowhere, two cars came flying up the street and slammed on the brakes in the middle of the street. Everyone started running into their houses, grabbing kids from outside, and running in, locking the doors. Even on the porch I was sitting on with Gee Mane's people, my extended family.

These guys jumped out of the cars and just started walking around in the middle of the street. My extended family left my ass on the porch and locked the door. But in all honesty, I did not even move from where I was sitting. I didn't move an inch either. My grandfather, Big Red, raised a man who knew how to stand. What had been done to me just didn't sit right with my soul.

He didn't have to say what he did about my glasses. I was working on getting a better pair anyway, I'm thinking.

One of the guys said it: "This nigga must think he is tough or something! You think you're too hard to run like those bitches, nigga?"

They started walking towards me. Cheese said, "Who do you think you are, nigga?!"

My glasses were sitting next to me, folded, on the cement porch. I picked my glasses up and unfolded them, putting them on, and saying, "I'm the guy with the very nice glasses, cheese!" I'm standing up, getting ready to get on the side of the cement porch. As I made the move, one of the guys yelled “He got a gun!” They all ran, jumped back in the car, and took off. But Cheese was hanging out of the back seat of the car with the back door open as it was speeding away.

Standing on the door jamb, “we will be back, BITCH ASS NIGGA!”

I sat back down on the porch and watch them speed off. Everyone came back outside, recapping everything they had witnessed. I didn't even say anything; I remained silent.

I came and said, "Let's go to the crib before these dudes come back."

“AND, THEN WHAT?” I yelled, frustrated. “I don't fuck with anyone! I stopped hustling and trying to do right. I even had my attorney, Lorence, create a music label for me to sign my artists. trying to be right. If I go to the house, they will just come there, and you guys would be in danger. I don't have any money anymore. You can't run and hide without money. This shit will end today. I'm going to push it to these NIGGAS, and we'll go on and see what they're built like, one way or another."

Then I hear some shouting coming from out of one of the fields: "WHAT'S UP NOW, NIGGA? What's up now?” I see Cheese yelling and waving a gun in the air. I ran, as did everyone else!

I pulled that fuckin' 40-cal Glock and started cutting them loose on that chicken shit ass bully actor. All that, what's up now, what's up now, SHIT is for a NIGGA looking to talk. Let's work, Nigga, and fuck the talking, was what I was thinking.

Cheese fell in the field without getting a shot off. I ran to the other field on the other side of the house, thinking that Cheese was down. I was expecting his crew to be coming through the opposite field. I knew I had to get over to that side fast and start firing on them before they made it through the field and set up by starting to spread out. I was surprised to get over to their side and not see any of his two car loads full of buddies.

I'm standing there scanning the field, looking for anything moving. “Wayne, Cheese is up and running towards Yvonne’s backyard.” I said.

I started running toward the abandoned car that was in the opposite field from where Cheese was laid, on the other side of Yvonne’s house. I didn't know what he may have been trying to get to through that field and the next block over. I thought I hit him when he went down.

I made it to the car and got low, equal to the passenger-side door. Waiting to ambush the bully fuckboy all over again, he came running full speed through Gee Mane’s mom's backyard, and I sprung up from the side of the car as he exited the yard fully into the field. I started cutting loose on him again, but I was looking to finish him this time. I shot until the gun locked back for a reload. As I'm dumping on Cheese, he shoots in the air two or three times as he does one of those western dances. similar to when the Cowboys tell the other guys to dance and start shooting at the ground.

I was shooting at Cheese from a distance of maybe 10 or 11 feet. Just the hood of a car and a few feet away, I didn't hit him once in two attempts. And I had every intention of someone dying that day—either him or myself. He's actually been shot, but by his own hand, not mine. After my second failed attempt at eliminating the neighborhood bully, He ran and hid in some bushes, according to what I was told later. He ended up shooting himself when a car like mine drove past the bushes he was hiding in.

Yvonne's husband asked me a question concerning that shootout I had in Hamburg a few days later. He asked me, "Wayne, I want to ask you some. I sat right here and watched you shoot it out with that boy. Then I see you run across right here, then off into the field, and go lean down by that car right there." he points to the car. "I just want to know one thing," he said, with a bewildered look on his face. How in the hell did you miss that boy? I was sitting here watching it all, and you were right dead smack up on him!"

I responded, "The Blessings of the creator was with us. God protects children and fools, as the saying goes, and the latter of the two applies to both of us: fools."

After being saved by the power of an animalistic rage within myself, I knew better from seeing so many in the past of that Reagan era fall based on animalistic egotism that had nothing to do with the basis of what we were all trying to accomplish: commerce. As the subject through the practice of business. But being the victim of so many bullies as a child, I needed to find the separation while moving forward and stop fighting the demons of the past, even if they deserved it in the present. I was taught by Larry Chambers that you cannot have your beef and get lots of money at the same time. To be effective at either, you must do one or the other.

Things just kept becoming more challenging for me. The highlight for me was the birth of my youngest daughter. I had to get a job to make sure I represented myself right. Being responsible for your family is necessary. There is no excuse for not making things happen for your family.

I was hired at a mortgage company and didn't know one thing about any of it either. I was drawn to it based off the fact you could create your own hours and you got paid for what you brought to the company. I signed a 50/50 contract with the company. I got my new little angels' mom a better car with my first check.

It wasn't long before I became the top earner in the struggling company. This was a predominantly white company. I started to buy lunch for the office two or three times a week. There was of course a dress code at the office also. Which I followed for a period of time. I switched my hours to later in the afternoon, just hours before the office closed. Therefore, I started to wear more relaxed attire based on the fact that I worked late into the night often. I was closing between 7 to 10 loans on an average month. I came in early one morning to pick up some paperwork, and a number of banks were there at the office promoting different programs their banks offered. This African American female from this one bank would always turn up her nose when seeing me come in late and not dressed the part. Which was warranted at times because I just looked homeless sometimes.

This one morning, I guess she had her feelings about this and asked another loan officer, "Does your boss know that he comes in the office dressed and looking like this," while she is pointing at me with this look of disdain.

The loan officer looked up to see whom she was referring to, then said, "SHIT," meaning he could come in here naked if he wanted to, then return back to his work. 10 minutes later, guess who decided to come introduce herself now? I'm never the one to hold grudges in business. I gave her about five loans right there as well. We actually became really good friends, and I even got to know her husband too. They were just really, really good people, even though it started off kind of rough.

A few months later, I met a real estate broker who had an interest in opening a mortgage company. looking for a partner to split the overhead of the office with. I met her through a friend who knew I had this interest as well. Her name was DJ, and we hit it off really well. I would be able to get 100% of my money outside of just office experiences, and any loan officers that came in would be split between the two of us.

I came out of the gate rolling, closing deals. I was making 15 to 20,000 a month at this point. I ended up meeting DJ's friend named Kevin. We ended up building a really close friendship. Kevin was an older gentleman that DJ had the hots for. He was the basis of almost all her business. Kevin started teaching me things about investing my money. I started to see the money I was making increase, I started to see a change in what I was making per month, which started to miraculously decrease for one reason or another having nothing to do with my production.

"Oh no, you are going to make more than me this month!" DJ shouted.

From that statement forward, my deal started to slow down. I was supposed to clear close to 50,000 that month. I ended up getting just a little over 35,000 that month. I also had loan officers ready to come in and bring business, but after that statement, she didn't agree to the loan officers anymore. I knew a change would have to be made in the near future.

Kevin was showing me a lot, and with all the money I was making, I started to bind up houses. I wasn't really even keeping money in my pocket anymore. I had to put that money to work. The plus to this is I was worth a few 100,000, following Kevin's plan. The downside is that I would go through periods of not having much end-of-month cash. Then, having work crews and making repairs was doing me in on the other end of things based on sometimes having to wait for closings or refinancings to happen on some of my properties.

Right at this moment, I get a call from my 15-month-old daughter's mother. She made me aware that the car I got her had been stolen. Things had gotten really rough on me, and on my new business, I wasn't planning as I spent money buying properties and repairing these properties. I had no idea about business credit, or even personal credit. Kevin tried to tell me about these windows of time where you have to float your business between additional earnings coming in. This ended up being a very taxing lesson learned.

My daughter's mother called me over to have a serious conversation. She started to express to me a few of her financial concerns and family problems that concerned her. Having her under a lot of stress, she was looking for me to have the answer. This was always the time I would tell her, "Calm down. I will take care of it."

I really did not have any answers for the financial problems at that moment. after just being lost for words. She just came out and asked me, "What are we going to do about these things?"

I responded by saying, "I don't know, Honey. I don't have any solutions right now."

She got really loud at me, not giving me the opportunity to explain to her that I was in between closings and I had some things coming, but I just needed a little time. “You don't have any idea?!”

I responded by saying, "I don't have any money on hand right now."

The scream that came from her said, "Well, you need to do something, Wayne!"

The only option is the street, and I don't know anyone anymore, so I said io her.

“Well, you need to do something, Wayne! Do something! I don't care what, but do something!”

The sound of the pain and stress she was under vibrated to the core of my soul. I just broke down and started crying. I loved this woman very much. She was my dream girl. I watched her for years and was always afraid to say anything to her. I even prayed to God that she would find favor with me. I would even drive my aunt's car up the block and hope she was on the porch. I finally took a shot one day, and she smiled at me.

Oh God, she smiled at me!

The most beautiful girl in the world finally chose me. I had to tell her about Big Red, my grandfather. How he rode with me in the buggy of his bike, whispering in my ear... ... the sacred ritual and what makes a man: providing, sacrificing, and accepting responsibility for family. I wanted to always make her proud of her choice. I want to have the answer to what was causing the other half of my soul distress. I have always had the answer. But not at this moment.

Lord God, please don't let her lose faith in my abilities as her man!

With my eyes red from crying and feeling like I fail myself as a man. I never wanted to feel this way again in my life. She gave herself to me and even decided that my life was worth reproducing. I will never feel this way again either. Big Red would not approve of my not being prepared.

The cell phone is ringing. 'Yo, Big Dawg" I said.

"What the FUCK is wrong with you, bro," Big Dawg stated.

"I'm over here fucked up, bro," I replied.

"What the hell is going on, little bro?" Big Dawg asked.

“I have spread myself really thin, and I have an emergency with my family right now. "I'm just crippled financially and totally wrapped up in my properties," I explained.

Big Dawg said, "I'm going to keep it totally 100 with you, bro." I don't have any money right now, but... Why don't you just come over here on the mile and run into me”

CHAPTER 4

"I DON'T HAVE ANY MONEY, BUT..........

"YO, BRO I AM on some 100 type SHIT now.......... I ain't trying to run into you and you stall me out." I expressed.

"LIL BRO, just come chop it up with me." Big Dawg said he started to laugh.

I'm headed over on the mile to go and talk with my brother Big Dawg. Thinking while I'm driving, this SOB is following one of America's top doctrines: never let a disaster go to waste. I'm sure Big Dawg has no clue of the doctrine, but he plans to take full advantage of the spot I'm in right now. I don't like what I know he was about to do to me. I really did this to myself, based on the lack of foresight. Not based on the lack of ability to foresee either.

'This fat ass nigga got the damn money too' I'm thinking.

I respect the game and he was better prepared than me, this time. Never break the rules, respect the next man's hustle and never knock the next man's hustle. Beware of all that count your money or the next. I was not going to count what wasn't mine; that's what Dee taught me years ago.

I arrived On the mile and my brother started to give me the details of, but........ now. The devil always lie in the details, but details is where I cut my teeth at very young age. My bro was no stranger to ability. Big Dawg went on to tell me that he really wanted to help me with the cash I needed to borrow.

"But....... I was thinking we can help each other" Big Dawg suggested.

"What do you have in mind bro?" I questioned as I gave him a stern look.

Big Dawg explained, "I have a shit load of marijuana that I need to move. Remember this Spanish dude name Frank, that I brought over to your house to use your Internet?"

" Man, I don't know nothing about marijuana!"

(From this point forward I will refer to marijuana as weed Or pounds.)

"Don't trip because they are our top flight rigs." he replied. Then Big Dawg pointed to some excessively big white bundles shaped like bales of hay.

Big Dawg told me that Frank has started to ship him loads weed. He had already started to move it. His concern was that he wasn't moving it at the pace that was to Frank's liking. Big Dawg also told me that those big bundles were called bales of weed. Each bale contained 25 pounds or so within it. He told me that he would charge me $925 a pound for a bale. I put the bale of weed in my car and headed home. Big Dawg told me that pounds of weed were going for 1000 to 1050 Dollars in the city. I have always worked with coke not weed.

$925 I would have had to pay my brother a little over 23,000 per bale. He advised me to let each pound go at $1000 per pound. He told me only to bring him 20,000 of the 23,000 off the bales. I would need to bring him 20,000 each off the two bales of weed that he gave me. I will clear 10,000 after I've moved two bales of weed. Arriving home but the pain from not measuring up to what I committed to in my heart was much greater.

My dream girl had just awakened, a sleeping giant. She was the one that pleaded with me to never sell drugs again. Then to just change that when things were challenging for a moment. I swear that I wouldn't allow myself to not measure up to what Big Red whispered in my ear while I sat in the buggy of his bike. An accountable man that didn't make excuses for not measuring up toward God made me to be: A MAN.

The need for her to believe in me was of utmost importance to me. I would now live by these words I deemed best. I would live and die by what I felt was best. I just didn't want to feel this level of ineptness again. But my love for her was deeper than I could put words to. She is just a little mean sometimes though............. With such a bad bad attitude!

I'm thinking of how to move this. I had to reach out to people who knew a thing or two about weed. I called my oldest daughter's mother and asked for her brother's number. I called him and asked him to swing by my house. Once Big I arrived, I told him my situation and showed him the bales of weed. BIG I asked me to excuse him for a minute so he could go make a few calls. While BIG I was making his calls, I was freaking out.

You don't know about these huge fucking things, you won't be able to move it, and making only $75 to $50 off each pound isn't worth my time; trying to store it There is no way it can be hidden at all!

Big I walked in and said, "Can you get another bale? I need two."

"Are you serious?" I asked while looking at Big I with disbelief.

"Bro I'ma need to take that one bale with me. I'ma come back with 50 racks of money for the bale I'm taking and another thing I want if you can grab it really fast. Can you get it though?" Big I questioned in a firm business tone,

"I got you." Was my response a Big I?

"Big Dawg, I'm outside" I called him from the driveway. I walked into the house and told him that I was about to bring him those 40 racks on the two we talked about. "And I need two more, bro."

Big Dawg said, "Man, you're back popping and fast too." He told me that he was going to give me 4 bales, but this would be at its regular price of $925. I left with the four bales and one straight to my house in Hamburg. BIG I dropped the 50 racks off, grabbed the extra one he had just paid for, and took another that he would owe me for the next morning. I shot the 40 at Big Dawg after taking my 10 racks. I received a call from Player D. He wanted to run and took me on the Burg.

Player D shows up, and his eyes get big when he sees the work. "Let me get one of them bales and I will be right back," Player D said. He returned with the money for the one he took and the last one I had. That's another 50 racks now. Player D told me he needed more. I told him I wasn't sure if I could or not. I told him I would call him

"Big Dawg, I'm outside"

He let me in, and I gave him $66,000 on the 69,000 and some change while I was with him. I gave Big Dawg every bit of his money I had in order to come closer to convincing him to pay me the one bill Big I still owes me. I told Big Dawg I would catch up with him in the morning on the rest owed to him.

Then I said, "I need more, bro."

"No, hell no, Wayne!" You're running through all my shit I was just trying to help you out! Don't you fuckin' Play with me, you Mutha Fucka! I'm running, and don't you try to stall me out, bro?" Big Dawg continued , "I will give you two more bales, but at $950 a pound! Don't bring your ass back for nothing or until Frank sends more."

Just two bales, but a growing demand for way more. I hit Player D and told him the situation. He told me that I needed to break them down into pounds now. He brought two really large bins and cut the bales open. Player D broke the weed, still shaped into a large bale, apart. Taking large zip lock plastic bags filled each with 450 grams of weed. Weighing a pound, I was able to see why everyone wanted the bales and not broken down into pounds. Mexico uses the Metric system of kilos when weighing. 1K is 2.2 pounds on state side. Therefore, 25 pound bales were actually about 27 pound apiece. Which helped me understand why I would most always see guys with the zip-lock plastic bags with weed in them. Dudes that get the bales never wanted to allow the street dudes to get the extras. Well, that would be changing soon for me. I didn't give a damn about the extras. This practice would be no different with any import company from abroad; the importing company keeps the extras commerce.

My R&B group stopped by to practice. The whole damn house smelled like weed and was very strong. They are practicing and arranging songs. They had another guy named Sam stop over. Sam used to sing in a former R&B group with one of the guys that's now in my group .

Sam came in and said, "DAMN, somebody got the good good stuff," meaning marijuana. Sam saw the bin with the pounds of weed in it. Sam asked me to let him get three of those. “I know someone who will grab these right now.”

I didn't believe him; he is a singer-dude, and don't know folks like this. I was only willing to let him take one. Well, my guys were singing, and Sam kept leaving and returning with pounds and money. My group would always practice for an hour and a half. Sam brought me almost 20 racks going back and forth within that time. It was late at this point, and I only had about 10 pounds left, so I let him take those overnight to pay me in the morning.

The next day, all my debts had been cleared. I want to see my brother Big Dawg, and when I cleared my end up with him, he looked at me and said, "NIGGA! You are fucking back! I've been trying to get you back with me, like when we were teenagers. I didn't know you would move that shit like that.” little did he know neither did I. “Bro, I need to know:

are you with me now? Can we put the band back together again?" Big Dawg expressed to me.

I reluctantly said, "Yeah, I guess." Then he started to catch me up to speed on things with Frank and Mario, Frank's brother.

Big Dawg told me that he was receiving 600 pounds from Frank. Out of that 600, he would get 300, and the white boy named JD would get the other 300. JD was from Arizona and was the one in charge of the load. JD would handle the semi when it came in, and Big Dawg and his dudes would hit the truck and unload it.

After listening to my brother tell me the order of operation, I didn't like the way things sounded. I was just coming on board and needed to see it actually function. It didn't sound organized at first hearing.

Big Dawg spoke again. "I need you to come along with me. in about a week. I want you to start running this. The load was on the road, and JD had just flown into the city. I spoke with JD, and he started telling me about the men and the money that can be made."

I asked him how often they didn't receive it. JD went on to tell me once a month and how fast the weed moves during that month. I'm thinking like once a month. Do you call that shit fast?

JD and my brother were splitting 600 pounds. I did a little over half of what my brother, Big Dawg, was getting from JD. The last time, I was just getting started. Not to mention I did that in a little over 24 hours.

The load arrives, and I'm present when they unload the truck. There was no order to this process. We split the work with JD, and he went to the west side of Detroit. Big Dawg and his crew of misfits headed to the eastside of Detroit. Once we made it back east, Big Dawg gave a bale to the three guys that were with us. He gave me four bales. I told him I needed more than those four bales. He spun me by telling me to wait until you get rid of the four bales and then come back. Then he even raised the price on me again, charging me $975 a pound! I felt like Big

Dawg was really screwing me over. But I know how to play the game. I knew that I improved JD's turn-around time.

I had also seen that the load was not 600 pounds anymore. I saw 32 bales; 24 bales would have equaled 600 pounds. There was an increase of 200 pounds. I could tell from the way JD was talking about the load when he landed, but call me crazy, he was looking directly at me when giving me details and messages from Frank. My brother was the one he had history with, and this was JD's first time seeing or talking to me. There was something afoot. And as usual, my big brother didn't see it. I just stayed silent and took the bullshit he was throwing my way.

I left with the four bales and headed to the Burg. I've reached out to my guys L DOG, Player D, Big I, and Sam. Between these guys, I had a little under $250,000 in cash. The issue is that I only had 100,000 worth of work, and I knew Big Dawg was going to try to act like he didn't have it. This is also why I didn't have issues with him taxing me so hard. This would make him give it up based on the additional profit he would gain.

"Big Dawg, I need to run into you on 911." I said it to myself. I walked in the house with a carry-on-size case. "There are the 975 racks I owe you on and a little over 146 additional racks here, as I'm staring right at him. What does 146 come out to be in work?"

Though he stated as he laughed, "Hee hee, hee hee. I need another 6 bales to complete this move here, bro."

"Well, Wayne, you know I don't have that much. Plus, you know I still have three bales in the streets too." He said.

"24 bales equal 600 pounds in total. I counted 23 in total, and I personally loaded 16 for you. If my math is correct, those three still in the street and the four I'm cashing you out for now would leave 9 bales remaining" with a very warm but aggressive smile.

Big Dawg looked at me in silence and said, "Hee hee hee."

I almost forgot who I was dealing with here. “Hee hee hee! I'm just going to give you the rest of them, bro.”

“The other nine” I said to let him know what I was expecting.

As I got ready to leave, Big Dawg said, "I guess we are going to just be out of work for the remainder of the month."

This is how my brother asked me a question about what he should do. I turned to him and said, "You need to put a call in to Frank and tell him you are all wrapped up."Frank is going to pull that other one from JD and give it to you. JD is not going to like this either. This will end up being the beginning of the end of him overseeing you, or he will become your enemy. Word of advice, I don't trust two of the three guys I saw you give that work to. When we pull that other work from JD, only tell the one and remain silent with the other two.”

"Why do you say that about them with two?" he said.

“Because those two have no intention of fully paying you. And you will need that window of time because things will be changing fast. Leave them on the old 30-day schedule. You can thank me for this maneuver later. It will save lives.”

Later that same night, Big Dawg called me. “ bro. Remember what you were saying to me earlier today? Well, I did that, and we got the green light! Hee hee hee hee, be ready to run into JD first thing. Will you be coming all the way and first thing two?”

This was basically him asking me if I would be paying off the rest of what I owed on the nine bales. "Sure," I replied.

The following morning, Big Dawg can't even get anyone to drive the van with the work in it. He is putting these guys to work, but they left him to drive the van with the work from JD. I told him that you are too important, you should never be left to do some shit like this by your crew. I drove the van to get the weed and back.

I told him, "Fuck those dudes!" I took all the risks, and I'm ready to get rid of them all too. I got rid of it all just as I said, and I ended up giving my brother like 700,000 off this load. I don't even think I made 18 racks off all that shit. Now if I would have broken everything down in pounds and not sold bales. I would have picked up an additional 50 or 60 racks, but it would have been a much slower turnover. I was playing chess with my brothers' bosses and setting in motion a chain of events. By allowing Big Dawg to think he was fooling me and charging me all this unnecessary money. This kept my brother busy, self-deceived, and drunk on his own ego. He was starting to think he was the architect of what was happening. He couldn't see the language I was speaking.

My investment in the houses will start to change, because the houses were just sitting there, and now the housing market is responding favorably to my properties. My dear friend Kevin had just bought a building that was once a bank. He wanted to open a real estate investment company there. Kevin was impressed with the fact that I fully committed to his guidance. Kevin asked if I wanted to go into business for myself. I was excited about the idea. I had to call my attorney, Lorence, and ask for his counsel . It turns out that he was super excited for me, saying, "Donnie, I'm finally getting you into something productive." Lorence was always on my bumper about establishing business outside of what I was doing. He started right away developing my company, my real estate investment company.

My cell phone rings. "Yo, little brother, let's go up to Capers and grab a steak. We need to chop it up on some 100 type shit."

"Big Dawg," I question. "Yeah, this is me. You over the way?" meaning are you close to your house?

"For sure," I answered.

"I will see you there in 20." and With that, he hang up.

Our team arrives in about 15 minutes. I'm sitting in the parking lot, and Big Dawg pulls up on me and pulls next to my parking spot. We get out of the car and head toward the entrance of Capers Restaurant.

I said, "What is this shit All about bro?”

“I got a situation on the table, and I need you to come sit down with me and talk." He responded. We walk into the restaurant, and he walks past the fuckin' hostess.

I'm looking and saying to myself, "What the fuck? What was that shit about Frank?"

CHAPTER 5

MY BROTHER'S KEEPER

FRANK AND ANOTHER LATINO guy were seated already. "MUTHA FUCKIN, Frank," I said! I couldn't believe he brought me into another situation blindly. I keep asking this fat motherfucker to not do this without giving me some kind of idea of what to expect.

Big Dawg and I are greeted by Frank and his heavyset friend. Frank introduced his friend to me as Mario. Mario was already told no by my brother, Big Dawg. These two were showing every tooth in their heads, just smiling at each other.

Frank began thanking me for attending on such short notice. Then Mario cut in and said, "Yeah, because Big Dawg was telling us he couldn't reach you for a couple of days." with a pause, looking for a response or some kind of reaction from me.

"Well, we had a chance to talk over a number of other options with our friend Big Dawg over those couple of days," Frank interjected. I looked frank and smiled after he made the statement, breaking that silent moment. Frank was much more polished and in favor of my brother, Big Dawg. Mario was the polar opposite of honest; he was very blunt and borderline rude. Clearly, I'm not a fan of my brother either.

Mario was looking for a possible division or looking to start 1. I was an instant fan of Mario's straight-forward style. But, it had to be made clear from the beginning: in this chess game, I'll be the one pushing pieces, not being pushed.

"We have noted the turnover rate has decreased over the last two or three shipments," Frank stated. "And the only addition to what has been going on based on a 30-day timetable is you, Wayne. Mario and I increase the load two or three times, with shorter and shorter turn-around times. We couldn't get much accomplished over the phone with Big Dawg. Now that we are here on an unscheduled visit... ... two days in the making." as Frank chuckled slightly.

My brother Big Dawg is silent with a very unsettled look on his face. Frank continues with catching me up to speed with the details of the last two days of conversation with Big Dawg, when I was not able to be reached. Frank wanted to increase to 1000 pounds on the next shipment and continue to increase by 500 pounds per shipment afterwards. He also made me aware of his target goal for us, which is 3500 to 4000 pounds, or basically 2 tons of marijuana. I didn't say anything while listening.

"Big Dawg was excited and agreed to our offer. Frank smiled while expressing this to me.

"But Big Dawg, I was told that there was no deal without confirmation of your knowing and agreeing," Mario stated while looking at my brother..

"I can't agree to something or disagree when this is not my relationship." I expressed, " However, if my brother agrees, I'm going to help him in whatever way he asks me to."

Frank looks at my brother and says, "What is it going to be, Big Dawg?"

"I already told you I agreed two days ago," said Big Dawg.

"We know you agreed, but you did not want to tell Wayne anything, Big Dawg. In order for there to be a deal, Wayne has to be your partner," Frank firmly states.

Big Dawg sits there with an angry look on his face and refuses to answer these terms. “What is it going to be, Big Dawg?” Frank asked in an agitated tone.

"This is bullshit, Big Dawg," Mario said. “You know we can't send you that much weed! Someone will freaking take it from you, Big Dawg! They're not going to fuck with him, my friend.” Mario states angrily in a tone of voice towards my brother.

Big Dawg, just set them down.

They're quiet for a moment longer. “See, this is what I'm always telling you, frank.” Mario started his case with passion.

“Fuck it, he can be my partner.” Big Dawg, exhaled.

Frank looked at me and said, "Wayne, you are Big Dawg's equal partner now. You are to handle the logistics of shipment, storing the marijuana, and protecting it.” I gave Frank a nod of my head in agreement. I had a number of issues with the agreement, but I stayed quiet for that moment.

After a little more detail on things, Big Dawg and I left the restaurant. Mario suggested that we all get together to celebrate at Hustler's adult entertainment on the grass if we run 8 mile that night. I have always been a huge fan of gentlemen's clubs. I knew there would be much more to this.

I expressed to Big Dawg the way he allowed himself to be viewed. I also told him that he runs things the best way. I just made him aware that I would support him. But I told Big Dawg that we needed to revisit the terms he agreed to with Frank and Mario. We could not allow those two to increase the amount of weed without lowering the price. The price needed to reflect the volume received. I didn't talk with Big Dawg about him not sharing that his friends wanted to have me in the discussion. I couldn't say I was in shock either, though.

We met up with Frank and Mario at the strip club. Big Dawg brought his crew of misfits to class twice, which I felt was an awfully bad idea. Knowing your team is a reflection of you, confirming Mario's assessment of you.

Mario spent most of the night talking to me. I took it upon myself to engage him in bringing the price down as the loads increased. I will say that I enjoyed the relationship with Mario. We seem to have always had heated exchanges. But we always kept business at the forefront, and we shot it straight from the hip. Needless to say, we argued about the lowering of the price. Mario's accent got worse as he argued. He often switched to Spanish in our heated exchanges. I wouldn't know what the hell he was saying as he moved between English, Spanish, and whatever other dialect he would come up with. I just repeated my version of some of the names he called me in Spanish back to him.

Mario and I came to an agreement after all. "Si you pinche Bandito," Mario agrees. "I'm not...PINCHE MARICON, TU BANDITO! OK, YOU FUCKING CROOK. BUT I'M NO FUCKING PUSHOVER, YOU CROOK!"

I didn't really enjoy myself too much that night. I have never been the smoking and drinking type.

"Big dawg, where is my candy?" Mario screams as he flicks his nose. Then you had a group of grown men—the same group of misfits I mentioned above. I'm just sitting there watching this circus of underworld dysfunction. I knew it wasn't good politics to leave early, but I was stuck for the moment. Looking at Mario flicking his nose and watching a Big Dawg group of misfits try to appear more gangster than the other I have never really been the type to be around crowds. Fortunately for me, Frank came up with the idea of going to another club. I excuse myself from that suggestion. Mario pulled me to the side before I went my own way. "My friend, make sure you are ready for next week," said Mario.

"Big Bro, I have no need for your guys anymore." I explain. "I have a group I will be using to hit the truck. I don't even need you there."

Big Dawg didn't have an issue with that at all. I know that we need to separate the crews that distribute and unload the work. With Big Dawg built, he couldn't sustain a hit by law enforcement; separation of functions was of the utmost importance; this became the first order of business.

Always act as if you are being watched. Gerald Lorence.

Moving accordingly has been the order of the day for me. This needed to be part of the thinking process of this group I put together. Also, cutting down on careless acts or actions I had no patience for anything less than a determined focus. This action was of the utmost importance to me. Everything and one spot needed to be transported from point A to point B. Without this successful action, there would be no C, D, E, F, G, etc. A big mistake during this transaction equals checkmate!

My guys are posted in the yard at 6:30 AM that morning. I'm on the jump-off (cell phone) with Big Dawg, and he tells me the truck is 20 minutes away. I settled the boys down because this will be the first time for them. telling them that there isn't any need to do a lot of thinking. Follow my instructions and watch everything flow.

"He is all yours now." Big Dawg cut communication. I hear the tractor-trailer pulling into the yard. Normally, the driver drops the trailer and takes off. Not under my watch; this would not be a lengthy process. My guys hit the tractor trailer like locusts in a field of vegetation.

I see it going to Big Dawg. I'm in a car about four car lengths behind the load. while there is one car directly behind the load. I'm in my feelings, PINCHE MARIO (FUCKING MARIO). The first load is supposed to be just 1000 pounds and forty bales. A total of 10 U-Haul boxe. I counted 15 boxes unloaded off the tractor trailer and loaded into the Uhaul. Each freakin' box had 100 pounds, for a total of 4 bales of weed. 10 boxes is 1000 pounds... but 15 boxes is 60 bales and a total of 1500 pounds of marijuana. Make no mistakes about it. This is the same process as one company making a shipment that's received by another company. Anything other than what's on the Bill of Lading is an issue. It's just our Bill of Lading was made verbally. Based on the illegal nature of the business, but make no mistake about it, it's still business principles: commerce.

The car I'm in flicks the high beams, and the car following right behind Uhaul is a signal to pull off, with the load. I jump in behind to take it into its being the dropping point. Another 10 minutes of driving after the original tale car drops off, we arrive. I hit Big Dawg with a WE GOOD, then hang up the jump off (CELL PHONE).

My team, which I am still developing, was on point. I hit those boys up, and they went to work. Big I grabbed 8 bales, Sam grabbed 4 bales, and I let Player D have one bale. Player D wasn't really a trustworthy person. Around this time, his name was coming up in a number of people's murders.

Player D's name was coming up in terms of giving up locations on guys when they were murdered and actually setting them up directly in other cases. My good brother Devan would often warn his then-beautiful wife about this character. Even though it took time to tell me long before I had anything to talk about, watch Player D because when someone gets robbed or killed, Player D just seems to have pulled off or just pulled up on the scene. Player D at one point used to be the one giving me work after my cousin Dee and Jan were killed. Which was not long after my guy FATMAN, my cousin Dee's best friend, made sure to keep me afloat, and I would never forget that. I was doing nothing super major at that time.

I also recall Devan once telling Gee and myself, "Y'all think player D is just such a great guy, because y'all ain't never had shit! You better get something, and you better be very careful dealing with him." These words were coming back to life for me as my favorite girl never hesitated to keep me on point during my rise and not wanting to see what happened to her husband Devan happened to me; that's his beautiful wife Kia.

Big Dawg wanted just 250 of the 1500 pounds that were sent. I reached out to L-Dog and gave him four bales to move. I ended up running to my incredibly good friend named Hustleman. Hustleman heard about some of the moves I was putting down. He ran into me and had a major issue. His source had just gone down, and he needed work. I showed him what I had, and he loved it. He then told me he wanted to buy 8 bales and asked me for another 4, saying he would catch up with me in the morning.

Three days passed, and Big Dawg hit me. "Yo, little bro, I don't have any weed left; only people owe me money. One of my guys is done, and I want to send him to you. He owes me $50,000, and I told him to give it to you, too."

"Gotcha, I replied. His guy came over to see me on the Burg. This wack ass nigga must have thought I was like my brother.

"Yo Wayne, I got 15,000 right here, but I need another bell because I got a dude that wants it right now, and he's got all the money on deck right now." my brother' s guy expressed tolmay me. I put my hand out to receive the money he had first; after receiving that, I extended my other hand, and he gave me a puzzled look. Then he asked me, "What's up?" with a concerned expression.

I responded with, "You said you had someone with money right now for another bale of weed, right?"

"I have to take it to him first."

"You won't be taking anything unless I have without money from this mysterious person, or you hand me the other 35 racks while you owe my brother, Either way you choose, but one or the other must hit my hand." I expressed adamantly. The freaking nigga stormed off in anger.

I'm thinking, *"Get the FUCK out of here with that weak ASS con act. Nigga, you've fucked up my brother's money and are trying to get more to try and make up!"*

I wanted to make sure that he canceled himself out like the majority of the guys my brother was dealing with, just being a good dude trying to make sure guys eat, and they're playing games, leaving him stuck with the ticket while they're out here moonlighting as real hustlers. Get the FUCK on with that neighborhood hustler mentality, FUCK BOY!

Everybody came back in and paid me. Hustleman, pay me for the four bales he owed me; he brought another $300,000 with him for 12 more bales. Big I and Sam cleaned up the other nine bales. I ended up talking with Big Dawg for just under 1.2 million words in a big travel suitcase.

Big Dawg, 25 was supposed to come off the price at 1000 pounds and drop 25 dollars for every additional 500 pounds. This is what Frank and Mario agreed to. Why did they send 1500 pounds when it was supposed to be just 1000 pounds first? Big Dawg was just happy with any increase in production or product. He wasn't thinking about how the more volume you move, the cheaper it gets from them.

"Hee hee hee, man, why are you tripping about that shit Big Dawg?"

"I'm going to get what they agreed to at the right number next time," I said as I walked away. This is another element of business, and this is actual business: anytime there is an increase in volume of any product, it must always be reflected in a reduction in price based on volume. These true attributes of business are not limited to legal or illegal business because it is all business: commerce.

"Taking you back to the exchange with his guy he sent to me, that owed him $50,000. Big Dawg never told me 50,000, and I was not supposed to do anything except accept the money he gave me. Big Dawg told me the guy owed him around $50,000. Which became 50,000, I knew this was a very emotional guy here. “You still owe 35,000, but after you handed me 15,000 for my brother.”

The guy responded, "I just gave you 15,000, and I only owe your brother 30,000 now, Wayne," he emotionally yelled.

As I got in my car, I heard, "PINCHE BANDITO’S, Frank, Mario, and... BIG DAWG!!”

"There is no greater joy than to deceive the deceiver." NICCOLO MACHIAVELLI

CHAPTER 6

ARIZONA BABY DOLL

WE LOST SO FREAKIN' much because we couldn't see the ebb and flow or a life current. I'm thinking as I'm driving. This fat fucker is more interested in holding me down and blocking me from something I clearly don't want. I don't give a fuck about him over-charging me. Big Dawg keeps thinking in pounds and bales, while I'm thinking in metric tons and moving volume. What he is doing to me now is of no importance. I'm going to leave him busy tricking me; this isn't important... for now! but we'll be of significant use soon.

Pulling into my driveway, I exit the car. Big Dawg is a very good person, but he just can't put sibling rivalries to the side for a moment. as I unlock my door and enter the house. “Why is it pitch black in this freaking house?” As I move cautiously to the dining room, thinking; “ where is the light switch?”

Breaking a major safety rule: always leave certain lights on in the house and never enter a house that's pitch black inside.I hear some slight movement; oh, shit, I'm fucked. I’m thinking.

"Yeah, yeah..........You better not fuckin move.." The voice whispers.

I stopped right in my fuckin tracks. "Yeah, Yeeees, Bitch, you better not fuckin move." just a little louder than a whisper now.

"As soon as this fuck gets a little closer upon me, I’m jumping out this fucking window," I said to myself.

"You didn't think I would catch you, huh? WELL I GOTCHA ASS NOW & YOU ARE MY SLUT!" The voice exclaimed very loudly.

" WHAT THE FUCK.........Tez??!!" ! My heart is racing as I rush to turn on the light in the dining room. "YOU FUCKING SON OF A BITCH!!! WHAT I TOLD YOU ABOUT THESE LIGHTS." as my eyes are adjusting to the sudden light." Oooooooooooh, Lord, We're Going to Jail! WHAT ARE YOU DOING TO THAT DAMN GIRL??"

Tez is down on his knees, but he's leaning back some, and the young lady is on her knees, leaning forward with her head face down in his lap; the young lady's hands are handcuffed behind Tez back. Tez is leaning backward while on his knees. The girl's head is her only way to keep balance.

Partly talking to me and the young lady, Tez said, "Yo, Wayne, it's cool man! Don't you fuckin move! You are still under arrest!" as he is thrusting on her face.

"This is fucking rape or something, and you are doing it in the front room of my FUCKIN house," I yelled.

"NAAAAAAW, she loves this shit here, man! Yeah, yeah, yeah. Don't you fuckin' stop because I'm not talking to the police chief either!" He says to her.

"OH HELL NAW NIGGA!" I got really upset. "DON'T YOU FUCKIN MAKE ME YOUR CO DEFENDANT IN YOUR FREAKY ASS FETISHES."

" Baby, tell him that you're cool with this," as he grabs the back of her hair, pulling her free to speak. With tears rolling down one of her eyes and she is trying to gather herself together to speak to me.

"yes, this has become a norm for us.". as she shyly giggles.

Tez grabs the hair of this young lady and plants it back in his lap, saying, "You know you are a three-time felon and you're facing life! WORK WORK!" He yells to her,

"Tez! Don't you see me standing right here?" as I push him over on his side.

He gets upset with me and says, "Come on, Maaaan, don't fuck this up! WE GOT A REALLY GOOD THING GOING HERE!"

"Tez! I'm about to go order something to eat. Don't be here when I get back."

As I walk out the door, he says to the young lady, "Where did you put the key to the handcuffs?" We've got to get out of here!"

Big Dawg and I received a few loads at 1500 pounds and two at 2000 pounds, and now I am in pretty much full control of all operations. The loads coming in and Big Dawg would take about 250 to 300 pounds off the load. I did away with the Big Dawgs crew because they didn't pay. They eliminated themselves. I was just amazed at how his guys just flat out wouldn't pay all of what they owed Big Dawg. That was short lived with me though. I wasn't having anyone play games with the paper.

Big Dawg reached out to me and asked if I wanted to go down to Arizona with him. This was my second time turning him down on his invitation. I guess he forgot about his bragging about having to fly down to Phoenix to attend a huge party Frank had invited him to. But for some reason, he was not even boarding this flight to Phoenix. I also noted that shipments stopped coming as well. I pretty much figured out why he stopped coming to me: Big Dawg couldn't get in touch with me about the invite to this huge party in Phoenix. Big Dawg kept doing the same thing but expecting different results.

After a few weeks passed, Big Dawg wanted to be forthcoming with me on this Phoenix trip. only after I told him that I did not want to accompany him for the fourth time. "Come on, bro. You're on the bull-shit.. Frank hasn't sent anything else because we haven't come down to talk yet." Big Dawg admitted. "Buy the tickets." Asshole, with an evil eye. This is my fucking brother. Trying to pull all kinds of angles while shooting himself in the foot

Big Dawg got us on a flight out of Phoenix the next day. This was a 3 1/2- to 4-hour flight from Detroit to Phoenix. This budget baller actually booked coach tickets. I had the pleasure of being in the middle seat while he got the aisle seat. My brother is a very big dude (6'1" and a generous 375). He had to ask for an extra seat belt. I was in for a very long, 4-hour flight.

We landed in Phoenix after a very long flight for me. JD picked Big Dawg and I up from the airport. "Damn Wayne!! You missed a slamming party, and we still couldn't get you down here. We have been waiting on you." JD is smiling and adds me to their carefree conversation.

We got checked into the Hilton Hotel. JD made Big Dawg and myself aware of what to expect in the following days. We would get out on the town that night, and Mario would be along the following day to drive us to Tucson. During the ride, Mario would fill Big Dawg and in on several things.

That night, JD called Big Dawg and told him we should meet him down in the lobby. "Be ready to party." JD yells through the phone. Once we are picked up, JD heads to the strip club. As we are entering the club, I note its name: Body Shop.

"SENORAS HERMOSAS," I whisper as I look around the club. Latino mujeres everywhere I look

"Yo En Amor." JD had a short little Mexican fellow with him, and they've pretty much stayed with me. I would come to see how useful he was. A few of the girls didn't speak particularly good English. I begin to understand that in this world, I am a guest, and Spanish is the first language. There it is; it was the first time I felt in my element.

But it was a brand new adventure in a foreign land, or at least it felt that way. My little Spanish friend tapped me and said, "Look, amigo. This girl keeps looking at you." I turned my head to look in the direction of his finger. I see a cocoa complexion goddess. even complexion all over her body, with a refined shape that could only have been the work of a profound sculptor. I turned back to my friend.

"I think she is looking for someone behind me."

We continue to enjoy the night. Everyone was getting pretty wasted at this point. I'm not a drinker, but I was sitting down and enjoying the dancers I was receiving. "My friend, this girl is looking for you again." as he is pointing with his eyes. I looked over at the direction of his eyes. "Oh my God, this bad BITCH is looking right at me.". I'm looking at her in disbelief. I turned my eyes away in rejection of her aggressive, direct gaze at me.

I was back to enjoying the night, and I leaned over to my little friend, who was beginning to speak, and saw his eyes getting big and staring out in front of me. I follow his eyes; oh shit, she is headed toward me now... oh shit oh shit what the fuck! Damn, she is fine!

She is standing right in front of me as I'm seated in a VIP traditional style cushion single seat, like a loveseat but a single chair. I gathered myself and displayed a calm but quiet arrogance. And she stood in front of me with firm confidence. I examined her feet and moved slowly up her body to connect with her eyes. The look was not one of desire but more of "have a look" to inspect the level of quality.

Breaking the silent non-verbal standoff, "So what does a girl have to do in order to receive an invite?" she states with a hint of an attitude. allowing the question to linger a while arrogantly saying, "take it". She turns and seductively sits in my lap while placing her smooth, even coco-toned legs across me, putting her arm around my shoulders and leaning into the side of my head, releasing an airy "taken"

I smiled ever so lightly. BAD BABY...... BAD BAAAAAAAAAD BABY!!!! as my mind ran wild.

We started to talk and really connect with each other; she asked for my name and told me hers in exchange. I'm starting to allow myself to enjoy that moment. I would tastefully compliment her. I allowed her to see that I was impressed by her skin tone and found her incredibly soft to the touch. “Can I call you Baby Doll, Miss Perez?” I asked her. Her face lit up!

“Yes!” she replied. She stayed with me, on my lap, with her soft legs across me.

“Baby Doll, why haven't you moved since you accepted your invitation earlier?” I asked.

“When I said taken, I wasn't referring to when they were invited. I want it all; I took you.” With a sassy look on her face, shaking my head and smiling, "BAD ATTITUDE. BAD BAD ATTITUDE!" I was impressed, and her interest piqued my interest. Baby Doll and I exchange information. I did know how paramount she would be to my life. She literally changed my life. I left the club that night to get ready for a big day the following day.

“Big Dawg, I will arrive to get you guys in an hour. Be ready.” then Mario ends the cell call.

We are riding with Mario, and he appears very excited to see me. It just never appeared that he cared for my brother Big Dawg that much. Seems more like Mario tolerated my brother more than anything else. Mario seems to have a lot to talk about. Mario wants to discuss another increase in marijuana. He wanted to go from 2000 pounds to around 2 tons of weed now. We talked about a number of different subjects and concerns, but all related to the business at hand. Mario mostly talked, and Big Dawg responded to him generally.

I noticed that he was watching my facial expressions through the rearview mirror. This made me start to keep my facial expressions to a minimum. I did have moments when my brother would say or agree to things that weren't to my advantage today. I will turn my face towards the window as if I were looking across the desert, but out of view of Mario's rearview mirror.

Only to hear Big Dawg say, "Come, Mario, why in the hell do you keep playing with the passenger side mirror? The only thing I can see through it is the back of the truck! Man, you are so crazy! Hee hee hee hee." Big Dawg found it amusing Mario had another angle on me that I had not considered. which was a particularly good indication of things to come.

Donnie always maintains an even, balanced tone while engaged in official conversation. Your voice oscillates and is active for two-and-a-half octaves based on questions and statements presented to you in conversation. teaching moment by Gerald Lorence.

"Wayne, you are too fucking quiet, my friend! Big Dawg and I have been talking about the business, but you never say nothing," Mario said while looking at me in the rearview mirror. "But don't worry, my friend! I have something very special just for you, my friend."Mario is stating all these things with excitement in his voice. "You will not be able to be quiet for much longer. I'm going to take you right now to the candy store! Yes, my friend, the candy store! Not my kind of candy," he says, as he flicks his nose. "But candy, I know you like. We are going to be there in 20 minutes. I'm going to introduce you to a vampire bitch! This is why you will no longer be able to be quiet. The vampire is going to bite you. You are going to scream loudly. She is going to bite your dick, my friend!"

When Mario makes this statement, my eyes get huge in shock! Mario continues, "I called her a vampire bitch because she will suck you dry like a vampire! She is going to do this to you, and you will scream. She is going to suck your huge dick dry! Yes, she is going to suck your big, huge black dick!"

"Mario, you got one for me too," Big Dawg said in a concerned tone.

We arrived at the candy store, and Mario took us in, where Frank's nephew was waiting for us. Wayne This is the vampire bitch I told you about. You make sure you take very, very good care of my best friend here." Mario said to the young lady. He placed his arm around me.

Sssssssshid, she would not be biting me, the first thing that crossed my mind. Wasn't really a big concern because I could depend on my brother to display his most consistent talent: jumping his ass right in the middle! Big Dawg was on her ass tighter, then a small bathing suit on the long ride back from the beach.

The lady Mario had for me had been handcuffed by Big Dawg. She had a friend of hers attend to me. This pretty blonde with a heavy British accent was a refreshing change for me. We talked about a number of things, including England. She spent a lot of time talking about family, too. I looked over at Big Dawg and saw he was sitting at another table talking to Mario's vampire. Big Dawg is nursing this one beer. I had like eight beers on the table, and my British lady friend had a number of shots lined up for her to drink.

"Why do I have all these beers that I didn't order?" I asked as the waiter was dropping off more. My friend pointed me in the direction of a few Mexican gentlemen sitting at a table off to the right of me. was lifting their drinks to me and smiling. I gave the gentleman a nod and lifted one of the many drinks in front of me. OK, that explains these drinks that we just received.

What about the rest, I asked myself, why did I ask that question?

She started pointing in every direction in the bar, it seemed. I smiled and lifted beers in acknowledgement that these guys' had sent me. I had a puzzled look, and she read it, saying, "These are signs of respect and may even be a way to introduce themselves to you."

“Well, I'm not the man; he is.” as I pointed in my brother's direction.

"Well, that's not what they see when they look at the both of you," she states with her heavy British accent.

“Well, I won't be jumping my brother, and that's that.” in a very matter-of-fact way.

She replied, “there is no need to be concerned with jumping anyone. Those different tables I pointed to are not working together and are independent of the group your brother is with”

“Confused now, aren't you with Mario too?" I asked.

“Oh no, dear! with a big chuckle, she responded. She went on to tell me that Miss Vampire dated Mario some years back and still considers him a very good friend. But she made it clear she had a vastly different opinion of him and with . According to my British friend, she was just doing Miss Vampire a favor by sitting with me for her. She then began to explain who these separate groups were. I told her I was not really ready for the level of being the head of anything.

“That will change at some point soon, she said.

“how can you be so sure? I questioned her.

“You have that "it" factor written all over you. It's clear that I'm not the only one who sees it either. "How many beers do you see on your brother's table?" she asked, pointing to Big Dawg's table with her eyes.

Frank's nephew came to Big Dawg and told him that we needed to go. I made sure that my British friend had a very good night. “I hoped this was a reflection of my appreciation for your time today.” I said as I shook her hand. She smiled brightly after a slight glance at her hand. She gave me some valuable information. which was expressed in my handshake with her.

Frank had someone bring Big Dawg an A3 series BMW, to drive while we were in town. I looked at that little car and then looked at Big Dawg.

"This is going to be a very long ride." I say it aloud.

"You know these things don't actually drive that bad, though." Expressed Big Dawg with a very big smile.

Big Dawg and I had a short meeting with Mario that night. He informed us that Frank will be along the next day. However Frank would bring us back to Phoenix to catch an early flight back to Detroit. Mario was jumping on the road to see the semi off that night. We were told that the tractor trailer would have 3500 pounds on it.

Baby Doll called me that night, and we had some small talk. I had to make her aware that I wouldn't be able to see her as planned when I returned to Phoenix. But I promised her I would be returning to Phoenix shortly. She wasn't very happy with the last-minute decision either.

Frank was there early in the morning. We hit the road and was updated on a late minute adjustment. Frank started talking directly to me concerning this actual load. I gave him a plan for how it would be stored. The process of moving it. Projected timeframe that the account would be satisfied. I also started to give him a forward leaning view of coming challenges and concerns. But, I also gave him my view on how to address them. Frank started this conversation asking me aggressive questions. Not talking to Big Dawg or allowing his input.

By the time we got to the base of the conversation, I was in total control of it. Frank was dead silent and just listened, nodding his head and agreeing as I talked. When I concluded, there was a silence and Frank had a deep thought look on his face. And then he spoke, "Wayne I really liked the way you think about the business."

"Yeah, we stayed up almost all last night putting those ideas together, Frank." Big Dawg stated. "I'm happy that you like them too..... hee hee hee hee hee."

CHAPTER 7
MEXICALI

AFTER LANDING AT DETROIT Metro Airport, I will not fly coach next to this dude again! I had to be pinned in between Big Dawg and the side of the plane for about four hours. Big Dawg and I had 24 to 36 hours before the tractor trailer arrived. I was busy putting the team together to receive this load of 3500 to 4000 pounds of marijuana under the agreement that had been arranged with Frank on the ride to the Phoenix airport from Tucson. Beat the organizer and he would receive a $100,000 loan. This loan was advanced to us so we could plan to receive larger loads. The money would be repaid in $25,000 increments for each subsequent load.

I was tasked with buying vans in U-Haul style trucks. I had to also make sure we were able to receive, store, and supply the work. The more sensitive concern was the money. Finding somewhere to store the money, counting the money, and receiving the money, all while keeping it separate from the marijuana,

The money would also have to be shipped in a special manner. The currency would be shipped in $25,000 Saran bags wrapped in duct taped gray squared bricks of money. But within the $25,000 bundles of money there would be five $5000 rubber band stacks of money. Each $5000 was in an increment of $1000, with a rubber band on each one.

My team included L DOG, I AM, Loc Boc, BIG I, and Vito. Each guy had their own team under them. This didn't include Vito, though. The

Hustle Man was a good friend of mine, but he was more of an independent contractor. The Hustle Man had his own crew of guys outside of mine.

Within 36 hours, Big Dawg and I received the tractor trailer containing 4000 pounds of marijuana. Hustleman gave me 500,000 for 1000 pounds. BIG I took 500 pounds with 200,000 toward his balance. I AM took 250 and put 100,000 towards his balance. Loc Boc took just 50 pounds because he was more concerned with getting every dime he could. Player D got rid of about 300,000. L. DOG brought in 100,000 also.

Within a 24-hour period, I had about 1.4 million that had to be counted by me that night. I had 3500 of the 4000 pounds of marijuana, and Big Dawg had the other 500 pounds. My bill was a little over 3.1million at $900 a pound. The number should have been $800 a pound, per our understanding, with a $25 drop for every additional 500 pounds.

"Big Dawg, what's my number?" I asked.

"I don't know, man! What are you thinking, little bro?" Big Dawg asked.

"I don't call it." I said firmly. In my mind, I knew he wanted to fuck me like a normal person. I was not going to play that game with him. "Give me a price and allow me to move out,"

"Guess I'm going to look out this time. Just give me $925 on each. That's cool for you, bro?" Big Dawg asked as he focused in on my face. I turned and walked away. "With those numbers, I may need to run into you first thing in the morning."

I went to the BURG and began to break down the money to count it. With I started counting Player D's money first. I separated the money into piles of hundreds, 50, 20s, 10s, etc. I started with Player D's money because he will try you and bring short money. Player D was supposed to have 300,000 right here, but the ship was only at 290,000, or $10,000 off. I made a note of the score and kept it moving. I started counting by myself at about 11 p.m. that night.

Counting by hand; it took me counting all night, until about 1:00 AM in the morning. I kept catching cramps in the balls of my hands.

"Big Dawg, I'm headed that way." so I ended the call. I pulled into the driveway as I called Big Dawg Cell, let it ring twice, then hung up. The door opens, and Big Dawg steps out with that Russian-style AK-47. Don't get it messed up; the big boy was nice with that joint too. I pulled out the large travel-sized suitcase. It can hold about 1.2 to 1.3 inside; I had 1.5 in this case. The 500,000 that my nigga Hustleman brought was mostly all large.

"What's your way of enabling me to fit more inside the suitcase? Damn little bro! What the hell have you got in this bitch?" Big Dawg said as he grabbed eight.

"I was able to fit 1 1/2 in that joint." I told him, laughing at the look on his face.

"Mostly large, Big Dawg question. half large and the rest mixed, I said.

"Yo, you're not going to chill, so we can chop it up some. I only need your opinion on a few things," Big Dawg said with urgency in his voice. "I got major numbers in the street, and most of it is about to come in right now too. Plus, somebody gave me an extra 100,000. I've got to figure that out because somebody might be trying to make a move on me."

I return to the Burg. I could not be gone long; I was in major violation of every law. I had all the bales of weed in my basement, and I counted the money upstairs overnight in my room. This is a death sentence if you get robbed, and it's an open and shut case if the police raid you. One of the few first rules is: Money and drugs are never met. This is a loss you never want to take. usually spell disaster.

It's been a little over a week, and I've wrapped everything up on my end of things. I turned in a little less than 3.1 million at $900 a pound. Big Dawg was trying to tell me I owe him another $25 off each pound. I agree that he did say $925, but not that I would pay it. I had something for him too... just wasn't time for it yet. I in turn asked him about what the price is supposed to be per the agreement. Big dawg didn't want to talk anymore concerning that subject all of a sudden.

I received a call from Kevin, telling me he had found a building that he was going to buy on Kelly, right off Moross. At one point, the building was a bank. Kevin also told me that I had a number of buyers for a few of my properties. The title company will be in touch with me very soon to close. I called Lorence and told him I would need to see him in the early part of the following week.

Four closings will then occur that week, with checks totaling a little over $600,000. I called Lorence to make sure he was in his office. "I'm en route to your office." I told him.

"Donnie, I will see you when you arrive," Lorence said in a monotone voice.

I arrived at Lorence's office, and we embraced as usual. We entered his office, and I had a blank look on my face. "Donnie, are you OK?" he asked out of concern, but with a concerned look in his face as well. I handed him the envelopes with the four checks in them.

"I don't know what to do with them." as I'm looking back lost.

"Donnie, you have to put these in your corporate account now, Mr. Lorence." Looking at my very last facial expression, he nudged. "Come on, Donnie. Let's go downstairs and open your account up now," said Lorence.

Lorence had known me since I was 20 years old. He could see in my face that I didn't know how to open an account or write a check. He took me to the bank and showed me how to open a bank account. Then he took me back to his office and showed me how to write a check and balance my checkbook as well. “Donnie, 600,000 is a lot. Too much to have and just one account," he expressed.

Got together with Kevin to ride over to the building he just purchased. He went in, and he started to give me his vision for how he was looking to build it out. Kevin scheduled a meeting with a real estate broker who was a real heavyweight. This broker would buy bundles of houses directly from the banks. Kevin had the first pick of the houses he would get before he listed them. He would call the broker and tell him he wanted a property, and it was done. With no money at that time, the broker just wanted to settle up on everything once a month. After meeting with the broker, we want to look at houses. I picked out five or six really nice houses that day, too. We also had to find people to staff the new office.

Baby Doll called me Kevin, and we separated after a half day of work. Baby Doll and I had been building on a consistent basis at this point. She was constantly asking when I was returning to Arizona to see her. She told me how she was ready for a more serious relationship. Baby Doll proceeded to ask me why I have been so moody during the interactions we have had, and I told her, in a roundabout way, why or what my issues were.

Baby Doll would often cut me off by saying, "Baby, I understand, and I just can't wait to see you!" which I had come to understand as: *"I can follow your ideas without you fully expressing them, and certain things are better talked about in person."* This woman would end up teaching me SO MUCH!

“Wayne” Kevin called out. "You have a new baby now... When are you going to buy a really nice home and place your girl and new child in it?”

I was not even thinking along these lines. I had a blank look on my face.

“NIGGA, I figured you hadn't even thought that far ahead yet.”

"I'ma start looking into that for you," Kevin said. As my cell phone began to ring, I answered it.

”Yo, the babies are on the bus, and we'll be here tomorrow," Big Dawg said. This was in reference to the bales of marijuana that were on the semi truck and were enroute. I hung up without saying a thing. The turnaround was super fast on their end for some reason. This sent a number of red flags up in my head. We touched down, and things went as they normally do. There was starting to be a lot of bad blood toward Frank on my end.

Frank avoided speaking with me because of my ‘No Bullshit’ style. Frank was all bullshit, just like Big Dawg too. I was also noting that Big Dawg always appears to leave a nice balance after all the money was supposed to be in. Big Dawg was only dealing with one dude now. This dude was pretty good at moving about 350 to 400 pounds a week. But Big Dawg would always take 500 from the load. 500 pounds. With Big Dawg not always paying, I was always paying his full balance off. Nothing close to the number Big Dawg was supposed to pay though.

MARICON BANDITO’S

"I knew something was afoot," I said. I had a little over 500 pounds of very poor-quality weed. “These motherfuckers are going to pay for fuckin with me this time," I said to myself. “Big dawg, I need to run into you.” and then I hung up the cell phone.

Pulling up, I hit Big Dawg just so the phone number showed up. Big Dawg comes out and helps me with the two large suitcases. “That's 2.7 on that. But check this out—I'm done on that ticket, 2.7 million on what I owed toward the 3500 pounds I had. And I won't be bringing in 3.1 this time.”

Big Dawg is looking concerned and confused. “Did you know these dudes sent some very bad stuff we mixed in with the good?” I asked.

Big Dawg looked directly into my eyes before answering "no, I didn't know."

"Well, I'm going to give it a final count on what we have left, but it's about 500 or so. But it's trash." I said.

Back on the bus, we went into the basement to get a final count. There was about a 100 100-pound U-Haul box everywhere. The first order of business was to get rid of all these empty boxes.

"What the fuck?! Something can't be right! SHIT!" I said it with confused anger! I have to figure this shit out!

After a few hours of sitting in deep thought. I hit up Big Dawg. "did you run through them numbers yet??" Meaning did you count the money that I just brought you.

"Man you know I can't run through that shit that fast." Big Dawg said with a chuckle. "Is there something wrong though?"

"I was just trying to make sure our account matched." I answered. Big Dawg told me he would hit me soon as he was done.

My cell phone rang; it's Baby Doll. As I put the cell phone to my ear, baby, I need you to get on a flight to come see me! I have someone I want you to meet." Baby Doll said so sweetly.

"I'm in the middle of my workout, honey." I responded.

"Awwwwww baby! I really needed to see you at some point soon" Baby Doll said sadly.

"Give me a week, and I will be headed your way, honey."

I'm beating myself up, but I know my account was good for what I owed. I gave Big Dawg 2.7, and I should have 5 100-pound boxes left with something in them... Out of the 35 boxes in my basement, only 22 are empty! I counted 13 boxes with four bales of weed in each box. The other eight boxes are all my profit. sitting in a chair and staring at the wall emotionless. "What the hell is wrong with you, man? working on the force within you?" Tez felt he said some super funny stuff. "OK, dude, you are starting to freak me out now, bro." Tez's face WENT SERIOUS!

I slowly said, "Tez. I think this time next week... I will have made my first $1,000,000."

"DAAAAAAAAAAAMN, Straight up..........you're going to let me see it?" Tez asked, the latter part with a whisper.

The following morning, Big Dawg called and said, "Yo, that thing isn't right!" meaning that the money was incorrect.

My heart rate increased." you are fucking nuts; my numbers are always on point," I shouted.

"Well, not this time. You were like $20 off, and since I kinda like you a little.......... I thought I would let it slide. Next time you may not be so lucky though, hee hee hee hee!" I just hung up the freakin' phone on him.

Big Dawg called me back. "Yo, real talk, what are we going to do about that other (500 pounds)?"

My reply? "I'm not going to do SHIT with it. Tell them it's accounted for, and I will load it back up on the truck and return it with their money!"

Big Dawg was silent for a moment. "Do you think we should really do that?"

I responded, "This is the only option."

Big Dawg ends up calling me back and forth, trying to say it was good like the rest. My reply was, "Well, they shouldn't have any problem when they get it back then."

Once they saw I was serious, They have started negotiating the price now. I hailed and didn't start softening my tongue until we got to $500 a pound. We finally settled on $400 a pound. agreed to give them $200,000 for the 500 pounds at $400 a pound. Which I negotiated would be paid over the next two loads and payments of 100,000 per load until completed.

The weed was not of the same grade as a larger amount, but it wasn't anything that couldn't be fixed. I just wasn't willing to fix it for them. I fixed it for myself! Truth be told, the weed was still good but not worth the price. But it would have taken mixing it or just letting the street dry up a little. It would still go for a price. I finally got the chance to get back. Some of what was stolen from me just by refusing to fix their efforts to deceive me again.

Frank just wanted me to commit to the 200,000, and I knew the value of my word. I would just keep all 13 boxes as my profit. I'm just giving them $100,000 off my profit on each of the next two loads. I told Big Dawg to slow that next load because I needed a break to get some of my money off the street. which would cause the street to dry up in an almost desperate state. I was able to get $1000 for each pound. bringing me a little under 1.3 million that was mine just off those two loads.

" Tez, take all the dollar bills and $5 bills. Put them in a garbage bag for the night." I told him. "we were going to the Sting strip club." I

drove out to Eastland Mall to get something to wear that night. I hadn't been combing my hair or beard. I was looking homeless too. I walked past a Treasures jewelry store, and a rose gold watch caught my eye. I went into the store by myself. The guy in the store yells, "We are about to close!" with a look of disdain on his face.

I said calmly, but noticing his face, "I plan to purchase something if you allow me to." I asked to see a few pieces. The gentleman looks like he's ready to throw me out of the store. I asked him to pull the watch from the display case. He gave me a kind of crazy look. He pulled the watch from the case. I extended my hand for the watch while asking the price. I believe he told me $5000 or something of that nature. Then he asked me for my ID before he allowed me to handle the watch. This is a young man from India, but he is well groomed and up on his fashion. I pulled a $5000 stack from my pocket and set it on the counter.

“Will this address your concerns, sir?”

His face lit up and his voice got high: "Oh, sir, there are no concerns at all! but, yes, this is just fine by the way, my name is Jay!” I can't even recall the name of the damn watch either. The only reason I got it was to highlight his behavior towards me. But it was the beginning of a great friendship and brotherhood.

driving from the east and thinking *Oh, my new reality now. I would be a marked man with that type of money living in the city.*

I called a lady friend of mine at the time. She had been telling me I needed to move. Her Uncle Sam was an interior designer when I was ready to make a move. I asked her to arrange a meeting. But I didn't really have time to find anything. I will need him to handle everything.

I got the team together for a night out at the Sting Strip Club on the West Side of Detroit. We hit the club like 20 deep. That night. I rented out VIP for the night and all the booths along the sides of the entire gentlemen's club. My crew only consisted of four guys; the rest of the guys that were there were important parts of each individual guy's team. Tez's job was to handle the garbage bag of money. I told the girls they couldn't ask my guys for any money. Just dance, and Tez will be around to tip it down. They didn't get paid! They got paid for the song and tipped heavily during the song too. Every time I hit the Sting, I would give Maria a heads up that I would be in, and she would make all the arrangements to make sure that I was good.

Few days later, I was on a flight, first class, to Arizona. Baby Doll picked me up from the airport. She was really happy to see me, too. We went to eat and talk more. She told me that there was someone I needed to meet. She also told me that she wanted to be totally honest with me. The Latino gentleman that I would be meeting was named Brian, and he was her boyfriend growing up. But, he knew about us, according to Baby Doll.

Baby Doll drove to Scottsdale to a very upscale hotel called the Phoenician. I believe it was like $2,000 or $3,000 a night, depending on the room she picked. They drove us on a golf cart to the building our room was in. Brian was brought to come meet me the following day

The next morning, the Baby Doll wanted to be treated as such. She took me to a Scottsdale mall, and she had her way with my pockets. I had to remind her that you can only fly under 10,000. I had 20, all large. Lorence would have a fit if he knew the shit right here. "Spend what you want for whatever I don't have with me. Just put it on your credit card, and I will have the money put in your account before I leave." I whispered to her.

Right on cue, we arrived back at the hotel. Shortly after Brian showed up, wearing an all-white linen outfit with black open-toe sandals, it appeared to be Gucci.

This fucker is a bit overdressed.

Testosterone was definitely going to be a major part of this meeting. "Would you care to have something to eat, my friend?" I asked with a very warm smile.

"No, no, thank you." With a pause extending his hand to me. "Please excuse my forwardness."

"Thank you," I said as I shook his hand. "And you are—"

"Well, let's just say Brian. It's much easier to say," he said with a smile. "Wayne, my childhood friend, tells me a lot of great things about you." Brian was smiling but trying to read my reaction.

"In which I hope you will be willing to share with me later." I responded and caused a big laugh from everyone.

Baby Doll says, "You guys don't. You don't need me in your way, so I will run off to do some girly girl things."

. We started out pretty straightforwardly. “What is the nature of your interests, my friend?”

“A long-term relationship within the reality of limitless possibilities.” I responded.

I knew Brian was nothing more than someone with a number of contacts across the border. Baby Doll already put me up on his character. Brian was nothing more than a fuck up. But he had a number of relatives who had deep relationships in Mexico. His father was a Jefe and a respected man many years ago. I was clear that this would be his basic use. But he wanted to try to project himself as a big shot. There isn't any money in having a pissing contest with him.

“ I'm looking to deal in volume when it comes to weed.” I suggested.

“What type of money are we talking about?” Brian set up some in the chair.

“What type of money are we talking, as he sat up some in the cha ir.What type of quality and at what priced based on large volumes ?” was my reply. "There is money, or I wouldn't be dating your very, very beautiful childhood friend, now would I?" I continued. with a nod of his head in agreement.

"She is a very select investor. with a keen eye for rare talent. Wayne, what kind of volume are we talking about? One or two metric tons to start, Brian?”

"Start, Brian" I replied. There was a pause for thought.

Then Brian said, “I'm assuming that you already have an active market? You do know that this is not a very small request, Wayne.” Brain continued with noticed stress in his voice.

I replied with a reassuring tone, "Brian, the market is reality! And the request is not small, but it is nothing a dependable, healthy relationship can handle.”

“Wayne, it is a pleasure to have met you today! I have to leave now to make a number of calls. We will be in touch shortly.” Brian expressed, "We shook hands again, but stopped just short of the door, “Wayne, You wouldn't have any issue crossing or re-entering the country," Brian asked.

“No issues at all.” I answered with a huge smile on my face.

“Brian seemed to be really excited after meeting with you, baby,!” Baby Doll yelled as she came in the door.

“Are you going to tell me some of the great things you told your *‘Childhood Boo’* About me?” I said it in a childish tone.

"The outcome of your meeting should speak for itself," she replied in a very sharp tone.

I ran and gave her a big hug. But she didn't break a smile at all. “What's wrong with you? You know I was only teasing you, honey," I said in a very concerned tone.

“I want to know when you are going to start FUCKING ME!” Baby Doll said with a hand placed on her hips.

WHAT THE FUCK I thought as I looked at her in shock! I had to think fast here! “Wow, honey. Please tell me this isn't what this is all about here. I pray that this isn't how you view me," I said emotionally.

“No no no honey...... I'm sorry! I didn't mean it the way it came out," Baby Doll said. “I'm on steroids to get ready for my female bodybuilding competition coming up soon. The side effects make me really horny at times, and my anger and emotions go crazy at times. Then I haven't had a black boyfriend for SO many years. Black men don't really look at black women out here.” she expressed emotional frustration.

I was shocked, seriously, by her outburst. I had kind of noticed that she was looking a little extra toned. I told her something should happen, and it would take its natural course. “I'm not trying to handle you like an object of selfish pleasure, Baby Doll.”

I didn't want that kind of relationship with her. Plus, this girl was of the greatest value to me. As I have always said, if you want to ruin a good friendship or business relationship, add pussy and dick to the equation; it will ruin it every time. I didn't need any animal affection to fuck up possible millions of dollars. I would buy her whatever she thought she wanted. Sex would not be on the table for the foreseeable future.

"Baby, I need you to come sit down here with me. I have something I need to tell you." Baby Doll's voice got super serious. My mind is racing now; I hope she isn't about to tell me she was formerly a he? I'm looking kind of crazy now.

"Calm down, baby. You are acting like I'm going to rape you or something." We both laughed at her statement.

Then I said, in a humorous but concerned tone, "You are SOOOOOOO silly! I know you wouldn't be thinking anything like that... ... would you?"

"BAAAAAABY Listen to me! The guys your brother has been working with are no good." she said to me. I'm looking confused.

"Do you know them or something?" I asked.

"I don't only know them, but their whole family too." She informed me that she had been engaged to their uncle for a very long time. She was just over there at their grandmother's house a few weeks ago. And she was beseeching their uncle not to kill them because they robbed a load he gave them.

"We can't be talking about the same people." as I assured her.

"I'm talking about Frank and his fat, dark skin, Mario. And they are not freakin' brothers either!' She said.

I think them steroids are kicking in again, I was saying to myself.

"Calm down, baby doll, I believe you. You are just hitting me with so much," I said.

She had my full attention now. She went on to tell me more about the load they said was just caught by the feds. Frank gave his uncle fake, confiscated documents to prove the load had been caught. After listening to her, that sounds a lot like the load I just finished, which would explain why it came so fast and at such a reduced price, as well as the different grades of marijuana. The ship was all profit for them. "Anyway. PINCHE EL DIABLOS." I say it under my breath.

"Baby, I know what you can do. You just don't know what it's worth yet. But I do," Baby Doll spoke. "Brian isn't on the level that you are. He will try to act like a big shot and like a badass. He gets small stuff and messes it up, baby. But his family has a long history with moving drugs across the border ever since he and I were kids" Her information was good and she kept going. "Brian is going to take you across to meet some Jefes. Know that he is really doing this for himself. Even thought it will seem like he is only trying to help you. No one over there will deal with him anymore. But he knows they will, just to get their hands on you." She is looking at me very seriously while talking.

"I don't understand why they..."

"You will understand if you stop trying to talk and listen to me." Baby Doll cuts me off from showing my greenness. "Mexican men don't like you, Wayne. And don't allow any Mexican American male, like Brian, to make you believe so either." As she continues to teach me. "These are the three reasons they don't and won't ever like you and are jealous of you: 1. Their women love you. 2. Your dick is bigger than theirs. 3. Third, and most important, they cannot work the streets better than you." Commerce.

"Baby always keep this in mind when dealing with Mexicans." She paused to make sure I was focused directly on her. "Rule of thumb: all Mexicans lie, and all Mexicans are very, very greedy!" Damn, she really took me to school.

I had no possible way of understanding what she had seen in me at that moment, or how those words would become my gospel.

CHAPTER 8

TIJUANA CARTEL

BACK IN DETROIT AND excited about a number of possibilities Vito is on his way by the house. I was more interested in getting some rest. For some reason, Vito couldn't wait and needed to speak with me right away.

Vito arrived with his normal shenanigans— "Man, Big Dawg is tripping on me again! I'm in no mood to advocate for him, Nigga, if your ass doesn't get to the point of my interest and fast!" With a shocked look, Big Dawg discussed some major issues.

I looked at Vito as if to say, "Continue."

"Man BIG SEXY was on the road with them numbers (money) and got pulled over by them people (PULLED OVER BY LAW ENFORCEMENT). They locked Big Sexy up, and they are holding him." Vito said.

Vito went on to tell me the problem was that Frank called Big Dawg to tell him what happened and that his life was in danger.With Frank, people didn't believe his account of what happened. Frank needed to send another load ASAP to start paying for the loss of cash from Big Sexy. Big Dawg doesn't know how to tell you because I was so upset about this past load. Big Dawg, know you said you needed a break.

"Baby Doll, you are a heaven sent," I whisper to myself as Vito is talking.

I replied, "Vito the merciful! You have come to bring the message that will save Frank. Could this thing that you are doing or telling me be an olive branch for our brother so that you may win his forgiveness? You owe Big Dawg about 10,000." I told Vito. He agreed with the dollar amount. I continued, "I'm going to buy your debt. But this conversation never happened. Are we clear?"

"Hell fuck yeah! I'M TOTALLY CLEAR! Here is a little something else you may want to know," Vito said. "Mo Green will be home really soon too."

The information that Vito brought me was of great value. confirmed what I wanted to believe about Baby Doll. I didn't need Big Dawg to know; I knew about his concern about how he would approach me on the subject. I needed this to drag out some so I could turn this into a plus factor.

Never allow a crisis to go to waste. Winston Churchill

The time had come for me to treat myself a little. I was in love with that 745LI BMW. I reached out to Lay concerning it. We were finding a really good space with each other. I asked her to go get the car for me, and I would give her $20,000 and give her the money FOR 3 years' payments up front. She agreed but never followed through on it. My uncle Sam was over, telling me that he found me a really nice place that was also discussed. I was having a fit because she gave me her word. I finally told my Uncle Sam that I would go with the place that he found based on his liking it. I was more interested in venting my anger with her at him.

The following day, Uncle Sam stopped by. Nephew, I need you to come outside. I have something I need to show you. I walked out of the house and dropped my cell phone. My uncle was standing beside that platinum-colored spaceship (745LI BMW). I was totally caught off guard by him. I didn't ask my uncle to do this, but I made sure he knew how happy I was. I gave him what all Divas like: money.

The next day, I drove the spaceship to the shop for a major overhaul. I dropped her off to return later. Kevin called me and asked that I meet him at a certain address. This is something he does when he finds a property he is excited about.

I pulled up to meet Kevin, and he showed me this really nice house, "yo! I bet you are going to grab this one here!" I said, showing my excitement for Kevin.

Kevin replied, "No!" YOU ASSHOLE! You just grabbed it! You are going to buy this house for your girl. This is where she is going to raise your little girl until you guys figure out something better. But she does not deserve to be renting anything while she has your child, PERIOD!"

I always loved him deeply from that day forward for being a very good friend, helping guide me, being a better man, and other ways that clearly had not crossed my mind. Kevin continued, "I had already opened the office. You need to get ready to put your staff in place. I will have to add people as well, and I will keep you in mind during my search." Kevin added.

I called Uncle Sam up and told him I had another project for him to oversee for me. I needed him to go into this new house that Kevin had found for me and tear everything out and redesign everything in the home.

Big Dawg finally reached out to me. He wanted to get together and sit down to talk about a few things. He was getting a little upset because I kept pushing the date back. I had a very good reason for attempting to stall him. Baby Doll called me and asked me to return to Arizona but be prepared to stay at least a week or two, at minimum. Big Dawg was pretty much trying to catch me however he could talk with me now. I put that chase to an end, not wanting to insult anyone, even if they were trying to do so to me. Big dawg, I'm outside, and as always, I ended the call.

"Man you are hard to catch up with," Big Dawg stated with a hint of frustration in his voice. He went on to explain the situation in detail. also expressing that he felt compelled to come to Frank's aid. I agreed to help him but would have to wait until I returned from visiting Baby Doll in Arizona. He got really upset with me and said, "Damn! Can't you see I need your help? My guy is in some serious trouble." Big Dawg is yelling at the top of his voice.

I wanted to tell him the truth, but leaving him in the dark was best for now. "Bro!! I gotcha, man!"

Misplaced loyalty made Big Dawg predictable to be used financially. This was commerce again, and he made it loyalty; the two are independent of each other. I was beginning to learn that, but I had no idea I would have a doctorate before it was all said and done.

"I will be back within a week. And I will have the guys on point and ready to rip through that shit." I told Big Dawg with reassurance in my tone. I flew out a couple of days later, headed to Arizona. This time I brought I AM along with me.

Coming from California, I AM and I landed in Arizona after a long flight. We got checked in at a nice hotel, the Hilton Hotel. Baby Doll comes to see me and I AM meeting her for the first time. Man, she is a very pretty girl!

"She looks kind of buff, though," I AM said while looking bewildered. I didn't even respond to him. I would never hear the end of it if he knew she was on steroids.

"Baby, Brian is going to be coming to see you tomorrow. He seemed like he was really excited too." Baby Doll said while smiling from ear to ear.

After a night's rest, there was a knock at the door. "Who in the hell could be at this door this early?" as I'm looking out the little peephole.

"Brian," while I'm swinging the door open.

"Amigo!! Get your shit, we have to go! Now!!" Brian said it with a smile on his face.

"Hey! Hey! HEEEEEY!" I yelled as I was waking up. "What are you talking about? You never said we were going to be taking another trip requiring our SHIT!"

Brian replied, "Who is your friend, Wayne?"

"Oh, this is a friend that I have known for a long time. His name is Sam, but I call him I AM from the kids book." I responded as Sam stepped forward with his hand extended. Brian didn't reply or extend his hand to Sam.

"What does he do that could-"

I cut Brian off. "Be more than your wildest dreams could imagine?" Brian's face did not change based on what I said, so I continued. "When you think of Sam, I AM thinking of the green from the market that will purchase a shit load of bacon and ham."

Brian's face had an instant smile as he grabbed Sam, hugging him, and said, "I freaking love green that I can purchase large amounts of egg and ham with a side of bacon! Let's go, let's go, amigos! We have some very important people waiting for us in Mexico." Brian yelled, while jumping up and down smiling. "Now I have two black guys and not just one!"

After a long ride, we crossed the Mexico border. The first thing I knew was that there was a difference in smell. There was a clear and noticeable difference. I didn't know what to expect from this visit. I did ask for this. I maybe should have been clearer on the details of getting it, though. We pulled up to a nice house after entering Mexico and driving about 1/2 hour or so. Brian looked at me. "My friend, where is your jewelry? You have to put it on now." I started to put my bracelet and watch on. I guess I'm part of the props for his performance, I'm thinking.

A Latino guy comes out of the house to welcome Brian. This gentleman was wearing very tight jeans, ostrich skin cowboy boots, a nice buttoned-up very white shirt, and a belt with a very large belt buckle. a very confident gentleman, but he didn't seem overly confident or excited to see Brian. From reading his body language, I'm led to believe Boots only area of interest was the two black guys with him.

Brian walked off to decide with Boots. I noted that Boots keep his eyes on me, and I AM. He often looked at my jewelry but never really gave Brian eye contact. Brian, finally looking our way and spoke: " my MI AMigos, how are you guys doing? Do you need something to drink?"

I AM, and I smiled really big. "No thank you! We are doing fine."

The smile that came over Boots' face was huge. Boots just became a fan of ham and a side of bacon. "I AM," I remarked. "Why wasn't Boots smiling at you and me until Brian asked you if you needed some water." I AM asked.

At this point forward, as initially, I will refer to Brian's friend here as "Boots." Boots told him to ask us those questions. He wanted to see how we would respond to Brian. He doesn't really trust Brian, and there wouldn't have been a meeting without us. "I AM," I told him in a whisper. "They are walking towards us now." I slowly turn my head in their direction, but, still talking. "Boots is going to want to shake our hand if they have a deal. Make sure you shake his hand firmly and with a warm smile. Boots will be still looking at our interaction with Brian, giving me & I AM instructions."

Boots came, shook our hands, and wanted to interact with us more. showing a sense of humor while Brian translates. I'm watching as Boots force a close-up of the interaction with Brian and us as he directs the flow of discussion between our little group. which ended up going over very well.

We left Boot's house and headed to check in at a hotel. I asked Brian a number of questions, but he stayed pretty vague other than saying we have a very big possible meeting tomorrow, which was the most we could get Brian to say. It was starting to be clear that I would be dealing with an incorrigible actor. The history that Baby Doll warned me about appeared to still be very consistent, and this would just serve as the first marker of things to come while dealing with Brian, which would be a lot easier to say.

Brian checked us into a nice hotel to get ready for a little nightlife in Mexico. We ordered room service and took a little risk. Brian called me and I AM when as well as mine. "Let's get ready to see the ladies!" I didn't have any idea what was in store for me.

We hit the strip club in Tijuana that night. 'MUCHA MUCHACHA GUAPA NOCHAS', and I plan to let my hair down. We are seated in a very big booth that may hold eight or nine people. It was only us three, but we were expecting a lot of company. I ordered drinks for everyone but was surprised to find that the Mexican beer that is often drunk in America is really not known over in Mexico.

Brian started to get a lot of women coming his way. But I noted that they were all pointing at myself and I AM. I chose one or two of the best ones there. Then I would ask for his assistance with the language. Then I would see that he would take her from me. which I'm pretty sure once he told them that we worked for him and he was a big shot, in which the reality was the polar opposite. No one was worse than Big Dawg when it came to these types of things. I just didn't know this behavior transcended cultures. I noted that I AM sitting there and not allowing anyone to sit next to him or dance for him. Every time I look over his shoulder, he is buying roses, bears, rabbits, and dogs.

"Man, why are you doing this? You keep buying all this shit!" I said.

"You know they are going to keep bringing it because you are buying it." in my efforts to not allow him to be hustled with all these ugly stuffed animals.

“Do you see that fine MUTHA FUCKA right there?” I AM pointed to a young lady in the center stage "Bro, I don't want anybody but her, and I will wait." he said with a serious look on his face.

Before I could blink an eye, I was surrounded by three MUJERES. I later found out they were the friends of the young lady, Mr. Bigshot. Brian jacks me. The ladies were drinking and kept hitting me; damn, they hit hard, I'm thinking. They are yelling back and forth to each other across from me: "MUY GRANDE!"

Then the other one would yell back, "SI," "MUY GRANDE!"

One of the young ladies disappeared under the table. Where the hell is she? Then the one on the right hit me and said, "Muy grande, si?" and shaking her head yes.

I shook my head yes in return to her shaking her head at me yes. Then, out of nowhere, the lady under the table reappeared, very excited and animated. “Brian,” yells my lady friend, "The three of them really really like you!" I just smiled and shook my head yes! because that appeared to be the thing to do, just shake your head yes and say, "SI!"

Then, 1, 2, 3, 4, 5, 6, and 7 hands started reaching under the table and grabbing at my manhood. "OH SHIT, OH SHIT, OH SHIT!" I was surprised, with my eyes bulging out of my head in shock. I think I figured out what these three frisky ladies were talking about now!

I looked over to Brian to try and understand what just happened. He was laughing his head off. I AM little friend finally came over, and he gave her a shit load of things he collected for her while waiting for her period. Brian translated a number of things for him, and this pause helped settle these hellcats down some. Or so I thought! One of the girls grabbed my hand and started pulling me to get up. I finally started shaking my head the other way.

"NOOOOOOOOO, HELL NO!" I said to her as she pulled in the opposite direction.

"She just wants to give you a VIP dance, my friend" Brian spoke while the young lady with him was looking sad for her friend. "She really likes you. All three of them, like you." Brian continued.

"I just know all three of them—they better not show up!" I yelled back at Brian!

I followed in to where the young lady was pulling my hand. I paid the guy in the front of the VIP section. She took me into one of the private booths that had a black curtain hanging in front of it. The young lady started dancing for me, and I started to relax somewhat. But she started grinding in my lap a lot, constantly pushing the curtain back looking out of the booth. Next thing I knew, she had my actual manhood in her hand "Sssssssssi."

"MUY MUY MUY GRANDE," as if she had struck gold! She began to sing with prolific intentions within the mic. I started to have overwhelming feelings of love for her now; she was nefariously anointed with a supertalent. She was still looking out the curtains, and I could understand why. I'm about to freakin' go to jail in Mexico, which was my fear when she first started! My fear became a secondary thought with every passing moment. "Fuck it, I'll pay the bail!"

She jumped up in an effort to get in the saddle, and I stopped her relentless drive to be the mythological expression of Europa and Peri. This was a very rough ride, and safety is of the utmost importance.

"CASCO MAMA GUAPA"

"Por favor, Mama!" She found the rhythm in clashing notes and clenched her fist. The African God pulled her from the saddle by her hair while speaking softly to her soul in a hermetic love language of my innate genetic tongue. Standing her up and redirecting her attention by guiding her head by her hair to the spot reserved for the human posterior in the booth. "You are mine for this moment, and I'm going to grind your soul from your thoughts."

I knew this was the realization of her dreams. In this dream, I was God, and that booth was her holy of holies. She was locked in my pleasurable will and enduring the pain of her body senses being played in a key of divinity. I would forever be frozen in her mind's eye, and she would be loved over and over and over in her hermetic bliss of the clashing notes of that supra rhythm of this African phallic love for God.

I turned her around and kissed her on the forehead. We exited her chambers of love to reenter the club. Her friends rushed up to and surrounded her as I walked back to our booth, and I'm thinking with a smile on my face that they're probably surprised she returned in one piece!

Now we have more women at our booth and standing. But, it was time to leave and get rest for the following day's big meeting. I AM and I were still short on details concerning this meeting. which would be something that would not change with Brian. The following morning came fast.

Brian called both I AM and I. “I just received a call from those guys. We have to leave now to go meet them. They are waiting for us, just now.”

After a short ride, we pulled into the parking lot of what appeared to be a nightclub. We exited the car and approached the building as someone opened the door to greet us. Brian started his big-shot walk and demeanor. There were three Latino gentlemen with the normal Mexican drug dealer look of nice cowboy boots, very tight jeans, button-up shirts, big belt buckles, and cowboy hats. There was a fourth gentleman that stood out to me. He had an American style of dress.

Gucci loafers, Gucci jeans, and a button-up shirt. No huge belt buckles, but a Gucci belt and vintage Gucci handbag. He did meet with I AM and I. Asked was it our first time in Mexico, and how did we like it? He also stated that he looked forward to a very good working relationship with us. He left the club shortly after. He was someone of importance based on how everyone reacted to his presence.

We were taken over to a table and served drinks. I got pretty much the same feeling as I did with Boots. These three guys didn't seem to care for Brian. I could sense some bad blood and very deep mistrust.

"Amigos this guy right here, say that you want to do some business with us," he said, looking at both of his partners at the table.

"Yes, we would like to discuss this possibility with you and your friends," I replied.

The Jeep and the three gentlemen started to speak in Spanish with Brian for a moment.

"Amigo, we are excited about doing some business with you. We want to get more business back out east, my friend. How much would you be looking to start with and how long before you finish?" As the three focused on my face, I would not feel comfortable stating a certain amount at this point. My interest is more so in the terms of our understanding and quality of the marijuana, and with an equally focused look, I looked at this gentleman.

"What's the matter with your friend? He doesn't talk." the gentleman sitting to the right of the one in the center refers to I AM.

"I'm the JEFE (the boss)" I said in a firm tone with a direct, confident gaze to the right. He (I AM) has no authorization in matters; but, outside of that, he is exceptional at executing my directions, with a smile emerging on my face.

“I understood, amigo.” The gentleman in the center nodded. The gentlemen continued speaking. “the weed is very good, my friend. We would also like to send you 1500, my friend.”

I replied, "I will be done in two weeks. If the quality is what you say.” I knew it would only take a week, but dates are very important. It is always good to never break your agreement upon deadlines. It's the same as if you receive some form of personal or business credit and go past 30 days late. The difference in this case is, the process I just negotiated is classified as Business credit with Net 14, 30 and 60.... etc.: days until you pay a balance. The process is the same for clothing brand, appliances, food brands...etc.: distributer or retail store must negotiate net terms of credit; The drug dealer is a businessman operating under this same principle, but it’s illegal ONLY BECAUSE YOU DON’T POSSESS A LICENSE TO SELL THAT PRODUCT! Explained in underworld terms using the different cultural mafia’s description: you have to wet the bosses (The Government’s) beak. Also, the gentleman to the right of the one in the center was testing me. He wanted to see the relationship and look for weaknesses in it between me and myself.

I followed up with, "What number are we talking about for those 1500?" (about 1500 pounds of marijuana), the gentleman started to speak with Brian in Spanish. There appeared to be some disagreement in their exchange.

“Amigo, this guy (Brian) here is saying some things that are not right. But I would like to have $700 a pound. Is this good for you, my friend?” The gentleman asked me.

I paused for a moment and responded, "I don't have a problem with that number. But if you look to increase at a later date, I would like to discuss a different price based on that increase.”

The general responded, "SI, SI, me amigo! I want to tell you something, my friend. The gentleman continues, "I only ask for several hundred dollars for those 1500 pounds and nothing more, my friend."

I noticed the gentleman on the right cut his eye at Brian. I knew there was something afoot on Brian's end, and they didn't want to be mixed in with his BS. They started to speak in Spanish with Brian again.

"OK, we are going to... How do you say?" I broke for Spanish with Brian. "Brian, say, borrow."

The gentleman responds, "SI, We are going to borrow you those 1500 pounds for two weeks. But you will have to pay for the driver, my friend. This will come off the price for those 1,500, SI?"

I quickly responded, "SI, SI," to my friends, as they all started laughing.

"The driver is getting $100 a pound for those 1500 pounds." He said.

"That won't be a problem." I responded. "Will we get to see the weed now?"

"Oh, my friend, I barely forgot to tell you," the gentleman said, "that we have not moved this thing up to the border." a break for Spanish among the three of them. "Some of our loads will start arriving in town in a few days."

Brian cut in quickly, "we can wait in town to see it."

I also agreed. while knowing that the load from Frank will be arriving in Detroit soon too. They had a few more drinks, and everyone was smiling. We hammered out all the other details, and they made me aware they would be in touch very soon.

After having a very successful meeting, We returned to the hotel. I'm in my room in disbelief over what I just witnessed. My cell phone rang, and I freaked out that I got reception. I answered but didn't say anything.

"I know this is your ass on the other end." Big Dawg yells.

"Damn, I didn't know who this was, bro." I replied.

“"Why haven't you been answering your phone? I have been calling you for about three or four days now. Man, Baby Doll got your head's gone. Stop chasing that pussy and get your ass back here. The babies will be on the bus really soon," Big Dawg said with concern in his voice.

"I will move my flight up to get back in about two or three days," I replied.

"Naw, fuck that! I'm booking your flight back from this end myself. I don't trust your ass," Big Dawg said. "For all I know, you may not even be in Phoenix because your phone has been acting crazy. It's like some Spanish phone company on it. Had me kind of wondering for a minute... but shh! Hee hee hee! You know you've got to get up early in the morning to fool me," he said with arrogance in his voice.

"Yeah, you have always been a tough cookie to get past," I replied.

"Hee hee hee! I know, can't fool me," he answered in an inane tone. "I'm going to hit you early tomorrow with your flight info and with I AM'S info too," Big Dawg added.

I went to his room and told him what was going on. I added that we had to get back stateside fast. We spoke with Brian and made arrangements to get on the road early the next morning. Brian already knew we had a load that would be coming soon back home next morning; we were on the road while it was still dark out.

"As soon as you get reception, I need you to start scrambling those niggas up there. Tell them I AM, you know we would be touching down soon. I need them to have money on hand from their people. Also, make them fully aware of the situation — I'm pressed for cash! I'm in a bad situation, and I need them to personally blow the doors off their safes and bring their own actual money also. Be very clear when expressing these words to them: 'I will take it personally if my request isn't fully addressed; I dictated these instructions that I will express to our team.'"

"I need to see what my guys are made of. Things appear to be changing, with a lot of future promises. I need to see if these boys can produce under pressure. And also find out who was only looking out for their own interests."

We arrive in Phoenix, and Big Dawg called with new flight information that had I AM and I. Big Dawg moved it up one day based on what Mario told him about the babies on the bus. And on the road that following afternoon, I told him, 'We are flying out the next morning on a red eye.'"

Brian suggested that we celebrate the two deals we cut in Mexico by going to a gentlemen's strip club. We partied hard that night, but I was taken aback by a young lady named Sheila. She was a thick and sexy white girl from Phoenix, and I found her very attractive. I asked her to sit with me for the rest of the night, but she reminded me that she was there to work and wouldn't allow me to lie to her all night.

Curious, I asked her how much she would make on an average night. Sheila told me she worked between 1000 to 1500 hours a week because she refused to work too hard. We both laughed, and I offered her $2,000 for the remainder of her work hours that night. She accepted, and when it was time for her to report to the stage, I paid off the manager for the rest of her night off and even blessed the DJ.

Sheila and I clicked that night, and I invited her back to my room. We had a great time just talking and acting like kids. I didn't make any advances, and Sheila seemed to appreciate that. When I got sleepy, I asked her to leave, and she was surprised that I didn't try anything. "DAMN, THIS IS A FIRST," she said with intrigue.

Later on, I took a red-eye flight back to Detroit with I AM. What up doe!

CHAPTER 9

TIJUANA CARTEL 2

I RETURNED TO THE city feeling down. "Coming back to this place is so depressing. There's just a dark cloud over this city. Compared to other cities, it's like going back in time," I reflected.

As soon as I arrived, Big Dawg called to inform me that the babies were on the road, and he needed me to be in rare form. He also mentioned that Frank would hold the trailer in town for a day to return with as much money as possible.

"Do you have those guys on point with what I'm looking to see?!" I asked I AM. "They all know, and that's for sure," I AM replied.

My team performed like the Showtime Lakers, and within hours, they had me about 2.5. "Yo, I need to run into you, and you already know what I mean when the work is in town," I told Big Dawg.

"MAAAAAAAN, I know you're going to help me count all this shit here," Big Dawg pleaded. "Nope! Wayne, we've got to get this counted and on that truck,"

“OOOOOOOOH......... WE WE, so you are French now, I replied teasing him. I showed up and performed in the fashion previously promised. now I'm exiting stage left, as I walked out,

As I walked out, I heard him yell, "YOOUUUUUSE A DIIIIIIRTY MUTHA FUCKA!!!!"

Late that night a number showed up on my cell phone, I just got a call from my friend on the other side, Brian said. I will need you to come pick me up from the airport. I will have my uncle with me too. See you in a couple days, and I will give you details. Now make sure you have that ready for the driver too, Brian expressed.

The next morning, I asked Tez to ride with me somewhere. While driving, I called I AM and BIG I to meet me at the burg. As I pulled into the parking lot, they pulled the spaceship out of the shop. She rolled out with her platinum-colored body sitting on 22-inch Giovanni rims on Pirelli run-flat tires. The wheels had a 3-inch lip on the front and a 6-inch lip on the rear and were staged so there would be no rubbing. When they turned her towards me and rolled her up right in front of the car I was in, the chrome from her lips was shining as she drove towards me. Tez screamed at the top of his lungs, "OH MY GOD!!! "THAT BITCH BLOWS KISSES AT YOU WHILE SHE CRAWLING TO YOU." But to me, she looked like she was pouting. She just looked so, so spoiled, and I could tell from looking at her that she had a very, very bad attitude.

CHAPTER 10

SHE HAS A VERY VERY BAD ATTITUDE.........

I HOPPED INTO THE spaceship and headed to the burg to meet with I AM and BIG I. I had to put on a song fitting for this occasion, finally being introduced to the power of my thoughts in the form of this lovely lady's (BMW 745 LI) seduction by my favorite artist, Usher. I rode to the smooth lyrics and mellow harmonies of this phenomenal vocalist, feeling the power of his delivery flow through my custom system. You could feel the harmonies as they filled the air, and the sound was so clean and powerfully displayed. Two batteries were in my custom-built trunk to ensure that Usher's premium performance was well received. I was about to shake the bricks loose on your porch, while honey glazing your ears with every single sound within the song delivered clearly to your eardrums.

Later that night, Brian called and informed me that he received a call from his friend on the other side and that he needed me to pick him up from the airport with his uncle. Brian asked me to have all the details ready for the driver.

I met I AM and BIG I and updated them on the opportunity we had with Brian flying in with his uncle in a few days. I instructed BIG I to reach out to hustle man and explained to them the importance of this opportunity and what I was expecting from them. This was to be kept between I AM, BIG I, and hustle man only, and I didn't want anyone to know about this new relationship. I was waiting to hear more from Brian before disclosing anything.

Uncle Sam called me, needing money to start putting together the place he had found for me. Kevin gave me an update on the office and told me that I needed to come in to interview a few people for my company. I also needed to start putting together work crews for my properties. Hustle Man contacted me through BIG I and told me that he was excited about this new relationship, but he needed to tell me a few things that I was not aware of yet.

The following morning, I AM and I drove to Metro Airport to pick up Brian and his uncle, while BIG I got a suite at the Omni hotel, which was located on the Detroit River. I had an understanding with the hotel that allowed for a special arrangement. BIG I also contacted Hustle Man.

When Brian and his uncle landed, I stood by the luggage claim, waiting for them to appear. Finally, I saw Brian, along with a short, chubby older Mexican man. Brian's uncle had on dirty overalls and his hands were rough and his face aged by what appeared to be years in the sun. It was clear that he was a farmer and refused to dress in any other fashion. Brian explained that his uncle was all business The semi would be released to us only on his approval. "Nephew, we are here now. I need to see if your friends are set up and ready." It was clear that Brian was not in charge of anything.

"Yo, I AM. Hit BIG I and see if he has handled that yet. Also, tell him to meet us at Hustle Man's spot."

I called Hustle Man on his cell, "What's good bro. Change of plans for a moment. I just grabbed my KIN folks from the PORT (AIRPORT), and they want to see that we are built like I told them." I described it to Hustle Man.

"We can make that happen."

"What do you need me to do, Hustle Man? I ask.

"Can we run into each other over at your gym then?" I add.

"Gotcha," Hustle Man answers as he hangs up.

Meeting Hustle Man at his gym was basically saying I needed to meet him at one of his storehouses that he worked out of.

I AM pulled up, and Hustle Man, along with BIG I, was already there. Hustle Man and BIG I were standing outside waiting for us. When we exited the car with Brian and his uncle, a number of gunmen appeared, securing the outside area. Brian's uncle seemed a little uncomfortable at the surprise.

"I told Brian, don't get excited. They're with us," I said as I looked over at his uncle. "ESTA BEIN," Brian said in Spanish. The uncle returned a nervous smile.

Hustle Man took I AM, BIG I, myself, Brian, and his uncle into his gym. We took a tour and ended up in the basement level of Hustle Man's place. There was about a ton of marijuana in bales sitting in the center of the room, and Brian's uncle had a very huge smile come over his face.

"Brian, the trust that I'm asking for...," I pointed my finger at the word. "It's trust that I currently enjoy." Brian translated what I was saying to his uncle in Spanish.

"I control the bigger end of this city's market. I also reach the outer cities within the state. I can expand more inside the state! We currently have people coming from outside the state. And I would also love to entertain conversations in other states. This is why a good relationship is important to my vision of expansion," I dictated as Brian translated to his uncle.

I believe the reason Brian's uncle got nervous when he saw the gunmen is that American Mexicans often tell Mexicans from Mexico that "All Blacks rob and jack people." It's a tactic to keep themselves as middlemen between the Mexicans from Mexico, pushing them out and doing exactly what these American Mexicans were doing: dealing directly with black folks that really control the market and cutting them out as the predominant middleman.

Commerce, the GM dealership is not GM, The Gucci retail store in not Gucci, The Bank is not the Federal Reserve and The American Mexican is not The Mexican Cartel..... Therefore, you are paying a tax every step away from the actual brand itself. BIG I told Hustle Man that I wanted him to get a room down at the Omni hotel also. I sent BIG I to make a few more arrangements for our guests. We got into the car, and I told I AM to make a few more stops to show that we were set up to handle large volumes of work. Brian's uncle didn't speak English, but he was damn good at writing addresses, street names, and directions. But what I was showing was a skeleton of a much deeper organization.

I AM pulled up at Eastland Mall, and we went inside. We went over to Treasures Jewelry Store, and I saw my good brother Jay. I AM and I looked at a few pieces also. I ended up purchasing Brian's uncle some really nice things to take back to Mexico with him. I was being a very good host to my guests. I also saw that American fashion was valued, based on the fashion-conscious gentlemen at the nightclub in Tijuana. It was also important for him to see me inside my element as THE JEFE. The farmer wasn't interested in fashion, but it would stimulate plenty of conversation at home.

We ended up at the Omni hotel that night because Brian's uncle needed rest. I had Tez bring our spaceship down to the hotel, where BIG I, Tez, myself, and Brian hit up the STING strip club. Prior to going, I called Kiwi, a special girl who always had my best interests at heart. I asked her to make arrangements for our group and she reserved the whole VIP area for us. She also put 10 bottles on ice to chill and gave out wristbands to the best-looking ladies that night. She informed the bouncers to only allow those with special wristbands into our section.

Whenever I came into the club Maria would always make sure I didn't get overrun by strippers. I would later find out that the girls would get word that I was coming and on a particular night and they would call around the city to their friends to tell them I was going to be there. So 30 or 40 females would be at the club waiting for us to come in which caused me to accept Kiwi suggestions to start giving wristbands out.

That night, I hit the club hard and ended up spending about 30 racks, although we were supposedly taking it easy. The following morning, Hustle Man called my room and asked me to come down to his room to order some room service. He wanted to have a long talk with me. Over breakfast, he informed me that the work we showed Brian and his uncle wasn't just for me. He pointed out that the wrapping was the same and that the numbers written on the sides of each bale were also the same.

I was confused and Hustle man explained that a load had come into town and was working with a crew called NOTHIN II LOSE, which my brother BIG Dawg had worked with before. BIG Dawg's job was to drive Frank around when he and sometimes Mario came to town. Frank had been trying to collect hundreds of thousands of dollars from the NOTHING I LOSE crew and had sent my brother to handle the job. This is why Big Dawg kept bringing Frank by my house. Trying to convince Frank he could handle the work, unbeknownst to me. The issue was that Frank had sent a load to that crew while I was away in Mexico, but he had given them a cheaper price.

Hustle man continued, "Wayne, word is that your brother is doing the same shit them NOTHIN II LOSE dudes were doing and carrying really high balances." He also revealed that a white boy from Arizona named JD had been working as the middle man to help those guys get back in with Frank. Hustle man anticipated this move and that's why he was making the moves he was now.

I asked Hustle man what his plans were at this point, but he refused to answer, saying, "Don't ask me any crazy shit like that. Why the hell do you think I'm telling you this shit now?"

Hustle man was not only a business associate but also a trusted friend. He played a key role in helping me negotiate with the Tijuana cartel and other parties in the future. I could rely on him for financial support, borrowing as much as half a million or even a million dollars without hesitation. Despite his emotional outbursts and occasional threats to beat me up, he was a loyal and dependable guy. Our personal friendship was separate from our business dealings, and we never let loyalty cloud our judgment when it came to making tough decisions. I appreciated the fact that he took on this job simply as a matter of business, and that he had informed me of what was going on purely out of a sense of loyalty, rather than any financial interest. For us, it was always about the bottom line and not about blind loyalty to the hood.

This is what I knew so far: the "nothing to lose" crew never moved the volume of work I did. No one moved the mutha fuckin shit with the speed I did. I anticipated this move and stacked the deck in my favor. My cousin DIRT was the key figure in that crew. Dirt stored and protected the loads for them, and he was also their enforcer. I also knew that my cousin and Hustle man didn't always have the best relationship because they were both the same type of personalities. They provided the same service for two of the biggest crews in the city and always felt they would have to see each other one day. They looked at each other as a threat. I saw this situation as a great problem to have.

Hustle man was a big part of what I was putting together. He often helped free me up so I wouldn't have to cover all the expenses on new growth options. We were pretty damn good friends, and to my cousin, we came up together and literally wore the same clothes at times. As I stated above, they were both very, very good people at the end of the day. And with me being the nucleus between the two, there would be no threats, only love and lots and lots of money to be made!

With me in the middle, there would be no violence because we were businessmen and entrepreneurs, and our main interest was getting the money. All that other crazy shit was for the suckers. All of us being from the 80s, violence brought down so many crews because them people are not going to have you shooting, killing, and all that violent shit. They will lock your ass up and figure it out later. But when you are businessmen, even though you may be doing illegal business, they'll build the case first and bring the charges against you when they have it all put together. For me, it was never personal. They were going to do their job to catch me, and it was my job not to get caught.

The bottom line is that I created a new and blossoming market with major growth upside over what was apparent. Frank wanted to steal something he didn't create. His answer was to shift to the "nothing to lose" crew at a cheaper price, thinking the market would shift outright. But Frank didn't have the guts to shut BIG Dawg down either. I knew he would not have the balls to do this outright because the volume of product we were moving through us gave him more power back home as a major earner with guys that work fast! Frank would not be able to get this from the "nothing to lose" crew. Frank thought giving a cheaper price to the "tax-type" dudes would help this transition, but the extra room on price never made it to the street.

Frank's weakness was his greed and willingness to steal from all ends. He didn't care for people that had the ability to process complete ideas. The side effect of this was he became just as my brother was for him... dangerously predictable.

"I need you to swing by and see my cousin DIRT. Let him know that I will be to see him soon. Give him an idea of what it is. Leave all details for me to deal with him on," I requested I AM.

I was aware that my cousin was unhappy with the guys he was working with because they had their foot on his neck and weren't allowing him to make much. He often came to me upset about it. Asking I AM to deliver the message carried some risk of the new secret load getting out, but I figured this was more of a form of controlled chaos that could lead to positive blowback for me. I AM would just plant an idea and my cousin's own nature would do the rest independent of outside.

Mario, Frank's brother, would become an unwitting ally for me because of his dislike for Frank's decision-making. I sensed a myopic view from Mario, which could be useful in time. BIG Dawg made a lot of bad moves and had many quixotic choices that were not based in reality, which removed him from what would become the perfect expression.

Returning to my room, I went into deep thought. Brian came down to my room and informed me that his uncle was very impressed with what he saw. Brian also added that the semi with the work was headed our way. He wanted to get some ladies to come down to party, and I was starting to see what Baby Doll told me about Brian - he was a horn dog. I called a pretty good female friend of mine who was a stripper. We were just friends, but there was never anything sexual between us. I told her that I had some good friends in town and needed to bring in some girls who were up for it. I instructed her to bring some top-end girls with upscale costumes.

Ebony came down to the Omni hotel with a few friends. I told her to just come and dress up but she was to just sit around and look good. The room had two floors in it. The girls got dressed and came out, and I was very impressed, as was Brian. But Ebony had on an Angel costume with really, really huge colorful wings. I was totally caught off guard by this.

The boys just went at it like a pack of wolves, and the women seemed to be up for the challenge too. I just kept talking with Ebony and telling her how nice her outfit was. Ebony was interested in me and had been for some time too. She was a very good looking young lady with a very, very large posterior.

"Yeah, yeah, BIG I" I screamed as I heard a loud smacking sound.

"I thought I told you to look across the river at Canada! Don't look back at me! Keep your hands on the wall and look at Canada," BIG I at the person responsible. Ebony just kept walking back and forth in front of me and dancing in a really slow grinding type motion. She started walking up the stairs while dancing slowly.

I just fucking lost it! I was already rock hard, and she was looking like a colorful quail! But now, I was the quail hunter. I ran up the stairs and went into action. The wings on Ebony's Angel costume started to lose feathers, and the wings were in rapid motion now. I got so excited I opened the door and Ebony lost a wing on her outfit. Afterward, Ebony and I finished our dance. I was running up and down the stairs in my birthday suit. Brian was on the first floor with a couple of ladies at this point. I jumped up on the landing overlooking the first floor. I started pumping and whining the air with my manhood at full attention and screaming.

Brian looked up and yelled with his Latino accent, "What the fuck are you doing?" as he put his arm over his head and said, "Go somewhere and put that thing up!"

After all the male bonding, Brian told me that the load would be pulling in the following night. His uncle had not been coming out because he wasn't feeling that good. Brian also advised me that someone would be arriving a few hours ahead of the load to talk with me.

I went to Hustle Man'sroom and told him I would need $150,000 from him by the morning. He agreed to do so. I told BIG I that I needed him to put a team together to unload the semi the following night. I AM would have the money for the driver. I would have the uncle and Brian with me.

The following morning, Brian told me that we needed to meet the car that was a few hours ahead of the semi. We ended up driving to Chalmers and Harper on the eastside of Detroit. We pulled into the KFC parking lot and sat there as Brian gave directions to the car coming to meet us. Next thing I knew, a Spanish guy came walking across the KFC parking lot. He started smiling as he got into the back seat of the spaceship. "My friend, this fucking car totally kicks ass!" he started speaking in Spanish to Brian and his uncle. "My friend, the old man was right. You are doing very well up here. Your car is kick ass too," he said as he looked around in the car. The Spanish man started exiting the car and said, "We will see you tonight."

It was a night when the semi was running late, and they were waiting for it to arrive. I was driving a spaceship with Brian, his uncle, and a Spanish guy. BIG I was in a white work van with a few more guys waiting to hit and unload the truck. I had 150,000 to pay the driver as agreed, and the guy riding with me was in control of the driver and the drop spot. We were communicating through Nextel two way with I am, BIG I , and Hustle man. Brian's uncle was in contact with Mexico, and the spaceship was the mobile command center.

We were in an area with all office buildings, and the drop spot they chose for the driver was no longer available. I had to find a place nearby former drops, but they screwed up on this pretty bad. The truck couldn't go too far off route because of the tracker on it. Brian suggested, "Yo, tell your guy in the back seat that I don't give a FUCK what he thinks anymore! He already FUCKED UP the most important part of the deal. Pull the FUCKIN truck behind that FUCKIN building, and my guys will have that SHIT off in less than 15 minutes. Or I'm blowing the spot and taken my boys back in. And I'm going to put all your ASSES out, and you can all ride back to Mexico with that FUCKIN two-hour late driver and his DUMB ASS," pointing to the guy in the back. The Spanish-speaking man talked to the driver while circling the block.

"Yo, the driver is circling the block," I said very nervous to Big I over the two-way. "Did you see that move I pulled at the back of the spot?" I asked over the two-way. Big I replied, "FO SHO!"

"I need you to get your guys in position to shoot that move as soon as that thing pulls up there. We have 10 to 15 minutes tops," I said. We saw the white van getting into position. Brian was biting his nails.

"You good?" I asked I AM over the two-way. He replied, "Yes, Sir." The semi was coming back up the street. I used the two-way to let my number come across Big I's phone, letting him know to get his guys ready to hit the semi.

The truck pulled in and you could hear a pin drop. It was so quiet in the car. "Beep beep..." Big I indicated that the transfer was a success. The phone rang with a guy in the back seat. Excited screaming and yelling filled the car as the driver relayed the same information.

"I need you to check that," I told Big I. "My friend, where is the money?" the Spanish guy asked. I responded, "Everything is OK. He is checking in... Spanish speaking."

"Beep beep... talk to me," I said over the two-way. "I'm trying to find something to cut the bale so I can see it," Big I replied. "My friend, you have it now! We need the money, my friend!" the Spanish guy said, getting a little upset.

"Beep beep... Do you see the driver yet?" I asked I AM. "Yes, and I'm just waiting on you now," I AM responded, waiting for me to give him the green light to pay the driver.

There was very loud yelling and anger from the Spanish guy in the back seat now. "PAY THE FUCKIN' MONEY!! PAY THE FUCKIN' MONEY

NOW!!!" he shouted. In the back seat, yelling behind me while I was driving. I looked over at Brian, and he looked as white as a ghost from fear.

"Beep beep... bro, you are killing me over here. I need an answer, bro," I said firmly but calmly. You never want to pass the pressure you are receiving onto your guys in the middle of shooting a move.

"Are you OK over there?" Big I asked.

"Brian, you need to snap out of that bitch-ass fear and tell that dumb fuck behind me to shut the fuck up so I can give my guys instructions! They are getting nervous, and things are going to get bad quick!" Brian was talking very loudly in Spanish. Then Uncle started getting loud, and everything got dead silent. I'm assuming Uncle told them to shut up and allow me to work.

"Beep beep! Beep beep!" from Big I, and now I AM and Hustle Man. "Everything is good on my end, bro. I just need you to tell me something," I answered very relaxed and calm to Big I.

"Man, are you good?" Big I asked very aggressively.

"Big fella, I'm just peachy. Now, can I get my answer for the 20th time?" I asked in an aggressive tone toward him.

"Damn, bro... My bad," Big I said with a much softer tone. "I'm not crazy about what I see, but it will go," Big I said.

"Yo, you good to go? Go over to Hustle Man's way right after," I told I AM to pay the driver and then meet up with the guys afterward. "Enroute," I said to Hustle Man as the phone in the back of me started ringing. Spanish speaking in the car. "Everything is OK for everyone now," Brian said. There was silence in the car.

"This car totally kicks ass, my friend!" came a voice from the back seat of the spaceship.

CHAPTER 11

ROCKY POINT MEXICO

BRIAN AND HIS UNCLE boarded a flight heading back Out West, disappointed with the quality of weed they had acquired. However, they managed to make some money with a little extra effort. The load was paid off in full before it even started moving. To spread the wealth, I had I AM give some of the action to his cousin DIRT as well.

But things took a suspicious turn when Brian requested additional money based on an extra tax. I remembered the warning given by the gentleman in Tijuana at Table 2 about this. Brian asked for an extra 40,000 and spun a bullshit story to explain it. I had his doubts but ultimately handed over the cash.

Uncle Sam caught up with me and took me to Somerset Mall in Troy, Michigan. My uncle, a true diva with fashion sense, interior design skills, and seduction techniques, wanted to share some ideas for my place. We entered the Bang and Olsen store where I couldn't resist and ended up picking out several items worth just over $130,000.

Meanwhile, Baby Doll was thrilled to hear about my successful deals with two groups. She wanted to be spoiled and rightly so, and I didn't hesitate to fulfill her wishes. She expressed interest in investing in a group that opened workout gyms throughout Phoenix, Arizona, and I provided her with the money she needed to start the first gym and purchase equipment. The initial investment was around $50,000, which helped her secure a contract to open multiple gyms within the investment group.

Baby Doll had a bodybuilding competition coming up in California and she wanted her family members to attend. She asked me to pay for their travel expenses and also wanted us to visit Disney World after the competition for her niece and nephew. She also mentioned that she wanted us to have some quality time together during those days. I agreed to her plan and offered to pay for everything.

"I would love to meet your family and make them feel welcomed," I replied. Baby Doll was excited and happy to hear that.

"My mom wants me to slow down and find a good black man," she shared. I found her sweet and pretty , but couldn't help but feel intimidate by her muscular physique as she prepared for her body building competition. She was of great value, and I knew I didn't want sex to mess things up between us. Sex just wasn't that important to me and never really have been.

Baby Doll then brought up Brian, my friend who had shared some private details about me with her. "He told me about the party and your dancing too," she said. She reminded me of the three issues that Mexican men have with black men, which I had forgotten. "It doesn't matter how much money we make together or how friendly they get with us, these issues will always be there," she warned me. She also shared some vulgar comments that Brian had made about me. She said I'm looking forward to my personal performance of this dance in California she said with excitement! she wanted to see the African phallic love God, HUH??! I was arrogantly thinking.

Meanwhile, I had been working on a house for my daughter's mother. I had faced a lot of problems with her concerning the house. She was giving me a hard time with moving in, which hurt my feelings.

However, with the help of my uncle and Kevin, I was able to put the house together.

A little over a month had passed, and Frank was back, ready to send Big Dawg another load. I wasn't too keen on working with these guys anymore since they had already sent two loads to my cousin's people since the last time he sent Big Dawg. However, the two loads they sent didn't even come close to equaling the one load that Frank sent to Big Dawg.

I already knew that Frank would try to make amends after his attempt to steal the market from me, but I didn't want to work with him anymore. The success of my philosophy relied on players buying into the idea of cheaper prices for consumers and moving large volumes to make big money over short periods of time. This was based on the business principle of offering the best quality at the lowest price, even though many would argue against it. Let's say it takes a month to remove a couple of metric tons of marijuana or cocaine. If I can remove the same volume three or four times within the same time span, I can make more money than my competitors and my team can make more money too. Increasing speed during that 30-day window is a direct signal that the product is entering other markets. The key to this philosophy is to increase market value while making some profit off the consumer, but the main focus is to obtain compensation from corporations who have a lot more money. The political power that comes with this compensation is beyond measure and is simply commerce, not folklore or mythical tales of loyalty. At the end of the day, it's just business, and I am an entrepreneur.

The word "loyal" dates back to the 1530s and originally referred to the qualities of true faithfulness and allegiance among subjects of sovereigns or governments. Its French origin is traced back to "loyal" or "leal," which meant "of good quality," "faithful," "honorable," "law-abiding," "legitimate," or "born in wedlock." This information is derived from the online etymology dictionary.

Historically, loyalty was never just given, it was always earned. The sovereign, be it a king or government, expected loyalty from their subjects. The question is, in today's mentality, are you a boss or a subject? This is how the word was originally used.

According to the theory of the evolution of the word "loyalty," you owed loyalty to your king or government based on the opportunities for safety, ways to earn a living, health and well-being, and so on, all provided to you under the law. In return, your loyalty was required.

Within its original meaning, the word "loyal" or "loyalty" was used in reference to subjects, not kings, queens, or governments. You show your loyalty by following the law. Therefore, if you consider yourself to be a boss, you are getting a return on your investment in your subjects, and that is their loyalty towards you and your agenda.

The basis of your return to your boss, sovereign, or even company, is expressed by you following the law or policies set forth by those entities in exchange for what they provide you. Sovereignty is about law and legality, and these are intertwined with commerce, business, money, loyalty, and royalty. All of these fall under the law.

I instigated a major dispute over pricing. I was well aware that Frank had tried and failed to remain true to his nature, that pinche bandito. Despite this, I knew that the pressure was still on Frank to move the same volume of product in the same amount of time. Frank had swindled his uncle, taking advantage of the rapid pace at which he was moving the product. This placed the same pressure on Frank's uncle from his bosses, as Babydoll had taught me that all Mexicans are greedy.

Frank knew that he could rip off his uncle without any repercussions. His uncle's bosses were not willing to lose the large, rapid influx of income over some stolen money that could be repaid, and the account would remain active. Frank's leverage was his control of the account. However, he was starting to realize that I understood the business and that I would use that leverage against him. Frank attempted to escape by finding another venue, the "nothing to lose" crew in the same market, to steal that leverage. However, Frank did not anticipate that the philosophy and ideology that I got my guys to buy into were so strong that simply switching the venue would have a reverse effect. And it did.

So, in layman's terms, it's now my turn. And, as they say, whenever you break up with a pretty girl at the dance and you want to come back, you have to bring gifts!

When the work arrived, I intentionally slowed down the process, much to the frustration of Frank and Big Dawg. Frank complained to Big Dawg, saying that they were supposed to work quickly. But I didn't care about their complaints because I knew they were both involved in the deception. Eventually, I finished the work in about three weeks and it was time for my date with Baby Doll.

I submitted everything except for $100,000, which was part of my profit. For the first time, I paid myself first before anything else. Then, I AM and I hopped on a flight to Arizona where everything was arranged by Baby Doll. She was going to California for a competition, and her family was going to Disney World after the event. I even planned to perform my phallic love God dance for her, but I was worried about how to get past her muscular physique.

When we landed in Phoenix, Brian picked us up from the airport. I called Baby Doll to let her know that I arrived safely and she was thrilled. Brian knew everything about my plans with Baby Doll and asked if I had been to a competition like that before. I told him I hadn't. I wasn't paying much attention to him because I suspected he had already sold me out to Baby Doll.

Brian pleaded with me to change our plans and go to Mexico instead, but I had already promised Baby Doll and her entire family that we would go to California. I admitted to Brian that everything had already been paid for and I had given my word to Baby Doll, but my voice was tinged with frustration.

I AM and I got Brian to drop us at the hotel. I had a brief conversation with Baby Doll before agreeing to meet up with her the following afternoon to leave with her family. After that, I called Sheila to let her know I was in town. We spent some time together and picked up where we left off the last time we were together. "When we were together and we talked about everything; nothing to do with money. Sheila stayed pretty late before heading home to be with her girls.

The following morning, I was having breakfast in my hotel room with I AM when we heard a knock on the door. I AM got up to answer it and to our surprise, it was Brian. However, I wasn't surprised at all. Brian's face was filled with desperation as he expressed his disapproval.

"NO! YOU CAN'T FUCKIN DO THIS! YOU CAN'T FUCKING GO THROUGH WITH THIS, WAYNE!" Brian yelled.

I calmly responded, "Brian, I don't care what you say. My mind is set and I'm keeping my word. I'm not going to embarrass Baby Doll in front of her whole family."

"FUCK THEM!" Brian yelled back. "They are getting a free paid vacation that includes all kinds of first-class treatment! I AM, you have to stop your friend from doing this," Brian pleaded, looking to I AM for support.

"My friend, why didn't she come and see you last night?" Brian asked.

"I talked to Baby Doll last night and this morning too. And I'm going to tell you why! SHE LOOKS LIKE A MAN NOW, MY FRIEND!!!! SHE LOOKS JUST LIKE A FUCKIN MAAAAN NOW, MY FRIEND!!! She looks like a fuckin man now," I AM said in shock.

"YEAH, I AM," Brian continued to yell. "This dirty mutha fucka didn't stop there either! DID HE TELL YOU THAT HIS SWEET BABY DOLL WAS USING STEROIDS TOO??!"

I AM shook his head no, looking like he had seen a ghost. Brian continued his emotional outburst, "Wayne, you are going somewhere with a bunch of people you don't even know. Just to watch this lady's daughter walking out on a stage in high heels, LOOKING LIKE A MAN!!! I hope you don't think you are going to see pretty ladies in swimsuits. Noooooooo, they will look like big buff men in swimsuits & stilettos. And their clitoris grows when they're on steroids. Imagine a bunch of dudes walking around in heels and swimsuits and they're on the hard. Oh, this is what it will look like," Brian explained.

I was really starting to get concerned now and asked Brian, "Have you been to one of these things before?"

"How do you think I got so many details?" Brian replied. "I got tricked into going with her before. Let's go to Mexico right now! Boots is waiting for us to meet him in a few days. We can go on vacation for a few days and party with some really nice girls. Then go meet with Boots. He wants to discuss some business with you. My friend, you won't make it back in time," Brian expressed.

I was starting to see Brian's point: MONEY!! "Well, Brian, I think you may be right about this now. After all, I did pay for everything. I'm going to call her now to let her know," I said.

But before I could make the call, Brian cut in, "ARE YOU FUCKIN CRAZY!! We have to just take off now & run!! You call her & she will know that I talked you out of it! Brian, I AM, and I were on the road to Mexico!"

We ended up at a beautiful resort situated right off the Pacific Ocean, or at least that's what I thought. I had rented what seemed like a timeshare, with four fully furnished bedrooms, an all-glass oceanside view, and a huge balcony that was also furnished. After settling in and getting some rest, we decided to start fresh the following morning.

Late the next morning, as we were getting ready to explore, I looked out the balcony and saw the beautiful ocean filled with people. Brian suggested we go to a really nice restaurant in town, pointing up in a direction. However, I AM didn't seem to like what he saw up there. "Man, I ain't going up there!! That fucking place is sitting on the edge of a fucking cliff, Wayne!!" I AM yelled from the back seat.

We arrived at the upscale restaurant despite I AM's doomsday predictions about its location on the edge of a cliff. As we entered, the place was packed with tourists. The host, speaking in Spanish, seemed to be turning us away, claiming that they were full. Brian disagreed with him, and that's when an older, well-dressed Spanish gentleman caught my attention. He was watching us, particularly I AM and me, and I could tell he knew American fashion based on his stylish attire.

I decided to impress him and applied additional pressure on my arm, revealing my Ulysses Nardin navy blue and rose gold watch. The gentleman sprang into action and moved towards us, shouting "Mi amigos, mi amigos!"

He hugged me first, then I AM, and extended his hand to Brian. He scolded the host and led us upstairs, saying, "Forgive me, these young people only understand what they see every day. The locals can't afford to visit places like this. I entertain tours and have done so here for 30 years."

He assigned us a waiter who only served our table and made sure we had a wonderful view of the ocean. "Mi genti will be making sure your visit will be fully enjoyed. I'm sure there is much to enjoy tonight, and thank you for choosing my place," he said. He left us, giving additional instructions to his staff to make sure this mistake is never repeated.

As we sat down, I noticed there weren't any apparent Mexicans in the restaurant, only Caucasians. Brian asked me if I had been there before, but I answered in the negative. Later, I would learn that most Mexicans had never seen African Americans. Mexicans were mostly people of color, varying in shades of brown, and very dark in some cases. These young people may have only seen Black people on TV if they had access to a TV.

However, the older gentleman, whom I had taken a liking to, seemed to have a different impression. Seeing a Spanish man and two Black men, he might have thought we were in the cartel business.

After a delicious meal, we left the upscale restaurant and headed back to the resort to unwind. Brian shared some of the business that needed to be handled during our trip, but we planned to spend the next two or three days relaxing at the resort.

As nighttime fell, we visited various strip clubs. I AM became infatuated with one young lady and invited her back to the resort. Brian had to make arrangements for both of them to get past security.

Next, Brian took us to a number of brothels, and he and I AM went wild in one Mexican brothel. I sat there waiting for them, but they seemed to be trying to hook up with every woman in the place. I was uncomfortable with the women trying to lure me into the back and eventually stormed out. To my surprise, they even sent a feminine young man after me.

Sex is a significant part of Spanish culture, and it was clear to me that I was not familiar with their customs. I stood on the main street trying to process what had just happened. Suddenly, I noticed a silver Range Rover driving towards me. It was an unusual sight on the busy Mexican street. As the truck approached, the driver and I locked eyes, and I felt a moment of recognition. "We're looking into each other's souls, Frank?"

I said aloud, half-jokingly. The truck passed, and I shook off the idea that it could be Frank, reminding myself that I was in Mexico, after all.

Finally, we returned to the resort, and I retired to my room, which had a balcony overlooking the ocean. It was a dark night, and the only thing visible was the white foam of the waves crashing against the shore. I took in the cool breeze and reflected on the events of the day.

After returning to my room and enjoying the wonderful breeze blowing off of the ocean, I lay down to rest. However, I was soon awakened by the sound of heavy breathing, moans, and high heels rocking back and forth on a concrete balcony. "Those are two fuckin' horn dogs," I whispered to myself as I turned over.

The morning sun rose early and we walked up the street from the resort to rent some 3-4 wheelers. Excitement filled us as we hopped on and headed straight for the desert. We rode for hours, the wind whipping through our hair, and the sand spraying behind us. At one point, as I was riding, I looked down and saw a little green bush move. Suddenly, a mouse or rat ran out, and I freaked out and jumped off the four-wheeler. The vehicle flipped over, and I found myself on one side of the machine, face down in the sand with my arms stretched out. Brian and I AM pulled up to help, but I AM was laughing too hard to be of any help.

"Man, your fat ass was sliding across the desert floor! When you stopped, we couldn't see anything but a big cloud of dust," I AM joked.

I looked up and spat out a mouthful of sand. We got back on the four-wheelers, and while riding, we saw a freshly laid road and couldn't resist the temptation. We hopped onto the road and started flying. The tires were throwing tar back up on us, but we didn't care. Suddenly, we saw lights behind us - it was the police pulling us over. They started speaking to Brian in Spanish, and he told us they were going to arrest us for damaging private property. Brian spoke some more with the police, and then said, "When they come to you, just hand them any kind of card but put $10 of American dollars folded up under the card."

We were handed a ticket-shaped piece of paper with our password for the day written on it. We were free to break traffic laws for the rest of the day. If we were pulled over again, all we had to do was give them the password, and we'd be let go.

After this close encounter, we stopped by a drugstore. Brian was looking to buy some Viagra-type pills, which shocked me that they sold them over the counter. I asked about steroids as well, and it seemed like they sold everything over the counter. A middle-aged Spanish woman waited on us, and I started noticing her looking at me and smiling while showing me different Viagra-type pills.

"Brian, why does she keep looking at me and smiling while talking about these pills? Did you tell her I want them or something?" I asked.

Brian acted like he was translating, and then a Spanish man walked up to assist the woman with our order. He started to show Brian the steroids and tell him how to take them. Then, the man behind the counter pointed at I AM and myself while talking to Brian.

"He's telling me that I may not want to go to the beach with you guys if we all do the treatment. He said you guys are going to make me look like I have not been doing anything," Brian translated.

While the man was talking to Brian, the middle-aged woman was shaking these pills at me. She came over to me, and the gentleman started talking to her about what she was showing me. They got into a heated exchange, and I was concerned for the woman because she seemed really upset.

"What's going on with these two, Brian?" I asked.

Brian responded while laughing. "The gentleman is telling her to get away from you with those pills that don't work. She started yelling at him, saying that she's a woman, so she knows what works and what doesn't work that good. Unless someone has been using these pills on you, then you know nothing. But in case they have, use these. He will make you feel much better and for longer with these."

As she tossed the pills to the gentleman behind the counter, Brian finished explaining.

After hearing the translation, I AM and I looked at each other and started saying to the middle-aged lady, "SI SI SI, MUCHO MUCHO!!!" The lady started to laugh at our reactions. I wasn't in the market for any of those pills, but the way she was reacting, I became fully interested in them at that point. I don't know how the other ones were that the guy behind the counter was suggesting, but she wasn't lying about the ones she was talking about. Oh my God!

We jumped on the 4 Wheelers with some steroids and a SHIT LOAD of the blue, weird-shaped, no-name happy fun time pills. We returned back to the resort and had a few good Mexican-style meals. We knew that we had to be on the road early the next morning.

The following morning, we got a late start, but it didn't take long to get together and hit the road. Our destination was Tijuana to meet up with Boots. After arriving in Tijuana, we checked into a hotel and then drove to Boots' house. He was excited to see us again, and after we had a little something to eat, we headed to a nightclub.

Once we arrived, we met up with another group, and I noticed that there were guys with us, but they appeared to be maintaining a perimeter around us. The line at the nightclub was long, and it was still packed. A special entrance was made for our group, and a little lady was allowed closer to our group. One of the perimeter guys yelled something over, and as our group stopped, Boots yelled something back, and the young lady was let through. She went up to I AM and handed him a number and said, "I love you." Boots translated the remainder of what the young lady had to say to I AM.

Our group entered the club with what I had figured out were armed bodyguards. They cleared a big area for us to walk directly to the VIP section. We partied hard up in the VIP section, and wild women were waiting in line to be rotated up by the bodyguards. I asked about the heavy guard presence around us that night, and Brian made me aware that this was normal in Mexico. He also told me that the club owner was just kidnapped the night before in broad daylight at the intersection in front of the nightclub. I was shocked that things like that were so common over there. Brian corrected me, saying, "No, it's only common in Tijuana because the cartels allow it. You would never see that in a city like Juarez because the next day, you will find the kidnappers hanging from an overpass with a sign pinned to them."

Boots came over and started to talk to Brian. Brian turned to me and said, "Wayne, I forgot to tell you that you still owe Boots $2000 more from that last shipment." I knew it was most likely money that Brian owed Boots. I gave Brian a little hell over it, but I paid it directly to Boots. I saw that Boots' friend was named Chewy, and I could see that the heavy guard presence was really more attentive towards him. I found out later that night that Chewy represented a number of farmers in that region of the country that wanted to have their products on the American market.

I ended up having a conversation with Baby Doll about my absence and explained to her that I couldn't miss the important meeting. I didn't want to disappoint anyone, and it was crucial that we didn't let that opportunity slip away. Baby Doll understood my reasoning and supported my decision. However, she also expressed her frustration about the investment group she was a part of not fulfilling their financial obligations towards the workout and fitness centers they had invested in.

In a spoiled voice, she requested that I buy out three of the centers for her. I assured her that I would take care of it and asked her to let me know what she needed. "Consider it done," I told her.

I spent the night in Phoenix and got a chance to see Sheila, which was one of the biggest highlights of my entire visit to Phoenix, AZ. She was a wonderful soul, and I just hated that she stayed so far away because we had so much fun together just doing the simplest things. I had never dated a white girl before, and I never thought I would, but our friendship was refreshing and almost pure.

We started becoming intimate with each other, and it was almost like I had to force her to take money from me. She never once asked me for a dime or even insinuated as much. I often wished things could have been different so I could have fully had the opportunity to enjoy a serious long-term relationship with her. She really had a kind heart.

The next morning, I was on my way back to Detroit from Phoenix when I AM asked me about what Brian had told me regarding the 500 pounds of marijuana that Chewy was supposedly crossing for him. I paused to consider what I AM had asked and explained to him that Chewy only spoke to us because we were at the negotiating table. Brian had negotiated a deal with Chewy for access to me and the market I created, and the 500 pounds were Chewy's payment to Brian with a promise of a continued relationship moving forward. However, I also told I AM that Brian had no intention of just handing me over like that because he knew he was a major problem. He could keep cashing in and robbing Chewy while dangling me as bait.

Based on what Baby Doll had told me about Brian and what I was learning, he only had a few moves he could pull, and I had the deck stacked against him, except for one. I had to play along and play his hand all the way out. At this point, I had a few irons in the fire, and they were clearly working. Chewy came out of the shadows and was willing to invest big on the promise of a relationship.

There was a buzz that had started about me on the other side of the border, and I knew I would be able to cash it in at the right moment. I was determined to keep it clean and play the game straight, while staying true to one of my mottos: "There is no greater joy than to deceive the deceiver"

As we walked into the airport, my phone rang. "Hey man!" Big Dawg said on the other end. "Man, I've been calling you like crazy for the last few days. Were you in Mexico... Rocky Point, Mexico?" he chuckled.

CHAPTER 12

BUENO ESTRATEGA

GOOD STRATEGIST

UPON MY RETURN TO Detroit from Phoenix, it became apparent that news of my activities had spread. Despite this, I was prepared for any fallout that may arise. I had a number of pressing issues to attend to, some of which required me to navigate different cultures and environments with ease.

One day, while walking through the airport, my phone rang. "Big Dawg, now understands why," the Spanish speaking woman kept coming on my phone every time you were in Phoenix" I was actually in Mexico all those times. confirmed that I had, and he explained that Frank had seen me there and was concerned.

It was time for me to meet with Big Dawg and address any potential issues. pulled up to the house as usual and called Big Dawg on my cell phone. When I entered the house, I could tell that Big Dawg was stressed about an issue with Frank. I tried to make small talk with him, but he asked me why I never told him that I was going to Mexico. He explained that Frank had asked him if he knew where I was, and he had told him that I was in Phoenix visiting a friend. But then Frank saw me on a corner in Mexico and asked why Big Dawg had lied to him. Big Dawg told me that he still owed Frank money, and I still owed $100,000 of what he owed. I asked sarcastically if I should go get the money and bring it to him, but Big Dawg said that the embarrassment was the issue, not the money.

Big Dawg then told me that Frank had given him a hard time about me being in Mexico and had been yelling about how I was not loyal. I felt like Frank was just quoting someone else to express his own feelings. But Big Dawg seemed to be expressing his own feelings, and I reminded him about his past concerns with Frank. Frank would deal with Big Dawg for a short period of time and then switch back to his "nothing to lose" crew. This caused Big Dawg to suffer as he waited for Frank to return. This was not exclusive to my brother, as the other crew members were also waiting for Frank's return and begging him to send something else for them. Big Dawg would complain to me about this all the time, but his answer was always to not upset Frank. This made me angry because Frank fostered a sense of fear that held these guys prisoner. It was clear that Frank and my brother and the "nothing to lose" crew were playing out of two separate playbooks. Frank's bottom line was business only, while my brother and his crew's bottom line was loyalty, which made them predictable and subject to brutality and misuse.

When I joined my brother, Big Dawg, I noticed their reaction to the fast turnaround of cash paid to Frank. I got my first example of the belief that "all Mexicans are greedy." This is why I pushed for a cheaper price at every turn and introduced a more profit-centered philosophy based on volume. This was not unique, but rather just a different approach to business. I wanted to make sure that Frank's history would not repeat itself on my watch, so I kept him busy with a serious flow of cash that came at him fast. Frank would not have the luxury of vacillating with my brother while I controlled things from behind.

I asked Big Dawg what loyalty to Frank had ever profited him. My loyalty was expressed through the unfair taxes that I paid under his leadership to Frank and Mario for too long. I couldn't leave his ill-willed efforts out of this Congress of despicable ineptness, even though this was not a sibling struggle between him and me. Disclosing my intentions or whereabouts would have caused him to act predictably and impaired my efforts to end this embarrassment to his manhood. I also mentioned the six or seven zeros that could be earned behind my most honorable foresight.

I then informed Big Dawg about Frank's recent actions, including ending at least two or three loads to his nemesis just across town. I also informed him about the emergency Frank was in, in which BIG SEXY supposed to have had a run in with the feds, was about paying off the money from that load Frank jacked and it was found out. Frank had paid off Halo, who he had jacked, and was found out. During this time, Frank had also sent a load to Big Dawg and his crew and had given them a cheaper price. I helped Big Dawg understand that these were efforts to steal the increased market that I had created.

"Now, my big-hearted brother... I have your two BFF's check in, but unfortunately, there isn't any money left in checkmate at this point."

I proceeded to tell Big Dawg how I had created airtight relationships in his nemesis group and another crosscheck to his nemesis if they chose to be dishonest. "I knew we would come up with something!!" he exclaimed with a chuckle, but I gave him a disapproving look. He wanted to know my sources, but I disregarded his questions and instead told him how to address the issue at hand with Frank.

"Frank told me he wasn't going to deal with me anymore unless you agree to come back on board," Big Dawg told me.

I assured him not to be concerned with the things Frank was saying. "I'll be sending Frank an indirect signal to help enlighten him on the position he's played himself into. You just let Frank know that you will work this out with me soon," I told Big Dawg.

As I got up to leave, I got into my car and drove back towards home. About halfway there, I looked at my Rolex and said to myself, "Frank should have received his indirect signal and realized the position he's put himself in by now."

"Frank, man, you ain't going to believe this shit here... but don't worry about him though... hee hee hee hee!!" I said as I spoke to Frank.

This is a glaringly obvious example of misplaced loyalty.

"Loyalty benefits the ruler, not the ruled." - Wayne.

A few weeks had passed with back and forth conversations between Big Dawg, Frank, and myself. I was working on several different options on my end when I received a frantic call from Brian.

"Wayne, I'm in a bad spot... these guys from Tijuana are all over my back about some money I owe them," Brian said with a stressed voice, sounding more anxious than he did when dealing with Baby Doll.

"Yo, yo, calm down, dude," I replied, sensing the urgency of the situation. I knew this would be an issue when Brian received money from me, which was supposed to be paid to the Tijuana guys. Plus, I hadn't heard anything else from them after that successful transaction. I knew Brian had a lot to do with this too.

"Could you help me out, and I swear I will get you back," Brian pleaded with me. I really didn't want to help this snake, but I wasn't entirely in the position of holding all the cards yet.

"How much will this favor set me back this time?" I asked, trying to gauge the situation.

Brian went on to tell me he owed $50,000 to these guys, which turned out to be a problem since Brian was in Arizona at the time. I personally knew how Brian could be when afraid.

"How do you plan to get the $50,000 to them?" I asked, trying to assess Brian's plan, as I wasn't willing to give him anything personally.

"They are going to send someone from Tijuana over to you," Brian said quickly.

A smile came over my face. I guess in a case where my friend's safety was in question, I had to make sure he was safe. I stated with a heavy heart, burdened by the thought of interfering with the work of divine karma - Brian's safety was more important.

I had a conversation with the Tijuana guys, and we came to an understanding that someone would fly to Detroit, and I would meet with them. The person would arrive at the Metro International Airport and stay at a hotel nearby. Brian would give me a call with the hotel and room number for me to meet with this person. "Just go to the room and throw the money on his face! Don't even let him talk to you, my friend," Brian stressed. He was really bothered by the fact that these guys in Tijuana didn't give him a chance and how this would be handled.

The following day, I received a call that the Tijuana representative had landed and was instructed to head to the airport, where I would receive further instructions. Myself, Big I, and I AM got in the car and drove towards the airport. As we got closer, Brian kept reminding me not to let the Tijuana guy talk to me and to throw the money on his face.

When we arrived at the hotel, Brian confirmed that we had reached the correct location and provided me with the room number. As I approached the door, it swung open and the gentleman welcomed us inside. I AM and I stepped in, and my cell phone started to ring constantly. I looked and it was Brian as I figured.

“Please have a seat my friends.” The gentleman asked. My cell is still ringing like crazy. I AM pulled the $50,000 out of his pocket, all large, while we were still standing. I looked at I AM to hand the gentleman the money. I pulled my cell phone out. “Please, don't answer that just yet my friend, " the gentleman said urgently. I AM had his hand extended with the money. The gentleman paid no attention to the money.

“That is your friend calling for you over and over again. He doesn't want you talking with me.” The gentleman explained as he gently pushed I AM's hand holding the money back towards the pocket it came out of, this gesture got my attention. "My name is Orlando, and I work with the Tijuana cartel."

Orlando explained that he was not interested in the money and that Brian was just going to rob me. He warned me that Brian was not to be trusted and was only looking out for himself. At that moment, my walkie-talkie went off with Brian's voice calling out for me. Orlando instructed me to tell Brian that I was walking from the lobby and to wait for me.

I nodded to I AM to hand over the money, but Orlando ignored it, saying that my friend's call was more urgent. He then proceeded to explain the situation to me, and his words left an impression on me. I realized that loyalty was something valued on both sides of the border and that Brian was not displaying it.

"I'm walking from this place. You need to wait for me, my friend," I demanded in a scolding voice. "This is what I'm going to do for you, my friend. Please take this number for my cell phone. The only thing I ask is for you to save it in a safe place. You will be needing it soon, my friend, Orlando Stadium."

"Let me tell you something. The bandito is just using you to help himself. He is going to use you to rob people, but he will never let anyone get to you or you to them. His family has a lot of respect in Tijuana, my friend. This is the only reason he's still alive today. We forced this thing about the money because we know history all too well. Tijuana likes the way you guys do business. Keep my number in a safe place...you will see for yourself. Then call me, my friend," Orlando repeated.

I stood up and grabbed money from I AM, handing it to Orlando. He looked at me with a strange look, and I said with a half smile, "I don't jump...and I'm not like this bandito either, Orlando."

Orlando had a huge smile, and said, "Maybe my message had maybe got through to you." He accepted the $50,000 from me, saying, "This will come off our next load we do together."

As I AM and I walked out the door, I warned Orlando, "Make sure you don't lose that number. Let me tell you something. Be careful this guy doesn't get something for you and then rob you for it. The pinchi bandito will blame you for it. If someone sends something for you, don't give it to this guy. He would just blame you...as he tried to do with these $50,000, my friend," Orlando warned.

We left the hotel and I called Brian, cooking up a story I knew he would love to hear. This was the break I was looking for with Orlando. I had no idea what a cartel was, and still didn't fully understand after he told me. When first meeting Orlando, I wanted to appear as if I was following Brian's instructions. Can never be too safe. I wanted to see if this was what I was thinking in the way of a break. I needed to make sure my calculations were spot on.

From the meeting with Boots and meeting Chewy, within my mind, was the success in handling that first load and problem-solving too. Then to have the absence of them after that one load didn't make sense to me. I needed to appear not totally sold and effort to position myself for future talks. Also to show credibility and character. The timing was not right to jump on this offer just yet. I needed to let a few more promising possibilities develop. A premature act would only show up in the returns as such.

CHAPTER 13

THE RIDE

THE NEXT MORNING, MY phone rang, interrupting my half-asleep state. I answered to hear Big Dawg on the other end, barely able to contain his excitement.

"What's good, big bro?" I greeted him groggily.

"I've been talking with Mario and Frank heavy the last couple of days," he exclaimed. "They're giving a very large party, and Mario invited you and me to come down. He wants to broker peace between you and Frank. They're both saying this can be worked out, and nothing is off the table for discussion."

I could hear the honor in Big Dawg's voice as he delivered the message. "I'm going to book the flights for us now," he added. "I'll have to fly in a day or two after you. I can fly out tomorrow."

As he spoke, I couldn't shake the feeling that this was all too orchestrated, like a page out of Brian's book. We would show up as guests of honor, only to be used by Frank in front of his JEFEs. I wasn't going to be walked out at this party as if I were a Triple Crown-winning horse ready to be studded out.

"I'm going to fly out tomorrow and will just meet you down there," I quickly replied.

"Sounds good, bro," Big Dawg accepted.

After hanging up with him, I placed a call to Baby Doll, aware that I would be flying into Phoenix within a few days. I needed to get with her and seek her counsel on a number of issues. She also warned me that Brian would most likely be trying to get with me and go to Mexico.

"Just be prepared in case you need to crossover with no notice," Baby Doll advised.

I called up I Am and Big I, "Yo, pack your stuff, we gotta move to shoot in a couple of days." We jumped on a flight to Phoenix, with a vacation in mind. I was really looking forward to seeing Sheila and had no plans to attend Frank's party. It appeared that Mario had sensed my unpredictability in my interactions with Frank and was considering postponing it.

Once we landed, we headed straight to the hotel to check in. Sheila had already booked a few rooms for us. I made sure to let her know how much I appreciated her. She was truly my sunshine in Phoenix.

"Wayne, Frank, and Mario decided to change their plans and have a few friends come to Frank's ranch in Mexico instead of throwing a party," Big Dawg informed me excitedly. These friends were Mexican nationals who may have had issues crossing into the states, and I had a feeling there was something more to this idea.

I didn't care for Frank because of how he treated my brother, always trying to pray on desperation and not minding being the author of it himself. My issue was with Frank, period. Personal feelings were not something I typically dealt with, but this was my exception. I wouldn't allow myself to be part of Frank's self-grandeur Ponzi scheme.

When Big Dawg tried to find me, he would naturally do what he always does in my life, cutting me out and he never disappoints. These were his people, and he should be the one dealing with them. Mario and I may fight all the time, but we can still get things done. I didn't have the patience for Frank.

I met up with Big I and I Am, and as usual, we hit up the gentlemen's club. I had a VIP membership that worked in any of their affiliate clubs across Arizona, and we knew how to have a good time. I Am got attached to one of the dancers and started buying her flowers, while Big I and I joked around and pretended that Brian was being cheap. Later that night, Brian told me that he had spoken with Chewy and that we were invited to a face-to-face meeting. I knew we'd be leaving early the next morning.

When I checked my phone, I saw that Big Dawg had called me three times and an hour and a half had passed since the first call. I figured he was enjoying his moment in front of Frank, Mario, and their friends. I called Baby Doll and asked her to meet me at the hotel.

After arriving at the hotel, Baby Doll was waiting for me. She had stopped taking steroids and was transitioning back to the Baby Doll I met some time back. I started talking to her about a number of things, including some important issues I was having trouble with. My phone was ringing non-stop, but I pretended not to notice. Baby Doll was getting upset and asked me if everything was okay. I assured her that everything was great, but she could see that I was lying.

She was about to leave when she realized that my phone was ringing because someone was trying to get a hold of me. She assumed it was a woman and got angry. I"What's wrong? What is all this about, sweetheart?" I asked out of desperation.

"Baby, it's clear that your ass for tonight is trying to get over here to see you pretty bad. I guess she is going to get to see the dance before I do. And, why not, even Brian got to see it first," she said softly but disappointedly.

"That's not a woman, Baby Doll, I pleaded," as the cell phone kept ringing.

"Oh... I'm more than sure it's not just one. There's more than likely three or four calling at once," Baby Doll sternly stated.

"That's just Big Dawg calling me like that," I said.

Baby Doll paused, looking at my face, and said, "Baby, why would he keep calling you like that though?" I grabbed her and turned her away from the door while explaining, "I told you about the so-called party Frank and Mario were doing, and then not doing."

"Baby Doll responded, "You never told me that, but it got to where it didn't happen?"

"Baby, well why is your brother still down here and not headed home? My cell is back ringing; Frank changed it to a small get-together over at his ranch in Mexico," I said.

Baby Doll yells, "At his ranch in Mexico?!"

Suddenly, Baby Doll grabbed my phone and handed it to me. It was Big Dawg on the other end, yelling at me for not answering his calls. Big Dawg started to ask me questions about business over the phone. The only thing I could hear was my attorney Lorence's voice saying, "Never discuss business over the phone and never give or accept orders over the phone." I didn't give direct answers to anything. Big Dawg started talking reckless, meaning saying things he should not say about illegal activity, over the regular cell phone and not the walkie-talkie. Finally, it dawned on me that Frank was negotiating with me through Big Dawg. Baby Doll is quiet but listening very closely. Once I figured this out, it became purposely difficult to negotiate, with Baby Doll whispering, "Baby, Frank or Mario is listening in on the conversation."

We negotiated the price down to $800 a pound, with no funny business from Big Dawg or anyone else. I wanted to get it down to $700, but settled for $750. As we were talking, Big Dawg mentioned that Frank had loaned me $100,000 that I had never paid back. Baby Doll grabbed my mouth and told me not to say another word. She whispered in my ear aggressively, "Don't you FUCKIN say another word other than what I tell you in your EAR."

She then asked Big Dawg where he was, and he said he was with Frank's nephew, headed to Frank's ranch. “we are headed to Frank's ranch. Can you believe he got us lost. He’s driven to his uncle’s ranch a million times before. Now he wants to get lost all of a sudden.” Baby Doll face went blank. “We have been driving around lost in the Mexican desert in the pitch black for the last 35 to 40 minutes. He is just so stupid....... he he he he he!!”

"Baby Doll, agree, agree, agree... don't say SHIT other than you agree," said Baby Doll urgently.

"Yeah, you know how backwards Frank's nephew can be. Tell Frank how does he want to work out those $100,000," I said, following Baby Doll's instructions. The $100,000 that Frank had loaned us had been paid shortly after he'd loaned it for us to get trucks and places to store work.

"Let's stay at $800 a pound with $25 tax with each pound until those $100,000 is repaid," Big Dawg repeated.

"I agree," I replied.

Big Dawg yelled at Frank's nephew, "Man, we done drove past this DAMN road 100 times since we've been lost out here in the desert. Now you figure out to turn down this road. Wayne, can you believe he done found the DAMN road now?"

"Man... he is SOOOOOO stupid... Hee hee hee hee hee!!"

After an agreement was made and I had a good idea my brother was safe, I cut the call. "Big Dawg, make sure you run into me soon as you cross back over into the states," I demanded.

Baby Doll took me through what happened. She explained that Frank and Mario were mostly on the nephew's cellphone listening. "Baby, Frank may have had a number of important people at his ranch to meet you," Baby Doll said.

The $100,000 had been paid back by me in a manner agreed to with Frank on the ride to Phoenix from Tucson over a year ago. Vito had told me sometime back that Big Dawg always carried a balance over to other loads. I also found over the course of working under Big Dawg, he never kept records, let alone kept up with balances of previous loads. Frank would always attempt to trick him up and cook the books on Big Dawg. They had a very high success rate until I came along.

Baby Doll left when Big Dawg was headed my way.

Once Big Dawg arrived, he told me that a few people he had never seen before were at the ranch. It was a relaxed setting. Frank introduced Big Dawg to another gentleman, in which there was a conversation of past unpaid balances. I did not press more details with Big Dawg at that time. My brother never had a problem with creating stories on the spot. I didn't need his creativity at this moment. The closest thing I could get to the truth was paramount. Big Dawg moved off the subject of unpaid balances pretty rapidly.

Big Dawg went right to the subject of most interest two of these unnamed gentlemen: white or cocaine. Make sure you pay attention to this one little part because this will return deeper into the story.

I moved off that subject even faster than Big Dawg and his unpaid balances. Big Dawg kept trying to have a conversation about the white. I entertain Big Dawgs effort with, why not take these subjects in order presented to me then: Unpaid prior and current balances, then the white.

CHAPTER 14

NEVER SAY, NEVER

"Big Dawg is on a flight back East. Praise be to the God there aren't any deserts for him to get lost in over that way. Big I, Brian and I were driving towards the border for a meeting with Chewy set up for the following day. We planned to follow our normal ritual of visiting strip clubs once we got into town. As we crossed the border, we noticed the many American franchises that were present. Brian pulled into one of these restaurants, but I noticed something very different this time.

There was an older man and his little girl in the parking lot. It was an extremely hot day, and the little girl was working very hard to help her father. Even Big I, myself, and Brian were discussing how hard she was working. I looked at her sandals to try and get an idea of their standard of living, but they were in very bad shape. Her father's shoes were not any better.

Brian gave the little Mexican man some change, and we sat down to eat. I had a lot of questions about what I would be seeing, but I couldn't stop watching how the Mexican man was doing everything he could to comfort and praise his daughter. I was struck by the fact that she stopped working and just stared at me when I stepped out of the car. Her father touched her with a little shake and spoke to her in Spanish, apologizing for her behavior. Brian translated.

As I looked out the window at the little girl and her father, it reminded me of my own childhood in Black Bottom Detroit. Despite all the love my grandfather gave me, I too had very bad shoes and often went barefoot to play outside. I only had one pair of shoes that worked for school. My grandfather, who I thought was my father for many years, would put me in the buggy of his bike and we would ride as he talked to me in my ear.

As we left the restaurant after eating, the little girl stopped working and started staring at me again. Brian started translating for her father, who said he had never seen her act like this before and was very sorry. I walked over to the little girl and she kept looking directly at my face. "Hola nina," I said, after asking Brian how to say hello to her. "Hola senor," the little girl replied. My eyes teared up and I stuck my hand in my pocket, grabbing a bill to hand to her. She took the money and looked down at it with both hands. I turned and walked away before the big American drug dealer tough guy wouldn't be able to control my emotions any longer. I started walking towards the car. There was a moment of silence and then I heard yelling of excitement from her father. I looked back and he picked her up and hugged her tightly. We sat in the car and watched him for a moment. Her father packed up and carried his things in one hand and his baby girl's hand in the other. As he walked away, after what became maybe a great month for his family, the little girl just kept looking back at the car we were in. Brian pulled off and the car was silent for about two or three minutes.

"Wayne, you just made a young American black man somewhere a very lucky man one day," Brian said, his tone subdued. "The old man said that he just lost his wife last month. And it hurts him that he has to bring her to help him and to catch up while still making sure her little siblings don't have to miss any meals. And she has been wonderful about helping. But it is not what he promised their mother for them."

To this day, I don't know what I gave the little girl or if it was just one bill or two. I know I always carried large bills, hundreds and fifties, across the border when I went. I have always just prayed that it helped his family. We checked into a hotel and got a little rest for that night's action.

We headed to the club to fuck up some money. As we walked in, we were greeted by beautiful ladies. The bar gave us a waiter, but I told Brian that we didn't want a male waiter. Brian responded that we wouldn't have a waiter at all then, as male waiters are the norm in Mexico. Big I went to the VIP room with a young lady, and I and Brian were enjoying ourselves. I noticed an exceptionally beautiful Latino goddess and asked Brian about her. He asked our waiter, who told us that she was a featured dancer from Mexico City.

Big I had just returned, and the young lady came back to continue dancing for him. "Yo, man, you gone keep her with you all night?" I asked Big I.

He shook his head yes with excitement. I pointed Big I attention over to the Latino goddess that had me out of my mind. "FUCK HER MAN." But I noticed he was sweating on his forehead when he returned from VIP. As I turned towards Brian, our waitress ran through the club. My heart rate increased, and I wondered what was going on. The waiter was running full speed, and as the Latino goddess was walking down the stairs, he scooped her up and set her down right in front of me. She grabbed my hand and led me through the club while everybody started clapping for me.

I paid the bouncer for the VIP, and she pulled me to the end of the hall where a mirrored wall popped open. She led me to a small room with a bed and a fan in the wall. She said something in Spanish, and I replied, "No comprende." She started to write her cell number down, and after going back and forth for a moment, she repeated, "Yo quiero que me llamas," which means "I want you to call me."

She handed me the paper with her number, and I was ecstatic. "Hell yeah, I will call you!" I yelled. I was visibly shaking from desire, and the African phallic love god clashed in passion with this Latino Helen of Troy. We were in that little booth for so long that the bouncer came knocking because we were locked in a timeless embrace.

After being pried from the little room, the bouncer was extremely upset and started yelling and acting out. However, Ulysses Grant was able to calm him down without saying a word. We left shortly after my encounter with the Latino goddess. She had told Brian that she would be flying back to Mexico City in two days and wanted to see me before she left. I considered asking her to come to our room that night, but decided against it because we had important plans the next morning with Chewy. Brian was discouraging me as well and warned me about the drug trafficking and cartel activity in Mexico City. It was common for women to be used to recruit for the cartels, which was most likely her interest in me. Brian knew this as well. At the time, I had no idea that Mexico City would play a significant role in my future.

We hit the road with Brian driving, and arrived at a little hole-in-the-wall restaurant in a very small town. Chewy arrived in a similar fashion to when we first saw each other at the club, but this was our first official meeting. Boots was also present.

Chewy greeted me warmly and we sat down in a corner section of the restaurant, while the other guys were seated about 10 feet away. Much of the talking was done in Spanish, with Brian translating. Chewy apologized for not being able to make it all the way into town to meet me as agreed upon earlier.

Chewy was very direct and made it clear that he wanted to work with me. He represented a number of farmers who wanted to get their product into the American market, and he was in need of someone who could handle four or five metric tons of product to start, able to handle half to a full semi load with product.

Chewy started asking questions about our setup and capacity to hold large quantities, securing product and currency, and asked about the locations of some of our drop spots from the summer. I was giving Chewy ideas, but they were not actually my drop spots. I started to wonder who Chewy was giving this information to over the walkie-talkie, as this person seemed to know these areas.

Chewy explained that he had someone giving the info to someone over the walkie-talkie, and that he couldn't make it to me because he was working a deal with a farmer a few towns over. "This farmer is for you, my friend," Chewy said. "I know people who have worked with you, other than who you see here. You work very good and your guys are good. But the locations you are giving me are for someone who doesn't know how to work, my friend. Please, let's work! Give me one of your good places now," Brian translated, looking nervous.

I nodded and gave them a real drop spot. There was a lot of Spanish talking over the walkie-talkie. "Now I think I know you now, my friend," Brian translated from Chewy, and then Chewy talked about the business and the area, locations of other trucking companies in the area as well. Everybody was smiling.

After we finished eating and some small talk, we left the restaurant. Chewy embraced me and Brian translated for him that he would be in my town soon. We had a great meeting and headed back to the hotel to relax. I had plans to call up my Latino goddess for an exciting night before she headed back to Mexico City.

A few hours later, the guys wanted to go grab something to eat at a local taco stand. I placed my order just not to be difficult, as I was often accused of by the guys. "Let's get the full Mexican experience this time," Big I yelled at me. However, once they arrived back at the house, everyone had what they wanted except for me. The stand had closed, so I had to take what was left. I wasn't a happy camper and tried not to be difficult, but I wasn't pleased with what they brought me.

I had beef fajitas with corn tortillas at the local Taco stand, but for some reason, the food didn't taste right to me. Then I started to doubt myself, thinking, "How is Mexican food supposed to taste anyway? I wouldn't really know." I was trying to deceive myself based on other people's comments because I had said before that I would never eat from those stands.

A few hours later, my stomach started to act up, ruining my plans with my Latino goddess that night. I had to cancel our breakfast date the following morning. Everything I had in my stomach was in rapid mass exodus mode, and I felt like I had food poisoning. "I told you we should never eat at those fucking stands!!" I yelled at the guys. We were having major trust issues. To quote America's greatest president, Ronald Reagan, "Trust, but verify," especially when it comes to anything having to do with my posterior. I had to stay close to a toilet and keep a fresh change of clothes nearby.

That night was bad, and the following morning got even worse. I had moments when the pain in my abdomen was so intense that I had to grit my teeth and clutch the blankets and sheets to my face. Brian called EMS to the hotel where we were staying.

On a separate note, Ronald Reagan and George Bush are considered the golden age of hustlers from the streets dealing in cocaine.

The EMS arrived, and we were faced with a different set of challenges. We realized that we were in another country, and the EMS technicians were small men compared to American standards. Even their stretcher was small, and they commented that I was huge compared to them, being a black guy. There is an unspoken folklore or myth that black men are super dominant figures with a masculine nature, which I believe to be true to a degree but not exclusive to one race. I feel that this played a huge part in the events that followed, leading to the hospital and throughout this illness.

The EMS technicians tried to move me from the bed to the stretcher but were not strong enough to do so. I was helped to my feet and placed on the gurney by my own efforts. I was being rushed through the halls of the hotel, spilling over the edges of the gurney as well. We were taken down in the elevator and rushed through the lobby towards the stairs, then the sense of urgency stopped. The gurney stopped at the stairs after it was let down. I heard numbers in Spanish - "uno, dos, tres". I felt an effort or two to lift me, but then there was no more effort. I opened my eyes and noticed the EMS technicians shaking their heads frantically, saying "no y mas" and refusing to try to lift me anymore. Brian was yelling at them to lift me, but they kept shaking their heads and saying "no y mas".

"Get the fuck out the way then, you fucker! Let me grab him!" Brian yelled to I AM and Big I. "On 3! One, 2, 3!" I was snatched right up into the air by I AM and Big I, only to hear thunderous hand clapping, screaming of excitement, and whistling. I later found out that I AM and Big I had on football jerseys at the time, which explained why people thought we were players for the American professional football team. I guess this explains why I was listening to "Los Raiders". I was then placed in the EMS and rushed to the hospital.

I arrived at the hospital, and as soon as the doors of the EMS opened, there were about ten medical personnel ready to lift me off the stretcher. I was pulled from the EMS, and the wheels came down from under the stretcher just as they started pushing me. Suddenly, the damn stretcher started to tilt and fall sideways while they were pushing it. It was too top-heavy and started to bend to one side. There was a lot of yelling, and an extra man ran to grab the stretcher from collapsing on one side. I thought to myself, "Oh my God, these folks are going to kill me."

They wanted to put me in a wheelchair, but all the wheelchairs were too small. Finally, they brought a regular size wheelchair like the ones in the states. I was wheeled into a large room and transferred to a newer hospital stretcher. There were maybe three nurses in the room when I was wheeled in, but as time passed, I saw maybe six or seven more nurses join them. A doctor came over to speak to me, but he didn't speak any English. He left, and when I looked to my right, I saw all ten nurses smiling and giggling. Three more doctors came in, and one of them spoke some broken English. He told me that a doctor who spoke much better English was on the way back to the hospital.

I explained my symptoms as best as I could, and I was instructed to use the restroom but not to flush because they needed a sample.

I needed to use the restroom urgently, and as soon as I made a move, a group of people rushed to assist me. By now, the group had grown to 15 people. I managed to make it to the restroom, but I had to squeeze my cheeks tightly to prevent an accident. Just as I was about to let it rip, I looked up and saw three nurses staring directly at me. I couldn't help but laugh, and the nurses rushed out of the restroom.

After I finished, an older nurse came to collect my clothes and give me a gown to change into. However, when she saw the group of women outside the door, she quickly closed all the curtains around me for privacy. Another older nurse returned to take my blood and insert an IV into my arm, and she was quite rough with me. After she left, I tried to rest, but nurses kept coming in and out from behind the curtains to check my clipboard and take more blood.

In the midst of all this, I kept feeling like someone was watching me. Whenever I opened my eyes, I couldn't see anyone, but I noticed the curtains moving. So, I decided to sit up and watch to prove to myself that I wasn't losing it. As it turned out, seven different nurses had been trying to sneak a peek at me.

After the third nurse came to take more blood, I started getting upset because they were stabbing my arm. The fourth nurse came to get more blood and I made sure she knew I wasn't happy about the repeated stabbings and blood being taken. When the fifth nurse came, I said, "No más señora," as I put my hand over the area they were drawing blood from, which was now bruised. The nurse smacked my hand and I jumped back in shock. "This bitch is crazy!" I whispered to myself, trying not to make any sudden movements. "This woman is dangerous," I thought, my eyes wide with shock.

The nurse started talking shit to me with her badly broken English, "You cry! You cry!" as she stabbed my arm again, making me jump a little and cry out like a baby. She looked me in the eyes and said, "Yo sicario" (I'm a hitman).

The nurse laughed at me and said, "No no, you baby!" I was speechless for a moment, and then I said, pointing to myself with the free arm that had not been hijacked, "You got a bad attitude, lady...a bad baaaad attitude."

I was eventually moved to a different area of the hospital, and placed in a room for some privacy. I was put in a wheelchair and pushed through the halls, and it seemed like every doorway had nurses standing and watching me along the way. I even had a few waves from some of them as I passed by.

Once I was placed in my room, I was wondering where in the hell Brian and my guys were. I thought they must have gotten lost. Later on, I found out that those fuckers were actually back at the hotel, taking pictures with fans, signing autographs, exchanging cell phone numbers with ladies, and even bringing a few back to my room for drinks and room service.

The three doctors returned with an additional doctor who spoke English well compared to the others. She explained to me that I had food poisoning, but I would need to undergo a number of other tests. She also informed me that I would be held overnight for observation. This doctor was very nice, much different from the abusive nurses. She even gave me her cell phone number and home phone number.

She also made me aware she had the number to the room phone that was given for my personal use. "I will be calling to check on you throughout the night. Also, call me, and don't worry, I don't have a husband or boyfriend," she said, giving a small laugh followed by a pleasant smile.

I nervously smiled back, glancing at the other doctor to try to understand if this was normal. The three other doctors looked at me with a blank smile on their faces. "What the hell! They don't know what she just said to me," I finally figured out.

As the tests began, the doctors seemed to be putting me on every machine in the hospital. They scanned my brain, they had me stand in front of a machine shirtless while they swung a machine in front of my chest and scanned it. They even gave me an ultrasound like I've seen used on pregnant women. I was even laying there looking at the screen with them too as they were smiling and laughing. We never found anything in there either, I may add.

Later on, Brian and the guys finally showed up. They were concerned about my condition and asked me about the doctors and tests. Brian became furious when he saw how many tests were being performed and how much it would cost. He yelled at the nurses, asking what they had done to me and calling them out for running up my medical bill.

As my clothes were brought in, Brian urged me to change and leave the hospital immediately. However, I reminded him that the doctor had ordered me to be held overnight for observation, and I didn't want to risk my health.They are doing a Mexican medical GANG BANG on your wallet!!" Brian said. "Put your clothes on and we're going to get out of here." Brian said with urgency in his voice.

I got dressed and we began to leave the hospital. As we walked, I noticed there were nurses everywhere. "What didn't I expect was Los Raiders and agent, had come to visit their sick American friend. Lord only knows what they told them I was; Maybe the ballboy or their cook!" I joked. The nurses, who were previously all dressed down, were now wearing their best uniforms. "They are saying you look much better with your clothes on," Brian translated, trying to make sense of their comments.

We turned down a shorter hallway that led to another show hall, which in turn led to the sign-out area. "Let's run for it!" Brian exclaimed, bolting towards a side exit door. The famous Los Raiders were right behind him, sprinting down the hallway. I stood there, stunned, as they disappeared through the door.

Brian turned to look for me, then stopped running. "What is wrong with you? We have to run and get out of here," he said urgently, motioning for me to follow him.

"I'm not running out any side door exit," I said firmly, feeling disgusted with Brian. "My friend, this is Mexico!!" I continued.

"They don't bill you later like they do in America! You will have to pay in full after treatment!" Brian warned.

I guess that was the deal breaker for Los Raiders, because they ran out of the side exit door at full speed. "I guess it's just you and me now, Brian. And I will need you to translate for me at the desk so I can pay what I owe," I said, resigned to my fate.

As we made our way through the hospital, we passed by nurses who were now all done up and looked completely different from before. "They are saying you look much better with your clothes on," Brian translated for me, causing me to feel a bit confused.

We turned down a shorter hall, which led to another hall that ultimately led to the sign-out area. Suddenly, Brian exclaimed, "Let's run for it!" and started sprinting towards a side door exit. I could hear the footsteps of Los Raiders, who had come to visit me in the hospital, close behind him.

However, I couldn't bring myself to run. "I'm not running out any side door exit," I said with disgust. Brian turned to me, exasperated. "What is wrong with you? We have to run and get out of here!" he pleaded with me.

Meanwhile, Los Raiders were gasping for breath after their sprint. "My friend, this is Mexico!" Brian explained. "They don't bill you later like they do in America! You will have to pay in full after treatment!"

It seemed like this explanation was the deal breaker for Los Raiders, who ran out of the side door exit at full speed. "I guess it's just you and me now, Brian," I said. "And I will be needing a translator at this desk so I can pay what I owe."

As we left the hospital, I could feel the warm Mexican sun on my face and a sense of relief that I was finally on the road to recovery. "Let's grab something to eat," I suggested to Brian as we walked to the car. "I could really go for some tacos right about now."

Brian nodded in agreement and we drove to a local taqueria. The smell of grilled meat and spices filled the air as we stepped inside. I ordered a plate of tacos al pastor and savored every bite, feeling grateful for the simple pleasure of a good meal.

Afterward, we stopped at a nearby pharmacy to pick up some supplies. As we walked down the aisles, Brian pointed out various medications that might be helpful for my ongoing symptoms. "I think we should get a few of these just in case," he said, holding up a bottle of antacids.

"Good idea," I replied, grabbing a few other items from the shelves.

Back at the hotel, I felt myself starting to relax. It had been a stressful few days, but I was finally feeling like myself again. However, my relief was short-lived as my symptoms began to flare up once more.

"I don't think this medicine is working," I told Brian, feeling frustrated.

He looked at me with concern. "We have to get you back to the States and to an American hospital," he said firmly. "This isn't something we can mess around with."

I knew he was right. I loaded up on the medication to try and slow down the effects of my illness, but it was clear that we needed to get moving.

We hit the road and I watched as the Mexican landscape rolled by outside the car window. The sun was setting in the sky, casting a warm glow over everything. Despite my discomfort, I couldn't help but appreciate the beauty of the moment.

As we crossed the border back into the United States, I felt a sense of relief wash over me. We were finally back on familiar ground, and I knew that help was just around the corner.

Upon arriving back in Phoenix, Arizona, I was taken to the emergency room and rushed in on a wheelchair. However, things seemed to slow down once I entered the hospital. I explained my symptoms and was admitted, but I could sense that the nurses weren't as urgent as I was. Blood was taken from me and I was told not to flush the toilet when I used the restroom. This lack of urgency was frustrating for me, and I was starting to get upset with the situation.

As I used the restroom and alerted the nurse, she came in and got a sample in a very extreme, rough but calm manner. I was in tears from the intense pain, which was four or five times worse than what I had experienced in Mexico. Suddenly, the nurse burst into the room, moving quickly with two additional nurses and IV equipment. They were shouting about how many CC's of this and that they needed, and I was freaking out at this point.

All I could see were needles and medicine bottles being handed around at a rapid pace. I had to wipe the tears from my eyes just to see if this was the same nurse that I was upset with earlier.

OH SHIT, THAT IS HER," I think to myself. "WHAT THE HELL IS GOING ON, AND WHY ARE YOU MOVING SO FAST ALL OF A SUDDEN?" I point to the super calm nurse, who wasn't so calm at this moment. "Am I about to die?" I asked.

"The doctor looked at your sample, and while looking, he told me to get in here right away and give you these four shots because you are in excruciating pain. Which will be given to you through your IV. But, this one will need to be given to you on the side of your buttocks," the nurse said to me as she revealed a needle that appeared to be as long as my forearm.

"What you are receiving through the IV will cause you to sleep and relieve you of the excruciating pain that you're experiencing now. This will give other medications time to take effect," the nurse explained before adding, "The doctor will be in to explain further details at some point. And to answer your earlier question; You are not going to be dying under my care, Mr. Thompkins," she said with a very warm smile.

After a few hours of painless sleep, I woke up to the doctor looking at my chart. "Mr. Thompkins, I'm happy to see you resting so peacefully," the doctor stated. "I have looked in on you a couple of times before having this chance to speak with you," the doctor added.

The doctor continued to explain the details of the medication that had been given to me by the nurses. "Mr. Thompkins, my records show that you were diagnosed with food poisoning at a Mexican medical hospital?" the doctor asked, to which I confirmed. "Well, Mr. Thompkins, once I looked at your stool sample, I noticed an infestation of parasites...but not just any parasites, Mr. Thompkins. You inherited the most aggressive types," the doctor explained, playing with a serious tone.

"The most aggressive types?" I repeated with a bewildered look on my face.

The doctor paused for a moment before answering, "Let's just say, Mr. Thompkins, that if you had stayed in Mexico and continued taking the medicine prescribed to make your symptoms bearable, after five days, you would be wearing a colostomy bag for the rest of your life."

I was shocked. "The slimy substance that I'm sure you saw a lot of when looking down after you relieved yourself...those were pieces of your intestines that the parasites were still eating. Mr. Thompkins, you were literally being eaten alive," the doctor stated with a concerned tone. "I really couldn't believe what I was seeing. I have never actually seen those parasites active outside of a controlled setting," he added.

The doctor went on to explain that he had given me large doses of medication to clear out the parasites from my infected intestines, but he was concerned about the large number of eggs that remained and could hatch later. He gave me some very strong medicine to address that concern once I returned to Detroit. Then he pulled up a seat and began to ask me questions about the care I had received in Mexico. He seemed to enjoy hearing the story of my experience.

"Thank you for explaining everything to me, Doctor," I said, feeling a mix of relief and disbelief. "I never thought something like this could happen to me."

The doctor smiled, "You're in good hands now, Mr. Thompkins. We'll make sure you get the best care possible and are on the road to a full recovery."

After leaving the hospital, we flew back to Detroit. “I need to go up to my office to address a number of issues. Big Dawg came up to my office an called me so I could come out in the parking lot to meet with him. I came out the office to see what he wanted.

'"What in the fuck happened to you!! You've lost a lot of weight since I last saw you in Arizona," he exclaimed. I explained to him about the parasites. "Man...........SHIT!! I need to catch that for about a week then!" Big Dawg said with excitement, which I ignored.

"I always say I would never ever eat from one of those stands," I added, reciting the old saying, "they always warn against: never saying never." Big Dawg agreed, "You know what! That is a very true statement because you said you would never work with Frank again too!!" He said with a huge smile on his face. "Frank will have a semi here in a few days....... you and your crew will be ready, right?!" Big Dawg sarcastically added to the list.

I gave him a very nasty look and turned to walk away when I heard him say something under his breath.

"Never say never, right?? Hee hee hee hee hee!!"

CHAPTER 15

THE END, THAT BEGINS

IT WAS A COLD morning and I wasn't feeling good about the lesson I had learned. I couldn't shake off the memory of Big Red whispering in my ear when I was a child, "When a man gives his word, there cannot ever be a question of follow through." It was a time when deals were done with a handshake, and a man's word was his bond.

But I had a job to do, and I needed to focus. I rallied my crew and we hit the truck, unloading the work and ripping through 3500 pounds in just three days. My team was well-seasoned and our speed would become my signature. I didn't want to give law enforcement any window for investigation, but I didn't yet realize the true value of my talent.

Word of my efficiency and reliability started to spread across the border but as Big Dawg's little brother Frank and Mario's circles, I was known as Wayne from Detroit to others. But my real name would be clarified at an unexpected time and day in the future.

Vito, the broke Italian, showed up at my front door with a sarcastic greeting, reminding me that Mo Green would be coming home in a few days and we needed to talk. I knew this day was coming and I wasn't sure how I would handle it when it arrived. Mo Green had caused some suspicion on my name in the streets when he went in to start his state bid. Being labeled as a snitch or an informant in the street was the worst thing that could happen to someone. It hurt my feelings deeply, and it also killed my earning and hustling ability until the streets sorted through the madness and arrived at their own conclusion.

The labeling was deadly because there was no way to prove the accusations false. The harder one tried, the more suspicious they looked. The best defense was no defense, so I went to my corner and sat down, waiting for the streets to come up with their answer. It took some time, but the streets usually figured it out, sometimes accurately and often times not. In my case, I was eventually vindicated.

I couldn't emphatically state that Mo Green started the rumor because these rumors always took on a life of their own. However, I was upset that he could have cleared it up. Instead, he called the Detroit narcotics officers to raid my house at 4:00 AM, causing me to bear the cost of repairs and having to call up Lorence to represent me. It wasn't a secret that this particular guy was responsible for locking up a number of guys in our area. But, after thinking about it, I realized that this was Mo Green's first bid and maybe he just wanted to block everything outside. I was looking to find out more about it.

Good lawyering on the part of Lorence resulted in the charges being dropped against me. He became my attorney for life, even though I didn't have the money to reward his efforts and unbelievable results on my behalf. But, this was a much different day for me now. Lorence would have everything he wanted, including all paid-for vacations four times a year and everything in between too.

This day marked a significant change for me, as seven years had passed since I had experienced anything like it. I was in the final stages of putting the finishing touches on my new place, which would provide me with much-needed protection from potential threats. However, there was one issue that made me uncomfortable. I had known Mo Green since he was 13 years old, and I had played a significant role in his life, getting him his first date, first sexual encounter, and first girlfriend.

I began to consider alternative ways to check if he had made any changes while in prison. I decided to ask Vito for help. "Vito, I need you to take $1000 to Mo Green's aunt so they can throw him a coming home party," I instructed him. "Once he get home, I'll give you some money to give to Mo Green. I need you to check on him and let me know how he's doing."

"It's essential that you and Mo Green's family believe that this is something you're doing independently of me," I emphasized to Vito. "This has to be about your love for him, not about me." Although I knew Vito wasn't going to mention me even if I told him to, I needed to make sure that this was entirely separate from me. This flaw in Vito's character could be useful, however, as letting him be his normal self could be beneficial.

After donating to Vito's favorite charity to ensure that Mo Green's coming home celebration was fully funded, I sent him on his way. Additionally, I believed that Player D would be useful in this situation, as he had a reputation that made him a good deflection. I needed to make it clear that the assistance we were providing was on its own merit and directly from the individuals appearing to give it.

After about a week, Vito returned to me with an update on Mo Green. He told me that Mo Green had come home to nothing and was in need of additional assistance. My heart went out to him, and I felt a sense of responsibility since I had practically raised him. I couldn't just leave him in a bad situation after serving time in prison. I was convinced that I would help him, but I had to do it from the shadows and observe from afar.

I know it might seem unorthodox and even creepy that I wanted to observe someone so close to me, but I had my reasons. I wanted to make sure that Mo Green received all the help he needed, but at the same time, I was involved in something that was rapidly growing and needed to be protected. I understood that loyalty and business were two separate things and had to be dealt with independently for my own safety.

The next day, I contacted Player D, a guy who had caused me a lot of trouble in the past. I offered to give him work again, but with one condition: he had to work with Mo Green without revealing the source of the work. This was a common issue in the hood where every man wanted to be seen as a boss. But in this case, it would work to my advantage. I promised to give Player D four bales of marijuana, and he would then give Mo Green 20 pounds, including an extra bale that he would not be charged for. He could keep the extra 5 pounds, and I would also waive $10,000 off the $40,000 he owed me. This was a generous offer that I knew I would never see the money for, but it was worth it to keep the operation going smoothly.

"I'm glad to hear that Player D came through for us," I said to Vito over the phone. "I'll have to give him some extra props next time I see him."

"Yeah, man. He's a solid dude. He gave Mo 10 pounds of the weed, just to help him out. Real stand-up guy," Vito replied.

"That's good to hear. I'm glad he's back on his feet. Look, Vito, next time Mo wants to meet up, let him know that I'm willing to talk. I want to see how he's doing and see if there's anything else we can do to help him out."

"Alright, I'll let him know. I think he'll appreciate that. You always take care of your people, Lil bro."

"I try my best," I said with a chuckle. "Thanks, Vito. Let me know if anything else comes up."

"Will do. Stay up, man."

I was spending my first night in my place. I was so busy I never even got a chance to see it as he was putting it together for me. I didn't even know how to get to the place or even where it was. My uncle would just come by and tell me the money he needed, and I would just give it to him. The actual night I went home for the first night, he had to put the address in the navigation system in one of my vehicles to take me to the house.

I picked up my very good friend KK to come out and spend the night with me for my first night. I actually had anxiety about going and seeing my place for the first time. We were really close, and I knew she would be a great support system for me. When I got the opportunity to walk into my place, I was speechless. "This is insane, KK. I can't believe this is my place," I said as we walked through the door.

KK looked around and nodded, impressed. "Your uncle really outdid himself," she said, admiring the furniture and decor. "I know," I replied, still in shock. I was totally lost for words and became extremely emotional. I literally started to cry because I had never seen anything like that in person, only in magazines. I recall myself just crying insanely, while expressing that I didn't feel comfortable there and that I felt like I was in somebody else's place.

KK being the sweetheart that she has always been just hugged me and helped me believe that I was worth everything that I was experiencing, which I never forgot. We spent the rest of the night exploring the house and testing out the home theater system. As we settled into our comfortable beds, I couldn't help but think about how far I had come. Coming from Black Bottom Detroit to this... Wow!!

"Player D started to really fuck over me at this point. The money he was starting to owe me was becoming unacceptable. I had to cut him off for good now. Allowing him to owe anything else would have caused me to have to address these types of issues in a totally different fashion than necessary. Certain amounts of money can't go unaddressed in the streets. One of the best courses of action is the cut-off option. In most cases, this avoids unnecessary violence that you don't want to be known for - law enforcement ain't buying it,"

"Neither did I ever feel it was really necessary based on the business aspect because your hustle will be short-lived and at the root of it, most of that violent shit is centered in ego, it has nothing to actually do with the business. I was actually advised by the cartels that if someone runs off or messes up below a certain amount of money, just don't deal with them anymore. Player D was actually beyond that certain amount and really had no other uses outside of his hustling ability. He just wasn't worth it anymore," I said, shaking my head.

"That's smart. You have to protect yourself and your business," my friend agreed.

"The danger is being viewed as sweet. It's a death sentence in the streets!" I exclaimed.

Shortly after moving off the Burg, someone broke into the house on Hamburg.

As I walked through my former house, I couldn't help but feel violated. Someone had broken in, but nothing was taken. It was clear that whoever did this must have thought I was naive enough to turn my old home into a stash house. I had a few ideas of who could be responsible, but I knew that the tools of expression were worthless in this situation. What I was interested in was finding out who the designer behind this was.

I made some calls and arranged to meet with some associates. One of them, Vito, had made arrangements for me to meet with Mo Green at an Applebee's near Eastland Mall for lunch. The meeting started off slow, but I was eager to push him on a wide range of topics. I wanted to see if he had anything to do with the break-in, or if he knew who did.

As we talked, I could sense a change in his demeanor. He seemed more mature and level-headed than I remembered. I offered him a chance to work directly with me, and after we arrived at a comfortable understanding on business, I asked him a question that had been weighing on me: "Mo Green, do you know or did you hear of anyone that may have broken into my house?"

He looked me directly in the eyes and denied having any knowledge of the break-in. With that weight off my chest, we headed over to Eastland Mall for some shopping. First, we went to my brother J's jewelry store, Treasures. I picked out some nice pieces for Mo Green, then we went across the way to Al Wissam to grab him a leather jacket. In Detroit's dope boy culture, it's essential to rock a few nice leather jackets, and Mo Green was already known for his collection of 10 to 15 jackets that guys would come steal without him even noticing.

A few more loads came in over that summer, from Frank and Mario," Mo Green said excitedly, "Within a matter of months, I was all the way up. I purchased four new cars within like two months, and a host of other things very nice lifestyle additions. Which I knew it would take me no time to get back into rare form. I was a totally new beast on my hustle game now. An animal."

"That's what I like to hear," I replied with a smile, "After all the hard work, it's finally paying off for you."

Mo Green nodded, "Yeah, man. And it's all thanks to you."

I waved off his gratitude, "Nah, don't thank me. You put in the work and made it happen. I just facilitated the connections."

Mo Green chuckled, "Alright, alright. But I still appreciate it, man."

As we sat there discussing our success, I couldn't help but think about the issues with Frank. "Listen, Mo Green. I need to talk to you about something."

"What's up?" he asked, sensing the seriousness in my tone.

"I've been having some problems with Frank lately. He wants to keep increasing the amount of work per load, but at the same high price. And he's been mixing cheaper quality product in each load to rip us off," I explained.

Mo Green's expression turned serious, "That's not cool. What do you want to do about it?"

"I think it's time we start looking for a new supplier," I replied, "And I have a feeling Chewy may be ready to make a move our way."

Mo Green nodded in agreement, "Alright, let's do it. We need to stay on top of this game."

We finished up our conversation and headed out, ready to take our hustle to the next level.

"I began to go to my office more at this point," I said to Mo over lunch. "Refusing to deal with Frank anymore now."

"Anyway, Brian started flying into Detroit more and hanging out with me."

Mo Green even picked up a little house from a relative and needed some of my company's vendors to assist your effort with material and repairs."

Mo smiled. "Yeah, that was a good deal. And then I started calling your assistant as if she were an employee of mine. Sorry about that."

I waved it off. "No worries, man. But as time preceded, you started to really do very well with buying properties under your company too."

Mo grinned. "Yeah, I'm building up my empire."

We finished our lunch and went our separate ways. Little did I know, that this stoppage would be for some time. Which gave me much more time to just work at my office. Where I was truly happy for once. Even Lorence my attorney was proud of me for once. Brian had just grabbed a flight back to Arizona from hanging out with me that week.

Around this time, I began to do a lot of self-reflection. I knew that if the truth were ever told about me and how I earned a living, and my true feelings on the subject and myself, it would come as a shock to many. I never liked selling drugs at all... I even cried many days in private, concerning what I did. I was never really a popular person, and Lord knows I wasn't a ladies' man either. I didn't like crowds or really interact with people. I often say that life chose me. I was pushing all this weed, but couldn't tell you the difference in what good, bad, or OK weed was by looking at it. Truth be told, I never sold any of the drugs I was entrusted with... I will soon find myself!

As I sat there lost in thought, my phone beeped, signaling a new message. I looked down and saw it was from Mo Green.

Mo Green: Hey man, you good? I haven't heard from you in a minute.

Me: Yeah, I'm good. Just been busy with some personal stuff.

Mo Green: Alright, just checking. You know you can always hit me up if you need anything.

Me: I appreciate that, Mo. I'll keep that in mind.

Mo Green: No doubt. Take care, bro.

After the brief exchange with Mo Green, I continued to reflect on my life and the choices I had made. I knew I needed to make a change, but I wasn't sure how. It was a difficult realization to come to, but it was one that I knew I couldn't ignore any longer.

ME: Yo, What up Doe??

Brian: My friend! (Urgently) I just received a call from Chewy & he is in trouble!

Me: Tell me, My friend??!

Brian: Chewy has a load with over 5 metric tons on it, headed to Chicago right now. But, he was just told that his guys that are there to receive it on the other end just got hit by the feds.

Me: OH SHIT....THIS ISN'T GOOD!!

Brian: Chewy wants to know can he reroute the semi to you and you unload the truck, store the 5 tons until the following day. Then another semi will arrive under your control to pick the load up. And you are free to take as much as you would like to move.

Me: How soon are we talking about??!

Brian: My friend if you agree to help! I will be to you today and Chewy will cross over from Mexico tonight. We will pick him up in the morning at the airport.

Me: I trust that you will give me more info when I pick you up tonight at the airport.

Brian: Thank you, My Friend!! I will call you back with my flight info.

I knew this was the break I was looking for here. But not reading the signs correct will cost me. And misplaced loyalty would be the basis of this blindness. One thing was clear...... I put together a team that was season and knew how to move at whatever pace I called.

Beep, BEEP, BEEP.......

I AM: Whats up Home Boy!

Me: We got action!

I AM: REAL TALK! WHEN??!

ME: With in a matter of days. But,we have to get lined up, 911 tho!

I AM: Yo, something aint right with this Big Homie......Chewy!

Me: Ssssssssssssshid, everything is right with this!! He will be here soon. And, we coming in hot(: The Load.) & HEAVY!

I AM: We gone need to pull up??! (Somewhere to unload the semi??)

Me: FO SHO! (HELL YEAH!)

I AM: GOTCHA!

Me: ALL NEW JACKS! GIVE ONE , GET ONE, BUT ON MY CALL ONLY. (all new two-way radios phones. When you give them their phones, they must give you their old one to get a new one. Only hand them out when I give the okay ONLY!)

I picked up Brian from the airport that evening and he updated me on the situation as we drove, but I cut him off from giving too many details while in the vehicle. I remembered a statement from Laurence, "Always assume you are being watched or listened to."

The next day, I took Brian, I AM, and BIG I to a restaurant called Benihana in Dearborn. After eating, Brian and I headed to the airport to pick up Chewy while using the time at the restaurant to catch I AM and BIG I up to speed on what they needed to know and address any issues that may arise.

We pulled up in separate vehicles, with Brian and myself in one and I AM and BIG I in another. As we walked towards the entrance of the restaurant, we were joking and laughing with each other. Suddenly, I noticed two sets of eyes staring at me with a hostile look. I AM and BIG I also noticed this from the sudden pause in our conversation and laughter. Two Latino men were looking at me with a menacing stare, but I maintained a carefree and non-threatening demeanor.

"Hello Wayne!" Frank said in a confrontational tone, with a hint of anger on his face. Mario's angry expression quickly turned into a questioning one as he looked at Brian up and down. "I see you're showing your friends our town," Frank said, glancing at Brian. "Wow, was that Arizona sun a bit much on your already tan complexion, Mario? A change of climate would address that issue, huh!"

I replied to Frank's comment about our city, nodding at Mario. "BIG I, why don't you take Brian in and get seats for the four of us. You know lunchtime is pretty busy at this spot," I said, giving BIG I a relaxed smile and a wink.

As they headed towards the entrance, Frank's face turned red, and he said, "When are you going to pay me my money, Wayne!"

I replied matter-of-factly, "I can get that to you later on today, Frank."

A confused look came over Frank's face, and he asked, "You have a little over $600,000 for me now?"

I was shocked at the amount and replied, "600,000! Man, I don't owe you no $600,000! I owe you $70,000!"

Mario was getting more agitated in the background, shouting at Frank, "I told you that Big Dawg was lying to you! But, noooooo, you don't listen to me!"

Frank looked at me, still confused, and said, "Your brother told me that you owe me those $600,000, Wayne."

I replied in a firm but insulted voice, "He could not have told you anything like that concerning me, Frank. I have $70,000 for you, and after I get done with my business, I can get that to you."

Mario and I exchanged numbers so that we could meet later for them to receive the money I owed them from past deals. "Wayne, how are we going to deal with those $600,000?" Frank asked me with a humble tone.

"My friend, I don't know how you and Big Dawg are going to handle those $600,000. But, I guess you will be able to subtract my $70,000 from it," I replied as I turned to walk away with I AM. I stopped short and turned back to Frank, "I do think we need to all get together so you can get the truth. Then you will be able to see what Mario was telling you before the man has a heart attack over there."

I continued to explain, "This is a perfect example of the benefit you get when being second in command, as you've seen in the case with Big Dawg and DD. Nevertheless, it's part of the job description, but always remember the very old saying, 'Shit rolls downhill'."

CHAPTER 16

THE END THAT BEGINS PART 2

AFTER NOTICING MARIO'S ACTIONS, I knew something was up. It was too colorful and telling. After finishing our meal and informing I AM and BIG I about the urgent situation at hand, we parted ways for the moment. Brian and I went to the airport to pick up Chewy.

When Chewy arrived, he seemed genuinely happy to see me. "My friend, I'm sorry for causing you problems," he expressed with shame.

"Don't worry! Everything has been arranged," I replied. I proceeded to drive Chewy around and show him the arrangements that I had set up to store his low and keep it secure until the following day when it would be loaded onto another semi.

Little did Chewy know that once the load dropped, he would be loading the dinero for it the following day.

"Well, my understanding was that the load would come in the following day. But that night, Chewy shared that info with Brian in Spanish and he translated it to me. I instantly hit I AM on the next-tel two-way."

"Beep beep beep. What's good, big fella?" I AM answered.

"Yo. Let's put those guys on point," I responded.

I AM in turn responded with, "Gotcha. Only you and BIG I on me. But everything you and BIG I see, I see."

This meant programming the numbers and phones where the top guys always have each other's numbers and code names already programmed in the phones when handed out to the guys. Only I AM and BIG I would have access to me via those phones. Everyone's number would be in my phone though. And whatever numbers I AM and BIG I had on their phones, they better be in mine as well.

I AM responded with, "Done."

Brian translated everything I said to Chewy, who was from Mexico and only dealt with American Mexicans. He had an issue with Chewy because Chewy didn't want to stay in a hotel in Detroit. Chewy was afraid of blacks because of stories American Mexicans would tell Mexicans from Mexico about them always robbing people. While it was true to a degree, the lie was that all blacks robbed, which was not true. The lie was very useful for American Mexicans because it kept them in control as middlemen. They could rob and blame it on the blacks.

So we wanted to get a hotel around the whites, which is fine. Out West. But in the Midwest and East Coast? He was a wetback. Brian and Chewy was not. Aware Of the history of Detroit and its surrounding white communities. And eight mile was like the gun line. I made the mistake of allowing them to tell me what they wanted to do and let it go. Not knowing that the rules state. When in Rome, do as the Romans do. the underground rules for anyone visiting on business from Mexico, I was in control, PERIOD! I allowed them to check in a hotel at 10 and a half in Gratiot.

Very bad move.

The next day, around noon, I arrived at the hotel. As I walked down the hallway, the strong smell of marijuana smoke filled my nostrils. I knocked on the door, and a heavily tattooed, overweight Mexican man answered, "What's up, homie!" as the smoke engulfed me. I thought to myself, "What the hell?"

As I walked in, Brian introduced me to this long-haired, mustached, gangster-looking Mexican man as Chewy, his childhood friend who had just been released after serving a 15-year sentence in California State Penitentiary. I turned to shake his hand, but he jumped out of the cloud of smoke and hugged me, yelling, "What up, fool!"

"Brian, we really need to talk outside," I said after warmly greeting Fu Manchu.

"Shoot. Roll one up, fool! You smoke, right? You gotta smoke, fool. All the bruthas smoke," Fu Manchu said, laughing confidently while looking around at Brian and Chewy. I shook my head in the negative, indicating that I did not smoke as Brian started to move towards the door so we could talk outside.

"He's a brotha... right?!" Fu Manchu whispered to Brian, as if I wasn't standing there, looking at him, and looking extra confused.

"Yo, Brian!! What the fuck are you doing, man? I told you that these white people up here in Michigan are very, very racist!! Then we got the load coming today. We don't need this shit right here, right now, man!" I exclaimed as we stepped outside the hotel room. Chewy walked out to join us as well.

"About that load later on tonight. It was about to be dropped in Chicago anyway," Chewy said, trying to ease the tension.

I gave Brian a disapproving look, but before I could say anything, Chewy continued speaking. "I hope you are not too upset with me. When I return to Mexico, I will be loading up, and I will be back to you here in two weeks," he said.

Chewy expressed that he was happy he came up to see how we handle the type of work he is used to working with. Brian continued to translate for Chewy and offered us an invitation to come to Vegas with him to watch his friend's fight at the MGM.

"His fight is the main event, and we are going to be in the back with him before the fight. Then we are going to have a lot of women back in his room after the fight too. I'm going to pay for everything, and I'm going to return all the money you spent to help me with my problem too," Brian said, trying to persuade us to go.

I was upset and declined to go, hoping not to offend Chewy. Chewy kept trying to change my mind, but I stuck to my guns and refused.

I thought it was best to not come between Brian and his friend. I didn't want to be a dirty snake like Brian. Chewy also let me know that he had been working with Brian for some time, and even suggested that Brian return me the money he had spent on his behalf. It was becoming clear that Brian was hindering progress. However, my loyalty to the game, as I understood it, was becoming more and more of a liability. I was allowing this bandito to take away my significant political capital.

I tried once again to emphasize to Chewy and Brian that we needed to move out of the hotel due to the addition of Fu Man Chu and his smoke clouds. But my plea fell on deaf ears. Nonetheless, I rented a car a few days ago and I will move Chewy now, Brian added with arrogance, wanting to have a pissing contest at a bad time and the worst possible subject: security.

Brian and Chewy flew down to Vegas and enjoyed Sin City under the spotlight on Chewy's friend being the featured fight on the ticket. After returning from the fight, they both returned to Detroit.

Brian called me that morning while I was in the office. “My friend come so we can go to breakfast”.

I asked, “Where are you guys at now?"

Brian says slowly, "We are at the same place”

I said in clear frustration, "I'll see you in a sec, dumb fuck.."

As Brian had a blind need to appear as an,” EL JEFE.” I arrived at the hotel shortly after Brian's call. Sitting in the parking lot and refusing to go inside again. Brian came down but without Chewy.

"Where's Chewy?" I asked as Brian entered my truck. I told Chewy that you and I needed to talk first, Brian answered. That answer confirmed to me. The bullshit was afoot. I allowed himself to be boxed out by Brian. As I had been warned this would happen, Chewy was trying to fight through it with no help from me. Brian and I walked into the IHOP restaurant. Which was bustling with people that morning. The hostess seated us in a mostly empty area. I was furious with Brian and determined to let him know that the nonsense he was pulling would have serious consequences. My intuition was on high alert, and I knew I needed to stay vigilant going off.

And my awareness needed to be heightened now.

“Always assume you are being watched,” Gerald Lorence.

Brian began to talk about future arrangements with Chewy, attempting to increase his end of things with an additional tax on the loads that will start coming to me in two weeks of their departure. Later that evening, Brian was trying to fast-talk me, but I could see the desperate part of him shining through his pseudo-calm. Brian is steady talking, and I have pretty much tuned him out. I'm deep into my thoughts and feeling the energy in the area. I'm seated with Brian at 12:00 o'clock, but there are three white men sitting alone in this part of the restaurant. Two of the three are seated in the mostly empty area that Brian and I are seated in, at 3:00 o'clock and 9:00 o'clock.

As I sit there deep in thought, Brian breaks the silence. "So, what do you think about the new arrangement with Chewy?" he asks. I pause for a moment, contemplating my response. "I think it's bullshit, Brian. You're trying to increase your cut by adding a tax on the lows that will start coming to me in two weeks of their departure," I say firmly.

Brian starts to defend himself, but I cut him off. "Save it, Brian. I can see the desperation in you shining through your pseudo calm," I say, my frustration mounting.

At that moment, I notice the zealot at three o'clock looking at us, but I try not to show any concern. Brian, however, seems oblivious to the situation. "Why did you choose this IHOP, Brian?" I ask, my suspicion growing.

"I don't know. Chewy and I have been coming here every morning for breakfast," he replies.

I nod my head in confirmation of what I'm seeing. "Why? You don't like IHOP, my friend?" Brian asks, laughing.

I look at him, trying to contain my anger. "Clearly not as much as you and your clandestine associates, fucker!" I think to myself. The zealot continues to stare at us, his blue eyes locked and intense.

My mind races as I try to figure out how to get out of this situation without being blamed for it. "Three o'clock is locked, cocked, and ready to rock. And Zealot is super dangerous," I think to myself. "Brian will blame me for everything to avoid responsibility and admitting he fucked up by not following my directions."

I can't help but think about the label that could be put on me, just because I'm a black man. "Brian is a Mexican American. And in the event anything ever goes wrong, BLAME: EL ASQUEROSO NEGRO!" I think to myself, feeling the weight of the unfair stereotype.

"Yo, this waitress is taking too long with our order. And I don't think I can get my pants legs any higher from your bullshit!!" I exclaimed, slowly getting up from the table with a smile on my face. "Then, I want to agitate 3 o'clock, 9 o'clock or the one near the entrance of the IHOP."

As soon as Brian and I got into the truck, I started in on him. "Exposing your simple game, since it appears that there's nothing that will stop you from prolonging this transaction," I said in an irritated tone.

Brian tried to defend himself, but I wasn't having it. "Plus, I need you out of my truck as soon as I pull up to the hotel. And you can get your chickenshit ass out of my truck before I kick your ass all through this parking lot," I demanded.

Brian's eyes widened in fear as he quickly got out of the truck. "Alright, alright, I'll go," he muttered before walking away. I took a deep breath and started the engine, ready to get this deal over with and move on.

I jumped down on the expressway after I kicked the bum out of my truck, driving in the far left lane and checking my mirrors for any potential tails. About a mile out from the hotel, I noticed a cruiser zooming down the expressway with its lights flashing and engine roaring. The car was moving so fast that it made the surrounding vehicles look like they were going backwards. Though I was already driving at a high speed, I knew they were after me, and I didn't want to get caught with Brian, the snake. I couldn't let him pin his fuck up on me.

I didn't hit the brakes because I didn't want to show my brake lights. Instead, I simply took my foot off the gas and let the truck slow down on its own. I assumed they had no idea who I was since I had never been to that IHOP with them or even stayed at that hotel. But when a black man shows up around Mexicans, it's always assumed to be a drug deal.

"This will be my close-up now," I thought to myself.

As I expected, the cruiser pulled behind me in the far left lane with its lights flashing. I knew it was our signal to comply and move to the right. The cruiser moved first and cleared the way for me to pull over to the shoulder safely. Two local officers approached, one on my driver's side and the other on my passenger side. I rolled my window down and the officer on my driver's side asked for the usual information. I could see the officer on the passenger side looking in the back of my truck and back seat, but I didn't turn my head and kept my hands in plain sight on the steering wheel at 10 and two. Whenever he requested something, I asked for permission before reaching for it.

It wasn't long before the officer asked the question I was expecting. The correct response to the question should always be "NO, minus a search warrant."

As I sat in my truck on the side of the road, two officers approached from either side. "Can we see your license and registration, please?" one of them asked. I handed over the documents, keeping my hands in plain sight on the steering wheel.

The officers began looking through the back of my truck and the back seat. I didn't want to give them any reason to suspect me, so I asked permission before reaching for anything they requested. As they searched, I knew that Brian's involvement in drug deals could cause me trouble. I didn't know if he was already involved with someone in Michigan, but I didn't want to be caught in the middle of it.

Suddenly, one of the officers called for a supervisor and a canine unit. My heart raced as I imagined what they might find. The supervisor would most likely give permission for a search, but I couldn't let that happen. I needed this process to move along without any red flags on law enforcement end. Without thinking, I broke the rule and said, "I don't mind, sure!"

The officers continued their search, but it was just a quick look in open areas of my truck. They didn't check under the seats or the glove compartment. They were looking for major amounts of cash or bundle size items. After the search, they allowed me back in my truck and told me, "We pulled you over because you didn't have on your seat belt."

The officer even helped me snap my seat belt in place. I couldn't believe how good he was at shoveling me the bullshit excuse. I was just happy that I didn't get caught. The officer then added, "I'm going to just let you go with a warning this time."

"Wow, thanks," I said, grateful to be let off the hook. I drove away, relieved and eager to get on with my day.

I rolled back into the city towards my office, feeling bothered about how all this unfolded within a small window of time. I stopped by one of my OG's places to help me unpack the events. My OG breathed on me and told me that oftentimes when the feds are building a case, they don't want to alert their presence. They will employ the assistance of local law enforcement. Most common, are our traffic stops or so they would like you to believe. That tactic had just been used on me.

My OG also told me I wasn't the focus either. Brian was a snake, but I didn't want to see him get messed up with the feds, though. My OG advised me to stay away after I said, "I gotta hit my dude and let him know what's up!"

"When them folks, the Feds, get on you, youngin', ain't shit your phone call, now, is going to do for them. But get yourself off in their conspiracy if they got you on the phone, or if one of them is an informant," my old G pleaded with me.

Driving back to my office, I went against my OG's advice...

The sound of my two-way radio beeps, and I quickly grab it to call Brian.

Brian: WHY ARE YOU CALLING ME!! (Brian yells in fear.)

Me: WHAT THE FUCK DO YOU MEAN WHY AM I CALLING YOU!!

Brian: NO NO, THE POLICE HAS CHEWY'S FRIEND PULLED OVER ON THE EXPRESSWAY

AND IT LOOKS LIKE THEY HAVE THE GAS TANK DROPPED!!

Me: Chewy's friend Fu Man Chu?!!

Brian: SI!!

Me: I didn't know Chewy had a fuckin car up here??!

Brian: He brought the car and flew his buddy up to drive it back to AZ for him.

Me: Are you okay tho?!

Brian: SI! Chewy and I are in a cab headed to the airport.

Me: I was calling you to tell you I got pulled over when I was leaving you as well.

Brian: (speaking in Spanish telling Chewy what I said.) Thank you, for telling us my friend. I will call

you to let you know if we make it back to AZ.

Me: I will wait for you

However, that call never came...

Baby Doll called me later and asked for more details about what happened. I explained the whole incident step-by-step, including how Brian was supposed to return the money he owed me. She informed me that Brian was already in debt with Chewy and had planned to use the money he owed me to pay off that debt. Chewy had instructed Brian to pay me with that money, but Brian had lied and said that he had already paid me.

Baby Doll also warned me that Brian might use this as an excuse to avoid speaking with me until he could come up with the money. She said that he would probably try to get his act together and stop messing up before reaching out to me again to clear his debt and potentially get more work through me. Baby Doll promised to contact me again once she had more information.

I was furious about this, but I managed to keep my composure at the IHOP. In the following weeks, my two-way radio kept receiving alerts from Brian's number every few days, but he wouldn't say anything. He was just checking to see if the number was still active, trying to play games and give the impression that there was still hope. But he would soon find out that "this NIGGA doesn’t deal in hope."

After a few weeks, Baby Doll called me back and gave me an update. Apparently, Chewy had still sent the trailer to Chicago, but to some guys in the same crew who had not been picked up yet. They had sent him the final payment for the previous load, which had been driven over from Chicago to Chewy in Detroit. The payment was hidden in a stash in the gas tank. Baby Doll also told me that Chewy was getting desperate for our relationship, but Brian had plans to run up a large bill with Chewy before bringing me back into the picture. According to Baby Doll, Chewy wasn't going to play along with Brian's games for much longer.

"Chewy is not going to put up with him for too much longer," she said. "Everyone knows the game he plays. Chewy will have his ass in the desert for the wild dogs."

After a few more weeks of Brian playing phone games, he finally wanted to talk. He gave me an excuse that he and Chewy needed to make sure they knew where everything was coming from. Then he told me that Chewy was ready to work, but had gone way up on the price to pay off his large debt, just as Baby Doll had predicted. I wasn't interested in dealing with Chewy, especially not after the reckless, greedy shit he pulled that put me in the middle of some shit going on in another state.

Reluctantly, I agreed to all of Brian's terms. "Okay, I'm going to call Chewy tonight and let him know you're ready," Brian said. "But I'll call you tomorrow when I'm going to meet with him. He's going to want to say hi to you."

The following morning, Brian called me to confirm if I was ready to answer the radio when he pulled up to meet Chewy in about 15 minutes. "I'm just waiting for you, my friend," I replied. Brian advised me that if Chewy asked about the money from the last time, I should tell him everything is fine and just take it from the first load that will be delivered to me soon. He also mentioned that the money should have earned some interest by now. I asked if we could work it out, and Brian assured me that everyone was okay.

He then warned me to be careful, as Chewy was going to try to rob me on the price to pay off his debt, and still make a profit on me. But I was more interested in the fact that Chewy might put Brian in the desert with the wild dogs.

I waited anxiously for Brian's call, and when it came, I answered the radio immediately. He put Chewy on the line, who greeted me warmly and asked how I was doing. Chewy then got straight to business, telling me the new price, which was much higher than what we had agreed on before. I tried to negotiate, but Chewy wasn't having it. He made it clear that this was his final offer.

Feeling like I had no choice, I agreed to the new price, knowing that Chewy was using me to pay off Brian's debt. But at least I would finally be getting some work and making some money.

After Brian and I stopped talking on the radio, I opened the back of the phone and pulled out the SIM card. I broke it up and flushed it down the toilet. Then I broke the phone and ended the chapter of my life involving Brian.

I'm sure Brian and Chewy had a wonderful meeting...

As the famous quote goes, "Oh, what a tangled web we weave when first we practice to deceive!" by Walter Scott.

Beep beep beep......

???: Hola

Me: Hola.... Orlando??....

Orlando: SI..........

Me: This is Wayne, a former friend of the pinche Bandito.

Orlando: HOLA, MI AMIGO!!!!!

Danny

Me: HOLA HOLA ORLANDO!!!

Orlando: I was starting to think that the Pinchi bandito found Christos!

Me: NO, NO, MY FRIEND!! I FINALLY MET EL PINCHI DIABLO!!

Orlando: I hate to say this, my friend...... I hope you didn't lose too much with this guy?!

Me: I'm okay, my friend...... I'm really okay NOW!

Orlando: SI, SI, MI AMIGO! Are you still there and ready?!

Me: SI, ALWAYS!!

Orlando: I need to call these guys right now!! They're going to be so happy now, my friend!! I can tell you now they're going to send me to you...... OKAY?!

Me: My friend! I'm waiting for you eagerly!

I had a very good conversation with Orlando, but I was also nervous about dealing directly with him instead of going through someone else. Despite my worries, we talked often over the next few days, waiting for flight information.

But then, I got a call from Mario. He wanted to meet and talk. I agreed, and we planned to meet at Fishbones restaurant in Greektown, downtown Detroit.

I made sure to bring $50,000 of the $70,000 I owed these guys. I went out of my way to get the smallest denominations possible, so I had to use a garbage bag to carry it all. But I wanted to make sure the full amount was represented.

I entered the restaurant and saw Mario seated at the bar as I entered and turned to the right. I took up a seat next to him at the bar.

"How are you doing, Wayne?" Mario asked.

"I'm doing just peachy," I replied. It felt like small talk, but I had no plans to sit there bullshitting with Mario. I had given my word that I would address what I owe, and other than that, we wouldn't be talking.

"Yo, I got 50,000 of that for you in the car," I told Mario.

"Thank you. When you leave, I'm going to have a few more drinks. Could you just put it in the armrest of my car when you leave out?" Mario asked, giving me the details of where he was parked.

"Sure thing," I replied with a smile. I knew I owed another 20,000, but I knew Mario would not want to insult me by asking about it. He wanted something from me.

"Wayne, you know that you and I talk straight to each other when we talk. Why do you keep fighting to work under Big Dawg? I just don't understand this. You are the only reason these things are going so great, Wayne. My brother Frank is afraid to work directly with you. Besides all the things your brother tells him that you say about him. Wayne. How can you stay loyal to someone that is trying to hurt you? I defend you more than your own brother..." Mario paused and waited for my response while taking up his drink, still looking forward.

"I do love my brother. However, the use of the word loyal in this conversation is misplaced... Mario, I AM a businessman. At the end of the day, when it comes to our business dealings, my brother Big Dawg is the devil," I explained.

"I know," Mario said. "Maybe one day soon, you will be in need of a much better devil. I think I may know of a very, very good one just for you too!" He looked at me and started laughing loudly. "My friend, I really think we would do some good business together. Maybe not now for you, understand. Just one day," Mario added.

"I guess in this business, there is always a need for a very, very good devil. Just one would do for me right now," I responded with a smile.

"Please, no one needs to know the details of our meeting here. Let this stay between one good devil to another," Mario pleaded.

As I began to leave, Mario said, "Be expecting my brother to call Big Dawg for a meeting between you guys. Don't allow your brother to lie to you about this. My brother will be calling in two or three days. Maybe a little more."

That night, I received a call from Orlando informing me that he would be landing in Detroit the following day. The next day, around noon, I received another call from him, but to my surprise, he was already in Detroit. With his direct style of speaking, Orlando asked, "When will we be able to discuss things, my friend?" I told him that we could meet at Capers Steakhouse on the Eastside of Detroit that evening. I also reached out to I AM and BIG I to join me.

We arrived at Capers around 6:00 or 7:00 PM that evening, and Orlando was already seated in the back corner of the restaurant, waiting for us. He insisted that he would find his way, and he did just that. The four of us exchanged pleasantries about our first encounter that led to the very moment. Orlando's phone kept ringing in his two-way radio as well, and I AM and I exchanged glances again. Orlando caught the glance this time and answered the call right away, apologizing for the interruption.

After the call, Orlando expressed his apprehensiveness and told us that he was being pressured to be nice to me so that I would come back to work with them. I asked him when we could begin discussing the numbers, to which he replied, "My friend, I don't have authorization to discuss amounts or prices with you."

I held a poker face but was really lost and didn't know what to say. Orlando broke the deafening silence and said, "My Jefes would like you to come back to Tijuana to negotiate these things with them personally." I looked at I AM and BIG I, unsure of what to do next.

They both just looked away and down. I could see they didn't agree with this idea. With some aggression in my voice, I stated, "Orlando, you tell me when you are to arrive in my town. Then you call me and you are here before you tell me you are to arrive in my town. I offered to come to your hotel and bring you to this restaurant tonight, but you insist on coming here yourself.......... You arrived well before me and my guys, and I was informed you have been here 45 minutes prior to our arriving," I conclude my statement with a slow, sarcastic laughter. "My dear friend Orlando, you wouldn't even allow me the pleasure of knowing where your hotel is for the next few days.......... But you want me to trust and accompany you back to Mexico?..... I would have felt better if you would have asked me this question over the radio. Then to come here and negotiate with no authorization," I expressed in an insulted sarcastic fashion.

Orlando responded with a very reassuring tone. "Wayne, I did not come here to do any of those things you say........ I was sent here for you as insurance, my friend. I have checked out of my hotel and my luggage are in the car now. I was sent here as your hostage. I will do and go with whomever you tell me to. Your guys can hold me here until you feel safe. And within your return.........."

Lost for words again. I sat in silence while staring at Orlando and what would appear to be deep thought, questioning his truthfulness. Truth was, I wasn't prepared for this and I was lost. The silence. I did not need to appear as if I was as inexperienced as I was. I needed to make a decision, but I needed time to think this through.

"Orlando, I will need to get back with you on this. I will give you a call tomorrow with an answer. Uh, blah me to pick up the check and I will call you with a place you can meet me," I said.

Orlando's response was confused, "My friend. I don't think you un derstand......... I belong to you now. I have to go with your guys until you decide," as he slid the two-way radio to me.

"You have to call my JEFE'S and tell them what you just told me, but also that you have me, my friend," Orlando said. Orlando could see that I was green as well as being lost and not knowing the next steps to take.

And being as gracious as he was, he decided to give me a step-by-step action of what I needed to do next.

I took Orlando's radio and began to speak with his head face. I was surprised to find someone on the other end who spoke very good English to translate. They were very excited to speak with me and a group was actually present. They gave me a very generous price and agreed to return the $50,000 I paid on behalf of the pinche bandito Brian. The actual reason for them wanting my presence was for me to see the actual marijuana before it was shipped to me.

"My friends, since you have shown me your kindness, I don't see a need for distrust in the beginning of what I hope would be a good relationship that lasts for many years. Just as you have returned those $50,000 that the bandito robbed from me, I will be returning your friend back to you. I have to settle some things here, but I will be there with you in a week from tonight," I concluded our conversation.

Six days after our conversation, BIG I and I landed in Arizona where two Latino gentlemen were waiting for us at the airport. They drove us straight to the border and after several hours of driving, we crossed it and Orlando and his friend Danny were there to receive us. We had already been checked into a hotel for the night. After dropping off our luggage, we were taken to the same restaurant I had visited with Brian before. We were greeted and then taken to the back where I was shown some bales of marijuana. I allowed BIG I to check the quantity and quality of the product, and I was asked to mark all the bales that I approved of. These were the ones that would be sent to me in the States.

We didn't spend more than 35 or 40 minutes at the restaurant. Orlando and Danny then took us to a very nice upscale bar with many beautiful women. I ordered the Mariachi to sing and play for the ladies who were entertaining us that night. BIG I disappeared with one of the women, but I needed to be seen as there for business only. So, I had the Mariachi play my favorite song, "Guantanamera," repeatedly. They didn't mind the work, and I made it even better by paying them in American dollars.

After our trip to Mexico, Danny was very hospitable towards me and I asked him a lot of questions. His favorite one was, "Do you like to deal in the white, my friend?" I knew he was referring to cocaine, but I didn't want to deal with it anymore. So, I politely responded, "No, no, my friend."

Once we arrived back in Detroit after our two-day trip, BIG I and I went our separate ways. Arrangements needed to be made for the load that was being shipped on the truck while we watched prior to leaving Mexico.

After checking my messages, I saw that I had several missed calls from Big Dawg. I remembered what Mario had told me about Frank calling for a meeting with Big Dawg and me. I decided to call Big Dawg back.

Me: Hey, Big Dawg.

Big Dawg: Man, it's been hard to catch up with you!

Me: Well, at least you're being honest this time. laughs

Big Dawg: I never lie, it's just that sometimes things get a little blurry. If you know what I mean. laughs

Big Dawg then informed me that Frank had called him and wanted to meet with us. He didn't have any idea what it was about, but he seemed excited. Big Dawg promised to call me back after contacting Frank for a meeting point.

Later, I headed over to pick up Big Dawg as Frank wanted to meet us at a gas station near Wayne State University. We had to hurry because Frank had a flight to catch, according to my brother.

It took us about 15 to 20 minutes to reach the gas station where we were meeting Frank. As I pulled into the station, I locked eyes with

Frank who appeared shocked by my new truck. Big Dawg and I jumped out of my truck and into Frank's. My brother spoke up, "Hey, Frank!" with joy, but Frank kept his eyes straight and didn't respond, visibly upset.

I didn't care to speak as I didn't care for Frank anyway. I took pride in the fact that Frank was upset by my success independent of him. Finally, Frank spoke up, "When are you going to pay me my money?" My brother just sat there silently. Frank continued, "It's time to tell me that it was your brother that caused all this thing, right?!" He almost sounded as if he was pleading.

Big Dawg repeated what he had told Frank before, but Frank was looking for a "gotcha" moment with Big Dawg's help. "Go ahead and just say it, Big Dawg. He is right here, right now." Frank yelled as he turned slightly in his seat to point at me in the back seat.

Big Dawg just sat there in silence. "Big Dawg, just say it! Big Dawg!!" Frank yelled. "Big Dawg? Big Dawg!" My brother just remained silent.

It became clear that Frank already knew he would never receive that much money from my brother. Despite lying on me and possibly putting my life in danger, I wanted to stop the verbal assault on my brother's manhood. Frank kept demanding my brother pay him and even made Big Dawg make promises he knew he couldn't fulfill.

I let the friends carry on a little longer, and Frank continued to demand payment. I pointed out that my brother had no money and that the debt was mostly before I started working with them. I made it clear that my brother had stolen nothing from him, and that he was responsible for giving my brother work while knowing that some of the guys were not paying him.

I suggested that Frank agree to a reasonable number and expect to be repaid back. I reminded him that he was just as responsible as Big Dawg, and that he had even made Big Dawg accept me as his partner.

Frank knew someone would take the work from him, but they wouldn't do that to me. He had added more money than what my brother owed just because my brother would agree, and I told him that he was robbing from his own Jefe.

I knew this game very well and I said all this in a matter-of-fact tone. It was time for Frank to face the facts and come to a reasonable agreement.

Frank sat for a moment before speaking, "Wayne, you're right. I know your brother was really easygoing." He paused again before continuing, "I will agree to forgive some of what Big Dawg owes me, only if you agree to help him pay the agreed-upon amount later." Frank looked in his rearview mirror at me.

I replied, "I'll be willing to have the conversation once I see the final number agreed upon, Frank."

Frank then asked, "Can we also agree that there is room for everyone to earn some profit in this business? I know your cousin is a very important part of my other friends' team in this city." I was shocked that he would admit in front of my brother that I had him in checkmate, but I still understood that there wasn't any money in checkmate.

I replied, "I'm an agreeable person, Frank. With agreeable people. I look forward to hearing from you soon on the final numbers, my friend."

I turned to my brother and said, "Let's go, Big Fella."

After that encounter with Frank, I never heard from him or Mario again, but their presence always lingered in my mind.

Over the next six weeks, I received two substantial loads from my friends in Tijuana. The price was good, and I made sure to keep it at street value to remain "agreeable" to those concerned.

However, things started to slow down with the Tijuana relationship as they began pressuring me to accept cocaine. I refused and as a result, they started slowing down on the marijuana loads.

Then one day, Danny called me to say that my friend Orlando was no longer working with the Tijuana cartel, but he had given him my number. Danny expressed that he would still like to maintain our relationship in Mexico, and I agreed to continue doing business with him.

A few weeks had passed with no movement from his friends in Mexico. Danny called me again and informed him that he was leaving the Tijuana cartel and moving back to Ciudad Juarez. However, he still wanted to help ne find something nice in Juarez.

I accepted the offer when Danny told him that he would be given a Chewyce: either accept white or not receive any more marijuana.

Shortly after getting a call from Danny, I received another call from the cartel. He was surprised because he had resisted dealing with white. The caller informed him that someone had been sent from Tijuana to establish business up north and that he would receive information on his next load of marijuana.

That night, I went to Fishbones restaurant in downtown Detroit. As I entered the seated area, he spotted two Latino men seated at a table for four. One of the gentlemen waved him over to the table. I recalled meeting him when he returned a load of weed that the cartel had sent him when he first started working with them. The cartel had sent him low-quality weed, thinking he would be their garbage man. However, they came to an understanding when I gave them the bad weed back.

I was greeted by the gentleman and seated at a table with two Latino men. One of them waved at me and introduced me to the older man who was the Cartel center cross, who spoke English fluently. The subject of the meeting was once again about white, but I made it clear that I wasn't interested in dealing with it.

I then turned to the man who brought the older Spanish gentleman to see me and asked about the load that the Tijuana guys said they would have information on for me. He told me that we were discussing that load right now and that if we made a deal, he would tell me the time of the load's arrival and include a load of weed for me, but no white. "No white, no weed...my friend," he said with an arrogant smile.

I had a negative impression of the man who claimed to be the "plug" since the first time we met. He had that typical "I'm the boss, and you are beneath me" attitude. But I played along to be a good sport. When it came to negotiations, I knew the older Spanish gentleman would not agree to my terms. However, I restated my stance and said that I had no interest in dealing with cocaine. If I were to consider it, I would need to see it at no more than $16,000 per piece. The Spanish gentleman immediately accepted my offer, but the other man, whom I referred to as "Fuck Boy," cut in quickly, speaking in Spanish. He was shocked that the Spanish gentleman had agreed so fast, and so was I. It was clear that Fuck Boy wasn't going to let me get a good deal, as he had been ripping off his crew in Ohio.

This incident is an example of how Mexican cartels trying to do business often get their deals sabotaged by Mexican Americans like Fuck Boy, whose existence depends on the cartels never having a direct line to the consumer through black people. He saw me as a threat to his livelihood and power, but what he didn't understand was that I had seen his type before. It's a constant repetition of the same game, played over and over again.

The meeting ended abruptly after that exchange. As we walked out together, Fuck Boy turned to me and said, "Orlando is no longer with the cartel. And the guys over there told me to tell you not to answer or talk with him anymore. Also, change your radio tomorrow and call those guys over there with the new number." Then he added, "And break the old radio."

The next morning, I changed phones and called Danny with the new number. I then broke the old phone and tossed the relationship with the Tijuana cartel out of my truck's window with the damn phone.

The following day, I returned to my office and continued doing business as usual, helping people and managing my properties. Over time, my company had acquired around 70 different properties in Detroit and its surrounding subcommunities. In total, we had probably owned upwards of 100 properties.

Dealing with the disorganized Tijuana Cartel had become quite taxing. The product was inconsistent at best, and there was no accountability for these inconsistencies. It seemed to me that everyone who did business in the Mexicali and Tijuana region of the country operated in this manner - lawless and rogue for the most part. The appearance of being a cartel seemed to be more important than actually running an organized operation.

The behavior of hustling drugs was something I learned out of necessity. I had a difficult upbringing and losing my mother at the age of three was especially hard. In many cultures, the loss of a mother was considered a death sentence for a child. I truly believe that if it weren't for Big Red, I wouldn't have made it. When my mother passed away at 18, there were no government programs available to assist me. I had no interest in anything after Big Red started to succumb to life's cycles. Growing up, I had contempt for women in my heart due to the anti-mothering figures in my life, such as my stepmother, grandmother, and some aunts. Big Red became my savior and protector from those personalities. I want to clarify that not all of my aunts were antagonistic toward me; some of them provided mothering qualities, and I don't want to isolate them. But we were struggling financially, and they had many children of their own to care for, so they were limited in what they could do. Father time placed limits on the amount of love and protection Big Red could provide, but he did his best for me.

My life was undergoing significant changes, and my perspective was shifting. I was deeply in love with the mother of my youngest daughter. She could be incredibly sweet, but in an instant, she could become hostile. She didn't care about fashion or style, and she knew nothing about these things. I prayed to God for this woman and asked for a combination of my stepmother, grandmother, and certain aunts all in one person. But I discovered that I was a child again in her hands, taking in all her hostile ways just for those brief moments of affection. She became my driving force, even though she often said things like, "You're not this, you're not that. Who do you think you are? You will never be or do this, that, or the other."

I often left her feeling angry and full of fire, thinking, "She has the worst attitude ever!" I was determined to show her what I was capable of. Imma show that Bitch!!!

I eventually came to accept the fact that I was fighting my own demons from the past, not her. I was trying to prove something to the women who hurt me and who had passed away. Meanwhile, she was fighting similar demons - always wanting to be a daddy's girl, but her father kept leaving and running the streets. And that's what I was doing too, in a way.

She was always on my back about leaving drugs alone, but it was difficult to do when there might be a financial need for it. She had a famous saying, "Head for the fucking hills, buddy!! Be a fucking man!" that would shake me to my core. This was the first law of Big Red's - there was no excuse for this action ever. So, I tried to leave drugs alone, but I still had to produce in other ways.

This woman believed in me and supported me when I had nothing. She even brought me clothes and food against her mother's wishes. She gave me a chance when her mother pointed out my disheveled appearance. She defended me to her mother while keeping my secret, saying "He doesn't have any buttons on his shirt."

I was in a really good space at this time. I was good at navigating the politics of the drug world, but I never liked dealing with it. Even though I was exceptionally good at it, I never had any real desire to be a part of it. I didn't feel any pressure to continue dealing with drugs anymore.

I had the opportunity to renovate houses and sell them, and was able to give some of my properties to single mothers with children. It was a joy to be able to help provide Christmas gifts, school clothes, shoes, and food for these families. At times, I even paid for their gas and electricity bills so they could have heat and light during the cold Michigan winters. I don't want to paint myself as a saint, as I was just trying to save myself and act out the kindness I wished for as a child. Unfortunately, no one ever showed up for me.

Danny, on the other hand, was persistent and continued calling me for a year and a half to two years. I had no interest in talking about drugs anymore, and he didn't force the issue. Instead, we talked about traveling and family, including his wife who he described as an "evil dictator," which I could relate to.

Danny, like myself, always had an adventurous spirit and ideas. One day, he excitedly told me about his friend who had just returned to town. "My friend, my very, very good friend, is back in town now. I have been telling Tano much about you too, my friend. Tano works all across Mexico, and no one bothers with him either. He wants to meet with you too," Danny said. However, I wasn't interested and made excuses. Danny wasn't pushy and seemed to understand.

At that time, my life was going well, despite being unemployed. I gave my friend a job and even hired my own sons to work during the summer, to teach them the value of work ethics. I also gave a job to one of my son's uncles. Occasionally, I would fly to Baltimore to visit Smoochie, who had become a father figure to me.

However, things took a turn for the worse when the housing market began to decline rapidly, and money became scarce. I had several employees who depended on their jobs to support their families, and I couldn't bear to let them go. I continued to hold on to them, even though it wasn't healthy for my business. As the business came to a halt, I paid my employees out of my savings because they had become like family to me.

Danny was still calling and talking about his good friend Tano. "My friend, I need you to do something for me," he said urgently. "Just come to Juarez to meet with Tano. Listen to him only. He is a good friend. Your visit will help me get some work from him for myself too."

As Danny spoke, his worries were evident. His wife was ready to leave him again, and I was starting to wonder if I may be forced to rethink some things for myself.

After listening to his plea, I responded, "Give me about two weeks, and I will be with you in Juarez, my friend." I could sense the urgency in his voice, and wanted to help him out.

With that, Danny expressed his gratitude, and the conversation ended. I knew that I had to act fast to make the trip to Juarez:, and I was prepared to do whatever it takes to help my friend in need.

CHAPTER 17

CIUDAD JUÁREZ

IT WAS A SCORCHING hot summer day when I landed at the El Paso Airport. The airport was small and dwarfed in comparison to the Dallas International Airport, which I always enjoyed during my layovers. Little did I know that my layovers at that airport would be the first of many flights, and I would become well-known to a number of vendors there.

After landing, I powered up my two-way radio Nextel phone and hit the alert button to inform Danny that I had arrived. I knew he would give me some time to make it to the baggage claim area. While looking around at all the military flying in and out of the airport, I heard my friend's voice come from my two-way radio. I quickly responded, even though I knew it was a no-no to answer without waiting for a response. Danny had been trying to contact me for five minutes and was starting to worry.

He informed me that there were two guys waiting for me outside the airport, giving me the make and color of the car. I claimed my baggage and proceeded outside, where I saw the vehicle parked in the scribe with two Latino gentlemen inside.

As I entered the car, I noticed a distinctive smell in the air. As we got closer to the border, the smell became stronger. I would come to call this smell the "smell of Mexico," which, in the years to come, would bring butterfly-type feelings in my stomach, similar to the ones you get before a big game or a fight where you're not too sure of the outcome.

We crossed the border into Mexico without any delay. In contrast, the entry into the state had long lines that extended all the way across the large bridge and into Mexico, with a strong security presence. However, entering Mexico might only have a police pickup truck with officers standing on the back.

Danny had already arranged a room for me at the Holiday Inn hotel in Juarez. "Damn, they have Holiday Inns over here too," I exclaimed in amazement.

Danny welcomed me warmly and said, "My friend, I need you to ride with me. My wife is going to kill me. I have to pick up my daughter from private school. My daughter will tell on me again!" I looked at Danny in disbelief and thought, "Danny? Really?!"

After picking up Danny's daughter from a Catholic school, Danny tried to engage her in conversation, but she seemed unresponsive. Danny kept talking, but she didn't say a word in response. "Oooooh, fuck me," Danny cried out in frustration. "Are you okay, Danny?" I asked. "She fucking told! I know it," Danny whispered. "How do you know?" I asked. "She's not talking to me," Danny explained. "I'm not worried this time, my friend. Her telling will do nothing to me. I have a secret weapon on my side this time. Do you know what my secret weapon is?" Danny said with an evil smile as he pulled into the gates of his home and saw his beautiful wife exiting from the porch, walking towards the car with an unhappy expression. Without waiting for me to ask, Danny answered, "You are my secret weapon," with a huge smile across his face and waving at his wife frantically through the windshield of the car while pointing at me with his thumb.

As we watched his wife's eyes focus on the passenger seat where I was sitting, her smile grew bigger than Danny's. She approached the car, and Danny introduced me to her before taking me into his house to meet his whole family.

Danny took me to a restaurant called Montana Steakhouse after I met his family. We had a good meal and discussed the meeting scheduled for the next day. Later, I went back to my hotel room to rest for the busy day ahead.

The following morning, Danny arrived at my hotel room early and hurried me to get dressed. He then took me through the hotel lobby and an internet novelty shop and led me to a bar. Inside, we walked towards a well-dressed man in his 50s named Tano. "Tano, this is my friend Wayne." Danny introduced me to the gentleman. He greeted me with a firm handshake and asked if I was a Wolverine.

When I confirmed that I was, Tano mentioned how he enjoyed winter and always wanted to visit Michigan, as he frequently visited Chicago. He then turned to Danny and asked if he was keeping his wife happy, to which they both laughed and confirmed.

We ordered food and engaged in small talk, and Tano began to inquire about my business interests. I shared my interests, and Tano assured me that he could make it happen for me, and volume would not be an issue for him.

Tano moved from the subject of marijuana just as quickly as he cleared up any concerns about his ability to fulfill volumes needed. 'Wayne, my greatest interest is cocaine,' Tano said after answering my business interest. 'You do have a history in white, I'm sure,' Tano asked based on my persistence in only discussing marijuana. 'My history is in white, Tano,' I responded.

'What do you look for in appearance when you open a kilo of white that would indicate quality?' Tano continued with a rhetorical question. 'I believe it is called fish scale, Wayne. When the fish scales or flake is the sign that shows that it has been treated. Pure cocaine that comes from the leaf would surprise you. It looks just like the washing powder you use to wash your clothes, my friend,' Tano explained with a professor's tone.

We continued to talk more but concerning business. Tano went on to ask me questions about how I would handle interactions with law enforcement and listened to my every word. 'Wayne, I was just doing business with someone stateside recently. We had done business for some time and never had any issues. One day this person had a run-in with your government, which is just part of the business. We asked for any paperwork confirming his loss. With proof of these things, we can't hold you to account for these things, after proper proof. The individual told us he had a total loss. Then gave the documentation to confirm. What he didn't know is that we employ investigators of our own. However, we found out that there was a loss taken, but not total. We had to bring him across... Which was most unfortunate, a wonderful relationship lost to unnecessary lies,' Tano explained, giving pause for a moment.

'Wayne, I would like to do business with you,' he said with a bright and ambitious smile."

I lowballed Tano on the price of the white, but it didn't work as well as before. I told him I would need at least $16 per kilo to consider it, but I would be willing to accept an even higher price for the marijuana. Tano could tell that I was trying to avoid the white. He countered my offer and even lowered the price to $17 per kilo, and he offered as much volume of weed as I could handle. At this point, Danny jumped in and asked for a moment to work out his end of the deal with his friend.

Tano agreed to let Danny call him later with an answer to his offer. Tano knew what Danny was doing, and I was relieved that Danny had my back. I realized that I needed to grow up fast and negotiate my own terms because these deals would be made in my blood.

Tano had a rare personality type. He was an aesthetically refined gentleman, and negotiating with him was very different. It was almost like engaging with a political figure or some branch of government. Danny would become my new teacher, and he would take me to different meetings throughout the day, but nothing on the level of what I experienced in the meeting with Tano.

The following day, I crossed back into the United States and flew back to Detroit from El Paso. Over the next month, things got progressively worse. I had to lay off two work crews, which broke my heart. The next morning, my assistant Camara came into my office and started talking my ear off. My executive assistant Gina was out of the office, and I didn't have anyone to run Camara away for me. I tried to put on a tough boss act, but I wasn't feeling as tough as I once did. Gina was the only one who could truly put me in my place. My attorney, Lorence, loved her too, and I valued her greatly. He warned me to keep my assistants happy because good assistants were hard to come by, and someone was always trying to steal them.

That morning, Camara was on me, and Camara wanted to tell me about her weekend. She showed me her Facebook page and mentioned that she had a friend who I used to see briefly, and that's how I ended up hiring her. I wasn't too keen on hiring Camara, but Gina convinced me that she was the most qualified candidate. Gina had interviewed a bunch of people, and Camara stood out. Despite my reservations, I ended up hiring her.

As Camara pulled up her page, I couldn't help but think, "Her fucking friend put her up to this. This type of shit is what I told Gina would happen."

Camara exclaimed, "Look, Mr. Thompkins, those are all girls' night out pics. And my friend was executed that night," referring to her friend who twisted her to hire her.

I looked at the screen with very little interest until I focused on the screen with renewed intense interest while whispering in my head, "Oh my fucking God... that's really her."

Camara looked at me with excitement and said, "Yes, that's really her, and ain't she cute?" referring to her friend. Camara observed my focus, replacing her excitement for her friend with a confused look on her face. "I told you she would be in the picture, boss," she said with a confused look in her eyes.

"No, no, you did tell me she would be in the picture, Camara," I replied, snapping out of the trance-like gaze I was in. "But who is that right there?" I asked, pointing to the screen.

Camara looked and said, "Oh, that's your ex-boo's other BFF besides me. Her name is Mena. Do you know her or something?"

I was caught up in the moment, trying to figure out exactly where I knew her from. Then, I had a flashback. He had dragged me out of the house shortly after he and Snoop completed high school. I was depressed and stuck in the house for some time after Lawrence got the charges dropped against me in the Moe Green situation. Tez and I were at a club when I saw this very light-complexioned version of the best of my imagination. I was speechless, caught up in my fantasies. I was nothing near what I was becoming. I built up some serious courage just to approach her, but it wasn't enough because I could not get my feet to move. And, Tez was nowhere to be found, which was not unusual for him. Tez were always and forever more becoming the ambassador to that errant part of myself that would have never seen the light of day.

After being a wallflower all night, the club was about to close, and I found Tez. We were exiting the club on Eight Mile and walking to my car. I looked to my right and saw her again while talking with Tez. I totally lost track of our conversation. Tez said, "What the fuck is wrong with you, NIGGA!! man, there she goes again..." as he pointed to her with his eyes. Tez made me aware that he knew her from Osborne High School and then told me she had a dude that treated her bad and how she would work and take care of him.

I was still just looking at her, speechless and walking blindly. "Ah, Mena!" Tez yelled as he ran over to her. "

Oh, shit. Oh shit. What the fuck are you doing, you fucking asshole!" I saw it, but it was too late. He was over there talking to her and pointing at me now. Tez would just spring into action because he knew I wouldn't. Tez waved me over and introduced me to the reflection of my imagination. We walked and shared some small talk until she got in her car. I handed her my number and maybe a $100 bill folded inside.

She looked at it and said, "Thank you! But, I can't accept this because I'm in a relationship."

"Well, just keep it anyway. Just in case," I replied with a smile.

Mena smiled as she handed the money back to me. "I won't be calling. It wouldn't be right for me to accept this, fully knowing that," she said before turning and walking back to her car with her friends. Watching her leave, I felt like she was just as elusive as a dream, driving away into the hollows of my mind. "She'll always be stuck in my mind, like a melody of a song that you just cannot find. That's just how she is and has always been through high school as well," Tez added, snapping me out of my flashback.

"Oh my fucking God, that's really her," I exclaimed. The melodic sound of her voice started to play in my mind again, haunting me. "She had the right attitude," I said to myself.

Camara repeated her question, "You know her or something?" I was still looking at the picture when I replied, "We have met in the past."

"OK! OK! Enough! OK! Enough!" I interrupted myself, trying to snap out of my thoughts. "Let's get some work done today now. And, no playing games on the computer or personal phone calls! Just because

Gina ain't here, because I will tell, and I don't mind adding shit either," I said, trying to sound tough and focused on the task at hand.

Danny called and asked me to return to Juarez, "Rapido mi amigo," Danny pleaded. I booked a flight out that same week, and I brought BIG I along this time. We would be looking at weed this time for sure, and I didn't know good weed from bad, so BIG I would be needed for that.

We landed in El Paso about a week later, and after the baggage claim, there was a car waiting to take me and BIG I across the border. Just like last time, we checked into the Holiday Inn, and shortly after, Danny came by the hotel.

We dropped our bags and headed back out the door with Danny. After two days of having several meetings concerning weed and seeing sample after sample of very low quality, I was starting to feel that Danny had the fix in on these arrangements and meetings. Danny disclosed that he had a very huge meeting that had just not happened yet. "Just don't worry, my friend. I have the best for last," Danny promised with an unsure look on his face.

For me to come with him for a moment, but alone. We left BIG I at the hotel. Danny and I got into his car and drove about an hour. I have someone I want you to talk to again, Danny said, without any details on the "again" part.

We pulled up to this ridiculously huge walled mansion. The entrance gate was grand, a circle driveway entrance at the end of a long, straight driveway. This house had Greek pillars and a welcoming double door. The door swung open, and there stood an old friend, or so it was starting to feel. "TANO, MY FRIEND!! I'm not surprised at all," I said before he could say anything. Tano was happy to see me, and Danny just smiled.

Tano gave me a tour of his home that was still under construction. The entrance had a Rotunda style to it with marble heated floors. A circular staircase hugged the Rotunda shape of the entrance area on both sides, leading to the top. Tano was quick to point out the handrails, all handmade and beaten by my friend.

As we went up the stairs, there were landings with statues of different Greek Gods highlighted with lighting shining on them. "What do you think of the White Bull there, Wayne?" Tano pointed to one statue featured by the brightest of the lights on it.

"You mean Europa, Tano?" I asked just to make Tano aware. I was cultured somewhat, but I knew it wasn't Europa.

"Yes," Tano exclaimed with unmeasured excitement. "I see you are familiar with Greek mythology. But it's Zeus. Europa was a Princess kidnapped by Zeus, featuring himself as a white, massive, beautiful bull. I agree with that, knowing that Europe decided to take this Princess of Phoenicia name, once it decided to create a seventh continent when there was only originally six and naming the 7th Europe. After this goddess, Europa. Well, I'm still hopeful that I may be able to abduct the Lady of Liberty, as Zeus did Europa the Princess. She will bring us much fortune, Wayne!" Tano exclaimed.

Tano's home was very exquisite, cultured, and refined. As he continued to give me a tour, he took me into his master bedroom with a ceiling featuring Michelangelo's Sistine Chapel Masterpiece, The Creation of Adam. On the main floor, there was a big sculpture of another Michelangelo work, of King David from the David and Goliath Biblical story.

Tano went on to give me some details of his plans for our relationship. I was always very fond of Tano, but there didn't appear to be a Mexico-centric bone in his body. Tano didn't move, talk, or share similar interests as everyone with similar clandestine business interests. He carried an unspoken presence of a clandestine and punitive nature. I just had a gut feeling that this would run much deeper than drugs.

After the walk-through at Tano's house, we headed back to the hotel. Danny told me that he was waiting for someone to come into town to meet with me. "This will be a very big meeting for us both," my friend Danny stressed.

The following day, BIG I and I had a flight to catch. Things didn't look promising. Up early and packed up our things so that we could get ready to cross back over into the states. Danny came to see us off and expressed how bad he felt about this final meeting.

BIG I and I loaded our things into the cab, then headed toward the border. We were in traffic, lined up to cross the bridge from Mexico toward the actual border. Danny was in traffic on foot. He ran up the line of waiting cars to our cab. "Come, my friend! Grab your things from here now. Those guys are in town now and ready for us," Danny said while breathing hard.

We jumped from the taxi and started running down the bridge toward the waiting car, pulling our bags. "This is not America here. You don't see black guys with luggage running through the streets of Mexico every day, and never away from the US border." We made it back to Danny's car, and he sped off.

Danny drove us to a neighborhood that was difficult to describe. We waited in a small shack-type house with several young guys. Suddenly, the two-way radio beeped, and the young guys pulled out semi-automatic rifles and pistols from every corner of the room and ran out the door. BIG I started to panic, but Danny reassured him that everything was alright. The young guys were just setting up a perimeter to protect us from whoever was coming to see us.

After a few minutes, a man walked in, and the room went silent. He was like a rock star. His name was Flaco, but I later learned that his real name was Amando Nunez Meza, also known as Mac 11. He had on dark sunglasses, a tight blue jean outfit, and spiked hair. When he walked in, the whole place came to a standstill.

I watched Danny, and he seemed nervous. One of the guys put a bale of weed on the table, and another cut a big triangle in the top and pulled it back to reveal the product. BIG I looked at it and exclaimed, "Yes, this is the shit right here?"

Danny asked in translation, "How much can you do?" BIG I yelled, "Whatever they want to send!" Danny translated, and the guy smiled.

However, Flaco had a different question. "¿Y el blanco?" he asked Danny.

"Can you move the white too?" Danny translated.

BIG I yelled out that we could do both with ease. Before I could stop him, Danny started to translate what BIG I had said. Flaco smiled finally, but then I had to correct what BIG I said, and Danny looked at me twice before translating.

Flaco's smile vanished, and he said, "Nah. Nothing else now."

We made a deal for the weed, but Flaco never spoke or reacted again. We got a high price because BIG I kept talking over me, but at least we had a deal in place for some pretty good weed.

BIG I and I were in a taxi, heading back to the bridge again. We had to spend a night at the Embassy Suites Hotel in El Paso, and we would miss our flight. "BIG I, do you have anyone ready to move the work you agreed to back there?" I asked him. He answered no, as I expected. I asked the same question about the white, and got the same answer.

I also asked him if he had money to cover any mistakes. We both knew the answer to this question. “The only thing you were brought to do was to check the weed. You were to answer no questions other than the ones he asked me.” I expressed in a calm but firm tone. I knew BIG I did not mean any harm, but that hood shit, he knew. It didn't translate well across the border, where the deal seemed pretty simple and enjoyable while making them. They're made in blood. Payment for mistakes? Would be accepted in blood.

I knew that the smile on Flacco's face that turned to a frown was most likely the deal-breaker. We flew back to Detroit the following day. Two months after the fact, we never received a load.

Headed back to Ciudad Juarez at Danny's request, I went through the same steps after landing, determined not to make the same mistakes as before. This time, I brought I AM along, knowing he could handle these situations. Danny arrived at the hotel after a couple of hours, and it seemed like he and I AM hit it off better than Big I. We followed Danny downstairs to the lobby, where a van was waiting for us.

The driver didn't speak English and seemed somewhat concerned as he looked at me through the rearview mirror several times. I mirrored Danny's laughter when he jokingly mentioned the driver's suspicion of us being DEA. The driver's uncertain smile showed he was still unsure.

We arrived at a walled home, and upon entering, I noticed beer and liquor bottles scattered around. There was a table with a white powder-like substance, seemingly cocaine. The driver went to get a kilo of cocaine wrapped in gray duct tape, and Danny asked me to test it. I AM and I examined the product, and I AM praised its quality.

As the driver and Danny prepared lines to test the cocaine, I noticed the driver becoming increasingly nervous. When he handed me the bill to sniff the cocaine, I hesitated, and I AM refused to accept it. Spanish-speaking erupted between the driver and Danny, with Danny explaining that the driver accused us of being DEA because we didn't sample the coke.

I reassured the driver that we were there for business and not to party. Danny then mentioned another concern the driver had, wondering why I didn't act like other black guys. I AM and I looked at each other, knowing this guy had never encountered a black person before.

Overall, it was a tense situation, but we managed to resolve it and proceed with our business intentions.

A deal was cut for the white, with the promise of weed as well. Within three weeks of returning to Detroit, I received my first load, which consisted of only 10 bricks. I paid $16,500 per kilo, totaling $165,000. I gave the $165,000 to the driver immediately out of my own pocket and got them back on the road, hoping the next shipment would arrive soon. I planned to deal with getting my money out of the cocaine later. My crew hadn't been working, so I gave them the 10 bricks with a small tax on top. I still had no interest in dealing with cocaine, but it was becoming increasingly clear that unless I did, I would not be receiving any marijuana.

Despite my reservations, the crew was excited about the future possibilities. The next load would consist of 15 bricks and the guys on the road would drop off the money for the 10 and come back with the 15.

At the request of Danny, I was instructed to find a place for their guys to stay while they waited for me to finish each load. I suggested buying beds, stoves, refrigerators, plate sets, and bed sets. But the guys in Juarez didn't want me to spoil them and risk them not coming back. Instead, they asked for sleeping bags without pillows and to have them sleep on the floor. I was to buy only bread, milk, beans, eggs, tortillas, flour or corn, and no meat. They were not allowed to drink until the weekend, and only beer was permitted.

The next load with 15 bricks arrived, and my guys had buyers ready, so I didn't need to use any of my own money this time. The drivers stayed a night in the house, and I set out early the next morning back to Juarez. The price I received was $17,000. I stuck to my usual line, insisting on at least $16,000 per kilo. Eventually, we settled on $16,500 per kilo, with the promise of weed to follow.

Danny reached out to me to express how excited those guys were with my performance. "They are going to do something very nice for you now, my friend. They are going to send you 25 of the white," Danny said, his voice filled with pride.

"No, no, no, my friend...I would not take anything over those 15 at 16-5, or meaning $16,500. Those guys are coming to my town and are coming right back to you, right away, my friend," I responded. "OK, tell me, my friend," Danny asked. "I need $16,000 per for those 25, mi Amigo," I demanded.

The guys were back on the road and on their way to me with the 25 already, and I was threatening to send them back if I didn't get the price that I wanted. Needless to say, the price was changed, 25 at 16 per.

The trick is to act as if sending you larger amounts of work is doing a favor for you. Yes, it does create a larger return, but it also creates a larger mandatory minimum and increases your guidelines for federal sentencing. They are not your friend and won't respect you for not knowing the business. With an increase in workload, the fucking price MUST come down, PERIOD!! There is an exception to this rule, but you don't need to know it just yet. Keep reading...

Again, I will repeat for the sake of beating this into your memory: "This is business. It has nothing to do with the myth of American loyalty. The concept of business and loyalty are independent of each other."

"LOYALTY and COMMERCE are two separate entities: When the two are combined, the former is used as a tool to drive down the price of labor. NO FREE LOYALTY!!" - Donald Thompkins

At the time, the street price for a kilo was around $23-24,000. I sold mine for $18,000 per kilo, allowing my guys to put no more than $1,000 on each one. This was well below the market value at the time, but I didn't care. I wasn't going to sit on that C4 and risk getting jammed up by the authorities. I also needed to protect my team from getting caught trying to break it down to make every dime possible. My mentor, Larry Chambers, would call this ineffective business and the opposite of capitalism. But that wasn't a concern for me. I knew that the cartels, which were my financial institution, had way more money than these street guys. My focus was to get the cartel's money by forcing them down on the price. This gave me more leverage and political capital on their end.

After the street got over the fear of my bricks being fake or serious, re rocked. The thought of what I had just created was overwhelming.

The next five trips went pretty much the same way. My guys were blowing through that shit. I started breaking my own rules and slowing my guys down. The streets were talking and I didn't need my guys getting hot that fast.

The Juarez guys were coming once a week with 25 bricks, which equalled 100 per month. It was about to increase to twice a week, but not without another reduction in price rule of thumb. I was starting to get work that a number of crews in my city desired but was causing them to desire a sit-down meeting with me. The problem was, no one really knew me, but I knew it wouldn't be long before they did.

The voices were getting louder, "Them niggas is fucking up the game!"

No one else could move their work. Things got bad to the degree of people refusing to buy from anyone but my guys. They would wait if we were out at the time. Soon, other crews started to come over to buy my cocaine, which was much cheaper and way better quantity and quality-wise. The same way I got it from Mexico was the same way I made my guys push it.

The side effect of this success was that there was no more talk of weed on the Mexico side, and no more talk stateside from my guys as well.

BEEP BEEP BEEP

Me: Yes! Go ahead.

Danny: Ooooooh, my friend. I need something from you.

Me: Tell me, my friend!

Danny: Those guys up there at the house you get for them! They are over there fighting! They are even outside in the driveway and backyard. This is not good!

Me: Yes! This is very, very bad, my friend.

Danny: These guys are here with me now. They are asking can you send two of your guys over to this place?

Me: OK! What do you want my guys to do?

Danny: My friend, these guys have drunk too much. They must have sneaked or something. But they will deal with them soon. Just send your guys to make them go back in the house.

Me: I have two of my close guys for this. Don't worry!

Danny: My friend! Also tell your guys to make them go to sleep. (Silence. And I hear Spanish speaking.) My friend, these guys say that you have any problem. Have your guys kick them in their ass. It's OK!

Me: Don't worry, my friend!

I sent my guys I AM and Loc Boc over to the house. Those guys were shitfaced drunk, too. My guys got them inside and told them to go to bed. I instructed them to wait a bit and make sure they were asleep, and to take all the alcohol they were drinking as well.

Another six loads came over the next four weeks. They started running a group up when the other group was on the road coming back. The guys in Juarez sent up a guy with rank among them to stay at the house and control their people. I didn't want my guys having to discipline their people. That was their fucking job and they needed to babysit it. This guy they sent spoke manageable English as well. I knew something was up.

I decided that I needed a break. I never liked not being out of work every now and then. I flew to Baltimore, MD to see my pops. This one flight caused me to fall in love with the city. It may have just been because of what it represented for me. I went to town for a break, and my pops, Smoochie and I really bonded over the years. I never really had a father, and this great man never had a son, just two daughters that he loved dearly too. He also began to love me just as much. And I wanted to be closer to that. I even had two sisters now as well. I was a very happy camper.

The actual flight time from Detroit to Baltimore was less than 45 minutes.I found myself frequently traveling back and forth between loads to Baltimore with I AM accompanying me every time.He even met a nice young lady named Michelle from Baltimore and would fly there to see her on his own. Meanwhile, I became a regular at the Norma Jean strip club and developed an interest in a dancer named Charlie. Additionally, I bonded with my sister Candy's man, Sleepy, who I called "Slick" due to his ability to make money.

I AM and I agreed that it was time to find a place in Baltimore. Flying between Detroit and Baltimore became routine for us, with occasional trips to Ciudad Juarez.

However, the speed at which my guys were moving the 25 bricks became an issue. When the load arrived, there was enough money for 50 bricks sitting there. I told Danny that I needed a supplier who could keep up with my pace.

Baltimore had become my playground away from home, but I couldn't fly with the amount of money I was carrying through an airport. Slick and I talked more and more about this and he expressed interest in getting involved in the business in Baltimore. Danny was negotiating meetings with other suppliers who could handle the demand in Detroit and possibly Baltimore.

I received a call on my two-way radio and answered promptly.

Me: Hello, what's up?

I AM: Do you know the head guy from the house?

Me: Okay?

I AM: I need you to come over to the N, right quick. He is saying the money was not right when it got across. They sent him over here with a message, but only for you.

Me: I'm coming that way, 911

I rushed over to Novara Street and I was furious. I knew the money I sent over was correct. I even had my guys sit down with this guy and he recounted everything they did at the same time.

When I arrived, the Spanish guy was smiling. "¿También, mi amigo? You worry too much, my friend," he said. I was confused, but I instinctively knew this had nothing to do with the money being short. I turned to I AM and said, "Send the guys to Starters Restaurant and give them a big order to pick up. Tell them to order once they get there though. Only one person I want here with us is Loc Boc. Put him on the door, and no one comes in until I say so."

After a moment, we continued with the conversation. Only after I AM pushed the guys out the door, leaving only Loc Boc. "You seem very happy for someone speaking for some upset Jefes," I said. "No, no. Todo está muy bien, Jefe!" the Spanish guy responded, calling me boss now.

"I need to speak to the Jefe only for this!" I said. Smiling at the bullshit I said, the Spanish guy replied, "Jefe, my Jefes want to become amigos with you now."

"But, my friend, we are already amigos," I responded while acting confused to force him to say it. "¡Sí, Jefe! You are very good Jefe, with my Jefes," the Spanish guy said.

"Do you have authorization for what you say?!" I asked in disbelief. "¡Sí, sí, Jefe!" the Spanish guy responded with excitement. "Your Jefes are asking me to jump, Danny, my friend?" I asked.

With a serious face, the Spanish guy responded, "Jefes should talk to the Jefe. There is no longer a need for your friend Danny, Jefe."

"He is not a Jefe and should not be speaking as a Jefe with Jefes," I said firmly.

CHAPTER 18

BALTIMORE

IT WAS A WARM evening in the bustling city of Tijuana, Mexico. I was sitting at a restaurant, enjoying a meal with some of my associates. As we were about to finish our dinner, Rojo, a local businessman, approached our table.

"My friend," he said as he greeted us with a smile. "Do I owe your Jefe's something?"

I was taken aback by his question. "No, no! My Jefe's are very, very happy for the work your guys do," he continued with a sly grin.

But then, his tone shifted. "Tell me something, my friend," he said with a hint of suspicion. "Why do your Jefe's concern themselves with my people? Do I tell them that you are not a Jefe and should not be speaking to me?"

I was insulted by his insinuation. "I'm the Jefe, and Danny has my authorization to speak for me," I responded sternly.

Rojo quickly backed down. "I understand this, my friend. You are in, right what you say," he said, shaking his head in disbelief at my loyalty.

He then asked me a favor. "Do you give your amigo authority to add 1000 each? For you, my friend. I really need amigos like you! You are paying 16 each, and you should be paying $15,500 each, my friend."

I was hesitant to agree to his request. "I don't know if I want to be amigos with you now," I said, partly jokingly.

Rojo looked at me with concern. "Look," he said, "You tell me that mi amigo Danny is robbing me for 1000 each. But you are only going to rob me for $500 each., huh Rojo?"

We all erupted into laughter as Rojo shrugged his shoulders and admitted, "This why I wish for to be your amigo so bad! It's for those 500 each," he said with a little laugh.

I couldn't help but join in the laughter. "Pinche bandito!" I exclaimed, falling out of character.

As we all calmed down, I told Rojo, "I'm sorry. I would not jump my friend. Tell your Jefe's they will be hearing from me soon."

With that, Rojo left our table, and we continued our dinner, still chuckling at the amusing encounter. It was just another day in the life of a Jefe in Tijuana.

After the surprise encounter with the Juarez guy, I immediately called Danny to inform him about what happened. He listened quietly and advised me to take my time and make a decision. I assured him that our partnership was still intact despite what had just happened. During our conversation, I could hear the concern in Danny's voice. He didn't like the situation, but he would still respect my decision. Although I was disappointed about not getting the price I wanted, I couldn't be upset with Danny for making his money. After all, I got the number I wanted at 16 per kilo. I was taught not to count the next man's money, and Danny was doing an amazing job for me.

I told Danny that I wouldn't jump him and I had informed the Juarez guys about it as well. However, I insisted on getting those 15 per kilo and I was flying to Baltimore tomorrow. Fix this and call me with those fifteen per Danny I stated. I made it clear that I wasn't upset with Danny for making his money, but I had learned that loyalty wasn't free. He didn't steal anything from me, and the payment he received could be considered a finder's fee coupled with managing. I gave Danny my loyalty, but I also expected something in return. Let's just call the payment of $1000 that Danny received as a loyalty tax, which I was sure he would pass on because it's just business.

The next day, I AM and I arrived in Baltimore. I was excited to see my pops and I AM his lady friend Michelle. We had made plans to meet up at Michael's Café in Timonium, which was about 30 minutes outside of Baltimore.

After enjoying dinner with my pops and Michelle, I AM left with Michelle. During dinner I AM made plans to look for a place to stay in Owings Mills, which was a middle to upper-class neighborhood just 10 miles from the Ravens training facility. He found some nice townhouses and even discovered that a few Ravens players lived just up the street. Later, after dinner Pops dropped me off at the hotel so that I could get some rest from the flight.

The next day, I AM met up with me and pops who informed him that he found a nice place in Owings Mills for them to stay in. Excited about our new home we decided to celebrate by visiting Norma Jean's strip club, where I was going to meet Charlie. Charlie introduced I AM to her friend Cinnamon, who I AM was interested in, but he was also known for being cheap.We went to the club with my Pops, Smoochie, his best friend Shorty and his friend Big Cody. Cody was a bail bondsman in Baltimore and was in love with Charlie.

Despites Cody's initial attitude , I made sure he had a good time, spending around $10,000 in just two hours at the club.I just never liked the way she looked at him in those small little moments. I noticed that she didn't seem to be very interested in him, Which can be common when a girl feels you are wasting her time and they are trying to work. Nevertheless, I AM would often drop around $800 to $1000 on her, while getting drunk in the process.

After a few hours of enjoying the club we left and headed back to our hotel. The next morning I AM and I were going to see the place he had chosen for us in Owings Mills.

Beep Beep Beep ....I answered my two-way, it was Danny.

Me: Yes, go ahead......

Danny: Hey, my friend....... How are you?

Me: Bien Bien (Good, Good.)

Danny: I have something nice for you, my friend.

Me: with those guys?

Danny: No, my friend, don't worry for those guys. When can you be here with me? I have something for you, where you are now?

Me: I will be there with you very soon, my friend.

The following day I informed I AM about my plans to leave Baltimore I left him behind to finalize everything with the house After taking care of business, I flew back to Detroit and arrived in Juarez four days later. Danny came to pick me up at the Holiday Inn where I usually stayed, but this time, he arrived in a van with a paranoid demeanor. Danny instructed me to sit in the back and drew the shades to prevent anyone from seeing me. The driver of the van was a young man named Jesus who greeted me with excellent English and praised my work. While appreciative of the compliments, I was concerned about the secrecy surrounding my visit.

During the ride, Danny asked me about my business, and Jesus listened intently without saying a word. We eventually arrived at the topic of Baltimore, and Jesus became more involved in the conversation. He offered to take care of Baltimore for me, which was music to my ears. Jesus and I negotiated prices per kilo, and he matched the $16,000 rate in Baltimore, which was a very competitive price for heroin in the area. We had a deal for Baltimore.

"No, my friend, let me tell you how I fixed this thing with those guys who wanted to jump you," Danny said. "I made sure you got your $15,000, and I've been sneaking you around to avoid their surveillance. They've been watching me ever since you knocked them out, and they're calling me now with a deal for you for $300,000."

As Danny's phone rang, he continued, "I haven't given them an answer yet." He answered the phone and spoke in Spanish, then hung up and turned to me with a big smile. "But everything's okay now! I'll sell to you for $300,000, just barely right now, my friend."

Jesus interjected, "Fool, you can't speak to them anymore! You'll have to hand over your phone when they give you the $300,000."

Danny responded, "I had to have him here with me now to sell him. I'll give them this old radio with my new number and still talk to him." He took my radio and programmed his new number into it, then hit the button to alert his phone with my number.

Jesus shook his head and laughed. "You're crazy, fool!"

Feeling concerned for Danny, I said, "I'm starting to feel bad for you."

"Don't feel bad for me, my friend," Danny said seriously. "Feel bad for them."

Danny explained that he needed me there with him to do the deal, so he could give me his number. I knew that being there with him was important to ensure that the deal for $300,000 went through and was foolproof. Danny needed to make sure that I was really with him and couldn't throw him under the bus. From that point forward, I would talk directly with Rojo and his Jefe's. I would keep my relationship with Danny a secret and would receive my 15% commission. But, I also had my deal for Baltimore as icing on the cake.

It's ironic how there are major differences between business in the US and business on the other side of the border. In the underworld on this side of the border, it is a red flag when someone is counting your money, watching what you're making, or clocking it. This is like a form of heresy, one of the biggest violations that you could make in the underworld. So following this expectation, it means that it wasn't my business how much money Danny was selling me for the $300,000, and I would be in violation to count that since I got everything that I asked for. But the exact opposite is correct. Danny was making me aware of how much he was selling me for or selling my contract for and gave me the option to request some of those proceeds, which I was actually entitled to as being brought in on the actual process.

This is a classic case of the differential outlook between cultures and how one thing could be the rule of thumb in one country and the total opposite in the other. I was clear that the mistake that Rojo and his bosses made would cost them. Therefore, I placed the loyalty tax on Danny and took the thousand dollars that he was receiving per. Little did I know that that was peanuts because he leaned in on them by the mistake they made and cost them little over a quarter million for my contract.

Again, I will state as I have stated so many times, this is business and nothing more, but exactly that, business. This is how these individuals and cartels handle the whole process. It is not their fault because you don't understand the culture over there and know how good business operates. But at the end of the day, it costs you immensely by not knowing exactly how business is operated and what you're entitled to, which is no different than what happens over here in this country. When rappers or entertainers go into entertainment and get ripped off for everything, including their shirt, it's business.

I'm sure Danny had his hands in this Baltimore deal as well, but the guy was damn good at fulfilling my requests as a super sports or entertainment agent.

After flying back to Detroit, I met with I AM who updated me about the house in Owings Mills. I gave him some money to get basic needs for the house in Baltimore, and he flew back out to make arrangements. I told him we had a deal for Baltimore, and I planned to arrive before the load got there.

Rojo contacted me and said the first load at 15 per had arrived, and another load would leave in two days heading for Detroit. They couldn't supply me with more, and my guys noticed they started playing with the quality of the cocaine too. What they didn't know was that I was already an expert at playing this quality game, having dealt with Frank and Mario that made me extremely seasoned in turning the tables and making a mistake or come up for me.

Danny radioed me to let me know that the load had crossed and would be in Baltimore shortly. The next morning, I was on a flight to Baltimore.

Pops picked me up from the airport and we went to Ruth's Chris over on Water St to eat. I AM would meet us over there. I ordered two orders of veal chops cooked medium, with sweet potato casserole and asparagus. We had a certain waitress that we always requested. Once Millie became our regular waitress, I asked her, "Do you want the gratuity included or do you want me to tip you separately? Choose wisely now," I said with a smile. Millie chose for me to tip her.

I ate at Ruth's Chris like three to four times a week and always tipped Millie no less than $150 to $200 for just I AM and myself, and any additional people who joined us. The starting point for her tip would be $250 and up. Plus, she had a thing for I AM, which didn't come as a surprise. We became so well known at Ruth's Chris that even the head chef would come out and greet us, even bringing our dessert out as a gift from him personally. I always made sure he knew we appreciated his welcoming gestures, even if we were there three or four times a week.

One of my very good friends came by to break bread with us at Ruth's Chris. After leaving the restaurant, we split up with Pops. I let Slick know that the load was on its way and that we had something ready to receive it. I told Slick that it was something like 10 bricks to get him started, and that the next trip would have 20.

The load came in without issue, and Slick went to work. I told Danny to send someone over to Detroit. When I returned, I would pay for those ten bricks over there. I needed some money I could play with over in Baltimore anyway.

As the money came in from Slick, we started to put the house in Owings Mills together. I had a custom-built pool table put on the first floor, along with stand-up arcade games like Mr. and Mrs. Pacman, Galaxy, and Centipede. We also had plasma TVs on all the floors and Xbox and PlayStation consoles on every level.

When all the money was in, we went to Norma Jeans to celebrate the first successful load down in Baltimore. I think I spent a fortune that night. I AM was all over Cinnimon, and I could still see the hate in her eyes. Charlie and I had a great time, and she ended up calling me later that night and came by my room. The love God was ever present in me, and I did a man's deed to Charlie on that night. It was an undisciplined deed, though.

Chapter 19

UN AMIGO DE MI AMIGO DE MI OTRO AMIGO (A FRIEND OF A FRIEND OF A FRIEND).

I returned to Detroit and stayed put for a few weeks. During this time, I received a number of shipments from Rojo. However, the quality was much different without Danny there to check it before these guys shipped it to me. I started to experience issues with quality as well as general tricks and schemes from these guys. I soon realized that they were just looking to rob me now that they felt I had no other option since they believed Danny was really out of the picture. This misstep would return to haunt them very soon.

During this time, I became pretty good friends with a young lady who worked at the T-Mobile store. I would often forget to pay my cell phone bill, which led to my service being interrupted. She would often call to remind me about my bills.

Danny sent a carrier up to Detroit to receive the funds I owed him from Baltimore. It must be made clear that while Danny represented my interests in Mexico, we were also partners together inside loads. I would split the cost of the product with him that I would also get rid of stateside. Oftentimes, this is how we would build up a number of markets I would look to enter. We would then look for a supply source once I built a predictable demand there.

After paying Danny for his part of the Baltimore load I sent, I went back to Baltimore to establish a real footprint for us there now. There was a rapidly growing demand and our new supplier, Jesus, was ready to start sending bigger loads. Things were really changing for the better for me, but I had no idea of how much it would become almost overnight. A perfect storm was coming and up to this point was just the dress rehearsal.

I started working on Tez's rap album as I promised I would do for months. We were at Underground Studios, owned by my very good friend Kevin Holivor. Tez had been talking to me about running into Kamaya recently. The last time I saw her, she was a very young girl being managed by a good friend of mine who had passed away some years ago.

Tez told me Kamaya was going on and on about this major up-and-coming manager named Woo, whom I knew from years past out of Atlanta when I was managing R&B acts. Woo was also a D boy just like me. Kamaya desperately wanted to be managed by him and used her knowledge of me as leverage to reconnect with Woo, who was looking to reconnect after so many years.

While I was happy to hear about and maybe even see Kamaya, I wasn't excited about seeing Woo again based on our last interaction, which wasn't horribly bad but we often disagreed. I declined to see Kamaya based on the news that Woo was in town with his R&B group One Chance, signed to US records owned by Usher, whom I happen to be a superfan of even to this day. Woo's group was opening up for Trey Songz in downtown Detroit.

I told Tez we could meet with Kamaya after Woo had left town. However, while Tez was in the sound booth recording, Kamaya walked into the studio. I gave her a very big hug, glancing over her shoulder towards the sound booth. Tez was refusing our contact with me, which was a good reason to.

After catching up with Kamaya, I found out Woo would be coming to town with his group One Chance, which was on tour as an opening act for Trey Songz. Kamaya begged me to meet Woo when he came to town because it would help her career efforts with him. She was my very good friend Ray's favorite, and he loved her like his own child. I agreed, and Ted, who had cut his own deal with Kamaya to get her in front of me at the studio, would cut many more deals in the future.

I flew back to Baltimore and was picked up by I AM at the airport. We headed to Michaels Cafe to eat and talk about new developments. My pop and his best friend, who was like a brother Shorty,joined us as well. As expected, Slick walked in - he was my guy, a real money-getting dude. We discussed business, and I informed him about the home in Owing Mills and the first load from Jesus that would arrive in a matter of days. There would be 20 kilos, and I would let him see them at $21 per kilo. I was receiving them at $15 per kilo. The price in the Detroit market was between $24,000 to $25,000. The further east you travel, the price increases. Baltimore's market price was about $28,000.

There would be two trucks with 10 kilos cut in half, matched up by numbers 1-1, 2-2, 3-3, etc. The drugs would be transported in the block of the engine of the truck. Drugs would come out, and money would go in. The trucks would arrive 35 to 45 minutes apart. After business was expressed, we just enjoyed each other's company. My pops and his best friend Shorty joined us at the table.

Slick then told us a story about a female stripper at a gentlemen's club named Norma Jeans. When he mentioned her name, I glanced at I AM. Slick continued with his story and how a very good friend of his was enjoying a friends-with-benefits relationship that had been interrupted by some out-of-town dudes who were taking care of her very, very well. Slick told his very good friend to move on because he didn't think she would be back anytime soon.

Finishing his statement, he said, "Big Bro, I ain't in your business, nor will I ask you yours. All I know is that I fucks with you and what I want to do for myself, I want for you. Baltimore is a heroin town, and dudes from out of town are targeted. Dudes like you - good dudes - don't exist anymore. The bitch's name is Charlie, and she's got a nigga she fucks with that she puts on from out of town to rob. Be careful, big bro. I would hate to have to pull up on this bitch. I have all the ops on her already."

Couple days later, the load came in as scheduled, and everything was moving smoothly. I had I AM fly in a couple of trusted guys to help guard the money that would come back in off the streets. Slick, DJ, and Jay, who was I AM's brother, joined us. Slick warned them about potential dangers, especially from females trying to set them up for robberies. With our guys present, I returned to Detroit for the next month, knowing the shipments would be taken care of.

Back in the studio with Tez, Kamaya showed up, and I was always happy to see her. Later, I agreed to meet up with Woo despite my initial reservations. We met at a Hilton Hotel in downtown Detroit, and Woo was all smiles. He suggested helping with Tez's album and even introduced the idea of moving the work down to Atlanta. I was surprised I hadn't considered this option earlier, blinded by past disagreements. Woo and I had different approaches to business, but we respected each other and decided to collaborate.

I agreed to go to Atlanta and cut some records with Tez while exploring Woo's vision and potential team. After Woo's show that night, we hit the Sting Gentlemen Club. The next day, I headed back to Baltimore with I AM. Arriving there, Charlie greeted me, and after taking care of her needs, we enjoyed each other's company at Nautilus Cafe, our favorite spot for breakfast. I AM insisted on introducing me to a new guy he had met, but I had reservations about him, as I didn't trust him entirely. We had recently cut ties with another associate in Baltimore, following my rule of never keeping all our eggs in one basket. However, I always ensured that I had at least three guys I could rely on whenever I operated in a new town.

I AM kept reminding me that his father grew up with my pops and knew him all his life. Although my pops liked this kid, something about him didn't sit right with me. He seemed like a lower level hustler, which could bring problems later on. I couldn't quite put my finger on it at the time.

One day, we were all seated when Zip walked in. I AM introduced him to me and Zip went over to hug my father. Zip filled my pops in on how his father was doing, but as we started talking business, my pop quickly realized that Zip was in over his head. He didn't have a clear idea of his market or the quantity he could move within a week. I AM was embarrassed, but my pop continued to talk to Zip about his father. We asked for the check and Zip blurted out a warning to be careful at the strip club.

Throughout the interaction, my pops, Shorty, and I remained mostly silent, Zip knew that I didn't care for him at all. "Yo, I want you dudes to be careful if you go to the strip club," he warned. I paused and asked, "Why? Is there something we should be aware of, Zips?" I had not spoken more than two words to this dude the whole time. He was happy to have my interest and talking with him now. "You all are from Detroit, right?" he asked. "Yeah, there is a female at Norma Jeans named Charlie, and she sets niggas up to be robbed," Zips explained.

My pop dropped his head, and Shorty looked on as if to say, "Keep talking," so I knew Zips had already told him. My pops never liked Charlie because of all the money I would give her. Then a good friend of his was in love with her and felt he had a chance with her until I came around. He started telling my pops everything he knew or heard. My father knows me well, and he knows I reward folks with information for me, true or false. Then his timing and developing a severe case of rapid word vomit was telling.

I gave Zips a serious look and said, "Really?" in a questioning tone. He was seeing daylight at the end of the tunnel now. My pop asked him if he was sure, and Shorty repeated the question. Zips went on to express that Charlie had a dude that she takes care of from her dancing money. What he does is get street teams to come in and rob out-of-town dudes that she set up. He just happened to know the dude her boyfriend often employs.

He went on to explain that the boyfriend had already made contact several times with his friend, but his friend told him that Charlie is refusing to give this out-of-town guy up now. According to her boyfriend, Zips stated, "My homie told me. After a while, he gave up asking Charlie's boyfriend because he started saying shit like, 'Man, to be honest, I don't want shit to happen to him either! He's a real good dude, and he is breaking her off, so good shit done got better for me too!! She doesn't even embarrass a nigga no more, either. We are good!!'"

I looked at pop and then stated to Zips, "Thanks for looking out, family." I AM gave Zips a big smile while saying, "Keep your phone close. We will run into you later." Zips smiled even bigger, "Yo, I will keep my eye and ear to the street on that too," referring to Charlie.

After hearing what Zip had to say about Charlie's schemes, I couldn't help but feel uneasy. My father, on the other hand, seemed to take the news in stride. He knew the game well and had seen it all before.

As we left the restaurant, my father turned to me and said, "Son, this is just the way things are in this business. You always have to watch your back and be careful who you trust. But don't worry, we'll handle it."

I knew my father was right, but the thought of being set up and robbed left a bad taste in my mouth. I made a mental note to be extra vigilant during our visit to Norma Jeans.

Over the next few days, we went about our business, working on deals and making connections in Baltimore. We even went to Norma Jeans, but I made sure to keep my guard up and watch my surroundings.

As we prepared to leave and head back to Detroit, I couldn't help but feel relieved. We had made it through the trip unscathed, and I was grateful for my father's guidance and expertise.

But I also knew that this was just the beginning. In this business, there would always be people like Charlie and Zip trying to pull a fast one. It was up to us to stay one step ahead and protect ourselves at all times.

I and I AM walked to the car in silence. Then, I AM spoke up, "We have to find a way to get a lien on that dude, Charlie's boyfriend, and talk to him directly ourselves."

"Well, that shouldn't be too hard to do," I sarcastically replied. "You just gave him a job."

Zip was a Jack boy, and my father couldn't see past the little boy he once knew. He was trying to protect me and get me away from a girl whom he believed gave me too much money. However, the word Zip was spreading made me realize that he could be a valuable ally or a deadly enemy. I had no choice but to play it by ear.

I AM was Dip's biggest supporter and thought he was the coolest. He was unable to see that he would have been Dip's first target.

What no one could see was that Charlie was my most valuable asset in that town. Well, everyone believed Charlie had my mind gone with sex. Most every time I went to a room with Charlie, I gave her large sums of money and we just talked and acted silly, like kids laughing. I allowed Charlie to see she could just get the money minus any physical activity between myself and her. What she wanted she got, so why was there a reason to have me robbed when her whole life was getting better without asking in a lot of cases? She could get all the money herself without having to split it.

I'm not saying that it's not a dangerous game or that it wasn't a gamble. But it became in her best interest to protect me and prolong this as long as she could. Rule of thumb: the strip club females are the best at reading their clients, which come from every walk of life, and it's their job to play off into their fantasies. Most important, they have their finger on the pulse of the underworld in that city.

You need a clear look from both sides, the good and the ugly: get the finest and the ugliest strippers and the best gentlemen's clubs in town. You will get a clear view of both sides of the coin, the city and Charlie. The ugly stripper's ambition doesn't match her reality. She doesn't have good or great nights at work. You changed that and she will tell you everything about the pretty one, because in most cases she hates her. Keep your fucking cock in your pants. It's not good for business.

This game had a lot of deadly moving parts. Reading them in real time and correctly was of paramount importance.

The following day, my attorney Lorence called me up and greeted me with his usual question, "Donnie, where are you?" I replied that I was in Baltimore, heading to Ruth Chris down off Pier 5. Lorence then told me his wife's recommendation, "My wife told me to tell you to have the cowboy steak." We chuckled, and he proceeded to tell me that he needed to see me once I got back in town.

My earnings in Baltimore were growing rapidly now. Pops took me to see a very good family friend at Mano Schwartz Furs to get fitted for a chinchilla coat. The coat was tailored with a Russian-style hat and gloves made of chinchilla fur. After being fitted by many, I had to return to get the numbers together to ship it back once the next load arrived.

I was making so much at this time that what I would send back was getting smaller and smaller compared to what I was making. I made the proper arrangements and was on another flight back to Detroit.

Loc Boc came to pick me up from the airport, and as we were driving, my two-way radio started beeping like crazy. It was Danny trying to reach me urgently.

Me: Yes, go ahead.

Danny: My friend, I have been trying to get you! I need you in Juarez, Rapido!

Me: My friend, give me two days and I will be there with you.

Danny: OK, I'll wait for you, my friend.

I had to quickly make arrangements for a shipment coming in from Rojo for Detroit and book a flight to El Paso, TX. I AM Oversaw that load that came in for Detroit. We then headed to Novara which was Loc Boc's house and also our command center.

Moe, Big I, and L Dog came in to grab their bags and hit the street, while Rico, another hard-hitter who was more like an independent contractor, joined us. On the day of my flight out, my two-way radio beeped again, and it was Tez.

Me: What up doe?!

Tez: Yo, I got 250 over here for you ($250,000).

Me: You need to call I AM with that.

Tez: He keeps saying he's tied up right now.

Me: Well, wait then, Nigga! You know I don't ride around with large sums of money, PERIOD!

Tez: You're right! I do know that. But what you don't know is that I met this bad Bitch last night... I'm starting to feel some kind of way about her after last night. I'll call her Karate, Clem!

Me: Karate Clem?...

Tez: Yeah, 'cause when she's making love, it's like she's throwing karate! And I think I love her...

Me: I'm on my way right now!!

I had to be at the airport, but now I had $250,000, mostly in large bills, stacked in a triple grocery bag. I was driving and needed to find a place to stash the money. This was my personal money and I didn't want it mixed with the ticket money. My cell phone rang and it was the girl from T-Mobile.

Me: "What up Doe?"

Mobile: "Is it that time of the month again?"

Me: "Yeah, I'm about to pull up. Could you come out and grab it from me? I'm actually in kind of a rush."

Mobile: "Sure thing!"

I pulled up and she came out of the store and jumped in the car. "Listen," I stated, "I'm going to pay my bill, but I need your help with something." She looked concerned. I assured her that it was nothing major as I reached my hand in the back seat behind the passenger seat on the floor. "And, you make sure you get yourself something nice for helping me out," I said, exposing the grocery bag of cash and dropping it in her lap.

"Oh, my God, is this real, Wayne?!" she exclaimed, looking like she had just seen a ghost.

"Yes, it's real, and just take whatever you need for yourself and pay my bill too," I said, pushing her towards the door, patting her on the back and shoulder

. She started yelling and about to cry, "Wayne, where am I supposed to put this? I just got to work. I can't leave for hours!!"

"Just put it under your desk. Nobody will know it's there but you, and buy yourself something nice, really nice," I said, getting her almost all the way out of the car now.

"How long do I have to hold this?" she asked.

"Oh, just for a few hours. I'll be right back," I said with a smile. I got her out of the car and instantly turned my phone off. I was off to the airport now, finally!

I landed in El Paso, Texas, and turned on my two-way radio. It was going crazy.

Beep. Beep. Beep.

Me: What up doe?

Slick: Big Bro, this ya, man.

Me: What's good, baby?

Slick: Yo, your folks you sent over this way are going to get robbed., Big Bro.

Me: Damn, what's good, bro?

Slick: These Niggas got a bunch of bitches up in the crib, Big Bro. But I took care of it for you! I put

them out Big Bro. I can't stay, but you need to get somebody up here.

Me: I'm on it bro. And thank you, family!

I reached out to I AM and told him to reach out to those dudes over there. Then wrap that thing up with Rojo, catch a flight that way and post Loc Boc up with them fools to keep them in order.

I walked out of the El Paso Airport and inhaled the air......... I can smell Mexico in the air. I hit Danny to

make him aware I have just landed and should be crossing soon. I jumped in a car and was taken to the

Holiday Inn over in Juarez, Mexico. Danny had a key waiting for me at the front desk.

As I walked into the hotel room, I saw Danny sitting at the table with a map laid out in front of him. He stood up as I walked in and gave me a big hug. "Thank you for coming, my friend," he said.

"No problem, Danny. What's going on?" I asked, looking at the map.

Danny pointed to a location on the map. "This is where the shipment is supposed to come in. But we've heard that there might be some trouble. We need your help to make sure everything goes smoothly."

"Alright, let's do it," I said, ready to get to work.

Danny and I spent the next few hours going over the plan and making sure everything was in place. We had a team of men stationed at various points along the route to keep an eye out for any trouble.

As night fell, we got word that the shipment was on its way. Danny and I took our positions, waiting for the trucks to arrive. It was a tense few minutes as we watched the trucks approach.

But everything went smoothly. The trucks pulled up, and we quickly unloaded the cargo. As soon as it was safely in our possession, we breathed a sigh of relief.

"That was too close," Danny said, shaking his head.

"Yeah, but we got it done," I replied, feeling a sense of satisfaction.

We spent the next few hours celebrating our success before I finally headed back to the hotel room to get some rest. As I lay in bed, I couldn't help but think about the risks we had taken and the danger we had faced. But I also felt a sense of pride knowing that we had come out on top.

This was pretty much like my last visit, riding in a van with shades down, going from one place to the next. Danny had informed me that this was the meeting of meetings, and Jesus had helped set it up for us. Jesus wanted to do more business since things were going well in Baltimore. Later that day, Danny showed up with Jesus. Jesus pulled out a few pounds of Kush weed, which were sealed in numbered freezer bags. He told me to make a small cut to see and smell it, but warned me to be careful because the smell was strong enough to fill the room and hallways. He handed me a list of other strains and we cut a deal for me to import this Kush, which was connected to the bigger deal Jesus was arranging.

Danny and Jesus moved me to a different hotel that day because it was hard for Danny to move around without being watched. Jesus then took me to an upscale Chinese restaurant where I met with Jesus, and Danny showed up later. I later found out that this side of town was controlled by the Juarez Cartel, and the Rojo Band of banditos weren't allowed to move around freely there without permission first. The meeting was to try and get a meeting with a boss in the Juarez Cartel via a representative of the cartel. When he arrived, I recognized him from a year or two before when I was talking too much to Flacco about bales of weed. This time, a deal was cut pretty fast and the gentleman stood up, shook my hand, and stated in broken English, "I look forward to making much US money for you, my friend?" with a huge smile.

Danny informed me that a date would be given in weeks or months to come, but no one knew more than that. I later found out that Jesus' first words to me were in Spanish, "¿Puedes mover mucha blanca? (Can you move lots of white?) We will see soon, very soon!"

CHAPTER 20

NORMA JEANS

RING, RING, RING.

Me: "What's up Doe?"

Mobile: "OMG, where have you been?" (crying) "Are you OK? You didn't answer your phone, why? Why did you do this to me NIGGA?!"

Me: "Woah, woah!! I'm sorry, but this was something out of my control!"

Mobile: "Who leaves a person with a quarter $1,000,000 and refuses or turns the phone off?"

Me: "I can't give you details, but I really had no choice at the time. Did you buy yourself something nice though?"

Mobile: "Fuck you, Wayne!! Come get this fucking money, because I know something very nice that will cost a fraction of what it appears you don't want."

My real estate investment company had to be closed based on the market crash. I had to let a number of my employees go, and that really hurt me. I knew they needed their jobs with me. I had seen so many of them grow and succeed with their earnings. There wasn't anything I could do... I was really leaving it open for them. My executive assistant was really running my company for me while being overseen by my mentor Kevin.

I made Gina my personal assistant now because she really knew how to take care of me, and Lorence loved her. He hated everybody! Plus, I had a few deals that I needed her to close before I shut down.

I'm fighting with Rojo based on the poor quality of the coke. My pace and their inability to supply me was just getting embarrassing now. I didn't have much time to fight based on a flight I had to catch with Tez down in ATL to get with Woo.

Beep. Beep. Beep...

Danny: "Go ahead, my friend."

Me: "Have you got things ready for Atlanta, my friend?"

Danny: "Don't worry, my friend."

Me: "I will call you when I'm there, my friend?"

Danny: "I will wait for you, my friend."

Touchdown and Woo put Tez in the studio with one of US Records' producers up at Daplyn studio. DJ Polo, Michael Cox, Rock City, etc. had studios up there. Woo and I hit Strokers Gentlemen's Club to discuss some business concerning the first shipment coming to Atlanta.

The following day, Woo had me ride with him up to Silent Sound Studio, owned by Babyface and LA Reed. I was dressed in Eastside upscale dope boy fashion jeans, a gold-studded belt, a leather jacket, full Gator Lucchese cowboy boots, and a Gator-nose hat. I wore a rose gold presidential Rolex with a diamond bezel and platinum-framed Cartier glasses. Walking into the studio with Eric and Woo, we waited to meet someone. After a short while, a dark-skinned dude came around the corner with a very hard, angry expression on his face. Woo walked towards this guy with excitement that he didn't bother returning. This guy stayed locked in on me as Woo kicked it with him. I would later come to know this dude as Kinky B of CTE.

Woo had a number of his guys come around giving me an idea of what they could move. The understanding I got was that there had been a major void after Big Meech was taken. I couldn't help but feel pride because them boys were Detroit Boys too. The guys I met were upset because the Spanish boys had all the work and were running the numbers up on them and playing with the work.

The following day, a small load of thirty came into town. Woo was shocked and didn't even know that it was coming...... Beep. Beep. Beep.

Danny: Go ahead.

Me: How are things my friend?

Danny: You have a safe trip, my friend?

Me: SI SI

Danny: I will be there with you in two days, my friend.

Me: Ok, I wait for you.

Woo guys didn't lie. That shit was gone in less than an hour. Woo wet his beak well and was ready for more but was upset when I said I had to return to Baltimore. I would return to Baltimore to meet this real estate agent my pop arranged for me via a good real estate friend of his. This gentleman's name was Major. His grandfather was a very prominent judge in Baltimore at one point. Major took us to see a number of very nice properties, but one of the places really impressed me. A new Ritz Carlton residence at Inner Harbor, Baltimore.

The Ritz Carlton residence had high ceilings, a spacious living area, and a beautiful view of the harbor. The kitchen had top-of-the-line appliances and marble countertops. The bedrooms had large windows with a stunning view of the city skyline. The master suite had a walk-in closet and a luxurious bathroom with a jacuzzi tub and a steam shower. The building had amenities such as a gym, a pool, and a rooftop terrace with a panoramic view.

I immediately made an offer on the property, and Major helped me negotiate a good deal. I was thrilled to be living in such a luxurious place and being neighbors with the Smiths.

However, my excitement was short-lived as I received a call from Woo, who was in a panic. The shipment had been intercepted, and he was afraid that the authorities were closing in on us. I told him to lay low and that I would fly down to Atlanta to handle the situation.

I quickly packed my bags and headed to the airport, hoping to resolve the issue before it got any worse.

The phone kept ringing, and when I answered it, I was shocked to hear the voice of my dream girl, Mena. She was calling to check me about trying to date one of her friends, but it wasn't true. However, I hung up out of fear when she started to get upset. Seeing the look on my face, my friend I Am moved over and asked if I was okay. I wasn't, as I had been wanting Mena for years, but my efforts had always failed.

I Am snatched the phone from me and answered it. He knew I wouldn't, but he also knew how much I wanted Mena. I finally got to speak with her and ended up talking to her for four hours, trying to win her over again. Mena told me that she couldn't because of my past relationship with her close friend, but I expressed that we could start a relationship in Baltimore and not know each other in Detroit. I even offered to fly her out to spend time with me at my new place in Baltimore.

During our conversation, my favorite song came on the radio: "I'd Die Without You" by PM Dawn. Mena told me she would think about my offer, but she did invite me to her shop for a pedicure and manicure. That was one of the happiest moments of my life at the time.

After being consumed with the idea of love, I totally missed the showing of the place at the Ritz Carlton. Thank God for I AM making that decision and selecting that place for me.

I AM was invited to attend a party, which he claimed was business-related and he wanted me to join him. I had no interest in partying; that was more I AM's favorite pastime, not mine. However, he convinced me to come, saying that he wanted my advice on how to deal with his new snake.

The party took place in what appeared to be an old school building. Security was heavy, but Zip, I AM's associate, didn't allow anyone to touch us, and I guess he thought this would impress us. I AM was a fan and was impressed, but I didn't care for Zip at all. It was very clear to me that his efforts were towards me, trying to allow us to see his crew.

Zip was a jack boy and operated a crew of the same. These dudes moved with a different deadly swag. However, I AM couldn't read this off these guys. Zip took us to meet his lady, a very fair-skinned young lady who looked well cared for.

Zip ran off with I AM, leaving me and his lady together in a private section away from anyone else. This move was familiar to me and let me know he was having problems reading me. She began a graceful but delicate dance with me, with the sole purpose of uncovering a vulnerability in me that Zip couldn't.

Normally, I wouldn't bother to engage in such purposeless activity, but this was very different because I AM's life depended on this dance. She would be drunk after I dazzled her with my mental footwork and deep embrace of her local understanding, unpacked on an international table. I mind-fucked her and left her caring more for my interest than his mental hit job he left her to perform, and with a much better handle on who he really was.

I AM was with me in a private area and wanted to discuss the night's events. As we were re-entering the building, a man shoved past us aggressively. I AM exchanged words with him, but I could tell the man was trying to escalate the situation. I stopped I AM, knowing that this man was seeking a particular outcome. The man then pulled out a large hunting knife and said, "Nigga, your man saved you from getting this hung and you bitch!"

Just then, Zip appeared from the building, seemingly having been informed of the situation by his crew. Zip yelled at the man, "What the fuck are you doing, fronting my people off you Bitch Ass Nigga." The man appeared terrified and spun around, seeing Zip and his crew.

Knife guy: "Oh shit.! Zip, I didn't know these were your people!"

Zip: "Yo! Did this bitch ass threaten y'all?!" (talking to me and Sam on the side)

Knife guy: "Zip!! Bro, I didn't know these were your people, I swear!"

Zip: "I AM, just tell me! Nod your head or something!!"

Knife guy: "Yo man! I'm so, so sorry!! Zip, I didn't know, PLEASE!!!!"

Zip pulled out a .40 caliber handgun from his back, and his eyes took on a blank stare that I had seen many times before. It was the look of a man losing his humanity, becoming the Angel of Death. I AM was lost in Zip's eyes, and I could see that he was ready to sign the man's death warrant. Meanwhile, the knife guy was crying and visibly shaking, knowing that his end had come.

Me: "NO HE DID NOT!!!!!!" As I stepped in front of the guy..... I AM breaks from Zip's trance.

I AM: "NAW, he good man........ Looking down now."

Knife guy: "I told you, Zip! We had a misunderstanding! Only because I didn't know, but I never threatened anybody!!"

Zip: "Bitch, the big homie saved yo ass! I was about to push your shit back, bitch. Get the fuck out of town! I better not see or hear you have been anywhere for the next couple of weeks. Bitchass NIGGA! Y'all see that nigga anywhere in town? Put one in his shit!! (Talking to his crew.) Until I say he good! Bitch, I will be in contact letting you know that this pass My big homie gave you gonna cost. Get the fuck on before I change my mind."

Knife guy breaks into a Usain Bolt-type sprint out of there. I AM, Zip, and myself are walking toward the parking lot.

"Big homie, please don't step in the line of fire like that. Zip says it. I will say I have never seen that before though. Big homie, you've been around some real shit before. You're a real nigga," Zip said in disbelief.

I AM had got us in a very bad spot with these guys just dealing with them. Zip knew that I knew what he was trying to do there. If I AM had nodded or said yes, Zip would have put one in that kid's head. Which wasn't how I did or wanted to do business.

It was clear that if Zip had pulled the trigger, it would have created a debt that I AM would never have been able to pay. More of that kind of business would have only eaten away at our reputation. I knew a faceoff with Zip Was inevitable, but for the time being, it was safer to keep him close than to push him away.

However, I couldn't afford to let my guard down. Zip would try to get closer to I AM, not to build a relationship with him but to gather information on me. I needed to be careful about what I shared with I AM, at least until I could fix the situation.

My father along with his friend Shorty was increasingly worried about my safety given I AM's bad choices and erratic behavior. Despite this, business was still moving well, and my father wanted to take me back up to Mano Swartz to pick up my chinchilla. I needed to make arrangements for that upon my return.

As soon as we landed back in Detroit, I made my way to Mena's salon where she worked as a nail tech.

I AM arrived at the nail salon and parked my BMW 745LI in front. As I walked in, the salon was filled with women. I made my way towards Mena's area, taking in all of the women's beauty. In the past, I had always tried to use my money to impress Mena, but it never worked. I couldn't even get her to have a conversation with me. My mental ability and persuasion were my superpowers, but it seemed like Mena was equally gifted, if not more so.

Mena politely asked me to take off my shoes and socks, but I refused. When she called me "hunnie," I melted into my seat. She looked into my eyes and I became lost in her gaze. She got up and started gathering her things, beckoning me to follow her into a back room. She closed the door and locked it behind us, as I sat on the couch and she took a seat in front of me on a folding chair.

Mena sweetly smiled and asked me to give her my foot, to which I reluctantly complied.

As I sat in the nail tech's chair, I couldn't help but notice Mena's bad attitude. Despite my mental charm and persuasive abilities, I couldn't seem to win her over. Even as she removed my shoes and socks, she kept a distance between her large breasts and my feet. She had a way of touching my soul, and I was almost begging for a chance with her. But she wouldn't say yes or no, and only accepted her price and a modest tip.

It hurt my male ego to discover that Mena had the ability to neutralize all my superpowers and gifts. She seemed to want nothing more than to break me, to defeat my ego. But I knew that my ego was just one of the many masses that came with my job description, and that I was more than what people perceived me to be.

I had two great fears from my childhood that drove me to insane measures: the fear of poverty and not being able to provide for my children, and the fear of becoming like my father. If only Mena could see the real me.

As I left the salon, I knew that there would be issues with the shipment arriving in a couple of days. But I was determined to face them head on and prove myself to Mena, and to myself.

I AM: Bro, the streets are saying this shit ain't locking up.

I AM: I'm fucking tired of playing this game. Call Rojo over.

I AM: I'm going to hit him up now.

Beep. Beep. Beep...

Me: What are you into?

Mo Green: Shit! What's good?

Me: I need you to swing by Loc Boc's spot right fast.

Mo Green: Headed your way, 911.

I arrived at the same time as Rojo. I had a very heated exchange with him concerning the poor quality of the cocaine. I made it clear that I had no intentions of allowing him and his Jefes to screw me over. Rojo and his Juarez Jefes thought I had no other options.

Me: Rojo, this shit ain't locking up. This shit ain't even locking up on the straight drop!! And my folks are complaining about the shit not jumping back! (Straight drop basically means that it's being cooked straight up without any additional additives being added. Jumping back basically means that when you cook the cocaine, you're losing grams.)

Rojo: Jefe, I have spoken with my Jefes and they are saying your people are lying to you. Jefe! It was tested and each kilo is 98%, Jefe.

Me: Well, I have one here, Rojo! (Mo Green walks in and pulls out a kilo) Cut a triangle in the top. Mo Green, hand me the Pyrex pot and I want to see you make it lock up and not lose a gram, Rojo.

Rojo: Jefe, I don't know these things. (As he says, placing the Pyrex pot gently on the stove.) I see you guys do it in American movies. Only Jefe.

I knew those guys across the border knew nothing about whipping the cocaine. This is why I called Mo Green. His wrist was platinum when it came to cooking the white.

Me: If you agree, I will have my guy cook and you tell your Jefes what you see over the radio.

Rojo: Si, my friend.

Mo Green begins to cook it popcorn style, catching it at the top with hardly any baking soda. Mo Green is hitting it with the beat fork, whipping it. I'm giving Rojo hell the whole time.

Me: It doesn't take this long to lock up, Rojo! Your Jefes have lied to you about those 98% each!!

Rojo is talking on the two-way radio and he is visibly stressed now. He is walking in and out of the kitchen and I swear it seems like Mo Green took off a piece of clothing every time Rojo re-entered the kitchen. I mean, the shit was bad, but it was not nearly that bad. Mo Green was putting down an Oscar award-winning performance, and I had to be the best supporting actor now.

Rojo's bosses had cut the coke with some synthetic coke, or that's what it was starting to be called back across the border. Rojo didn't know that the traditional cold water to harden wasn't working. Warm to hot water from the tap would work to lock it up. The streets hadn't been faced with this and I will have to send Mo Green, one of our main folks, to show them. Mo Green was NOT a rookie and I knew this would cost me handsomely. Rojo's bosses were forced to renegotiate the price now.

Me: Rojo, I'm going to give this back to you, my friend. Tell those guys over there to send those guys back with this.

Rojo: Jefe, my Jefes are asking what will you give them for each to fix this.

Me: NO Y MAS, ROJO! No more, Rojo, no more.

Rojo: Jefe, there must have been a mistake, and my boss is going to make the guys responsible pay. We are not going to fight over the price, Jefe.

I glance over towards the kitchen to see a slight smile on the half-naked Mo Green's face in the kitchen as he puts his clothes back on.

Me: Well, let me see, my friend. Because this was very bad and cost me money, Rojo. All mistakes on their end have to cost them. If you don't make it cost them, they will keep doing it and depend on you to fix it while they take the discount, just because you don't know and understand the business aspect of this. This is how you ensure that the middleman or transport people keep their hands off your product.

I later found out that Rojo was the mastermind behind the botched cocaine deal, or at least he had to pay for it. They raided his home and took valuables to compensate for their losses. When mistakes are made, someone always has to pay.

Issues in transportation and logistics are common in any business, whether it's food or drugs. The shipping company always absorbs the loss. It's just business at its core, not some secret society.

Despite the setback, I still made a nice profit off those fools. I contacted my interior decorator, Uncle Sam, and had him fly to Baltimore to spruce up my place. I also called my girl Kiwi to make arrangements for us at the Sting Gentlemen's Club.

Kiwi was my connection to the West side of Detroit, where I kept my ear to the street and a finger on the pulse of the city. She was special to me, and I made sure she knew it. There was no secret that Westside guys didn't care for Eastside dudes. We were looked at as savages and inhumane. But the most renowned drug dealers in Detroit's history came from the East side, and that was a fact.

I booked all the VIP booths for me and my guys at the Sting Gentlemen's Club and left their crews to be seated in the other VIP booths. I fucked up around 40 thousand dollars that night, and as Tez would say, "When the Winning Team shows up, baby, you don't have to ask for it." Shout out to Big New!

After wrapping up things in Detroit, I flew to Baltimore to meet up with my Uncle Sam and attend a few appointments with tailors and

Mano Swartz with my father. On my first night, I went to Norma Jeans Gentlemen's Club with Mo Green and Tez. We had a great time in the VIP section, but I could sense that things were becoming unsafe. Charlie, the woman I was seeing, was trying to get my attention, but I kept a distance from her as I knew it was necessary at the moment. Despite this, I still made sure to provide for her.

The next morning, I headed to Pier 5 to meet up with Slick at Ruth's Chris Steakhouse. Slick was my guy, and we had talked about expanding and running all the work through him. However, I needed to see his right-hand man first. I wanted to bring in a semi at some point, but I knew that the gift I wanted to give my brother could be a life-threatening curse, and the energy of his selection for right-hand man was very bad.

The energy I got off Zip was the same energy I would later call the "Baltimore nigga vibe." Don't get it twisted though, there are some good dudes down in Baltimore, real thorough dudes who know how to get money. I have major respect for them and at one point, looked at it as a home away from home. However, there was this one particular group with that Baltimore type of energy that you could see the envy all over their faces. It's well known that Baltimore dudes and females don't like out of town dudes trying to move in on their town, even though I was just the plug for them. The plan was to hand everything over to Slick and snatch I AM out of there and let Zip figure out what happened for himself. Slick was from a totally different part of Baltimore and trust me when I tell you my dude is nothing to be messed with. Let's make sure we understand that. That being said, the bad vibes off Slick's friend could be useful. The envy was enough to give pause, but it was a non-starter for the moment.

Slick: Big Bruh, you know this is Ruth's Chris, right?

Me: Really?! Looking around, just noticing we were the only black people there.

This caused me to recall an event that happened there a few weeks back. Up to that point, I had been going to that same Ruth's Chris at least three to four times a week when I was in town. The waitress, valet, hostess, and head cook loved me, I Am, and Pop. I tipped each one very, very well every time I came. I always wore a wifebeater tank top-style undershirt there. Lorence told me not to do that and to wear a suit jacket like the policy requests, but I kept doing it anyway and didn't tell him.

As we walked into Ruth Chris around noon, I noticed a well-dressed gentleman staring at me. I ignored it and we placed our order. The gentleman politely introduced himself as the district manager of Ruth Chris and informed me of the dress code that required a sport jacket. He offered me one but I had skin exposed, so I couldn't use it that day. He asked us to finish our drink and appetizers and then leave. He politely walked away after that.

While standing near the exit area, I saw a number of employees talking to him. Suddenly, the head chef came out and started yelling at the poor man. We were wrapping up our meal when Mr. District Manager showed up again and apologized to me. He asked me to stay and explained how I was very popular with the staff there. He even said he might have to leave with me if I didn't accept his apology and remain with them. I accepted his apology and suggested we both stay a little while longer. He then asked if I was a professional athlete, maybe with the Ravens.

Later, I discussed with Slick about his friend and the vibes I was getting from him. I shared my thoughts about the Baltimore type group and how their envy was all over their faces. Slick assured me of his friend's youthfulness but also warned me that the streets were talking, and Charlie was upset that she protected me, but maybe she should have let things happen. I realized that Slick had a good point, which should have been more than obvious to me.

Pops, Shorty and I headed up to Mano Swartz to try on my new tailored Chinchilla coat, hat in gloves.

After talking with Richard, like we often do when I see him. His staff was bringing out some additional furs, he made for other clients. I totally fell in love with this ladies hooded Coyote jacket. I gravitated

over to it. Richard saw the look in my eyes......Well, who is going to be the lucky lady, Wayne? I have a young lady I have been after for years. I think I may be interested in something like this for her. You appear to really like this piece a lot. What is this young lady' name?

I politely declined to tell Richard the young lady's name, as it was a personal matter. He understood and we continued to talk about the fur jacket. Richard told me that it was made of high-quality coyote fur and that it was both stylish and practical for cold weather. He also mentioned that it was quite expensive, but he was willing to give me a discount as a loyal customer.

After thinking it over, I decided to buy the jacket for the special lady in my life. Richard helped me with the payment process, and we discussed how to properly care for the jacket. As always, Richard provided exceptional customer service and I left feeling satisfied with my purchase.

As we were leaving, Pops reminded me that we had to make a stop at the bank before heading back to the hotel. We got in the car and made our way to the bank, unaware of the events that would unfold next. Business was moving along smoothly. Just a couple of days before we had to return to Detroit, another load was to arrive from Rojo.

Under normal circumstances, it wouldn't be a big deal, but given the current situation, I needed to be present. I AM approached me about going out with him and the guys (Mo Green and Tez) to hit Norma Jeans. However, based on the information Slick gave me about how

Charlie was feeling, I didn't think it was a good idea. I didn't want anything to change between us, at least not for a while. I didn't want Charlie to feel like I was completely abandoning her.

Disregarding her feelings, I rationalized that this was just business and not personal. Zip, one of our associates, informed me that there was an important business opportunity that required my presence and urged me to come along with him and the guys to Norma Jeans. Despite my initial reluctance due to the tension with Charlie, I eventually agreed to go. Upon arrival, Zip greeted us and I noticed Charlie sitting alone at the far end of the VIP section, visibly upset and refusing to perform. Eventually, she signaled for Zip to come over and started buying him drinks. As they conversed, Charlie's emotions shifted from animated to melancholic, with occasional tears, while placing her hand high on Zip's upper thigh at times. I refrained from engaging with any dancers that night, mindful of Charlie's unstable emotional state. After a while, Zip came over to sit next to me and informed me that Charlie was willing to leave her current partner and be with me. He even signed his name on my leg multiple times as a sign of his endorsement.

I watched as Zip motioned his signature on my leg over and over, writing "Zip, a real ass nigga" on my leg. I didn't even talk to this dude, but I let him have his moment without overly reassuring him, all while processing everything he was saying.

In my mind, I couldn't help but think about what his girl had warned me about. She had told me to be careful of a woman named Charlie, whom Zip swore he never slept with but had once knocked my tooth out over. Charlie had been emotionally unstable at the club and was making motions to the waitress every time Zip's glass got low. It was clear to me that she wanted something from me - maybe to come to Detroit where she knew no one but me, and in return advocate for Zipto receive a major promotion.

But it wasn't just Charlie's intentions that concerned me. She had been venting to different people about making a grave mistake and not allowing me to be robbed, and her emotions were getting the best of her. There were plenty of people around trying to take advantage of that, and I knew that I was hearing that an attempt was afoot again. Everyone was waiting on Charlie to make a move, but little did they know, so was I. I Beep. Beep. Beep......

LOC BOC: Yo, big guy....... These guys brought more garbage in here again.

Me: You didn't let it hit the streets, right?

LOC. BOC.: No, I did what you said. Dropped it and it did the same.

Me: Tell Rojo, I will be flying back that way tomorrow noon. He needs to be gone and return that beat upshit to him. LOC BOC.

Me and the guys are headed to the Baltimore International Airport to fly back into Detroit. It seemed that everything was just happening. All at the same time.........

Beep. Beep. Beep.......

Me: Go ahead.

Danny: My friend! Those guys just called me. They are coming into town, and they are ready for this big meeting. I need you here Rapido Rapido, My friend!

Me: I'm going to fly back into my town barely right now from this place over here. Soon as I get to my town. The next day I will be to see you. Rapido, My friend!

We touched down at the McNamara International Airport in Romulus, Mi. Now me and the guys are headed back into the city. I was in the process of making the arrangements to get a flight going out for I AM, Big I. and myself to Juarez, Mexico. I didn't even have time for a sit down with my guys to discuss the new developments. Over in Baltimore. I had to bed down for a good night's sleep and be ready to fly out the following morning. In the wee hours of the morning on the following day.

Beep. Beep. Beep.........

Me: What’s up I AM?

I AM: The Guys up in Baltimore just tried to rob our spot. Jay and Ol boy had a shootout with the intruder, but he got away. Luckily, they didn't get anything. but our guys are in custody right now.

Me: Did you say the intruder was a singular person or multiple people?

I AM: Just one person.

Me: Well, it seems like they underestimated us. They must not have known that we're not to be messed with. But this was definitely a rogue act. One person doesn't just pull off a heist like this alone. This was some renegade type of stuff.

I AM: Yeah, I agree, But this is a major issue......... What's our next move?.......

I AM was at serious risk, and I needed to be careful about disregarding Charlie's feelings and not making things too personal. This was a business, after all.

Me: What's up, I AM?

I AM: The guys up in Baltimore just tried to rob our spot. Jay and Ol boy had a shootout with the intruder, but he got away. Luckily, they didn't get anything. But our guys are in custody right now.

Me: Did you say the intruder was a singular person or multiple people?

I AM: Just one person.

Me: Well, it seems like they underestimated us. They must not have known that we're not to be messed with. But this was definitely a rogue act. One person doesn't just pull off a heist like this alone. This was some renegade type of stuff.

I AM: Yeah, I agree. But this is a major issue. What's our next move?

I AM was at serious risk, and I needed to be careful about disregarding Charlie's feelings and not making things too personal. This was a business, after all.

CHAPTER 21

JUAREZ CARTEL

BEEP. BEEP. BEEP.........

Me: What the fuck?...

I AM: The guys up in B-more just had a botched robbery attempt and a shootout inside the house. My guys are in custody, but no one was hurt seriously on our end.

Me: Shit, I have a flight booked for Juarez, Mexico at noon. I can't push the call from Danny or he'll suspect something's up.

I AM: What's the move?

Me: I need you to get on a red-eye flight and contact attorney Warren Brown ASAP. We need to make sure the guys have legal representation and a bail bondsman on hand. If the locals get their hands on my money, the feds will be all over us. Let's start thinking about pulling out of B-more work-wise. We have to maintain control of the situation.

I AM: Understood. I'm sorry I'll miss the trip.

Me: It's all good. I'll hit you up as soon as I touchdown.

BIG I and I were on the way to the airport to fly out to Juarez to meet up with Danny when they received a call from I AM. He informed them that their guys had been released on bail that morning after going to court, and that he would spend another day or two in B-more to put his ear to the street before returning with the guys.

After a 5 1/2 to 6-hour journey, BIG I and I arrived in El Paso and took a taxi across the border to check in at the Holiday Inn. Danny appeared looking excited and informed them that this meeting was the meeting of all meetings, and that they would be in a good position if everything was successful. However, he didn't offer any further explanation.

Days passed with no meaning or explanation other than waiting for a call from the "office," which frustrated BIG I. He was starting to get upset, wondering what the hell Danny meant by "office." They were in another country wasting time, and he had just taken a $500,000 loss, with Danny losing close to $100,000 that he didn't even know about.

Danny came to the hotel late in the evening, as it was turning to twilight outside. "Let's go, my friend. We must hurry!" he said. BIG I and I quickly jumped into the car with him and he sped off.

We pulled into a Burger King parking lot and parked. Danny sat there looking super nervous, not saying a word. Suddenly, a huge pickup truck pulled into the parking lot at high speed, followed by another car. Both vehicles had guys jumping out, brandishing weapons in the Burger King. The car stopped some distance away from us.

Danny got out of the car and I followed his lead. I looked back for BIG I to try to calm him down, knowing he would be scared shitless at this sight. However, I didn't see him anywhere. He was still in the fucking car. I waited for him to come out.Danny got into the front of the truck, while BIG I and I were ushered to the back. BIG I struggled to get into the back row of the truck due to his size, but managed to push the back door open wider. As we were all loaded into the truck, I noticed automatic rifles mounted everywhere. The men spoke Spanish, and Danny turned to me and said that we would need to put black bags over our heads, as the armed men held them up. BIG I looked at me, his eyes starting to water up. I reassured him and put the bag over my head, thinking that it was too late for regrets and second-guessing.

Danny instructed us to lean our heads forward on the back of the headrest in front of us. The guy sitting next to me guided my head towards the back of the headrest, and I felt a hand on the back of my head, ensuring it stayed in place. We drove for a few minutes with the black bags over our heads, and BIG I started whispering to me in a shaky voice that he would never come back to this country with me again. I was worried that we might not make it out of this alive. BIG I continued, saying that if he made it out alive, he would stop selling drugs and start going to church with his mom. He asked the Lord to keep the person next to him away from him, as it was all his idea and he wasn't trustworthy.

My eyes tried to adjust to the dim light of the garage, feeling like a bright summer night after having that black bag snatched off my head like that. Someone screamed at me, "AQUI AQUI AQUI!!"

"¡My friend! ¿Is your hermano okay?" Danny asked with concern in his voice.

I responded in an embarrassed tone, giving an excuse, "Sí, my friend! Don't worry for him. He is just Catholic." But then I heard a unison sound of more than one, "Iiiiiiiiieeeeeeeee!!" As if to say, "Oooooooh, now we understand!" Silence came over the remaining 15-to-20-minute ride.

Within maybe the last five minutes of that ride, a cadence of beeps from the two-way radios in the truck with another party that wasn't. The call and response of beeps between the two-way Radio Nextel phones steadily increased. My mind tried to keep count between them, but I couldn't. Inwards, a wild imagination was going on inside of me. I had to just accept that this was a type of Morse code.

The truck started to slow down, and a number of turns were made. Coming to almost complete stops, then proceeding very slowly over these huge speed bumps... We were in a residential neighborhood. We must be very close to this house. I was thinking. The truck slowed, then made a fast turn up into a garage. I could hear the automatic garage doors beginning to close. Doors were slamming, and loud Spanish speaking was going on. I heard our door open, the bag was snatched off my head, and my eyes tried to adjust to the dim light of the garage, but it felt like a bright summer night sun after having that black bag snatched off my head like that.

"AQUI AQUI AQUI!" was being screamed at me, which basically meant "here, right now" or "let's go this way."

I noticed the guy holding the door open from being in the back seat next to me on our 20-minute joyride. The door was open just feet from the three cement steps that led to the unfamiliar face that stood to the side on the top stair, which led to the next open door leading down this dark hallway to the inner house. I was helped out of the truck as my foot hit the first step, and I noticed the automatic rifles in the right hand, pointed down, of the unfamiliar face. "AQUI AQUI AQUI," they yelled every step of the way up what felt like the view of an infinity pool, never-ending, or so it seemed.

I got to the end of this hall and did not see a face I knew. "Where the fuck is Danny? Shit, where is BIG I?!" I asked myself a million questions at what appeared to me as lightning speed. I made it to a big open space. The wall to my left continued out into the open room, while the wall to my right disappeared, opening up this big dining room type area. The yelling stopped, but the automatic rifles didn't. There were just pointing directions with their free hands, fingers pointing me to another big but furnished room just around that wall to my left.

To my left, this room was very dim. Men standing around, but only two in this room. I could see nickel-plated .45 caliber pistols and the waistlines of their very tight jeans and big belt buckles. Button-up shirts and expensive skin cowboy boots. There was a full-length couch against the back wall of this room. There was Danny already seated on my far right very corner of that couch. There was a man sitting on the left, but his right part of the couch. He was leaning back, relaxed, but purposely leaned back in the shadows. This living room-style couch set featured the long couch with Danny sitting.

One of the gunmen gestured towards a love seat on the left side of the room for me to sit on. It was located about 10 to 12 feet away from where Danny was seated on the long couch, with the gentleman in the shadows on the right. BIG I was seated across the room from me. One gunman stood between BIG I and the gentleman on the right side of the long couch, while another stood near me on the left. A third gunman walked in and stood in the middle of the room, without a gun but casually dressed. He was bald-headed and dressed in an American style of clothing, and will be referred to as "Bald Head".

The lighting in the room was turned up, and the gentleman on the right of the couch quickly grabbed something off the coffee table in front of him and dimmed the lights back down, giving someone a nasty look. He then leaned back into the shadows. There was a moment of silence before Bald Head began to speak, standing in the center of the room. Danny also started to speak, with all conversation between Bald Head and Danny in Spanish. Danny repeated his Spanish statements in English for my benefit.

"We have been working together for two years now, Chief," Danny said. "We are so happy that you were able to meet with us today. We are having problems finding someone that can supply enough to keep my friend here working. He has been working in Detroit, Baltimore, and we just added Atlanta."

Bald Head responded to Danny in Spanish, and the Jefe Chief remained silent. He appeared to be staring directly at me while Danny and Bald Head talked.

Chief finally spoke, and everyone fell silent. He spoke softly, and Danny began to translate his words to me. Chief's English was barely broken, and he asked, "Where do you wish for me to do business with you?" I replied, "I would like to work with you in my hometown of Detroit." Bald Head then translated what I said to the Chief. The meeting continued in this manner, with Danny translating for me, and Bald Head translating for the Chief.

Chief asked, "How much are you moving there now?" I responded, "I'm moving 25 kilos within a few hours of them bringing them to me. I receive two shipments of 25 every three days, but within the matter of hours, they are back on the road with full payment." Bald Head translated what I said to the Chief. Danny spoke in Spanish and then translated for me, "Chief, this is why we are happy that you were willing to have time for us. I was hoping that you could help us with 50 in Detroit. And, you see that my friend is also able to work in other markets too, chief." There was some Spanish-speaking between Bald Head and Danny. Chief still appeared to be locked in an unrelenting stare at me.

Chief then asked, "How long will it take you with those 50?" Danny translated for me, and I replied, "I'm sure it shouldn't take me longer than a week to complete." Bald Head translated what I said to the Chief. However, Chief didn't seem to pay attention to Danny's translations and directed all his questions to me. This form of negotiation was new to me, and usually, Big Eye would try to answer every question. But today, he remained silent.

Bald Head translated the chief's questions to me as Danny appeared to be in shock from being cut off by the chief.

"I would find out later that Flacco is actually the Chief's little brother," I thought to myself.

Chief: "Are you willing to work with me in these other places too?"

Me: "I don't see any reason why not, based on everything going well in Detroit," I replied, and Bald Head did the honors of translating.

Chief: "Are you willing to work with me only?"

Me: "No."

There was a moment of silence after my answer. Bald Head took over translating for me and the chief, while Danny remained quiet. I noticed that Danny was sliding over more and more, but the fear and concern were all over his face.

The chief replied to my answer: "I was thinking these guys can't keep work for you?"

"Yes, they are having problems," I replied.

"Why not be done with them?" the chief asked.

"My hope is for this one day. I just don't think this is that day yet," I replied.

"Would you have a problem with making those 50 for your town 100 now?" the chief asked.

"With a little more time, it's doable," I replied. Danny was looking at me in shock, sliding over in his seat.

"How long will it take for you to complete 150?" the chief asked.

"Well, this depends on the number per, but guessing three weeks," I replied.

Bald head is still translating between the chief and I. The pace of the negotiation has really picked up and getting tensed.

Chief: 200. Would be good for you?! Danny, jumps in at this point., thank you, chief........, this may be way too much. I think those 50 will be more than enough just for this first time. Chief, please. Danny, Pleads.

Chief: is this what your friend here say is true?

I started to shake my head with a little chuckle, while waving my index finger back and forth as if to. Say, I see what you are up to.

Me: those 200 is to make sure I don't have time to work. The other guys. As I started to laugh, softly, like you, little devil. I saw teeth from a big smile that cut through the Dim light. As it came. Over Chief face.

Danny, was sitting on the small cushion that was in front of the arm of the couch now.

Chief: so, the 200 won't be too much? And His smiled, got bigger.

Me: that depends on how much you like me? After a little back and forth in Spanish, between Ball Head and Chief.

Chief: 18.

Me: At 50 Kilos?

Chief: At 200?

Me: at 50 kilos.

Chief: 150 At 18.

Me: 100 at 17. Bald head jumped into object strongly.

Chief: 150 at 18.

Me: Chief, you are Starting to make me feel like I'm not the pretty girl at the dance anymore. 17 At 100.

The chief lean forward while sitting on the very edge of the couch now. He grabbed the lighting and turned it. All the way up now. To allow me to see he was clearly laughing. And, also revealing a gold plated huge ass pistol in his lap. Bald head is very vocal in Spanish. Danny has a look of clear shock and amazement. On his face.

Chief.: 150 at 17.5. While still clearly laughing. And Bald Head is bitching.

Me: chief, I'm doing better than that price now. I'm willing to do 75 at. 17.5. As I dropped my head and disappointment.

Chief: 150 at 17.

Me: I quickly raised my head and put my thumb and index finger together In front of my chest as if I was twisting my nipples. And said, I'm starting to feel. Pretty again! 100 at 17.

Bald head isn't translating anymore and appears to be trying to stop the chief. Which wasn't a problem, because Danny took back over. This part of things chief is laughing and everyone is laughing with him and appearing to be enjoying the engagement as If there was a rooster fight taking place.

Chief: 125 at 17. Stated slowly. With an evil smile on his face now.

* All Mexicans are greedy came to my mind.

Me: 200 at 16......... Said in a similar tone.

The chief sat up straight and looked me directly in the eyes, and bald head protested again. I did the nipple thing again, and the room erupted in laughter.

The chief accepted the deal, and I asked him what would happen if I had trouble paying him back. He asked me which I would prefer, time to pay or death. The room fell silent, and I said I would prefer time to pay.

The deal was complete, and Danny was pushed to the side as a translator. I realized there was much more going on than what was apparent to the watching eye.

Bald Head began discussing logistics with me, specifically the details of crossing and moving from El Paso to Detroit. He was moving fast and giving me a lot of details, and then started asking me questions that I didn't know how to answer, concerning truck stops and other specifics. I looked at Danny for help, but he said nothing. I felt like Danny had abandoned me in this negotiation, but what I didn't realize was that I had really abandoned him.

Chief engaged me directly, which was out of the format of the normal negotiation. I didn't understand or know that this was different. Chief started staring at me to get a read on me, then set out to prove his theory. He wanted to see if I could handle some pressure. I'm sure he hadn't heard no from anyone in a very long time. Chief was most impressed with my ability to read maneuvers in real time. He wanted me for himself, but Bald Head didn't see this and had set out to expose my greenness. Danny understood what was going on and wouldn't speak.

Bald Head looked at me and said he could get the 200 kilos to Ohio for me, but couldn't bring it any further. He had been trying to get me to come all the way down to El Paso to pick it up, but I didn't have the special vehicles or drivers for such a trip. I turned to plead my case to Chief, but it became clear that Bald Head was trying to kill the deal I had negotiated with the chief. When I turned towards Chief, Danny jumped in to translate.

" Chief, I can move those 200 in maybe three weeks. I wasn't making much with those other guys based on the small amounts of work. I can afford to purchase and have cars made for this. I also haven't had a chance to screen someone for a job like this. I promise that I will once I work a few times with you, Chief." I said.

Bald Head spoke in Spanish to the Chief, then turned to me and said, "Well, my friend, I don't know what to tell you now. Maybe once you have transportation, you can come back. Next time you need to make sure you are ready to work on a level like this. I'm sorry, my friend..." with a sarcastic smile on his face after giving me his lecture.

Chief finally spoke, "No, we will take it all the way to him in Detroit," after Danny translated it for me. "Thank you, Chief...Thank you!" I said this with passion.

Chief said a few final words in Spanish. Danny started to tell the Chief about those guys that gave him the $300,000 for me. Chief told a few of his guys to go over to their office to tell them that I work with him now. They must not cause problems for themselves by fooling around with Danny.

CHAPTER 22

BALD HEAD

As I drove up 94 E from the airport, I couldn't help but reflect on what had just happened. I was still in shock from being grilled by the Chief, and I wasn't sure what to make of my relationship with Bald Head. It was clear that we didn't care for each other, and the feeling seemed to be mutual. Despite all of this, I managed to keep my nerves during the meeting with Chief, but now that it was over, I was left feeling shaken.

BIG I: I swear you'll never get me over there again. I promise, God, if I got out, I would never go back!

Me: And how many times have you lied to God? Right. I wonder.

BIG I: (After a brief pause...) That's my point! I ain't going to lie anymore, though!

Rojo and his bosses were fully aware that their attempt at the double cross of Danny was met with the triple cross from me and Danny. We played to their egos once Chief sent his guys over to their office.

I pulled up in the driveway to have a sit-down with my guys at LOC BOC House. There were a lot of things that had to be changed and arrangements made. I AM still catching up to speed on more information I received concerning what happened in B-more. Warren Brown did an excellent job getting the charges dropped against Jay and Dee. They just had to pay a small fine for discharging a weapon inside the city limits. But the gun charges that were placed on them were thrown out. To a person that doesn't know, that sounds extremely exciting and good. But being a seasoned vet with these types of things, I know that when this type of stuff happens, it's a red flag and an indication that the feds are involved or may indict soon.

The counter move is to completely withdraw from the area. Accept all losses incurred as a form of paying your dues. Make no mistake, the charges will be tallied and added to your bill later, extending your tab. This is why it's crucial to avoid any unnecessary violence, as it will only escalate your situation. Those people, meaning the Feds or Local Law enforcement, will apprehend you and determine all your charges later. YOU BECOME A THREAT TO PUBLIC SAFETY!

The Feds are also driven by greed; why charge you with just a part of what you're doing when they can stop it all? Jurisdiction may slow down the process, but it will ultimately lead to your downfall.

Hence, it is imperative that you are perceived as a businessman involved in criminal activities and not a violent criminal. This is not criminal advice but an explanation of the process that could lead to your demise. You should reevaluate: The Feds and Local Law enforcement have complete control, deciding when and how to apprehend you, without any doubt!

For those considering transitioning from a criminal lifestyle, take note that the underlying principles of business are the same, whether it's legal or illegal. The only difference lies in legality: being licensed or unlicensed. However, the core principles of business remain consistent. Moreover, it's essential to understand that the process of charging and facing charges is essentially a financial transaction in our commerce-driven world. In its simplest terms: IT'S ALL COMMERCE!

We also got more information concerning how this rogue individual came about. As I had already heard, Charlie was venting to people and there were a number of people trying to make arrangements to come and rob me. Since she got cold feet the first time, I guess she ended up getting cold feet the second time and somebody just got pissed off and went rogue and got a big surprise. I really did believe that Charlie wanted to try and attempt to start a whole new life after causing so much harm. But I've seen it happen so many times before, and it's always consistent within the underworld. Once you become known for a certain thing, you can never outlive that reputation.

We had a lot of times just laughing and having fun, being silly. I'm sure if she had a chance to change a lot of things in the past, she would have. Life just doesn't work that way, though.

The next couple of days were spent setting up a bigger network, including storehouses for the white and a separate system for protecting the money. My main three guys could pick up their bags from another location, and the money would be dropped off at 4 different counting locations. All these systems had to run independently and without knowledge of each other.

After the setup, we took a break to relax and have some fun while making money. After touching down in Atlanta, we went to check in at Strokers, Woo, E, and my guys. While there, Tez had a crazy look on his face and told me to go get I AM. I looked around frantically and asked what was wrong. Tez pointed towards the restroom, where I AM was.

As I walked towards the restroom with my bodyguards and Tez, I AM was standing too close to a urinal and singing to a guy who was relieving himself. I confronted I AM, asking what he was doing, and he spun around, shocked to see me. The guy he was bothering threw his head back in relief as if thanking God.

I AM explained that he was singing the lead singer's part of Jagged Edge, thinking he could jog his memory. I asked him why he thought it was appropriate to do so while the guy was relieving himself. I then escorted I AM out of the restroom, and the gentleman escaped. I AM is a big R&B fan and also sings himself, so he felt he needed to be discovered.

Afterwards, I AM joked with Tez, calling him a motherfucker for that situation.

The following day, work came in fast and went just as quickly. Atlanta was a major hub for the Southern region. The little I had coming was literally nothing. What became clear was that I could take my time. Big Meech was a Detroit nigga, as I often heard, which I was already well aware of from back in the days. One thing was clear, this was his time, and he left that money-making machine well-oiled too. What I noted was that dudes came with their money and weren't looking or expecting handouts. They were happy to just get quality work once.

I also found it weird that black dope boys wanted to buy black. Meech was gone and the Spanish boys were holding all the work. The brothers felt they were being taken advantage of by them too. I wanted to keep it light and party down there with Woo, Keith, Pretty Boy, I AM, Tez, and myself. We hit the 300 Bowling Alley and had a really good time. Then Keith told Woo that Usher had rented the Ten Pin VIP Bowling Alley out and wanted them to come through and bring his group, One Chance.

I wasn't sure how this would go based on an earlier crossing of paths with Usher. He called Woo, and the group Woo got Keith to sign up under Usher's label, US Records, for One Chance. Usher rented out a basketball gym after hours and invited one of the guys to come down. I basically chilled out on the side, but Tamika was there with him as well, and we conversed during the game they played. It was just harmless conversation, mostly joking. Usher didn't say anything to me, but some glances I got were interesting, though it could be taken out of context.

We arrived deep at Atlantic Station and entered. Everyone got their bowling shoes, which I covered. I got a size 17 bowling shoe and walked around buying women drinks and looking them in their eyes hard, getting their attention. Then, looking down at my feet as they followed my eyes, I tapped my size 17 shoe on the floor and smiled at them when they looked up. I got a huge laugh out of them. I was dope boy fresh. I had my bracelet with 60 carats invisible set rose gold with a rose gold presidential Rolex with the Rolex diamonds clean. You couldn't even take a picture of them. I mean, I was everywhere in that bowling alley.

Jazze Pha walked over to me and said, "So that's how you feel! Oh boy!!" as he commented on my jewelry. We engaged in some small talk, and it appeared he also knew Kamaya .

I guess I was doing a little too much, to say the least. But I had noticed Usher sitting over on lane one with a bottle of champagne, drinking by himself, perhaps lost in deep thought. Out of nowhere, I had a bright idea.

Me: Waiter, bottles of champagne for everyone!

By this time, I was back in my black Gator boots with the Gator nose sitting up off the toe of the boot. Woo's Group One Chance loved me because I showed them a lot of love. There were a few women I had my eye on, and I was stunting super hard. I was just straight up on my Detroit Dboy shit.

One female was dark-skinned with a wonderful shape, but she seemed to be with older black men. Actually, there were a number of older black dudes in there that night, and all had nice-looking young women with them. My moves didn't seem to be working for me. I shifted my attention to a group of light-skinned, very pretty, and professionally dressed ladies. I sent a bottle over to them and focused on two that I was trying to decide how to approach.

Corey: Yo, what's up, Big Homie?! You ain't gonna believe this hoe-ass shit. This dude called me over to him, asking me, "Who are you?".... I asked him, "What do you mean? That's the Big Homie!"

Me: (confused.) Who asked you that shit, Lil homie?!

Corey: That motherfucker. (Pointing at Usher.)

Me: Are you serious, Lil homie?!

Corey: Yeah, Big Homie! He was about to have them put you out! I had to flip out on him and tell him everybody fucks with you hard! He doesn't like how you move, but I had to tell him that's just what you do everywhere we go. You look out!

Me: Good looking, Lil homie. While thinking, let me go sit my ass down somewhere, fast!

Usher could have gotten the security's ass torn up in there that night. I wasn't on any shit like that, though, so I fell back.

Beep. Beep. Beep....... Yeah, go ahead.

Danny: My friend, we have a problem.

Me: Tell me, my friend?

Danny: My friend the Chief wants you to send one of your friends. To be here with him while you are working out there.

Me: What the FUCK Danny? We have never worked like this before!

Danny: Yeah, I'm sorry, my friend. But this is much, much bigger.

Me: I will call you when I get back to my town.

Danny knew I was pissed. I knew something wasn't right with this. Chief was upfront and very clear about what he wanted and expected from this deal. I could also remember how more uncomfortable Danny was after Chief started moving past those fifty bricks that he wanted. I had nothing but a gut feeling, and I wanted to gamble on my gut feeling being correct. This wasn't smart on a deal this big....I would have to figure this one out, and I had no one I was able to send for something like this?

I sauntered over to the two the two light skinned women and sat in the middle of the couch, putting my feet up on the table in front of them I leaned back and put my arm. around the back of the couch, charming them with my slick talk and making them laugh. One of the women, a brown skin dressed to the nines in high heel Giuseppe boots and a big Hermes bag, caught my eye. She was making small, funny comments that had everyone laughing, but when she turned her playful teasing on me, it became a back-and -forth battle. However, I noticed that the other women were starting to back off and reject my advances, except for one.

As the night began to wind down, we all found ourselves in front of the 10 Pins VIP Bowling Lanes, trying to decide whose house to go to next to continue the party. The young lady who had been shutting me down all night walked past me and started with me again. We exchanged a few more funny comments as she walked towards the corner of the cross on the side of ESPN Sports bar. As she crossed, she yelled something back at me, and I couldn't resist responding.

"Come here for a minute, Wayne," she called out as I walked towards her. "Put my number in your phone," she said, snatching my phone and hitting send. "I don't trust your ass, Nigga, because I know you won't call. No, I have your number. And, oh yeah...don't waste your time with the light-skinned pretty girl. She isn't on your level, Wayne. She would be a waste of time." With that, she handed me back my phone and walked away.

Bitch! Who does she think she is?! She has a very, very bad attitude..

I'm on Novara street sitting at the pool table talking with I AM, Moe Green, Dirt and BIG I. The issue is my circle of people was enlarged and I couldn't just send anyone since Danny Little brother had spent a lot of time up in The D with us during the Rojo dealings. Before they paid Danny off, they knew my crew and I needed these guys and their extended teams. We were really struggling to figure this out and we had no answers. I turn to the guys and I said that all we had to do Is fine someone that-----

LOC BOC: listen! I don't know who you Niggas think you are!! Parking your fucking cars all over my fucking grass! I'm gonna put you Niggas out my shit and Wayne, don't get mad at me! Then tell me that I'm overreacting about this!

We are exchanging quick glances at each other while he is acting in normal fashion; Bursting in the house, yelling and. Cursing at people. But now we are all staring at him.

LOCBOC: why all Y'all Niggas staring at me?! as a smile comes over his face. I'm serious, y'all wrong Bro!

I AM: you got anything planned major over the next week or two? As we all start to smile now Back at him.

LOC BOC arrived in El Paso. And taken across....... Beep. Beep. Beep......

Bald head: Do you have the drop spot, my friend? When do you contact the drive? It's under your responsibility Coming off the freeway until he is back on it. Bringing white or returning with cash?

Danny has LOC BOC checking in with me often. I'm still unsettled by the fact I know this is fucking Danny's doing! I just couldn't prove it at the moment.

Beep. Beep. Beep...

Bald head asked, "Do you have the drop spot, my friend? When you do, correct it. And the driver? It's under your responsibility from coming off the freeway until he is back on it. Bringing white or returning with cash?"

Danny had LOC BOC checking in with me often, and I was still unsettled by the fact that I knew it was Danny's doing, but I couldn't prove it at the moment.

The truck issue was resolved, and I AM went to the truck stop to pick up the driver and show him the route to the drop spot. BIG I secured the location, and my cousin Dirt brought three carloads of guys as backup. If needed, they were ready to intervene with force.

To verify the delivery, I was present when the driver unloaded 198 kilos from the compartment over the fifth wheel of his trailer. He was supposed to deliver 200 kilos, but he claimed the amount had been changed.

The driver tried to hand his two-way radio to I AM so he could confirm the delivery, but I signaled to I AM not to take the phone and held up two fingers to indicate that we were short by two kilos.

The driver became upset and started swearing, but I AM and I remained firm. The driver thought I AM was a Jefe with the power to authorize the delivery, but I AM refused to take the phone.

As the driver was arguing with I AM, his two-way radio beeped. It was Ball Head, trying to reach him. The driver stopped talking and looked at me in shock when he heard a two-way radio sound coming from me.

I AM quickly explained to the driver that the radio was from my boss, Chief, who was checking if he had delivered the full amount. The driver handed over the remaining 198 kilos, and I confirmed the delivery with Chief. I still suspected that Danny was behind the missing two kilos, but I couldn't prove it yet.

The driver spins around quickly while stating, "My friend, I swear..." as he appears to be searching again. "Oooooooh, mi amigo!! I think I feel something! I think it may be those two! Si SI it's those two, Jefe!!" holding them up so I could see them. Then looking to I AM.

Driver: "You were right! I barely just found them. It's very dark. In that place there, my friend." Looking at me with a concerned look. "I'm sorry for your time, Jefe... I will know better every time now." With a nervous smile.

Beep, beep. Beep, beep...

Me: "Go ahead."

Danny: "My friend, the chief is calling! This Ballhead guy is telling his shit too, Chief!"

The driver smiles at me and gives me the two thumbs up!

Me: "No, my friend, everything is fine. I have those 200 and I called you."

Danny: "OK, my friend, I'll wait for you!"

We hit the freeway and came up deep East Chalmers exit and road the service drive to Maryland St. I gave 25 bricks a piece out to my guys: I AM's guy Mack, Moe Green, and BIG I. The game plan was once you finish with all numbers in on those 25, you had free access to the 125 left. Them boys got it popping! Chief and I agreed to a three-week turn around time, which I knew wouldn't take me that long. Six days in, my guys brought in 2.8 at $18,500 apiece. When I was seeing them at 16,000 a piece. The price in the city was between 24 to 25,000 a piece. I was at 19.5 and kept the guys' price at 21 to 21,500 apiece.

I want you to pass some of that profit off to the street. I had a hard time at first because no one thought my work was real! Guys needed to finger fuck them first. They were used to the Rojo whole stuff that came in halves. Once they've seen that, the ship was jumping back. We couldn't keep it. But during that time when people were skeptical of us, the pace of the sales was unpredictable. Moe Green came to me with lying stories of how someone was cheaper than us and I dropped $1000 to 18.5, but I got it back from Rojo Jefe's.

Once I found out, I never said anything for a couple of loads. Then, I took it back by capping the peak sales price at $1000 less than before. Fucket, I couldn't miss it, but I had to swing the heavy hammer on them for trying the bullshit on me. We will just give it to the street. Shortly after speaking with Danny, beep, beep, beep...

Bald head: Go ahead, my friend.

Me: I need you guys to come now. I have never held this much of someone else's money and I'm nervous.

Bald head: Don't worry, my friend. I will be there with you soon.

Me: My friend, I need to ask you something.

Bald head: Tell me?

Me: How is my friend? I hope he is okay, my friend.

Bald head: Your friend? You mean Danny, my friend? You lost the number for his radio, my friend?

Me: No, my friend. The chief asked Danny to have me send...

Bald head: Ooooooh, my friend!!?? No, he is doing fine, my friend. I just spoke with LOC BOC, and he was complaining about the place he was being held. Being cold at night, missing windows. This had me really upset, but he needed to take this for the team.

The Semi arrived and I AM went out to meet the driver. Also to make sure the driver made it down on the freeway. Then, I AM hitting me on the two-way. "That's done... Beep. Beep. Beep..."

Bald head: Go ahead, my friend.

Me: I'm done. The driver is yours.

Bald head: Thank you, my friend. Chief told me to tell you he understands that you were nervous being your first time. But, we have to complete things from now on so it doesn't become confusing. It's just better that way.

Me: I understand.

I left off at 400,000 and was told to complete that with the money I turned in on the next load, which I was almost done with anyway.

Bald head: My friend, let me tell you something.

Me: Go ahead, my friend.

Bald head: The chief never asked for your friend, my friend. I told him what you asked me about your friend too. Danny is no good, my friend. The chief just sent some Sicarios to get your friend from Danny right now. Chief will have him call you soon as he has him settled. Danny is your friend, and I don't know why he would do this to you, my friend.

I asked Bald Head to thank the chief for me. I never mentioned this to Danny. What Bald Head was attempting was clear, and this is where I would start to share these events with Danny. Not this time. The writing was starting to become clear. Danny wasn't slow by far, and I know he was seeing it as well. Just all at my expense, my loyalty to my friend.

I spoke with LOC. BOC, and the changes were in his voice. The chief put him in a very, very nice hotel, which he couldn't pronounce in Spanish. I could understand Danny's fear, if this was really fear. This was a power move at my expense to project power and total control over me, but outwardly so. Jefe move! Danny just didn't know I was a quick study, and he just crossed a line that could have been in LOCBOC's blood. The bullshit begins, but this time, I have some of my own to sling around!

Danny just didn't know I was a quick study. What I was starting to see now would cost me dearly throughout my life. Unconditional loyalty would be a liability, and very dangerously so too! I would have to prepare my mind for what I saw coming. This time, Bald Head would be Rojo. But both would be after those $500 to $1000 per Kilo.

Still upset I just pulled the triple cross to dissent and defend my friend Danny's backside, ensuring he came out on top and riches on all ends. Now to have him pulling the bullshit on me! Another semi pulled in with 150. Despite the 150 came out, I had, I AM have the driver put those $400,000 that I owe. This impressed the chief that I sent it ahead of time.

Long story short, I completed 350 bricks in that initial three weeks from those first 200. LOCBOC arrived back to The D before I AM loaded. The money for those 150 bricks. I think chief again after he returned. My buddy back to me. This was more so to thank him for his trust in me, and so he would be aware that I was aware he got LOC BOC back to me after I got the next load and with intentions to have him back before I fully paid him for the first one. To make sure I understood it wasn't him. Chief and I were creating a symbolic way of communication.

LOC BOC: "Weezy, man, I need to kick it with you when you get a minute. It's some deep shit that I know you can understand better than me."

I needed to take a pause after those stressful three weeks and kind of blew. LOC. BOC off. I needed to get away and process everything that was happening at lightning speed. I had just gained a new best friend: Bald head. "You have to be careful with Danny, my friend. People are starting to whisper about very, very bad things he is doing here!"

What Danny didn't know was that I was already seeing the changes in him. Another move or two from him and I would see the end game. There were only about three outcomes at this point and one included Bald Head and the chief being in on it with Danny.

I landed in Baltimore to address some unfinished business. I needed to see Pop about getting with Major to move into a really nice place right off the golf course where Tiger Woods was said to have played a number of times. My guy Slick had some info off the streets about who was behind all the robbery bullshit. I still had business with Danny in Baltimore and Atlanta, and I needed to get another load in Baltimore for Slick too.

With so many things to get done in Baltimore, it should have caused me stress, but the thought of making arrangements to fly Mena in first class on my next trip to Baltimore put me at ease. Ruth Chris made me aware of the special requests that I was allowed to make, so I set an appointment to have them arrange a candlelight dinner for Mena and myself alone in the restaurant, free of patriots, with only my special waitress and chef who always treated me well.

Tez approached me with news, "Yo, big bro, you do know Mena went on a date with Snoop last night?? But something just ain't right about this. You know, I told you I went to school with her. I think she is using Snoop to fuck with you. They are going out again, and she's cool with me going too. I will get to the bottom of this for you."

I would find out from Tez that he was correct on Mena's Intentions. Just to be honest, as he is the majority of the time. Tez can call the dice before they stop, he's just that damn good. She wasn't really interested in my cousin Snoop, she just wanted revenge on me for being a womanizer. Years ago, I had tried to get to know Mena better but ended up dating one of her friends named Hunnie. Mena found out about me and the T-Mobile girl getting close, and it seemed like it was building up to a mental battle. I was hoping I was wrong, but Tez's instincts were usually correct.

Despite the situation with Mena , I had to focus on my to-do list and get back to Detroit. I had made all the arrangements for Mena 's visit and needed to handle everything else before seeing her. Recently, I had purchased the new S 550 long wheelbase, which was only released in limited amounts by Benz. I was the only one in Detroit with it at the time, and it would be another two years before they would become more common on the streets. I had dealt with an Arab gentleman to acquire the car, as the white dealers didn't want to see a Black man driving it. One dealer had only one and was holding it for some CEO, but I managed to get it by putting $30,000 upfront. The Arab car dealer was happy to make the deal, but the looks from the white dealers could kill.

I pulled up to Mena 's aunt's house in style, dressed in a tailored raw silk leisure suit with Maury soft bottom gate shoes and a matching

Gator belt. I wanted to make a statement. Mena begged me to come in for a second, and I hesitated but knew she probably had someone she wanted me to meet, like her aunt or female cousins. I parked the car and left the door wide open, thinking to myself, "That's that new thing...they won't even know how to put it in gear!"

Just before I stepped into the house, I showed off my platinum and gold watch with a mother of pearl face and 25 VVS stones around the bezel, along with half carat canary yellow diamonds. It was just a light flex, nothing too flashy.

Mena 's mom exclaimed, "Oooooh Mena !! This is a grown man!!! This ain't no little boy!! Oh my God, he looks just like Levert (R&B singer)." She couldn't resist touching and grabbing me.

I teased her, "Okay now, woman! You over here touching and grabbing on me? You gonna get yourself in trouble!" We laughed together while Mena looked visibly upset and embarrassed.

Mena's, Mom: well, bring it on! I'm grown.!! I ain't gonna play with you like her. As she pointed at Mena.

Mena yelling... MA! MA! What are you doing! MA! MA! Looking upset and embarrassed at the same time!

Meeting Mena 's mom was a surprise for me, but we connected instantly. From that day forward, our communication would start on a good note.

Mena told me, "You know, the earrings and fur that you sent me arrived at her house. I got off work from the bank and went straight to her house. She answered the door in the fur and earrings."

Getting the chance to connect with her was starting to put my mind at ease about what Tez had told me. We walked into one of my favorite restaurants, and as usual, the valet guys kept my car parked out front for me.

The restaurant was packed, and there was a 35-minute wait, but it never bothered me. I was seated right away. Suddenly, the owner's brother came out, visibly upset, and demanded that I be removed from my table and wait like the others. Mena looked uncomfortable as the owner's brother made somewhat of a scene. It appeared that I was seated before even him and his wife. I touched Mena's hand to reassure her that there was no need to move. With a nod, soft wink, and smile, I knew it wouldn't take long before someone would overrule him. This was familiar territory for me.

Soon, the general manager emerged from the back and made it over to me to apologize for the misunderstanding.

GM: "I don't know who he thinks he is. He set himself up to get embarrassed in front of his wife. You will never have that issue again, big bro."

Me: "How is the team doing?"

It's always best to stay modest in situations like that. Gloating is distasteful.

GM: "They are doing great! Their faces just lit up when I brought out their new uniforms. But when I brought out their shoes, they went crazy, big bro!! Thank you so, so much!"

Me: "God is good, family."

I was fortunate enough to assist with a young group in an athletic program that he ran. Mena was a real humanitarian-type person. This made her feel a little better about staying seated because the gentleman had a good point about the whole waiting in line thing. He was just extremely colorful and disrespectful, which took away from a valid point that he had. This turned into a night from hell and one of the reasons why I wanted to date Mena in another state and not Detroit.

Mena didn't approve of my lifestyle. I started receiving bottles of champagne and drinks at my table, which was embarrassing as the waitress brought them over and pointed out compliments from people I didn't know. I don't drink, and I was trying to eat and maintain good conversation, but I had people starting to walk over to the table to say hi and introduce their dates to me.

In some cases, They said; "I know you don't know me, but I'm so-and-so's friend, and I've seen you at this place or that."

One guy walked up with his buddy, thinking he was doing me a favor by introducing himself and saying, "Yo big homie!! Word on the street is you're calling in airstrikes! Put me on, baby!!" Needless to say, I didn't even know who this guy was.

I knew I had to speed up the night, as it wasn't going as planned with Mena . Plus, it could have turned into a safety issue for her. I carried a .40 caliber coat with a rubber pistol handgrip, which I legally carried as I had no criminal record, not even a parking ticket. However, this wasn't a plus with Mena .

The valet ran to get my keys as they seemed to be coming out. I then saw a childhood friend, DeBoy Mickey, who I used to tease for his light skin. We hugged tightly, happy to see each other after years of not crossing paths. Mike could clearly see that we had a lot of history. After all, he was the first person I met at the eventful field night.

Deboy Mickey asked, "What's been going on with you? I heard your investment company is doing well. I need to exchange information; I'm looking to get into the market up here in The D. As in Detroit. There are some nice investment opportunities down my way as well now!"

Deboy Mickey was an upscale hustler like my guys in Baltimore. We had a whole conversation about investments, but respectfully avoided talking about drugs in front of our ladies. Deboy Mickey had a major foothold in Ohio, and I wouldn't mind getting involved and making some profit.

I apologized to Mena and asked for a do-over, but this time flying her out to Baltimore. She appeared happy to know I was taking her feelings into consideration and agreed. I gave her a hug and a kiss on the forehead after walking her to the door. I jumped back in the car and heard a beep.

Tez called, "What's up, big bro?"

I replied, "Yo, I just ran into my guy Deboy Mickey. I need you to take his number down and meet him tomorrow. He has some possible investment options for us down his way. I have a flight first thing tomorrow."

Tez said, "I got you, big bro."

I AM and I headed directly to my favorite spots to be, THE STRIP CLUB, with Woo and Eric joining us for a night of entertainment. We had a load coming in the following day. After an intriguing night out, it was time for business, but this load wasn't going to last long. The demand for the white we were bringing into Atlanta was rapidly increasing. Woo was on my case because the small load of 50 bricks wasn't even lasting a couple of hours after it was dropped. I knew what needed to be done, but I didn't plan on coming into Atlanta with a heavy load. I just wanted to use Atlanta as my playground while helping my dude Woo out at the same time.

I was then contacted by my friend Jewels.

Jewels: Let's go get something to eat.

Me: That's cool! When do you want to go?

Jewels: Wait! What do you have on right now??

Me: I have LV shoes and Year of the Dog 800-dollar pants.

Jewels: Oh no, hunnie! We can't do that! What size suit jacket do you wear??

Me: .... I don't know?! (Feeling lost)

Jewels: You look like you could be a 52 or 54. Listen, I'm going to call one of my friends and have him open up his shop so we can go get you a suit jacket. He doesn't open on Sundays, but he is going to open up for us. We are going somewhere really nice, and you can't wear that stuff you have on now.

Me: Feeling shocked, lost, and embarrassed all at once, I say, "Listen, what I tell you about tryna treat me like I'm your bitch! Stop tryna make me your bitch!" as I hang up on her once again.

Uncle Sam contacted me about the furniture I wanted to put in the house in Maryland. I made him aware of my other place. I need him to move on just two or three minutes from the Governor's mansion called The Rocca. But first, I need Uncle Sam to head to Baltimore, at my place at The Ritz Carlton, and get everything set for my big date with Mena coming up shortly.

I was starting to notice a significant change in the dynamics of our business arrangement with Chief, courtesy of Bald Head's ambitions. Bald Head started contacting me directly about loads coming into The D, instead of going through Danny for logistics and money matters. Danny, on the other hand, began acting strangely, adopting a more authoritative tone, even though we were supposed to be partners. It was becoming evident that our understanding of loyalty was vastly different, and I realized that loyalty might not be as valued in the Spanish-speaking Mexican underworld culture as it is in the American or urban context.

I knew I needed to adapt quickly and master the blurred lines between the black and gray areas of this business. The 48 Laws of Power gave me the rules to power, but true mastery lay in understanding the exceptions to those rules, much like a seasoned Roman senator.

Touching down in Baltimore for my big date with Mena, I was filled with excitement. I wanted to show her how much I valued and appreciated her, especially considering her past abusive relationship. I wanted her to see her worth and how much she meant to me. Uncle Sam had everything arranged for my special night, and he headed to Atlanta to receive the custom furniture I ordered for my place there.

However, my excitement turned to concern when my Pop Smoochie called me a few hours later.

Smoochie: Son, is everything okay with your lady friend??

Me: WHY?! WHAT'S WRONG??! My heart skipped a beat!

Smoochie: The car service called and said the driver was waiting with the sign for Mena, but she never approached him. Did she miss the flight or something??

Me: I don't think so... I think she would have called me if something like that happened. Last I spoke to her, she was on her way to the airport, Pop.

Well, after calling several times with no answer, I was in a state of shock at the possibilities while hoping nothing went wrong. I just ended up going out with my pops and hitting the concert with my bodyguards, making the best of what was supposed to be a night to remember... which it was after getting a voicemail message making it clear that I had been stood up. That was a very long night for me too.

"I AM" flew in the following day because we had a light load coming in that was going to be handed over to my guy Slick. I received a call from my very good friend Jewels.

Jewels: Where are you? Are you in town right now?

Me: Nah, I'm out in Baltimore.

Jewels: Really! I love it out there. Have you tried the crab cakes out there yet?

Me: Yes, they are like nowhere else outside of one spot up in NY at The Marriott Marquis in Time Square, but still not quite Maryland crab cakes though.

She went on to tell me about different experiences out in Baltimore with several of her girlfriends that she identified as her BITCHES. Continuing to ask me about different things, "Have you done this and that?" I was feeling defeated as I answered all her questions with, "No, I have never done that before."

Jewels: OH MY GOD NIGGA I FUCKS WITH YOU, FUCKS WITH YOU!!

Me: Wide-eyed with a shocked look on my face as I answer the question, "Thank you??!"

Jewels: Most niggas be lying about shit like they've done everything under the moon just to get there to find out they hadn't done a damn thing! This is why I fucks with you so hard because you are just real and don't mind just being honest! I FUCKIN LOVE THAT ABOUT YOU! Listen, why don't you call down a few of your homies, and I'm going to call down a few of MY BAD BITCHES from California. I'm going to lease a house right off the lake in the Hamptons where Puffy and ETC are right up the street for the weekend.

Me: I don't even know what your girls looking like, and ain't no one trying to fuck up some major numbers on women that's less than desirable.

Jewels: I guess you didn't hear me when I said, "I'm calling down some of MY BAD BITCHES." They are paying their own way the whole time down here! You just make sure that your niggas know how to keep their mouth shut about everything that happens over the weekend.

This became apparent that Lady Jewels had other plans for me. I wasn't going to let her BAD BITCHES loose on my crew to give them a once over after a week of fucking and Lord knows what else............THIS WAS AN INTERVIEW!

Me: I would love to take you up on your offer at a later date, but the next couple of weeks are going to be very demanding for me and the guys. I will reach back out to you just before I touch back down in Atlanta, Jewels... I gave a light chuckle.

Back in The D with my game face on and ready to receive this load Bald Head told me would be arriving a few days prior. Still, with a heavy heart from the night before being stood up by Mena in Baltimore, the loads were coming faster and faster. I was starting to notice that I was being questioned about my whereabouts and my timing with arriving state to state before loads arrived. "I AM" informed me that between the loads, the drivers were different, which is not normal.

Danny started calling me right around similar timing that Bald Head would be contacting me and with different loads. Starting to pay closer attention to this pattern, I was looking for the stamp on the bricks to be different, but they weren't. They all had the crown stamp. The crown stamp would be equivalent to a car or a certain product being made at the same factory. These issues were starting to escalate, and Bald Head and Danny would begin saying nasty things about each other.

I know that Danny went to The Chief to complain about Bald Head circumventing the system that was put in place for the logistics of the loads arriving to me. Whenever loads came from Bald Head via The Chief, there was never anything less than 200 to 250 or more. The loads Danny was authorizing had odd numbers like 90 or 125 bricks of cocaine when they were always even numbers and consistently the same in most cases not that small.

Danny progressively got more and more aggressive when communicating with me over the two-way radio. Paying attention to the inconsistencies in his aggression, at times sounding much more passive, I came to settle on a conclusion. One day he calls, giving instructions and demanding, but the tone was much different on this day, with a certain hubris that was foreign to Danny's voice and personality. I knew at that moment he had someone of authority in front of him, and he was trying to make an impression with the Big Jefe (Boss) maneuver.

What makes this important is that he would be recognized as representation for me in Mexico, giving him the power to negotiate deals on my behalf. It is important to recognize this because deals can be cut on your behalf, and you can be sold, or the contract can be sold with major money exchanged without you knowing anything. The old number you called will be dead. You have just been sold! He wasn't going to pull a Rojo move on me this time, though. Danny's instruction to me was interesting at best.

Danny: We will be there with you with those 125 tomorrow, my friend. Let me tell you something, my friend.

Me: Go ahead.

Danny: You are not to take White from that Bald Head motherfucker anymore, my friend.

I didn't respond to that. I just let him have that moment. This wasn't anything we agreed to, and it appeared that the nature of our relationship changed unbeknownst to me. What I don't think he understood was the maturation of Wayne: There would be no more Rojo deals without wetting my beak. I was prepared to do business directly at the table or away from it: My LOYALTY TAX must be addressed first.

What was evident to me based on Danny's last conversation with me was that he was dealing with a different entity outside of The Chief and Bald Head, but from the same factory. More importantly, the market I developed was of utmost value to Danny, which seemed to be the basis of that two-way radio conversation in the interest of this Phantom gentleman, which I could care less about. I had no understanding with this new gentleman. Danny wanted to keep the money part of their conversation secret.

Those 125 bricks came in as scheduled, and we did what we always do. Just this time, the money would be returned $100,000 short. Danny asked about the $100,000 bucks, and I made him aware that I had an issue that I would fix and deal with those $100,000 later. It wasn't a big issue at all for Danny. He said, "Don't worry yourself, my friend. We will figure it out later." This was, for sure, a different entity that Danny was answering to because The Chief only wants his money once complete, and if there is any issue, the paperwork of that issue must be loaded in the suitcases that contain the balance. The $100,000 just became my secret. My beak was a little dry, I guess.

Beep beep beep....

Bald Head: Go ahead, my friend.

Me: I need to ask you something, my friend.

Bald Head: Tell me, my friend.

Me: I believe I want to come over with The Chief now, my friend.

The feud between Bald Head and Danny is escalating, and they are now making threats of bodily harm towards each other, leaving me in an uncomfortable position. Danny wants me to stop accepting anything from Bald Head, but I remind him that we are partners and have an employer-employee understanding. He expresses concern for his safety and asks me to promise to inform him if Bald Head plans anything against him, which I do. This becomes one of many agreements we make as we face various challenges.

Despite the difficulties, Mena and I are slowly rebuilding our relationship after the heartbreaking incident in Baltimore. She has concerns about my lifestyle and my involvement in the streets. However, she doesn't know the full extent of my activities and the various successful businesses I run. I try to maintain this illusion to keep her safe, but I know that the streets are beginning to talk. We spend more time together, mostly at my place.

The following morning, I want to do something different with Mena . She had expressed interest in legally carrying a gun and going to the gun range. I have a permit to legally carry a gun in Michigan and know a shop owner's son from where I have purchased some of my guns. We visit the shop, and Mena , who is stunning with her curvy figure, light complexion, and large breasts, is impressed when the son greets me warmly by name.

Things were going great between Mena and me, and I wanted to do something a little different with her. Since I had a permit to legally carry guns in Michigan, I took her to a gun range. Mena was impressed by a few of the guns I had and often spoke with me about wanting to legally carry as well as go to the gun range. I knew all about guns and frequented the range often, knowing the owner of the shop quite well. We walked in, and the owner's son greeted me warmly, calling me by name, which impressed Mena .

We had several guns on the counter, and I told her the best one for her that doesn't have too much kick. I proceeded to tell her that we could go to the back so she could squeeze off a few rounds if I wasn't in a rush. As we were looking at the guns, the owner, an older gentleman, came around the corner. His son engaged him in conversation, and I later understood why.

Me: How are you this morning, sir?

Shop Owner: How are you this morning, young lady? What are you looking at there? Totally disregarding my morning greetings.

Mena : I'm kind of confused between these two right here. As she touched the two guns, I started to interject my expertise.

Owner: Yes, I saw you on the surveillance camera in the back. BOY! You were being told a bunch of BULL CRAP out here! With a smirk on his face. Don't you worry your curious soul because I came out here to save your pretty little ear from so much BULL SHIT. Grab this gun right here. How does that feel to you, honey? Giving me a nasty look.

Mena : I don't know. I think this is the right way.

Owner: No, you're holding it the wrong way. The gun is going to fly out of your hands. As he grabbed her hands, repositioning her grip. Now how is that there?

Mena : WOW! That's different there.

Owner: Well, that's because I've never been interested in taking his classes or going to his range. He's not exactly the most welcoming person, if you catch my drift. Plus, I prefer to go to other ranges that have better facilities and more experienced instructors.

Me: Yeah, Mena , don't listen to him. He's just trying to stir up trouble.

Mena : Okay, I trust you. But I'm still interested in taking those classes he mentioned. It sounds like a great opportunity to learn how to defend myself.

Me: Absolutely, we can look into that for you. Just be careful around that old man, he's always trying to pull one over on people.

Mena : Got it. Thanks for looking out for me.

As we walked out of the store, I couldn't help but feel a sense of relief. Despite the awkward encounter with the owner, Mena seemed excited about the prospect of learning how to shoot and defend herself. Maybe this would be the start of a new hobby for us both.

Me: What does he know? Just as he admitted to you, HE IS NEVER THERE! Ironically, that's when I'm there squeezing off mad rounds! I TELL YOU THIS...... I'M TOTALLY DONE WITH THAT PLACE NOW THOUGH!

Barely making it out of that situation, Mena was gracious enough to act like she believed me. Little did I know that I would be receiving a call from Bald Head with a message.

Bald Head: My friend, The Chief wants you to fly down to El Paso. I will pick you up, and we will cross... I told The Chief what you said, and he wants to talk with you face-to-face about this.

I needed to fly out 911 to El Paso. I told Mena that I needed to fly to Maryland on business, and I would return in a few days. She decided to stay at my house while I was gone. I got with "I AM" to tell him I think our big break had come. He drove me to the airport, and we had a new set of two-way radios we would communicate on while I was gone.

Arriving in El Paso, the smell of Mexico filled my nose. Bald Head was there to pick me up, and we headed directly to the border for Mexico. We entered the state of Chihuahua in the city of Juarez. Bald Head drove us to Ciudad Juarez International Airport, and we boarded an Aeromexico flight to only God knows where. I wasn't told, and I didn't feel very comfortable asking either.

This flight made several stops in what appeared to be some rather remote areas. After leaving the international airport in Juarez, this was the real Mexico that you don't see on Telemundo. The plane was landing and taking off on all dirt runways, shocking me but not saying much while looking at the weeds growing in some instances all over the runway. The plane is about half full of people mostly getting off the plane, and no one boarding, really freaking me out even more to the fact that no one even knows where I AM. The pace at which people are getting off this plane, Bald Head and I may be the only two left to onboard.

Bald Head, my acquaintance, informed me that he had to disembark at the next town to attend to some business for The Chief. He assured me that there was no need to worry since the subsequent stop would be my final destination, and some friendly individuals would be waiting for me there to take me to The Chief. Bald Head further reassured me that he would be arriving soon after me.

As I nodded in agreement with his instructions, I couldn't help but think that this was my first time outside of Juarez, and I was being left alone. I had a sinking feeling in my gut.

As expected, I was the only passenger left on the plane. I walked down the stairs and headed towards the lone shack, which appeared to be in the middle of nowhere. There was only one tiny conveyor belt that resembled a dog's door, and it circled outside and came back inside through another dog's door. I noticed a man grabbing my bag from the plane and walking away with it.

In a panic, I muttered to myself, "SHIIIIIIIIIIID!!! HE CAN HAVE THAT FUCKING BAG!" I even turned in the opposite direction to distance myself from it as if it wasn't mine.

Suddenly, a friendly voice caught my attention. "Hola amigo," a man standing by the exit door waved at me. He informed me that he was there to take me to The Chief and gestured towards a car waiting outside. I was relieved to see my bag being put into the trunk. The driver and I sat in the backseat alone, while the other gentlemen hopped into the car behind us. They were probably Sicarios, I thought to myself.

The car ride seemed to last forever. Finally, we arrived at a restaurant in the middle of nowhere, which made me feel even more uneasy. The location was FUCKIN OVA MY DAMN NERVES THO!!

The Sicarios guided me into the restaurant where Bald Head greeted me with a smile, "Don't worry, my friend. The Chief is waiting for you now," he directed me towards a dark-skinned man who stood up from his seat. I recognized him as The Chief, but he sat in the shadows the first time we met, so I couldn't recall all his features. Bald Head advised me not to stare at him, so I avoided looking directly at him.

The Chief spoke in Spanish, and Bald Head translated for us. "Joe told me you wanted to talk about leaving Danny," The Chief said.

I replied, "Yes, Chief, I just want to be able to work and do good business."

"I understand what's troubling you," The Chief said. "Danny has gone to work with my cousin, and he thinks I don't know. Danny brought you over and has control over who you work with. My cousin gave him a job in the factory because of you, my friend. This will do a lot for our factory, or so he thinks."

"Chief, I don't want any trouble," I said. "I really like the way we work together, and I choose who I work with. Danny doesn't have the authority to choose or set prices for me."

"I called Danny, and he knows that you are here now with me," The Chief said. "When I do business, I try to be fair because I don't like secrets and lies. Things don't end well when this happens, my friend. I look forward to working with you. Danny was being paid from everything you did with us, my friend. We will come to another agreement that works for everyone involved."

Me: Danny is my friend, Chief. I don't believe in cutting people out to make business. Unfortunately, I was forced to work with someone outside of our agreement.

During our negotiations, we came to a good understanding of what the future would hold for our business relationship. However, this was only the beginning of pseudo-Jefes trying to profit off my work. They used the so-called American urban concept of loyalty as leverage to blind me from millions being made using my efforts and ingenuity as an asset for their own benefit.

It's important to note that The Chief called me down personally to negotiate with me based on a different understanding we had arrived at. Wanting to ensure that Danny still received something, I left money on the table, which Bald Head was able to slide in and take because I didn't negotiate for it. Money that I should have made the cartel pay was paid by me because I didn't know how to negotiate for myself.

I was taught the American urban street ideology of "never count what's on the next man's desk" by Larry Chambers. He told me that any man who is always looking or counting what you earn is jealous of you and should be considered a serious threat to your life.

These rules saved my life in so many situations and still stand as law, but there is an exception to that rule. Larry Chambers taught me that was my money, and these lessons helped me understand business. We were doing the same thing that Fortune 500 companies do, discussing compensation for actual contracts even though verbal. When I executed those 200 or so kilos of cocaine, it was clear that Danny only wanted 50 kilos of cocaine from the Chief per our initial negotiation. That contract became worth a lot more money, which I didn't understand, and Danny leveraged that contract that I outperformed for more money and political favor with The Chief's cousin.

After a rather event-filled experience, I arrived back in The D. I met with the guys to discuss some of the new adjustments that would need to be made to comply with our new deal. The Chief also made me aware that he would be wanting to increase the quantity of cocaine being shipped out to me. Danny and I spoke shortly after, but interestingly, he never brought up me going down to have a sit-down with The Chief. Neither did he ever speak to me about anything having to do with The D again. He kept his position with what I would come to understand was The Juarez Cartel. It was naïve to believe that all was well. Battle lines were being drawn.

Business in Atlanta was really starting to pick up fast now. Danny and I were still working together in Atlanta and Maryland. We did a few more loads, but things were starting to slow down based on most all factories closing for the holidays. The shutdown really starts to happen in November until February. That would be different if you really had relationships high up in the Cartels, though. That being the case, you can receive your last load in December and be back at it as early as mid to later January. We used that time to party and fuck up some serious bread. I flew a number of our friends in from other states for New Year's. I had on Chinchilla everything too.

I was feeling relaxed and looking forward to the next year, hoping to do things differently once work started again. Bald Head had informed me that The Chief wanted to see me after we completed the first two or three loads. However, that time hadn't come yet, and Mena made me feel like a king once I got home. Sometimes I would mention things I forgot to do or didn't have time for, but she had already taken care of them for me. She completed me in every way possible. One evening, while having dinner together, Mena opened up to me about her thoughts.

Mena : Wayne, you've slept with all of my friends. When I first went out with you, my intention was to teach you a lesson. I didn't like how you could treat women with such disregard. They couldn't handle you mentally, and I could see right through everything you were doing. My goal was to break you down emotionally.

Me: I think your assessment is a bit unfair. I met you years before I even knew any of them, Mena . You turned me down, even after I tried to pay you to take my number. You gave me my money back, even though I told you to keep it to make me feel better. I dated two of your friends, and that's how I ran into you through them. I didn't know you guys were friends, Mena . I treated them well, but their intentions were very different than mine, unfortunately. They didn't really care about me; money was their focus, and they did well for themselves based on their intentions.

Mena : I know this may sound crazy, and I can't believe I'm about to say this, but... I feel, no, I know that they did you wrong. I totally misjudged you. You are one of, if not the only genuine man I have ever met. You have a very good heart, and you really try to help people. You just want to be loved, and the little things that make you happy are some of the most effortless things to provide.

Hearing this brought me to my knees mentally. I had never had anyone who understood me in my life. Losing my mother at 3 years old, I suffered immensely growing up. I always felt like an alien from another planet with an intergalactic culture. Mena 's willingness to reciprocate my efforts and take time to care was something new to me. I never considered myself a drug dealer because they never accepted me. This was the story of my life, constantly being reminded of how different I was from actual existence.

I AM and I arrived in Atlanta to meet up with my friend Woo. Danny was sending a small load up that way. Woo wanted to talk to me about investing in one of his artists, so we headed to Doppler Studio to listen to the artist cut a few records. He wanted to rent out studios A&B, but we had to settle for B&C studios. I was just hanging out with my friends Woo and Keith Thomas. There were also A&Rs from several labels, presidents of Universal, Usher, Kinky B, and producers like Bryan Michael Cox and DJ Polo.

I invited my friend James Terry and his wife Miko to come up and network. They are a songwriting team, and James turned to me and said, "Bro, do you know how much power is up in here right now?!" James was networking while Miko and I were standing in the hallway to the right of the main hallway leading to studio B. Just past me, continuing down the main hall was B. Cox studio, and Usher was in there listening to some records for his album that was rumored to be opening soon.

I saw a very pretty white woman walk into Doppler Studio. She had curves for days, and I was thinking to myself. Suddenly, Usher came by, yelling, "Alicia!!" Miko looked as Usher hugged her tightly and said, "That's Alicia Keys!"

Me: "DAMN I THOUGHT THAT WAS A THICK ASS WHITE GIRL!" as we both laughed!

We continued to catch up because we hadn't seen each other in some time. Usher walked back past us, and Woo yelled to me that he would be right back. Out of the corner of my right eye, I saw someone take a big step out, made a military turn right towards Miko and me, and we both stopped talking, looking in that direction, noticing it was Usher. He took another big step, stopping right in the middle of the hallway between me and Miko as we're looking at him. Then he started physically spinning right between us like a top & VERY FAST, then stopped on a dime still faced forward then walked off.

Me: "The fuck he do that shit for?!"

We both started laughing hard about seeing some shit like that. The shit was funny, but that shit was super impressive! I was telling Miko that I would have hit every damn thing in that hallway & fell at the end for the finale.

After an event-filled night, I met Uncle Sam over at my new place that he was putting together for me. I wanted to follow up on his progress. My new place was called The Rocca, just a 2- or three-minute drive from the Governor's Mansion. I had a place on the top floor of the building. Uncle Sam was showing me the progress made, which wasn't much at all. I heard a knock at the door. I proceeded to answer the door, and it was a small Jewish woman there.

Jewish Lady: Boy this is nice! As she pushes pass me entering the house, talking with a heavy Boston /New York accent.

She introduces herself as my new recently divorced neighbor. Which I would find that my definition of recently divorced and hers differed greatly. Promptly expressing to me that she was a very aware neighbor And wasn't into dealing with any shenanigans on that floor based on her extreme interest in everybody's goings and comings even who with.

The Jewish Lady exclaimed, "This is a very quiet neighborhood. People are very friendly, and many families have been here for generations. It's a wealthy area. You do know your neighbor to your immediate right is a whore She's blonde, wears 6-inch heels, and has a number of interesting gentlemen that she brings in from time to time. I've already reported her to upper management."

I ended up becoming best friends with the Jewish Lady during my time at The Rocca, although it wasn't entirely voluntary. She was always full of life and had the latest gossip. How did I get so lucky? I guess I just had to make the most of it.

I returned to The D to prepare for the first load of 6 coming in soon, according to Bald Head. He also informed me that The Chief wanted to see me after we completed a few loads but no later than the end of February. I was having trouble getting enough work for Atlanta from Danny. I didn't want to push him too hard for more because I knew certain amounts had to be authorized first. This would mean that The Chief would know because it's the same factory and is involved in high-level dealings with the logistics for The Juarez Cartel. I knew that at some point, this could become an issue, given how I knew The Chief could be with wanting everything. This was something he tried to maneuver when I first met him.

Back in The D, we were set to display the lightning speed of the new year. "I AM" needed to fly over to B'More to catch a light load and make sure it got to Slick. I put things in place for him to control that because it was becoming challenging to go over there. I still had a bad taste in my mouth about what had happened over there in the past. Slick could handle that since it was his town.

"I AM" returned to The D only to find us halfway done with that particular load. Bald Head was shipping these loads back-to-back, not even leaving any time for a break in between. It seemed to me that my days of calling the loads in were negotiated away without me knowing. The Chief was in full control and dictated the pace now.

Bald Head: My Friend, The Chief will be moving closer to the border. I'm waiting for you here My Friend.

Me: I will be there with you, My Friend.

I AM met the Semi Truck that came in to pick up two large travel suitcases filled with US currency. Now the money is headed towards the border and it's my turn to start moving towards the border as well. Big I drove me to the airport to catch my flight to El Paso to meet Bald Head and cross the border. We crossed and Bald Head drove for about 45 minutes until we reached a street that was blocked off.

Bald Head spoke to them in Spanish before being allowed to pass. Shortly we pulled up to a house with a lot of armed men outside. The house was walled off from the other homes on the street.

We entered through the gate, and I saw the Chief getting into a five series BMW. The Sicarios opened the doors to Bald Heads truck, while some other men opened the doors on the BMW The Chief was driving. Bald Head told me to sit in the front with The Chief as he got into the back.

There were two cars and two pickup trucks, for a total of five vehicles. The pickup trucks had three guys inside the cab and the back filled with Sicarios. The cars were also loaded. The Chief had a motorcade of bodyguards. The Chief started asking me how's my trip as Bald Head was sitting on the front of the back seat between me and The Chief translating for both of us. The Chief also questioned how was business going? Was the product up to my expectations?? "I couldn't be happier," I expressed. The conversation continued heavily until we arrived at this restaurant.

Bald Head and I followed The Chief into the restaurant, where we were shown to a private room upstairs. The atmosphere was tense, with Sicarios posted at every corner, keeping a watchful eye on our surroundings. The Chief seemed to be in his element, with an air of authority that demanded respect.

As we sat down, The Chief poured us some tequila and proposed a toast. We raised our glasses, and he welcomed me into his inner circle, expressing his confidence in our partnership. He spoke highly of my reputation and the value I brought to the business, acknowledging the growing demand for the product I was delivering.

During the meal, The Chief shared stories of his rise in the cartel, tales of power and influence that both fascinated and intimidated me. He spoke about loyalty, trust, and the consequences of betrayal, making it clear that he expected complete loyalty from his associates.

Bald Head chimed in, telling The Chief about my market expansion and the connections I had made, earning me nods of approval from The Chief. I could sense that I was being vetted, and every word I spoke was being analyzed.

After the meal, The Chief extended an invitation to his private estate, which was situated in the outskirts of Ciudad Juarez. He wanted to show me something, and I accepted, feeling a mix of curiosity and caution.

Arriving at the estate, I was taken aback by its opulence. It was a sprawling compound, complete with luxurious amenities and heavy security. The Chief led me to a room filled with stacks of cash, weapons, and drugs. It was an impressive display of wealth and power, and The Chief made it clear that this was only a glimpse of what he controlled.

He turned to me, his gaze piercing, and said, "You see, my friend, loyalty is everything in this world. I trust you, and you must trust me. Together, we can achieve great success, but betrayal is not an option."

I nodded, understanding the gravity of his words. The message was clear - I had entered a world where trust and loyalty were paramount, and any misstep could be deadly.

After being introduced to the devil, our discussions turned to other matters, and I soon realized that this would become a regular occurrence at the beginning and end of each year. The Chief would lay out his plans for the upcoming year, review the progress made, and strategize for the future.

The Chief inquired, "Are you working with Danny in other places, My Friend?"

I replied, "Yes, Chief. Danny and I are still working together in Atlanta and Baltimore."

He looked at me, shaking his head slightly, as if processing the information with a deep sense of contemplation.

As the night wore on, The Chief's men showed me to my quarters on the estate, and I tried to process everything I had experienced. The weight of the situation settled on my shoulders, and I knew that from this point on, my life and business would be forever intertwined with the dangerous world of the Mexican drug cartel.

Bald Head welcomed me to the table and introduced me to some of The Chief's associates. The table was filled with food, drinks, and laughter. The Chief ordered for everyone, and the food was outstanding. I couldn't help but notice the amount of security present in the restaurant, it was clear The Chief was taking no chances. After the meal, The Chief invited me to his villa for a nightcap. Bald Head followed us to The Chief's villa, and we entered through the back door. The inside of the villa was spacious and elegantly decorated. The Chief offered me a drink and we sat down in the living room. The Chief began to ask me more questions about my business and what my plans were for the future. I kept my answers vague, not wanting to reveal too much information. The Chief seemed satisfied and even offered to introduce me to some of his contacts in Colombia. After a few more drinks, I thanked The Chief for his hospitality and said my goodbyes. Bald Head drove me to my hotel, and I fell into a deep sleep, exhausted from the day's events.

Entering the restaurant parking lot, I observed the perimeter was already secured by Sicarios, not to mention the ones with us. Once inside, we were directed to our area and seated. I sat with The Chief, Bald Head, and Junior, who was The Chief's personal bodyguard that went everywhere with him, even sleeping in the same room while traveling. Junior also controlled The Chief's Sicarios. He spoke very bad English, but it didn't stop him from trying.

We had a serious feast at this restaurant, with them eating clams and squeezing limes on them before eating, almost using lime with everything including beer. I tried ordering myself a Coke but ended up mistakenly asking for cocaine. The Chief asked me about America and how I liked it. After answering his question, I in turn asked him if he would like to visit America one day. He had a good laugh over that question and responded, "No, no, the only interest I have in America is the money!"

During our conversations and laughter, I noticed The Chief suddenly stopped talking and laughing, staring at me with a penetrating gaze, almost looking through my soul. I tried to act as if I didn't notice, but it was becoming hard to do. Everyone stopped talking and laughing too, and The Chief began speaking to me in a serious tone, with Bald Head translating.

The Chief said, "You are more important than you think you are... You are much, much more important than you could even imagine." I felt lost and confused by this statement, looking for reassurance in Bald Head's eyes, but he looked down and away.

The Chief: I need you to promise me this.... Promise me you WILL NOT ever throw me under the bridge. Promise me right now, My Friend. PROMISE!

His stare became more intense and voice slightly elevating. With everyone staring at me waiting for my answer to this VERY INTENSE question.

Me: Chief, I am your soldier and I promise I would NEVER IMAGINE throwing you under the bridge EVER! I PROMISE YOU THIS CHIEF.

.After Bald Heads translation everyone starts to clap, whistle, cheer and laugh .

The Chief: Good. Keep that going, but make sure you prioritize our business over everything else. Remember, you made a promise to me. And I expect you to keep it.

Me: Yes, Chief. I understand. Our business comes first, always.

Bald Head nodded in agreement, and the other men at the table murmured their assent. It was clear that this promise was not to be taken lightly.

The next morning, as I woke up in the lavish quarters provided by The Chief, the weight of my decision weighed heavily on my mind. The reality of the situation hit me like a ton of bricks - I had willingly entered a world where loyalty and betrayal were matters of life and death.

I couldn't shake the feeling of unease in my stomach, knowing that my life now depended on upholding my end of the bargain. There was no turning back; I had committed myself to this path, and there was no escape. This was a realm where contracts were sealed in blood, and any breach of trust could lead to dire consequences.

As I prepared to leave the estate, The Chief's men accompanied me, ensuring my safety, but also silently reminding me of my new reality. The world I once knew had faded into the background, replaced by a dangerous dance of power, money, and loyalty.

Back in Atlanta, I returned to my operations, knowing that I had entered a new chapter of my life - one that demanded a higher level of caution and awareness. Every move I made had to be calculated, and every decision carried immense consequences.

I continued to work closely with Bald Head, navigating the complex dynamics of this new arrangement. The market I had built was now a valuable asset for The Chief, and I used this leverage to protect myself as best I could. But in the world of cartels and power, nothing was certain, and my loyalty would be continually tested.

I remained true to my word and upheld my commitment to The Chief, but I couldn't shake the nagging feeling that I was living on borrowed time. The fine line between trust and betrayal became clearer each day, and I learned to navigate it with caution, treading carefully to avoid attracting unwanted attention.

The success of my operations continued, but I couldn't escape the dark cloud that hung over me - the knowledge that I had entered a world where danger lurked around every corner. I kept my emotions and fears buried deep, as showing any signs of weakness in this ruthless world was not an option.

As I moved forward, I focused on maintaining my integrity and honoring my commitments, knowing that one wrong move could lead to irreparable consequences. The path I had chosen was treacherous, but I had to survive and protect the ones I cared about.

In the heart of this dangerous game, I sought to find some semblance of balance - a way to navigate the blurred lines between loyalty, survival, and the unyielding demands of the cartel world. I was now fully immersed in a world where trust was scarce, and the consequences of my actions had become my constant companion. My life had forever changed, and I had to walk the tightrope, knowing that one misstep could be my last.

As we finished our meal, the conversation shifted to more lighthearted topics. The Chief talked about his family, and I shared stories of my own. We laughed and joked, and for a moment, it felt like any other dinner with friends. But the weight of the promise I had made hung over me, a constant reminder of the dangerous game I had entered.

After dinner, we said our goodbyes and The Chief and his entourage left. Bald Head and I headed back to the border, but not before making a detour to drop off some packages at a safe house. As we drove, I couldn't help but wonder what the future held for me in this world of organized crime. But one thing was certain - I had made a promise, and I would do whatever it took to keep it.

Chief was seeking a closer relationship with me and closely monitoring any other business dealings I had outside of our arrangement. Those days of operating independently were numbered from that day forward. I tried to get Bald Head to explain Chief's request for me to promise not to throw him under the bridge, but he feigned ignorance, and at that point, it didn't seem to matter anymore—I was committed.

Back in The D, "I AM" picked me up from the airport after the long flight. I needed time to think, and I went home to gather my thoughts. The phone rang, and it was Danny.

Me: Yes, go ahead.

Danny: How are you, my friend?

Me: Doing okay, My Friend. How is your wife and the kids, Danny?

Danny: They are fine, My Friend. You know my wife is a crazy bitch, My Friend. My fucking daughter told her I was late to pick her up from school again. I tried to even offer my daughter money to just take it easy. My Friend, can you believe that she would not even negotiate a price. She just kept silent the whole ride. These kids My Friend....... I'm her father and she wouldn't even respect me enough to just negotiate a price. My son is a good kid, we negotiate all the time. My Friend, he has respect!

Me: I guess you are out of the house for a while now, My Friend.

Danny: Yeah. But the money you sent me from Baltimore should be here tomorrow. You know she will let me back in the house when I have money, My Friend.

Me: Well, My Friend, tell those drivers that when they go back to Baltimore next time, my other guy will be there for them.

Danny: I wanted to tell you that I will be sending these guys to you in Atlanta first, then to that other place you just told me about, My Friend.

Me: I'm just waiting for you, My Friend.

Danny: My Friend, I need to ask you a favor.

Me: Tell me, My Friend.

Danny: Promise me that if The Chief ever wants trouble for me, you'll look out for me, My Friend.

I assured Danny that I always have his best interests at heart. I also requested the same favor from him, wondering why all these sudden promises and alliances were cropping up. The dynamics were shifting, and I couldn't help but question the motives behind these new developments.

Danny: They are doing well, thanks for asking. So, how did it go with The Chief? Did everything go smoothly?

Me: Yeah, everything went well. It was an intense meeting, to say the least, but we made it through.

Danny: That's good to hear. Listen, I wanted to talk to you about something. I have a job that I think you might be interested in. It's a big one, but the payoff will be worth it.

Me: Okay, tell me more.

Danny: I can't really discuss it over the phone, but how about we meet up tomorrow and I can give you the details?

Me: Sounds good. Where should we meet?

Danny: Let's meet at our usual spot, the coffee shop on 5th and Main. How does that sound?

Me: Perfect, I'll be there at 10 am.

Danny: Great, see you then.

With that, the call ended, and I sat there thinking about the job Danny had mentioned. I knew it was going to be risky, but the potential payoff was too good to pass up. I had a lot to consider, but for now, I needed some rest. I headed to bed, knowing that tomorrow was going to be another long day.

Danny responded, "My Friend, you don't have to worry about me. I've got your back always. We are in this together." I thanked him for his loyalty and assured him that I would do the same for him. We ended the conversation and I was left with my thoughts once again.

It was becoming clear to me that this business was not just about making money. It was about loyalty, trust, and relationships. I knew I had to be careful and keep my eyes open at all times. But for now, I had work to do. I had to prepare for the arrival of Danny's guys and make sure everything was in order. The next few days were going to be busy, but I was ready for the challenge.

The load that Chief mentioned arrived a few days after my return to the city. Each kilo had a crown stamp on it, making it one of the most sought-after items in the city. The crown stamp is equivalent to the Kellogg's, Delmont, or Nestle stamp on their products. It indicates which factory or cartel in Mexico the kilo came from. This is a clear example of why selling drugs is not only a crime but also a commercial crime. The entire process is called manufacturing.

The streets were starting to buzz with talk about us. As a result, there was a lot of jealousy from other street guys. We heard that we were disrupting the market on the streets. I was selling the bricks to my guys for 18,500 each, while the street price was around 24,500. I believe my guys were selling them for between 20,500 and 21,500. This caused other street groups to complain about not being able to sell their products. I didn't want to put my guys in danger because of a jealous individual. So, I decided to slow down the rate at which we called in the loads to give these guys a window of time to move their products. We were working in several states, so it didn't hurt us at all. At that time, I still had control over the pace at which we moved, but that had been negotiated away from me without my knowledge. I kept note of who the complainers were, just in case strange things started happening. Although we didn't want it to come to that, if it could be avoided, we didn't want to involve the FEDS in any shooting or killing. We wanted to do good business without any unnecessary drama.

The Chief had sent me some very high-quality cocaine which was highly demanded on the streets. The word was that it was "JUMPIN OUT THE GYM," meaning that when cooked, the weight increased greatly. I instructed my guys not to cut the bricks and serve them as they were received from Mexico. However, other crews were getting their hands on our drugs and cutting them, then reselling them. They would then come to us to purchase our uncut cocaine, cut it, compress it into bricks, and rewrap it. Despite the cutting, our drugs were still better than the bricks other guys had.

I could see that this was going to become an issue soon.

Maybe we should add a story about hitting the sting operation and then going to Jay to pick up my jewelry before hitting The Rhino. While in the jewelry store, some hoodlum started talking shit to me about my gun.

We were doing well, with loads coming in hot and heavy. I asked for a break to reorganize our storage capacity and figure out where to store the increasing cash. Bald Head called me with a surprise load that The Chief had instructed him to send. I didn't really believe Bald Head, as his behavior was starting to remind me of Jefe's. Bald Head was attempting to become like Jefe of me already.

When I received the load, I was upset about it.

Bald Head said to me, "My Friend, you need to put together 500,000 and give it to the driver. The driver is still waiting." I asked him under whose authorization this was, knowing that it would upset him, and it did.

Bald Head replied, "What do you mean, My Friend?! I don't need authorization from anyone. I sent this thing to you, My Friend." I told him that I couldn't do it because he didn't have the authorization for it.

Bald Head got angry but tried to control his voice. It was clear that he felt undermined by me, and he was right. I knew that the money he was asking for was more than what the driver would have received, and he was trying to get an advance. He had also been taking liberties and speaking on my behalf with Chief, which made me think he was trying to become my new Danny. I suspected that he may have even told Chief that he convinced me to leave Danny.

I wanted to make Bald Head beholden to me because he clearly knew things, like what happened at that table, but wouldn't tell me. I was starting to understand my worth, and I knew he wanted to stay in the loop with me because it gave him power, among other things. After this fight, he would need to be of value to me as well as Chief.

"All Mexicans are greedy," as Baby Doll once told me. After going back and forth in intense disagreement, Bald Head told me in a somewhat threatening tone, "My Friend, you really need to get those 500,000 to that driver."

This was a dangerous gamble I was taking, but I deeply believed that Chief would see through Bald Head's maneuver and give me the upper hand. Bald Head was playing into my hand, and my money was on him not being smart enough to see what I was doing to him.

Me: "I REALLY need to get those 500,000 to the Driver?! Like I said, I'm sorry for you, My Friend. I have not completed this thing here and I feel REALLY sorry for you!"

Bald Head was very upset, but he didn't respond to my last comment. There was about 10 minutes that passed...... Beep Beep Beep.......

Junior (Chief's Main Bodyguard and translator in important times to communicate with me):

Me: Yes, go ahead.

Junior: This is Junior calling for the Chief, My Friend. The Chief is here listening to you now.

Me: Okay, My Friend. Hola, Chief!

Junior: The Chief says, "that he is not happy with you for lying. He wants to remind you that he DOESN'T like liars, My Friend."

Me: Junior, did you say "lying," Junior?? Junior's English is the worst.

Junior: Yes, The Chief said, "he does not like liars," My Friend.

Me: Junior, I don't lie! I don't ever lie....... Who did I lie to, Junior?! My voice was showing shock, confusion, and insult. Chief, I don't understand? I have never lied...... I don't ever lie, even if it could harm to tell the truth! There was a pause for a moment. Chief.......

Junior: The Chief is here, My Friend. The Chief says that he didn't mean "lie," that was the wrong word. (The Chief is seeing that something wasn't right by the way I responded. Therefore, he changed his approach sensing something wasn't right.) The Chief said, Bald Head called him. What happened with you and Bald Head?

Me: Chief, Bald Head told me to give this guy up here with me now (The Driver) 500,000. I told him that he doesn't have authorization.

Chief, you told me to not send any money not completed again Chief. Chief, this Bald Head guy tries to talk to me like he is my Jefe (Boss). This guy is not my Jefe. You are my Jefe. I only have one Jefe, and that's you, Chief. My Jefe told me to never send anything not complete, so I told him I feel sorry for him, for those 500,000.

Junior: The Chief has a big smile, My Friend. The Chief said, "You are right," My Friend. He said, "He should have called to give you authorization for those 500,000.

Yeah, yeah, I was brown-nosing right there, while creating a little drama to make it interesting. This went well while putting Bald Head on notice: I'm no longer Pussy, I'm looking to fuck.

Me: I'm sending my guy to see this guy with those 500,000 right now, Chief.

Junior: The Chief thanks you, My Friend.

I AM went out to meet the driver and gave him the 500,000 that Chief instructed me to deliver. Shortly after that experience, we turned on money, and from that load, things had progressed to the point that I needed to get permission to travel or even have a break. The response would always be, "Ah, I don't know, My Friend. I think we will be there with you soon," which sometimes was the case, but oftentimes it was just to have me in place purely for convenience, just in case.

This time I decided not to ask; I just took off for Atlanta. I AM and I arrived in Atlanta with another load from Danny not far away. Keith, Woo, and myself went down to Atlantic Station to have something to eat and discuss business. We walked into a restaurant (I can't remember the name of the restaurant). Woo made the comment while looking towards the bar, "Oh my God, Candy has a big ass on her!" Looking in that direction, I was very impressed with her posterior myself. Plus, she has always been a very nice-looking woman to me anyway. Being perfectly honest, I would have loved to take my shot at her that night, but Woo told me, "You may have a chance because she loves D-Boy's," with a laugh.

We got down to business and had an extensive conversation about the music industry, specifically the money that can be made from publishing. Woo suggested forming a company, and Keith came up with the name BE-LY publishing, which stood for beats and lyrics, reflecting the creation of songs. Our plan was to sign artists and acquire the legal portion of their publishing in exchange for a certain amount of proceeds upfront. We had a list of potential artists, including Writer Robbie of One Chance, producer Mad Scientist, Rock City, producer Pretty Boi, production team Outsyders, writer Kamaya , among others. We agreed in principle that night and planned to revisit the subject in detail later, targeting whom we would sign first.

We finished the load that Danny sent to Atlanta within two days of its arrival. Woo was upset that the amount of work brought wasn't enough and didn't last for more than 24 hours after arriving. However, I couldn't explain to him the real situation and the potential issues that could arise from it. I knew that the amount of work Danny was bringing could increase significantly, but I also knew that if it did, The Chief would want a cut of it. Bald Head called, attempting to make amends after our little argument.

Bald Head: MY FRIEEEEEEND!! HOW ARE YOU DOIN MY FRIEND! (Bald Head's smile can be heard through the two-way radio). My friend, I think I should tell you something, but please don't tell the Chief that I told you this. The Chief is starting to get mad at you, my friend. He says that your money is starting to always be short when you send it, my friend. He said that it was very small amounts, but it is starting to grow little by little, my friend.

Me: That can't be, my friend! This must be those guys counting for you over there.

Bald Head: I don't know, my friend. I'm just calling to tell you that there is a problem with the Chief. Let me tell you something.

Me: Tell me.

Bald Head: Don't say to the Chief when he calls, "It is probably those guys, my friend." That would be VERY BAD. You can say whatever you want to me, my friend, because you know I won't say anything. Just don't say that thing to the Chief, please, my friend. Just tell him you didn't know and thank him for telling you. Say that you will look into it.

found it very interesting that Bald Head was now warning me about Chief's growing dissatisfaction with my money transfers. He assured me that my secrets were safe with him and that he would never tell on me. It seemed like lying about the missing $500,000 was a nicer alternative than actually telling on me. Junior called me just as he had warned me he would, and I repeated what he told me to say, which calmed everything down. I asked Chief how much I needed to repay, and he told me it wasn't anything significant, but it was slowly starting to increase. At the time, I didn't catch on to what he was trying to tell me. What I didn't know was that this wouldn't be the last time I would have this issue.

Bald Head's warning really helped me out. I wouldn't have been prepared for that call without the heads up from him. After our pissing contest didn't turn out how he had intended, he must have observed something that he had seen before but didn't like the outcome. He wanted to form an alliance of some kind, or so it appeared.

I spoke with my friend "The Jewelry Lady" about an opportunity that she thought I might be interested in. She asked, "You want to make a quick 100,000?" I told her I wasn't really interested, but asked what she had going on anyway. She informed me that there was a demand for my car (a new 2006 S550 Benz) in South Africa. If I gave her my car to put on a container as soon as it undocks, she would give me $100,000 for it. I understood what she was doing. She wanted to show me that she could create profitable situations for me while still testing me out. It was clear that she wanted to ally with me and the different teams I worked with. I was starting to become interested in a possible relationship with her, but she was clearly way over my head in a lot of different areas. The woman had serious money. To be honest, I was intimidated by her, but also impressed at the same time.

Beep beep beep.

Bald Head's warning about Chief knowing my location in Atlanta came as a shock. It became clear that Chief had someone spying on Danny and his cousin, which explained how Chief knew when I received work from Danny. When Chief asked if I was "still working with Danny," I confirmed and disclosed their work location as well. Bald Head advised me to leave soon since Chief had just crossed what he needed to send for them.

CHAPTER 23

VINCENTE CARRILLO FUENTES

I AM AND I quickly got on the freeway and headed back to Detroit 911. We didn't have much time according to Bald Head's instructions. The loads being sent by The Chief were getting bigger and more frequent, which was confusing to me. I couldn't understand why he was increasing the pace and quantity so much. It soon became apparent that the Chief didn't want his cousin or Danny to receive any credit for the labor of me or any of my affiliates in Atlanta or Baltimore. I later found out why this was such a big issue for him. Chief had a significant amount of power in The Juarez Cartel, just below the actual boss Vincente Carrillo Fuentes. He would have known about anything leaving Mexico from The Juarez Cartel, and his authorization would be necessary. I realized that the Chief would not have allowed Danny and his cousin to ship anything to me in Baltimore or Atlanta without his authorization. My guess was that the authorization had to come directly from the boss himself.

As I was lost in thought, my two-way radio beeped.

Bald Head: my friend, you have a very big problem again. Chief is so angry the money is not right again but this time it's more the usual missing my friend. Don't say nothing that I told you please, my friend. You must do something to fix this my friend. This is becoming very bad, especially right now.

Me: This is a lie my friend. I know everything has been right every time since you told me that Junior was going to call me for the Chief to talk to me. I swear this is not true My Friend.

Me: Okay, Bald Head, I understand. I will take care of it. Can you tell me what the specific issue is so that I can address it?

Bald Head: My friend, I don't know the details of the issue, but Chief is saying that the money is not right, and it's more than the usual missing. You need to figure out what's going on and fix it before it becomes a bigger problem.

Me: Alright, I will try to get to the bottom of this and make sure everything is sorted out. Thank you for letting me know, Bald Head.

Bald Head: No problem, my friend. Just be careful, and remember that Chief is very powerful. You don't want to cross him or make him angry. Good luck, my friend.

Beep beep beep.

I was already dealing with so many concerns, and the money shortage couldn't have been on my end. I had previous experiences with my brother Big Dawg and drivers stealing money before it was turned in, leaving him responsible for the missing funds. He couldn't prove that he initially paid, and he didn't argue the point. I never understood why he didn't, unless he was in on it, which may have been the case. Nevertheless, I wasn't involved in any theft, and my motto was to pay what I owed.

What was clear to me was that I was dealing with a sophisticated underworld business organization, and they operated like any other legitimate business. So, I had to ask I AM to recount all the money before we handed it over to the driver for transport. I didn't have a lot of time to deal with trying to smoke out whoever may have been taking the money. I was still in disbelief, thinking that it was either the driver or someone in the cartel.

However, my mistake was thinking that I was being blamed personally, which wasn't true. The message they were trying to send was different, and I would find out shortly. But until then, I had to inform the counters that I was aware that the money wasn't always correct and to be more conscious when counting.

Another issue of great concern at the time was that the work wasn't moving at the same pace as before. This put me in an uncomfortable position since The Chief knew my pace and was sending loads without asking if I was prepared. At this point, there was nothing I could do, and I turned to one of my close friends, Moe Green, for help. He was like a brother to me, and I asked him to put his ear to the street and find out what the numbers on the street were for the work. There was no reason for our pace to change without a valid reason. The only reasons for a slowdown would be limited supply, price, or price fluctuations. However, the streets didn't seem to be flooded with product, and no one was heavier than our team, PERIOD!

Asking someone to do what I asked of Moe Green required a very high level of trust. It was essential to do a price check, just like any franchise or major department chain would do. I asked Moe Green to check when it was important to me, and I would make decisions to raise or drop the price based on his word. Moe Green came back and told me that everyone out in the street had our price, and in some cases, it was lower than ours by $500. I immediately dropped the price by $1000 from 18.5 to 17.5 for my guys so they could remain competitive.

Although the pace picked up a little, it wasn't enough to shake a stick at, which still had me confused. I was in a quagmire because my pace slowing down would seem suspicious across the border. This could put me in a lot of danger because the chief would start to think I was taking other loads up in Detroit from his cousin and Danny. I was compensating out of my pocket, with the help of friends at times, putting a million to 1.5 million with what I had on the truck to send back to Mexico. I would receive another load but still would not have my money back out before I had more work and a fresh bill.

It became clear that the chief did not want me back down in Atlanta for good reason. But if he suspected I was taking shipments from his cousin and Danny, he would believe his boss Fuentes was giving the authorization without his knowledge to send them to me up in Detroit. I learned that situations like this created a death sentence for him because the revenue he brought in could be covered, making him expendable. That would make me a serious threat to his life.

One day, I AM pulled me to the side and told me why things were so slow. It had nothing to do with the original price of 18.5 that I was charging our guys, not including or even considering what they charged on the street or to their crews. Come to find out, the reason things were moving slow was that they were being greedy and colluded together without my knowledge to start selling at the actual market price of 24 to 24.5, which was $2000 higher than what they were originally at, 22 to 22.5.

Moe Green lied to me about a phantom group having a cheaper price than us. Unfortunately, when I dropped $1000 on them, they didn't even have enough sense to pass on the savings. This really shocked me, but I had to see that these guys really had no idea the danger they were putting me in, and that I needed to put rules in place for more control over these guys.

I called a meeting and gave all those fuckers a talking to. Letting them know that I knew the bullshit they were pulling on me, and that they had an agreement amongst themselves, which made it clear they could care less about the well-being of the collective or me. I told them that I had a good mind to go to Atlanta or Baltimore and stay gone for a few months to teach them a lesson. I told them that I would cut them all off without them even knowing they were cut off by just disappearing, allowing the city to dry up.

I told Moe Green that he violated my trust for what was equivalent to nothing. I set the price for the street at 18.5 and not a dime over. I would leave their number at 17.5, where they could make $1000 off every brick they sold. I would also give each guy 50 bricks apiece once the loads arrived. The rest would sit until the first guy comes in with the completed ticket for his 50 bricks, then he would have access to the rest of the bricks sitting, which would often be 100-250 sitting. No one else would have access to the extra bricks until he completed his ticket of the complete 50 bricks. Then he could join in on getting rid of the extras.

Just in case there was someone that still had some of his original 50, and everything was done, including the extras, the whole team could pull from whatever that one person had left of those fifty. The first time you get caught not done, whatever guy took of your original 50, you wouldn't make the full $1000 of each one, he was only obligated to give you $500 of that $1000.

When the load came back in and you had a bag that was cut down by 15 bricks to 35 bricks, you still ended up holding after you got cut down. Then you don't need to be on the A team; you would get moved to the B or C team.

Prices would go up, and the quality would come down if anyone broke anything down until ALL money for everything was in to I AM. Breaking the bricks down into smaller increments slows down the speed and increases the number of people that my guys are in contact with, which leads to law enforcement. Anyone that needs to buy smaller increments is either dealing in crack or supplying someone that deals in crack. The crack dealer always makes the most money, but he's also on the frontline, which makes him the initial informant for Law

Enforcement looking to get a hold to try and flip people up the food chain to the bigger fish. I also put a stop to anyone sending drugs out of town just to sell for more money. If you can't get it in town, then you don't need it.

I created a farm system to develop new talent. Once all the money was in and loaded on the truck gone, I would have a few bricks left that I would let guys break up and feed some promising guys that I felt had the ability to grow. This was a system set up to expose my guys since it was clear that I had to insulate myself and become collude proof against greed and a form of unionization."

I learned a valuable lesson that was scary, to say the least. I was receiving a crash course in the international drug trafficking business and had to adjust on the fly while being vulnerable from so many angles. It was extremely difficult to keep myself out of harm's way as my life could be in danger for the simplest concerns. The American urban concept and arrogance left me hopeless in my efforts to have these guys understand. I didn't have a reference point to teach from on the subject. I had very seasoned hustlers, and the hubris of exceptionalism was my issue. Needing to become a dictator was the only way this could be done, and that was clearly not the way I wanted to do business. It sucks to be me!

A small break finally came, which was well-needed. I had to find a way to address a number of issues with my guys. A system needed to be put in place that would allow me to be aware of what my guys were always doing. Bald Head actually called me this time with instructions from the Chief not to leave The D.

Bald Head said, "I know you want to get out of there for a break, my friend. The Chief is having some big meetings and will be leaving town. If you want to leave, I won't say anything, and I will give you a warning when Chief gets ready to cross something like last time, my friend."

Bald Head didn't have to tell me twice! Sam and I hit the road for Atlanta. I had a meeting with Woo and Keith concerning the incorporation of Be-Ly publishing.

We arrived in Atlanta and got straight to business. Woo, Keith, and I met with Monica Ewing to finalize the paperwork for Be-Ly Publishing (Beats & Lyrics Publishing). We also had a meeting with a producer and a writer to decide whom we wanted to target first. After about a week of making good progress, I received a call from Bald Head.

Bald Head: The Chief wants to see you, My Friend.

Me: What's wrong, My Friend?!

Bald Head: Chief said he needs to see you right away, My Friend.

He had an official tone, so I knew there was no need to ask him any questions. I expressed my concern about crossing the border frequently and how it would look if my name kept showing up there since I'm from Michigan. I didn't give him a date for when I would be down there.

Bald Head: My Friend, you have to tell me something because they keep calling me, asking if I've talked to you. I keep telling them that I'm having problems contacting you and just give me a chance. I'm calling you now because The Chief just called personally, My Friend. I told him the same, so he will be calling you soon. Don't tell him that you talked to me, please, My Friend.

I assured him that I wouldn't do anything to compromise our relationship. Bald Head advised me on what to say, but he also stressed that some major changes were coming. And then, the call ended.

Me: Yes, go head

Junior: My Friend, you talk to this guy......Bald Head?

Me: No no, My Friend. I barely just charge my radio. This battery is no good My Friend.

Junior called me on the radio to translate for The Chief. I pretended not to know Bald Head, but when I tried to explain my reluctance to cross the border so often, it didn't work. Junior relayed The Chief's understanding and appreciation for our business, but he couldn't promise that things would be different.

I asked for a few days' notice before heading down to the border, and The Chief agreed. I didn't want to leave any flight records, so I drove straight there from Atlanta. I still had a lot of questions and concerns, but I knew I had to face whatever was coming.

Bald Head and I landed and arrived at a restaurant called The Montana where we met Chief, Junior, and some other gentlemen I didn't know. Chief hugged me with a big smile on his face and told me that some changes were coming and that he needed me to be on my A-game for the next few months. He explained that the money shortage issue in the past would stop for some time but start again with slightly higher amounts each time. Chief warned me about upcoming changes that might confuse me, and he needed me to trust him and keep doing well.

Although I didn't understand his language, I could sense the urgency in his tone. I realized that we had some strange connection, which he recognized before I did. I agreed to everything he said, and since he was asking for a lot, I thought it was a great opportunity to ask for something that never happens. I asked the Chief if I could have an extra load after the shutdown in late November for a favor.

Chief replied with a big smile, "Don't worry, my friend." It was my kind of meeting, quick and efficient. However, I didn't understand why the Chief couldn't have said everything over the radio. It became clear after I returned to The D.

Chief asked me if I was still working with Danny, and I replied, "Yes, Chief, we are still working together in Atlanta and Baltimore." Chief warned me to be careful with Danny as he was causing problems he shouldn't be in.

We embraced as Bald Head and I headed for the door. Didn't take long to get to the border but the wait to cross was like forever. After crossing, Bald Head confided in me that Chief had told him to find a guy working with Danny on the U.S. side of the border and tell him not to help Danny with stopping his loads from crossing. The Chief told me to take a screwdriver and stab him in his ass cheeks three or four times with it, so every time he tried to sit down, he would remember what Chief said.

Bald Head told me that he wasn't always with Chief, and that Chief killed his boss and almost everyone in their whole group. After Chief killed everyone, Bald Head was told that he worked for Chief now. He quickly added that the Chief is a very good man, even better than his previous boss.

Bald Head took me to a hotel to stay overnight in El Paso and catch a flight out the next morning. Before we parted ways, he made me promise to tell him if I knew or heard about any harm coming to him, and he promised the same to me. It seemed like everyone around Chief needed some kind of life insurance or advanced warning.

After touching down in The D, I quickly received the work and we got to work with our signature Lightning Speed. We turned in all the money and waited for the next move. I was surprised that we were on hold for a minute since I had already gotten the guys ready to steamroll through 600 to 700 within that month. I messaged "I AM" to see if we could run off to Atlanta quickly. I planned to call BaldHead on the two-way the following day to see if anything had already crossed or to give me a heads up before they crossed something so I could get back before the truck arrived in town.

I arrived at Novara, which was Loc Boc's house and where I would stay whenever I came into the city. As part of my normal routine, we were working in case of emergencies, just in case I needed to make any critical decisions. Suddenly, I heard a beep from my phone.

Me: Go ahead.

I AM: Yo, I know this is a crazy question, but did something come in for us??

Me: Did you hit a truck that I didn't know about or something? (I responded sarcastically but was confused by the question.)

I AM: Naw, that's why I asked, just in case you knew something I didn't. You know you don't tell me everything, Brian. Moe Green and BIG I hit me up asking me this crazy question. The issue is that guys on their teams are saying that their people are calling them, complaining about our bricks?!

Me: That's impossible because we are on hold right now... with a VERY PUZZLED SOUND.

I AM: YEAH, I KNOW, but their guys let them see the work they brought, and it has the same stamps and wrapping. However, the work looks different.

Me: Tell them niggas to put their ear to the street, then run into me and you on The Novara Street in a couple of hours. I need you to 911 this way, though. I AM pulled up on me shortly after our conversation. We put our heads together but came up with nothing. The team pulled up on Novara: Moe Green, BIG I, Mack, Loc Boc, and The Bone. Moe Green, BIG I, and Mack were my kingmakers. Loc Boc and The Bone handled my farm system, developing guys while being my eyes and ears on my Kingmakers.

After hearing everyone's input about the issue with knock-off bricks using our Crown stamp, we suspected that someone may have duplicated it and used it on their work. However, we were still puzzled as to how they had the same wrapping as us. The city was flooded with these fake bricks, making it difficult to narrow down where they were coming from.

I had to calm my team down and remind them that finding out who did it was impossible, as it could lead to unnecessary violence and retribution. I also knew that we were making enemies because of our success in the business, which could lead to envy and jealousy from rival teams.

I had to assess the situation and determine if we needed to reinforce our defenses against potential threats. However, I still couldn't explain why the knock-off bricks had the exact same stamp and wrapping as ours.

Bald Head contacted me, and we had work to do in town in a couple of days. I didn't want to mention anything to him about the situation, as I didn't want to alarm anyone and risk attracting unwanted attention from our enemies. Instead, I decided to investigate further and gather more information before taking any action.

Faced with a slow-moving issue, I realized I had to explain the situation to The Chief, or he may think I'm involved with Danny and his cousin. However, I was hesitant to do so, as I couldn't be sure if this was Danny's work. I would usually call Danny for advice, but this time I needed to handle things myself.

Then, Bald Head called me, and I explained the situation to him. He was silent for a moment before advising me to call The Chief.

Me: "I need your help, My Friend. I think someone up here has duplicated our Crown Stamp. The city is filled with this stuff, and it's very bad. This has guys afraid to buy now without wanting to finger fuck them first. Everyone knows now that our stuff is still the real one, but that brought A LOT of the fake one, which is no good, My Friend..."

Bald Head: Silence

Me: "My Friend?!"

Bald Head: "My Friend... I think you need to call The Chief."

Bald Head had hinted that something was going on, but he couldn't tell me directly. When I called Junior and explained the situation to him, he reassured me that everything was fine and that it was just a matter of the t-shirts. They were being made at the same factory as our Crown Stamp, which was causing confusion in the streets.

My emotions got the best of me, and I went crazy on the two-way radio, berating Junior for why they would ruin the market I created for that brand. I showed my entire frustration on that radio. Then the radio opened, meaning someone held the button to speak but didn't say anything. The button was held again, and I heard The Chief's voice in Spanish. His tone was usually happy sounding, but this time it was different. Then Junior's voice came across the two-way radio translating what The Chief said.

Junior: I DIDN'T DO IT TO YOU... SO WHY ARE YOU SO CONCERNED?

This question is a perfect representation of the different sides of this business. There is a clear and always present gray area that appears suddenly, and life and death are the reflection of what you choose. The ambiguous nature of this question, the tone of voice while delivering it, even though it was in Spanish... It was clear that this was not a question, and no answer to Chief's ambiguous question was the only answer.

I remained silent, which was clear in my mind that this was the only course of action that could be taken. The market that I had established in this market, making The Crown a trust brand that consistently performed taking the guesswork of mistrust when it came to quality, out of the equation. The Crown stamp on The Bricks of Cocaine became as your Jordan shoes of today on the market that consistently leave the consumer of today TRYING TO WIN THE OPPORTUNITY TO PUR-

CHASE, versus the arrogance of the value of their buying power & what it historically provides.

The Urban Businessman's goal is to achieve the so-called," PLUG OR CONNECT." Depending on the level of," THE PLUG or CONNECT," is equivalent to Michael Jordan negotiating a shoe deal from The Nike Brand. The courtship and negotiation process in principle are the same, REALLY. When the deal is agreed to, Jordan becomes an asset of The Nike Shoe Brand. Nike is "THE BRAND," not Jordan....... The actual power lay with The Brand Creator, NOT THE ASSET, which in this example is Michael Jordan. Now Jordan out performs the expectations of his contract, which raises the overall value of The Nike Brand. Jordan as an asset of The Nike Brand opened different markets that were not available to that Brand prior to acquiring him as an asset. The performance of this now enormously powerful asset, The Nike Brand Leveraged this newfound leverage into many languages and cultures worldwide. Giving secondary power to a behemoth of a secondary resell market via Stock X and Goat etc. of Nike Brand shoes bearing the name of that brand's most powerful asset posts his career, bearing his name: Jordan.

These business principles remain the same, regardless of the commodity at the center of the exchange. However, I had underestimated the power and influence of The Juarez Cartel, particularly as The Brand Creator.

The Chief, representing The Brand, offered me a direct deal as an Urban Businessman, a rare and unprecedented opportunity for a Black man at that time. I exceeded the expectations set in our agreement and successfully established The Juarez Cartel brand in my market. I created a highly influential secondary resale market, with its reach extending throughout Michigan and even into the main hub of Chicago. Unbeknownst to me, The Chief capitalized on this success by leveraging our agreement and the market I created, positioning it as a valuable asset for The Juarez Cartel. He then made a move to connect with another more powerful cartel, The Sinaloa Cartel, and its leader, The OL Man Mayo, who hailed from the state of Durango, just like The Chief.

It became clear to me who was in control of all activity, and that I would need to trust The Chief's plan. Moving forward, I knew no one was going to hold my hand, and I had to catch on to indications as they became clear in real time.

It took some time to get rid of the first load of bricks, but after completing it, I immediately received another load stamped with the Ferrari symbol. From that point on, I never saw another Crown brick again. I realized that the stamp on these t-shirts was from a different factory. The Chief had used the leverage I created to negotiate a much more lucrative deal with The Sinaloa Cartel, destroying the market I had created for The Juarez Cartel and their assets. This maneuver gave me more power and credibility in my market, but Danny and his cousin would not be able to return. The Chief was sending the loads in fast, and I was responsible for returning 3 to 4 million dollars at a time. The work was becoming taxing on my stress levels, and I couldn't afford to make any mistakes with that kind of money.

There is no calling The Chief after a loss with the complaint that" I'm just having a bad day....You do not have bad days with money like that because those kinds of mistakes are fatal.

Mena became even more valuable to me because she treated me so well. It seemed like whenever I came home and saw her, all my stress disappeared throughout my whole body. She was starting to feel like she wanted more from me now.

Mena : Wayne, I was thinking about you and Honey's friendship. I am not comfortable with this anymore. We have been seeing each other for some time now. This is really feeling like it could work out for us, Wayne.

Me: Wow... with a huge smile on my face.

Mena : I am just going to go out to lunch with Honey tomorrow and I'm just going to tell her that we are together. I refuse to keep sneaking around hoping no one sees us together. She did not know what she had, and it sucks to be her right now.

Me: Are you sure you want to do this?? (I was so sooooo happy, but this was the wrong thing to say.)

Mena : Yes, Wayne....... I'm not going to be playing any games with that bitch when it comes to you. If she messes with me, calls you or gets in your face, I'm going to beat her ass. I will make that very clear to her too.

Me: Mena , you have been friends since you were little girls, and I don't think you should resort to fighting over a guy.

Unfortunately, what I did next ended up being a fatal mistake. My intentions were pure, as I simply didn't want my girlfriend getting into any fights over something that wasn't even her concern. But my judgment was off, and it didn't come across the way I intended. I was never good at expressing my emotions accurately, even when I meant well. Mena thought I wasn't serious, but I truly was.

My lifestyle consumed me, and I was always trying to anticipate threats from the streets, the border, the DEA, and those close to me. It's painful to admit, but I didn't have enough mental capacity left to anticipate my own problems and desires.

The money I was making was becoming an issue, too. I had too much of it and nowhere to put it. Just then, my phone beeped.

Moe Green: "Hey, homie. Can you swing by my mom's house real quick?"

Me: "Are you okay?" (concerned)

Moe Green: "Yeah, everything's good, homie. Just need a quick favor."

I arrived at Corbett Street on the eastside of Detroit and saw Moe Green standing out front with Weezy, who was part of another hustling team on the east side. They were also getting a bag out of Chicago. Weezy had asked Moe Green if he could hold fifty bricks overnight because he had some buyers coming into town, but Moe Green told him he needed to get the okay directly from me.

I usually worked through my network to avoid getting caught on the tail end of someone else's indictment, but Weezy was someone I knew from growing up with Moe Green and his family. He had worked hard to earn his success.

The exchange was interesting because Moe Green would ask me a question in front of Weezy, then he would tell Weezy what I said even though he heard me say it. Weezy would then ask Moe Green a question about what he just told him, and Moe Green would turn to me to ask me what Weezy said, even though I had heard the question when Weezy asked it.

Moe Green: Yo, Homie, Weezy is asking me to front him fifty of those thangs until tomorrow around this time. I told him that I would have to ask you, but he thinks I'm just stalling him out.

Me: Are you sure he'll be all the way in by tomorrow, Moe Green?

Moe Green: Nigga, are you sure you're going to be all the way in by tomorrow, AssHole? You thought I was on the bullshit, but now you see.

Weezy: Yeah, I'll have about twenty of them gone in a couple of hours, and I'll run back into you with that. I have the other guy coming in in the wee hours of the night for the other thirty. I'll be on your head first thing. What are you going to let me see them at, though, Mo?

Moe Green: He said he may not need all that time, but this time tomorrow to be sure. What's the number on that going to be, though? I'm okay with him seeing it at my number too, Homie.

Me: You good with him at your number?

Moe Green: Yeah, because this nigga thinks I'm lying to his ass about the number I'm seeing them at, so I want his ass to see I ain't lying to him.

Me: Well, 17.5 is good with me, but don't come to me asking for shit later because you gave yours away, fat-ass nigga!

Moe Green: Weezy, did you hear that shit, nigga? I told you that was my number, and you also heard the nigga tell me not to come at him for shit later too. You're gonna have to look out, nigga.

Weezy: Whatever, nigga! Charge that shit to the game! Ima knock that shit off that ticket when you jacked me way back when. Bitch, I thought you were lying about seeing them at that number, though! My guy ain't letting me see them at nothing near that fucking number. Dude's letting me see them at 22.5 to 23, Moe Green

I sped off while they talked, but he was clearly irate about this. But he would find out soon enough the reason. The end of 2006 was rapidly approaching, and the yearly slowdown was starting to come in while everyone started to cross to enjoy the Christmas holiday season. We had some breathing room to sneak off to the south, and that we did. We got a chance to get with my guys and start signing some artists to Be-Ly Publishing. Got with Woo and Keith Thomas to work on who we would sign first out of all our options. I was doing this whole venture because my dude Woo wanted to make it happen. I didn't know shit about this kind of stuff at all. I loved music and always have been a fan of the whole creation process. Our opinions varied on whom we would sign first.

Woo, Keith, and I were heavily involved in the music scene. While I strongly believed in the talent of The OutSyders, Woo and Keith felt that they needed some development. However, I was a huge fan of their music, and after some back and forth, Woo and Keith agreed to my gut feeling. Our next step was to provide them with a workspace to create music as per our contractual agreement. We were informed by Woo that Kinky B of CTE had informed him about Jeezy selling his house in Alpharetta, which had a full studio that came with it, making it an ideal place to work. Woo convinced Keith to purchase the house from Jeezy, and we were set to go.

Woo had several R&B groups with projects that were open at the time. The plan was to cut records for these artists at the house and then bill the labels for the studio time. He also had a producer named Sounds and a roster of other talented individuals he was developing, including One Chance and Sounds, who were signed to US Records, owned by Usher Raymond, through Keith Thomas's efforts as an A&R for US Records. Ray Raney, a female group, was signed to Def Jam Records, and Woo's most valuable talent, Tamela, had the voice of an angel.

Keith Thomas was an A&R for US Records and best known as Usher Raymond's best friend. Keith and Usher came into the industry together as noticeably young teenagers, and Keith was exceptionally talented with music and had an ear for hit records. He had an artist/producer named Pretty Boi Fresh.

I think it should be clear by now that I received another load while I was in town, and it turned out to be the last one for the year down in Atlanta.

Finally, Uncle Sam completed work on my place at The Rocca in Atlanta. I was excited to have my own place there instead of staying in hotels every time I visited. I was starting to develop a fondness for the city, and I learned that Keith was quite the party animal. While I was in Atlanta with I AM, we managed to accomplish a lot, but the volume of work coming in was becoming overwhelming, and Woo was putting pressure on me to address it.

Back in Detroit, I was preparing to receive the last loads of the year. The Chief had promised me one load in December, which was crucial because there is always a drought during this time. Prices skyrocket, and buyers are desperate due to the holidays and the shutdown of all drug factories across the border for observance. We had a few loads that came in just before Thanksgiving and two more at the beginning of December, and this would mark the end until the following year.

Successfully completing these loads and receiving the extra load in December as promised by The Chief, I was quite satisfied. I could now put my pirate patch over my eye during the drought and take advantage of higher prices.

Beep Beep.

Me: Go ahead My friend.

Bald Head: My Friend the Chief has a very big gift he saved for you, My Friend!

Me: Tell Me My Friend??!

Bald Head: The Chief just told me to send you one more so you can have a very nice Christmas. This is a gift from The Chief only for you, My Friend!

Me: Are you sure because Christmas is only like 5 or 6 days away when you make it here to me, My Friend.

Bald Head: yes, I know My Friend. That's why The Chief needs to be done faster for favor, My Friend. This is what The Chief tells me to say to you.

Me: Okay I wait for you, My Friend.

The truck was already on his way. Bald Head was talking to me concerning the shipment. As normal we unloaded the truck, but this would be a little different. I did something a little different I made an offer to my very special customers, an exclusive offer to buy what I had as a gift to them since there would be no more drugs in the city or surrounding for the next month or so with a catch, they had to put together money to buy it all or I will give the streets access to it. I was not disappointed these guys showed up in a major way normally the money is in three to four suitcases. Each suitcase holds about 1.3 to 1.5 million dollars apiece. This is with the denominations of 20-, 50- and 100-dollar bills. These guys were so exciting to get access to this load exclusive access that they went into their personal money. I filled one large suitcase and a small travel size suitcase with everything I owed, I had mostly hundreds and some fifties no other smaller denominations Beep Beep Beep!

Beep beep.

Bald Head: Go ahead, My Friend?

Me: My Friend, is this guy still here??

Bald Head: No, he just left, My Friend. Is something wrong?

Me: Yes, I need you to send this guy back because I'm done. My guys are counting the money right now. I AM is ready to go to this guy in about an hour, My Friend.

Bald Head....... (Silent)

Me: What do you say, My Friend??!

Bald Head: GOD DAMN, MY FRIEND!! WHAT THE FUCK DID YOU DO, MY FRIEND!! OMG, I HAVE TO CALL CHIEF!! HE'S GOING TO BE SHOCKED and SO HAPPY, MY FRIEND!! I'm sending this guy back to you right now, after I tell The Chief! The truck returned to the drop spot for I AM to deliver the money to the driver.

Beep beep beep.........

Bald Head: My Friend, this guy says, are you sure that is all the suitcases??

Me: Don't worry, My Friend. That's all 100's and just a few fifties, My Friend. Don't worry!

Bald Head: My Friend, The Chief was in a big meeting and I had those guys over there tell him anyway because I knew this would make him incredibly happy. The Chief came out of the meeting to call me back and told me to tell you thank you. He is very happy, My Friend. He wants to know if he can call you right now?

Me: Of course... But is everything okay, Jose?

Bald Head: Yes, he just wants to thank you himself... You just made him very happy! You couldn't have done this at a better time, My Friend.

The Chief had Junior call me and he spoke in Spanish thanking me. Right after, Junior translated his appreciation to me in English. The interesting thing about this is that I always knew The Chief was happy with my performance, but he never thanked me before, which was strange to me. I appreciated it, but it was strange. What would be even more strange was that The Chief called me back on the two-way radio and thanked me again in Spanish but added his Chief thanks me as well. As always, Junior translated this message to me in English.

Beep Beep Beep...

Me: Go ahead, My Friend...

Bald Head: My Friend, OMG, The Chief's Chief just called me! (Sounding like a serious super groupie) He told me to tell you that he personally thanks you, My Friend! This is huge, My Friend! This never happens ever, My Friend.

I was extremely puzzled by the statement that The Chief's Chief thanked me. I couldn't understand who this person was or why they were thanking me. I had always thought that The Chief was the biggest person in the organization, so I couldn't comprehend the significance of this additional Chief thanking me. However, I would soon find out what it all meant.

After Christmas, I had some free time and decided to head down to Atlanta. I met up with my friend Woo and Keith, and we spent some time in the studio cutting records for One Chance. We also discussed finalizing the deal on The CTE house so that our artists and producers could start creating there. Keith and I then did what we do best and went to the Onyx Gentlemen's club.

After the New Year, I moved into my place in Atlanta. We looked at a number of different talents to target during the 2007 New Year. I watched Woo's development process for his other artists, and I learned that it was an arduous process that involved more than just recording. Showmanship was also constantly emphasized.

Before I knew it, Danny called me with a small load of about twenty bricks that he wanted to get rid of in Atlanta. It was a simple transaction, with his guys pulling in with the drugs and then turning right around with the money.

Bald Head sent the first load of the year from The Chief, and two more followed shortly after. Then, I received a call that I was expecting but hoping would not come. Beep Beep...

Bald Head: My Friend, The Chief is looking for you.

I booked a flight to El Paso, TX again, and I AM and I jumped on a plane with a short layover at Dallas International Airport. We then boarded a propeller plane, which I hated, over to the El Paso airport, which was small compared to other airports. I'm sure most of the business that the airport received was from the cartels and military personnel.

Bald Head was waiting for I AM and I outside so we could cross over into Mexico. We headed straight for the Juarez Airport to catch another flight to what I would find out to be the State of Durango. This flight was different because Bald Head asked for our real names this time. I AM and I looked at each other in confusion because we always flew with Bald Head, never needing to do anything like this. I got upset with Bald Head and asked him why he needed our actual names this time.

I was also confused about why we needed to fly out. Where was The Chief? We always met The Chief in Juarez, even if he needed to move up towards the border for our meetings. Bald Head insisted that this was just the way it needed to be this time. It was a clear indication that something was much different this time around.

Finally, I gave in and agreed to give my full name, and I AM followed suit. Bald Head went off to purchase the ticket. I told I AM that Bald Head was calling in our names so they could run a check on us. This reminded me of the conversation I had with Tonal years before on a similar topic of verifying different clients' identities.

Accepting a sudden new reality, I knew clearance would be evident soon enough. Boarding yet another flight headed to an unknown destination, the experience was similar to other flights I had taken in Mexico. The seats were ridiculously small, as were the aisles on the planes, which meant I needed a couple of extended seat belts. These people sure had ways of letting you know you were not in control of anything.

Once we reached our destination, indicated by Bald Head proceeding toward the front of the plane, we were received in the normal fashion of the disciples of death, sicarios (hitmen). Two cars, including the one Bald Head, I AM, and I were riding in, arrived at a restaurant where The Chief was waiting to receive us. The Chief stood up as I approached and embraced me in the normal fashion for him and me. I noticed that he never interacted or even talked to I AM when he came with me. He asked about our flight, but only looked at me while Bald Head was translating.

The Chief started to make clear the importance of this meeting.

Chief: I need you to start buying guns and send them back with the money, Hermano.

Me: What caliber of pistol or rifle should I buy, Chief? And how many should I send?

Chief: Any and every kind you can find. Don't stop buying all that you can, My Hermano.

I nodded in confirmation. My mind was going wild wondering how I would get out of this one. I knew that all guns were registered to their owners and could be traced back to their origins. One thing was clear to me - the type of guys who always picked me up at the airport were not the big game type hunters I had seen on American TV.

"Any and every kind you can find. Don't stop buying all that you can, my Hermano," the Chief replied.

As Bald Head began translating, the Chief locked in on my face, and I tried not to make any facial expressions that could be questioned or read. I had learned from Danny to always answer questions with as few words as possible. How ironic that his advice would be practiced to perfection on hearing about his impending death. The Chief then said calmly and relaxed, "Hermano... I'm going to kill Danny." I just nonchalantly nodded my head in confirmation.

The Chief spoke calmly as he revealed his plans to me. He explained that Danny was causing many problems and that he had been a good friend to him. He had provided Danny with a house in a gated community, cars, and paid for everything in his home. He had even paid for his daughter to attend a prestigious Catholic school to keep his wife happy.

I maintained my poker face and kept my eyes locked on his face, not allowing them to wander or blink. The Chief then instructed me to cut all ties with Danny and to let him know if I needed anything, he would be there for me.

The Chief called for Bald Head and instructed him to accompany me wherever I needed to go, along with the Sicarios. As we prepared to leave the restaurant, the Sicarios got ready, and the Chief's BMW was parked out front with the doors open. Bald Head got in the back seat, and I sat in the front seat next to the Chief. I AM was in another car as usual whenever we saw The Chief.

I was struck by the size of the group gathered at the abandoned zoo. It was clear that The Chief had been busy recruiting, and the level of organization was impressive. As we sat at the picnic table, I couldn't help but wonder what was going on. The Chief seemed tense, and Junior and his group were on high alert. I tried to keep my composure, but the situation was getting more intense by the minute.

After a few minutes, The Chief returned with the older gentleman. They sat down at a nearby table and began talking in hushed tones. I couldn't make out what they were saying, but the atmosphere was tense. The Chief seemed to be trying to keep things under control, but I could tell that he was on edge.

As the conversation continued, I noticed that the older gentleman had a certain air of authority about him. He seemed to be in charge of the large group of men that had gathered with him. They were all armed, and it was clear that they were not to be taken lightly.

After a while, The Chief stood up and motioned for us to follow him. We walked over to where Junior and his group were standing, and The Chief began speaking to them in Spanish. I couldn't understand everything he was saying, but it was clear that he was giving them orders.

As we walked through the group of men, I couldn't help but feel a sense of danger. These were not the kind of men I wanted to cross, and I knew that things could turn ugly in an instant. I kept my head down and tried to stay focused on the task at hand.

After a few minutes, The Chief turned to us and motioned for us to follow him. We walked through a maze of corridors until we came to a large room. The Chief turned to us and said, "This is where the real work begins." I didn't know what he meant, but I had a feeling that things were about to get a lot more complicated.

Me: Bald Head, what is that damn sound?!

Bald Head: What sound, my friend?

Me: This sound... right... here! points finger in the direction of the sound

Bald Head: That's a lion roaring, my friend! laughs This used to be a zoo right here. It was closed, but they moved the lions to the far end of the zoo. points in the distance

Me: That can't be that far because we can still hear them.

Bald Head: My friend, you can hear a lion's roar for miles.

The Chief was talking with this gentleman for a couple of hours. Bald Head informed I AM and myself that this was The Durango Zoo in the city of Durango, located in the state of Durango.

Bald Head: My friend, The Chief is waving to you. Wave back, my friend!

I waved back just as energetically as the Chief was waving, but I noted the old gentleman was waving just as hard. It wasn't clear what that was all about, but based on the interesting selection of this meeting place, it must have been of grave importance. Things were quickly wrapped up at a rushed pace on both ends. Both groups headed towards separate exits as we left the zoo.

I loaded into the vehicle with the Chief, while Sam joined Junior and the sicarios in another vehicle. Our drive to the destination took about 30 to 40 minutes, and we arrived in a residential neighborhood. As we slowed down, children started running towards the Chief's vehicle. He had a beaming smile on his face as he exited the vehicle, and I followed suit. The sicarios that were riding in the back of the pickup truck provided security as we walked towards a house, with the Chief handing out money to the young kids and buying whatever they had in their hands to sell him.

As we left the fields and headed back towards the vehicles, we passed an area behind the farmhouse where the marijuana was being processed and dried. The area was huge, with marijuana plants in different phases of drying out. After viewing the processing and how the product was moved to the market, we loaded back up in Flaco's Suburban and headed out towards the main road that brought us in.

Instead of going back the same way, Flaco drove through the rest of the field, across the farmer's front yard, and directly into more fields. We continued to drive off-road through empty fields for a couple of hours.

After walking for about 20 or 25 rolls of corn, I could sense the strong smell of fertilizer with my experienced nose. The plants were towering above us with extremely big buds dripping with oil, and the ground was curved with plants as far as the eye could see. I couldn't believe what I was seeing, and I couldn't understand why I needed to see this to do my job. I reached out and grabbed a big bud on top of a plant, not knowing that it was marijuana until I smelled it. The sticky sap-type oil was all over my hand, and I wasn't dressed for this occasion in my Coogi short outfit, Coogi socks, and Ferragamo riding slippers.

As we left the fields, we moved towards the processing and drying area for the marijuana at the back of the house. The area was huge with plants in different phases of the drying-out process. After viewing the processing, we loaded back up in Flaco's Suburban and continued driving off-road through fields for what seemed like hours. The grass ranged from very tall to medium and short, and I didn't understand how Flaco even knew where he was going. There wasn't a single landmark in sight to help us navigate, and we just kept driving without any direction.

As we drove, I noticed a river up ahead and pointed it out to I AM. He was concerned about finding a bridge or crossing point, but I had a strange feeling that we weren't slowing down to cross. I AM became more and more anxious, and I gestured towards Flaco's friend to calm him down. But he kept looking at I AM and trying to reassure him with his broken English. I told I AM to relax, but he was worried because he couldn't swim and the river was moving too fast.

Flaco and his friend caught on to what was happening and started to laugh, picking up speed. I AM was freaking out, and I was getting scared too. As it became clear that they didn't have a bridge in mind, they slowed down on the bank of the river and drove down into it.

We drove slowly but steadily as the water continued to rise up the side of the suburban. It was clear that this suburban was not just an ordinary one, judging from its performance on that dirt road alone. But now, with the water coming up to the lower to middle part of the glass on the truck, it felt like we were totally submerged, even though it may not have been that high. We made it across to the other side without issue, and Flaco's friend looked back to check on I AM. I looked at him and pointed towards I AM to indicate that he worried for nothing.

ME: You know that shit wasn't Gangsta, RIGHT??!

I AM: Mmmmmman.........MUTHA FUCK YOU!!!!

Another 15 or 20 minutes after crossing the river, we arrived at a camp. The chief had just arrived as well, along with Bald Head and Junior. I AM and I exited the vehicle as the chief waved us over towards him. A man rushed out to greet the chief and seemed extremely happy, much like the effect the chief seemed to have on all these folks. The gentleman started to lead us, pointing and describing things to the chief. The camp was separated into four different areas, all adjacent to a small but decent-sized shack with a metal tin roof. I guessed this could be considered the office or something of that nature. We entered and there were several older women, like grandmas, cooking on a makeshift oven-type huge flat grill. Stacked high along each was food supplies of 100 to maybe 200-pound sacks of flour, beans, powdered milk, and cereal. Bald Head explained that the women were responsible for cooking for everyone at the camp, and the supplies were what their daily diet consisted of, with no exceptions. The chief told Bald Head to tell us to look around and check the place out. I observed Junior and how everyone in the camp was running up to him like he was a person of great significance, almost like a boss type figure.

I AM walked off in a different direction with Bald Head, while Junior caught up with me to explain the layout of the camp. According to him, each of the four adjacent parts of the camp had separate functions for processing marijuana. The first area was where the weed was brought in and further separated according to the drying-out process. The second area contained weed that was almost ready to be trimmed. The third area was mostly for women who did the trimming, and the fourth area was for marijuana that had been trimmed of its stems, with only the buds ready to be baled. This is where the weed was weighed and wrapped into 25-kilo bales. They used the metric system, which gave an extra four or five grams per kilo when converted to pounds.

Junior walked with me on purpose and started to connect with me on a personal level.

Junior: My friend, you know The Chief is a very, very big jefe!

Me: Yes, my friend, I know this even more now.

Junior: Do you know that you are a very big jefe now too, my friend?

I stopped and looked at Junior with a confused expression, not really understanding the moment I was in, with all the unnecessary touring of production facilities.

Junior said to me, "Yes, my friend! You are a very big jefe too now. No one can tell you nothing now, jefe. You are over Bald Head, me, and everybody here at this place. Now we must listen to you, jefe. Look at how everyone looks here to you now." I stopped to see what Junior was saying, and everyone else stopped and looked at him, even whispering to each other. Then I understood why Junior wanted to walk with me and be seen as well. Junior said, "Jefe, you know that I used to live in this place too for many years. The Chief saved me from here. Therefore, I owe him my life, jefe! These are my people, and they don't have anything, jefe. They will never be lucky like me. I try to help them as much as I can because they need things. I was like them too..."

I could see the concern on Junior's face as he witnessed people walking around on the ground with no shoes. Most of them didn't have shoes, not even young children as young as 3 or 4 years old, walking around barefoot or sitting next to their young mothers or grandmothers. This sight hurt the protagonist's soul badly, and he knew that Junior could see it too. This is where Junior started to bond strongly with me and would become a strong ally of mine.

Junior: Jefe, if there's anything you need, just let me know. I'll always be here for you, my friend. And don't worry, we'll take care of those people in the camp. We may not be able to change their whole world, but we can make a difference in their lives.

I nodded, feeling grateful for Junior's offer of friendship and support. Despite our shared profession, we were able to connect on a deeper level and recognize the humanity in each other.

As we continued walking through the camp, I couldn't shake off the images of the poverty and struggle that surrounded us. It was a stark reminder of the harsh reality that many people in the world faced, and it made me feel a sense of responsibility to help in any way that I could.

My offer to send clothes back to the camp was a small gesture, but it was something that could make a difference in someone's life. And his offer to design a t-shirt for me was a reminder that even in the world of drug trafficking, there were ways to show kindness and appreciation to others.

The memories of my own childhood and the struggles that led me to this point weighed heavy on my mind. But in that moment, I felt a glimmer of hope that maybe, just maybe, I could use my position as a Jefe to make a positive impact on the world around me.

Some yelling disrupted the peacefulness of the camp, and Junior turned to me, "Jefe, our Jefe is calling for you now." We quickly made our way to the front of the camp, where we loaded up and left, heading back to the hotel just outside of Durango. During the ride, Bald Head remarked, "My friend, you won't be able to fly back with those clothes you're wearing now. You should never have gone into those fields. That smell will never come out. It doesn't matter how much you wash them, they're ruined now, my friend," ending with a chuckle.

At the hotel, the Chief reviewed everything that was discussed on the trip, emphasizing the importance of preparing for the increase in volume on two fronts, and performance was crucial. The next morning, it was time to head to the airport and fly back to Juarez city, so we could cross back into the States. As I handed Junior most of my clothes, including my weed-infused outfit, shoes, socks, and even my underwear, I realized that they couldn't make the flight. "This is something for your family back at the camp, Junior," I said. His face lit up with a big smile, and emotions filled his eyes.

"Jefe, you know I went back with them last night," Junior said. "They had a lot of questions about you guys. They've never seen Black people before. They were confused because you guys were the same color as us, but your clothes and hair were different. I told them you were from America. They'll be very happy for these clothes. I'll tell them they're from you, Jefe. American clothes!"

We flew out of Durango airport, with several stops along the way, and finally arrived at Juarez International Airport. After a few hours of crossing the US border, we headed straight for El Paso airport to catch another flight to Detroit, Michigan.

As soon as we entered the vehicle, we started working the two-way radios heavily. I AM was going the hardest because he had to arrange to hit the trunk and unload it. Bald Head warned us that the driver would arrive before we did, and there were 300 bricks in this load, already increased by about 100.

I wasn't overly concerned because I had heard that the streets were drying up. That was music to my ears because I didn't have to hear a shitload of crying from dudes with small bags complaining about not being able to move anything. I wanted to rip so I could get back to ATL.

My team is seasoned, and we did the normal two-step. We knocked that thing down with all money in and counted; four days turnaround. Moved all the street, of course, 10 or better, no breakdowns, and no super whale purchases. Beep beep beep...

Bald Head: Go ahead.

Me: I need you to send those guys... We're ready.

Bald Head: GODDAMN, MY FRIEND!

I laughed, knowing the Chief would be happy, and our stock was increasing even more than before.

Bald Head: I will send these guys to you now. My Friend, the Chief, was barely just getting ready to cross now. I will do you a favor and tell you just before he crosses.

When I wanted to leave town, I would often have to ask if I could go, and it was always, "I don't know, My friend! Because we are going to be there with you soon." Which meant "NO, YOU CAN'T!" Bald Head would do this for me so I could run off for a little R and R, just as I would cover for him at times too. I was not going to leave this time. My plan was to wait until that next load came in, then I would leave it in I AM's hands as I run off to ATL.

After a week of waiting to hear from Bald Head, I was becoming a little restless. I had a lot of things that I needed to address down in ATL. I was in consistent communication with Woo and Keith, but the question was always, "When are you going to be back this way, Big Homie?!" Beep Beep Beep.........

Danny: My friend.......

Me: Go ahead, my friend.

Danny: You are very busy these days, My Friend.

Me: No, never too busy for my very good friend.

Danny: When are we going to work again, my friend? I'm ready to come to you now. I can be there with you in two days. My Friend, I'm starting to think you are not wanting to work with me and avoiding.

It was clear that Danny was becoming impatient and was expecting a response from me. I knew I had to make a decision, but I also had to make sure that I didn't jeopardize any of my current business relationships.

Me: Danny, I appreciate your eagerness, but things are a bit complicated right now. I have a lot going on, and I need to make sure that everything is in order before we can work together again.

Danny: My Friend, I understand that you are busy, but I have been waiting for this opportunity for a long time now. I need to know when we can work together again.

Me: Danny, I understand your frustration, but I need to make sure that everything is in order before we can proceed. Give me a few days to figure things out, and I will get back to you.

Danny: Okay, my Friend. But please don't keep me waiting for too long. I need to know when we can start working together again.

Me: I hear you, Danny. I will let you know as soon as I have some news.

I hung up the phone, feeling a bit stressed out. It seemed like everyone wanted a piece of me, and I wasn't sure how I was going to handle everything. I needed to take a break and clear my head. I decided to take a walk and think things over.

Danny: The Chief has been making some moves that I don't agree with. He's been cutting corners and taking risks that are not worth it. I've tried to talk to him about it, but he doesn't listen. He's become more ruthless and paranoid. He's been accusing me of things that I haven't done. I'm afraid he might try to eliminate me to cover his tracks.

Me: I see. That's a serious accusation, my friend. Have you considered leaving the organization and starting fresh somewhere else?

Danny: I can't just leave, my friend. I have a family and I owe a lot of money to the cartel. If I leave, they will come after me and my loved ones. I need to find a way to protect myself and my family.

Me: I understand. You're in a difficult situation, my friend. I will do what I can to help you. Let me talk to the Chief and see what's going on. I will try to find a solution that works for everyone.

Danny: Thank you, my friend. I appreciate your help. Be careful, though. The Chief is not to be trusted these days. Keep your guard up.

Me: I will. Take care, my friend. I will be in touch soon.

Danny: Don't feel sorry for me...... You should feel sorry for him My Friend...

The two-way radio went dead after that statement. This situation was getting serious, or maybe it already had. There was clearly a mole on the Chief's end. I felt terrible about lying to Danny about something so serious, but telling him the truth would have definitely jeopardized my safety. Beep Beep Beep......

Bald Head: We will be there with you soon, my friend......

The work arrived as Bald Head said it would, and the load had increased again to a little over 500 units. It became clear that I needed to prepare for this increase in work. I told I AM and my cousin Dirt that I needed to find a place to cut some compartments into about four vehicles. These compartments would be used to store some of the work when things escalated. I didn't want any automated stash spots because the state troopers and Feds had some type of wand that they could wave around in the vehicle, making anything with power open. In Detroit, it was known to cut stash spots into vehicles, but guys were getting fancy, wanting everything automated. I was sticking with the old-school method, so we had to find someone who still knew this old trade.

As planned, I took off for ATL after a couple of days of making sure everything was set. I AM was in total control of everything in my absence. It was almost like autopilot with the guys now. My problem was that I needed to get some work back down in the ATL. The Danny situation was too dangerous at this point. Bald Head never mentioned getting anything down there in The ATL. I'm sure it was a set-up too. However, I'm also sure that Bald Head didn't want anything to do with it, period!

Arrived in Atlanta, and I was thrilled to be there. However, I couldn't shake off the stress, knowing I wasn't supposed to be there without proper authorization. Nevertheless, I had important business to attend to with Keith and Woo. We met with Woo's attorney, Monica Ewing, to structure Be-Ly Publishing and start signing artists, writers, and producers. I ended up footing the bill for all the legal costs, even though we were equal partners. It was agreed that I would hold Key Man clauses in the contracts with artists signed to Be-Ly Publishing, and I would also be responsible for financing the deals with signing artists.

Our first signing was the Outsyders Production team, consisting of Ervin and Dean. Our schedules were jam-packed as we moved from studio to studio, working with different artists that Woo and Keith had signed to various major record labels like US Records, J Records, and Def Jam Records. I ended up financing much of what the labels didn't cover. Beep Beep Beep......

Bald Head: My Friend! The Chief is going to be calling you right now. I'm calling to warn you because I know you are down there with your friends. Chief is going to tell you to rush down now.

Me: Bald Head, you know I can't come down there now! We are working......

Bald Head: I understand My Friend, but he said it was urgent. He wouldn't tell me why. I just wanted to give you a heads up. Be careful, My Friend.

Me: Thank you, Bald Head. I appreciate you looking out for me. I'll see what I can do, but I can't make any promises.

After the call, I couldn't help but feel uneasy. The Chief never called me during a job, especially not to come down to Mexico. Something was definitely up, and I needed to find out what it was before I made any moves. I decided to call up my contacts down in Mexico and see if they knew anything.

I finally got through to one of my sources, who informed me that there had been a big bust at the border, and the Chief's operation had been compromised. He needed to get out of the country fast, and he wanted me to come down and help him.

I was torn between my loyalty to the Chief and my own safety. I knew that if I went down there, I could be walking into a trap. But if I didn't go, the Chief might see it as a betrayal.

I decided to take a chance and go down there. I made sure to bring some backup, just in case things went sideways. When I arrived, the Chief told me that we needed to move all of our product out of the country as quickly as possible.

We worked non-stop for the next few days, moving everything we could out of Mexico and into the United States. It was dangerous work, but we managed to get it done. In the end, we made it out alive and with all of our product intact.

I learned a valuable lesson from that experience. Loyalty is important, but so is self-preservation. I needed to be more careful in the future and make sure that I wasn't putting myself in harm's way for someone else's gain.

Bald Head: I understand, my friend. I'm just warning you, and don't tell him I told you, but you should rush back up there because he's going to tell you to come RAPIDO.

This was never normal for something like this to happen in the middle of a load. We are always instructed to come after all the money is out of the street and on a semi headed back. I have even had situations where as soon as the money was loaded and we ensured the semi got on the freeway (which meant it was no longer my responsibility. Nothing can happen to that truck or that driver once he comes up off that freeway to drop a load or to pick up money. Once he is back on the freeway, it's out of my hands).

Beep Beep...

Junior: How are you, my friend?

Me: I'm okay, Junior. How are you, my friend?

Junior: I'm okay, my friend. The Chief is here listening to you now, my friend. The Chief says that he needs you to come down Rapido!

Me: Junior, I don't understand... Ask the Chief, doesn't he want me to come as soon as I see this guy that Bald Head sends here?

Junior: (the radio opens so I can hear the Chief's voice, and Junior translates.) My friend, the Chief, said don't worry. Everything will be okay over there, but he needs you here... (Junior stops talking, and the two-way radio remains open, and I hear the Chief's voice) RAPIDO RAPIDO HERMANO!!!

Me: Yes, Chief! I will be there with you very soon, Chief.

Something was very wrong; this was not normal protocol! Bald Head would usually give me some details per our agreement. He was tight-lipped; the only thing he would tell me is that it had nothing to do with me being in any danger. Why do I need to keep fucking going down there!!! I just fucking left from down there!! I can't keep jumping these flights like this without setting off red flags!!

Beep Beep...

I AM: What's up, buddy?

Me: I have to jump another flight over that way again!

I AM: We're working; we can't do that shit!

Me: The Chief called me directly.

I AM: OH...... SHIT!! He called you DIRECTLY??! You good?

Me: Bald Head told me it ain't got shit to do with me. I need you to come down here to swoop me 911 tho.

I AM: On my way...... I'm coming with you tho so book me a flight with you. You good with that?

Me: I'm gonna have the girl book the tickets for us.

This was crazy flying into a situation that I didn't have a fucking clue what was goin' on. I AM and I land back in El Paso, TX approximately 36 hours after the call from the Chief. We retrieve our bags from baggage claim after I use my two-way radio to alert Bald Head that we arrived. He makes me aware that there are two vehicles outside of the baggage claim area waiting to transport I AM and I across the border. Bald Head tells me the sicarios would bring us directly to the Juarez airport where he would be waiting on us with tickets to fly out. This whole interaction would be an additional item to place on the list of extremely abnormal behavior contrary to past practice. We cross the border into Juarez as Bald Head had made me aware of what happened.

Upon arriving at the airport, the sicarios pull our bags from the vehicles about the time we exit them. We head towards the entry of the airport where Bald Head would be waiting for I AM and I. As soon as I lay eyes on Bald Head, I am on his ass about all the strange events that are occurring at a rapid pace without explanation.

For some reason or another, Bald Head remained very tight-lipped and didn't disclose much about what was happening. However, that didn't stop me from trying to get some idea of what the fuck was going on. He reassured me that it had nothing to do with me, but reminded me of our agreement, a form of insurance policy that he had not forgotten and would honor in all circumstances. He suspiciously looked at me for the same confirmation that my efforts would be reciprocated on my end, which I quickly affirmed.

Whatever the case may be, Bald Head seemed very nervous and looked around a lot, which probably explained why the sicarios picked us up at the El Paso airport. "My friend, things are changing fast and I don't want any trouble for maybe saying too much," Bald Head expressed to me. "I promise I will tell you more once this thing is over because there are certain things I don't know yet, but what I do know is when things like this start to happen, it means something. I don't say anything right now because it could be very dangerous to be wrong," Bald Head added.

We boarded AeroMexico airlines as usual and flew for about 45 minutes to an hour, with two stops along the way. I couldn't tell you where we landed, just that we were retrieved by sicarios and taken to a restaurant where we were received by the chief. Some pleasantries were exchanged as well as hugs as normal, and we had something to eat as was customary in situations like this.

The chief tried to act as normal as usual, but there was clearly a heightened sense of awareness due to the large increase of security both inside and outside of the restaurant. After eating, we quickly scurried to the vehicles, with Bald Head and I riding with the chief while I AM rode with Junior, second in command of the Sicarios. This time, I AM would ride with Junior for the first time.

I witnessed a different type of protocol now; Junior was personally responsible for the chief's safety. These were intense times, which was evident by the level of security I was witnessing. Junior would not leave the chief's side throughout this duration, even to the point of being wherever the chief was, even in the same room while he was sleeping. Junior would not leave the chief's side, period. This security detail was much different based on the level of high powered rifles that were visibly apparent on the sicarios. Under normal circumstances you always see some high-power rifles but mostly high caliber pistols. This situation was very different because it seemed that everyone had high powered rifles and pistols. We also travel at very high rates of speed now in tight formation. This road trip wasn't just for a couple of hours we or driving through the night at very high rates of speed.

The Chief was driving, I was in the passenger seat, Bald Head was seated behind me and Junior behind the Chief. I did a lot of off and on dozing off during this ride. One time I woke up when the rate of speed started to slow down and Chiefs' car started to pull over on the shoulder of the freeway. The lights of the federalist police had the whole car lit up inside and out. I was shocked and didn't really know what to think. I knew the Chief carried a gold plated forty-five caliber pistol and he had a Mac 10 in the back with Junior who also had a 45-caliber pistol nickel plated. I didn't know if Bald Head had a pistol or not, but under the circumstances I would have to assume he was also armed. I knew better than to look back into the lights based on my experience on the eastside of Detroit. I kept my head straight only attempting to use my peripheral vision once the nickel-plated chrome of Juniors 45 was pulled out, catching it.

Bald Head chambered something behind me. Chief adjusted his side only visible to me, slightly pulling his shirt on that side up.The officer slowly walked up to the vehicle on the driver's side. I'm assuming he asked for the Chief's paperwork to the vehicle etc. the Chief handed the officer what he requested but kept his head straight forward. There was dead silence. I could sense Junior getting a little itchy; Bald Head was whispering something in Spanish to Junior, some of the words I noticed," take it easy my friend." Junior was making some very slight grunting sounds in almost like disagreement. Suddenly, the officer's whole tone changed from official to very friendly and excited. The officer immediately started to apologize to the Chief stating he would not have pulled him if he would have known it was him. The Chief's whole demeanor changed as he appeared to console the officer. The officer seemed very nervous, but the chief reassured him he was okay based on the translation.

Bald Head started to whisper in my ear now that things were relaxed. The chief handed the officer some money, and the officer emphatically thanked him for it. Before leaving, the officer bent all the way down, looked over at me, then paused. Then he pointed at me and said something, and everyone in the car started to laugh wildly from the comment. I started to look around, wondering what was said. Bald Head had translated everything else but that, ironically. I asked Bald Head what was said by the officer, but he wouldn't reply. I started asking Junior what the officer said, but he tried to respond with his very badly broken English. Then the chief said something, and I'm assuming he told Bald Head to tell me.

Bald Head: "This guy said, 'DAMN! THAT'S A BIG FUCKER!! Be careful, chief, he may fucking eat you!!'"

Then they all started to laugh again as if the chief and Junior could understand very well what Bald Head was saying to me in English. "You MUTHA FUCKERS got fat jokes in Spanish too, HUH," I thought to myself.

After a long night of driving, we finally arrived back at the Durango Zoo. The routine was the same as before, with Junior and a few sicarios accompanying the chief to meet with the older gentleman in the white cowboy hat. They spent a couple of hours talking, and I later found out that the man was Ol Man Mayo, or El Mayo (Ismael Zambada-Garcia). Everything was repeated, including the chief and Ol Man Mayo waving enthusiastically, and Bald Head telling me to wave back, even though I was already waving. It was just like déjà vu.

We loaded back into the vehicles as before, and Chief seemed extremely happy, even more so than during the entire duration of our ride down. We drove for about an hour to reach a different hotel, and it was nothing short of luxurious. The staff's uniforms were elegant, and the service was top-notch. The rooms, the amenities, everything about it was on another level. I AM and I had a room right next to the Chief, and Junior slept in the room with him as well. I wasn't sure where Bald Head slept for the night, but what was clear was the heavy security presence – sicarios were stationed on the same floor, and outside our doors as well as in the lobby.

The treatment we received was like that of rock stars – a mix of respect, intimidation, and compensation. It was mind-boggling how we seemed to be invisible to the authorities, like they didn't see us. This was a culture shock of unimaginable proportions.

The next morning came early, as Bald Head rushed us to go down and have breakfast. We were taken to a dining hall that was truly exquisite, adorned with chandeliers, mural paintings from the 15th and 16th centuries, and gold fixtures everywhere. The buffet breakfast had a wide array of delicious food and fruit. I whispered to I AM, "I don't think this is open to the public," and he seemed to agree without saying much.

To my surprise, our party had grown overnight, and there were several new faces – individuals who seemed just as interested in us as we were in seeing them. One gentleman approached I AM and me and just made himself at home. He started talking to us as if we were old friends, and we found ourselves responding in kind, as if we had known him for decades. The whole situation was surreal and intriguing, leaving us with many unanswered questions.

As I often said, "When in Rome, do as the Romans do!" Just knowing this business like I was starting to know it, things just didn't happen by coincidence. It wasn't lost on me that we were two black men sitting in the presence of maybe 15 or 20 Hispanic gentlemen. All eyes were on us. Everyone in that room knew we were in the same line of business, and they understood we weren't there just taking in the sights of the city. What was never expressed but understood was that they knew not to approach and force this big Nikolai Russian-looking dude to just come sit down and start a full conversation and speak pretty good English.

Need I mention that the skill set required for this line of work had nothing to do with the standard of education and being bilingual because we all spoke the same language: money and shitloads of it. When you get to the level of the big Jefe's, this was a much more diverse crowd of eclectic individuals that had several skill sets. Now, in and around these guys, you will see a diverse level of some form of education and charisma, always. You often knew them by just a sense of belonging, entitlement, and unearthly arrogance. A kind of God complex in a few cases.

As usual, my senses never seemed to fail me. I would find out that Ol Nikolai was the Junior for one of the Beltran Leyva brothers. They joined us overnight at the hotel, which ended up being a rendezvous point in the state of Durango that is run by Ol man Mayo. Full disclosure, I must be honest. I did not know the level or how deep I had raised two in this cartel. The type of individuals I was meeting, greeting, and befriending, I could not comprehend at the time because of the lack of awareness of how and what cartels were.

Outside of hearing what was equivalent to local drug dealers or king-pins based on the level I had arrived at and the tall tales of their drug expeditions, which summed up to just driving out of town or flying a few states over for their so-called pull up or connect, this clearly wasn't that. There was nothing and no one who could prepare me based on their prior knowledge for what I was experiencing or would come to know - that I was in the presence of clinical psychopaths, serial killers, perverts, and sadistic-minded personalities.

CHAPTER 24

CULIACAN, SINALOA

THERE WAS FRIENDLY CONVERSATION going on with Nikolai, just in general. Which was clearly a tactic just to feel us out, I am sure. There is never any wasted action or just general kindness or conversation with individuals like this; there is always an objective. I AM and I represented an American market that was wide open, and who would not want that. I will later come to understand just how important I was, as The Chief had referred to some time back with this statement, "you are much more important than you think you are!"

There was another interesting character at the meeting who caught my attention. He seemed to be purposely trying to get noticed without making direct contact. He wore all black and had jet black hair, reminding me of Johnny Cash. Once he settled down to eat, he sat parallel to me and made sure to lock eyes with me.

I didn't see The Chief or Junior, but I knew Junior was likely with The Chief wherever he was. Bald Head could be seen occasionally, but he kept to the shadows to make sure no one got too close.

As we were leaving, Reyes suddenly appeared and embraced me as if we were long lost friends. This caught Bald Head off guard, as he knew there was no prior relationship between us. I knew this was all for show to try and impress The Chief. It was the beginning of Reye's move to become a big Jefe, but I wasn't impressed. I knew that Bald Head was already acting as a middleman and interpreting for me, but he was just trying to earn a finder's fee. Junior had already made it clear that I was Bald Head's Jefe, so Reyes attempts to insert himself were futile.

We quickly got into the vehicles and sped off at a rapid pace. I was becoming desensitized to the large number of sicarios and the security detail. The countless pickup trucks with armed sicarios in the back were becoming the norm. It was as if I was being indoctrinated into becoming an American Narco, coming from Black Bottom Detroit Lower East Side. We drove for hours, and I lost track of time. I had no idea that we had entered Sinaloa cartel territory, and that the Crown T-shirts had been replaced with Ferrari symbol T-shirts, which were loads of T-shirts that the chief had taken from the Sinaloa cartel. I soon learned what Junior had meant by "the Chiefs' Chief" and how the chief was the goose that laid the golden eggs. This was high stakes, and I was a pawn being pushed to the middle of the board, just as Danny had done with Rojo, and then saved his own skin by handing me over to a higher bidder, the chief representing the Juarez Cartel. However, the man in the big white hat at the zoo was about to change everything.

Finally, we arrived at a beautiful town right off the Pacific Ocean with beachfront properties, beaches, and upscale hotels. The area was secured, and we walked along the beachfront area, going in and out of tourist shops. I was encouraged to buy some souvenirs, which I did. I purchased several Mazatlán T-shirts, postcards, mugs, and fitted caps.

After buying several trinkets, I discovered the reason for the tourists' moments. Several sicarios along with Bald Head went ahead and booked rooms and another exclusive hotel right off the beach of the Pacific Ocean. Upon their return we all loaded back up in the vehicles and headed a little way down the strip. We pulled into a parking garage. Our entourage was very deep but as we continued deeper into the parking structure it began to thin out the higher we got. This led me to believe the sicarios were setting up checkpoints throughout the whole parking structure. What was becoming customary was once we stopped people were separated into small groups to talk this was no different. There were several discussions. I did not know what was stated because of course the first language was Spanish with which I was not familiar. Bald Head would translate but oftentimes he would do selective translating some things that would translate some things I just was not supposed to hear because he did not translate.

We had to be standing out in that parking structure for an hour and a half or so at this point. There were still cars pulling in adding to the separate groups, even to our big Jefe group. Two-way radios started to go off; guys were scrambling and started to move really fast which caused me to be alarmed. I was starting to feel as if there was some danger or something about to pop off but from reading the eyes of the sicarios I started to notice the rapid movement was just in preparation in anticipation of someone's arrival.

Within 5 minutes of the chaos a black Hummer started to pull up into the area that we were standing. I noticed that a certain crowd started to move away from the black Hummer while some of the groups started to combine into one moving towards the black Hummer. This black Hummer was trailed by several vehicles that also had sicarios that set up a perimeter inside of our perimeter for whomever was in this black Hummer. The doors of the Hummer were opened as several people jumped out, but I noticed one was noticeably short with flip flops and a man bag wearing a baseball cap. The Chief says something to Bald Head and Bald Head then instructed I AM and I to follow him. Bald Head led us toward the hotel, but this short guy's eyes followed us locking eyes with me as he nodded, in turn I nodded back

After following Bald Head, I AM & I were led into the hotel and up to a suite on one of the upper floors. The short man in flip flops was already inside, along with several other men who appeared to be high-ranking members of the cartel. Bald Head made introductions, and I learned that the short man was indeed The Chief of the Sinaloa Cartel.

The Chief seemed friendly and personable, speaking in English with a heavy accent. He explained that he had heard good things about me from the Juarez Cartel and that he was interested in working with me on some upcoming business deals. I was surprised by the offer, but I knew better than to turn down such an opportunity.

Over the next few hours, we discussed various details of the business deals, with Bald Head translating when necessary. I was impressed by The Chief's knowledge and expertise in the industry, and I could tell that he was someone to be taken seriously.

As the meeting came to a close, The Chief invited me to stay in Mazatlán for a few days and enjoy the sights and sounds of the town. He assured me that everything was taken care of and that I would be safe and well taken care of.

Feeling grateful and a bit overwhelmed by the turn of events, I thanked The Chief and his associates and left the suite with Bald Head and I AM. As we walked back to our own hotel, I couldn't help but think about how my life had taken such a strange and unexpected turn. But at the same time, I felt excited about the possibilities that lay ahead and eager to see what the future held.

"You already know I started on Bald Head. I had a million and one questions, but he couldn't answer them fast enough. Unfortunately, he wasn't even trying to answer them either.

'Yo, yo man, who in the fuck was that?!' I asked. 'Why did everybody start freaking out, even The Chief? Did that short dude know who were because he fucking nodded and smiled at me?'

Bald Head just kept walking, not even giving me eye contact. I got a little beside myself, not taking into consideration that it was something he wasn't supposed to share at the time. 'Oh, you Mutha Fucka, you'll pay for this! Do not call me in the future asking me what The Chief told me about nothing, because I am not gonna tell you, SHIT!! I threatened him. This always got Bald Head's attention.

Bald Head had the capacity to always end up in some shit and find himself asking me, 'My friend, could you tell The Chief this or that for me because he is going to fire me, I just know it, again my friend.'

Bald Head: 'My friend, you know I will tell you anything, but there are some things I just can't tell you right now. But I will tell you everything. You already know this,' Bald Head replied. 'That short guy was the chiefs', Chief.'

'What the fuck is this "Chiefs', Chief" shit again?!' I was becoming increasingly confused about this description. Even to the point of wondering if I had the appropriate definition for chief, 'That means boss, RIGHT?' I recalled being told by Danny that The Chief was the most powerful, so how could he have a chief?"

Nevertheless, Bald Head directed us to our rooms and advised us to relax, informing us that everything was fine and to contact him via his two-way radio if we needed anything. It was clear that he wasn't going to answer many questions at that moment, so I settled in and got some sleep.

The following morning, Bald Head came to my room and told me that he had to be careful because everyone was watching everyone else. He informed me that some significant meetings were taking place, both at that moment and throughout the night, with the Beltran Leyva brothers, the Los Mazatlecos Jefes, and others in attendance. According to him, changes were going to happen quickly, and he seemed happy about it.

Bald Head's two-way radio went off, and after a brief conversation, he jumped to his feet and said, "We must hurry to the parking structure; they are waiting for us there." We quickly put on our clothes and headed out the door, with me reminding Bald Head about breakfast. "My friend, we will eat something at the top of the mountain," Bald Head stated as he rushed out the door before us...

Me: "TOP OF THE FUCKIN' MOUNTAIN??!!"

There were so many vehicles that I lost count. I'm sure there were over thirty, maybe even forty or more. From what Bald Head had told me, there were at least three or four cartel groups at this hotel. Our group had about 10 to 15 vehicles and pickup trucks. Bald Head explained that they decided to split up some of the vehicles to avoid congesting the roads too much while going through the mountains. That didn't make much sense to me, but then again, the word "mountain" caught my attention again.

What I would soon find out is that this was going to be the ride of my life. I was warned that I might get dizzy on this ride through the mountains, and if it got really bad, I should stick my head out the window to regurgitate because there might not be a place to pull over during most of the journey. This was one of the worst rides I had ever been on in my life. It felt like a ride at some type of amusement park. The road was a single two-way road with traffic going up the mountain and traffic coming down. This road was shared with cows, donkeys, chickens, dogs, and all other kinds of animals. The cows walked around as if they were children with no one attending to them, and they would walk in the main road, causing us to creep behind them until they decided to move to the side or reached an area where they could move to the side. Sometimes, they stopped in the middle of the road.

The road we were on was also shared with semi-trucks and all other kinds of vehicles, even some pulled by horseback. This ride was about four and a half to five hours of swerving around corners as deep as some points or often like a roller coaster, causing the dizziness that was described to me. Going around these curves was so steep that the semi-trailers would fall over on the mountains. There were no railings or barricades to keep your vehicle from falling off the side of the mountain on your way down while swinging around these curves. This infamous mountain road between Mazatlán and the state of Sinaloa is called "THE DEVIL'S SPINE!" I guess that can give you an idea of what this fucking road is like.

After a few hours of driving through the twists and turns of the mountain road, we finally reached the top where it was snowing. There was a small hut where they were making breakfast burritos and fajitas. Bald Head had mentioned this place earlier, but I had no idea what he was talking about. As we approached, I saw a grandmotherly woman cooking the food, and a flamboyant person serving the men. It was shocking to see how the men were treating this person, making catcalls and whistling as they twirled around. It became clear to me that sex was a significant part of their culture, and love was expressed in different ways.

After eating the spicy fajitas, I realized there was no restroom around, so I had to use the mountain as my personal restroom. We got back on the road and started our descent down the mountain. The ride down was just as challenging as the ride up, if not more.

Finally, we landed on the other side of the mountain, in the city of Culiacan, Sinaloa. We pulled into a hotel with similar arrangements as before, with carriers waiting for us upon arrival. The hotel consisted of a few buildings, but we were directed to the back of the grounds where a building was reserved for cartel members. There were sicarios that raised the gate leading to the building we were occupying. We had individual rooms with separate outside entrances on two levels of the building, with a lot of space but dirt in front of the building. There were cement walkways and stairs leading upstairs, and several tables where sicarios would gather to drink, gamble, and listen to music all night. Many were also standing outside the building in groups, heavily armed.

This was the point in which the Johnny Cash look alike dressed in all black decided to start talking. He asked me how the experience riding through the Devil's Spine for the first time was. That was the right subject to strike with me at that moment because I had a laundry list of difficult experiences that will scar my memory forever. Not knowing his name, I named him Black Shirt from that point forward. Interesting fact to me is that he did not have an accent at all and spoke very good English. He had a somewhat refined presence about him that reminded me of the gentleman I had met years before through Danny named Tano. There was no confusion about the fact that he was somebody exactly,who he was I do not know but I would find out more as time would proceed. Black Shirt was in pursuit of a much deeper relationship with us which it would not take him long to show his hand. He stayed in proximity to us through that whole trip as well as Bald Head oftentimes translating for us when Bald Head was not available.

After checking into our rooms, we loaded up and headed out again, this time with a smaller group of sicarios. We drove for about half an hour into the heart of Culiacan, Sinaloa.

We arrived at a large house, with tall walls that appeared to be 10 to 12 feet high, and a sliding steel gate that could only accommodate a few cars. The house was divided into four or five condominium-style living quarters, each with a significant amount of square footage. As we entered one of the condominiums, we found that there was very little furniture, just a few fold out chairs arranged in a large circle. We were invited to take a seat, and as more people arrived, the circle grew larger.

People stared at us in amazement, a reaction that was familiar to me from my frequent visits to Mexico.

The trips to Mexicali with Brian and a few of his friends had that look of amazement in their eyes which led to Boots setting up a meeting with Orlando and Danny, leading to me working with the Tijuana cartel. After meeting Danny that led to the city of Juarez and working with several organizations in that city before Danny finally taking me to meet The Chief. The Chief via Danny brought me into the Juarez cartel. Now The Chief was taking and parading his prized horse on display in front of the Sinaloa cartel; I just didn't know it yet! One thing was undeniable was the stare of amazement that came from Narcos just seeing Black men over there in Mexico.

Baby Doll had warned me that Mexican men were jealous of Black men because they couldn't work the streets like we could. Some of the stares were friendly, but others were filled with jealousy, envy, dislike and feeling we did not belong; that was what was behind a number of those smiles which Baby Doll told me we would see one day.

As we sat in the circle, a group of muscular men walked in wearing tight T-shirts and strutted around as if they were the most muscular men in the world. They soon realized, however, that they were not as muscle-bound as they initially thought. One of them, a man named Reyes, tried to put on a fake smile, but it was not very convincing. It was clear that not everyone appreciated our presence, and some felt that we did not belong there.

Little did I know at the time that this encounter would lead to my involvement with the Juarez cartel, as I would eventually meet The Chief and be brought into the cartel. But for now, all I could do was sit and endure the stares and whispers of those around me.

We will talk about that more with him soon. None of this bothered me because one thing is for sure and certain - these people were the best of the best at what they did, and they could sense any insecurities in you. There had to be an obnoxious type of arrogance that you carry or a borderline God complex. Part of this I had naturally, but the latter part I would just have to win an Oscar for.

As before, there were a lot of people coming in and out of this condominium, and after moving around a little myself, I observed that they were going in and out of the majority of the condominiums in the whole complex. The Chief, via Junior, would have me introduced to a selective group of these individuals, not many though. Black Shirt would make sure he was hovering somewhere around just in case somebody wanted to speak. He could interpret, but mostly to make sure no one tried to get close to us for his own selfish reasons, which I would find out at some point soon.

We were just sitting there for hours, and I did not understand why. Then Bald Head said to us that we needed to load up because we were going to get something to eat. I loaded up in the vehicle with The Chief as always, with Bald Head in the back seat. We drove not too far away to some restaurant. When we arrived, there was already security there on the outside as well as strategically placed and obviously placed inside of the restaurant. They had booked the whole entire restaurant because people just kept coming and kept coming, and we were just eating while these guys were drinking their asses off.

Junior sat between I AM & I, and he was really feeling good. He was talking to us a lot, laughing, and hugging us, just really performing for all the onlookers that were still amazed. He even yelled at the top of his lungs as he pointed at guys saying to them, "DO YOU WANT A PROBLEM WITH ME?!"

I couldn't even count the number of times Junior yelled at the guys around us, asking if they wanted a problem with him. Everyone would deny it and drop their heads. We spent hours at the restaurant, with all-you-can-eat and all-you-can-drink. Even though I didn't drink, The Chief kept sending me drinks, which I had to remind him I don't drink. He then ordered me some softer drinks from a Mexican perspective, and even a few shots of Baileys Irish cream liquor, which I reluctantly accepted to not offend him in front of everyone.

Me: Yo! I AM, you'll have to handle this one because you know I don't mess around with this stuff. The Chief wants to show us off, but we need to get into party mode.

This was I AM's area of expertise when it came to partying, drinking, and acting a fool. Under normal circumstances, I wouldn't have allowed it, but in this case, his talent was needed. Junior called out I AM and I for a game of shooter. It was a round in a big steel drum with a small basketball, and the rules were that every time you missed a shot, you had to take a shot of liquor. The ball went around in circles, and these guys were damn good, as if they played the game often. I AM couldn't hit the side of a barn with a brick, so he was knocking down a lot of shots of liquor. Knowing how much he loves liquor, and how he described Mexican tequila as being a lot smoother than American purchased tequila, I suspected he might be missing them on purpose, almost as if he was throwing them back.

I couldn't count the number of times The Chief yelled at us to get into party mode. Sometimes, he would even turn around behind him as he was sitting and shout to the guys behind us. But everyone would just say no in some drastic form and drop their heads.

He was drinking so many damn shots of liquor until these guys started getting afraid for him, telling him that he should slow down. But I AM, being in true form, was a clown, and they really enjoyed him.

Enough for me and him accomplishing what I needed to accomplish and making Chief happy because everybody enjoyed him in me based on him. Refusing to stop drinking and telling everybody in a loud slurring voice that, "THIS AIN'T SHIT! CAN'T NONE OF Y'ALL DRINK MORE THAN ME! THIS SHIT IS LIKE WATER TO ME!!" Even though most of them didn't know what he was saying, they still appeared to enjoy it.

Not stopping there, he had to make them aware that his whole family drinks, and this is a normal ritual, and he was experienced. They warned me that I may be asked to stop him because he was not going to feel it right now, but it would hit him hard later. Therefore, I stopped I AM. We loaded up again and headed back to the hotel, not to the condominiums. When we arrived back at the hotel, I was blown away by the number of cars and people all standing outside around the hotels on the balconies of the hotels. There may have even been some people on the damn roof. It reminded you of a big corporate meeting or convention somewhere; it was crawling with Narcos and sicarios. Every hotel, restaurant....etc. was rented out & all expenses billed to the corporation of the Sinaloa Federation.

After getting I AM into the room with the help of our new shadow, Black Shirt nearby just looking without being too close or seeming overly interested in us personally. I AM was laying down, that tequila was starting to creep up on him as Junior and the sicarios warned. There was a knock at the door. I got up to go answer thinking it was Bald Head. When I opened the door, I saw it was Junior asking me to step out on the balcony. I stepped out looking in the direction he was pointing....... There was a lengthy line of very pretty Latino ladies. One thing you will do a lot of when visiting is eat and fuck. Seems like every time you stop anywhere for a brief period of time you are offered food or pussy;

sometimes both! I was starting to feel stressed out with all that was going on that I didn't understand. I was forced to come back across the border in such short notice, still not knowing why really. I had close to a ton of cocaine over in the states, Chief threatening to kill Danny; while Danny is advising me; I should feel bad for Chief not him. Now I'm at the Narcos's Convention of world domination with a line of beautiful Latino women.

As I stood on the balcony with Junior, I couldn't help but feel overwhelmed by the situation. The sight of the line of women was both alluring and unsettling at the same time. It seemed like a constant reminder of the dangerous world I had stumbled into. The thought of indulging in the pleasures that were being offered to me was tempting, but I knew deep down that it was a slippery slope. I couldn't afford to let my guard down, not even for a moment.

Junior noticed my hesitation and placed a reassuring hand on my shoulder. "Don't worry, amigo," he said with a smile. "They are all very clean and very good at what they do. You won't regret it."

I nodded, still unsure of what to do. I didn't want to offend anyone or make the wrong decision. I was about to ask Junior for his advice when I noticed a new face in the crowd. She was beautiful, with long dark hair and bright green eyes. She stood out from the rest, and I couldn't help but feel drawn to her. Without even thinking, I pointed at her and said, "I'll take her."

The other girls started whispering amongst themselves, and I could sense a nervous energy building. The girl I had chosen looked at me with a mixture of fear and defiance. I could tell that she wasn't happy with the situation, but I didn't know how to handle it.

That's when I noticed Black Shirt standing nearby, watching the scene unfold. He seemed to understand what was happening and stepped forward to help.

"My friend," he said in a calm voice, "perhaps you should let the girl choose for herself. It's not right to force her into something she doesn't want to do."

I felt a wave of embarrassment wash over me. I had been so caught up in my own desires that I had forgotten to consider the feelings of others. I apologized to the girl and let her go. The other girls seemed relieved, and the tension in the air dissipated.

Junior patted me on the back. "Don't worry about it, amigo. It happens to the best of us. Just remember to always treat people with respect, no matter what the situation."

I nodded, grateful for his words of wisdom. Even in the midst of chaos and danger, there were still moments of clarity and humanity. I knew that I still had much to learn, but I was willing to try.

Now I find myself at the Narco's Convention of world domination, surrounded by a line of beautiful Latino women. Another new face appears, inviting me to pick one. I assume this is the American urban definition of a pimp. The girls start whispering to each other with nervous body language. I realize what's going on, and I don't feel like having sex. This was my perfect excuse. I point to the most nervous-looking girl, and she responds with an emphatic shake of her head, "NO!" She starts speaking fast, explaining, I assume. I look down the rest of the line and see terror in the eyes of these girls - TERROR OF THE BIG BLACK MAN WITH THE SUPER DICK!!! My ego couldn't take it anymore, I needed to know the exact words of terror. I looked around for Junior to interpret what these terrified ladies were saying. Junior is busy laughing with all the other guys on the balcony and the ground, just getting a kick out of this, but Black Shirt is there to assist me.

Black Shirt: "My friend, they are saying that you are going to break their very small pussies. They say they can see you through your pants right now!"

When we arrived in the room, I changed into some cotton shorts with a t-shirt, but no underwear. Never being one to let a disaster go to waste, in the nature of a true capitalist, I put my manhood to virtual use. I start pointing at them one by one, placing my hands behind my head while pumping the air violently after pointing one out. My manhood swung this way and that! Needless to say, the girls broke rank and started running in different directions. The pimp guy held one of the girl's arms, pulling her back as she was on the ground, pulling in the opposite direction as he was yelling at her. The sicarios were chasing them while laughing. All you could hear was laughing, whistling, cheering, and some guys were mimicking me violently pumping the air too. The Chief had come out on the balcony and placed his arm around me as I stood over the girl the Pimp was holding. I grabbed her arm away from him to help her escape. Before I released her, I gave her a good scare with my thunder pumping! She started screaming as she turned to high tail it out of there. The Chief was laughing, the guys were cheering, and I was screaming the word they use for pussy, "Mustachhhiiiiiiiii!!!"

They called another and knocked on the door I came out fast as I looked down the line, knowing my audience was ready to be entertained.

I start yelling," MUSTACHHHHIIIIIII," the erupted in madness like a sporting event and I grab the invisible woman stance letting my manhood swing, slapping back and forth in my very loose shorts. They took off and ran just as the other line of girls did too. The Chief along with Junior came over to me as The Chief grabbed me again. The Chief offered me to go into his room and have his lover.

I'm thinking in my mind," that shit called rape back across!" I had to convince him without insulting him that I appreciate his offer, but I was kind of tired already and I AM was starting to get really sick now. I was thinking this was over now, I got another knock at the damn door. I answered, another damn line; this one was much longer. I looked; there the Pimp was again with more women. Where is he getting all these damn women from," SHIT!!" I hit the WWE performance again expecting the same result, these girls started to take a half step in the other direction but didn't run.

I was feeling like they were told in advance not to do so or something. To my surprise, one started walking towards me after stepping out of line. I was shook, and afraid at the same time," this bitch actually walking towards me!!" The guys really went BANANAS NOW!! The young lady was beautiful with a capital B too. I stopped my pumping as she grabbed my hand. The boys were cutting up, even shooting in the air, whistling, throwing kisses! I led her towards my room , knowing after all that hell I raised I had to do all that shit now.

She was just smiling at me with a huge smile too," BITCH IMA ABOUT TO SPLIT YO ASS IN HALF NA!!"

I AM was in the restroom throwing up all of his insides. I checked on him, as I told him I had action.

Me: I got a bad Mutha Fucka on deck Nigga! You get ya self together enough to come peep around the corn and see ya man laying down the BEAST FUCK!!

I came back around the corner and saw Momma jumping on the bed, showing off her impressive dance moves. She was better than some of the dancers I've seen in gentlemen's clubs back in the states. Her signature move was repeated frequently,I pulled the condom out and the jet black hair had me harder than an armored truck. I snatched her legs from under her and I started doing a grown man's deed to her at full strength. I was power driving her, giving her the blues and no cap (No Lie) . She could not handle it, But I think she liked the pain or something. She got me geeked up and super excited," man I think I'm her fantasy or something! Shit, she must think I'm sexy too!" Were the things that were going through my head. I gave her everything I had and she couldn't handle it, but I could tell she enjoyed the pain. I was feeling like a stud and thought I was her ultimate fantasy.

But things took a turn when the condom broke from the excitement of the moment. I panicked, realizing I didn't have any more. I stood up and walked towards the door, shouting to I AM if he had any. I opened the door and two guys stumbled in, probably eavesdropping on us. The Pimp quickly left the room upon seeing me naked, and I asked the guys if they had any condoms. As I looked out the door, I saw six or seven guys peeking through a gap in the curtains, with three of them stacked on top of each other. I asked if they had any condoms, but they quickly ran away. I was annoyed that they didn't even offer to give me one after watching the show.

I had to cut my intense sexual encounter short because I didn't have any more condoms, which ruined the moment for both of us. Meanwhile, I AM's condition was getting worse, and he seemed like he wasn't going to stop throwing up. The young lady must have informed the guys that I AM was sick in the restroom, prompting Bald Head and Junior to check on him. They brought some milk with them and told me to make I AM drink it, but he refused. I thought it would hurt him, but they assured me that it was a way to deal with liquor poisoning. We eventually forced him to drink it, and they told me to keep him in the restroom because he would start throwing up profusely, like he was possessed by demons. They also said that once he stopped, he would instantly start feeling better, which turned out to be true.

I spent a long night looking after I AM, and the whole room smelled like everything he had drunk and eaten the day before. Who would have thought that milk would be such an effective remedy for alcohol poisoning! The only side effect of that remedy is the rapid and intense regurgitation of what appears to be the person's insides.

Morning arrived quickly after a night filled with caring for I AM and moonlighting as the Phallic god of Black Bottom, Eastside Detroit!

We returned to the walled condos for another meeting with some others. This time, we didn't go back upstairs to the same condo from the previous night. Instead, we gathered in small circles throughout the medium-sized parking area outside of the condos. There were messengers who traveled between circles, passing messages and even pulling certain guys out of circles for side bar conversations.

Another car pulled into the walled gated area, and the pimp from the previous night emerged from the vehicle with a beautiful Latina goddess by his side. She was so stunningly beautiful that she didn't look real - like a refined wine, fine China, or the Mona Lisa in motion. It was apparent from her presence that she knew it, and the pimp walked into a ground-level condo with her in close tow. I had never seen anyone walking in or out of this particular condo before.

Everyone continued to interact as they were, but I noticed Chief's pausing in conversation, taking notice of the pimp with his eyes as he disappeared into the condo. I turned to I AM and told him about the pimp's endless lines of ladies from the night before. Just as I filled him in on some of last night's activities, the pimp came back out of the condo with the beautiful young lady. They stood to the side isolated from the groups, and the pimp was speaking to her along the side of our groups. Different guys in different meeting groups were keeping an eye on him, seeming like everyone was interested in him or the young lady. I figured it must be the guys wanting to put their bid in to have an audience with

Mona Lisa. I told I AM that I would give an arm and a leg for her. "I AM, I think I'm going to ask The Chief if I can have her! I want to see if they could sneak her across for me too." I couldn't keep my eyes off her, like everyone else was doing. Bald Head was unusually silent on the subject, and I was talking to I AM just as much as I was talking to Bald Head.

Me: "I AM! Why does he look right in my fucking face every time I try to get a sneak peek at the girl?"

I AM: I'm wondering why you haven't noticed that shit! Dude ain't took his eyes off you the entire time he's been standing there with her. You said when you opened the door last night, that he was the first one you saw....... And, I bet he didn't give you eye contact one time. DID HE??!

Pausing to think for a moment, but knowing I AM was correct.

Me: YOU.... MAN FUCK YOU....

I AM: Not at all! I KNOW!!

I looked back over towards Mona Lisa right at that moment.... The Pimp locked eyes with me again," SHIT, BRO! I THINK YOUR RIGHT!!" Bald Head overheard me, then asked me if I was okay. Turning to Bald Head," Hell Naw.... That dude is sweet on me, My friend!" Bald Head looked confused about the meaning of my statement. "That dude over there is gay,man," as Bald Head disregarded what I said. He just looked the other way as if I didn't say anything at all. I AM agree with me when it appeared Bald Head blew me off.

Bald Head turned to me after I repeated myself, right after I AM whispered to me," Man, he wants you bad! He ain't even trying to hide it anymore. Don't look because he is staring at you right now!" "My Friend, he is NOT gay," Bald Head exclaimed with emphasis. We started going back and forth as I AM and I was laughing, while making jokes. Chief noticed the energy we were going back and forth with.

Chief asked Bald Head what we were talking about based on the reaction of the whole circle started to laugh. I could only assume Bald Head told The Chief I felt the Pimp was gay and he kept staring at me. The guy's got a kick out of this apparently.

The Pimp: What are you guys laughing about??!

I bet you want to know how I know that's what the Pimp said, right?! Well, let me tell you what happened.....

The Pimp spoke very loudly, and instantly everyone stopped laughing abruptly, including the most powerful narco in Mexico, The Chief. This is what Danny had told me when we first went to meet him. There was dead silence from every group, and all eyes were staring at the ground except me. After witnessing that, I looked over in the Pimp's direction. He wasn't looking at me then; he was looking over all of the groups that were now silent. You could hear a mouse piss on cotton; it was so quiet. The Pimp said something, and then everyone started moving towards the vehicles as the big steel gate was being slid open.

Bald Head, My friend, said, "See, I told you that he wasn't gay."

We got into the car with The Chief, and he didn't mention anything that had just happened. The car was silent for the short ride we took to an Applebee's restaurant. We entered in the same fashion as always, but the Pimp and Mona Lisa went in first. Everyone was eating and drinking heavily. I ate, but not as much as usual. I was complaining, still not understanding why we needed to be there, bro.

We returned to the hotel again after spending a few hours at Applebee's. We repeated this for the next few days, the only difference being the places or what would be brought to us over at the condos. Every day over there, we saw different interesting people who had that big-time Narco Jefe look. We didn't see much of the Pimp after that last gathering at Applebee's.

One morning, I had finally had enough. We had just under a ton of cocaine back in the states, and we were just hanging out in Mexico with no clear purpose. I felt like it was Groundhog Day because we did the same things every day. That morning, we headed to a huge mall to settle down in what would be a food court area of malls back in the states. I was feeling restless, and I started talking more with The Chief, who knew how I was feeling. Bald Head was telling him about my concerns about being in Mexico while so much work was back in the states, but The Chief just kept telling me not to worry, while smiling.

As we sat in the mall, people were walking around very slowly, staring at us. A nice group had gathered around us, staring and often pointing at me and I Am. This was not new to me, as I had been coming to Mexico for years at this point. The sicarios had the perimeter secured, as always, but unbeknownst to me, we were safely in Sinaloa territory. The Chief waved in a group of young people who wanted pictures and autographs. The Chief really enjoyed the whole scene and excitement from the people.

At one point, I got upset with I AM because I felt like he was acting Hollywood towards the people who just wanted some pictures and autographs. After everything settled down, I AM made me aware that he wasn't acting funny at all. He called my attention to one of the groups that he refused to take a picture with.

"I AM: Just keep looking at them and tell me what you see.

Me: I don't see anything special, just some kids...

I AM: What?! Grabbing each other's asses, right? I can just imagine all the fun they'll have with your pictures! You have that universal appeal!

The Chief signaled for us to walk with him. As we walked through the mall, he strutted in and out of stores with I AM on one side and me on the other. The sicarios walked a little bit behind us, while people stood aside, pointing and looking in amazement at The Chief.

The two-way radio started to go off, and the guys informed The Chief of something urgent. We picked up our pace and headed back towards the food court area.

When we arrived back at the food court, I saw the Pimp sitting at the head of a long table, which the sicarios had put together. The Chief, Bald Head, I AM, and I sat right beside him, while Black Shirt listened very attentively. The conversation focused on me, as I answered a barrage of questions from the Pimp.

Bald Head translated some of what was being said to keep me informed, but there were certain things he would not translate. Most of the translation revolved around logistics, such as how to get the products to me in the markets I was currently in, and the volume or increase in volume that would be needed.

The Pimp was extremely impressed with what he heard, and he asked me if I could get into other areas of interest to him. I began to explain the other markets I could penetrate easily and some that would require more work but were still doable. The Chief and I had great chemistry, and he loved that I could catch on to a lot of what he was trying to do. So I started to exaggerate, even adding in things that I had no idea how to pull off."

Bald Head was translating, but I could tell by The Chief's facial expressions and subtle smiles that he wanted more information. I had mentioned to The Chief in the past that I was interested in obtaining keys of heroin for my Detroit market. This question was presented to the Pimp. The Pimp elaborated stating that they mostly had black tar heroin, but the Gulf Cartel was the one that had the keys of heroin. I knew for a fact that the Sinaloa Cartel had keys of heroin, but perhaps the volume that they were asking for was the issue

Bald Head wouldn't translate everything, so I gathered that there must have been an agreement between the two cartels that certain products or volumes would not be dealt with. It was not uncommon for one office (Cartel Plaza Boss) to contact another office (a different Cartel Plaza Boss) if one group was short on cocaine or other products. I assumed that this could go all the way to the top Narcos Jefe's as well. The Pimp was clearly not just a pimp, as he was at the head of the table taking inventory of amounts of product moved, markets owned, possibilities of markets to be added, and areas that Sinaloa would like to access, which all equated to the volume of drugs moved in tonnage.

After an extensive conversation, we returned to the hotel. The Chief appeared to be in an increasingly good mood, leading me to believe that the meeting went very well and my shit was effective in that process. Over the past few days, when we returned to the hotel, we would stay there until the beginning of the following day. This time was different; we were summoned back to the vehicles and returned to the walled condominiums. Once inside, we returned to the one where we would normally sit in a circle. People flowed in and out as they did on the initial day that we came to the same place. However, there seemed to be more of a matter-of-fact type of movement in the atmosphere, and people were moving with a purpose or so it seemed to me. I started to think that something was afoot once the Pimp showed up. We had not seen him there in a number of days. I couldn't put my finger on what was happening because I didn't even know why I was down there, but it appeared that whatever was going to happen would be centered around him.

The Chief was sitting next to me in the circle, and his spirits were high. He asked me to promise him that I would return back in November for a very big party that would be taking place. He expressed to me that it was of grave importance that I attended, and he seemed pretty happy about it. Within the course of that conversation, two-way radios started to go off everywhere, and guys started to move around extremely fast. The Chief grabbed my arm and pulled me with him, and I just followed suit. Everyone was moving extremely fast with a purpose, and I was almost freaking out because the Chief's whole demeanor changed. I didn't bother asking Bald Head anything because I knew he wasn't going to tell me anything, and he looked kind of nervous. Once I saw the Pimp on the move, I understood instantly that this was big.

We entered the vehicles and were on the road traveling at a pretty fast rate of speed. This was a very large group of vehicles, not just based on the ones inside of the walls, but there were a bunch of vehicles outside of the walls as well. I couldn't even assume the amount of vehicles based on the amount of dust that was flying all around once we exited the walls from the movement of vehicles everywhere. I'm thinking we had to drive maybe about half an hour or 45 minutes until we arrived at a farm. The gates to the farm were opened, and we started to pull in slowly. It was very dark on this farm; you couldn't see anything either way that you looked. This road, which was on private property, was maybe about the length of two football fields. I was starting to see a well-lit area at this point, maybe 100 to 150 yards up the road. We pulled into this area with the majority of the vehicles hanging back, leading me to believe those were the vehicles of the sicario on the perimeter. Everyone exited their vehicles, as there were dogs running around everywhere. This was clearly a farm based on observing all the farm equipment and things related to farming.

The interesting thing for me was that I couldn't see a house anywhere, but again, it was very dark, and visibility was poor. To the right of where we pulled in, there was a cemented area that had a pavilion-type structure with some tables. To the left, there appeared to be a sizable hut that looked like a small wind could easily blow it over. People were standing around in groups, having conversations that moved back and forth between other groups in conversation, right around the vehicles and to the right of the vehicles, near the cemented area. Our little group was there too, with some additional faces in a circle. After some time of standing and talking in our circle, much of our group left and moved about 30 yards behind our position, leaving only me and I AM.

As I saw Black Shirt out of my peripherals double back to where we were standing, he started talking in riddles that I couldn't understand. His tone changed to that of a warning while still questioning me, and he made direct eye contact with me up close, which he had never done before. At times, his eyes would wander to the left ever so slightly, causing me to turn to my right and say something to I AM without tipping off Black Shirt that I had noticed his eyes wandering. I AM and I exchanged a few words based on the conversation at hand. I cut my eyes to the left to have him follow my gaze and saw the Pimp standing there with Mona Lisa. I wanted I AM to be aware of the Pimp, as he had been before.

Now, in my mind, this was either some type of weird coincidence, especially with Black Shirt doubling back, or it was not. I AM stood to the back of me as I turned to face Black Shirt directly, shielding I AM from being seen by Black Shirt while he kept an eye on the Pimp and Mona Lisa. I AM would also be able to whisper to the back of my head what he was observing, if need be. Black Shirt continued.

Black Shirt: Are you sure this is what you want to do, my friend? You do know that these people you are dealing with here are very powerful!

Me: Yes, I know... I also know that The Chief is also very powerful.

Black Shirt: Yes, Chief is powerful too. But, my friend, these people are very powerful. These people control this state and the surrounding states. All of the politicians, state and federal, are paid by these people. They even have very long arms to politicians in the states through their friends here, my friend... Are you sure you want to do this because these are not people you can just disappear from, friend. Yes, The Chief is powerful, but he will not be able to help you with these people.

Me: Well, I'm a Big Boy.

This was stated with extreme sarcasm. I had to make sure that I sounded extremely arrogant and obnoxious at that. I turned away from him in a blowing him off type fashion. I AM started to point out to me that The Pimp was starting to stare again. I took a small glance in the pimp's direction and he was staring again! This was starting to get to me. I thought he had basically gathered himself over the last few days, but evidently not or was there something else afoot that I just wasn't aware of.

Speaking with I AM, telling him I'm under the impression that there were a lot of things that were not told to us. Right at this moment, there was a big semi-truck that poured into the farm and pulled right to the left of our parked vehicles, close to the big Hut-style barn. There were a number of guys that attended to the semi-truck, opening up the back doors of the trailer.

"Man, they just pulled a couple of guys out of that trailer! All they fucking had on was their draws, bro," I AM stated to me while being visibly shaken.

Black Shirt turned towards me and asked, "My Friend... Do you think it would be okay if I put a ton of marijuana on the truck to come to you too? I can give you a good price too!" I turned towards him while he was mid-sentence, noticing that he was looking straight ahead where I AM was also looking, at the back of the trailer where the naked guys were pulled from and taken toward the hut. It was clear to me now that negotiations about drugs or something related to it were going to take place.

Me: "That's not a problem for me at all. As long as you discuss it with the Chief first, My Friend."

Black Shirt: OH! OH, YES!! OF COURSE, MY FRIEND!!

The lying SON OF A BITCH!! Black Shirt's tone of voice went up two to three octaves once I mentioned the Chief. It made me think of the Chief repeatedly warning me, "DON'T THROW ME UNDER THE BRIDGE!" My stress levels started to climb in my chest, and my senses were on high alert. I realized that this was why Black Shirt had been sticking so close to I AM and me. He was waiting for this moment.

I kept all my thoughts to myself, not wanting to make I AM uncomfortable. If my hunch was correct, and all these moving parts were connected, the Chief would be a dead man if I showed any signs of listening to Black Shirts offers. Bald Head was leaving us open for this guy to interact with us too, and it was apparent at this point. Bald Head was still upset about the Chief killing his former boss. However, I would keep Black Shirt and Bald Head's secret. After all, I was a business professional - a true capitalist

I AM: Oh shit! Don't look, but here he comes, and he got her with him too!

That wasn't much of a FUCKEN warning because soon as I looked up the pimp was right in front of me with Mona Lisa to his left. How convenient, Black Shirt Is always in the right place at the right time. You just can't make shit like this up how perfectly they just fall in alignment. The Pimp stood in front of me without saying a word as he looked me up and down and turned into Mona Lisa saying something. Mona Lisa smiled and said something in turn to the Pimp.

Pimp: What's the matter??...... You don't like Rolex??

While showing me his Presidential Rolex, with the Rolex diamonds on his arm. They both had a sadistic smile on their face of temptation. I lifted up my arm and showed I was wearing a Submariner Rolex. expressed it was something casual, not flashy yet stylish that I could fly without bringing attention to myself.

Black Shirt was translating all of this between me and the Pimp making the Pimp aware that I had a rose gold presidential with the Rolex diamonds. He said something else to Mona Lisa as she started to smile very hard letting out a little giggle. This giggle concerns me greatly. Mona Lisa nodded her head yes.

Pimp: You are a Jefe! I think that you should have a nice Rolex from me now.

I'm feeling nervous as FUCK at this point. I got someone else tryna make me " THEIR BITCH", I'm thinking nervously in my head. I could feel the tension rising as the Pimp and Mona Lisa continued to try and tempt me with the Rolex. I knew I had to stay strong and not let them get the best of me. Black Shirt was still translating everything, and I could tell he was getting uneasy too.

Black Shirt: My Friend, it is a very generous offer.

I could see the greed in his eyes, but I didn't want to judge him too quickly. He might just be trying to make some money for himself.

Me: Thank you, but I'm really not interested.

Pimp: Come on, don't be shy. It's a gift from me to you.

Mona Lisa continued to giggle, and I started to feel very uncomfortable. I knew I had to get out of there before things got out of hand.

Me: Look, I appreciate the offer, but I really have to go. Maybe we can talk about it another time.

With that, I turned and walked away, not looking back. I could feel their eyes on me, and I knew I had made the right decision. I needed to stay focused on my business and not get caught up in their temptations.

At this point, I was feeling extremely nervous. However, I was saved by the two-way radio that started going off. The pimp turned and ran back towards his initial position with Mona Lisa in tow. Bald Head came out of nowhere and grabbed me, pulling me back towards where the chief was standing on the cement, just to the right of the pavilion.

As I looked up, I saw lights coming down the private road towards our position. About four or five small pickup trucks pulled in by the vehicles. It was like the invasion of the munchkins; all of these short guys were walking around us at the same time. I noticed one of these guys from Mazatlán, the same guy who had nodded at me after exiting the black Hummer truck. He walked towards me and The Chief and nodded again at both of us. He was dressed in flip flops, no socks, a man bag over his shoulders, and a baseball cap. He looked kind of weird to me.

After a lot of commotion, things eventually settled down. A couple of guys grabbed two bales wrapped in silver foil and laid them on the table under the pavilion. The Chief started moving towards the tables, signaling me to follow. One guy walked up to the silver-wrapped bales and cut two big triangles inside the wrapping, exposing marijuana.

As I stepped forward to examine the marijuana, a man on the opposite side of the table stepped forward as well. He appeared to be the same guy we had seen at the zoo over in Durango, wearing overalls and a white cowboy hat, if I remembered correctly. The short guy with the man bag was standing to the left of him but far left, not really close, but the closest considering everyone else.

I looked around for The Chief and saw that he was standing behind me. The gentleman began to speak to us, asking us what we thought about the marijuana before us. I noticed that The Chief had become Danny in this situation, and I was to speak directly to his chief, as I did when Danny brought me in front of my chief.

The gentleman asked me what I thought of the marijuana. I told him that I thought it was of very good quality.

Ol Man Mayo: How much would you like?

Me: I could handle two or three tons to start. How much time?

Ol Man Mayo: How much time would you need?

Me: Once I get up to speed, I could do that every 7 to 10 days.

Ol Man Mayo: Could you handle a truck every week with 7 to 8 metric tons?

Me: I would need a little more space, but with some extra time, it's doable. Yes!

Ol Man Mayo: $500 a kilo good price for you?

Me: I agree.

I was so overwhelmed that I couldn't think straight. I was totally freaking out on the inside, but with a calm outward demeanor and a great poker face. When he said "metric tons," I wasn't familiar with the term when it comes to marijuana. I'm sure I could have negotiated the price down a little lower than the $500 per kilo, but I was too nervous during the negotiation. Eight metric tons of marijuana would be 17,600 pounds of marijuana.

The negotiations were straightforward, and there weren't a lot of games, really no back and forth, and believe me when I tell you this was intense. I think at this point, I started to understand what black shirt was trying to express to me. This was clearly a whole different level of sophistication and volume. Things wrapped up fairly quickly after prices were set. There wasn't much negotiating on the cocaine because the market pretty much set the prices for that. In most cases, all the proceeds from the sales of marijuana pretty much funded the transportation and overhead costs of the main featured product, which was cocaine. That's why I should have negotiated down further on the marijuana, seeing that there was always much more wiggle room to manipulate better odds in my favor.

This entire process marked the beginning of The Chief keeping his promise to me, as part of our verbal agreement for me not to "throw him under the bridge," as he put it. Bringing me along to negotiate my own terms on the marijuana was a way for him to verify that he would keep his word by allowing me to negotiate at the next level up.

As everyone dispersed to different vehicles, I rode with the Chief, with Bald Head in the back seat sitting close between us to translate. After turning onto the main road, the Chief suddenly slammed on the brakes, grabbing my knee as it was shaking uncontrollably.

Chief: CALM DOWN HERMANO!! CALM DOWN!! I HAVE FAITH IN YOU AND KNOW YOU CAN DO THIS!! LOOK AT IT AS THEY ARE GIVING IT TO ME AND I AM GIVING IT TO YOU!! I AM RESPONSIBLE FOR EVERYTHING, NOT YOU!! PLEASE JUST CALM DOWN, IT IS NO DIFFERENT THAN BEFORE!! YOU HAVE TO JUST CALM DOWN AND TRUST ME HERMANO!!

I nodded in agreement, indicating that I understood what he was saying and would try to calm down. However, I was completely unaware that my body was shaking outwardly, and my mind was in a state of panic.

Chief: I'm going to send you a ton of cocaine from my chief each month, and 500 kilos from me in the same shipment. I will also include an additional ton of marijuana in the same shipment as the 8 tons you will be receiving from my chief every seven to ten days. ALWAYS PAY ME FIRST BEFORE MY CHIEF!

As the car began moving again, I nodded in agreement, but I couldn't shake the feeling that this was only making me more nervous than before.

Chief: Starting in the second month, you will receive 2 tons a month from my Chief and 1 ton from me every month. The marijuana will remain the same, but always remember to pay me first. Don't worry if you are not finished every month with the two tons from my Chief in the beginning. It will continue to come to you every month. Just have money to send back with every truck that comes. I will send a separate truck for my money. After the first couple of months, you should be able to complete everything within that month. Don't worry if you can't for my Chief, just come close to finishing. I will take responsibility if you don't. Just keep paying me first, no matter what Hermano.

The emphasis on paying him first was overstated, to say the least. He continued to place the emphasis on paying him first, and there seemed to be an underlying message present.

Our group stopped at the end of the road, where there was a corner store. Everyone, for the most part, got out of the vehicles and filed into the store. Security, of course, set up a perimeter around the area where we stopped. Another group that was at the farm as well pulled in and entered the store. I was sitting in The Chief's car alone, replaying everything that just happened, along with the conversation The Chief had with me, wondering if I would be able to live up to his expectations.

Then, for some weird reason, I just had a feeling someone was staring at me. I slowly turned my head to the right, and my instincts were accurate, as they usually are. The damn Pimp was staring at me so intensely, I instantly felt uncomfortable. I quickly turned my head straight forward, just to at some point try to inadvertently look again to see if he was still staring, and, oh my God, he was. I would never have imagined, as a man, I would feel kind of horrible because this guy clearly appeared to be a superfreak of some kind that I didn't want to imagine.

We were heading back to the Devil's Spine, and I was relieved at the thought of returning to the safety of the hotel in Mazatlán, far away from the creepy Sinaloa pimp. However, The Chief's phone rang, and it was The Pimp on the other end, asking us to come back for a big party to celebrate the arrangements that had been made during our stay. What I didn't know was that this meeting was crucial, and they were discussing logistics for transporting metric tons of drugs from

Columbia to Panama City and Mexico City for distribution to various cartels, including Sinaloa and Beltran Leyva.

My portion of the shipment would be sent from Mexico City to Ciudad Juarez, then crossed into El Paso, TX, and finally forwarded to me via King Transport, owned by Bald Head's double-crossing partner Reyes, to various cities, including Detroit, MI, Baltimore, MD, and even Atlanta, GA, which was news to me.

Despite my protests, we turned around and headed back to the party, which meant being in the presence of my not-so-secret admirer, the Sinaloa pimp. I expressed my discomfort to Bald Head, but he and The Chief just laughed it off, not understanding the gravity of the situat ion.This guy thinks I'm hot and he wants me badly too!! I can see the shit in his eye!! They were just laughing uncontrollably! Just seems to be the funniest thing to them as if they didn't understand what the big deal was.

I soon found out that The Pimp was not just a pimp but one of the most crucial and intricate parts of the Sinaloa organization. I was merely an asset of significant value in more ways than one, and history was repeating itself as I had become nothing more than a bargaining chip, just as Danny had brought me to The Chief before.

Returning to the apartment complex was a stark contrast to our previous visit for the meeting at the farm. The security was much more stringent, with military-style checkpoints on roads leading towards the complex. As we approached, the security personnel stepped aside to let our vehicles pass through. Bald Head and the Chief were communicating in Morse code on their two-way radio, but our movement was not hindered. As we neared the complex, the security detail thinned out until only The Chief's and Junior's cars were allowed to enter the gated compound.

Exiting our vehicles, we were greeted by the Sinaloa Pimp, who immediately engaged in conversation with me. This was unlike our previous interactions, as he was much more friendly and engaging. I noticed that I had a new translator, Black Shirt, who seemed to be more comfortable around me than the others. Bald Head, Chief, and Junior were mingling with the other guests at the party. Reyes, who was a clout chaser, stayed close to me and I AM, which was not surprising. I was already aware of his true intentions from the beginning.

Sinaloa Pimp: I hear that you are coming back for the very big party in November Primo. I must take you around and show you our town. You are a Jefe with a lot of power now. A Jefe must dress and look the part. I will take care of you, don't worry Primo.

I'm thinking to myself," I guess I'm safe until I return in Novem ber...." This fucking guy was hitting on me, I guess. I didn't feel safe trusting my instincts at this point because so much was happening so fast, I needed the opportunity to just get away and decompress and go through some of this.

Sinaloa Pimp: Primo when you arrive back in your town be ready. We are going to send a guy up to you in Detroit. You will need to pick him up from the airport and show him the exits and freeway to your place where he will bring those things to you, Primo. This guy will be the actual driver coming over to your place. Then take this guy back to the airport because he will need to fly right back so we can be back over there with you soon after.

This shit is happening really fast and I'm not prepared for it at all but I'm keeping my game face on and I'm in full control of my body. Reyes muscled Black Shirt out for the translating position, cutting him off often trying to make himself a part of the process for his own purposes, I'm sure. Now At this point I finally figured out that my name had been changed to Primo while questioning myself," when did this happen."

Sinaloa Pimp: Listen Primo.... Our Chief wants you to purchase 3 Presidential Rolexes, A Cartier watch and a special made diamond and platinum bracelet for the party in November. I will get you the design before you are gone. Primo, once you become a Jefe you must wear a Presidential Rolex. This is a gift that our boss gives to all his Jefe's. You are a Jefe now Primo.

Reyes is still translating and has placed his arm around my fucking shoulders now. While trying to appear overjoyed for me. Reyes was the worst kind of Mexican narco because is from the class of American Mexicans that don't really care for Black men exactly what Baby Doll warned me about. He had a real problem with that fact that a Nigga made it this high BUT being the opportunist that he was....... he wasn't going to allow what he viewed as a disaster go to waste! I was the goose that laid the golden eggs and appearing to be a friend and trusted interpreter for me could put him in a power position to others that would be looking to undercut my Chief for the sake of our Chief.

Got an opportunity to breathe for a minute after the serious download of upcoming events and same sex flirting. I saw Bald Head stopping over to check on I AM & I.......

Me: I told you that fucking guy wants me baaaaaad!! Then you are going to fucking leave me out here as fair game. Let me find out that my actual ASS has been mortgaged off for a couple extra tons of cocaine and I ain't getting a fucking cut Bald Head!!

We exchanged some words back and forth with each other with him getting really upset with me, and not on his own behalf either.

Bald Head: My friend you really need to stop saying this thing about this guy!! This is not good for you my friend! I'm going to tell you why you need to stop this now. This guy is responsible for paying everyone in Mexico the government the federal rallies the police everyone my friend. He is very powerful very powerful my friend you don't need to be fucking around with this guy.

Well from that point the Sinaloa pimp was no longer the Sinaloa pimp he became the Sinaloa treasury secretary. A new epiphany had come over me and it became very clear that the Sinaloa treasury secretary was NEVER gay and an upstanding gentleman.

After this profound new understanding, I noticed Black Shirt walking towards I AM and me. The short guy who was negotiating with me over the marijuana at the farm was walking with Black Shirt towards our position. I knew he was important because of the stir at the farm when he showed up, but he didn't seem to have more power than the taller guy with the cowboy hat. I was about to have a formal introduction to my Chief, which I anticipated would have great significance. Rerez was also making his way towards us, but this time he was not trying to muscle in. Black Shirt was translating as Chapo began speaking to me.

Chapo: My Primo! I'm happy to finally meet you after talking through the radio all the time. Mayito was telling me that you, Primo, are the first Black guy I have ever done business with. I had some dealings with one many years ago in the early '90s and late '80s maybe. I shipped him loads, and he always paid. He was never short, and we never had problems. He paid for the last load I sent him and just disappeared. I never heard of him anymore. We never spoke one time, but we had very good business.

After a pause of reflection, he smiled. Reyes tried to put his arm around my shoulders again.

Chapo: Primo, in this business... always remember, this right here! Must always, MUST ALWAYS... end up in the hand of a Black Man

I was in disbelief. Everything Baby Doll had told me so many years ago was proven to be true at the very top of the food chain. Just hearing that the man at the top knew that none of this could be possible without the ability of the Black man to do what he does in and for the business, BLEW MY MIND. It was equivalent to Steve Jobs saying that the African American community is paramount to the global brand that Apple has become.

I allowed my mind to wander about how many companies and brands we were quintessential or paramount to establishing as brands. We have missed so many opportunities by not noticing the value we bring to so many products and how we are globally looked at to determine what's cool, what's fashionable, what's entertaining in music, sports, fashion, etc. We never leverage that political and physical capital into a come up for our people. Because someone is leveraging it even if you don't. It's going to be paid out to the Brains, Rojo's, Tijuana Fuck Boy's, Danny's, Bald Head's, Reyes's, and Black Shirts of the world; that doesn't represent the best interest of you and your community..... And they're not supposed to either! Because it's all COMMERCE at the end of the day.

This party that I did not want to attend ended up becoming very valuable to me on so many levels. However, I think the Chief had seen enough with everyone coming over to speak with I AM and myself. Not too long thereafter, he made the decision for us to start our journey through the Devil's Spine on the other side of the mountain for the night.

Traveling through the Devil's Spine was going to be just as challenging as it was initially when we traveled through it. The dizzy spells of going back and forth giving me the whole rollercoaster experience was very challenging. The Chief started to ask me questions about some of those people that were at the party, asking for my opinions on them, what I thought about them, some of the people that I talked to as well as some of the people that I did not speak with.

It was clear to me that he wanted to see how well I could read people without actually speaking to them or interacting with them. Noticing as I gave my observations on several individuals, he listened tentatively to all the words that I was saying, often nodding his head in confirmation at times. His eyes squinted as he called into question the things I said, and he smiled in approval leaving me to feel like I had passed his test.

Back in the state of Michigan after landing at the McNamara International Airport. I AM and I are standing at the baggage claim waiting for our luggage as I recap on a few things that happened during our visit. revisiting the words that just continued to replay in my mind over and over again," This here must always end up in the hands of a black man." Most importantly the individual it was stated by, I asked I AM what his thoughts on the statement.

I AM: Yeah, that kinda shocked me to hear that come out of his mouth. That's close to the stuff the body building chick you were in love with put you up on.

Me: I wasn't in love with Baby Doll.....But yes she did point that out long ago.

I AM: Were you actually dead ass about wanting your cut if Chief & Bald Head had a separate negotiation going on involving you physically??

ME: You fucking right I was DEAD ASS BRO! We have come up short too many times not picking up on all these side deals these folks are cutting based on our abilities.

I AM: But you willing to let a Nigga fuck...... For your cut of some extra coke Bro??! I mean you the one getting pounded for it......It should be yours, RIGHT??!

With a sincere but very concerned look on his face as if I will really be selling myself short here.

Me: WTF ARE YOU TALKING ABOUT!!! HELL, NAW I AINT ON NO SHIT LIKE THAT ASSHOLE!!! You know what the fuck I meant when I said that shit man.

With a sincere but very concerned look on his face as if I will really be selling myself short here.

Me: WTF ARE YOU TALKING ABOUT!!! HELL, NAW I AINT ON NO SHIT LIKE THAT

ASSHOLE!!! You know what the fuck I meant when I said that shit man.

I AM: Yeah, you're right...... I knew what you meant. You was gone .... Take that SHIT FOR THE TEAM BABY!!

Me: THE FUCK!! FUCK YOU AND THE TEAM!!! Don't know what the hell you thought!!

I AM: That your ass was worth tons of coke. Once you gave up the ass.... You wanted your cut of the payment!

Me: Yeah okay......You just make sure you get to Jay and order that Jewelry 911 or The Secretary is going to have yours for free!

We got in pretty late so the plan the following morning was to reach out to the guys so they could pull in the money off the street. We had to get ready to put those numbers together so we could get them on a truck that would arrive in a couple of days. I AM had to head to the airport to pick up the driver that the Sinaloa Treasurer Secretary told us he would be arriving, and we were already getting calls about the jewelry everything was going to plan.

The money came in off the streets. I AM picked up the guy from Sinaloa, showed him what he needed to see and took him right back to the airport as instructed. There was a mad scramble to secure more space for the major increase of marijuana and cocaine. There were a number of arrangements that had to be made on a level that I wasn't anticipating which wasn't the issue but the time span in which I had to do it left me a little concerned. Waiting on the marijuana to arrive after seven days we were starting to get a little concerned about the delay. This wasn't normal, especially when instructions are given from the very top. The balance that has been previously owed on the initial load had already been paid. this would of course push back the turn of cocaine that was coming or so I thought wishful thinking of course because it was a possibility that both could arrive back-to-back a logistical and storage nightmare for me.

Beep Beep Beep.......

Bald Head: Yes, go ahead my friend.........

Me: My Friend, where are those guys?? There has been no communication my Friend

Me: Alright, well let's hope they show up soon. We need to get this shipment moving as soon as possible.

Bald Head: Yeah, I hear you my friend. I'll make some calls and see what's going on.

Me: Alright, keep me posted.

Bald Head: Will do my friend.

I hung up the phone and took a deep breath. This was the nature of the business, unpredictable and constantly changing. I had to be on my toes at all times, ready to adapt to any situation that came my way. As I waited for updates from Bald Head, I couldn't help but think about the risks involved in this line of work. One mistake could cost me everything. But the potential rewards were just too great to ignore.

I continued to make arrangements and coordinate with the various people involved in the operation. It was a delicate dance, trying to keep everyone happy and on the same page. But I was determined to make it work.

Finally, after what felt like an eternity, I received a call from Bald Head.

Bald Head: Hey my friend, good news. The guys just arrived and they're ready to unload.

Me: Thank god. Alright, I'll be there as soon as I can.

Bald Head: Sounds good my friend. See you soon.

Me: I'm going to call Junior and talk to the Chief, my friend!

Bald Head: Please don't, my friend!

Me: You're lying to me, my friend!! Tell me what's going on!

Bald Head: The Chief is very sick, my friend...

Me: He will be okay, right??... My friend?

Bald Head: I don't know, my friend... This is very bad. We don't know if he will even make it..

CHAPTER 25

THE CHIEF IS VERY SICK

AFTER BALD HEAD'S FINAL statement, our conversation ended abruptly. We were both at a loss for words and knew there was no need for further discussion. The loss of the Chief would have a significant impact on both of us and the uncharted territory that awaited us was uncertain. However, I had come to recognize that the Chief was a man who valued power over greed and was willing to share the spoils with those he trusted. The Chief's name, Mayito, which meant black or dark-skinned in Spanish, spoke volumes to me. Despite being in territories never occupied by black men, the Chief had forged a connection with me that others wanted but were too afraid to cross due to political purposes or clear racism.

Although I had questions swirling in my mind about the sudden illness of the Chief and the secrecy surrounding it, I was conflicted and puzzled by the news I had received from Bald Head. The urgency with which I was pressed to arrive and the veil of secrecy made me doubt that the Chief had simply succumbed to some form of sickness. But I knew that everything was on hold for the near future and that war was on the horizon. This was precisely what the Chief had warned me about with his "don't throw me under the bridge" statements.

As the night dragged on, I received some welcome news from Mena. We had a lengthy conversation, and she finally came to the conclusion I had prayed for - that I could be a quality man and prove myself to her. She chose me, and there was no better feeling at that moment than knowing how she made me feel as a man.

She made me aware that she was going to be honest and get her things from the other gentleman's home that she was dealing with. She was going to make it clear to him that they were done, and she was making a full commitment to me. I applauded that decision because it was one that she arrived at independently, not based on me pushing her in that direction. Even though deep in my heart, there was nothing I wanted more, my ego would never allow me to verbalize that to her anyway.

That night we connected in a major way. We opened up to each other and were honest about how we saw each other and our projections for the future. The understanding we had was that the following day she would get up, go to work, and shortly thereafter, she would meet up with this gentleman to retrieve her things and give him her decision.

The following morning, I did what I usually did every morning. I went over to Novara St. Hot Nuts, and he would see me pull up. His job was to have the door open as soon as my foot hit the top stair. I had already reached out to I AM to make him aware that the guys were to meet me that morning for a sit-down to discuss the major shift in plans for the near future. Just when I realized...

Beep Beep Beep......

Bald Head: "How are you, my friend?"

Me: "I'm doing okay, I guess. Just over here worried about The Chief."

Bald Head: "I'm going to tell you something, my friend. I was told not to tell you anything

Me: Please tell me.

Bald Head: The Chief was ambushed by his cousins from the Juárez Cartel the day after we returned from Sinaloa.

Me: But my friend, The Chief is powerful... How could this happen?

Bald Head: You don't understand, my friend...

Me: Tell me what happened.

Bald Head: The Chief was with The Juarez Cartel for a long time. The Juarez Cartel is the Carrillo-Fuentes brothers. Look for Google, my friend. It can tell you. Remember when we were in the Devil's Spine & Chief was talking to you about those guys??

Me: Yes, go ahead.

Bald Head: The phone was ringing & he answer but was saying nothing, just listening my friend.

Me: yes, I was wondering because he just changed attitudes really fast my friend.

Bald Head: Yeah! Those guys were talking to him barely right then my friend. Telling the Chief,' no don't do this we are Familia. Just come on back to Juarez we can work this out like men where everyone can be happy."

I just pushed the two-way radio button see he could hear the line open but silence on my end, I WAS SHOCKED!!

Bald Head: Yeah, my friend this is really bad. The Chief went to meet up with those guys to work this out. Those guys were standing there, but the Sicario just came out and shot up all the Chief's body guards, the cars and everything my friend. They did not know the Chiefs car was bullet proofed. They killed almost everyone on the Chiefs security. They hit the Chief a few times but Junior got Chief back in the car to get away.

Me:.....

Bald Head: I was barely just telling the Chief not to trust those guys. They are known for this type of problem, my friend. The Chief is not good but he wanted me to tell you so you would know.

ME: I'm really worried for the Chief, my friend.......

Bald Head: We just have to wait to see, my friend. Let me tell you something my friend.

Me: Tell me, My Friend.

Bald Head: You have to be careful too, my friend. With the Chief down, things are going to be in flux for a while. Other groups are going to try to make a move on our territory, and they may see you as vulnerable. You need to make sure you have your own security and keep your guard up. We'll keep an eye out for you too, but you need to be careful, my friend.

Bald Head said to me, "You need to start saving more money soon. Don't waste your money on things you don't need. There's going to be a very bad war over here soon, my friend."

I replied, "I don't think it will last very long. Maybe a year or two, my friend?"

Bald Head responded, "I don't think you understand. The war will last for years, my friend. Like 5 to 10 years or more... This is really getting bad now. Remember I told you the Chief killed my last boss in that war. Which was nothing compared to what looks like is going to happen now, my friend. Listen, start to prepare."

This was a lot to take in, and the rest of the day was particularly challenging for me. Mena called me and told me she was on her way to meet with the gentleman she had mentioned earlier and retrieve her things. She said she would call me right after, which was welcome news. A few hours later, Bald Head called me back to give me an update on the Chief, letting me know that he would make it. The future was still uncertain, and I still didn't fully comprehend what war really meant, but I was about to find out soon enough.

Phone rings, her name showed up on my screen, I was instantly excited, thinking she was calling me to give me an update. I answered the phone in a manly but excited tone, saying,

Me: “What up doe?"

Mena: "Yo, man, I ain't goin'... NO WHERE!"

Me: "WHO THE FUCK IS DIS??!!!"

Mena: "DIS, DARRELL!!"

This was a major violation for me or any hustler. Allowing someone else to use your phone and call me puts me at risk. This was an extremely messy situation that I have seen take down many hustlers before, and in some cases, it had cost them their lives. I had to take an overly aggressive tone to get my point across, but I measured my words so as not to put business at risk or scare someone to the point that they would go to the authorities.

Me: Nigga! Do you know whose phone you just called? The mistake you just made! You would rather have gone into a drug store and drunk everything with crossbones on it than do what you just did.

Darrell: I know who you are, Wayne... I have a lot of respect for you, and I'm sorry to be calling your phone like this... but I love her Wayne!

I was taken aback. This guy knew my actual name, took the aggressiveness out of his voice, and even apologized for calling my phone. But then he screamed, "BUT I LOVE HER WAYNE!" This guy was dangerous and emotionally unstable. My first instinct was to send a few Headhunters up to the barbershop where he worked, but then I remembered what my mentor Larry 'Marlow' Chambers had taught me as a young teenager: real power is the power not to use it.

I couldn't help but think back to my own experiences as a young man, walking the girl home from school, carrying her books, and buying her candy with my last bit of money. I always seemed to lose the girl to someone with better family support or financing, or they would put me in the friend zone. If I ever had the chance to be one of those guys, I swore I would not transfer the same disregard that I was subjected to.

But this situation was different. I loved Mena too, and I knew that this unstable person posed a danger to her. Plus, if he ran to the feds just to get me out of the way, it could mean an earlier than expected prison sentence for me.

Me: Dig this right here, D... I'm going to give you a pass on this one, my boy. Don't you ever, and I mean ever, call my phone again, my guy. As for ol' girl, you got that. I am totally done with it, and I'm sure you are letting her hear this too.

Darrell: Thank you, Wayne! Thank you!! I'm sorry about this again too.

I hung up the phone, relieved that the situation had been resolved for now. But I knew that I couldn't let my guard down. In this game, you never knew who was going to come at you, and when.

It was clear that Darrell was just an average guy, but I later found out that he was raised in the church, with his father being a pastor. You could hear this in the way we spoke. That night, Mena still came to be with me, but I had major concerns about her even allowing that to happen. She expressed that she was honest with me about everything she did, and I should have understood that there was a possibility he could act out.

The following day, I called my guys back together for another sit-down. They weren't too receptive to the news that we needed to start trying to put money aside because of a possible war. Like me, they didn't fully understand the depth of the situation and what that really meant. I often made the mistake of giving my guys money to pay their bills when loads didn't come in, which was essentially enabling them to continue being irresponsible with their money. Often, shortly after a load would be done, between their gambling, tricking with females, and paying off car notes and mortgages, they were dead broke. This led to the issue that's at hand now. I didn't know how long the chief would be down, but I did get information from Ballhead that he would make it, so that was a definite plus.

The last few days were filled with drama. I felt like my gut and emotions were taking another ride through the devil's spine, but the rollercoaster wasn't there yet. In the middle of the conversation with my guys, my two-way radio goes off.

Beep beep beep...

Me: Yeah, go ahead...

Danny: How are you, my friend?

Me: I'm okay. How are you and the kids, my friend?

Danny: I'm okay, and the kids are fine. But, my friend, I really need your help.

Me: Tell me, my friend.

Danny: You know my wife is always giving me problems. I have like 50 that I need help with. One of my guys that I deal with down in Miami just had problems, and you know I still must pay for this problem. These are bad, and you know how my wife is when I don't have money for too long.

This was an issue for me all in itself because I'm not supposed to be talking to Danny anymore. The Chief wants to kill Danny, not excluding the fact that Danny works directly with the Juarez cartel that just tried to kill the Chief. After telling Danny to give me a minute, something was going on here, and Danny was lying, most likely trying to get me to take something from him because he knew I wasn't working or maybe I had not been working.

Danny got the position with the Juarez cartel based on the fact that he brokered the deal that brought me to the cartel, and he also tried to pull me away from the Chief once he got his position to pretty much do the same thing he did to Reyes. That was the reason he was sending me cocaine at the same time the Chief was in the beginning, trying to double-cross the Chief with the Fuentes brothers. Most likely, he was attempting to pull this same thing again.

I brought this to the table, making the guys aware of what was going on and asking them what I should do. Needless to say, all of them agreed that I should take the 50 from him and then just don't pay him. I knew why they wanted me to take it because they were broke, being greedy, thinking about themselves, and not thinking about the fact that I could be killed even though they knew there was a slight possibility or a risk.

I AM was the only one to put it on the table despite the ridicule and scorn he received for even bringing it up. "Home Boy....... How do you know this ain't a set up? Bro, it's too much going on right now to risk that shit," I AM said.

I AM was totally right, and the guys were totally wrong. The risk factor was too great, the dynamics of what was going on ran too deep, and the politics of the matter would take too long to explain. Shit they really did not need to know anyway. I AM would always tell me, "Don't let your misplaced loyalty to Danny get you killed, Home Boy."

Me: How long until those 50 are ready and what's the price we're looking at?

Danny: I know you work fast, my friend. My guys can be up there to you in two days. Another couple of days is good for you at 16, my friend.

Me: I work fast, so I need a fast address to make sure they arrive in a couple of days, my friend. How about two days at 15?

Danny: Okay, my friend. I will send these guys to you up there. I will just have them wait for you two days, okay, my friend?

Me: I'll wait for you, my friend.

It became clear to me that this was a set-up. There was no way Danny could afford to give me those 50 at 15 if he owed the cartel for the loss in Miami. The price to cross in Juarez was 12, and with an additional cost to cross into El Paso, the price would be 13, meaning his profit would only be $2000. He either stole this work or this was a setup. I immediately called Bald Head to make him aware that Danny had just offered me some white and to let the Chief know. Unbeknownst to me, Bald Head was in front of the Chief and he told me to hold on as he informed the Chief.

Bald Head: My friend... The Chief is smiling very big right now. MY FRIEND!! THE CHIEF KNEW!! THE CHIEF KNEW ALREADY, MY FRIEND!!!! THE CHIEF IS SMILING SO BIG FOR YOU RIGHT NOW, MY FRIEND!!! HE FUCKING KNEW IT ALL ALONG!!!

I was happy that the Chief was happy, but visibly, I couldn't show it. This situation was getting stressful, and the games that these people played made it clear to me that loyalty was a liability and could get you killed quickly. Loyalty would be used against you in this game. These guys were playing out of a different playbook, and as they say, "if you know, you know." The downside to that is if you didn't know, everybody would know BECAUSE YOU WOULD BE DEAD!! This would be one of the many war stories told when revisiting their greatness.

Bald Head called to inform me that Danny had blocked another load from crossing the border, but the Chief was sending his men up to me soon. At first, I was confused about how Danny could block loads that the Chief was trying to cross through Juarez to El Paso, but I eventually came to understand the politics and structure of the cartels.

The Carrillo-Fuentes brothers controlled the Juarez cartel and, therefore, the city of Juarez or the Plaza of Juarez. Any other cartel or underground organization that wanted to cross through the territory or operate within it had to pay the Juarez cartel because they owned the Plaza. They had certain days when they were allowed to cross, and if it wasn't their day, they couldn't cross. To obtain control of a Plaza, large payment arrangements had to be made with the government, which was essentially snitching or cooperating with the government.

Danny introduced me to the Chief, who was at the very top of the Juarez cartel, in exchange for a prestigious position in the cartel and some monetary proceeds for eventually selling what they referred to as my contract. Just as Danny had done with Rojo when he ripped them off and ran to the Chief with me as a bargaining chip. Danny's plan was to get inside the Juarez cartel and then pull me back to his side after demonstrating my value. That would be his leverage in dealing directly with the Carrillo-Fuentes brothers and the Chief. This is why he was sending me loads when the Chief was a few chapters back; he was showing the Brothers I could do two or three times what the Chief was sending me at that time.

Trusting I would remain "LOYAL" to him as I did twice before. This is when he attempted to turn into my Jefe in front of one of the Carrillo Brothers in his attempted coup d'état on the Chief....... All at my expense not offering his partner a dime (LOYALTY TAX) as he scaled up but had me at risk of being killed the whole time. Danny's new job with the Juarez cartel was to ensure that any and everyone one crossing had received authorization to do so. Blocking the Chiefs load again was another attempt add getting me to receive or accept work from him again which he could then use as more leverage to show he had a way to backdoor the Chief.

The whole effort was to take away any leverage the Chief had with Sinaloa by placing a higher-level producer on the table as well as his skill at war. Since their attempt at killing him did not work they attempted to pull me again to ensure that he couldn't deliver on his promise with Sinaloa and in turn be killed by them.

The Chief wanted my loyalty, which was appealing to him. However, I learned that loyalty was dangerous on this side of the border because it made you predictable. Everyone was using any additional leverage to put themselves in better positions and your loyalty made you predictable in their negotiations for more leverage for themselves, even at the point of making you the fall guy.

Eventually, the work started to come in fast, and I received 400 kilos of cocaine at $16,000 apiece, as the Chief had termed it. I realized that across this border, these people were doing business by all means necessary, and every tool was on the table to secure their bottom line. The playbook that was useful in the states did not apply over here, and I had to learn that quickly. My senses, foresight, and intuition were at an extreme value in this game, and no one gave you a heads up unless it was financially beneficial. No one was a liability, and everyone had a use, even if it was dying.

The Chief offered to "loan" a certain percentage of the 400 kilos of cocaine that were delivered to Detroit at a price of $13,000 per kilo. There were two options available to me - I could either take them at $12,000 apiece at the Juarez price before the shipment was crossed, but I would be responsible for that percentage if the shipment was caught crossing. Alternatively, I could take it at $13,000 apiece at the El Paso price after that percentage had crossed, but if it was caught coming to me in Detroit, Baltimore, or Atlanta, I would be responsible for it.

Crossing cocaine at that time cost $1,000 per kilo and crossing marijuana cost $100 per pound, although it could have been cheaper. The Chief gave me one week to finish the load in Detroit, which meant I had to turn in all the money and have it on a truck headed back towards the border within seven days. The stress of owing that much money made it difficult for me to sleep, especially since I knew that Jack boys typically operated at night.

To mitigate the risk, I had a rule that all my guys had to be off the street before nightfall and no one could transact any business or receive money after dark. When the bag was in town, there was no partying, hanging out, or visiting girlfriends - everyone had to be home, and I would verify that. Mena was an important person in my life during this time, as she had a calming effect on me and made me feel that everything was going to be okay. We would talk about things other than business, and she knew all the right things to say to put me at ease. Money wasn't a major concern for her, which at times felt like a liability on my end because it just wasn't important to her.

As our relationship grew closer, Mena started coming over to my house every night, even when I went to Mexico. I would leave her with keys to the house, which was not like me to do. One particular night, she started complaining about her home. It was right off an alley and she didn't feel safe. The guys across the street from her continued to make passes at her, and she had seen mice in the house the week before. The house wasn't big enough for the furniture she wanted to place in it, and she just needed to move. But she didn't have anywhere that she liked.

We were on our second load without a break, and I was a couple of days from having to put that money on the truck. But I was about two tickets off or two million off. We were in bed, and she was sitting up going on and on. I was tired and kept suggesting things, but she kept turning them down. I got frustrated and jumped up out of bed, went into the closet and pulled out a brick of money which consisted of $5000 stacks. I tossed one of them on the bed to her and said:

Me: "Please, just take that and find a place. That should get you anywhere you like. Once you choose the place, let me know, and we can go pick out whatever furniture you want. Just please, I need to get some rest."

She looked at the money, hit the bed, stared at it for a minute, and then looked at me with a confused expression. I never kept large sums of money at my house per Attorney Lorence instructions.

Attorney Lorence had warned me: "Donnie, never keep large sums of money at your home. No more than 2 or 3 grand in all large bills."

Mena had been dropping hints that she wanted to move in with me, but my mind was consumed with my lifestyle and I missed it. I didn't realize that she didn't approve of my lifestyle and wouldn't understand it. Despite that, she took good care of me, going grocery shopping and even helping me shower when I was too tired to do it myself. But my life was full of drama and dealing with shady individuals, so I couldn't give Mena the attention she deserved.

On the outside, I appeared cool and collected, but inside, I was under a lot of stress. There were so many moving parts to my business dealings, both on this side of the border and across it. Everyone had their own agenda, and some of them were more nefarious than others. The cocaine trade was booming, and I was receiving much more than I had initially.

Luckily, I had a duplex owned by my partner Kevin's real estate investment company, which served as a safe space for me to retreat to when things got too hectic. But I knew I needed to make changes in my life if I wanted to keep Mena in it.

One side of the duplex was occupied by my money counters, who I had trained using a color-coded system. If there was any discrepancy in the money, I could ask them what color rubber bands were used to wrap it and identify who had counted it. On the other side, we stored large amounts of money in travel-sized suitcases after they had been counted and packaged. This was one stop before the final safe house and transfer to a semi-truck. The purpose of the duplex was to have two separate addresses, which would require two separate search warrants if necessary. It also served as a trap for anyone attempting to pull a Jack move on one side while we were operating out of the other. Additionally, I kept an extra house nearby in case of emergencies, as there could be no mistakes when dealing with such large sums of money.

However, I soon discovered that my money counters could not count past $500, and only one of them was able to count up to $1,000. They were unable to use the money columns correctly, even when I preset them. I tried having them count manually, but this only partially solved the issue. When we started receiving larger amounts of work, they were unable to keep up. I had to lay them off for some time until there was enough work to bring them back. When they returned, the sums of money they had to count were much larger, and they were coming in much more quickly than before.

As they began counting the money, I had just turned in a number of suitcases heading towards the border.

Bald Head told me that my guys had sent the wrong amount of money for the next load, which was much larger than any previous shipment. The Chief was furious and had instructed Bald Head to tell me to wait until the correct amount was sent and to fly down to Mexico to verify the money when it arrived. The money was to be deposited in a bank in Mexico, and I would have to inspect it to ensure it was packed the same way he had sent it. If it wasn't, the Chief would have the driver killed in front of me. If it was, My friend you would be taken to the bank to watch the money being counted. Bald Head warned Me that if the money was not right, the consequences would be severe.

I realized that if the money was not packed correctly, he would have to return to Detroit and find out which of his men was stealing. He would have to make an example of that person, just as the Chief would have done with the driver. Bald Head agreed to accompany me back to Detroit to verify that the problem had been addressed.

Bald Head explained to me that the Chief's theory was that anyone who stole in this type of situation would eventually try to set up or kill the person they stole from to get the money. Bald Head also shared the story of the last money counter who was caught stealing. As soon as they identified the culprit, the other men sprayed him with bullets and dragged his body out to the back.

Bald Head helped me devise a plan to avoid this difficult scenario. Bald Head warned me of the danger he was in and the potential consequences of failing to meet the Chief's expectations. Bald Head's warning allowed me to prepare and avoid any potential danger.

Bald Head advised me to ensure that everything is correct for the next money that will be sent down and to pack the money from the previous load that wasn't packed correctly in something similar to the correct packing. This plan was successful as the chief was satisfied with the explanation that the money was missed due to a mistake by my guys. I AM recounted the money after each of the guys to find out who was stealing, and they discovered that one of the guys' money was continuously coming up short. After pulling the guy aside, he got emotional and revealed that he didn't really know how to count, and his little cousin had been helping him by correcting his mistakes before the money made it over to us. The little cousin was setting him up to make it look like he was stealing, not caring about the outcome for him at all. We found out that the little cousin was taking money to go out with a girl and buying her expensive gifts without understanding the severity of his actions.

After getting my head out of the lion's mouth due to my little cousin's selfishness and lack of understanding about the position he had put me and himself in, I decided to go to my trusted jewelry guy, Jay. He makes all types of custom pieces and cleans diamonds for me. I headed to his place immediately after touching down in the city to order the jewelry pieces the Sinaloa Treasury Secretary had asked me to purchase for my

Chief. I requested for three presidential Rolexes, a Cartier watch, and a platinum flowered diamond bracelet that Jay could design.

To ensure the safe delivery of the jewelry, I asked I AM to drive Loc Boc to the airport so he could fly down to Bald Head and take the jewelry across. I knew I had to be cautious and take all the necessary measures to ensure everything went smoothly, especially after what had happened earlier with my cousin.

I was on Novara street late that same day, around 12:00 o'clock at night. I found myself sitting on the front part of a house with some pretty big chairs outside on it. Despite being in the middle of the hood, I felt safe and just wanted to sit out there by myself to enjoy the breeze and look up at the clear night sky with the shiny stars. As I sat there, I played a lot of things in my head with Mena, the close call with the money being short, and the increase in work in the fast-paced life of getting rid of it.

Initially, I was able to control our pace, making sure that we were out sometimes just to cool off. However, the game had changed, and I was no longer in control of the pace or the volume. I was just stuck in a position reacting other than dictating, which was the actual reality of that life. I was just being protected from it by Danny.

On this particular block, most of the street guys shot out the streetlights, and the street was very dark. The only thing that was lit up was Gratiot. There was a corner store right on the end of Novara and Gratiot. Directly across the street was a strip mall or strip of commercial buildings that were vacant. There was a space between the end of the commercial buildings and an old credit union on the other side of that gap, which exposed the alley behind, but everything over there was vacant.

As I was deep in thought, just staring straight ahead at nothing, trying to process so many things on the porch in an attempt to go home to Mena with a clear edge for once, I noticed some headlights. The vehicle quickly shut off its lights, dropping my attention to it. I stared at the vehicle, pondering through my mental rolodex, thinking to myself:

Me: "There has never been a motherfucking car there before. All of those fucking buildings are vacant, no one ever goes up that alley, and what is a car doing in that alley anyway just sitting?"

I called hot nuts out and began to ask him questions about whether he had ever seen a car sitting over there and pointed the car out to him. Hot nuts said no because he frequents the front porch quite a bit with binoculars looking down the street at the women going in and out of the corner store, not to mention just to watch for law enforcement. But he was very observant, and he confirmed exactly what I was thinking.

My spidey senses started to crawl, and I began to feel that something was not right.

The next day, I went down Novara St. as usual, with Hot Nuts opening the door for him. I would post up and make short runs here and there, as he had done before. Having been in the streets and dealing with narcotics from an early age, I knew that my awareness always had to be high. Marlowe, his mentor, had taught him that when arriving at a location, it was essential to be aware of the cars behind you, three to four car lengths back. If you ever thought you were being followed, you should turn off and drive through the neighborhoods, taking neighborhood routes to your destination.

This would make it easier to note if you kept seeing the same vehicles. Getting on the freeway and increasing your speed to high rates was another way of noticing if you were being tailed. These were normal precautions in street life, based on the volume of hustling you were doing or the volume of interpreted hustling you were doing, which made you a target for the Jack boy based on how powerful you were. That was most certainly a death sentence.

Over the course of a couple of days after the headlight incident on Gratiot, I started to notice that I was being tailed by a number of different vehicles. What stood out was that the majority of the tails were white men and white females in an all-black city, which was extremely interesting. So I started taking routes through neighborhoods with no busy streets wherever I was going, and I would continuously see these same vehicles either on the outskirts of the neighborhoods or one vehicle coming in and out to track me. I told the guys what I was seeing and experiencing, including the headlight situation, but they blew him off like I was just paranoid, as usual.

As a precaution, I had Hot Nuts drive all of their vehicles up to a muffler shop that was friendly with them. I had all the vehicles lifted up, and the underbelly was checked for tracking devices. This was something my team up in Baltimore had done before and after the robbery situation up there. One time, they found a tracking device, and the guys were discussing how to pull it off and put it on the back of a school bus. As they were discussing and contemplating what to do, the DEA pulled up and finished the thought for them. The DEA made them aware that pulling any tracking device off a vehicle and placing it anywhere other than where the government intended would be considered destruction of federal property, and they could be prosecuted for it. The DEA advised them to stop watching so many mob movies!

As the days went by, I started to feel like I was being tailed more and more. It seemed like they had increased the number of tails on me and were blatantly following me much closer through the neighborhoods. What was interesting was that all the tails were white people, which struck me as odd in an all-black city. So, I called up my guys, I AM and Mo Green, to come meet me on Hamburg down the street from my old residence.

I also took the time to point out that Loc Boc kept getting pulled over almost like every day and most of the time with a warning. This is one of the very main tactics that the DEA or federal agencies use, this frequent traffic stops by local law enforcement to not trigger you that they are onto you, about to execute some type of operation against you.

They pulled up shortly after I called them, and we had a conversation outside the vehicles. I explained what I was experiencing, but they kept looking at each other like I was crazy. I got frustrated with them and started describing some of the vehicles that were following me, including an old Ford pickup truck with a white guy in it with a bandana tied around his head. Just as I was describing it, the same truck turned onto Hamburg and drove past us. I pointed it out to them, but they still wanted to believe it was a coincidence.

The next day, I did my usual routine of getting in my spaceship and heading towards the city. My place at the time was on 19 and Garfield in Clinton Township, so I would jump on the 94 freeway and maintain the speed limit, which was 65 at the time. As I made my way down 94, I passed the 696 Freeway merging onto 94 West. I looked to my right since I was in the slow lane to see if any cars were trying to merge, but there were none. However, I noticed a GMC Pontiac wide-track type vehicle sitting on the shoulder of the entry point from 696 into 94 East. This was unusual, and my sense of awareness was heightened at this point.

I stared for a moment and locked eyes with the individual in the vehicle. In my mind, he seemed pretty interested in me, which made me even more unsure. To test my theory, I increased my speed to 75 miles an hour, which was just 10 miles above the flow of traffic. I wanted to see if the individual would continue to follow me, and if so, it would confirm my suspicions that I was being tailed.

There I was staring at him through his rearview mirror. I swear this Joker had to turn beet red and you could tell he was 38 hot. His brake lights illuminated, and he started to slow down and as he slowed, I slowed down behind him. He moved to the right lane, and I moved to the right lane behind him, then he moved back to the middle lane, and I moved back to the middle lane behind him. As I mentioned the freeway isn't super but it's busy. I'm thinking at this point we might be driving 35 to 30 miles an hour going back and forth from lane to lane as he's trying to get me from behind him and it's clear to see that he's starting to use colorful language not towards me though but I'm sure about. Cars are passing by as well as semi-trucks blowing their horns at us as we continue our delicate dance of egoism. He's in the far-left lane at this point and I'm behind him. He's reduced his speed to maybe 25 to 20 miles an hour. My exit is coming up and it's been fun but I have shit to do so I moved into the middle lane and now he's behind me. I slow down even further and I'm going maybe 15 to 10 miles an hour and he's right staring at me in my review at this point, but I refuse to give him the pleasure of looking back. My objective was to move extremely slow until the far-right lane totally clears just before my exit, not giving him much room to maneuver.

I had plans to stump on the gas and shoot from the middle lane across the far-right lane and straight up the ramp. So my moment came I stomped on the gas and did exactly as I planned but this motherfucker was pretty good he was dead on my ass so I reduced my speed back down to 20 to 15 miles an hour and stared in my rearview at him all the way up the ramp. We came up on the Morang or Moross exit that leads to Saint John's hospital. At the top of the ramp, I hit the gas again and shot back over to the right lane where I will be taking a right turn onto Morang. But I slowed down again rolled my window down and looked out of my driver side window putting my right arm out the window as he was in the left lane looking directly at me and I waved my finger from right to left as if to give him an indication that trying to clandestinely trail me was a BIG NO NO.

After this rather eventful experience that I just had I pulled up on Novaro. The guys were already there. I talked to them about what just happened to me on 94 E, they were in total shock. We all knew that under normal circumstances you don't see the feds until they want you to see him and when they want you to see him is pretty much a countdown from that point, they got you. I was already under a great deal of stress. Now I was really under stress because we just received another shipment, and we were wrapping up the ends of it. I think at that point we may have maybe another 100 bricks to go, and a shit load of money stored. I just didn't need any issues at that point, so we had to start moving differently since we knew we were being watched. I was very seasoned. My team was seasoned and we knew how to work while being under investigation. My whole wish was just to wrap things up and then fly to the town. I had been instructed a couple of days earlier by Bald Head that once I turned the money in for this last load I needed to get ready to jump on the flight and head down that way for this big party in November. Loc Boc had already delivered the jewelry down to those guys months ago so now there was nothing left but the big party.My biggest concern was being run up on by the DEA.I knew that was spelled the end of my relationship with the cartel or plug. When you have fed problems or DEA problems that's when the phones go dead and so is the relationship.

September the 13th Loc Boc had a run to make going to meet with one of the guys that worked with him on his team. I had a system in place, that all of my guys had two way radios. Any one of us during business hours per se that left the house had to be in constant contact with someone in the house. This was to ensure that that individual was OK not being harmed in any way. Most importantly outside of the harmed part, in case they were taken into custody or had any police interaction. As I stated earlier Loc Boc was constantly being pulled over and today would be no different. This particular time he was taken into custody for an apparent traffic violation. He was missing for about 3 hours, as we continued to hit him on the two way his phone would beep then it was off which should have been a red flag. I was meeting with my interior decorator giving him money to continue working on my place down in Atlanta.

Hot Nuts: HERE THEY COME!!!!!

Hot Nuts yelled from the front porch as he peered through the binoculars. Which I'm sure most people reading this door would wonder," okay, who is coming??!" Only if you were in the streets would you fully understand just who ," THEY ", are that was coming. Just know that this would qualify as one of the worst days of your life, total nightmare type shit.

Everyone in the house jumped up and started moving around really fast. I was sitting at the pool table coming out with money to give to the guy dealing with my interior decorator. I stood up and looked out of the side window just to see cars driving extremely fast through the lot up on the side of the house. Most of the cars look kind of familiar to me over the last couple of weeks seeing them in my rearview. Mo Green was interested in what I was looking at. which we all know he doesn't have a very good history of knowing how to handle these type of things

Mo Green: YO!!! WHO THE FUCK IS THAT HOMIE??!!!!

Me: It's them!

Mo Green: WHO THE FUCK IS THEM THO HOMIE??!!!

Me: NIGGA!!!!! IT'S THEM!!!!!!!

Mo Green: Ooooooooooh SHIT IT'S THEM!!!!!

Mo Green, yelled that as he was running in the opposite direction pulling objects from his pocket and throwing them this way and that. I calmly told everyone to come to the pool table and pull everything from their pockets and put it in the center of the pool table. Everyone came to the pool table and put money or whatever they had of value in the middle of the pool table. I ensured everyone followed my instructions, making them aware as Attorney Lorence has always taught me: If there is ever a raid, obey protocol whoever has the most money in their pocket is the leader and any illegal substance found of any type, even weapons will all be placed on him. Therefore with the money or things of value being placed in the middle of the table and everyone steps away from the table they can't place anything on anyone.

Before they rushed in everyone had assumed the position with their hands on the wall leaning forward and feet spread. We had already assumed the position Because we knew what was coming. They secured hot nuts on the porch and rushed into the property and secured the property as well. After that we heard a whole bunch of different guys yell secured secured secured. DPD: Are y'all sure we got the right house....... MAN, I BET WE HIT THE WRONG DAMN HOUSE!!! THIS CAN NOT BE THE HOUSE! BECAUSE THESE DAMN GUY'S LOOK LIKE THEIR DOING EXTREMELY BAD!! THEY SAID, BIG TIME DRUG DEALERS, THESE GUYS ARE THE ONES USING IT I BET YOU WE FUCKED UP AGAIN!!! Another individual stated go ahead and call them and tell them the property has been secured.

A second set of officers came into the house at this point. Stating." we got it from here guys. Thank you and awesome police work." The initial group packed up and left while the second group took over. Shortly after the exchange another gentleman walked in.......

Head DEA: GGGGGGGGOD DAMN!!! You Boys made one hell of an impression on those other officers that just exited. And, I would not have believed it if I hadn't seen this my Goddamn self!! You boys were already in the assumed position with ya hands on the walls, legs spread. You are hospitable & gentlemen like!

We were already handcuffed and the head officer instructed the other officers to seat us all on the couch. They began to prep us so they could take pictures of us individually and as a group as we sat on the couch. After asking hot nuts if his dorag was being worn for religious purposes, when he answered in the negative they started to remove it. Hot nuts started to argue and curse the officers saying all types of shit which was typical behavior in the hood towards law enforcement.

Me: Yo, Hot Nuts chill Bro. We don't do that...... Let them people do their job.

Head DEA: You know you guys have been gentlemen throughout the whole process. Take the cuffs off those guys in there. Continue to be perfect gentlemen & we will be out of your way shortly. Other than these 60 fucken phones, a few registered guns and about 60 thousand in cash in the middle of the pool table that no one seems to know anything about...... We'll be wrapping up soon & I'm sure you guys won't mind me getting this big pile of cash out the middle of your pool table. I'm sure it has been in your way here.

One of the guys kept asking the officers who are you? Who are you with?. No one ever answered him, they just ignored his question. One of the officers kept asking me, "So where's your money?" You may as well just go ahead and tell us where's your money because we're gonna find it anyway it's just a cat and mouse game we always find it. I'm assuming because my demeanor was pretty calm the same officer said to me well your friend keeps asking," We're the DEA." while pausing after stating that looking directly into my face for a reaction.

Me: Yes, officer....... I know.

He looked really puzzled by my answer because he didn't get his GOTCHA MOMENT out of me.

DEA: Oh yeah! How did you know that??!

Me: It's on your badge sir.

That officer went on to ask me if the BMW in the backyard was my vehicle. I told him no but it's not my vehicle. He proceeded to tell me that was my vehicle because it appears that everybody listens to me so I must be the one in charge. I interned and stated to him that he was concerned once he ran the plate on the vehicle. Which shortly after he did run the plate and the car wasn't registered to me so that appeared to satisfy him. The BMW was registered to the gentleman coming to pick the money up from me or the interior decorator, who was a legit businessman with no illegal ties to anything. But for some reason This gentleman would not stop, he had a hard on for me. He began to tell me that I'm destroying my community with the selling of illegal narcotics. I'm the reason the house is Or looking the way that they

are in the neighborhood. Word destroying the property value causing kids to be on drugs and we are infesting our communities with violence. I begin by asking the officer why was drugs illegal. The officer told me it was illegal because of what it does to the neighborhoods and to people in general. I told him that I respectfully disagree And that was not the reason. I asked him the question again......

DEA: It's because you are breaking the law!

Me: Well, if a person were to be selling drugs, they would be breaking the law. Drugs are illegal because it is an act of commerce & taxes must be paid on all forms of commerce. Rather you are selling Pussy, cigarettes or lemonade on the corner, if it is not taxed it is illegal. All those other things you stated could be considered propaganda and rhetoric in support of something.

DEA: This isn't propaganda or rhetoric, these are all things we see every day.

Me: These are the same concerns that were attributed to marijuana in the sixties & seventies. When our country had their crusades under the same rhetoric. Now it is other substances of concern that this same rhetoric has been slapped on now. What I want to know is what are you going to be saying when marijuana is legalized, ONCE the tax break down is accepted by congress. Then the Government will be selling it...... Please keep that same energy Sir.

DEA: Our government will NEVER BE A PART OF DESTROYING OUR COMMUNITIES, SCHOOLS & CHILDREN!! Marijuana will never be legalized in this country! You sound insane!

Me: Are you saying this has never happened before??.....

DEA: YES, THAT'S WHAT I'M SAYING! YOU ARE REALLY A SICKO BROTHER! LOL !

Me: What about prohibition??!

He looked at one of his fellow officers who nodded in the affirmative to my question as he turned to walk away. There is an officer that walked in at about the middle of our exchange, leaning up against the wall listening to us. He is plain clothed but listening attentively.

DEA: WELL, WELL, I'LL FUCKEN RESIGN!! I'LL JUST FUCKEN RESIGN IF THAT EVER FUCKING HAPPENS!!!

Me: You may need to start drawing it up, because it's going to happen & you are going to remember the conversation too.

The agent with the street clothes started to speak at this point. He started by saying that this whole conversation was well above their pay grade. As he made a statement toward me while asking me a question.

Det. DEA: That's a REALLY nice BMW in the backyard. Would you like to get some of your things out of it before we take it?? I'm pretty sure it's going to be forfeited or the dealer is going to steal it back from you if it's not paid off already.

DEA: OH! That's not his BMW...... That's the other guy over there.

Still trying to be a hard ass towards me after our respectful exchange of thoughts. The Plain Clothed agent looked him off & restated his question to me.

Det. DEA: As, I was asking you Sir...... Would you like to get some of your things before they put it on the flatbed out there now.

I just shook my head, no. He went directly to the point he was looking to make all along to me. Clearly he knew much more about me then I was aware of at that moment.

Det. DEA: It's actually a pleasure and an honor to finally meet you Sir. I didn't think it was any of you guys from the 80's still out here in the street playing at this level anymore. You are from the Chamber's crew at the very beginning of the crack era. Billie Joe & Larry Chamber's..... The Chamber Brother's.

He just continued to ramble on talking about the 80s and the different legendary names inside the city of Detroit mentioning Demetrius Holloway, Maserati Rick, White Boy Rick, the Brown brothers of the Best Friends Crew, the Chambers brothers, Clifford Jones etc. He was just going into detail & speaking glowingly about that era when he just joined the DEA. Often stopping to remind the other agents that they weren't out of grade school as of yet. That this was the era of real street hustlers that made big money kill you quick. But it was about the hustle, it was about making money, it was never about the color that a person wore or any of the stuff that they were going through and that what he described as the new generation of hustler. He was describing in order and a form of honor among thieves as he would state these guys weren't soft. He was just standing there just telling a bunch of war stories but felt he was in an element speaking with someone from the era that knew what he was talking about. To me he really sounded like he just missed that era of the streets which was weird to me but in a weird way I understood exactly what he was saying. Then the BULLSHIT began......

Det. DEA: Where is your phone?? They already have sent them downtown. I wanted to give you your phone or one of your phones back. You know, so we can talk a little more.

Me: I appreciate you wanting to give me one of my phones back. You already know that phone would not be used anymore because you would be on it. Respectful, Sir, there is nothing for you & I to talk about. All communication from this point forward would be between you and my attorney only.

Det.DEA: No No, I respect that...... That's the ol skool way, but I know you understand that is my job. I must try, but I really respect that...... You do not really hear that often anymore these days. I just wanted these younger guys to hear what that sounds like, from an era of guys that meant it. I'm going to put my number on the search warrant just in case you reconsider for whatever reason. I don't need to tell you this because you know how this goes......... We will be in touch.......

After the DEA exited the house on Novara. I placed a call to Attorney Lorence. He asked me a series of questions as he normally does about the events and what happened leading up to the raid during the raid etc. I made him aware of exactly what happened; that I took control of the guys and gave them instructions of what to do according to all the teachings that he had given me over the years when dealing with law enforcement. After hours after I was done disclosing all the events that had occurred.

Attorney Lorence: Donnie, I could just kiss you right now! You did very well! I will reach out to the US Attorney, but we need to meet. Make sure you have the Search Warrant with you as well.

I was in a hotel room while speaking with Attorney Lorence. I had to replay all the events leading up to what happened to try to put a handle on exactly where this may have come from. How did this man know that I was formerly a part of the Chambers organization when I was much younger? There aren't many people that even know that about me.

Attorney Lorence showed up to meet with me in my hotel room. He had a bunch of different questions for me while also making me aware of how I needed to move over the next 30 days. He made me aware that the indictment would be sealed for 30 days for what reason I don't know. Attorney Lorence made sure I understood that they would still be around investigating and seeing what else they could dig up or find to add to the case. I gave him a list of names of all the individuals that were in the house at the time of the raid.

Attorney Lorence was the head attorney on the Appeals network system with several attorneys up under him. He always made me aware that if there was an evident investigation I would need to make sure that I got all of my guys' attorneys up under him so I could know exactly what was going on with the other guys and indication of knowing who was going to flip first. He never allowed me to believe even way back then that all of my guys were going to stand strong. He was always a realist with me, making sure that I knew that someone a number of someones always flip. He also told me to never give or receive instructions over a phone that was the basis of a conspiracy always.

Attorney Lorence: Donnie, you never put your freedom in another person's hands. You expect everyone to tell on you & ALWAYS operate as you are being watched or someone is listening to you.

It didn't take long to get to his favorite subject. Well Donnie we're going to need since this is a federal case about 20,000 apiece for each one of you guys. This will retain an attorney for all of them and a separate attorney for all of them. As I always discuss with you I can't represent no one but you because that would be a conflict of interest. Also it would be a dead giveaway if I showed up at the courthouse for a bunch of random guys dealing with drugs they would connect it all to you. Now Donnie ....

Attorney Lorence: I don't want to insult you so, I'm going to need Forty thousand for you. As you well know....... As your attorney for many years now. I would never insult you.

I had never been in a position before where I really had that desire to be insulted but for some reason I guess he just refused. I would have had no problem with making an exception for that one time though. I AM arrived with the cure to my attorney's ailment, which was nothing more than a treatment. I made sure I made him aware that in time I would find a way to cure him of this ailment

Me: At some point we will need to stop treating your symptoms & start killing this germ.

Attorney Lorence would just laugh when I would make this statement because he knew I was telling him in my own way that I knew some of these prices or a contribution to his favorite charity. Understanding that a very good attorney it's like a beautiful woman or a valuable personal assistance: you gotta keep them happy.

After speaking with Attorney Lorence I went straight to the protocol which included me reaching out to Bald Head. I knew this would be the last or next to the last time that I spoke with him or dealt with the Chief. I felt the one ace I had up my sleeve is that I owe them a lot of money and I was damn sure they would want that money. I told Bald Head what happened and the exact steps that I was taking, making him aware that I had not taken any losses but I still had a little over 100 bricks of cocaine left. He made me aware as I was expecting that he will contact the chief and update him. The issue for me was that they took all of the phones in the house including my phones, most importantly the yellow and black Nextel phone the chief had given me personally.

I had an extensive conversation with I AM concerning the way we needed to move while we were under investigation. This was not new to me, I had been a part of a number of large organizations from a kid right next to the actual leaders and they constantly poured knowledge into me concerning the laws and in they're terms preventative maintenance of your organization. The house that the DEA ran in on Novara was not a drug storage house, it was more of a chill house for me and my top guys to have a meeting in the other mind and consult during operations. There were never any drugs anywhere near that house or any crazy amounts of money that was brought to that house once it was picked up from different separate extensions of my guys' consumer base.

Leading up to the raid things slowed down for us in the streets for a minute but for some odd reason after that the sales started to increase. I had somewhat of an idea of the part of our organization that was under investigation so I limited access to the work to the part that wasn't. Within my structure that I developed the different crews that were touched were independent of others just for the purpose of someone going under investigation. It would be like springing a leak in your home and just turning the shut off valve for the parts affected while the water still flowed to the rest.

We got rid of the remainder of the work that we had but I had another problem at this point. I spoke to Bald Head and he made me aware that I would need to get another radio and give him the number because the Chief wanted to talk to me.........

Bald Head: This doesn't happen, My Friend! THIS NEVER HAPPENS EVER! When someone has problems like this, they never call them again. They throw the phone & just go to the next name on the list, My Friend. This never happens.......

The shock, amazement was clear in Bald Heads' voice but I couldn't help but notice the shock and amazed sound more like a disappointment. He appeared kind of upset about it for some odd reason. I found myself thinking, "am I crazy or Has this man been unpleasantly surprised by the communication with me not being cut off"; but why?? It still wasn't lost on me that over in Sinaloa Bald Head constantly left I AM and I unattended. Black Shirt had unprecedented access to us where he was able to have inappropriate conversations of business with us outside of the Chief.

The Chief and I had an opportunity to speak. I made him aware that we had taken no losses, that I was able to get rid of the rest of the product and I had the money secured. Interesting fact was that I had the money secured up to a week and a half prior to speaking to him but no one was coming to retrieve it from me. which I wasn't very upset about it because it would have made me a very rich man. The chief had a very conciliatory tone when dealing with me at that moment. For me he was just overly reaffirming the point that he is in support of me. Even to the point he asked me if I needed anything towards my attorney fees to just tell him how much. This shocked me. I was not expecting to hear this at all.......

Me:I don't know because it is so early.but I think 250,000 would be a good start.

The Chief: Just take what you need, I TRUST YOU. Don't worry Primo, because this is just part of our business...... These things are going to happen from time to time.

The Chief also asked that I put the search warrant inside of the suitcases that the money was being stored in when I shipped the money back across. This wasn't new to me because Tonald Had made me aware of the process that these organizations use to ensure that what you said really happened. This was also a receipt which would be used to clear any debt on my end.

The remaining fact was another two weeks went by. I'm still holding millions of their money and they would not send a truck to pick it up no matter how much I called and begged them to. Junior would just keep reassuring me that the truck is about to come and it should be to me any day now which was lies. Bald Head at this point didn't really seem to know anything, almost as if he was out of the loop until he finally admitted that he didn't know anything and they weren't really telling him anything either, while sounding a little nervous about that. There's only one person that I knew that could help me understand and navigate through this obstacle course. Beep Beep Beep........

Danny: Yes My Friend. Go ahead.

I explained to Danny my dilemma and what I was going through. That I had all this money based on what had happened to me with the DEA and that they weren't coming to pick it up regardless of how much they told me they were on their way and so on. I was scared shitless because I knew I was responsible for that money, I was responsible for all that fucking money.

Danny: You must call The Chief and say this right here my friend. I DON'T WANT ANY TROUBLE. I HAVE THIS THING UP HERE FOR YOU GUYS BUT I DON'T WANT ANY TROUBLE. You have to say it just like this, only. My Friend, there is someone the Chief doesn't trust and it's not you....... Why doesn't that Bald Head guy tell you. He must not have communication, My Friend. You need to maybe watch this guy, My Friend. Don't forget this guy never liked us in the beginning. He never wanted the Chief to deal with you. Now he sees he was wrong...... He is your best friend now. I told you a long time before to watch this Bald Head guy.

I called Junior and I did exactly as Danny had told me. I did not call Bald Head because it was clear that there was no communication with Bald Head and he didn't know anything for some odd reason. The response I got from Junior was totally different, almost was a pause and then I had direct communication with the chief after saying what Danny told me to say. Looking back at the response that I got I should have known that they knew for me to have that exact language I got it from someone. Within three days there was a truck that pulled in and I AM loaded it up with the money I owed The Chief.

After the truck pulled in and left with the money I made Bald Head aware that my bill was paid with The Chief. He was really shocked because his truck trucking company with Reyes was responsible for these transactions and he knew nothing about it. He knew he was in trouble with losing me so he decided to come forth with some information that he felt would keep him in good graces and show his value to me.

Bald Head: My Friend, I am going to tell you something.

Me: Tell me, My Friend.

Bald Head: These guys get mad on me because they say I tell you to much. I don't care because you are my friend, My Friend. I don't think you may come to the party right now because of what just happened up there with you. The party is very big party because these guys have agreed to go to war with the other cartels already, My Friend. We have Three members of Sinaloa in the new president of Mexico's cabinet now. There is a agreement between our cartel & the President of Mexico. This party is for this thing right here my friend. All that stuff you had your guy bring down here. These were gifts for this agreement, but only for the Rolex. The Cartier was a gift for The Chiefs, Chief Girlfriend LA VOZ. The bracelet was a wedding gift for the Chiefs, Chief new wife, My Friend. But there are problems inside of Sinaloa too. These guys are mad because the Chiefs, Chief makes everyone pay his girlfriend LA

VOZ something of every load they touch....... Even the Chief must pay too, My Friend. I really think the Chief is up to something. Has he said anything to you, My Friend?? I'm only telling you this because you are my friend & we protect each other My Friend.

This shit was really starting to get weird. There were a lot of moving parts and things were changing extremely fast. But this was only the beginning. Loc Boc had been trying to talk with me for some time stating that he had something to tell me about his time when he went across to Mexico that he just didn't understand. For the most part I kept blowing him off and not to be an asshole I just had a lot on my mind and I figured that it may have not been of any interest that needed my immediate attention at the time.

Based on all the madness that I was starting to observe I figured that it may have been time for me to sit down and hear what he had to say about what he noticed that was extremely weird over in Mexico when he was there. What he told me correlated with some of the information that I was starting to get, especially the information that Bald Head introduced me to. Loc Boc told me that when he was in Mexico that they gave him security and placed him in an exclusive hotel. The following morning, he went out for a walk in the city of Juarez to get some air around 11 in the morning. As he got close to the curb in his attempt to cross the street 5 or 6 SUV's all black with black tinted windows sped past stopping right in front of the hotel.

A bunch of men in suits with automatic weapons jumped out and secured the area. Once the area was secured the door was open and he saw a gentleman get out of the SUV and enter the hotel. He said he immediately went back into the hotel wondering what was going on while returning to his room. The gentlemen that were with him did not speak English, so he was going to the room to tell the one that did speak English exactly what he observed and start asking questions. The

English speaking sicario accompanied Loc Boc down to the lobby to see exactly what he was trying to describe to him. The sicario advised Loc Boc that It was the President of Mexico. He took Lock Boc into the dining area to sit down and have breakfast, maybe four or five tables over from the position of where the president was sitting according to Loc Boc.

Also Loc Boc advised me that after he returned to his room no longer than an hour later someone came up to the room encouraging them to come down to the lobby because the boss was down there waiting. Loc Boc Told me that this gentleman was often referred to as Chief. They jumped into several vehicles and went to another part of the city of Juarez where The Chief got out of the vehicle along with the sicarios and walked around through the neighborhood giving Loc Boc a tour of the neighborhood pointing out where he was going to build an arcade for the kids in the community and other community activity that cartel was putting in place for the community.

There were some additional details that he gave about a few other things but the one thing that just stood out to me was when the sicario told him that the SUV's featured the president of Mexico. I don't know how things go for security in Mexico, but I do know in America I'm pretty sure The President of the United States would not be in a hotel that the cartel is heavily moving through. Then the other thing that stood out was that as he described a gentleman called The Chief was at the same hotel. After what Loc Boc and Bald Head had just told me it was starting to get hard to see how these lines didn't cross.

After turning the money in to the chief for that last load I was just mostly relaxing. I would be lying if I were to say that it was not a major concern for me just having gone through that whole process and on a federal level. Everyone in the hood knows that if the feds put their hands on you for any reason you're going to do some time and it's not out of the norm for them to go away but they're like the Terminator they always return.

Bald Head was advising me that it may be safer for me to head down to Atlanta. Reaffirming to me that most likely there are one or more people inside of my organization that is cooperating with the government. According to him, the more I sit around them not knowing exactly who it was just gives them more opportunities to keep reporting things back on me to the government. Therefore he advised me to be somewhere that no one that is formally dealt with could give any information about my whereabouts and all my current activities. Which I thought was very good idea. I would just find out that there was a catch to it.......

Bald Head: When this type of thing happens, My Friend. Just anyone that you were dealing with before, don't deal with them anymore. This is what the cartels always do. Don't give the snitches anymore information to report. My Friend, you know that make up shit all the time too.

I was feeling this was a good change for me since I had business that I had entered in down there in Atlanta as far as music was concerned. I still had some money that was owed to me that was still in the street which I thought that I would actually get it back out of the street first before I took off. I think I may have had about a little over 400,000 still owed to me. Deep down inside I was really tired of the city and how the culture of the streets was just starting to really change. I also knew how much I loved Atlanta, I would have been happy never returning at that point.

Bald head was in constant contact with me over that deciding period that I was experiencing. I believe he may have been told that he needed to stick close to me to be reassuring and encouraging to me.

Beep Beep Beep........

Me: Go ahead......

Bald Head: Have you talked to The Chief, My Friend??

Me: No, My Friend..... Are you okay??

Bald Head: I don't know, My Friend. The Chief Just had Junior call me to tell me to come over across.This is not normal! I'm not supposed to go over there until next week.I don't know My Friend.

Bald head was extremely nervous; this was out of the norm according to him. His voice was shaking and everything, it totally freaked me out just listening to him. He wasn't sure if I knew something or not. The one thing that was totally clear he was super afraid. I didn't really catch on initially asking him why he is concerned. He wouldn't really answer, he will just continue to say that he doesn't know and that this isn't nor mal.He went on to advise me to please not change my phone number while he was across.Telling me that he may be over there for about a week but just please don't change my phone number. I was concerned why changing my number was so important to him. I did put forth a question concerning it. He in turn told me that if they take his phones while he is over there, he will no longer have any communication with me. Which at the time again I didn't understand why communication with me was so paramount? Moving forward it would become clearer why it was so paramount because I had become his lifeline. You could always bail yourself out almost any situation if you had a bigger and better money-making opportunities for whomever you may have been running to to save you from someone else. Just as Danny had done and the chief was currently doing, seems like Bald Head was trying to get in on the fun. He left me with a few words of advice.........

Bald Head: If I don't call you back in 5 days...... Just be careful & don't come over here if they ask you to cross, My Friend.

Over the five days that I was waiting to hear back from Bald Head, Attorney Lorence contacted me. He informed me that the US attorney asked the court for a 15 day extension in order to keep the indictment sealed. This really had me concerned, letting me know that the government informants must have really been working overtime making the government feel they needed additional time for whatever reason. I still had a little under 200,000 still in the street. I told Moe Green that he could have it because I was on my way to Atlanta. I informed him that I wouldn't be coming back anytime soon so spend it wisely, and I jumped on the road headed South.

A couple of days after arriving in Atlanta I heard from Bald Head. Bald Head was extremely happy, and he was also using the same two-way radios, so he didn't get his phone's took. I was concerned with what went on because I didn't know if I was under suspicion because of what had just happened to me. He assured me that it had nothing to do with me and he kept repeating it because I kept asking. After feeling he was lying to me, I started to really pressure him, and he kept assuring me that it had nothing to do with me, it was him. Pushing the envelope, I asked him why it would be him that would be under concern and for more details. He told me that the chief kept asking him the same questions centered around did he know anything leading up to or concerning the raid that happened to me.

Bald Head: My Friend he just kept asking me this question, while staring at me really hard. He even had Junior asking me questions while he just kept looking at me very hard. But it was me that he was concerned about. It had nothing to do with you.

Bald head was really enlightening me to a lot of things. Some of the things that he was saying and telling me was just telling me so much almost to the point you can't really believe what you're hearing because of the implications of what these things mean.The Chief called him over there and pretty much interrogated him was just really fucking weird to me. And why would he do that? What's really going on?

Me: Damn...... Could Bald Head be a government informant??.... . Naaaaw, this the fucking cartel his ass would be dead already.....May be?

I went to sleep that night with a lot on my mind as always. My mind just started to wonder back over so many conversations and different stories Bald Head told me about different things he's experienced. Like when he told me he was in Tennessee and they were sent up there to basically store the money from loads that the guys were doing down there. And at some point the hotel called law enforcement because they were suspicious. Law enforcement got a key and went into the room and saw very large sums of money. When they returned to the room law enforcement was there and he told me as if law enforcement extorted them and asked them for a certain amount of cash or they were going to lock them up and take it all.

That they had to call across to get clearance to take some of the money and pay the detectives. And they just stayed in the same hotel after paying the detectives. That story just never sat well with me. Another story he told me when we were flying together on a flight from Texas back to Detroit. He told me that he was on a similar flight but up to Chicago to rendezvous with the truck that was laden with a load of cocaine. And that as they were landing in Chicago they saw a military helicopter flying with a semi truck hanging from it and it was the truck they were supposed to be making the delivery of cocaine up to Chicago. I just thought to myself what a coincidence and how come all these coincidences seem to always go in your favor, but no this couldn't happen with the cartel.........HE WOULD BE DEAD ALREADY........

I got up the next morning still a little tense from the night before. But then I asked myself a question: Why the hell are you tense and all on edge? You're in Atlanta now, not Detroit. You can relax as Bald Head said and try to enjoy yourself. I called up Keith and kicked it with him a minute then we agreed to get together later on to go down to Atlanta station to have something to eat then go back to his house out in Alpharetta Georgia. Keith told me that I needed a Myspace page to be in the music industry so I got Tez to put me together one.

I never had any friends for the most part on stuff like that so when Tez made the page for me Keith and Pretty Boi Fresh and a number of others put me on their top friends list and I was getting a lot of friend requests and I was enjoying it. After getting off the phone with Keith I jumped right online to check my Myspace page to see how many new friend requests I had. That was the first morning I really didn't have many which was a surprise I had three. So by me being new to this whole experience, everybody that requested me as a friend I wanted to look at their page first to see if they were worthy because I was a music industry guy now full time. I checked each page like I just stated but one particular friend request was rather interesting.

I've seen a picture of the guy the whole backdrop of his page, which is the American flag. I'm thinking to myself damn this guy is super patriotic that's different. So as I look more at this page and the things about this gentleman. His hobby was catching the crook. His occupation was DEA....Damn.

DEA Guy: He had some song playing by a group named the Bare Naked Ladies and I think the name of the song was something about a crook or catching a crook or something. Well of course this had to be a coincidence and what the hell just because he works for the DEA doesn't make him a bad guy. He couldn't know nothing about me because that fucking shit is in Detroit I'm in Atlanta and I'm a full time industry music industry guy.

Needless to say I accepted his friend request and I moved on with the rest of my day or so that was my intention. I left the computer open, went to the restroom and came back just to see I had a message..........

DEA GUY: Thank you for accepting my friend request. Have you seen my page?

Me: Hey, New Friend....... You have a nice page.

DEA GUY: I added some new features to it. Check it out.

Once I looked back at his page I did see that he added some additional features. There was a number of messages on his page," Gina said the water bill is due, your daughter said that she needs some additional money for summer clothes and oh yeah your mom said don't forget she's cooking dinner this Sunday and she expects to see you." besides the messages he placed another message stating that I should give him a call soon. Of course that wasn't enough lower down toward the center of his page from his profile pic he had like a carousel motion of a picture of himself and a picture of me going around and around in a circle with two additional pictures. What I did was click the other two pictures that I didn't recognize just to see their pages and I guess he was after them too. Which I will go back later on to see those folks deleted their pages. I responded back to him after reading the messages that were on my phones that were confiscated by the DEA in the raid on Novara street in Detroit MI.

Me: Yeah, I just saw your new features you add to your page.

DEA Guy: COOL! What did you think??

Me: I think I look A LOT better than the guy right next to me.

Just in case you didn't know the guy right next to me on his carousel was him, the actual DEA agent. I had never seen this agent before, at least the profile picture of this agent which was a black man. After this exchange I immediately called attorney Lorence to update him on this whole Myspace fiasco that was going on. I told him step by step what was happening. I gave him the address to my Myspace as well as the other information he needed to look into it. I also told him about the exchange between me and this phantom DEA agent, the messages to me for me to get in contact with him as well as him putting the messages from my cell phone up on his page. Then I told him about the carousel with myself and the agent featured after I looked back at the agent's page. I told Lorence what my response was to him once he asked me about his new features on his page.........

Attorney Lorence: GOD DAM IT DONNIE!!!! (As he was fighting back laughter from being caught off guard from my response. into a more serious tone.) YOU CAN'T DO THAT! You don't want to make this personal. This does not need to be you against him thing. You do whatever it is that you do but you want to be respectful. This needs to be just another case that he must work and nothing more. DON'T RESPOND ANYMORE! PLEASE DONNIE!!

I went on to ask Lorence if there was something that we could do about him taunting me. He informed me that there was nothing that we could do because we didn't know if it was him or not, it wasn't his actual picture. And there were no laws in place at that time to do anything about that type of thing. He went on to tell me that I could put a page up," BUT, PLEASE DO NOT DO THAT;" stating that he plays with little boys and there will be nothing that he could do about it at that time.

Keith and I met up in Atlantic station to have something to eat. After we ate, we went out to his home in Alpharetta. This was the home that he purchased from Jeezy that featured a full studio in the basement and a nice stripper pole among a bunch of other wonderful features. Later that day there was a number recording session from different artists that Woo and Keith were managing at the time. I was invested in several of the artists that they had featured on their label. Woo, Keith and I were all partners of Be-Ly Publishing company. I was there that day just chilling with my guy and waiting for the Outsyders to come begin their session as well. I was already talking to I AM about what happened, and I showed him on my laptop. Keith just happened to come over and inquired about what we were looking at. I showed him, and he was still pretty much lost and we're like," yeah, that's cool Joe!" I had to explain to him that this was everything but cool then I started to explain to him what was really going on and he totally freaked out stating....

Keith: Are you serious Big Homie! Listen Big Homie....... Anything you do or that you are involved in PLEASE DON'T TELL ME! I don't want to see anything or know anything. Because I fucks with you hard Big Homie....... But I can't go to jail, I can't fight.... I'm just being honest Big Homie...... I'ma tell, Big Homie. I can't fight, I never could.

I AM and I just burst out laughing. We laughed so hard, but Keith was so serious about what he was saying. Not in a malicious way but more so in a heads-up type of way which at the end of the day you have to appreciate, and we did.

Thinking that the DEA agent was done with his taunting was pretty much wishful thinking. He would go on taunting me online until the actual indictment was unsealed after the 15 day extension that was granted to them. Every day he would leave messages for me to call him on his Myspace and he would change the backdrop to his page often. He even ended up posting a Myspace page of the actual Spanish guy whose name the yellow and black phone The Chief gave me was in. As Lorence instructed I did not respond to any of his antics. He put the Spanish guy, myself and him on his carousel going round and round with a Spanish song. The name of the song was Alante Alante. I asked Bald Head what that meant and what song was that and Bald Head told me it was a party song meaning Let's Go! Let's Go!, as in Let's Go it's time to have another drink.

I understood what he meant by let's go let's go meaning let's go let's go hurry up and give him a call. The picture that the DEA agent had posted up was a old profile picture of mine on Myspace but I guess he did enough digging and found the newer Myspace page that I had featuring me looking more like an artist leaning up against the spaceship and Benz with some Chrome Heart glasses on in my Detroit style of dress.

This became his picture that he will start to use from that moment forward. He did all kinds of crazy things while telling me to call him on this page. The closer we got to the 15 day extension running out he cleared his whole backdrop of his page out and pretty much took everything off his page except for a very small picture of of me leaning up against my BMW and Benz he placed me in the upper right hand corner of his page with a message you need to call me and I guess me being in the corner of his page was to let me know I was cornered or boxed in.

I still did not respond to any of his antics. I made Lorence aware of everything he was doing as he requested for me to do. Then the day finally came and Lorence gave me a call saying that he contacted the agent to receive the documents you requested and the agent was not responding. He called the US attorney to make the US attorney aware that the agent did not turn the documentation over after the government decided not to file the indictment against me.

The US attorney reached out to the agent and made the agent aware that he had to turn the document over and he made my attorney aware that we would be receiving THE SEALED INDICTMENT on the following Monday the call was placed to The US attorney on the Friday of the weekend leading up to Monday. The following day Lorence informed me that the whole process was over but don't be careless, but it was a good thing that I was in Atlanta and no longer in Detroit. I then asked him if he had the paperwork in hand he said no but the US attorney assured him that he would have it and that the agent did not respond because he was on assignment down in Texas.

Me: WTF!! ON ASSIGNMENT DOWN IN TEXAS!!!

Shocked by the news that Lorence just gave me, I return to the only source of communication that the DEA agent frequently used to subliminally communicate with me. His page had been totally redesigned; it was totally fitting for a dope boy. He went from the day before having my new dope boy profile picture as the total backdrop of his page making it a whole bunch of small size photos of me just all the way across the whole backdrop with me standing in front of the two vehicles. His song of choice was unique if I may say he picked the little Wayne song go ahead get your money little duffle bag boy.

My nerves instantly got bad. I started looking all around the club and ducking down thinking to myself is he here where he must have told the damn DJ to play that song. This was the same song that I had just listened to earlier on the DEA agent's page. Starting to settle down a little, I couldn't help but laugh not in a mocking way but some were more in respect because that guy was from the old school on the other side but nevertheless he didn't appear to be someone doing anything other than his job and I respected that.

This was time to party. I got the boys together and we headed out to the Onyx strip club. I know everyone in the videos talked about the girls of Magic City at that time and I often went there at first until I was introduced to them by beautiful women at the Onyx strip club. As I often say when you went in there for a dance these girls would interview you. They all had a professionally put together business plan of what they were trying to do outside of entertainment and each one of them needed at least 10,000 to start my type of place.

I called ahead to my waitress and made her aware that I wanted the whole VIP section over on the DJ side which is a normal area I get. I also told her I wanted bottles of Rose 10 to 15 bottles just sitting there and ice chilling with fruit ready when I get there. I've paid a few bouncers just to stand in front of the stairs on each end and not letting any of the girls up unless they were requested, unlike being overrun by them in Detroit. We went to that club and we went hard. I'm enjoying myself. I mean we really had a good time. I spotted one particular stripper named Desire. This girl was so beautiful she was slim and it looked like God just attached a beach ball to her backside cause that's how perfectly round it was as well as huge. When I first saw it all I could think of was one thing........

Beep Beep Beep....

CHAPTER 26

THE WAR

BEEP BEEP BEEP... JUNIOR approached me and said, "My Friend, the Chief needs to ask you a favor."The timing of this request was interesting as I was just starting to understand why they wanted me to relocate to Atlanta to "relax." Junior asked me, on the Chief's behalf, if I would be willing to work in Atlanta. I was taken aback by this question, as I was currently under indictment and couldn't believe they were asking me to work in another market. I explained to Junior that I didn't have a team or the necessary resources to fulfill their request, hoping to slow them down. However, Junior told me not to worry and said that the Chief really needed this favor.

Curious, I asked Junior how much the Chief needed me to do. Junior replied, "Don't worry, only 600, My Friend." I reiterated my concerns about not having a team or the resources to move things around, but Junior reassured me that it was okay. He went on to explain that I wouldn't need to handle all 600 myself. The Chief needed me to retrieve the 600 and hand off 200 to a Mexican member of the cartel named Pepe. This freaked me out, as I was not used to dealing with anyone when it came to handing off large quantities of cocaine, especially not with someone from another group, let alone a Mexican. I was concerned about the potential repercussions of dealing with members of other organizations, as they could easily get me wrapped up in an indictment if they were caught.

"I was totally outside of my comfort zone. I had never been in a scenario like this before," he said. "Unbeknownst to me that this was just the beginning, and this responsibility would grow. I will soon become the anointed 1, The Primera for the Sinaloa cartel in Atlanta GA."

"How did that happen?" I asked.

"I was basically talked into it, not really because I knew I didn't have a choice, but I had an idea where this was headed," he said. "That little voice inside of me that talks to me all the time that I try to get it to shut the hell up because it often tells me things and it's right most of the time. This was the beginning of; if the drugs didn't come to me first they could not come into the state or the hub for The Sinaloa cartel. Atlanta was the hub of that region for the Sinaloa cartel. Just like Chicago is the hub for the Midwest region, I will soon start to receive this kind of information by me being promoted in a way, I would need to know where not to move drugs and where I could move drugs, needing to have authorization to move into certain regions."

"Not long after I received that call, Bald Head showed up down in Atlanta and within two or three days after his arrival, the 600 keys of cocaine showed up," he continued. "I basically gave the instructions to I AM based off of what Bald Head had told me about how shipments were received down in that region. I got with what would become our team down there and picked up the 600. The instructions that were given, we had to get 250 keys to Pepe and another 100 keys to another gentleman."

"As the old saying goes, everything is on a need-to-know basis. This is pretty much how the cartel works," he said. "You never really get told anything directly, you must have a great 6th sense and foresight. This is how you move up the ranks. Because unless you're sitting directly in front of someone when they're given instructions which in most cases won't be the case, and even sometimes sitting in front of them, you better have that 6th sense, intuition, and foresight. Everyone speaks in incomplete sentences, riddles, and hints, and the foresight is needed to often save your own life."

Pepe and I had been set up for a big fight. This was scheduled to be a heavyweight slugfest; they even took bets over there in Sinaloa. Everyone including El Chapo betted against me except for The Chief, Junior, and Bald Head but nobody warned me, and nobody warned Pepe.

We both had 250 keys, but this was Pepe's market. He was the front runner and the favorite. We moved those 250 keys so quickly that I couldn't even tell you how we did it. We finished in less than a week. Later, I realized that this was the Big Meech effect.

What was impressive to me, and what I would soon find out, was that the black drug selling community shopped with the black drug selling community. The streets talk, and it wouldn't take long for the streets to know that there was a brother in town who had the bag, and all that business came directly to us just because we were black.

Dope boys often get a bad reputation, and I would be a fool to argue that it's not deserved in many cases. It's almost like because Congress has deemed this form of commerce illegal, then everything and all the practices that come from it are disqualified. In reality, black folks should be looking at the business model practiced by this entrepreneurial group outside of the needless violence and other misconceptions that the whole business community of drug dealers are painted with.

Outside of an act of Congress, which the Constitution gives the duty of managing all acts of commerce, these practices would be studied and emulated in almost every case. Each organization has its own methodologies of interacting in interstate commerce, and make no mistake about it, this is interstate commerce. America is a capitalist country, and the principles that are practiced, whether it's sex, loose cigarettes, drug dealing, etc., are all principles of capitalistic expression disqualified and prosecuted under title 27 dealing with commerce. The sale of drugs is a violation under the act of commerce.

People love to bring up that drug dealing destroys communities, destroys lives, and kills people. But I would like to challenge the reader to go back and look at the same things that were being said about liquor when it was illegal, marijuana when it was illegal, even the chain charge that was being held against black people when they were slaves, and even white people when they were slaves, even though they think that the distinction of indentured servant is different than slavery, but I digress.

Miraculously, whenever Congress chooses to make any of these things legal or create laws to protect them, each category where the human or substance was all commerce becomes glorious distinctions, and only the highest of accomplished individuals in the same categories that were formerly illegal but now praised and studied. It often reminds me of how free trade is looked upon as a great invention of Western society when it was given birth to by pirates, who in some cases were financed but effectively all used by Western countries against each other just off the record.

During the drug war in Mexico, it was all about commerce and getting the commodity - drugs - to market. The United States government declared war against its citizens classified under the war against drugs, but the war was really against access to commerce, especially for minority underserved communities. I hope that minority groups, especially blacks, stop buying into the propaganda that just because these were illegal acts, they were automatically wrong. Don't get me wrong, there are consequences to breaking the law, but I believe that we are harming ourselves by not looking at what these individuals did as just business practices and the pooling of funds by circulating these phones among a distinctive group.

The proceeds from the sale of drugs constantly rotated around within that community over and over again, all enriching themselves in the process because the majority of all the funds raised were all spent with each other. The comparison I'm about to draw is not to indicate that any of these other groups are participating or committing any illegal acts, but nevertheless, the principles of business practices are no different than the Jews, the Asians, the Irish, the Arabs, the Russians, the Indians, and the Hispanics. They find ways to circulate their capital amongst their own, which leads to economic empowerment and success politically, never the other way around.

As I learn more about business, I will see drugs in their appropriate context as a commodity. My purpose for writing this book is to make these distinctions and point out that all the street corner indoctrination propaganda and rhetoric being spewed to our young people as a form of hood patriotism and loyalty is nothing but a tool being wielded in the hand of the mentally and morally bankrupt, which leads back to nothing but another form of commerce: cheap labor. Our young people end up being used to carry out acts for the enrichment of a very few. I have been at the table, negotiating at the highest levels, and getting the very best prices to bring back to market for my homies to enrich themselves with, even at the detriment to my bottom line. All of it was nothing more than commerce. These sophists are doing no more than taking your zealous behavior and herding it altogether as a commodity and leveraging it to enrich themselves.

The chief decided to introduce me to a group of guys who were waiting to say hi to me. Bald Head, being his usual self, asked me to greet them and say "Hola." Although I found it a bit odd, I obliged and greeted about 15-20 guys who all had varying levels of excitement when saying hi to me. Afterwards, Bald Head explained that there was a bet going on about who would win between me and Pepe in the market. The Chief and Bald Head had bet on me and won, while everyone else had bet on Pepe, who happened to be Mexican like them. This win for The Chief led to a promotion where he was put in charge of shipments going to that particular hub. With his newfound powers, The Chief made me the Primera of that state, which was a major distinction since it was the major distribution point for the Sinaloa cartel in the region. It turns out that my ability to understand The Chief's vision and execute it quickly had made our relationship productive and tight.

Beep beep beep...

Bald Head: MY FRRRRRRRRRIEND!!!! HOW ARE YOU, MY FRIEND!!

Me: I'm okay, my Friend... Are you okay, my friend?

Bald Head: Yes, my Friend!! I have a few guys just right here that want to say hi to you, my Friend!

Me: ...

Ball Head: Please, my Friend. Just say hi to them, they are all lined up and just want to say hi to you. The Chiefs, Chief has given you the name Primo. He calls you his Cousin. So they are going to say Hola Primo. Just say Hola back to them, it will make them very happy, my friend.

Once again, I allowed Bald Head to use me for his own purposes. I think I may have said Hola to about 15 or 20 guys. They all had different levels of excitement when greeting me. So, of course, I made Ball Head give me some form of explanation. This is when he told me about the bet that was going on and how he and the chief won so much money because everybody bet against me.

I found out that this went over extremely well and that the chief received a promotion. He was given control of the shipment going to that particular hub, among a number of things, because he predicted that I would perform the way I did. It was pretty embarrassing for the other side. The chief had the goose that could lay the golden egg anywhere he placed him. Speaking in business terms, the chief identified the ability that I had and leveraged that ability against his boss's top guy and won big time, creating a much better financial position for himself - commerce.

With the Chief's new powers, he made me Primera of that state now. This was a major distinction as I stated above because that was the major distribution point for the Sinaloa cartel in that region. The drugs that were shipped into Atlanta would feed the majority of that region, with Atlanta being the pivot point to ship drugs into North Carolina, the Virginias, and other areas.

As I and Keith were celebrating their recent victory at the Onyx gentlemen's club, Bald Head pulled me aside to give him some advice and a warning about what was to come.

Bald Head: I'm not supposed to say nothing. This may be the last load you receive over at your place for a little while, My Friend. Things are getting very bad, and it's going to get worse now. We are not able to cross nothing no more. Also, don't say anything, but the Chief may send for you soon too.

Me: What do you mean, Bald Head? Can you explain?

Bald Head: Attorney Lorence has already informed you that things are getting really bad over there. The Mexican government is supporting the Sinaloa cartel, and several government agencies are now on the border. The alphabet boys and Homeland Security are all there. It's just not safe for you to go across that border anymore.

Me: I see. Thanks for letting me know, Bald Head.

After their conversation,Keith and I continued our night at the club. Desire, a waitress at the club, jumped into my lap as I ordered rose champagne for their VIP section. I was back in my element and felt good after this recent victory. We continued to party and enjoy the night, which normally would have included a visit to the 300 bowling alley for celebrity night on Sundays. Usher and Tomeka would often join them, along with other celebrities,to party and have a good time.

"This was on a Sunday. Normally Keith, Pretty Boy, I AM and myself would always go to the 300-bowling alley for celebrity night on Sundays. Usher had started showing up as well as a lot of other celebrities that we knew to party with us because we were going hard and everything was on me. So Usher would bring Tamika with him and sometimes the kids as well. This particular Sunday Tamika spoke with Keith about throwing her sister's baby shower party the follow-on Sunday at 300 bowling alley on our night. Everybody pretty much knew that we would be up at the 300 bowling alley on Sundays and I would cover the cost of everything.

The general manager became a very good friend of mine based on me coming in on Sundays and spending about 10 or 15,000 on food and whole bottles of patron and they would just flow. Which caused us to pick up a whole lot of people that we knew and didn't know from the music industry in some cases to come and enjoy the festivities. So, Keith set up the baby shower for Tamika the following Sunday at the bowling alley.

I kind of got upset with Keith about that because I knew what was going to happen. I was already paying for everything and in the Atlanta fashion you throw a party in the midst of an ongoing party and slip out on having to be responsible for the bill. Just for the record, I'm not trying to insinuate Tamika would have done any such a thing because she really seemed to be a stand-up sister and about her business. Now independent of that Keith would often get very belligerent with Usher because he would come in and enjoy the party with bringing people alone and heading out the back door without saying anything. Keith stopped him several times in his tracks stating.........

Keith: Damn nigga!! You ain't even gone tell the Big Homie, good looking or nothing??!

Which I didn't take personally because I knew that Usher didn't really care for me that much based off past interactions we've had. Soon I would find out a little more about the reasoning for this because Keith and I had become very close, I believe this may have been perceived as somewhat of a threat to Usher based on Keith and his childhood friendships. One thing was clear to me throughout all the interactions just exclusively at the 300-bowling alley, Usher starting to become a regular enjoying Sundays with us.

Based on my knowledge of this and past practice from partying with him that following Sunday I was going to be at the Onyx, and I made Keith aware of that. Keith decided that he will come along with me and the rest of the guys over to the Onyx after making the arrangements for Tamika and her sister's baby shower over at the 300-bowling alley on celebrity night in the VIP lines.

I had told I AM that I was going to make sure we gave the appropriate space for them to enjoy such a special occasion. That added with dude didn't appear to fuck with me like that..... I guess I was wrong though

Desire was the top dancer in the Onyx, and trust me when I tell you that there were some very beautiful women in that particular gentlemen's club. I would have other girls dance for me as Desire just sat there in the love seat talking. Every now and then, I would have her get up and dance for me. I never wanted her on top of me or straddling across me grinding on me. I always wanted her to stand back a little ways from me as she danced, so I could just appreciate God's artistry and genetic perfection accentuated by her curves. But I just couldn't enjoy a moment without some form of aggravation or threat of stress for some odd reason.

Keith came over to me and whispered in my ear that he had just gotten off the phone with Usher, and he wanted to know if it was OK for him to swing by and party with us. I told Keith it was cool; I didn't have a problem with Usher. What I did clarify to Keith was that I didn't want the whole baby shower party to crash our party. But if Usher and Tameka wanted to come through, that was cool with me because I really liked Tamika; I felt she was cool people.

After 30 minutes of enjoying Desire and having conversations with her, my attention was called towards the door. There was a huge group of people entering the Onyx and headed towards the VIP area that I had bought out for the night. I looked at the head of this group and saw Usher and Tamika. Needless to say, I was extremely hot. I looked over towards Keith, and he just dropped his head. I knew this was their intention last week Sunday at the bowling alley when they wanted to do the impromptu baby shower on that following Sunday. That's why I came to the Onyx with my guys, including Keith, which I felt was my guy as well. That whole party just flooded into the VIP area that we had rented out. I was really angry with Keith, but I understood his position because he still worked for US records, and Usher was not just his best friend, but also his boss.

I was looking forward to making a deal with Usher because he was working on his new album after being off for a number of years after his "Confessions" album. I wanted to give him money to book a number of dates from him once he entered back on tour. Partying with Usher and even Tamika at that point was starting to become normal because we were pretty much around each other all the time. So much so that Usher's bodyguard would ask me for certain directions because I had a number of bodyguards that I hired from down there, and then my street guys that were with me were also on guard.

Desire and I had so much security around us, so eventually when Usher came to hang out with us, he didn't bring security. He would have his kids and Tamika with him oftentimes too. But all of these other people just crowded in, just confirming what I had felt the Sunday before.

I made Keith aware that it was cool if no one came down into my area, sitting on or around my loveseat where me and Desire were sitting. Doing as I would normally do, getting a few dancers and having Desire stand up and dance for me every now and then. I looked up, and here comes Keith...

Keith: Yo Big Homie.......

Me: What's good, Keith??

Keith: The Big U wanted me to ask you can he get a few dances??

Me: Hell Yeah, Bro!

I told the girl that was dancing for me at that time to follow Keith down to the other end of my VIP section & give Usher a few dances.

Keith: Naw Big Homie...... Not her, he wants her.

Me: He wants Desire, Bro??! HELL, FUCK NAW KEITH! WHAT TYPE OF SHIT IS HE ON BRO!!

Keith: I know Big Homie! BUT, PLEASE BIG HOMIE.....PLEASE!!

I was feeling hot and wild, wondering why this guy was always messing with me. It seemed like he wanted whatever I had. Then, he put Keith in an uncomfortable position by having him come and ask me for him because, at the end of the day, he was still his boss. This reminded me of a few weeks back when I was talking to I AM and his brother Jay at 300. The music was extremely loud, and we were seated in comfortable chairs, with Jay in one and me sitting on the edge of a loveseat, leaning in towards each other and having an important conversation. Usher was sitting on the loveseat directly across from me at the total opposite end, sitting on the arm. As Jay and I were talking, in the middle of a serious conversation, we both heard, "Hey man, hey man, hey bro," as he yelled it over towards our direction. Eventually, Jay looked up in his direction, and I followed Jay's eyes, looking towards Usher.

Usher greeted me with, "Hey, Man. How are you?? Haven't seen you in a while, you good??!" Jay looked over at me with a puzzled expression on his face, probably wondering why Usher was acting like we hadn't just seen each other the week before. Jay jokingly asked if we had some sort of agreement or if Usher had an issue with me. I brushed it off and said it was nothing, but inside, I was thinking differently.

I didn't understand what was wrong with Usher; he just didn't seem to want to see me succeed. Thankfully, Keith, my real homie, was there for me. I asked Desire to go down and dance for Usher, even though she didn't want to because he was cheap. I knew I had bigger things at stake, so I insisted that she do it and come back after three or four songs. She expressed some reservations due to past experiences, but I convinced her it was for a bigger picture.

As Keith looked on freaking out, Desire eventually went down and danced for Usher, while Tamika watched. Keith was so grateful because he knew how much I was affected by Usher's gesture. I had the original girl that I thought Usher wanted, but it turned out he just wanted my connection to keep the money flowing.

I got up for a minute to walk over to the DJ and request some songs, but I overheard him shouting out the Mexican guys on the other side of the club who rented the VIP area. The DJ told everyone that they were the plug, stating that the Migos got the whole city on lock. Little did he know that they were getting the work from me, as I had become their new plug just a couple of days ago. I couldn't help but think, "if only you knew."

Back to my seat, I noticed a gentleman standing on the love seat and sitting on the headrest part in the middle, making it impossible for anyone to sit on the love seat. I politely asked the gentleman, who was obviously with the party that had come with Usher and Tamika, if he could move. He became hyper and disrespectful towards me, probably thinking that everything was paid for by Usher. I was already upset, so I got extremely aggressive with him, and my guys were ready to take action when Keith came running in and grabbed the guy, giving him a good understanding of who the actual host was. After this misunderstanding was cleared up, things settled down pretty quickly, and he was made aware that his sense of entitlement was misplaced. Just as things calmed down, Desire returned to me, and she didn't seem too pleased...

Me: What happened?

Desire: I knew I shouldn't have gone down there with him.

Me: What happened down there?

Desire: I just should have followed my gut feeling.

Me: What was she saying to you?

Desire: She was mostly talking about me to him.

I was shocked to hear what she was saying and she seemed embarrassed to tell me. I was more concerned about his response to his then-girlfriend, who would later become his wife. Desire said she was tired of the verbal abuse and decided to leave. When I asked about her compensation, I was shocked by what she told me. However, based on past experiences, I wasn't surprised, and it seemed that she wasn't either. Later, I would discover that they had an indirect connection, which was just one of many surprises I would encounter in the music industry.

I was having a blast partying with Keith and the guys, going out to eat and visiting labels in New York for One Chance, a male singing group managed by Woo on Keith's label. We met some beautiful young ladies who showed us around town and got us into exclusive clubs. One night, I embarrassed myself on the dance floor with a Puerto Rican girl who loved to dance, but I had no rhythm. The girls teased me about it for the rest of the trip. Keith was wild, even tongue kissing two same-sex ladies on a booth seat at one club.

While handling business in the music industry, I was in constant contact with Bald Head, who updated me on the escalating war and how badly they needed ammunition and weapons. The Sinaloa cartel was losing ground, and members were switching allegiances, stealing large amounts of cocaine from the cartel, causing them to take a financial hit. Bald Head urged me to get weapons and ammunition, but I didn't want to be involved in such cases.

Despite the seriousness of the situation, the party never stopped. We frequented Onyx and 300 bowling alleys on celebrity nights between recording for One Chance and Usher's albums. Keith was heavily involved in both, and I got to hear all the songs being submitted for Usher's album. I even heard the Mario song "You Should Let Me Love You" before it was sung by Mario. Usher had turned it down, but the writer insisted that it would only be sung by Usher or Mario, and we all know how that turned out.

I received a call on my two-way radio from Junior who informed me that Chief needed me to travel to a location within a couple of weeks, and I needed to start planning accordingly. I spoke with Bald Head about this, but I was hesitant to go based on what Atty Lorence had told me. I asked Bald Head for advice on how to handle the situation, but he didn't have any suggestions, and he seemed nervous even discussing it with me.

After some contemplation, I spoke with Junior again and explained that it was not a good time for me to go. However, he relayed to me that the Chief didn't care and that I needed to be there. Junior also instructed me to prepare and send some weapons and ammunition across. I was put off by the tone of Junior's communication and thought it was unusual because the Chief would always communicate with me directly, and Junior would just translate. Moreover, the Chief was never absent when Junior was speaking to me.

I AM, my colleague, expressed his desire to accompany me, but I was hesitant to bring him along. I had a feeling that I might not come back from the trip and didn't want to put him in harm's way. Although he didn't understand why I was being paranoid, I explained to him that I had some reservations about the trip, mainly because I knew that Danny's name was going to come up. As I was still in contact with Danny, I knew that he was an essential player in preventing Sinaloa's shipments from crossing into Juarez, and I was not optimistic about the outcome of my meeting with Chief.

The Chief always seemed to be in the know, and I recall a past incident where I had a disagreement with Bald Head because the Chief did not tolerate lies.

I went to see Atty Lorence and shared my dilemma with him. He advised me not to go, but I requested a copy of an article he had kept for me to read. I knew that I would need something to show Chief when I arrived to explain my concerns about the trip. Shortly after, I was informed that I would not be able to cross, and it would be better for me to fly directly from Michigan to Mexico City. This news came as a surprise to me, as I had no idea that the meeting was more significant than the previous one in Culiacan.

I tried to convince my colleague, I AM (Sam), that he should sit this trip out due to the danger involved. Atty Lorence had informed me about the increased presence of government law enforcement agencies along the border with Mexico, and I was worried about the risks. However, despite my best efforts, I AM insisted on joining me on the trip to Mexico City.

We had our tickets booked, flying directly from Romulus, Michigan, to Mexico City on Northwest Airlines. During the flight, I was quiet because I knew the danger that lay ahead. I couldn't shake off the feeling that I didn't have a choice in the matter. My mind kept going back to the last time I had crossed into Juarez with I AM and flown out of the Juarez airport. When we returned a few days later, we were held up in the airport, and Bald Head was acting extremely strange.

I approached Bald Head calmly and quietly, not wanting to alarm I AM, and asked him what was going on. But he was evasive, saying a lot of things without really telling me anything.

Bald Head: "My friend, we can't go out there. It's no good!"

I persisted in trying to find out what was happening, and eventually, Bald Head told me what was going on.

Bald Head: "No, no, my friend, listen...there are Sicarios out there waiting to kill us right now. We may have to board another flight and fly back out of here. They are waiting to kill us all."

I wasn't happy with his response, and the lack of confidence in his voice when he spoke about our safety didn't inspire much confidence in me either.

Bald Head: My Friend! The Chief is talking with them barely right now just to let you guys pass. Not for me though. The fucker Danny wants to kill me because he thinks I steal you from him for the Chief. I just know it My Friend. I know they won't want any problems with you guys. they would have big problems with the US Government because you guys are citizens I TOLD THEM, I ALSO A CITIZEN TOO BUT THEY DON'T CARE!! THEY DON'T FUCKING CARE ABOUT NOTHING MY FRRRRIEND!!!! We are friends,my friend they won't touch you guys any way; you have too much value. You must tell Danny it was you and not me if they get ready to kill me because it will be a very long night for me before they do. Danny is really going to fuck mmmmeeeee my friend!!!!

I would be remiss to not point out the fact that my friendship with Bald Head, according to him, was always invoked when he thought someone was going to or wanted to kill him. I don't know if you have noticed by now no matter what side somebody always wanted to kill him.

Nevertheless, we were allowed to leave the airport and cross without issue. Bald Head had to purchase another flight back out of the city of Juarez and return to the Chief which I've never seen him happier with that option.

This flight was a very uncomfortable flight for me knowing at that time; the details about what was happening at the airport I knew I could not tell I AM about them as well as the full scope of what we would be faced with when we touched down in Mexico City.

We landed in Mexico City, Mexico, and went on through customs. I noticed that everybody else's passport was stamped in the back, including I AM's, but for some reason, mine wasn't. I asked the customs agent about it, and he explained that sometimes they don't stamp the back of the passport when the government may not be friendly with that particular country. I understood that it might not be in my best interest to have that evidence stamped in the back of my passport.

Bald Head and a group of sicarios picked us up at the airport and took us to a nearby restaurant. When we arrived, Bald Head left us in the car with the driver and went into the restaurant. He returned shortly after and got back into the car with Sam and me. I knew something wasn't right, but I didn't ask any questions. The driver was likely listening to our conversations and the length of them, so I remained quiet.

Junior emerged first from the restaurant, followed by the Chief. The Chief got into his vehicle, and Junior got into the one right behind him, with us in the car behind Junior. This was unusual because I normally rode with the Chief and Bald Head. We were driving up the expressway when Chief's motorcade suddenly stopped in the middle of a busy freeway. Bald Head jumped out of the front passenger seat, ran up to the car head, and got in with the Chief, and then the motorcade continued.

I AM asked what was going on, and I signaled to the driver to relax. I explained to I AM that this was what I had warned him about back in the States and that it was important for him to remain calm and let me do all the talking if there was an issue. I also told him that I was more than sure that Bald Head was being questioned about us and other things we would soon find out.

We rode for a few hours, and I took the opportunity to go to sleep.

I AM: How in the fuck can you sleep at a time like this........

Me: Because I know that we're good. Just stick to the script and we Gucci.

I can't confirm what I had just told I AM, neither did I know the outcome that would be lying ahead for us, but I knew I couldn't express that concern to him. I needed him to do exactly what I asked him to do with confidence while giving his usual quote, "Damn Brain, I knew you were going to come up with something."

We eventually pulled into a gas station and the Chief, as well as Junior and a few others, went into the gas station. We were woken up by some knocking on the car window. It was Bald Head with a very huge smile on his face giving us the thumbs up as he ran off, returning back to the vehicle with the Chief.

I AM: What do you think the meaning of that was, Bro??

Me: Just what I told you already. We're good! Just stick to our game plan. I do ALL the talking.

I was lying. I did not know if we were good or not for sure. I knew that that was a good sign that things had the potential of being OK.

What I was starting to learn from separate conversations that Junior and I would have, was that Bald Head was falling out of favor, and his allegiance was in question. The Chief was very good at reading people and had to be in order to survive over there. Bald Head was not difficult to read. Bald Head often told me things not because he was trying to be my friend, as he would always put it, but oftentimes once he told me things, he would ask me what I thought about them. He would often say that the Chief and the guys over there would get mad at him for telling me too much. What they didn't know, but the Chief actually figured out, was that I did not need Bald Head to tell me anything. I could read it and put things together on my own based on how they were lining up. Often, the Chief would give him a message to tell me, to make sure he told me in that certain way. Bald Head would ask Chief to tell him what he meant by the statement he would give him to give me.

The Chief: Don't worry, Jose. Just tell him......He will know.

Bald Head was initially oblivious to this talent that I possessed until the Chief started to make use of it. Bald Head often delivered messages to me from the Chief that were about him and he didn't know it. Often asking me what it meant right after he told me, and I would spin him. It was starting to become clear to me, and I believe the Chief was starting to prepare me for life after Bald Head. But right now, it was my turn, and the focus was on I AM and my life.

Finally arriving at the top of this very huge hill, it was very dark outside at this point. The scenery from the top of this hill was just beautiful. There was a 360 view of the residents down below that were all lit up. It was really beautiful. I AM noticed the sound and he asked me...

Me: "Those are pigs, I AM."

"Well why are they so loud like that? Man, they are going crazy over there, they're making a lot of goddamn noise," he stated.

Me: "They're acting like that because they know these guys just arrived and they figure it's time to eat."

What I didn't tell I AM is the known fact to most, that pigs will eat anything and if they ate that night, we would be on the menu. Right in front of this mansion was a pool that hadn't been used for some time. There was dirty water, tree branches, and a number of other things that were just lying in this pool.

As we entered the house, it was apparent that there was no furniture in the house. We walked into this very huge dining room area with a smaller kitchenette type adjacent to it. The kitchenette area was pretty big itself but not as big as the dining room, but this is where a huge table was present. The sicarios started to put chairs around this very big table. One of the sicarios pointed to where Sam and I should be seated. I looked over at the Chief, the Chief nodded in affirmation that that is where we should sit, which was extremely unusual. No one told me what to do when I was around the Chief but the Chief, and if the Chief was not present, Junior or either Bald Head would be my guide but never telling me where to sit or anything of that nature.

The interesting thing about the seats was that our backs were facing the kitchenette area where the sicarios were preparing sweet biscuits and tea. As they were serving us the tea and sweet biscuits, there was a lot of hustling and bustling movement around us. I grabbed the edge of the table, placing my hands flat up underneath it, noticing that this table was extremely heavy and looking like it was carved out of a huge tree in two parts.

Which made me wonder, since the house had no furniture, what is really done on this huge table next to the dining room in a huge kitchen net area room? The Chief finally started to speak to me for the first time after arriving in Mexico City. When he started to talk, everyone stopped moving. The Chief usually starts by asking how the flight was and all the other pleasantries that are asked among a welcoming party.

This clearly was not that type of scenario. The Chief asked me about one particular shipment that had been sent to me some time ago. The shipments that I usually receive all have one stamp, and only one stamp on them. That stamp is usually the representation of the cartel, but this was not the case. These bricks had two different stamps on them - some border stamp of Mazda like the Mazda vehicle and a stamp of a dolphin were on these bricks.

The quality was absolutely horrible, which was not normal from any of these shipments that I received. It led me to believe at that time that those bricks had to come from another office and not ours. After some conversation and me explaining to the Chief what the problems were with the bricks and why I had fallen short of covering the whole cost, he then told me that he was doing a favor for a friend to help him out. He then asked someone a few questions, found out what his price was, and told me that I at least needed to pay him the amount that he received them at. This was unusual in itself. He never questioned me about something like this because I was never short, not intentionally anyway, and he knew that the quality on this particular product was horrible. I didn't take the option of offering to return them because I would never want to insult the Chief, as that would always be a maneuver to force a cheaper price. He moved from that subject while still remaining very dry with me...

The Chief: Have you spoken to Danny?...

I had been anticipating this question, knowing that it was crucial. The room was eerily silent, with no movement or whispering, unlike before the question was asked. The answer I gave would determine whether we would be spared by the Sinaloa cartel or end up as food for the pigs at night. I understood that giving the wrong answer could result in someone sneaking up from behind and knocking us off.

The Chief had already known the answer to the question even before he asked me. I was sure of it, as he had been aware of the bricks Danny had offered me some time ago. The only way he could have had such information was if he had a mole within the Carrillo Fuentes brothers' cartel who was still loyal to him and providing him with intel. The Mazda and dolphin stamped bricks that I had received could have belonged to the individual who had been passing information to the Chief from the Juarez cartel.

As the weight of the situation sank in, I lowered my head, creating a pause as if deep in thought. Then I slowly raised my head, looking the Chief straight in the eye.

Me: Yes. Yes, Chief I have spoken with Danny.........

The Chief just paused and stared at me for a moment. It's like that time period lasted for an eternity. He just continued to stare at me then his eyes wandered off to the right for a moment as if he was thinking. Bringing his eyes back dead center gazing into my eyes..........

The Chief: Okay. Let's move on, BUT DON'T HAVE NO COMMUNICATION, NO MORE WITH DANNY.

I knew it would be an extremely huge risk to tell the truth but, I also knew what telling a lie and being caught in that lie would do in the middle of a war. I do believe under the circumstances that I should have been dead at that moment but what was clear was that there was no one you could trust over on that end with everyone switching allegiances and having someone that was willing to tell the truth even at their own demise was a priceless value.

I do believe that deep down inside whereas the Chief then like be constantly communicating with Danny after he told me not to, he could appreciate and maybe even desired the loyalty and friendship that I still showed towards Danny. was an innate nature that he felt that he could also be the beneficiary of as well.

What I would find out is what he made clear to me so long ago when having me promise him that I would not throw him under the bridge; was that our destiny was tied to each other, and we were too deep in the race to try to switch horses. What made me so valuable was that it was understood what the black man was worth in that world having a direct connection to the market by passing the American Hispanics and having access directly to the market without the manipulation of the American Hispanic as the middleman.

The Chief could afford to deal with me a little differently than what he would deal with the Mexican national that was part of the cartel because he understood that stateside, we played out of a different book and loyalty was something within our book but absent from their book of business nothing more nothing less.

As the Chief proceeded and talked to me about some of the current events and what was happening over there in Mexico and a position that the Sinaloa cartel was in now. Junior called Bald Head signaling for him to follow him outside. The Chief began to talk at a more rapid pace at this point but towards me. The translators that have always translated conversations between me and the Chief were now gone outside Junior and Bald Head. The driver for I AM, and I started to translate for the Chief the Chief: Listen Primo, I'm going to send you more loads very soon. I will need for you to work fast.

I have made you Primera now and everything must come to you first now ONLY! I'm doing something for you Primo. I'm showing you can control everything. Don't tell anyone, but I'm going to give you better price. I'm going to give you one thousand off each from my money Primo. This can help you go even faster than before Primo. This is very important for everything...... Everything Primo".

I knew that this was a big opportunity for me. Being promoted to Primera meant that I was now at the top of the food chain and that everything would be coming directly to me. The Chief was showing me that he trusted me and that he was willing to reward me for my loyalty. It was a risky business, but the rewards were enormous. The thought of having an extra thousand dollars off each load was like a dream come true. I knew that this would put me in a strong position to expand my operations and take on even more business. I nodded my head in agreement with the Chief.

Me: Yes, Chief. I understand. I will work fast and make sure that everything comes to me first.

The Chief nodded his head and smiled.

The Chief: Good. You're a smart man, Primo. I know that you will not disappoint me.

We continued to talk for a little while longer, discussing the details of our business and what we needed to do to stay ahead of the competition. The Chief was a smart man, and I knew that he had my best interests at heart. As we finished our conversation, I got up to leave, knowing that I had a lot of work to do.

Me: Thank you, Chief. I won't let you down.

The Chief: I know you won't, Primo. Remember, everything must come to you first. Trust no one.

I nodded my head in agreement and walked out of the room, feeling like I had just been given the keys to the kingdom. I knew that this was just the beginning, and that there was still a long road ahead, but I was ready for whatever came my way.

I understood what the Chief was saying to me in this instance. There was a lot that was not said, but he knew that I would understand. In the language of commerce, he was basically telling me that through me, or for me, he was going to set up an empowerment zone. Oftentimes, empowerment zones are set up in black neighborhoods or minority neighborhoods, giving businesses huge tax incentives and even grants, in some cases, to relocate their businesses to impoverished areas that usually feature minority groups, mostly African American groups. We look at it as a positive incentive or explained to us as a positive incentive to help our neighborhoods when actually the group coming in and receiving these tax incentives and grants are not from our own but other ethnic groups that take these savings and profits made from our pockets and circulate this money back among themselves. The Chief recognized that I had access directly to the consumer, so bringing me into an area that was controlled by his own people and giving me a tax break/grant to bring my business acumen into this area would only increase his leverage to project himself into a highly valued position by his boss and his boss's boss over in Columbia.

I understood exactly what the Chief was saying. The Chief wanted control of the Juarez Plaza and control of that crossing point. He would use the political influence and additional manpower of the Sinaloa cartel to go back and get revenge on the Juarez cartel. I knew he wanted to create his own cartel, which was the reason he promised me, basically, my own connection in Columbia to receive directly from the Colombian cartels as long as I finished his products from them first, which he would be responsible for most likely getting them to me here in the states anyway. Essentially, he would repeat the same process that he did with Chapo by putting me on the table in negotiation and leveraging his ability as well with me as a representative to put himself in a power position. What he was actually doing was going to do the same thing Danny did in every case leading to me meeting The Chief. Now, the Chief was going to copy, paste and repeat... just at a higher level, still needing me to be loyal to him like I was with Danny when I enabled him to rip off Rojo.

This was the very first time I can say that I knew for sure that my life was in danger. I often wonder what would happen if I had lied about talking to Danny. Even though I don't think there was much to be left to imagine because the position of the sicarios behind Sam and me, and then the ceasing of movement, made it pretty clear that the observers wanted to make sure they understood their mark. The Chief started to talk extremely fast once Bald Head was removed from the room. I found that I had to lock in on what was being said by the driver to make sure I understood the ambiguous conversation, which seemed to be the basis of all of our conversations. There was no end in sight anytime soon either.

Sam and I were taken to an upscale hotel where we were going to stay for a few days. However, we didn't leave the hotel often, and this made me anxious. I didn't understand why my presence was needed so urgently when I was mostly just in my room.

The next evening, Bald Head and a few sicarios came to pick us up and took us to a fancy restaurant where we met with the Chief and some other important individuals. Reyes, whom I didn't like, was already seated when we arrived. After we finished eating, we moved to the lounge area, where they began discussing business. The main topic was the price of cocaine, and for some reason, Reyes seemed overly engaged in the conversation, which made me uncomfortable. He tried to get me to agree to certain numbers, but Bald Head didn't say anything, which wasn't normal. I suspected they were trying to run a maneuver on me. So, I decided to appear uninterested and blow Reyes off whenever he tried to manipulate me. He eventually stopped talking to me and turned his attention to Sam, who he thought had the authority to authorize deals, but Sam was unaware of Reyes' manipulations.

Reyes soon realized that Sam couldn't authorize anything and asked the Chief if he could send hydroponic marijuana to us in America. The

Chief agreed, and Reyes negotiated a price with us. He talked about shipping it to us directly from California at a good price. I negotiated with him in good faith because I knew the Chief was interested, but I didn't trust Reyes. We left the restaurant, but they split us up. I left with Bald Head and Reyes, and Sam was taken back to the hotel by the sicarios.

I was taken to a home somewhere in a neighborhood in Mexico City. It appeared to be a middle-class neighborhood. We entered the house fully furnished, nice furniture but nothing extravagant.

As we entered the living room Reyes walked in with his big Jefe swagger and started to speak with a somewhat heavy set female. This female looked as if she may have been the owner of the house with the lady of the house.

He walks in first with Bald Head in tow and I'm behind Bald Head. As Reyes projects this big cartel boss demeanor he arrogantly points to the left at a seat while turning around looking at me and re pointing to the same seat. The young lady looks directly at me and again I know what Reyes is trying to do.

Thinking to myself this fucking guy just won't give up he's constantly trying to make an impression at my expense not knowing that I understand what he's doing. I had just come to settle on the fact that Reyes was just a DUMB FUCK.

Being the asshole that I am, I looked directly at Reyes and then the young lady, as I went to the opposite side of the room to find a seat. The young lady looked at me with a shocked look on her face and burst into laughter at Reyes' expense. I even noticed that Bald Head found humor in it as well.

This whole conversation that they were having with this young lady was in Spanish. I couldn't really tell exactly what was being discussed except for certain keywords discussing cocaine as well as marijuana and some methamphetamine.

We were not there very long before leaving to head back to the hotel. The whole setup was nothing new to me if you were Black over in Mexico and from America you are extremely valuable.

Reyes just having me with him was a statement all on to itself he would be able to paint any picture that he wanted to pay with me standing there as verification of any truth or lie of exaggeration would have been accepted just with my presence. The arrangement he made with the Chief along with my relationship with Bald Head allowed him to be able to take me with him on whatever Ponzi scheme of leverage he was trying to project to that young lady.

I will later understand that this young lady was a daughter of a very powerful boss that Reyes was trying to get additional work from and give to me with the Chief's blessing as long as he paid the Chief his percentage. Where I thought that it was just concerning hydroponic marijuana there was really nothing off the table and the Chief will get a percentage of everything.

Much later I would find out that two hundred keys that were sent to me later on in Detroit were directly from Reyes and Bald Head. I received them for 16,000 apiece, they made four thousand dollars off of each of those bricks.

Right at Mexico City Mexico the price for a kilo of cocaine around that time may have cost between 6 to 8000 dollars apiece. I know after they subtract their 4000 off of each kilo of cocaine, they pay 12,000 overall, so if they're paying between 6 to 8000 at Mexico City price that $12,000 had to have the Chiefs fee in it and I'm sure it wasn't cheap.

Whatever the case may be, I'm sure Reyes and Bald Head were not upset about having $800,000 to split between the two of them, after a day and a half two days' wait. And of course the transportation would not have been an issue for Reyes because he owned a trucking company there was just no overhead for them two.

Again, playing out of the rule book stateside; you don't count what's on the next man's desk. I was familiar with all the pricing details of cocaine starting from its origin in Columbia, to the expenses incurred in crossing it by land or water into Mexico (though most of the time it was flown into Mexico City, Mexico airport). As the drug moved closer to the US border, the price would increase. However, I was supposed to have applied an additional tax on Reyes and Bald Head, which was not a part of the deal I had cut with the Chief. He made it clear that it wasn't coming from him either. I quickly learned that my code of conduct only applied in America, and in situations like these, it was important to adapt to the local customs. WHEN IN ROME, DO AS THE ROMANS DO!

Arriving back at the hotel with Bald Head, he walked me back up to my room. Upon entering, I saw that I was sitting on the bed, watching TV. Bald Head immediately started talking to Sam in a joking manner, asking him questions about how he liked working for me. Sam replied that he enjoyed working under me. Bald Head continued to ask him more questions in a joking manner, and whenever Sam gave him an answer, Bald Head would flip the answer around, egging him on as if he was joking to get more information out of him. Sam started taking the bait and went on and on about how he really didn't like how I wasn't paying him appropriately and how the other guys were dissatisfied, and so on.

Listening to Bald Head's cadence within his words, I began to sense that his rather persistent questioning and changing of pace in asking questions was a hit job being performed by Bald Head to fish a certain type of answer out of Sam. I cut in rather abruptly and started to really go at Sam while giving details of how much he gets paid, asking him each time I made a statement of clarification to verify whether it was the truth or not. Sam answered affirmatively to pretty much everything I was saying but, in some cases, elaborating on what I was saying.

I had to make sure that my clarification and questioning of Sam were not intimidating or appeared as if I was trying to cover something up.

After Bald Head got a better clarification, he seemed to abruptly need to leave all of a sudden. I turned towards Sam after Bald Head exited the room and told him that Bald Head was setting him up, that his questions were to test him and see if he was unhappy with his position to look for traces of jealousy or potential threat to me by him. I AM was really disturbed by the information I had just given him, and I reiterated to him that the next time I advise him to stay and not come along with me on these trips, it needed to be taken seriously. Even though I knew it was my fault and I should not have brought him with me, it was getting difficult to protect myself as well as him with all of the trickery and games of commerce that these guys were playing.

I knew at that moment that Bald Head was working for two sides and that he was becoming more and more of a threat, and I knew exactly how to solve that. Bald Head returned to the room a couple of hours later, extremely excited and jacked up. He used the name of the Chief's Chief for the first time while expressing to I AM and me what had him so excited.

Bald Head exclaimed, "My friend, Chapo is going to buy us some pussy! He told me to bring these brochures up here to let you guys pick whatever girl you may want. He's going to pay for it for us. He barely told me to bring this over to you guys right now. He said, 'Take this to my Primo.' Chapo is very happy with you, my friend, very happy."

In my mind, I couldn't help but notice how Bald Head was emphasizing how happy Chapo was with me. The interesting thing that stood out to me was that he finally used his name, something he had never done before despite referring to him countless times. Bald Head wanted to make sure that there was no mistake in who the message was coming from.

What I didn't know, and Bald Head didn't hesitate to explain, was that the women on the brochure were actually actresses and news-casters from major TV networks in Mexico, including Telemundo. We were being offered the chance to have sex with any one of these A and B list personalities, and Chapo was going to pay for it. I was taken aback by the offer, and I repeated what Bald Head had just told me. He confirmed that all these women were basically escorts for powerful cartel members, except for the wives and girlfriends of the big bosses in Mexico. He made sure I understood the significance of Chapo buying this kind of "pussy."

"Bald Head: Chapo is really, really happy with you, primo! I'm glad we're good friends, my friend!"

I declined the offer to pick one of the women from the brochure, and I AM followed suit. Bald Head was extremely upset because Chapo was buying for me. He kept asking me why I would turn down the best and most beautiful women in all of Mexico, especially since they were on TV. But I think what he really meant was, "Why would you do that to me?" Because now he wouldn't be able to have sex with one of the most beautiful women in Mexico, since Chapo was buying them for me. He persisted for an answer, so I told him that the women weren't thick enough for me. I like women who are very thick with a nice ass and huge tits.

This made him very angry, and he gave an emotional outburst. "Bald Head: No, my friend! You just like fat bitches! A bunch of fat bitches, that's all!" He pleaded with me to pick one so he could get one and fuck them both. He said he would tell Chapo that I wanted a particular woman, so if they asked me, I would know what she looked like. He assured me that he would fuck them both, and I agreed to pick one under the condition that it was a quid pro quo situation of my choosing. Bald Head was willing to agree to anything at that moment, and he did.

The next morning, Bald Head came in feeling like a new man. He wanted to give me all the details about the two beautiful women, but I asked him to spare me the details. I didn't want to indulge in the great honor being bestowed upon me, according to Bald Head. Based on how he was describing this gift, I knew it was coming from a place I didn't want to be a part of. Bald Head had already sold his soul to the devil, and it became clear that he had a separate agenda from the Chief's when we got to Culiacan. But it seemed like everyone had their own agenda, and it was all a game of leveraging and counter-leveraging, with someone else's leverage being leveraged for someone else.

When it came to prison talk, I wasn't going to be the new guy who came in with a bunch of snacks on my bed and started eating them, only to have Big Bubba show up later to retrieve his belongings that I had eaten. I didn't want to end up in the same position Bald Head had put himself in with me: quid pro quo!

"Why were you asking I AM those questions yesterday?" I asked Bald Head. His eyes grew extremely large, but he knew he had to answer because the favor I did for him could be fatal for him if he lied to Chapo. Bald Head was very uncomfortable with the question but, in true fashion, he replied, "My friend... We are friends, right, my friend? Listen, Sam (Sam is I AM), I was told to ask you these questions by the Chief. You didn't answer them right, but my friend covered for you, so I didn't tell the Chief that part. Maybe you should not answer questions because if a guy asks you something over here, Sam, it's for a reason. He is not your friend, like me and my friend (pointing at me). Don't worry; I didn't say anything. You are a good guy."

Later on, Bald Head pulled me aside when it was just him and me. He needed to make sure that I was clear on a few things for the future, of course. "My friend, maybe you don't need to bring Sam here with you anymore. I don't think it would be safe for him because, you know, you are my friend, my friend. The Chief does not like Sam. I don't know why, but my friend, please understand, he really does not like Sam. Do you understand, my friend?"

I AM and I arrived back in Atlanta, and I was super stressed from the events that had taken place while in Mexico City. I had anticipated pretty much what happened, but the pigs were a rude awakening for me. I was starting to really comprehend what this war really meant and that the loss of life was really real. Bald Head had really made an impression on me by giving me an inside perspective on where the Chief's head was concerning I AM. After a day of staying in the house, replaying all the events that had happened and the conversation that had transpired (and the lack of any, as well, from select individuals), my good friend Keith Thomas decided to stop by with his normal shenanigans. In my case, it was a blessing, allowing me to move my mind to other things because Keith was the polar opposite of anything street or illegal.

Keith walked into the room, excited to see his friend after a long absence.

"Damn big homie! Where the fuck you been? You just disappeared around this mutha fucka and wasn't even answering your phone," he exclaimed.

Keith went on to talk about a little white boy from Canada who could sing like Michael Jackson. He was convinced that this boy was the next big thing in the music industry and had even reached out to Usher to get him on board.

As Keith raved about the little white boy's talent, I couldn't help but think he was messing with me again. We had been having a long-running debate about who was the better entertainer between Michael

Jackson and Prince. While I was a big Prince fan, Keith always argued that Michael Jackson was the superior performer. He had even showed me a YouTube video of the two of them performing together, which had crushed my argument.

Now, Keith was trying to convince me that this little white boy was the next Michael Jackson. I wasn't even interested in giving him a listen, feeling that Keith had committed the highest form of blasphemy by comparing anyone to Michael Jackson, let alone a little white boy.

Despite my protests, Keith continued to talk excitedly about the boy's talent and his plans to make him a star. His enthusiasm was infectious, and I found myself getting caught up in his vision for the future. As we talked, my stress from the events in Mexico City began to fade away, replaced by a sense of excitement for what was to come.

Me: Man, you gotta be out of your got damn mind, nigga!! Can't nobody ever in life be the next Michael Jackson. Ever!! Then your chicken shit ass is going to come in here and tell me a little white boy that's still a kid is the next Michael Jackson?? You better get the fuck out of town before sundown!!

Keith didn't pay me any mind. He stayed focused, well, at least he sat down working the phones. He was relentless as well as focused until he heard from Usher that he spoke with this kid's father and was making arrangements to bring him over stateside to start recording right away with Pretty Boi Fresh.

I could not have been more wrong, and I wasn't wrong by a little bit either. Where I still say to this day, this kid could never be Michael Jackson, but the fucking kid turned out to be phenomenal after I said he couldn't even sing either. This little white boy behind the keyboard singing is known today by the name of Justin Bieber. Keith Thomas was instrumental in discovering this kid, to bring him to the attention of the owner of US records,Usher Raymond. Keith did all of this while working on One Chance's album, Woo.Usher's album had just opened up, and he was accepting songs and submitted him to submitting them to Usher at the same time.

Without missing a beat, we headed off to 300 bowling alley for celebrity night. Like I stated before, this was our ritual. We did this every Sunday when not interrupted, of course. We even went as far as getting custom bowling balls made. We were really serious about this bowling thing.

We went in, and we set up as normal. I sent a couple of my bodyguards out to the VIP area to go get some real attractive women and invite them into the back VIP area of VIP bowling lanes with us. They brought back three beautiful females. I started to talk with one. She was from New Orleans. Her best friend was from New Orleans too, I believe, and they had another young lady with them with a banging shape. She was drop-dead gorgeous.

Keith started to talk with my little friend's best friend, and Woo started to entertain the other young lady. We were really having a good time with these young ladies. Keith made me aware that Usher wanted to come party with us as well. He asked me if I could speak with the young ladies and make them aware that Usher was coming in through the back entrance and that he would be bowling with us on the lanes.

Just pretty much ask them to take it easy not to act out of character or make anybody feel uncomfortable. The short mean that wouldn't happen, which wasn't really a big surprise because in Atlanta, you see celebrities or entertainers all the time. It wasn't really new for them. My little friend expressed to me that sentiment exactly by stating, "Oh no, we would never do that. We're used to being around celebrities of that caliber."

Shortly thereafter, Usher did enter with one of his sons from his then-girlfriend but soon-to-be wife Tamika. We had a very good time as the girls promised. This wasn't a very big issue for them, they were used to it.

After a night of fun, Keith came over to my house once again, which was normal. He made me aware that my friend Toya's friend was actively dating the Indiana Pacers starting point guard. She was driving his convertible coupe 645 BMW. Which would be the beginning of them two characters coming over to my house, going into the backroom, enjoying each other's time. This was really crazy to me because seeing the actual car with the Indiana plates and this gentleman's last name on the plates, and my dude is banging his girl's brains out on a constant basis, and it wasn't about the money either.

Toya and I started really building and got pretty cool. I really liked her a lot, she was just extremely sexy to me, and she was a Scorpio. We just seemed to click. That whole group would meet up with us every Sunday at the 300, and we would have a really good time. We went on a few double dates together, but for some reason or another, sometimes it was hard for her to come out, and I didn't understand why. She would always tell me that she can't come because of her daughter.

I would offer to pay for babysitters and all types of things, and she would just tell me that it wasn't that. One particular time we were hanging out, and we really just started to talk, and she told me she really couldn't come out at certain times because her daughter would tell her father, and that her daughter was her life. I told her that she didn't have to be concerned because her daughter's father was taking care of all the bills.

I told her I will take care of all of her bills and to make sure that she was good and not messing up anything for herself. I will give her the money to pay all of her bills up for a year. "Fuck that nigga, Momma... You good! I gotcha, don't even trip on that lil shit he doin' fa you."

Being the lady that she was, she just thanked me for my offer of generosity and told me that that wouldn't be necessary at that point. I didn't like it, but I respected it because I really wanted to try to build something with her. The thing that I like the most about her, she really didn't talk much about herself or too much really going on with her, which is a really good sign when you are a street guy because if a woman isn't quick to tell you anything about herself or anyone she's around, which usually means she won't be quick to tell anything about you as well.

I went about a couple of weeks without seeing Keith, but he didn't miss a beat with his girlfriend though. They had a hell of a chemistry between them and evidently the rhythm was good as well. We hit the 300 again, this time she showed up with her friends and she was all up under me. She was taking so many pictures with me and asked me if it was okay for her to post them on her page. I was happy to hear that and it was not an issue with me at all. I felt that I really had a chance because something had changed dramatically. I told her with renewed confidence that my offer still stood, just let me know when, and it's done, whatever she needed, all up front too.

I had a really good time the night before, but my morning started early the following day. I got a call from Bald Head making me aware that he would be in town with some really good news for me very soon. Even though I was pretty sure what that good news would entail, I humored him with fake excitement. I was also looking forward to speaking with him because I had other concerns that I needed some clarification on.

Erving gave me a call, wanting to meet up with me so he could introduce me to a gentleman that they were considering to bring on as their manager. The agreement that we signed the Outsyders up under was strictly for publishing through BE-LY publishing, not management. We ended up meeting at a small coffee shop near my place at the Rocca, literally 4-5 minutes from the governor's mansion. We sat down and Erving did most of the talking while introducing me to this gentleman whose name was James Mason. I had seen this gentleman a few times around 300 bowling alley on celebrity night. I mostly saw him around or with Jazze Pha, a producer with Red Zone. I was familiar with Red Zone because they were attempting to sign the Outsyders to their production team at one point.

Woo was talking with them about assigning Erving and Dean of the Outsyders over to do production in their production studio. James Mason seems to always be around, and this is where I recognize his face from. The more interesting fact was that I just noticed how when we were out in public, he appeared to be staring at me extremely hard like he knew me. I will find out later that he did know of me and wanted to befriend me as well. Mason was speaking to me about the music industry and what he wanted to deal with the Outsyders as representation for them. Erving seemed comfortable with him and excited about the possibility, but wanted my blessings. Woo and Keith weren't interested in managing the guys, and as long as they were happy with the choice in Mason, that was okay with me.

I had so much on my mind at the time that I really wasn't there in the meeting and focused because there was just too much going on across the border, and I was starting to feel the presence of the government based on a lot of the strange things that were happening and with whom they were happening with. Bald Head was really a huge concern of mine. I just had a gut feeling about him for all the wrong reasons as well. Mason seemed to be a pretty cool guy, but he reeked of a street swagger that is unmistakable in my line of business. I wish I could tell you what was being discussed, but I was so out of it. After we wrapped up our meeting not too long after it actually started, I gave Erving my blessings, and I was off back to the house because Keith was on his way over.

As soon as Keith arrived, he was really excited and wanted to talk to me about last night at the 300-bowling alley and our experience with the girls. We sat down in the living room, and he started telling me about how much fun he had with his girlfriend and her friends. He said they danced the night away and that the chemistry between them was amazing. I could tell by the look on his face that he was really into her.

I asked him if he was still interested in the girl he was pursuing before, and he said he wasn't sure. He said he really liked her, but he didn't want to mess things up with his current girlfriend. I could understand his hesitation, but I also knew that he had a strong connection with the other girl.

We talked for a while about relationships and dating, and how complicated it can be sometimes. Keith was really open and honest with me, which I appreciated. He said he valued my opinion and wanted to know what I thought he should do.

I told him that he needed to follow his heart and do what felt right for him. I said that he should be honest with both girls and let them know how he feels. It might be difficult, but it would be better in the long run than leading them both on.

Keith seemed to take my advice to heart, and we spent the rest of the afternoon hanging out and talking about life. It was nice to catch up with him and see that he was doing well.

Keith: Nigga Roche!! Did you see Toya's Myspace page??! She got you all over her page Big Homie! Y'all hugged up too!!

I didn't have Toya's Myspace page information. For that matter I didn't even know what my space was, and I had to have Tez make the page for me. The only reason I even did it was because Keith informed me that in order to be in a music industry you had to have a Myspace or some type of social media presence. Keith always carried his laptop with him so he pulled up her page so I could see the pictures that she had posted of me and her and our whole little group. I started to feel really good because we looked like we were together, and she was really buying into the idea. I was kind of happy about that. I mean she had a lot of pictures up all over her Myspace page.

I'm scrolling through her pictures just scrolling scrolling and scrolling looking at all the wonderful pictures of me and her, Keith, and our whole group, but she put a lot of pictures up of her and I. Then I started to get into the pictures of her daughter at what appeared to be recent birthday party. I noticed a guy with dreadlocks in a lot of the pictures with her daughter and he just looked extremely familiar to me for some odd reason. My curiosity just got to me and I asked Keith a question after making a statement.

Me: Keith, her daughter just had a birthday party or something??

Keith: Yeah, it kinda looks like it, don't it Big Homie.

Me: Man this dude in the pictures with her daughter, kinda looks like Lil Wayne! Just a lil bite tho, not all that much but enough to make you do a double take tho.

Keith: Nigga, that is Lil Wayne!!! You didn't know her Baby Daddy was Lil Wayne??!

I didn't know that her baby daddy was Lil Wayne and neither did she tell me. She never made any insinuations or no hints about it either. That just reaffirmed the way I was feeling about her because she didn't feel the need to discuss that. She stood on her own merit and just showed that she was a beautiful person and I could appreciate that and I wanted that for myself. Just made me recall when I told her and her girlfriends that Usher was coming in and asked those guys to remain calm and not act out of the ordinary. Now I understood why she stated that," no we would never do that. we are around A and B list celebrities all the time." she could have easily just made me feel stupid for the statement but classy enough to not take advantage of the fact that I didn't know.

I was just so out of my element down there and the caliber of women that I was constantly around. Like in one particular case I hit on Sheree of Atlanta housewives and didn't even know it. One of the guys tried to tell me saying, you know her baby daddy is an ex NFL player?? I just thought she was beautiful and had a very big ass and hips with really pretty hair. We exchanged numbers and I just so happened to be switching phones a couple of days later because the load was coming in and tossed the phone. Nevertheless Keith made me aware that she didn't tell him either that her girlfriend that he was dating at the time was the one that told him. I guess he felt the need to give his friend those details because he's saying I was looking pretty confused by not knowing that.

Bald Head finally arrived down in Atlanta to come get with me. He updated me on the fact that our load would be in within the next couple of days. The arrangement in how these things were done will be changed slightly. He also made me aware that the way the money would be turned in would have to change. He spoke directly with I AM concerning the money counting part of things. He would actually illustrate the actual process to I AM. each package of the money would have to be vacuum sealed with the amount that was actually in the vacuum sealed pocket.

Each bundle of money would have to contain 100 bills of the same denomination. At the very end if the denominations needed to be mixed but still all had to contain 100 bills in each brick of money. But when that set of money was vacuum sealed on the outer side he would have to write mixed to indicate that there are different denominations of currency within that vacuum sealed portion of money but all still containing 100 bills in each set..

Bald Head went on to express that all of the monies from this point forward would be sent across and go directly to a certain bank. This made the process easier because each bundle could be grabbed and set a top and money counter without the money counters having to touch any buttons on the money counter at the banks that this money was being deposited directly into.

After this information Bald Head felt pretty good and he wanted to go out and party before the bag came in. He also made me aware that no one wanted to bet him and the Chief anymore on who would finish first between myself and Pepe. I guess all of the other guys got tired of losing because I was spanking Pepe's ass when it came to moving that work. My spot for strippers was the Onyx but Bald Head wanted to go to Shooters Alley gentlemen's club. We got to the club and in normal fashion we had a really good time. I met a stripper by the name of Montana.

Overtime Montana and I got pretty cool but she would always get pissed off with me because loads would come in when we had dates set and I would always stand her up and try to compensate her with money which she always accepted. But she actually told me she was starting to feel insecure like she was ugly or something which lord knows was not the case this woman was drop dead gorgeous. I just didn't really have the time and something always seemed to keep coming up but make no mistake about it she was so beautiful she was in a bunch of different videos but of course I didn't know that either.

That particular night Bald Head got extremely drunk. You could tell that he must have new a bunch of fucking drugs was about to come or becoming consistently for a minute' because he partied hard. This man got shit face drunk. He was so drunk to the point he just kept wanting to talk to me, but he was sitting on the other side of the stripper stage. The music was extremely loud, but he just kept yelling as if I was right next to him. I think he started to notice that I was ignoring him which made him on this occasion keep yelling to get my attention......

Bald Head: MY FRIEND!! MY FRIEND!! MY FRIEEEEEEEEEEND!!!!

Me: (Looking in his direction) ....??!

Bald Head: I need to tell you something, My Friend!

Me:....(I'm looking at him like, OKAY??!)

Bald Head: When you have MONEY......Even The DOGS will dance for you! BUT, when you have no money.......YOU WILL HAVE TO DANCE YOUR SEEEEEEEEEELF!!!!! (Stated with a heavy drunk Latino accent.)

Within a few days after partying at the gentlemen's club the load came. I AM was in charge of securing the load and taking it to his location where it will be stored. He was also responsible for taking care of our new responsibility of handing off a portion of the load that was designated for two other Mexican groups. This particular time it would be much different. We moved over five hundred bricks in one day not including what we had to hand off to the other groups.

Beep, Beep, Beep.......

Bald Head: Tell me, My Friend??....

Me: My Friend, I need for you to send those guys back.

Bald Head: Is everything okay, My Friend??!

Me: Everything is okay. Tell the Chief we are done barely just now, My Friend.

Bald Head:.........

Me: My Friend ??.......

Bald Head: GOD DAMN, MY FRIEND!!!

Bald Head was lost for words once again. He didn't understand how we could just come into another state and dominate the market like that my guy Woo, was the key to being able to move that much down there in Atlanta along with as I indicated before the Homie Big Meech effect. That market down there was wide open and the Mexicans had pretty much filled in the void directly now. So when the streets found out that there was another black man in town with the bag, black people shopped with black people and Woo had a team of guys that were plugged into the streets. Country boy was his hard hitter for the guys out in the country. But for the inner city, his guy named Sauce was the FUCKIN SUPER STAR, of a superstar line up. All of the Mexicans wanted Sauce and Pepe was the leading contender until I showed up. Sauce was Michael Jordan/ Kobe Bryan & Lebron James in their prime. That upscale hustler that I referred to earlier on in the book, concerning the different levels of hustles. Losing Sauce was a major blow to the Mexicans. Sauce got a chance to see that Pepe ended up with the same work we had, but he noticed we had it first.

Sauce began to recognize he always had his bag before Pepe even had anything. My brother Sauce was very sharp and peeped out the power structure had shifted making me aware......

Sauce: Big Dawg.... This is Atlanta, Black Hollywood. Once the streets find out we got the bag; Black gonna support Black.

I felt like moving that initial load was a mistake as it led to us receiving two more loads without a break in between. This caused a lot of pressure on the guys working on the streets, and the prices were creeping up higher and higher, which made me very angry. This caused a lot of distrust among the ranks, and I was overworked and starting to make mistakes. I noticed signs in I AM that he felt he was ready for a bigger role, which wasn't an issue for me as I wanted to move away from being the boss. I just wanted to be the electric socket for a well-oiled machine to plug into and run well, as Woo and Sauce represented, and this is what I was ready to do. However, I AM was not ready for this, and when I told him, he felt like I was holding him back. He did not know many things because I was shielding him from the pressures that did not go with his job description. I knew he could not handle the pressure, which was at a whole new level than what it initially was, and I was being baptized in it.

There was a series of loads that came in succession, and the pace was relentless. Normally, I disappear when loads are in, out of respect for what Keith asked me when I was going through the Myspace DEA agent fiasco. He would always respect that I would never give him details, just stating that I had business, and he would ask no more and wait for me to call him at that point. But this situation was a little more urgent for him, I assume. Keith had written the hook on the song "Love in the Club," and Ryan Lovett sang the song to demo it for Usher. Sounds, who was managed by Woo but signed to US records via Keith, did the "Love in the Club" remix under Keith's instructions. Ryan Lovett sang Usher's part, and one of the girls from Ray Renee demoed Beyonce's part. Keith was at my house discussing how he would get with Mark Pitts to have Usher, who was out of town at the time, to lay the vocals to the song down and send it over to Jay-Z in an effort to get Beyonce to lay her vocals down on the record. But at that particular point, the record was done, and the urgent issue was that Usher wanted Lil Wayne on the record.

Keith was concerned because Lil Wayne owed his label his album but was going around doing a lot of features at the time, making plenty of money off of that. The biggest issue, as I understood it, was that Lil Wayne was rather mercurial and couldn't be found. Keith contacted Toya, just trying his hand, and she agreed to help out. So while Keith was at my house basically trying to figure all of this out, while he had the completed record in his hands as far as the R&B vocals from Usher and Beyonce, Toya came with the information he wanted to hear and told him that Lil Wayne was in town at a studio where he was recording at that very moment. Keith rushed out, met up with Usher at the studio, and after booking a studio room in that same studio, he walked into Lil Wayne's studio session and worked his magic. Lil Wayne went directly over into Usher's session and laid down his vocals for the "Love in the Club" remix, and from my understanding, he did it in one take after just hearing the song playthrough one time.

The pressure was nonstop when it came to working. We finished an additional two loads not including the initial one. Yet there was another on the way. Bald Head was supposed to make it back to town, but he didn't. He asked me to cover for him and not let the Chief know that he wasn't there. I AM and I were on our way to my house from Woo's house after I got the two-way call with confirmation that the load was there in Atlanta waiting for pickup. I had no idea; evidently, Bald Head didn't either, which was not normal protocol, indicating that Bald Head may have been falling out of favor.

It was rainy, not very bad, but it was raining. I had just made I AM aware before we left Woo's house of what needed to be done, and he was just over the top, kind of high-strung and just going super-fast for some odd reason. When it rained in Atlanta, for some reason, it seemed the roads would get extremely slick. I kept advising I AM to slow down because he kept sliding while rushing when there was no need to rush because I would take the heat. But what I didn't understand was why he was rushing because I didn't tell him that there was a need to rush, and for some reason, I could not get through to him to settle him down, which was very unusual.

I had instructions from across the border that they did not want me around any drug transactions, any drugs, and any large sums of money. So I had to be dropped off at my house, and I will coordinate from my house, speaking directly to the bosses over in Mexico if the transaction had been made successfully. This was a very tense time throughout the whole transaction until things were safely in my hands. This is when you didn't need to have anything go wrong because you were the most vulnerable at this point.

Bald Head continuously called me because he was nervous because his ass wasn't where he was supposed to be. Then knowing how he freaks out dammit all the time, I knew what to pay attention to and what not to pay attention to with his antics. As I got out of the car, I told I AM again to slow down; you're going to end up making a mistake. In normal fashion, he would tell me that I'm paranoid, and I'm overthinking things as always.

I AM was leaving me to go over near the airport in Atlanta, and he was having the drivers and his whole crew that would transport the drugs as he oversaw the process while being in direct contact with me. I AM would speak to me if there were any issues or concerns, and I would speak directly to the bosses across through Bald Head, translating. If Bald Head was getting on my nerves, I could call directly to the Chief via Junior.

Things are starting to get really strange after I AM had took off heading toward the drop spot. The calls coming into me were becoming more and more frantic from Bald Head. I guess I can't overstate this enough this was highly unusual behavior. When Bald Head continuously calls me on the two-way I do not contact I AM because I know he cannot handle the pressure I just continue to spin Bald Head and tell him something but never letting the pressure make it over to I AM. But there was starting to be a very serious problem, the Chief was starting to call me now directly while sounding stressed. So when I got the call directly from the Chief via Junior I knew something had to be going on that was definitely not normal. I started to hit I AM on the two-way radio back to back but I was not getting a response from him. Not to mention I'm still receiving calls on the two-way radio from Bald Head and Junior at this point, as I continue to stall because I'm not hearing nothing back from I AM.

I AM: Damn bro I just had a BAD ASS accident!! I slid off the road down a steep embankment and hit a tree!!! I don't know how I'm still alive that tree damn near cut this damn car in two Bro!!

I have a severe problem now! The load is sitting there waiting with a little under a ton of cocaine in it and sicarios watching over the vehicle and timing is of an essence in a situation like this thing must go smoothly always or people start to freak out this is when mistakes happen people get trigger happy or nosy people start to notice suspicious things and call it in. The Chief is calling me like crazy now and his tone is not good it has gotten super aggressive now.

Me: Please Chief.... Just give me a minute this guy (I AM) is just barely calling me right now.

I knew that something was seriously wrong because at this point Bald Head stopped calling me altogether. This let me know that he was nervous and afraid because this appeared as if it was going really bad and fast.

I AM: I'm okay! I'm running along the shoulder on the freeway right now. I have to get to the next exit that's where I have my guys meeting me at. I can jump in with them. To get over to the drop spot.

Me: Bro this ain't good.... Are you sure you are, okay??!

I AM: Yeah! Bald Head just kept calling and calling me on the two-way tho!

Me: Just relax and keep your head in the game Bro. Let's get this thing wrapped up. We can figure the rest out later.

I'm kind of fucked up at this point based off what he just told me. He told me that Bald Head just kept calling him and calling him....... This was a very big problem because Bald Head was not supposed to have his number. Bald Head did not tell me that he had his number, he kept that a secret from me but why. This was not good at all, this was very bad very very bad.

Bald Head: Go ahead My, Friend.

Me: The Chief doesn't sound happy. I have to call him back barely right now....... Bald Head:.

Me: I AM just had a very bad car accident, just now! Bald Head:

Me: He is not any good under pressure but there was no pressure from me on him. I'm confused! I don't know what to tell the Chief about this right here, My Friend.

Bald Head knew what I was saying directly. This was a threat coming from me to him knowing by me saying that I knew what he had did and I was pretty pissed that he did it without informing me. My amazing concern was, was he just trying to jump (Cut me out and go to Sam because of his knowledge of my system), which wasn't a real concern of mine at that moment. I knew how I AM was starting to act with me as if he was entitled to more, as I stated above. This could be extremely dangerous, an indication of a plot on my life in circumstances like this. All kinds of thoughts were going through my mind. Even with those thoughts, it still wasn't my biggest concern; my biggest concern was a concern that I had in Mexico City: was Bald Head friend or foe? One thing was glaringly obvious: he was spying again, but for whom this time? I was hoping I was wrong, and all these things were just coincidence, but in my line of work, there's no such thing as mere coincidence.

Bald Head: "My Friend, I AM giving me his number so I was calling him earlier today. I knew that he ran off the road and almost killed himself."

Me: "That wasn't good, My Friend. He just gave it to you??"

Bald Head: "No....... I asked him for It, My Friend........"

Me: "Don't Worry Chief.... These guys are having some issues but I'm going to go fix this thing myself."

Junior: "You are going yourself My Friend??"

Me: "Yes! I'm barely leaving my house right now My Friend."

Junior: "The Chief is happy now. He says he knows that everything will be fine now."

Me: "Go Ahead"

Bald Head: "My Friend, My wife just called me and told me that four guys just showed up to my house asking for me. She sent them to the guest house in the back. I have to go there right now to see what they want, My Friend."

Me: "Just be careful, My Friend...... Are you going to be, okay??......."

Bald Head: "These guys were sent from over there My Friend. So, they had to sneak across the border to my place. The thing is no one told me they were coming to my place, My friend. This never happens without me knowing. But, I don't know......Let me just get here and see. I should call you back in no longer than 20 or 25 minutes. Just let me see, My friend."

Me: "Okay, I gotcha!"

Bald Head: "My Friend....... You are my friend, right My Friend??......"

Me: "Bald Head.........."

Bald Head: "Aaaaah, Yeah My Friend??"

Me: "My Friend you're okay...... Thank GOD MY FRIEND!!"

Bald Head: "My Friend....... The Chief sent them over here to me with no money. To tell me to get them over to Atlanta."

Me: "What they need over here My friend. You need me to make arrangements for them??"

Bald Head: "Well, yeah...... I may need you to send I AM to pick them up once I make these arrangements."

Me: "My Friend....... You are my friend, right My Friend??......"

Bald Head: "These guys are sneak over here to kill Sam, My Friend.........."

Me: "Are you fucking serious, My Friend?"

Bald Head: "Listen, My Friend! You need to call the Chief right now and do something. Talk to him, beg him because I have to get these guys over there RIGHT NOW TO YOU for, Sam! I had to tell them to be ready when I come back from getting my other house keys, but my wife was in the house walking around naked. They were going to follow me so I couldn't talk to you or something I don't know. I don't have a choice, I have to get them over there and right now, My Friend. You better convince the Chief or...........Yeah, I will need you to send I AM. You won't have a choice.........My Friend you won't."

I was shocked when Bald Head started to tell me this. I kind of thought he may have been joking at first because he kept pausing with like a slight little laughter in his voice. Until I finally figured out he was dead serious but the laughter was more of disbelief and maybe even shock. I didn't know how to feel about this. I was definitely in shock, but I had to work quickly and he made sure that I understood that.

I jumped right on a two-way and I called the Chief, and Junior answered.

Me: "CHIEF POR FAVOR, POR FAVOR!!! NO NECESITO PARA ESTA POR SAM, CHIEF POR FAVOR!!!"

That was the best I was able to come up with on such a short notice but under circumstances I had never attempted to speak that much Spanish to him before. I was just hoping that would help in my need to make sure I reached his heart and to give my guy a pass. After some time of begging, the Chief relented and made me aware that he knew Sam had given his number to Bald Head. He also made it clear that Bald Head had already expressed that I may not want to ever bring I AM back across again because that pass was just for that instance and don't bother next time.

This was just more stuff that I had in my head that I could not share with him. Me telling him often times that he wasn't ready; wasn't really because he didn't have a skill set. Not being able to work under pressure could change with added pressure overtime in his case. My pleading with him was in hopes that he would never do what he actually did would give his number to Bald Head. Not knowing that the closer he would have been thinking he was getting to his own situation, it would have been just that, a situation that he was certain to not make it back from.

Everything I was saying to him just kept falling on deaf ears for some reason or another because this situation was no different than Mexico City when I made Bald Head admit he was spying for the Chief with his line of questioning. He even advised I AM with always be cautious when someone over here is asking a question because no matter how friendly they sound, it's always for a reason.

This was not a very good time for me. I was experiencing some callous times mentally. It seems that the game was changing, and the stakes were raised. At a level, I didn't know I was prepared for at that time. For me, the risk of my own life was something I chose to do, but when others' lives were at stake for maybe naive things that they had done while not having a good handle on the level of the game we were playing. Nothing could have prepared us for what we were experiencing right now.

The challenging part for me was keeping all of this to myself; I could not share it with I AM. I got with Keith The following day, which helped relieve some of the stress, but subconsciously it was still there. He was sharing with me plans for Usher Video shoot out in California. He also invited me to come out. I felt it would be an excellent opportunity to build a better relationship with Mena.

I contacted my assistant and spared no expense with the arrangements made for this trip. I spoke with Mena, and I invited her down. She seemed excited to be a part of the whole process and see the videos to be shot. Keith told me they would be shooting "Moving Mountains" and "Love in the Club".

After a rather eventful meeting with Keith, my spirits were lifted. Woo had arranged for us to get together and go to a songwriting event. On our way to the venue, he made me aware that Usher was aware that I would be coming along and wasn't happy about it. I was confused, but I didn't really make a big stink about it at that time.

Woo wouldn't tell me much about the event we were going to, but when we arrived I was shocked. This place was filled with the who's of who in Atlanta. They were some of the best songwriters in the industry. This event was called by the management of Menudo, which had a TV series that they were trying to select who would be the new members of Menudo through a reality TV show. I believe the individual that came out was over the actual event said that they still had two final selections to go as far as the TV series was concerned. But we got the treat of being able to see who the last members were as they came out.

To perform for all of the songwriters that were in the venue as they were requesting them to start writing material for this Latin group. I can't recall what made me pull Woo out in the hall for a moment. Maybe something about a load that was about to come in or something of that nature. I just recalled starting to talk more about the issue of me not being welcome to the video shoot based on me being the street guy.

This is something I would typically not give a fuck about. Still, I was so stressed that I started expressing myself about not being happy about what I was doing, and I physically started to get emotional and cry. The pressure was taking a toll on me and I was being placed in a position that I wasn't used to because I'm not an over-emotional individual.

After that event I hooked back up with Keith. Keith told me about a party that Puffy was throwing in town at the club called Lucky's. I believe he told me it was Puffy's birthday party, and he was insisting that Usher come. I had made a date with Desi that particular night. Desi and I had been going out for a little while, and we were really enjoying each other. She arrived at my place, and Keith, Pretty Boi Fresh, Tez, and myself, and a few others headed to Lucky's. Once we arrived, we saw that Usher was already there, and they escorted us to the upper VIP area where Puffy and his entourage were. It was really packed up there in the VIP area. A lot of celebrities were also coming through to wish Puffy a happy birthday. They had several girls around on different stands, just dancing all throughout the room.

I was standing there holding Desi and just enjoying myself out of nowhere. Tez comes up to me. For a second, I thought he was looking directly at me, but it's almost as if he was looking through me.

Tez: Whatever you do, don't turn around.

Me: Man, what the fuck is wrong with you and what are you looking at?

Tez: Don't turn your ass around because Montana is behind you and she's staring right at your ass.

Me: Oh shit, are you serious, man? I was supposed to go on a date with her tonight and I didn't answer the fucking phone. I stood her up like three or four times back-to-back, and I promise I wouldn't do it again.

Tez: Well, you better figure it out 'cause here she comes, and she don't look happy.

Me: Yo, man, I need you to look out, man. Go up to her. Then run interference.

Well, that didn't work out for me too good because Tez turned around and tucked tail and got the hell out of town. Now I look out of my peripherals and Montana is standing right there, and she's not looking happy at all. I kept looking straight though.

Montana: Nigga, you see me standing here!!

Me: Hey Montana. Really nice outfit.

Montana: I'm naked.

Me: No, I just meant it was nice seeing you.

Montana: Don't play with me. I'm not one of these Atlanta Bitches. I am a Miami, Bitch. I will beat your ass, Nigga!

Me: Why are you acting like this?

Montana: I see you wanna play with me tonight. I told you I am a Miami Bitch. I will beat your ass. You are not going to keep playing with me. I know you saw my phone call.

As I moved away from Desi, I pulled Montana along with me. I noted that she was not looking at me the majority of the time she was talking, and she was becoming more and more agitated as she looked at Desi.

Me: Why are you acting like this? I'm trying to run a few plays, and you're fucking it up for me. Take this money right here and I'll give you a call tomorrow, and we'll talk more.

To this day, I don't know what I gave Montana, but it made her extremely happy, and she got her ass back onstage and started dancing again. Desi never mentioned it. We just continued to move forward with what we were doing. Thankfully for me, Usher had already gone over to see Puffy, and Puffy was starting to move toward the door at that point. We exited the VIP area and headed right out of the building. Now we're en route to Jermaine Dupri Club, the Velvet Rope.

We arrived at Jermaine Dupree club, and our bodyguards took us directly into the club. While entering the club, Pretty Boi Fresh had an opportunity to ask me a number of questions about my new lady friend.

Pretty Boi Fresh: Yo big Homie, who is your new friend?

Me: Her name is Desi.

Pretty Boi Fresh: I've never seen her before. What does she do?

Me: She's a model my guy.

Pretty Boi Fresh: Big Homie in New York, Los Angeles, and Atlanta; you have to be careful. All females are models according to them.

Pretty Boi Fresh was educating me with the way things go in these different cities. He knew that I didn't know the description of the word "MODEL" encapsulates an ambiguous meaning on I don't know how many levels.

I had a number of bodyguards. They led the way directly to the VIP area up on the second level, overlooking the club. There was a ramp going up toward the upper part where the VIP area was located. All of the patrons inside of the club could go anywhere inside of the club except for the VIP areas, which included one overlooking the club and one off to the side. Patrons could also stand along the ramp leading to the VIP area on the upper level overlooking the club.

Along this path, I noticed a young lady staring at me. As we walked past her, she even reached out and grabbed my hand. Desi observed this, but she didn't say anything as we walked along. I noticed Tez stopped and started speaking with a young lady right in her area.

We reached the top level and started enjoying ourselves with a number of other celebrities who were also in attendance.

As I was enjoying myself, I had that feeling like someone was just staring at me. So, I turned to the right and looked back toward the area where the VIP entrance was and saw the young lady standing there who grabbed my hand as we were coming up towards the entrance entering the VIP Area. I ended up locking eyes with her, and she waved at me seductively. Desi followed my eyes and saw the young lady waving as if she did not miss anything.

Jermaine Dupri made an announcement that he was going to be bringing together the Jackson five or something of that nature, and the crowd in the club went crazy once he stated that because this was during the time he was dating Janet Jackson, I believe. Right after this announcement, Jermaine Dupri, Usher, Nelly, Keith, myself, and our entourage headed downstairs to the VIP area off to the side.

Within this VIP area, there was a whole full bar that would cater to that VIP area that we were in along with a number of booths that were up on the stage.

As we were headed to that area, the young lady grabbed my hand again with Desi looking right at her, but this time she was much more aggressive with trying to talk to me, and I slightly pulled away. After getting a distance away, I noticed that it was her, but I also noticed that Tez was talking to a girlfriend of hers.

Jermaine Dupri had opened up his exclusive VIP area for us to enjoy. We filled the booths on the stage while the bodyguard stood along the stairs leading up to the stage. The crowd from the club was allowed to enter, but the bodyguards prevented them from coming up to the stage towards our booth. Usher was smoking a cigar, leaning against the wall while Nelly and Jermaine Dupri sat in the booth next to us. Keith, and our entourage sat in the two booths on the left.

I was in the booth closest to the wall on the left, and Desi was standing up in the booth with her back against the wall, and I leaned back against her. The bottles were flowing, and we were really enjoying ourselves that night.

Tez pulled my pants leg and directed my eyes towards the young lady who had been trying to communicate with me persistently that night. She was standing in front of two of our bodyguards, trying to get through, but they would not let her. I leaned down to Tez and whispered into his ear aggressively.

Me: "OK, you mother fucker, you sold me out on the last run. I need you to run interference. Don't let that bitch through. I saw you talking to her friend too. Don't let the bodyguards let her through. I'm not trying to fuck this up with Desi."

I started to relax and enjoy myself, knowing that I was in safe hands. But maybe 30 minutes after I gave Tez his instructions, I got another tug on my pants leg, and when I looked down, Tez was gone, and the young lady I was trying to avoid was in the spot where he was standing. My eyes panned over the crowd, and I saw the backside of Tez and the young lady grabbing my friend's arm as they headed out toward the open area in the club.

Me: "That dirty motherfucker!!"

The young lady stepped up on the booth seat, standing directly in front of me, and started slow dancing and grinding on me, looking me directly in my face. Now, don't forget, Desi was leaning up against the wall, standing with her back against the wall, and my back was laying on Desi as she was against the wall, and the young lady was leaning forward toward me, dancing on me and talking to me. She introduced herself.

Dream: "My name is Dream, as in, I would like to be your dream."

Me: ....

Dream: "I've been looking at your sexy ass all night, and that energy of a boss is just leaking out of your pores. Your swag is just so sexy, and I fuck with that hard."

Me: ....

At this point, I was shaking like a Las Vegas crap table. I didn't know what to think. I had never been in a situation like this before, and I was freaking out. Desi whispered in my right ear, as if she were coaching me.

Desi: Baby, this is Atlanta, and this is how women are. Go ahead.

This was a new experience and I think I may have been literally shaking because I wasn't looking at Desi, but she noticed that I guess I wasn't speaking. And she coached me through the process. Ain't that some sick shit?! Dream at this point looks around me. And extends her hand out to Desi and says.

Dream: Hi my name is Dream.. Nice to meet you.

Me:........

Dream: Sorry baby, but I had to introduce myself. I noticed that The THING kept looking at me.

She states this as she looks directly back into my eyes and starts to whine on me dancing while continuously talking to me. I pulled out my phone and I exchanged numbers with her, and I gave her some money to buy her some drinks or whatever she wanted for tonight. And told her to just give me a call later on that night. I guess that satisfied her and she exited the VIP area and I noticed Tez was peeking around the corner right at the edge of the VIP area, entering the open area of the club.

The club was getting ready to close. We were starting to exit out of the club with the bodyguards. When I noticed Desi seemed extremely uncomfortable for some reason or another. She asked me for my car keys and stated that she wanted to go sit in the car. I asked her what was wrong, and I was extremely confused by this. I told one of the bodyguards to go with her and I gave her the keys to go and sit in the car, but I was rather confused by why. Pretty Boi Fresh came up to me. And asked me where was Desi? I told him that she was extremely upset and wanted to go sit out in the car. I also expressed to him that I didn't understand why she wanted to do that. He then began to tell me why.

He asked me. "What did she do for a living?" He told me that Nelly's manager had approached her and got pretty aggressive with her because she was supposed to meet with him that night.

For some reason or another. He saw that I was still confused, but I didn't really think nothing much of it because that's sort of what managers do then? I mean, that's to be expected I guess, if she had a photo shoot or something. Then he made me aware of the reputation this manager had with a lot of the beautiful girls down in Atlanta. My guys came to me and were concerned about what was transpiring and wanted to pull up on Nelly manager.

One of my guys also made me aware that Nelly was supposed to have made some kind of suggestion that maybe we were dope boys or something. I wasn't totally sure because I didn't hear him say it, and I didn't want to cause a big issue because my guys were really drunk.

We started to exit the club because I could sense that things were about to really get crazy. So, I got my guys out of there.

Now we are standing in the parking lot over to a certain area closer to our vehicles, and Desi was sitting in the front passenger seat of my car. I guess there was some truth to what they were saying because Keith came over to me and looked at me and stated, "Big Homie where your Bitch at?!!"

Before I could respond to what he was saying, Keith took off running across the parking lot toward Nelly's car in which he and his manager were in. Keith stopped their car, snatched the passenger side door open where Nelly was sitting in the front passenger seat, and basically dove in the car screaming and yelling and cussing Nelly out, saying, "Where my Big Homie bitch at Nelly? What the fuck did you do with my Big Homie bitch?"

Nelly replied, "Man, Keith, what is wrong with you? She ain't in here, man. I told you, she ain't in here. She is in his car!"

Keith pulled back out of the vehicle and slammed the door of the Bentley that they were in as Nelly seemed to really enjoy laughing hysterically. Keith came back over to me and started to fill me in on what he knew about what happened with the whole Desi thing and that she was being managed by Nelly manager - pretty much what Pretty Boi Fresh had made me aware of. Keith told me that there were a lot of celebrities flying in town, and that may have been what Nelly's manager was really upset with Desi about.

Everybody decided to leave from there and head over to Usher's little brother's house, to continue the party as we would normally do. I got in the car, and I asked Desi about what happened, and she was kind of nonchalant, but she explained some things to me with her head down. She expressed to me that she wasn't really paying her manager any attention and that she was still going to stay with me for the night, but I could see that she was really torn. I wouldn't hate and I encouraged her that it was OK for her to go if she had some other things she needed to take care of; because who was I to judge anyone considering my lifestyle. She jumped at the opportunity and had her mother come to my place to retrieve her.

This just made me think back to when she would constantly say to me things like, "Do you wish that you could just start over again and move to another state?" I never really understood why she would constantly state that to me and almost suggest that I should move with her to another state just to start all over again. I do think we were starting to develop a connection. She was starting to bring her mother around me a whole lot, and we all would go out to eat, go bowling together, and do several activities. I didn't think too much about it. I just knew at some point we would talk about it more later or so I thought.

I didn't have much time to focus on all the things that went on the night before based on arrangements that were already made to fly out to California. I was waiting to hear from Mena based on the itinerary that was set about a week prior. I was supposed to pick her up at the airport, and the following day we would fly out with Keith and the rest of the entourage to California. The first video that was scheduled to be shot was called "Moving Mountains," which had already been scheduled along with "Love in the Club." Keith was really excited about "Love in the Club," seeing that he had written the chorus to the song. I was really starting to get concerned because I had spoken to Mena the day before and she assured me she would be on the flight. I even made additional arrangements for her to get to the airport without an issue. I was trying to avoid any mix up or disappointment, in which I had a history of receiving from her when it came to these types of arrangements. Being consistent to her nature for whatever reason, I was stood up once again.

This particular time I was really upset, pretty much livid about it, and I made sure that she knew that. This was extremely embarrassing because I told everyone that stood still long enough that she would be attending and made additional arrangements for her, as I had done a number of times before. This exit set off a heated exchange between me and her, and she decided to tell me that she didn't like my lifestyle, which I pretty much knew, and she was always clear about voicing that to me. But I didn't understand why she had accepted the arrangements that I had made. She went on to express that she was afraid of falling deeply in love with me based on my lifestyle, and I could be taken away at a moment's notice. She went on to give examples of jail and also being hurt in the street and may be murdered. And where would that leave her emotionally and mentally? She also expressed to me that she was very wary of my reputation and habit of becoming bored with women quickly, according to her.

I tried to assure her that that was not the case with her and that I felt very deeply for her, in which she told me that she believed me, and she knew that to be true. Her rebuttal was, "What about in five or six years, Wayne?" She basically just came out and said that the only way that she would start interacting with me on a level that I wanted her from that point forward was if I showed a commitment and married her. I promptly emotionally jumped at the opportunity, expressing to her that I would marry her so fast as if it were three weeks ago. After a number of additional questions to make sure that I was serious and not joking, which I confirmed that I was very serious, hearing the smile in her voice, she stated, "Well, Wayne, we are going to see."

I was really happy about that conversation, even though it ended with her not coming with me to California. And I also refused to go without her.

Without any notice, she called me a couple of days later and put her mother on the phone. Her mother expressed to me that she had heard that I wanted to marry her daughter. I expressed to her mother that is exactly what I wanted to do and hopefully she would give her blessing.

After her mother asked me a number of questions and I guess I answered the questions appropriately. Not to mention that her mother was already a very big fan of mine and we had developed a pretty good relationship. She handed Mena the phone back and stated.

Mena's mom.: Girl, I already told you he is a winner. Marry him.

Mena told me that she would call me back after she converse with her mother some more. I guess Mena's mother just flew into town and she wanted to share the news with her mother after she asked me a number of questions. I didn't want to rush the process and plus I was on cloud nine, so I was patient.

There was never a dull moment for me, and time just passed extremely fast for me on most all occasions. It was a good thing that I did not go to California because a load came just a couple of days after that conversation with Mena. I was not prepared, neither were my guys because we weren't expecting it. But I can't say that this is the first time that that ever happened.

Just in the fashion as I described before, we move through that load extremely fast, but what made this different is that the loads continue to come rapidly. I received a call from Bald Head and he was in the presence of the Chief when he called me.

He expressed to me that I was doing a very good job and the Chief was pleased with me, but also stated that the Chief wanted me to move faster. I was a little confused because we were moving extremely fast, at a faster pace than I had ever moved before, and I didn't understand the urgency.

I gave a little pushback, which was a little unorthodox for me, because that's not what you do in that type of situation with the boss sitting right there listening. I was already pushing my guys to damned.

And in order to move faster, I was pushing them to take less money for the volume of drugs that they were pushing. I was even almost to the point where I was cutting all the profit I would make out to move faster. It was clear to me that the Chief was leveling up, and I knew that he would make it up to me later.

But I was at a breaking point, and I didn't think I could push the guys any harder with getting less money without causing a revolt. The conversation over the two-way radio was a pretty much back and forth conversation, but after the last statement I made, the phones went silent.

The Chief.: You shut up! You shut your mouth right now!!

I was really shocked when the Chief told me to shut up and to shut my mouth right then. I didn't know how to respond, but I knew not to say anything else. Bald Head immediately started to translate for the Chief and told me that the Chief wanted me to shut up too and described what he was doing. The Chief put a napkin over his mouth and made a gesture from his neck like a noose was around his neck, hanging himself. He was trying to convey that he had spoken too fast and that by saying what he said, he was virtually hanging himself. It was clear that something was very different with him.

The Chief knew that I was important to him because I was the one who could help him make a lot of money. The rise he was making was because of my ability to do what I did with the white. I later learned that the cartels must pay the government quarterly, especially to be in control of plazas. The pressure to move faster was because payments needed to be made to the government, and oftentimes the money that I turned in was to meet those payments.

After the Chief made sure that there were no hard feelings on my part, he told Bald Head to make me aware that he needed me to be making it his way and crossing the border soon because he needed to see me in person. I agreed to come across at some point soon to see the Chief.

I called Danny to tell him what happened with the Chief, and he told me that the Chief was a different man now and was doing a lot of killing. He also told me that the Juarez Cartel was losing very badly at that point and that he was in fear for his life. Danny couldn't help but poke at me, saying that I shouldn't complain about the pressure of them asking for more speed from me since he shielded me from those things before.

My friend, this is just like you complain and want to go from Little League baseball to Major League Baseball. Then you start to complain about how hard they throw the ball.

You are in the major leagues now, my friend and this is what you wanted. I'm sorry for you. You must deal with it now, you moved me out the way. I can do nothing to help you. My friend. I knew that Danny was telling me the truth. And there was nothing that he could do. His hands were filled with trying to stay alive at this point. The baseball analogy was fitting, and it did make me laugh because he was absolutely right.

After the last load was completed, the Chief allowed me some time for R&R to get out and relax a little bit. Good news came in that the

Outsyders had secured the first single on Britney Spears new album with the song “Womanizer “ There was a whole lot of inside horse trading to get that song released since Woo, Keith, and I owned fifty percent of Outsyders Publishing for that record. There was a lot of back and forth discussion because the label was afraid that we may try to sue them if they released the record”.

No one wanted to sign the Outsyders in our BE-LY Publishing company we developed. I covered all expenses with the development of the company and funding for signing all talent. I even dropped my attorney from the developing of the company which turned around to cost me in a major way. BE-LY was screwed out of the publishing on the Britney Spears "Womanizer" record.

My understanding is that during the contract negotiations between Britney Spears' label and the Outsyders, James Mason incorporated The Outsyders name to bypass BE-LY Publishing. However, I was informed that James Mason offered millions of dollars in compensation when trying to negotiate with BE-LY Publishing. James Mason, along with others from the record company (whose involvement I am unsure of), were involved in this. All I knew at the time from the information I was given was that Woo killed the deal after discovering that James Mason intended to speak to me about the deal and his offer. James Mason was informed by Woo that he had the KEY MAN CLAUSE, and no one could override his decision.

He even produced the necessary paperwork to support his claim. Before this incident, I had a productive conversation with James Mason. The Outsyders had several other songs in the works for artists such as Usher, Rihanna, Chris Brown, and Ciara. My mistake was combining loyalty with business, as James Mason and Woo did not get along. Woo had informed me that I was entitled to the KEY MAN CLAUSE as the sole financial means of operation, according to our understanding.

However, if I truly had the KEY MAN CLAUSE, how could the beginning of many multi-million dollar deals, starting with the Womanizer record, be killed? I spoke to James Mason, and it didn't appear that he was trying to avoid paying or cutting our company out of the publishing we were entitled to. He did want to receive some credit, which I believed was due to him. The process was stalled for months, but when the time came for the release of the record Mr. Mason made the necessary move to release it.I would come to understand The Outsyders never officially claimed their name James Mason had the paperwork drawn up to claim the Outsyders name.

James Mason coerced one of the Outsyders to sign over the production, basically giving full control to a third member. The Outsyders was left with the understanding that James Mason would redirect all publishing monies due to Be-Ly publishing in effort to forgo their contract with Be-Ly publishing. As stated above even with the adjustments Brittney Spears record label was still apprehensive about moving forward with the record because they still felt they could be sued by Be-Ly Publishing. To ensure no repercussions they needed one of the Outsyders to sign an affidavit admitting that neither one of them participated in any production of the record.

My goal was to provide an opportunity for The Outsyders production team of Erving and Dean, two young men who I saw as talented and wanted to bless the world with their sound. Ervine and Dean they are not innocent which they would openly admit: As they would also readily admit it cost them the most ultimately in their efforts to ensure that Be-Ly received the publishing credit that they were under contract to give the monies back to Be-Ly publishing; since I was the sole financial investor in supporting signed talent and their publishing; It hurts my soul that egos and greed killed what could have been one of the greatest production team. My feelings were hurt even though I'm a street guy. My heart was in the right place. I was trying to help these young guys. I still love them to this very day. Being a street guy, we are used to taking losses and I guess this right here would be one of many examples.

I was screwed over so badly that I don't even have a Platinum Record for Womanizer to hang on my wall. But back to the story, during our usual Sunday ritual after bowling at 300 bowling alley, Pretty Boi Fresh pointed out that my old friend Desi was in the place, sitting to the side in silence. I hadn't heard from her in a while, and it was odd that she avoided me, seemingly ashamed of something.

Later, Pretty Boi informed me that Desi had started dating Idris Elba and moved to Florida. I won't speculate on how she met him, but I'm pretty sure it had something to do with our last night together at the club. Pretty Boi showed me a social media page that indicated she had been kicked out of Idris Elba's Florida home after he discovered that a baby she conceived was not his, as he had thought. This period was an emotional roller coaster for me, and little did I know that it was just the beginning and the roller coaster had no brakes.

CHAPTER 27

DETROIT 2

THE CHIEF MOVED CLOSER to the Juarez, El Paso border. This was so I would not have to travel into the inner parts of Mexico, and he just needed a quick meeting with me, and I had crossed at this point. I had been picked up by two sicarios and was enroute to meet with the Chief, but I had to go through several military style checkpoints. As we got closer to the residential area, there was no more talking on the two-way radio. The radio was just a series of clicks on the two-way radio, and I guess there was some type of Morse code or something. When I entered the residence, I entered toward the back of the residence, moving toward the front living room area. Once I reached the living room area, there was a kitchen style den attached to the living room area, and there were several gentlemen inside that area, and I noticed Black Shirt was also present. Black Shirt and I locked eyes, but he quickly averted his eyes in a different direction. I also noted that by all the windows there were men standing with automatic weapons and fatigues on. I was directed to a couch, where I sat on the right side of the couch. There was a love seat to the left of the couch, and the Chief was sitting directly on the side of that in a dining room chair.

The Chief started to speak with me, but his tone was extremely aggressive. Once the Chief started to speak, the man in the dining room stopped talking, and they were focused on exactly what the Chief was saying and my responses. The Chief's tone was extremely aggressive, much more than I had ever heard before, and almost stunningly so, I might add. He was barking orders about the speed he needed me to pick up and move things quicker, and that there would be no excuses, and basically like it was hell to tell the captain if I didn't and some heads would really roll, literally. I was becoming extremely uncomfortable, and I wasn't sure if this was something that I wanted to participate in any longer. It was really scary for me; of course, there was nothing I could say. I had to agree to everything that was being stated, and within the statements that he made, he told me that I would be receiving 500 keys within two weeks up in Detroit. He gave me just a number of days to be done with everything and money on the semi returning back.

I was pissed off to the highest of pistivity, but I could not show this or any mannerisms that reflected that. One thing was going through my mind. I was thinking that this guy must be out of his fucking mind, thinking that he's going to cross anything into America because George W Bush had already signed an executive order restricting all trucks coming into the United States from Mexico. But of course, I couldn't say anything. This was similar to when you were a child, and your parents are saying things to you, and you're saying all types of crazy things in return, but in your head. I guess I could be considered a tough guy at that time, but in my head.

Before I knew it, the two-way radio started to sound off like crazy. Seemed like everybody's two-way radio was going off at the same time. And then the guys in the dining room that we were sitting started to scramble and head for the door. Black Shirt was with these gentlemen that headed out of the door at a very rapid speed. The whole dining room area with these gentlemen were sitting cleared out along with some of the security. After these guys exited the house, the Chief yelled something toward the back of the house. Someone yelled back to him, and a few other people yelled, and I don't know what the hell they were saying because it was all in Spanish.

The Chief jumped up very fast from his seat and dragged his chair around the nightstand table to sit directly in front of me. He leaned forward and spoke rapidly to me, with one hand on each knee, in a totally different tone. He said he was suspicious of the guys sitting in the other room, didn't trust them, and that they were watching him. He apologized for his tone, but said it was necessary at the moment. However, his confidence and aggression were gone, and he seemed nervous and uncertain, which made me feel uneasy. The Chief and I spoke in our own language.

He told me that it was imperative that I move quickly with what he was sending me because he had a number of payoffs to do for his security team as well as some for the government. I didn't fully understand what he meant, but I knew from the way he spoke that it was a life-or-death type situation. Seeing Black Shirt there confirmed my suspicions, as Black Shirt had never worked in the Chief's interest from the day I met him. I recalled from when I was in Sinaloa that Bald Head seemed to purposely stay out of sight or move away, so Black Shirt could slide in for some uncertain reason.

The Chief virtually begged me to be done within a matter of days, emphasizing that it was totally imperative. He also made me aware that he was going to start a new cartel once these things got settled. He would do the same for me that he had cut a deal over in Colombia with Mayo Zambada and El Chapo. Speaking with them, he said that cocaine would be done first, which belonged to him, then any additional owed over to the cartels in Colombia would be done secondly. He also mentioned that the United States government had signed a treaty called the Meridia treaty with Mexico, and that we needed to stop using two-way radios and start using regular phone lines, as it was safer. However, even using regular cell phone lines, we could not talk for over 2 minutes because the phone calls would automatically be intercepted.

As he was filling me in on all these things at warp speed, the yelling inside the house started again. He yelled back a couple of things and then told me that we were in the meeting and he had to take off. As I stood up after the Chief, he offered me some pussy, telling me he had a very nice young lady upstairs that I could go enjoy myself with, but to make it brief before I left. I thanked him for his generosity but respectfully declined.

As we moved towards the back of the house, the gentleman who was sitting in the dining room watching every move and word followed us. These gentlemen pushed their way almost in front of the Chief to start extending their hands, which I shook. I noticed Black Shirt was the last to shake my hand but tried to hold it a little longer, indicating something. When I shook his hand, it was very wet from sweat, indicating he was super nervous for some reason. When I stated that I remembered him, he shook his head no, as if he did not know me, and almost snatched his hand out of my hand.

Now I fully understood what the Chief was trying to tell me and what those vultures were there doing, and I already knew what Black Shirt was up to or had a suspicion, but it was totally confirmed now. The Chief came up to me last and he extended his hand. So, to add some theater to everything that was going on and to show them fucks that anything that they had planned, they should reconsider.

I turned the Chief's hand over as I shook it, and I kissed his hand. The whole room erupted in cheers and whistles and loud screaming in excitement for what I had just done by showing my submission and loyalty to the Chief by kissing his hand. I had never seen the Chief smile so big and warm and confident at me, almost with his smile thanking me for what I had just done.

After leaving, there was a lot replaying in my mind and a lot that was said. I had an opportunity to kind of get a grasp of what was going on in the climate and how things were really changing over on that side of the border. A major part of the reasoning for the Chief needing to move fast, as expressed to me, was for his security and payments to the government. But all that was attached to the new position that he had received. He had become the head of logistics for the Sinaloa Cartel, and to him, becoming the head, he told me that I would have control of the Atlanta hub and control of Detroit.

What this basically meant was that in Atlanta, we controlled the southern region for the Sinaloa cartel, meaning all drugs came into Sinaloa and would disperse out to the states around, and all drugs from that cartel would have to come to me first, and I would distribute them. The same would be true for Detroit.

Cross back, but I was held up on the border for a very long time. I had to spend the night in El Paso because I missed my flight. There's so much going through my mind and at warp speed. I was rushed down for this meeting with Chief as he was working his way back up toward the border. I was told about this meeting while Bald Head was with the Chief. Even though Bald Head delivered the message, he was not allowed to be at the meeting, and I found that extremely strange. I flew down to El Paso by myself, and I was picked up by sicarios and taken across through the number of checkpoints that I had to go through in order to meet with the Chief. The interesting thing is, after all the weeks that we went through and the preparations made for me to meet with him. I was only there in his presence for maybe one-half an hour. And it abruptly ended. But the actual true meaning was made maybe only 15 minutes, 10 to 15 minutes after he pulled the chair around and was able to speak to me without the group.

Once I was checked into my hotel, ended up speaking to Mo Green for a moment and he made me aware of a number of things after I told him that we were supposed to be receiving 500 keys of cocaine up in Detroit within two weeks. I told him that I thought the Chief was out of his mind because there had been an executive order signed by George W Bush restricting all incoming imports from trucks from Mexico. Mo Green paused and then he made an interesting statement to me.

Mo Green: Homie, I don't know if you know this, but George W Bush and the President of Mexico, as well as the President of Canada did a joint interview over in Canada earlier today.

I didn't really understand what they had to do with the price of tea in China at the time. Nor did he elaborate much. But he was thinking that it could be possible. I thought him and the Chief were nuts, but I didn't elaborate much, again as I stated above. I had too many other things to think about.

I just could not get it out of my mind that this is the actual first meeting that I had with the Chief or over there at all, in any capacity. That Bald Head was not with me. He was always the translator for me and translator in between the Chief and myself. This particular time, the Chief had another translator there that I did not know that spoke extremely good English. And if you recall from earlier, I also made you guys aware that Black Shirt spoke extremely good English without an actual accent. And he was in the group that Chief was mostly concerned about. There was clearly something afoot and I believe that the Chief was starting to get more and more suspicious about or concerning Bald Head and I knew for myself from some suspicious things that happened in Sinaloa that something wasn't right.

Not to my surprise, Bald Head was calling me quite a bit. It took me some time to answer because I needed to compartmentalize everything that had happened to me and replay things back to prepare myself for conversation with him. I eventually ended up speaking with Bald Head, but it was clear that there were certain things that the Chief did not want me to share with Bald Head, so I kept those things confidential while trying to beat the grass and see what I could get out of Bald Head which he was always good at, giving me information just to ensure that his head wasn't on the chopping block again. After some small greetings, I asked Bald Head why was Black Shirt appearing so nervous and hands all sweaty once I saw him over at the meeting.

Bald Head: My friend. This guy was very nervous because The Chief just killed his brother maybe one or two weeks ago. My friend.

Bald Head went on to warn me of a number of things and to point out that the Chief was acting extremely strange, and things were really changing with the Chief right now. But at the same time, Bald Head was sounding just as nervous. As I expected, Bald Head will start to talk and release all sorts of information, but nothing could have prepared me for what he was about to tell me.

Bald Head: Let me tell you something, my friend. You must not tell Chief or no one that I told you this, my friend. The Chief used to be police for Juarez. Really, my friend? He still is policia. Because he never quit.

Once he told me that I was really starting to freak the fuck out. I did not know what to think. I was totally lost. I was fucking scared. I could not help myself but to think why the fuck is he giving me all of this information? All these little hints here and there, even about himself.

Well just as the Chief had stated within two weeks I had five hundred keys of cocaine in my possession in Detroit. As soon as the President entered back into the country, he did another executive order reversing his position on the borders in Mexico and the trucks flowing in I received the cocaine just as the Chief stated. I also ended up receiving another load down into Atlanta, which went just as fast or actually faster than what it did up in Detroit.

Bald Head called me with a message from the Chief. He was extremely happy with me because of the speed up in Detroit, doubled with the speed down in Atlanta, and I'm sure it helped him with his little issue that he told me about over in Mexico during our meeting. Chief also told him to show me this certain YouTube video that spoke about what was going on over there in Mexico and he told Ball Head to tell me and what Chief was very excited about, that they were starting to win the war now. Bald Head also couldn't wait for the opportunity to tell me a number of other things. He kept reiterating that the Chief was changing. He had made me aware that the authorities over in Juarez had told the Chief that a bar over there was holding a number of guys that were of interest to the Chief.

Bald Head: My friend, the Chief, just went to this bar. He called everyone out of the bar and had them line up. My friend, he shot, and he killed all of those guys that were lined up. All of them. My friend.

There was no doubt in my mind that he knew what Bald Head was up to. I was starting to see so many things just clearly now. This made me recall. When I was raided over on Novara St. and the Chief called him over across the border and asked him a lot of questions and held him over there for a number of days, just asking him question after question and looking really hard into his eyes after he asked him. The Chief had made so many attempts after that to switch me away from Bald Head and to someone else, but Bald Head would always come to me crying and begging me to help him get back into the Chief's good grace by making the Chief aware that I never liked the new guy and I wanted Bald Head back. It was becoming more and more clear to me that something just wasn't right with Bald Head and the Chief wanted to put me somewhere safe and away from Bald Head. But to be honest,

I was somewhat afraid to be away from Bald Head. And I guess I will get more into that reasoning later on.

I reached out to Danny because I was confused and needed some advice because I was freaking the fuck out and I didn't know how to handle what was going on, but I was in much too deep to try to get ideas. On bailing? Danny pretty much confirmed everything that Bald Head had told me but adding.a ffew of things, since he was on the other end of the war with the Carrillo brothers Juárez cartel. From Danny's perspective, being on the end with the Carrillo brothers They were telling him that the Sinaloa Cartel was being protected by the Government of Mexico and there were also whispers that the Sinaloa cartel also was given information to the US government.

Danny: Listen my friend. You need to watch this Bald Head guy. Remember, we never like Him. Don't trust this guy. They may be using this guy you know for to give information over here. My friend don't trust this guy. He's no good. don't forget we no like him, we never like him.

I knew that Danny wasn't lying to me, but this was getting deeper and deeper and I just. I just didn't know what to do. There was nothing I could do. I really had suspicions as I did some time back that Bald Head was an informant. Although the signs were there, and things were just. not adding up when he tells me stories. But everything that Danny was telling me. Pretty much fed into my suspicion. There were even times it was almost like Bald Head was telling me that he was. There were a couple of weeks that went by and there was no work after work being rapidly and consistently for a nice while.

Bald Head: My friend everyone is switching sides now. And running off with work. they're doing this just to steal because they know if they switch sides. to another cartel they will just have to give the cartel some of what they switch over with and keep the rest and that other cartel will give them protection. But listen friend my friend, I must tell you something. Chapo had one ton of cocaine at this meeting, and he was trying to see like who want to take it to move it and no one would take it. Everyone was afraid my friend. I'm just telling you, but the Chief stood up and he said that he would take them, he would take them all after silence and no one has said anything at the meeting. The Chief said that Primo will handle this for us.

This was also a strange time because Arturo of the Beltran Leyva brothers was starting to get suspicious, and I was hearing things. As if he was, he believed a number of shipments that were coming into Mexico for his group had been caught and Chapo was the reasoning for it. Things were rapidly changing and it didn't take long for me to get confirmation. That Arturo had left the federation because his brother was captured by the US government and he directly blamed Chapo for It.

I received the ton of cocaine in normal fashion, and my responsibility as the leader or the controller of that hub was to hand off to another guy or two. I was really starting to get more and more upset because they kept raising the price and I didn't understand why. It just wasn't normal, but this time it was really an issue because the quality of the cocaine was fucking horrible. This shit was really bad. It was so, so bad, but I had to find a way to get rid of it and it really took me much longer than what it would normally do. After some time of shucking and jiving, cutting all kinds of deals to do guys favors in the future just to take this stuff and not bring it back and try to work with it. I promised everything under the damn sun, but fortunately, I was able to finally get rid of it all and turn in the money for it. There was a big sigh of relief that came over me after this headache was gone. I was so, so happy, but I had a gut feeling that someone would be calling me, asking me for help because

I was hearing that the other people were not getting rid of any of it and were refusing to sell it.

My hunch was correct. It didn't take long before the two-way radio went off, and it was Junior asking me if I would be willing to help them out. I told him, emphasizing, "No, Hell No!!" I really liked Junior a lot, and I knew it wasn't him that was asking me, but I was really upset because I had really been fucked on this one. I made no money. I had been making no money because of this war. They were asking so much of me that I could not make money and cutting all types of deals, mortgaging off the future profits that would have been making just to get this shit sold, and then they're gonna shove a bunch of horrible drugs on me. There were a number of calls made to me, and I just stayed to my point of no. I did not want to deal with that headache again.

After about an hour and a half, two hours went by, I got that call that I knew was coming. It was the Chief. He asked me the same question that Junior had been asking me, but since it was him, of course, you know, I could not say no. I had to reluctantly say yes. The response I got through translation from the Chief totally blew my mind.

Junior.: My friend, the Chief, is telling me to tell you that those guys are coming up on your exit right now on their way to your place. They should be there in like maybe 4 minutes or something.

I was just flabbergasted at the actual thought of what just happened to me. The drugs were already on their way as I was saying no and refusing to take it. So, when I did finally say. Yes, it was actually coming up on the exit, so I really had no choice at all.

I didn't know what I was going to do. This stuff was really stressing me out. And they were making sure that I knew that they needed this money. I put in a call to my guy, Slick up in Baltimore and made him aware that I was really up against the wall, and I needed a favor. Big time. My idea was to send the work up to Baltimore because the stamp on the bricks still had a very good reputation and he was telling me that there was no work up here. So, I knew it would sell pretty fast and I was desperate, so I had to take this option.

I put the work on the road to Baltimore, which it would arrive that next morning early. Well, I was awakened the next morning, bright and early with someone speaking over the radio in Spanish to me, which didn't sound like a familiar voice, but it had a very threatening tone. And I would find out shortly thereafter who exactly the culprit was and the message to me and what they were saying.

Chapo: Get me my fucking money!!

There were so many twists and turns to this shit that was going on. I couldn't keep up with it, but I was totally bewildered with the fact that I had just received some drugs doing a favor and I was getting demand for the cash. In a matter of hours after I received it. This continued periodically throughout the whole day. I could not believe that this man was calling my phone personally, Demanding for his money. I had a really good idea what this was about. And it kind of lined up with a story I had just heard a couple of days before when all this infighting was going on amongst the federation members.

Chapo was having major problems with getting rid of that metric ton, and he tried to dump it off on the Chief, but Chapo had charged an exuberant amount of money and the Chief would not accept it, and. He told him that.......

The Chief: This price is too high for Primo. If you want to use Primo, you must bring the price down.

This would explain why the Chief stood up at that one meeting and said that he would do all the metric ton with me. Chapo must have capitulated on the price at that point. Which was a big favor to me because I would have surely not come back with the right money with the work being that bad.

A couple of days went by, and I could feel the pressure building up more and more. I felt like calling the Chief and complaining, but I knew it wouldn't do any good, and I could already predict what his response would be.

The Chief: Primo, don't worry. I'm doing something for you. You just don't see it right now."

The phone calls I received were becoming more aggressive and constant. Even Bald Head, who sounded nervous, was calling me now. I was getting really angry because I felt like I was being screwed over. Out of frustration, I snapped at Bald Head and told him to just tell them that I sent it up to Baltimore and was waiting for it.

Bald Head: No, no, my friend, I'm not going to tell them that. Because you did not have authorization to send anything over there, my friend. You don't understand they are not sending anything to that place to make the price go very high. And you messed that up my friend. For my friend, I'm not going to tell them that, and I suggest that you don't tell them that either, my friend. All I can tell you, my friend, is that nothing better not happen with his money or nothing, my friend. Because this is not going to be good for you. And please, my friend, don't even tell anyone that you told me this.

I have to admit that this conversation did not make me feel any better, nor did it make me feel safer. I had thought I was being innovative and making something happen out of nowhere, but now my life was in danger. I realized that I had unknowingly interfered with a marketing scheme to manipulate prices in another region of the country. It was like a crash course in real economics. But one thing was clear to me - Bald Head was extremely nervous and wanted nothing to do with what

I had done. He made it clear that any mistakes on the highway would make me a dead man.

Bald Head: My friend, do you remember that Mexican Russian guy? You know, the one that was with Arturo? They just killed him. They barely killed him, stripped him naked, and left him in front of the hotel where we had a big meeting. His body was really messed up and they threw him in the parking lot naked and dead my friend alone.

Bald Head added this information after scolding me for my mistake, which did not make me feel any better about the situation. I noticed that Chapo had stopped calling me, and now Bald Head was calling me, but he sounded extremely nervous. He tried to hide his nervousness, but he wasn't very good at it.

The following day, there was a knock at my door early in the morning. This was very unusual because there was no way to get into my area. I had state and federal senators in the same building, and armed guards patrolled the hallways. I opened the door and was surprised to see Bald Head. I asked him how he managed to get in, and then I noticed two Mexican gentlemen following closely behind him. Bald Head started talking to me as if he had no one with him, joking and laughing, while the two men spoke Spanish to him and he replied back. However, he didn't feel the need to introduce me to them.

I was on edge as I waited for Bald Head and his two companions to arrive. El Chapo had been calling me non-stop, threatening and yelling that he wanted his money. This time, I could hear him yelling over the radio, and soon after my phone stopped ringing, Bald Head's phone started. He was extremely nervous, asking me when I could possibly have the money. I assured him it would be arriving from Baltimore at any minute.

Bald Head gave me specific instructions on how to arrange the money. All large bills, no smaller than fifties, all facing one direction, and new bills. We also needed to get a small travel-sized suitcase, and the total amount of money that had to be added up to in the small suitcase was $500,000. This wasn't my first time doing something like this in Atlanta, but it was the first time I would be keeping a portion of the money. I would take $500,000 separately and have my guy separate the bills as instructed.

Finally, I got the call from I AM, letting me know everything had been arranged. I came out of my room to inform Bald Head, only to find two Mexican men lounging on my couch, shoes off, and snacking on my food. I couldn't help but think that this was cartel life. As I was talking to Bald Head, their phones started to chirp, and they got extremely serious. I noticed that they were trying not to look at me, and their total demeanor changed. At that point, I understood who they were and what they were there for.

Bald Head spoke to them in Spanish very fast, telling them we had to go and get the $500,000. We went downstairs to the parking garage and got into my S550. The two men got into the back seat, and Bald Head got in the passenger seat. We drove to rendezvous with I AM, who handed me the small suitcase with the money. Bald Head instructed me to put it into my trunk, which I did.

As we started driving, Chapo continued to call and yell that he wanted his money. The men in the backseat didn't say anything at all, and I couldn't see them when I tried to look in the rearview mirror. Suddenly, there was a loud, excruciating scream over the phone that sounded like Chief's voice. Bald Head's face went blank, and he looked totally lost. I nervously asked him who it was, but he didn't answer.

I was driving the car with Bald Head in the passenger seat, and he sounded extremely scared and nervous as he spoke. "That was the Chief, my friend," he said. "And he said it's not me, it's not me." The tone of his voice was melancholy, and he conveyed the message that the yelling and screaming were coming from El Chapo and not from the Chief.

As we arrived at a luxury hotel, Bald Head instructed me to back into a parking space. The guys in the back seat beeped the radio a few times, and then they got out to take a suitcase from the trunk. I didn't know who they gave it to, but a well-dressed gentleman in a suit appeared and took it from them.

After a few minutes of silence, Bald Head's phone rang, and it was the Chief's voice on the other end. "The Chief just told me to tell you that you are a very good man. A very, very good man," Bald Head said.

I didn't react to the compliment; instead, I kept my eyes straight ahead on the road. As we drove back to my place, the silence in the car was total until Bald Head's phone rang again. This time, the Chief's voice sounded calm and composed.

When we got to my parking garage, I saw blacked-out Yukon trucks in front of the gates. Bald Head and his two friends got out of the car, and he told me that he would be in contact. I didn't pull into the parking garage; instead, I watched as Bald Head and the others walked out of the area. At that point, I understood the deeper meaning of the Chief's message: "It ain't me. It ain't me!!!"

After that experience, I packed up and headed back to Detroit. It had been a while since I had returned home because the cartel needed me in place in case a load came through. But after what I had just heard, it was OK for me to come back. According to Bald Head:

Bald Head: My friend, things are really bad. I want to tell you something, but don't tell anyone that I told you this. My friend, there will be no work, no more work for a long time. Because the war is getting very bad.

I headed back to Detroit, but nothing could prepare me for what I was about to experience and learn about what I was involved in. This was turning out to be a very taxing war. As Bald Head had told me, there was no work and there was no sign of any work coming through as well.

Bald Head also advised me that I needed to slow down on spending money and start to save, but I did not listen. I continued to spend like crazy. I didn't quite understand exactly what he meant and what I was hearing about the different people that I knew being killed. I had no real grasp on what a war was in terms of actual war of that magnitude. I could only relate it to some local hood-type war that would, of course, not last nearly as long as what this war was doing. This war was lasting years, as Bald Head had told me that it would.

I started receiving a number of calls from people that did not have my two-way radio number but that I knew. Four to five months had passed with no signs of any type of work or even conversation about it. Bald Head stayed in contact with me through it all, but I received a phone call via two-way radio that I was not expecting, and it was from Reyes.

Reyes started the conversation with me trying to create a better rapport with me than what we initially had. He also told me that he could provide me with work and he also made me aware of the climate. What's going on? More so in Mexico and was saying that he basically had his own little area over in the Tijuana, Mexico area. He told me that he would be willing to work with me on very good prices on both marijuana as well as cocaine. But more importantly, he gave me information that he felt was to his benefit but confirmed what I already suspected.

Reyes: My friend. You do know that our friend. That guy, he's an informant. I know that this is your friend, my friend, but he's no good. He's been informing for a long time for the US government. I'm just telling you because you need to be careful, my friend. Also, my friend this guy was adding two thousand onto each one of those things that you received from the Chief.

The Chief was willing to give you those things for maybe 15,000 or 14,000, but this guy, he just greedy. He put so much money. On to you, my friend. The trucking company that was used was my trucking company. My friend, the only reason I'm telling you this is because it would be no problem.

For me to do something nice for you, my friend, something really nice. I'm not going to lie, my friend. I did receive some of the money, but I did not want to take that much from you because I understand that you are a good guy. And you did. You did very good business.

This is nothing new for me, I've been through so much at this point. I'm used to guys adding money on top of what I'm paying, so I had been broken into that already and I was not surprised. And the thing about Bald Head being an informant I already knew this. I had no proof of it, but now I had something to substantiate what I was suspicious of. I guess what I stated before that I would explain why I did not continue to communicate with him, and I kept him in play with everything I was involved in and why would I be or break the rule? With dealing with someone that I pretty much knew was an informant.

My biggest fear was experiencing everything that I experienced when crossing over into Mexico. There were a number of times I was not sure if I would return, and most people with common sense, which I did not have, would just not have gone. My biggest concern was if something happened to me, or I was killed or fed to pigs or whatever could have happened, that someone would be able to report to the US government exactly what happened to me and where my body was, just so my family would have closure.

Which I know most people reading this would just simply say, "if you were concerned about that, don't put yourself in that position where you could lose your life." For me, being born and raised in Black Bottom, Detroit on the eastside of Detroit, and experiencing poverty my whole life, I would rather have risked my life and ended up being killed than to continue to live in poverty and not have anything. I had seen so many generations of poverty that I just wanted to have nothing to do with it anymore, and I didn't know or have any answers that I could visually see where anyone turned out better.

Of course, you always hear the same line of education changes things and all this other stuff, but I've seen people with education, college degrees, and the whole nine, and they still suffered and were without. This was in the beginning of the hip hop era where you were starting to see beautiful women, nice cars, mansions, and all of that. We would later on find out as we got older that none of these things belong to these younger rappers in the beginning of the rap era. But I wanted to experience that type of life; I didn't mind dying in pursuit of it. Again, it defies all logic to most reading this, I'm sure, but just thank God you didn't have to experience it and have to make that choice.

Reyes had developed a case of word vomit and in most of his conversations was mostly trying to secure a relationship with me. But he also made me aware that my number was in great demand over there. That he had to pay a lot of money to get access to it. He also let me know that El Chapo thought very highly of me. Which I could care less about because my loyalty was to the Chief and I had made a promise to him that I did not plan to break. Even though I was understanding again, as I stated throughout the whole book, that loyalty is a liability. Beware of any leader that preaches the doctrine of loyalty: The word loyalty is only introduced to Subjects, for the sole purpose of bringing down the price of labor.

I spoke to Bald Head shortly after this conversation with Reyes. I made Bald Head aware that Reyes had made contact with me and was offering to work with me. Knowing Bald Head, I know it wouldn't take much for him to catch word vomit as well.

Bald Head: "My friend, I can't believe this guy actually called you. He barely just called you right now, huh? Listen, my friend, you be careful with this guy. The Chief is going to kill him. He double crossed the Chief really bad. He's over in the area over by Mexicali right now. The Chief has control of that area after he wiped out the Tijuana Cartel. My friend, and this guy he fucked the Chief.

One thing I knew for certain is that Reyes was not the only one attempting to fuck the Chief. One thing that was clear to me is that I was the goose that laid the golden egg to so many across the border. Reyes also confirmed this for me, but Reyes also made me aware of who was behind his phone call and that he would be attempting to be what Bald Head and Rojo was for me and trying to level up and get the leverage. By bringing me back to who initially wanted a relationship with me directly: Old man Mayo and El Chapo.

But of course, Bald Head would not be outdone by Reyes.

Bald Head: "My friend, listen to me. Don't worry yourself for this guy. He will be dead soon. Listen my friend, I know he will be dead very soon. This guy. We were very good friends, but he saw my wife one day last week and he acted like he didn't even see her. Then she went up onto his face and made him speak to her. And then she said he said some crazy things to my wife, telling my wife that, listen, do you know your husband is an informant for the US government? My friend. He did not even ask about my kids or how she was doing or nothing. My friend. But enough about that guy. I have something better for you, My friend. My friend. Do you remember the guy in the Black Shirt?

Well, he wanted me to tell you something. He wanted me to tell you that you know he heard that you've been waiting for work, and he doesn't understand why. And he does not like that he wants to give you some work right away. He will have work to you next week if you want, my friend. It is no problem for him. He told me to tell you that he will even come over there to where you are right now, my friend, and come and talk to you. Make a very good deal with you, my friend. I think you should think about it, because I'm not even going to lie, my friend. Things are bad for me too, and I could really use the work. But I mean, I'm not going to tell you what to do, you know, because I don't want you to get mad at me. But I mean, you should really think about it, my friend. "He's a good guy".

I was really starting to become overwhelmed once again cause it's like everything that I suspected or that crossed my mind about the fuckery that was going on was absolutely true and being confirmed now. This was Bald Head's plan from the very beginning. He was looking to fuck the Chief. But he wanted to have plausible deniability in the whole bullshit. I told Bald Head that I did not mind speaking with Black Shirt.

But I would not accept any work from Black Shirt unless it was coming from the Chief. I clearly knew that any offer Black Shirt was coming with. For me was not from the Chief and most likely indirectly from the federation absent of the Chief's knowledge.

Keep in mind I had been through this process so many times and I could give less than a fuck about loyalty, because I know. These gentlemen did not deal in loyalty, they dealt in business. I was leveraging my position, knowing that it would make it back to the Chief at some point that I had heard nothing from in many, many months.

My strategy was to also set Bald Head up because with him getting this meeting he would have more pressure applied on him from the federation, which in turn would make him deliver to me more information.

I did like Chief a lot because Chief was a darker skinned Mexican, not like the much lighter or white Mexicans that Is often seen in America or stateside. Which is not a reflection of the majority of the population of Mexico, which are brown or darker skinned people. Bald Head made me aware that he would be meeting up with Black Shirt and he would be crossing Black Shirt the following week and bringing him up to me on the eastside of Detroit.

The day had come that I was supposed to be speaking with Black Shirt stateside, but from El Paso, Texas shortly after Bald Head had crossed with him. Now this was very peculiar to me and I even asked Bald Head how is he going to cross? And he's a Mexican citizen. Bald Head just kept brushing me off and basically telling me don't worry about it, he has it all covered.

This was one of those weird kind of answers that, you know, you get from a person that don't wanna disclose certain information, but they are disclosing more than what they realize. Just like when he was telling me about his wife seen Reyes and him not speaking to his wife. Reyes told his wife that he was a U.S. Federal informant.

After expressing that to me, Bald Head went on to express how insulted and hurt he was that he did not ask about his children and how his wife was doing. As if the fucker just didn't tell me that the man told his wife to her face that Bald Head was a U.S. Federal Informant. But as the saying goes from my neck of the Woods: Game recognizes game, and this was starting to look familiar.

I placed a call to Bald Head to ask what was going on or why. I had heard nothing from him or spoke with Black Shirt. Bald Head pretty much answered right away and had a nonchalant tone.

Me: My friend, are you OK? Where's Black Shirt?

Bald Head: He got caught crossing the border.

Me: I thought you were crossing this guy. Where were you, my friend? Were you in the car too with him?

Bald Head: .... Silence........

This fucking guy never answered my question. I could tell that he hit the button on the two-way radio because the line opened and then it closed right back without him saying nothing. After that, he went on talking to me just about every day, not even bringing up Black Shirt again.

I knew what he had done, and I'm sure that he knew that I knew what he had done. He also knew that Reyes told me what he told his wife as well, and he never denied it.

I'm spending a lot of time watching the news now. CNN is reporting on the Cartel war across the border in Mexico. They're showing a lot of pictures of the different cartel bosses. I never knew any of these guys' names, but it seemed like every picture that they were fucking showing, it seemed like I knew every fucking body, and that was really starting to make me nervous.

I often told myself what you usually hear from older people of my generation or before, they say everybody has a twin. Convincing myself to believe that all those people and those pictures just look like somebody I've known before, I've met somewhere before I told myself this despite the fact of the major issues that were being reported over there.

I either had Bald Head or Danny's calling me, asking me was I aware of this or that? And I literally had just seen it on CNN, or I would know it before CNN reported it. As if things weren't strange enough my attorney Lorence called me.

Attorney Lorence: Donnie, did you watch the local news last night? The D.E.A agent that was killed in the car accident? That was the agent in charge of your case, Donnie...........

I was literally starting to feel like a character in a major motion picture, with a fourth or fifth dimensional ability to view myself while in it and thinking, this shit that's happening can't be normal or some type of coincidence!!

CHAPTER 28

EVEN THE DOGS, WILL DANCE

By late 2008, the Tijuana Cartel had been defeated by Chief "El Mayito." Shortly thereafter, Danny called me and informed me that the Chief had been promoted to the Head of logistics for the Sinaloa Cartel, with new responsibilities of crossing all products from South America to the lower parts of Mexico. A few days later, Bald Head contacted me with almost identical information, but with more details.

Bald Head said, "My friend, have you been watching CNN? They just killed Arturo. Did you see this on CNN, my friend?"

I replied, "He looks familiar, my friend, but I don't think I know this guy."

Bald Head said, "No, my friend, no. You do know this guy! You remember the Russian Mexican guy, the guy you always would say looks like a Russian? You remember this guy? He was the driver for Arturo. Arturo was at the same table with this guy. I know you remember him because he was the gym rat, always working out. You remember he talked to you, my friend? Yes, my friend. Yes, my friend. This is the guy that I'm talking about. Yeah, the Mexican Navy, they killed this guy after a really big shootout. Also, my friend, I'm calling to tell you that I will be there with you in maybe a week or so, I don't know the exact date my friend, but it will be soon. My friend, you know things are really bad over here. You should really think about getting a job or something. My friend."

I replied, "My friend, I wish you would stop bothering me and throwing this job thing in my face. I don't want a fucking job, my friend. It does not pay enough for me."

Bald Head: Also, the Chief now controls the Tijuana cartel's territory. He pushed them out, my friend, and he finally found that Reyes guy. The Chief searched high and low for him and finally caught him along with two other guys. The Chief killed all three of them, my friend. He left their bodies on this long road leading from Arizona to Mexicali, my friend. But the Chief really hated Reyes. Very badly, my friend, he cut everyone's head off, but he cut Reyes' body into pieces and left his head on top of the pile of parts.

What the hell is going on down there? Is what I thought to myself. He cut the damn man's body into pieces and placed his head on top of the parts so they could identify which heads belonged to what bodies. Information was starting to pick up and I was starting to receive a lot more calls over my two-way radio. Danny called me again a few days after I had the conversation with Bald Head.

Danny: My friend, I have something to tell you. My friend, uuuuhhh someone just came by my house looking for you.

Danny went on to tell me that someone had stopped by his home looking for me. Which I found that to be very interesting, seeing that I was in the northern United States, literally 5 minutes from Canada but someone stopped by his house looking for me? Danny lives in Juarez, Mexico! I knew that there was only one person that knew that I was talking to Danny. That one person also knew that I was extremely loyal to my friends and that I would continue to talk to Danny even though he told me he would kill me if I did, and that was the Chief. But I could not be totally sure that it wasn't El Chapo either because I knew that Bald Head was playing both ends of the stick. He would also give this information to El Chapo.

Danny told me that some guys were looking for me because they wanted to send something up to Detroit. I wasn't sure if it was the Chief, but I suspected it was him. Danny didn't give me many details, but I understood why he was being vague. What was interesting was that Bald Head didn't know anything about this contact being made through Danny. I reassured Danny that I was ready for whatever these guys wanted to send up to me. He said they would be coming to see me in a few days.

The transaction with these guys was different from any other cartel I had worked with before. They made me jump through a number of hoops, and I had to travel far to pick up the work. When I dispatched some guys to make the pick-up, they kept changing the drop location to make sure it wasn't a setup or that my guys weren't being followed. It was very strange and didn't make any sense to me at the time. But I'll explain it later.

Finally, after a few location switches, my guys received the work. It was only ten kilos of cocaine, which was a small amount, but it was the test load, so I wasn't too surprised or insulted. I didn't know the exact price per kilo at the time, but due to the war and severe drought in the market, prices were extremely high. Despite this, the profit margin was still good because of the high street prices. The loads started to come in every week, increasing slowly in amount, and all of my crew began to eat again. Trust between us also began to build.

I had been back in Detroit for almost a year at this point, and I was slowly starting to work again. Big Dawg was on my heels as well. He was constantly coming to see me speaking about the possibility of getting more marijuana, glorifying the old days. That should have prepared me for what was to come, but my mind was scattered and on so many things, dealing with the cartel and dealing with the new options that I was starting to receive via Danny.

Big Dawg: Man, you would never guess who I just talked to. I just got off the phone with Frank and Mario. They just called me out of nowhere. Can you believe that?

Of course, I didn't believe that. He was up to something the whole time, but I wouldn't let him know that I knew. I acted just as excited as he wanted or expected me to be. Big Dawg began to tell me that he was in discussion with those two assholes about possibly receiving some more marijuana from them. He knew how I personally felt about dealing with these two crooks, but I knew he was in a bad position and that he really needed some help as well, plus the additional money wouldn't hurt.

By that point, I had created an oversized and outrageous spending habit, and the money that I did have stashed was steadily decreasing, and I showed no sign of slowing down in my spending. But I knew it had been a while since Big Dawg had something from them. And I'm pretty sure it was because he owed them a nice amount of money, as he was known to do, of course. Out of all that time since I had been down in Atlanta, I don't think he had been working too much, if any at all. And I'm sure he knew that once he told them that I was back in town that they would immediately become interested. And I was pretty sure that's what he did.

As I continued to let Big Dawg talk, he slowly let out what I was expecting him to say, that Frank and Mario knew that I was back in town and they wanted to speak to me too, according to him, to see how I was doing. Which led to a number of phone conversations with Frank until it got to the point of me talking to Mario, and that's when you start to make dates and start working on prices and all that other good stuff.

Frank just wanted to know that I was really in town and that my brother Big Dawg was not lying to him. The next thing that he wanted to ensure was that I still have the ability to, as he would say, work fast.

I put his mind at ease and assured him that I still had the ability to work fast, that It wouldn't really be an issue for me at all. I was mostly sweet-talking his ear to make my brother Big Dawg happy.

It wouldn't be as fast as what it normally was some years back, but it still would be at lightning speed compared to how fast my brother moved his shipments. The conversation started off between Big Dawg and Mario, and Big Dawg started to make me aware of other things that Mario was telling him. That I knew were a bunch of lies as far as the price that he was trying to charge. So, I'm thinking to myself the whole time that these guys have not changed in their style, trying to gouge people, but Mario was not prepared for me, because he didn't know who I had evolved into. I knew the prices of all that shit from the price from over across the border and the price once it crosses over stateside.

During this time, I was having a number of conversations with Danny because the cocaine shipment were still coming to me. And I guess the anonymous gentleman that had come to Danny's house looking for me had felt more comfortable and was ready to start to increase the volume even more. Danny told me to preparing myself because they were going to start sending me 50 kilos at a time and the frequency was going to increase.

I turned the money in from the last shipment that I had and I was waiting for this new shipment to come in that would have the 50 kilos of cocaine., Before it arrived, Danny was to make me aware of exactly how the shipment will come and arrangements I would need to make in order to make the transaction effortlessly between the individuals bringing it. And my team receiving it.

Mario struck a nerve with me because I challenged him about the amount that he was charging. And then my brother had already told me the same thing that Mario kept saying. Listen, the prices of everything just went up and you need to check CNN. Check CNN.

This was just striking a nerve with me because I knew he didn't know shit about what was going on and he was being the worst actor in the world while trying to act like he was directly connected into what was going on and he was the big boss, and that he was experiencing the same thing with the war that was going on across the border.

Mario: Listen, you and Big Dawg don't understand. All I can tell you guys is just to watch CNN. There is a war going on that is very bad and my people are experiencing very high prices. So all I can tell you, I don't know what to tell you. Guys, you just have to watch CNN. There's nothing I can do for you.

Me: I wish you were in front of me right now with your lying ass. You don't know shit about what's going on across the border, nor does these loads of marijuana that you have anything to do with it, you fucking liar. I wish you were in front of me right now. I will smack your fucking face.

Mario: No, no, you are just saying this because we are on the phone right now. That is the only reason that you're saying this, because if I were there with you, you would not be saying none of this. All I'm going to say is you need to watch CNN. You really don't know nothing. You really don't know what's going on over here across the border. You really don't know.

Me: No, you listen, you fucking Bandito. I'm going to tell you how I know you don't know shit. Because for a kilo of marijuana over on that side of the border, it is only two hundred to $250. And as you move down toward the middle of Mexico, the price goes down even lower. You fucking asshole. And you keep telling me to watch CNN. I don't need to fucking watch CNN. Because I was there, Bandito. I drove through the devil's spine. I was there in Culiacan. I even took time to go to the zoo In Durango.

I knew that I didn't need to say anything else, just saying the things and the places that I had been. And also speaking of the Devil's Spine, cause no one knew that that was the name of the road in between Mazatlán and Culiacan Sinaloa. And this way he would know that me threatening to smack him was not just an empty threat because he knew what cartel was in that area and controlled that area and it had the effect that I expected it to have.

Mario: Oh, my friend, my friend. I don't wanna talk to you no more. I don't wanna talk to you no more.

You could hear the fear in this lying Bandito's voice. He instantly got off of the phone and turned it off out of fear. Big Dawg was sitting there as I was taking Mario out behind the woodshed, giving him what he rightfully deserved. My brother just had the sad droopy eyes. I began to talk to him and asked him what was wrong, and he shared with me as he was stating in his normal fashion, "I can't miss nothing I never had." Basically saying that he hadn't received the load yet so he can't miss it because he didn't have it. But I knew he just didn't want to tell me that he was really upset at me, but he didn't understand what I was doing. I told him to calm down. I started laughing at him and telling him, "Listen, he's going to call back, but he's gonna call around and do some checking," I said. "But what I just did for you, you don't recognize, but what I said to him is gonna really help things out. Watch and see."

After a couple of days, I had to get with a few of my guys and we had to go to a hotel. If I'm not mistaken, this hotel had to be in Dearborn, MI, not that far outside of Detroit. I was told that there would be a number of Indian Trail Buses that would be coming to this hotel. These buses would be filled with Mexican nationals coming across, but up to Michigan to gamble at the casinos. One of the bus drivers would have a suitcase, and in that suitcase, he would have 50 kilos of cocaine for me. The instructions were that I needed to rent a room in the hotel and give Danny the hotel room number, and one of the drivers would come to the hotel room and give the suitcase with the kilos of cocaine inside. But I put a twist on that because I didn't trust them just as much as they didn't trust me, so I booked the room and gave him the hotel room number. And I left the key at the front desk. This way, no one was in the hotel room and did not have to worry about too much funny business. So the exchange went fine, and this was how every exchange would happen for the coming weeks. And a number of times, it would increase twice a week.

I have to go speak with my guy Jay out at Eastland Mall because he wanted me to come into business with him at his jewelry store. Jay was a very good friend of mine, pretty much grew to being like my brother. But I expressed to Jay that I wanted him to take me over to India with him, what he always wanted to do anyway. But I made him aware that I needed to go over there, and I needed him to arrange for me to get a wife. I had been speaking with him about this for a very long time, but the arrangements were set and now it was time for me to accompany him to India. So, I was going up to the mall to follow up with him about that since he had already put in to purchase the tickets as well as the Visas to enter the country.

He made me aware that he made arrangements with three different families that we will be visiting that will close villages to the village where he was raised. He told me that I would have to be prepared to come in and basically sit on the floor and eat dinner with all the men. After dinner, the woman of the house will bring all of the young ladies into the room where all of the men in the village would be eating. And on command by the elder, the elder lady would tell the young ladies to drop their veil. And I will look at them and I would choose the one I wanted. He also made me aware that if I didn't find anyone attractive or that I really liked it, I didn't have to pick anyone at all, and we would just go to the next village out of the ones that he had arranged.

If I did find one attractive that I wanted to marry, then the young ladies would be told to put their veils back up and they will be instructed to leave the room as well as with the older lady that was instructing them. Then at that time, they would introduce me to her father, and then I will start to negotiating with her father for dowry, for the diary, for her hand. So I was really excited about this and I just couldn't wait to hear back about the visas being secured and exactly what date we will be ready to go.

After Jay informed me of the customs over there and what we would have to go through once we got in there, he told me that something strange had happened. He told me that his brother that had invited me was called to the embassy over there and they asked his brother a whole lot of questions about me.

Asking him if this was normal, I could tell by his expression that it wasn't. He confirmed that it was abnormal, which was a red flag, but I remained optimistic. Dealing with Danny, there were several setbacks, but things were going smoothly overall. Unfortunately, someone attempted to sabotage one of the loads, which slowed down my progress. Despite this setback, I was still making decent progress. However, when the truck came to collect the payment for that load, I wasn't completely prepared.

I had been dealing with Danny for a while now, but things were not going as smoothly as they had in the past. The quality of the cocaine was not up to our normal standards, and I was really angry about it. I was yelling, screaming, and cursing at Danny because of this. I wanted to make sure he knew how angry I was and that I expected him to fix the problem.

Danny was trying to calm me down and was telling me that he would check with the guys to see what was going on. He tried to reassure me that everything would be okay, but I wasn't having it. I continued to rant and rave, not really listening to anything Danny had to say. Finally, Danny had to raise his voice to get me to listen.

He told me to slow down and just listen carefully. He had spoken to the guy who had supplied the cocaine and he wanted me to know that he trusted me. Danny said that I could take as much time as I needed to fix the problem and just pay the guy whatever was fair. He even said that I didn't have to tell him right away. Danny kept repeating that the guy trusted me and that I didn't need to worry.

I realized that this situation was a perfect example of the hermetic type codes, where you have to decode and decipher the symbolism. The fact that someone trusted me enough to tell me to slow down, take my time, and pay whatever I felt was fair was significant. It meant that they knew who I was and had an extensive history with me. I knew immediately that it was the Chief.

The first load of marijuana was shipped by Mario and Frank, and after some adjustments were made, it was of good quality. But I knew it wouldn't last long with them. Soon enough, the fuckery began. They sent us about 1.5 tons of marijuana with 300 pounds of shake or loose marijuana that wasn't of the same quality as the rest. It looked like they had swept the dust from the marijuana and wrapped it up in the bale. When we opened the bale, it fell apart. I wasn't surprised, but I wasn't expecting it so soon. I knew that I had to make them pay.

I informed Big Dawg that we would be returning approximately 600 pounds of marijuana to them because it was not of the same quality as the rest.

After that one screw up on the quality, which I made right, and I paid what I felt that I owed off of the last balance, things were running pretty smoothly as far as the cocaine was concerned. I was starting to receive two loads a week, but in increments of 50 kilos. At times it will squeeze a little more in here or there, but the drivers on the Indian Trail buses did not feel comfortable with bringing over fifty kilos at a time. I rounded out at about maybe 500 or a little more kilos per month.

Danny also put me in contact with another group that was speaking back and forth with me as well as Danny. I got really pissed off with this, with this group of guys that I had never spoke with before, but I had an idea who they represented when they asked me for I AM phone number. This was a big no no and I didn't understand how they would have the balls to even ask for something like this. I made them aware that they did not need anyone number outside of me because no one had the authorization to make decisions other than me. They tried to give me some excuse, like it was just normal. I don't understand why they thought I would go for that, but I just thought that that was extremely weird. Extremely weird. They knew that I wasn't a rookie and normally when these attempts were we would be made, they would try to go around about and get the information that they wanted and not come directly to the actual person in charge. This was really weird. I just felt in my gut that this was some type of future setup or something; targeting I AM I didn't have any proof of it, but it was really weird.

Big Dawg came and expressed to me that Frank was really feeling bad about the episode that had happened with the portion of marijuana that was not any good. I knew this was bullshit, but this was a tactic that they were trying to pull, and I guess they didn't want me quitting too soon or whatever the nature was didn't really matter because they were gonna pay handsomely. Big Dawg made me aware of that. Frank would be calling within a short amount of time to speak with me directly. I knew my brother was getting uncomfortable with having to bring the two-way radio over to me and wait for calls just to have his people speak directly with me, but it wasn't too much that he could do about it.

Frank called and he was expressing how sorry he was about the mistake and of course it wasn't his fault. It must have been a mixed up and he started questioning me about the exact quality of the marijuana. He wasn't sounding normal; he was sounding rather friendly.

I remember that after that one screw up on the quality, which I made right, and paid what I felt I owed off of the last balance, things were running pretty smoothly as far as the cocaine was concerned. I was starting to receive two loads a week, but in increments of 50 Kilos. The drivers on the Indian Trail buses didn't feel comfortable bringing over fifty kilos at a time, so at times, they would squeeze a little more in here or there. I rounded out at about maybe 500 or a little more kilos per month.

Danny also put me in contact with another group that was speaking back and forth with me as well as him. I got really pissed off with this group of guys that I had never spoken with before, but I had an idea who they represented when they asked me for I AM phone number. This was a big no-no, and I didn't understand how they would have the balls to even ask for something like this. I made them aware that they did not need anyone's number outside of me because no one had the authorization to make decisions other than me. They tried to give me some excuse, like it was just normal, but I just thought that was extremely weird. They knew that I wasn't a rookie, and normally when these attempts were made, they would try to go around about and get the information they wanted and not come directly to the actual person in charge. This was really weird. I just felt in my gut that this was some type of future setup or something; targeting I AM. I didn't have any proof of it, but it was really weird.

Big Dawg came and expressed to me that Frank was really feeling bad about the episode that had happened with the portion of marijuana that was not any good. I knew this was bullshit, but this was a tactic that they were trying to pull, and I guess they didn't want me quitting too soon or whatever the nature was, didn't really matter because they were going to pay handsomely. Big Dawg made me aware of that. Frank would be calling within a short amount of time to speak with me directly. I knew my brother was getting uncomfortable with having to bring the two-way radio over to me and wait for calls just to have his people speak directly with me, but it wasn't too much that he could do about it.

Frank called, and he was expressing how sorry he was about the mistake, and of course, it wasn't his fault. It must have been a mixed-up, and he started questioning me about the exact quality of the marijuana. He wasn't sounding normal; he was sounding rather friendly. Much more than he would normally sound when speaking with me, knowing we didn't have a good relationship at all. But he just seemed really friendly and accommodating, and he would ask me questions and he would just let me talk, not cut in, and not really have too much of an opinion on anything that I was stating to him.

At this point, I've been around the world once and shook everybody's hand twice. I knew what was going on. He was asking me questions, but he had someone sitting there that he may have owed money to and allowed them to listen to me complain about the quality of the product. This was confirmed because he continued to talk, and he started to talk about different loads, maybe three or four loads back, and he was speaking as if these loads were consistently coming to me. And that there were issues, and that he was going to make it alright on that one conversation.

I knew then that someone was listening, and he wanted to use me as leverage to negotiate the price down for what the issue we were dealing with and most likely some other marijuana loads that he fucked up that had nothing to do with us.

But what it did allow me to see that he knew that I was much, much more seasoned than what I was before, and that I would catch on. But he knew that he would have to bust down with me at the end of the day. Bald Head was constantly in contact with me, basically just haven't talked about different things or whatever the case may be, filling me in on what was going on across the border while still promising me that he would be coming up to see me soon. Mario reached out to me. I had not spoken to him ever since. Our little spat over the phone. He started to ask me questions. That was out of the norm. But had nothing to do with our history in dealing with marijuana together, he started asking me about the white, other words, cocaine.

Mario: Hey my friend, I want to ask you something. Have you ever dealt with the white before?

After I answered him in the affirmative, he got extremely aggressive with his questioning. And was asking me was I interested in dealing with some again in the near future, and I also answered that in the affirmative. But just as Frank, I noticed that his cadence was different, and his tone of voice and he was asking questions. But when he asked questions, he held the line. Open on the two way a little too long.

This let me know that someone was sitting there with him, listening, but I continued to entertain him. He started to ask me about the prices that I would be willing to pay, and I gave him some outrageously low price that I knew was not accurate based on the war that was going on because I had Danny telling me what the prices were on that side of the border.

It was my attempt to bust his balls and to embarrass him a little but see the quality of the individual that he was sitting there with. To my surprise he agreed right away, and I know because I know how those things go. At that price he would have to get back to me because he would have to check up through the chain of command to see if it would be OK because I quote him a price so low.

Me: So, my friend tell me something. With this price. How much time will I be giving?

What this question asked, he was just a little too hyper and he did not even pay attention to the question I asked him because I was asking him for the terms at that price. I wanted to know if the time limit would be shorter because the price was so cheap. He gave me an answer, but it was the wrong one.

Mario: 200 my friend. I will send you two hundred!

There is no way he can offer that amount without having again authorization. And there's no one or no way he could give authorization that quick off of a conversation on the phone when he just found out the price which I quoted was well below the going rate over on the opposite side of the border. So just by him being so aggressive, agreeable on price and then the amount that he was talking about sending, which I know he did not have the power to send, that let me know that he was sitting there with someone that had direct connection with power. This made me recall a conversation that I had with Reyes. When he told me that the Chief had hid my number and there were people over on that side of the border that really wanted to find me and make contact with me. Mario did as I would have expected him to do.

When I threatened him, he went and started to ask questions. And somebody that he was sitting there with wanted to make sure and have verification that it was me without alarming me and this was affirmed with the shenanigans that Mario started to spew out of his mouth immediately, while screaming and yelling almost at the top of his lungs in excitement and joy. But first, I would answer his question in a fashion that I knew the person next to him wanted to know and that would affirm that it was me".

I told Mario that the task he had asked me to do was small and that I could complete it in a day and a half or two days at most. Mario seemed to be relieved and told me that he knew it was me all along. He reminded me of how long we have known each other, how he knows my family and how much they all love him. He also mentioned that he is very careful and always double-checks everything. I asked him again how much time he needed, but he didn't give me a direct answer and just told me not to worry and that he would be there with me in one week with the two hundred kilos of cocaine. I knew it would take longer, but he stayed in touch with me through my brother's Big Dawg.

I noticed that Frank was completely out of the picture and asked Mario about him, but he told me not to worry about Frank and spoke badly about him. It was clear that Mario was trying to push Frank out of the way and take over. This seemed to be working, as I stopped talking to Frank and started dealing directly with Mario.

Things were picking up, and I was getting a lot of valid offers from three different directions. One was from Danny, another from Frank, and Mario was also reaching out to me through Big Dawg about the white. Bald Head kept telling me that he would come up to see me in one week, but that kept getting pushed back. However, based on everything that was happening, I had a feeling that he would be coming up a lot sooner.

Me: Danny, I appreciate the update, but I have to be honest with you. I'm getting a little confused with all these different directions and players involved. I know the Chief is in control of the Tijuana area now, but there seem to be other players involved as well. Can you shed some light on this?

Danny: Yeah, man. It's getting pretty crazy out here. The Chief is definitely in control of Tijuana, but he's also expanding his territory to the south. He's working with some big players down in Colombia to get loads across the border. But there are also some other cartels that are trying to muscle in on our territory. We've been getting pressure from the Juarez cartel and some others.

Me: So, who else is involved besides the Chief and the Juarez cartel?

Danny: Well, there are a few players. There's Chapo, of course, but he's been keeping a low profile lately. And there's also Mayo, who's been trying to expand his territory as well. And then there are a bunch of smaller players who are trying to make a name for themselves.

Me: And how does Bald Head fit into all of this?

Danny: Bald Head is working with us, man. He's been helping us get loads across the border. But he's also got his own thing going on with the Sinaloa cartel. He's a smart guy, and he knows how to play both sides.

Me: Okay, I see. So, what's the plan going forward?

Danny: We're gonna keep sending loads your way, man. But we're gonna start using semi-trucks again to get them across. We've got some new drivers who are willing to take the risk. And we're gonna try to keep things as quiet as possible.

Me: Alright, sounds good. Just keep me in the loop, okay?

Danny: For sure, man. You're one of our top guys. We gotta keep you happy.

It's important to note that Danny was sending me loads from Juarez, Mexico, while Frank and Mario were operating in the Mexicali and Tijuana areas, just across the border from Arizona. I learned from Bald

Head that the Chief had taken control of the Tijuana territory after killing Reyes. Bald Head was dealing directly from Culiacan in the state of Sinaloa, Mexico. I was confused because the Chief was fighting with the Juarez cartel in the city of Juarez, but was also growing in power and handling logistics for loads coming into the lower part of Mexico through Panama City, Panama, from Colombia. It didn't make sense for him to be communicating with me from three different directions.

As I tried to piece together the information I had received from various sources, I couldn't help but feel like someone was trying to manipulate me. The three different directions the offers were coming from, each seemingly connected to a different cartel, had me feeling uneasy. Was someone trying to set me up or keep me in a certain position? I couldn't shake the feeling that something wasn't right.

Me: Man, if I didn't know any better, I would be thinking someone is trying to set me up or triangulate on me in some kind of way to make sure I'm kept or locked in a certain position. This is really weird.

Despite my confusion, I continued to receive updates from Danny, who informed me that the loads were about to increase and they would start sending semi-trucks across again soon.

Danny: My friend. I have very good news for you my friend. These guys barely just tell me that they are going to start sending you the trucks again, my friend. They told me to tell you that the next bus that comes. Is going to have the truck driver on it. You need to pick the truck driver up and you need to take the truck driver and show him the exits that he will need to come up on and show him the place that you have for him to come and bring this thing over to you my friend.

I was very happy to hear this news, but I was still a little confused because I asked Danny was I supposed to give the money to this truck driver that was coming up on the bus so that he could bring it back down there. Danny just told me no to hold on to it, but I was confused because I had been holding this money for like almost a month. because it was a very bad snowstorm.

But they had sent a couple of more loads of cocaine but not accepting the money. This was really weird. The Indian Trail bus came in as it normally would, but this time it did not have no load of cocaine on it just the truck driver. I was with my cousin Dirt, I AM. and myself. And we show the truck driver the exits that he would need to use in order to get to the drop spot. That we already had arranged for him to come to. This whole interaction may have took an hour, hour, and a half to take the guy, to show him everything and to bring him back to the hotel. In which he got out of the out of the vehicle. The guys were excited, and everything was set.

I was given the indication by the driver that it may be a pretty big load that was coming. Of course, the driver would not know about the details of what all the exact amount that was coming going to come. But he would have an idea of the load. Possibly, so in my mind, I was thinking that it had to be a ton or at least half of that. After all, I was already doing about 500 a month and that was pretty much taking it easy and not selling them whole.

They knew I could easily do more than that. No more than a couple of days after his meeting with the driver, Mario had Big Dawg bring the phone over to me and he made me aware that he would be up here to me within a matter of four or five days. He said the magic words that I was looking for, which was, He was just waiting for final authorization and confirm the amount of time that it would take me to complete.

The two hundred keys I had got excited with this additional news from Mario because hearing that authorization was the last thing that we were waiting on. I really got excited because I knew that this was as good as done and then on top of that I had another semi coming with approximately a ton more of cocaine on it. Not to mention that Bald Head was going to be coming soon and with all of this action going on and with the way I was figuring about these different angles, I knew Bald Head would be showing up soon.

I was starting to also think that maybe we're not ready, maybe that was pretty certain. That's if this cocaine came these other ways, that Bald Head was just coming up to see me. But it will be a clear indication that they were going to kill Bald Head.

It seemed like things were about to get even more complicated, and I couldn't help but wonder how much deeper I was getting into this world of drug trafficking.

As I pondered my next move, I couldn't help but feel a sense of unease and uncertainty. The stakes were getting higher, and I knew that any misstep could have serious consequences. But at the same time, the lure of the money and power was too strong to ignore. I just hoped that I could navigate these dangerous waters and come out on top.

I know I keep referring to Bald Head possibly being killed. There were a number of reasons for my speculation on this subject, but I was constantly receiving additional information. But the way this whole thing was starting to come together, it made me recall something that was going on at that actual time in the middle of these negotiations. And what I was recalling appeared to not have any direct correlation to what was going on with me, but at the exact timing that it was happening and the wordings that were being phrased within these deals gave a direct link to what I was recalling.

I had a very good friend named Kevin, which I referred to in the beginning of this story, who was my mentor with real estate. I was looking at purchasing a property that was being built on the banks of the city of Detroit River. The developer was looking to pull out of some properties because of financial constraints, and one of the properties that I was interested in buying, once it was fully developed, would be worth $2.3 million. I needed Kevin's opinion and professional outlook on the additional cost that I would incur by taking on this property outside of what I would have to pay the developer. Kevin, being the leverage that he was, needed some of my expertise at the time with the deal that he was trying to put together.

Kevin was the coach of a little league basketball team. On the little league team that he was coaching featured the son of a former NBA basketball player. This particular basketball player at one time played for the Detroit Pistons as well as the Chicago Bulls. He was now playing abroad, but on a professional level. Kevin and this gentleman developed a really close relationship that led into talking about additional things.

This gentleman was now playing for a team in Mexico. He started to make Kevin aware of some of the relationships that he was building down in Mexico and one of the relationships put him in position to maybe acquire some large sums of marijuana. Kevin wanted to pick my brain about the subject and me give him some negotiating tactics to probably win some type of agreement to get a load of marijuana. From these particular individuals. Agreed to assist Kevin in his quest to secure this contract. Even though I gave little merit to what he was saying. Because everybody that you hear of or that you know always have some great connect with the cartel that can deliver large sums of drugs but really never equates to anything.

I was blowing Kevin off, but I asked him, "OK, what area, what's the name of the cities and this type of things?"

I asked because I knew what cartels controlled which cities and so on and so forth. Just basically humoring him to get what I wanted out of him. To my surprise, Kevin started to give me some names of some cities and states that were very familiar, as in the city and state of Durango.

When he said this, this shocked me and I knew that he could not be lying because he knew nothing about this stuff. I had asked him to ask the gentleman this information and this was the name he came back with. My eyes got really big and I told Kevin that this was the area controlled by Sinaloa but directly by The Ol Man. Not to mention, Kevin had already mentioned to me that this gentleman was speaking to whomever he was speaking to about large sums of marijuana. Which made me recall the fields, the extensively huge fields, and the airfield with the smell of marijuana that I experienced when I was in Durango.

I began to explain to Kevin how imperative it was to handle this negotiation with care, and I emphasized to him that he should not use my name. Or tell this gentleman to use my name because someone will get hurt. Based on Reyes' information and what he told me prior to the Chief killing him, I informed Kevin of this. That the Chief was trying to hide my location from the rest of the cartel. So again, I kept emphasizing this to Kevin. Do not use my name as leverage to get the contract. Needless to say, after I started advising Kevin on what to tell this NBA player, things started to progress, but I started to notice that the amount of marijuana that was initially being talked about was starting to grow, and it grew to the point that they were talking about sending two tons of marijuana.

Again, there's that question that you're always looking for: who's given authorization to send this much marijuana? This type of authorization must come from the very top because no one wants to be responsible, if something goes wrong. No matter how much power you have, you cannot release the amount of marijuana that is currently being discussed without top-level approval. I started to curse Kevin because I knew that with that amount that they were discussing, there was no way you were going to send a load with that much marijuana with your first time dealing with someone on a brand-new contract, so

I told him that I knew that he used my name. He started to curse back at me, as we would often do with each other.

Kevin: I didn't use your motherfucking name. Fuck you. Your name doesn't mean shit. Don't nobody know you. My name is the one that matters now.

As he started to look at me and laugh with sarcasm in his voice. And begin to tell me why it matters? He's going to make sure that I'm compensated. Even if he did. All I could do was look at him as the crazy asshole that he was.

Me: OK, bitch, you better pay me good too!

Well, just before I got the information that I just covered, With Mario. About four or five days prior to that, I had heard Kevin tell me that the basketball player that was over in Mexico at the time told him to tell me that he was just waiting for final authorization. That the truck was at the farm, loaded up with the two tons of marijuana, and just waiting for the authorization to leave. I knew it would only take a matter of days before the marijuana would be in town. And then Kevin would be able to get with me to go look over this property, and I would be able to collect my funds from him for helping him deliver that contract. The interesting thing was that I was calling Kevin because I had the meeting set up with the developer, and Kevin was not returning my phone call. I was getting really pissed off because I knew in my mind that Kevin had received that load of marijuana and was avoiding me.

Which I would not have been surprised with, but I knew at some point I would see Kevin again and he would wet my beak like he was supposed to do. But that was just the type of shit that Kevin would do. But I was up against the wall now. I gave the developer so much money, and I was going to lose it if I didn't get back with him in a reasonable amount of time. At that point, a couple of days had passed, and I was blowing Kevin's line-up. I'm starting to leave really nasty messages, getting pretty irate with him, which is out of character for the most part. Kevin finally returns one of my phone calls, and he tells me that he's no more than 5–10 minutes away and that he will be pulling up at my place shortly.

Once he pulled up, he called me, and this was in the dead of winter. I opened the door for him to come in, but I noticed that he stayed close to his car. And would not even walk up the sidewalk toward the house. I turned to go back in the house, assuming that he was coming in, but he was yelling from the outside for me to come outside. Needless to say, this was really weird. I ended up coming out on the porch in the dead of winter. There was snow everywhere, and he was down on the sidewalk close to his car, trying to have a conversation that I was refusing to have with him outside when it was extremely cold, but I noticed.

He had an extremely weird look in his eyes. And his body language and his facial expression would be that of someone who would think you were trying to lure them into the house to do something to them. But I pretty much ignored all of that. And this was based on the fact that me and him never had any type of relationship that was threatening. That will make him even assume that the possibilities of anything like that could even happen with me. So basically, I told him either he was coming inside or staying outside, but I was not going to stay out there with him, so I returned back inside the house.

Left the door wide open. I knew that he would come up on the porch slowly and peek inside the house, so I had to make sure that I was sitting a nice distance away from the door, so at least he would stand inside the doorway with the nature of how he was acting. As I saw him, that's exactly what he did. He peered inside the door, looked around, and stepped inside the doorway. He closed the gate but left the big security door open as he stood by the door as if he might need to make a break for it or something. I'm looking at him, I'm talking to him, and I'm just laughing. I mean, I'm almost falling out laughing because of the way that he's acting. He's constantly looking at me, which is extremely weird. And not really saying anything but looking at me suspiciously if he sees he's trying to read me. And I'm just busy laughing at him because this was extremely funny.

Kevin: Man, your ass really don't know what's going on. I can't believe it. You really don't know. Me: Yeah, I know, I know. Your ass has lost your mother's fucking mind. (With laughter.)

Kevin: Man, you really don't know what the fuck just happened. Bitch, either you know and your ass is playing with me and you're trying to kill me, or you really don't know? Bitch, you're a bad motherfucker. You are a bad motherfucker! You told my dumb ass too. You told me!

He's making these statements. As you can tell, he's deep in thought, staring down at the floor but moving closer into the house at this point. He finally sits down. On the far end of the couch, but over closer to the door. He told me that he wanted me to listen to some of the messages that he had on his cell phone. He started to go through the messages on the cell phone, and he started to play the messages that this NBA player was leaving on his phone. Concerning the process of receiving that load of marijuana He let me hear a number of the messages and finally let me hear the one where the NBA player was saying that he was waiting for the final authorization, but the truck was loaded and ready to go.

He's pointing out the dates that are stated before each one of these messages. Are played. A couple of days went by, then the NBA player came back on with another message. The message was telling him that he had been traded to a team in Israel. And had been shipped out. That particular night, the authorization was supposed to come through from the owner of the team and be flown over there on a private jet to Israel. He told him that the authorization that came came in the form of somebody arriving and cutting off the head of the farmer. And that a bunch of sicarios were sent to the city to search around.

And the team owner told him he had to fly him out of there because a convoy of trucks was going around looking for him. Kevin knew nothing of the information that I had been receiving from Reyes. From Danny. And from Bald Head. This was more confirmation that there was a lot of infighting going on inside the Sinaloa Cartel, or, need I say, federation?

I was kind of confused because I didn't understand why or who would come into Durango and do something like that to one of the farmers. Because I knew that The Ol Man controlled basically all the marijuana crops. There. I knew Chief was trying to hide me and my information from the cartel for his own personal use, but I didn't think that he would do something like that to The Ol Man's friend. When that was basically like his mentor. So, this was more confirmation for me that Bald Head would be killed.

Because I know that he was not working on the Chief's behalf anymore and was working directly in the interest of El Chapo. I knew exactly what Black Shirt was up to, but he was representing Black Shirt. I knew Black Shirt was in the interest of El Chapo. And a direct threat to the Chief after the Chief killed his brother, and Bald Head was orchestrating all of this. Things were really getting weird! I received another call from Danny; it was starting to become clear that no one was going to come and retrieve the money from the last couple of loads I received.

Danny.: My friend, these guys are going to send a guy up there with you. They told me to give you the flight information for this guy that will be coming to see you in one week, and you will need to go and, you know, get this guy from the airport up there. I have the information right here for you right now, and he will buy you a ticket to fly in on Southwest Airlines. Sorry, my friend, sometimes I get these things confused. It's Southwest Airlines, my friend. When this guy gets to you, he will tell you everything. He will tell you what to do with those funds, and he will also tell you how much you are going to receive. Different, don't worry.

This was more good news. So, I had to make arrangements to get an outfit that I would wear to the airport to retrieve this guy. Then I would also have to make arrangements for him to stay somewhere. In the beginning, I would just allow him to stay with me so I could get a chance to really interrogate him and figure out where all this was going. Of course, interrogate him in a nice way. I spoke with Kevin, and he told me that the mansion would be a very good idea and a good investment. I sent my interior decorator, Uncle Sam, down to look at this place because it had an elevator, and I'll have to get contractors for all of these different things that need to be done. I would need him to do my interior decorating for me.

My two-way radio is like the hotline at this point. I'm getting calls from everywhere, consistent with everything that I've been hearing. Suddenly, Bald Head wants to call me.

Bald Head: My friend. I have very good news for you, my friend. I will be there to see you up there for maybe four or five days or something, my friend. Those guys in that place over there are going to be sending a guy up from there, and like one week for you to my friend, and I will be there with you when we get this guy from down there. Just one week, my friend. One week, that guy would be to us up there!

I was starting to really get excited with so much going on at once, but it was clear that something was going to come up short. As was receiving a consistent message from all three ends with another possible fourth end, and we know how that came to his conclusion, three were still alive with the climax of a week on all ends.

Everything appeared to be coming together just perfectly. There were a number of questions, but I figured I had the answers to the ones that were glaringly obvious in my head, and it all ended with the expiration of Bald Head. But again, that wasn't my business, and that was above my pay grade, so I would not be able to chime in or have an opinion on that. That was between them, and my job was just the business. At hand. After all, I had my own plans. My plans were to leave the United States of America and start to live abroad. My steps to doing that I was headed to India with my friend Jay, who was going to help me facilitate a marriage within a well-known tribe over there.

Then I was going to hit Brazil, get an apartment over there where I could do some relaxing from time to time, and I had a very old friend living in Puerto Vallarta, Mexico. He was waiting for me so I could come down and do a 100-year lease over there, break ground right off the Pacific Ocean, and get a very, very nice house built. The only thing I could do was continue to hear him constantly tell me that he was already in Puerto Vallarta, Mexico. Retired.

He just kept telling me, and I just kept hearing in my head over and over again, "Son, come over here. A bunch of Americans and Canadians are coming over here, but mostly all the black people that are coming over here are coming here to stay. You need to leave. Because all they're going to do is lock you up. That's all they ever try to do to us—lock us up."

I had gone back up to Eastland Mall to see Jay. He was expecting me to ask more questions about the visa. He informed me that he still didn't have an answer. And what was going on was extremely weird. He had never seen anything like this happen before. He told me that he had his cousin vouch for me, and they called his cousin up to the embassy and questioned him about me. He said after this he called, and he had a conversation and got kind of pushy with them about the visa process and asked him why it was taking so long, and they in turn told him that according to policy, they had up to 60 days to decide.

And they were not approving or denying my request, and they had 60 days to give an answer. When he told me that I knew something was wrong, I pretty much made him aware that I knew something was wrong.

But I didn't make a real big deal about it. I told him we'd just wait it out and see what happened. But I was pretty much ready to go and still had the families ready for me to choose one of their daughters so I could get married. But based on what was going on over in Mexico and everything that I was hearing,

And as that was being said to me, I knew that there was most likely An indictment of some time coming and that the government was influential in stopping the process of me being able to leave.

I was also in the process of arranging another huge party. And this one had to be really, really nice a huge party. And this one had to be really, really nice, upscale, and elegant. I made contact with my Uncle Sam, my interior decorator, and had him arrange something really nice. We would have occasional meetings for me to basically pay more money and more and more toward trying to arrange everything to make sure everything was perfect. I would have the whole team back together, and I would arrange for about 40 to 50 nice-looking women. For us to choose through as we party.

The day had come for Mario to make contact with us on the details of the two hundred kilos of cocaine that were on the way in, and as he stated, he was waiting for final authorization, which of course is always the last thing you hear before the shipment takes off. So Big Dawg came over, and I called him in to ask a question, asking him if he had heard from Mario and how much longer it would be before The shipment arrived.

Big Dawg: I don't know, man. I have been hitting him in the back. And his radio is off.

Me.: His radio is off, as in disconnected. Or turned off?

Big Dawg: as in turned off by him or someone.

This was extremely strange. Things like this never happen right in the middle of receiving authorization for a load to be shipped. **This was really weird again!**

I explained to Big Dawg how strange this really was, why it was so strange, the order of operation, and how things like this just don't happen. It doesn't happen. No one turns their phone off. Right in the middle of authorization being given. And someone turning their phone off is not like someone destroying the phone and throwing it away. That means the connection is over. For the phone to be turned off personally, that means that someone is not able to talk at that moment or no longer wants to talk at that moment, but in the middle of authorization being given and a load coming, this doesn't happen.

My thoughts were starting to settle on the fact, and it was becoming clear, Chapo and Ol Man Mayo were trying to box me into something. But I just didn't have enough evidence or circumstantial evidence to lock in totally on that assumption. Then I couldn't get it out of my head that this was being arranged and set up for the demise of Bald Head. Bald Head called me to discuss the up-and-coming meeting that was to take place, but he also started bringing up the fact that Chapo wanted him to express to me that we needed to take care of an old debt. Again, I thought this was strange because I did not owe that debt to Chapo. I owed that debt to The Chief, and that was the debt from the whole discussion when I was about to become a hefty snack for the pigs.

Bald Head went on to suggest, as he was starting to suggest more frequently now, that I should just stop everything and go ahead and get a job. I answered him in typical fashion, but he continued to push back, saying that I should really just go get a job, and a job is not a bad idea. After it appeared that I was adamant about not getting a fucking job, he went on to tell me that he would be seeing me soon, very soon, and that the guy was coming from down there, as he stated. Would be in tow in no more than a matter of days.

Now it was time to party. My uncle had arranged everything, and it was set to go off in a huge way. This was the party that was planned and organized for us to let our hair down and party hard before all of this work started pouring in and we became busy as hell. Mo Green had just gotten a new place, and we decided to turn it into a night spot. Which my Uncle Sam was incredibly good at doing.

He had movers come in and move all of the furniture out of the whole house. And ironically, he had a lot of upscale furniture brought in that was actually at the mayor's mansion the night before. I don't know how he pulled it off, but he also got about three or four of the chefs from MGM Grand Casino. Mo Green had a new construction crib built. And a four- or five-car garage, and they cleared the whole garage out and turned that into a kitchen. I mean, they had that fucking garage laid out with all those upscale grills and all kinds of shenanigans going on in there. You would never have known there was a garage. They had the MGM uniform,chef hats, chef preps, and all the rest. Then, on the interior of the house, we also had MGM waiters waiting on us, and it was nice. He also arranged for some of the members of the Detroit Symphony Orchestra to come in and create the music for us because they were laid off at the time. From what I understand, everyone was dressed up, it was by invitation only, and it was really an upscale event. If I'm not mistaken, I think I spent maybe a little over $50,000 or a little bit north of that figure. Everybody was so happy to see me throw another event.

I wanted this to be a night to remember. But to kick off a whole other idea with totally new ambitions of creating something bigger and worldwide at this point But I wanted this to be a mental marker of that first step, and everybody was dressed to the T. All the men had tailored suits. The next morning, I got up and started to make arrangements to get myself together to go to the airport, as Danny had instructed me. I had to go pick this gentleman up from the Southwest Airlines side of the airport. I had a very nice blue jeans outfit with a Ferragamo belt and loafers to match. With the traditional D-boy Cartier Buffs eyewear. Just as anticipated, I received a call from Danny, and I knew I wanted to just ensure that everything was going according to plan and that I would make it to the airport. But he was hitting me up just as I was leaving the room.

Danny: My friend, don't worry about this guy. He's not coming, my friend. Me: My friend, you say again!

Danny: My friend, don't worry about going to get this guy. This guy is not coming. He won't be there, my friend.

Me: I don't understand my friend. I'm barely going to get this guy right now, and then you just call me right now and say that this guy's not He won't be there. I don't understand, my friend. Tell me?

Danny: Yeah, my friend, I don't know. These guys barely just came to tell me right now that this guy is not going to be on the flight. I don't know my friend. I don't know.

Me: My friend. My friend, you know, this is not right. My friend, this is not right. This doesn't happen, my friend. Tell me? My friend, please tell me what's going on. This is not right. You know this is not right!

Danny: Yeah, I know my friend. But I don't know. I'm sorry, my friend. I'm sorry........

There has never been a time that Danny has not been able to tell me what is going on. He was my mentor. He taught me everything that I knew. About the cartels and how that whole business worked over there across the border. And he was never wrong. This man was the guru of that world, and he taught me very well, and I knew that this was not right. And he did not tell me anything else, as he would normally do if I was wrong.

This was the first time that he just said he did not know, and he said he was sorry, but the way he said he was sorry, I knew that that tone of voice was not right. and this guy was supposed to arrive and tell me what to do with all this money that I had been holding for them at this point for weeks and weeks. I just didn't understand. But one thing was very clear: It had come back to haunt me. The reason Danny did not tell me what was going on and explain it to me This was payback. For not telling him that the Chief was going to kill him, he was pleading with me, asking me, and I lied to him.

The following day, I received a call from Bald Head. He made me aware that he had just arrived in town. I was under the impression that it would take an additional few days for a representative from Sinaloa to come up to speak with me on behalf of the cartel. But it came as a surprise to me that Bald Head made me aware that the gentleman was actually with him and they were ready to meet. I made myself aware that it was a go. And they wanted to get ready to meet with us. I placed a call to Bald Head to find out exactly what hotel they were staying in so we could meet them at the hotel. But I was kind of shocked when Bald Head did not want to meet at the hotel because that's always the way it's done.

We would meet somewhere secluded based on what we needed to discuss. Bald Head told me that we would be meeting at a Buffalo Wild Wings in Troy, Michigan, of all places. I asked him about his selection, but he kept assuring me that it would be OK. I continued to give him pushback, stating that this did not make sense and that black people are not necessarily welcome sitting with Hispanics out in Troy, MI; at the very least, we'd stick out like a sore thumb.

BaldHead: My friend, I'm sorry, but this is where this guy chose; it's where he wants to meet my friend. I'm sorry.

There was nothing else that I could say because the individual that came up from Sinaloa was basically in charge. What must be understood is that this was highly unusual. Whenever anyone came into my town, whether it was to have a conversation or to bring a load, I was always in charge because I was responsible for anything that went wrong. This was not normal!

I and myself arrived at Buffalo Wild Wings. When we entered the Buffalo Wild Wings, the two hostesses were overly friendly to me, which I found extremely weird, but something just wasn't setting right within me just because of the place of this actual meeting and the high level of sensitivity of what would be discussed. I looked over to the right, and Bald Head waved. There was a Mexican gentleman sitting there with him. We joined them at the table.

I looked around and felt extremely uncomfortable, and I asked Bald Head why he would select the table basically right in the middle of the restaurant instead of one off in the corner or to the side. Then the gentleman from Sinaloa spoke up and told me, Do not worry, it's OK. There was just so much wrong with that setting and the placement of the table, and then I noticed people at the tables closest to us were having conversations that weren't flowing naturally. Those certain tables—one table at 9:00 o'clock, one table at 3:00 o'clock, and one table at 6:00 o'clock—these particular tables seemed to be a little bit too close. To our table. In the center.

Even though the other tables were further out and away. So, there was a lot I didn't say, and I basically followed suit with the pace of the conversation with just head nodding and short responses.

Sinaloa Man: "My friend, it is finally nice to sit here and meet the real deal. There is so much talk about you guys and the wonderful things that you do. It is really an honor for me to meet the real deal, my friend.

The Sinaloa gentleman continued to elaborate, making me aware that they wanted to send up a ton of cocaine on the first shipment. He began to discuss some numbers that I can't really recall at the moment, but what I do know is that I was not comfortable having that kind of conversation in the middle of Buffalo Wild Wings. Therefore, I did a lot of nodding. I turned down the ton on the first actual trip. And this is something that I had discussed with Bald Head: I wanted to maybe receive about 2 to 300. Initially.

This would give me an opportunity to have some funds to set up bigger and better places to store the majority of what was being shipped and also allow my guys to get a little money in their pockets. I knew if they saw that much work on the first load, they'd lose their fucking minds. The discussion continued with the Sinaloa gentlemen, and he told me that the first shipment would still need to be a ton, and shortly after that, it would need to increase. I asked him what the plans for the Atlanta market were, and he made me aware that we would be receiving 2 tons down in Atlanta. He also made me aware that I was being promoted, that I would have full control over all the cocaine that came into Michigan on behalf of the Sinaloa Cartel, and that I would continue to have control of the hub of Atlanta as well. I was really happy about what I heard.

These were all the things that I had asked for at the conclusion of this war. It started to seem as if I was getting everything that I wanted. From the answer that he gave me about Atlanta, I felt that was confirmation that Bald Head would definitely be killed shortly afterward. In a weird way, this made me settle down a bit. We were told that the work was on schedule. And that they will be getting in contact with us soon, and did we have the drop-off spot arranged? I answered the question affirmatively because we were all set to go on my end. The Sinaloa gentleman stated to me that they were really impressed across the border with how we worked when we were under federal investigation and were able to move 250 keys. And he kept emphasizing that we were the real D.E.A. I started to elaborate on this subject and tell him how my team was tight and knew how to move. Under those types of circumstances.

Me: My friend, for some reason you look extremely familiar. I know this may sound crazy, but I may have seen you over there in Culiacan. I don't know, but I seem to remember you from somewhere else inside the United States, my friend. I know this sounds crazy, but as they say, everybody has a twin, right?

The Sinaloa gentleman assured me that maybe it was his twin, and we all laughed it off, and he made the statement that most black people are used to hearing, but in reverse.

Sinaloa Man: Well, my friend, you know they say we all look alike.

Again, we all laughed it off, and I got up to leave. When we went into the parking lot to enter the vehicle, I felt a lot better. We got on the freeway and headed back to the east side of Detroit. But I was working the mirrors, and I noticed a gray truck. Normally I would have started to hit a lot of corners, but I thought maybe I was being a little paranoid. However, I did notice that this helicopter just continued to follow us, and once again, I started to think maybe I was just being paranoid.

The following day, Bald Head placed another call to me, making me aware that we would not be delivering at the location that I had given him. This really pissed me off, and I really gave him some hell for it. Once again, he invoked the Sinaloa gentleman. And how ironic that the place that he wanted to use as a drop-off point was Buffalo Wild Wings in Westland, MI. I made him aware that this was a damn suicide mission and that I would not be participating. Again, he told me that it was not him. It was the gentleman I put a call in to the Sinaloa gentleman I can't even recall what he told me. I don't think it made sense, but once he said that it was the call from across. What could I say?

I am, as always, in control of all shipments when they're getting ready to come in and all money going out. We got together with my cousin Dirt and the driver who would be driving the vehicle with the work in it. The plan was that there would not be a semi coming in that we would unload. The plan was that we would leave an empty vehicle in a certain parking lot that they designated and give them the description with the keys still in the vehicle. Someone would come and pick the vehicle up once my guys left, and they would load the vehicle and bring it back to the same identical spot.

Then put a call back into I AM, and I AM would come back and retrieve the vehicle. So once I dropped the vehicle off, he went to a restaurant not far away, which is typical of that type of arrangement. I AM continued to call me and tell me that something was not right. He just didn't feel right. I continued to press him and tell him that we had to move forward, that we did not have any choice, and to stop being paranoid. Even though. I will admit that I was feeling the same way.

The issue that I was dealing with is that I knew that this load was coming directly under Chapo's instructions, and I didn't have the authority to pull out of a shipment that was coming directly from him. I knew we would all be dead. I could do nothing but recall the same incident that almost cost I AM his life because that load was also directly from El Chapo.

I AM: Listen, man, something is not right. We are sitting in this restaurant, and there are a couple of white guys sitting in different spots staring at us extremely hard. Listen, man, I'm telling you something ain't right. You need to call this crap off.

Me: You need to just strap on your hard hat and tighten up your boots because we have to go through with this. I need you to tighten up because the guys are watching you, and if they see you being weak, then they're going to start freaking the fuck out, man.

I AM: I hear you, man, but something ain't right. This kind of setup is almost like the IHOP situation you went through with Brian. Man, I'm telling you. But OK.

God knows I wanted to call this off, but I did not have the authority to do so. I wanted to leave everything and just drop it and walk right away, and that was the right move. I was always a gut player, and usually my gut is right. But I just didn't feel I had the authorization because it was coming from El Chapo directly. Sam hit me on the two-way, making me aware that they were headed back for the pickup. The next click from the two-way radio would have been a notification that they were en route.

I AM: Man fuck. It's a fucking setup. It's a fucking setup. These motherfuckers are coming from everywhere. Bald Head set us the fuck up. Bro, it's a fucking setup.

Me: "Damn man, say that again."

I AM: bro. It's a fucking setup. Bald Head set us the fuck up. It's SUVs coming from every fucking place. They took down the driver before he even got to the actual vehicle. Dirt took off and maneuvered up out of their SUVs, trying to box us in.

Me: Where the fuck are y'all at?

I AM: We're leading them on a high-speed chase. We're jumping down on the freeway right now. God damn. It's a whole lot of them motherfuckers behind us. You don't see shit but lights.

Me: Yo man. Don't do that. Take the phones, remove the SIM cards, break them, and throw them out the window. Then break both of your phones and pull over. Tell Dirt to pull over. I'm not trying to see you guys hurt yourselves. Or fuck nobody else up. You already know what to do. Just hold tight. I'm going to get in contact with Lorence. And get somebody down there for you guys. Just be cool, bro. And tell dirt to pull the fuck over.

I would later find out that they pulled over. Shortly after, he got rid of the SIM cards out of the window. There were state troopers, local police, and the D.E.A. They had blocked the freeway off on both sides. The D.E.A ran up on the vehicle and pulled my cousin Dirt out as well as I AM. I AM said one of the D.E.A agents punched him in the jaw.Before a couple of other officers grabbed him.

D.E.A agent: Fuck them. They're bigger than BMF. These individuals are larger than BMF. You just don't know it. I have the fucking reports. They are larger than the BMF. Fuck them.

"After securing the area, the D.E.A agents placed I AM and my cousin Dirt in a vehicle. This vehicle was driven by one agent, I AM and my cousin Dirt in the back seat.

They were taken to a very small county, and within this county there was a small precinct. The exact precinct was never known, and this is a normal tactic to try to avoid attorneys being able to find their clients while they're trying to extract information from them. The ride was long but rather interesting. As they were getting close to the actual precinct in the small county, they were being taken to the D.E. An agent who was driving decided that he wanted to speak.

D.E.A agent: Whoever is involved in this is big. This was so big that there wasn't a lot of information given to us, but only what was necessary. What I can tell you from my experience and what I know is that whoever is involved in this is as big as, if not bigger than, BMF.

My mind is racing at this point. I did all the normal stuff that protocol will call for as far as getting in touch with my attorney, which was Lorence, and having him line up additional attorneys for my guys, but the first measure of business was to find out exactly where they were, and that was the issue, which was normal practice for something like this.

I replayed everything throughout my head, and the first thing that came to mind was "bald head." As I stated earlier, I was always suspicious and pretty much had confirmation that Bald Head was an informant. But I wasn't so sure about the gentleman from Sinaloa. I knew that they both were involved, but stating that the gentleman from Sinaloa was involved would implicate something totally different. I gave them both a call, read them both the riot act, and gave them plenty of help. Bald Head blamed it on the guy from across the border, the Sinaloa guy.

The Sinaloa guy said that he was unfamiliar with what was going on, but he would have to check with those across and get back to me, but it definitely was not him. I did what I always did over the years when I was at an impasse and couldn't figure out things that were going on: I called. My old, trusted, and good friend Danny

I wasn't prepared for what I had experienced. And it became clear why Danny was so apologetic to me about not having the answer that I knew he really had in our last conversation. Danny knew what was coming. And at this point, it was clear: Danny was gone.

At this point, it was clear what was going on, and it was clear that the three different directions of work that it appeared that I was about to receive were nothing more than a triangulation to box me in, like I figured. This was done to me by the guys across So, in my mind, there was no reason to try to start or continue cursing people and going through all these different changes, but to actually prepare. For what I knew was coming and what I had pretty much already mentally prepared myself for. I spoke back to Lorence. He made me aware that he had just gotten off the phone with I AM's lady.

She had been pulled over by the D.E.A., and they took her back to her home and asked her to open up the home so they could search for I AM, which was peculiar to me because they already had I AM in custody. I had all of my guys prepared with what to do in these types of cases, so she called my attorney. As I AM, surely advised her what to do in these types of scenarios. Lorence advised me that he got on the phone and spoke with the D.E.A. agent that was at her home. The D.E.A. agent asked Lorence, "Does he know my location?

Lorence told him that he did not, and he called the agent into question about how the agent was practicing going into houses and pulling people over and things of that sort. The D.E.A. agent made Lorence aware that he had an indictment for me or that there was an indictment for me. Lorence at that point asked the D.E.A. agent how he was able to pull that off because there had not been a grand jury hearing.

D.E.A. agent: We are executing an indictment and a warrant for the Western District of Texas. The indictment was done under secret indictment; it was filed and sealed on April 24th.

The agent promptly asked about my whereabouts again, and as expected, Lorence told him that he did not know where I was and promptly hung up the phone. After speaking with Lorence a little more and him advising me not to allow myself to be caught because that would add an additional charge to the charges that I would already be facing, the D.E.A. kept the number of my attorney and continued to call him to negotiate with him for my surrender. I called Bald Head again. But I changed my tone quite a bit and told him that I knew that he had nothing to do with it. Following the narrative that I had set, Bald Head began to go through all the possible scenarios of who it could be. Wow, continuously asking me what I was going to do—was I going to go on the run?

I knew that he knew that I was just playing a part and that he was fucking lying. His hands were dead smack in the middle of all of this shit. It just made me think back over all the time I have been talking to him and how his tone would be so different and he would be asking and saying all the right things and asking all the right questions.

But then other times he will call, and his whole tone is more personal, in contact with me, so to speak, and advising me. That man—maybe you should just get a job. I can understand so clearly now why there were two differences in tone and why he advised just getting the job—what he was really saying to me. On the one hand, the conversations that he was having with me were being recorded. So he could turn into his handler, leading up to what happened. The other conversations that he was having when he would constantly try to push and press me to get a job were the ones that were not being recorded; should I say those were the ones that were off the record?

Reflecting back on everything at this point pretty much lets me know that he really didn't want to do what he did. To me, he probably had another, ulterior idea of something he would like to put together after this whole process was over. And with me being an intricate part of his rise in the cartel, why not keep me active?

Having this past history with conversations with Bald Head kind of laid the guidelines for me, and talking to him now, he pretty much kept the same format. Lorence told me that the DA was trying to negotiate with him on my behalf for surrender. So with Bald Head constantly asking me, what was I going to do? Was I going to go on the run? He could help me because all these nice suggestions that he was making were on the record, so to speak, because he was asking these questions for the D.E.A.

So, I started telling Bald Head what I knew his handler wanted to hear: that I would be turning myself in. After Bald Head, it was pretty much assured. Or I could see through his conversation with me that his handlers were convinced that I would be turning myself in the following day because they heard it from my attorney as well; conversations went off the record.

Bald Head: My friend. I need you to listen to me. Please, my friend. You need to do what is best for you right now, my friend. The Chief. You told me to tell you to do what is best for you to get yourself home as quickly as possible, my friend. The chief says he does not care because he is in Mexico.

I started to get upset with Bald Head for his suggestion. And I started to become extremely belligerent with him. I had already made arrangements with Lorence, and he was assembling for me a legal team of three attorneys, including himself, not including the one that I would have for my guys. I told Bald Head there was no way. In hell, I would do anything like that. I don't care who suggested it.

Bald Head: No, my friend. You don't understand. Remember that you are my friend. And I told you I would tell you things. My friend, there are things that you don't understand, and there's no way for me to explain them to you right now. But we had a friendship that, if either one was in trouble, we would help each other, my friend. Protect yourself, my friend, and do what's best for you. Listen to me, my friend, please. Everyone has done it or is going to do it. You just don't understand, my friend. You just don't understand. It's not what you guys think over there.

This was really weird, and I could hear the sincerity in his voice, and I know for most of you reading this, that sounds crazy. That's funny, but there's a thin line in between the sincerity and the bullshit, and I could pretty much read the on-the-record conversations and the ones that were off. What he was reiterating to me was the pack that we had with each other to protect each other in case one knew that the other was about to be killed. The same exact pack that I broke with Danny, which allowed me to end up in a situation that I was in when Danny knew what was going to happen, but he did not advise me because I did not advise him.

When he was about to be killed. This shit was really getting more and more weird. Now this was the fucking kicker that blew my fucking mind, but let me know that something else was afoot, and the advice he was giving me from his understanding was sincere advice based on something that he knew that he couldn't express to me. At that moment.

Bald Head: My friend. I know that you're going to turn yourself in tomorrow. But I need you to do something for me. My friend, I need you to keep this phone number. Do not get rid of this phone number, my friend. So that you can still call me. So, we can still stay in touch, my friend. Make sure that you keep this phone number. Never throw this phone number away. I will never change it, my friend.

What the fuck is wrong with this dude? I was thinking. I'm about to go to prison, maybe for the rest of my life; I don't know, but I don't think it will be for a short period of time, and this jackass wants me to keep his phone number so we can stay in touch; this guy is a jackass. He was speaking to me as if we, at some point in the future, maybe in the near future, I don't know, would be able to reconnect and do some more of what we did before, all in a business-as-usual type tone. Why do I feel as though this is the end of the world, but dude sounds so nonchalant? This shit is weird.

That was the last conversation I had with Bald Head. Even though he continued to call me, I didn't want to talk with him anymore. Because he was really weirding me out, and I had already thought a bunch of things about him over the years. At that point, I was becoming more afraid of what else he might be willing to share with me. I turned myself in on May 4th. The indictment was executed by the D.E.A. of Detroit on behalf of the D.E.A. in the Western District of Texas on May 3rd. The following day, there was a court hearing downtown in Detroit at the US Federal Court building.

Lorence knew the US prosecutor. For like twenty odd years, according to the prosecutor. The prosecutor pretty much emphasized the same thing that the D.E.A. agents were telling me and my cousin Dirt. But it was apparent that he knew more than what the D.E.A. agents knew because he said this was one of the biggest cases he had ever seen. And told me that I knew who I was dealing with and that I had made it extremely high up in the rankings of some very, very dangerous people. And this was before we even went to court. He was speaking to me based on a relationship I had with my attorney. He told me that I would also be receiving a bond. But that the Western District of Texas already had someone waiting to appeal that decision as soon as it was made to not allow me to become free on bond.

The Western District of Texas would file paperwork to have him extradited to Texas. He asked me what I oppose and fight for. Extradition. I told him that if the Western District of Texas would guarantee me that, they would give me my bond rights. Once I reached the Western District of Texas, I would wave.

The US prosecutor got back with my attorney and told him that the Western District of Texas was willing to honor that request. The courtroom was cleared out before they read on the record what we were going to be charged with. There were just a few people in the audience, and out of those, a few were family members. The charges were basically a bunch of conspiracies to import over two tons of cocaine into the United States of America. Lorence made me aware that the US attorney, who was a good friend of his, allowed him to take all the records or minutes from the actual case with him down to Texas, where he would join me to fight this case as he was assembling my legal team of two more attorneys. I don't know what the significance of having the records or the minutes from the court case up in Michigan would have been, but he seemed pretty excited about it. But there was one question that I had that I asked Lorence. Which it seems like I just could not get an answer to.

Me: Lorence, I really don't think there were any drugs in that vehicle. They released the driver, and the driver said that he looked in the back of the vehicle before they took him down, and there was nothing in the vehicle. There was no cocaine in that vehicle. Did you see anything in the paperwork that indicated that there were drugs in the vehicle?

I didn't get a clear answer, and I can't say that I was surprised. Lorence was kind of sarcastic with me and the questions he asked in turn. It wasn't the first time he had gotten mad at me for, as he would say, trying to do his job, so I didn't take it too seriously.

Lorence: "Donnie, let me quarterback this."

There were a couple of days, and we were taken from Sanilac County Jail out to the McNamara International Airport. We were loaded on to Con Air, and from there we made a number of stops before arriving in Tolleson, Oklahoma. At that airport, they had a totally different taxi, which led to a separate area on the airport grounds where convicts were kept as you flew throughout the country. That was really a different experience there, to actually have cells and housing right at the airport and even have the actual onboarding and unboarding little ramp leading to and from the planes. We were not housed in Tulsa, Oklahoma, for long. We were back out of there in about three or four days.

Making a number of other stops before landing in El Paso, TX. We were unloaded, loaded onto a van, and taken to the holding facility.

We were taken to Chaparral, NM. After landing in El Paso, TX. The facility that we were to be housed in was on the White Sands Missile

Base. This was a very different experience for me; 98% of all the inmates in this facility were Mexican nationals caught trying to cross over into America illegally from Mexico.

They would be housed at this particular facility until they went through the legal process and were shipped back to Mexico. I believe there may have been a total of five or six black people in this facility. The rest were actually military servicemen who were arrested by the MPs off the base. It was nothing to wake up in the middle of the night and hear military helicopters landing at the back of this facility and shaking the whole building. The purpose of them landing in the back in the middle of the night was to bring in cartel bosses or different individuals from Mexico that had been extradited from Mexico into the United States.

I AM, and I will be taken back to the holding cells. That was a rather interesting process that I refused to participate in because Lorence was not here with me and my team of attorneys was not present as well. Which isn't a surprise, because as you're being moved through transit, the last people to know exactly where you are, of course, are attorneys and family, under the excuse of security. There were several things floating through my head. The first was the very nice sports jacket that the US Attorney wore. The next thing was the actual faces of all the other attorneys and other assistant US attorneys as their mouths dropped and eyes bulged out of their heads as Mrs. Kristal M. Wade read the factual basis of our case onto the record. As I stood there, I felt like one of the extremely bad guys in the Marvel movies as they stood in the courtroom. But there was only one constant that stayed in my mind.

Me: This assistant US attorney... She has a bad attitude. A bad, bad attitude...

Mrs. US Attorney had I AM really upset. Hearing that he would not be receiving a bond, and in the fashion that he heard it, it would be easier for you to shake hands with God than get a bond, he was becoming aggravated with me because I found humor in that. He was upset because he felt that he had been lied to. I pretty much knew that it was a lie, but the actual answer just intrigued me. And maybe I could be considered a sucker, but I loved Mrs. US Attorney's straightforward style and her very nice sports jacket.

US Marshall: Donald Thompkins, attorney visit

The US Marshall came to the bullpen, called my name out, and said that I had an attorney visit. Being naive to the process, I'm thinking to myself, "Damn, how did Lorence get here that fast? He must have already known that I was here. So, following normal protocol, I would have to turn around and cuff up before they pulled me out of the bullpen, but I was still shackled, hands to waist and ankle shackles. I had seen everybody else being pulled out of the bullpen and going into one of three rooms for attorney visits.

I was somewhat bewildered when they took me in the opposite direction to the elevators. They took me up maybe five or six floors, and we exited the elevator. The US Marshall took me to a room with two gentlemen sitting in it. I was already shackled; my hands were connected with a black box in between. Once entering the room, the marshals took the black box off me, disconnected me from my waist shackles, and connected my handcuffs to a mount on the table.

D.E.A. Agent One: Excuse me, Marshall, could you please disconnect him from the mount on the table? Also, could you take his handcuffs off?

US Marshall: Are you sure that you want to do this, sir?

D.E.A. Agent One: Yes, I'm more than sure this doesn't need to be that type of situation. Thank you.

US Marshall: OK, well, don't come screaming and crying if he attacks you.

This was a rather interesting exchange between the two gentlemen. I was kind of shocked myself that D.E.A. Agent One requested for my handcuffs to be taken off; that black box was kicking my ass, so I was appreciative of it. But that instantly let me know that something was afoot. The US Marshall removed my handcuffs, and he exited the room and closed the door behind him. The feeling in the room was somewhat awkward as I sat on one side of the table, staring at these two gentlemen. One is a Caucasian male, and the other is clearly a Hispanic male. They were staring back across the table, looking directly at me.

D.E.A. Agent One: I would like to begin this conversation with a statement, but off the record between us, if that's OK with you. The statement I'm about to make is in no way disrespectful to any race or culture.

I nodded in the affirmative. I agree that the statements that would be made would be off the record. However, I wasn't prepared for what was about to come.

D.E.A. Agent One: It feels damn good to be sitting across the table from a fucking American! As he smacks the table and pushes back from it, crosses his legs, and leans back in his chair. I fucking jumped when he smacked the table. I'm from the east side of Detroit, in the era where cops kicked criminals asses. It was almost kind of like a prerequisite in college; we had just come to understand it as part of the investigation back then. When he smacked the table, I thought that's where the ass-kicking part was supposed to start. But how the rest of the conversation went was just as surprising.

D.E.A. Agent One: You don't know how much me and my partner have been through over the last four or five years. I totally fucking swear. There has not been one individual that we talked to that was not a Mexican national, and we needed a fucking translator in here. I totally fucking swear to you. You are the first actual fucking American that we get a chance to speak to who was actually born in America, and we can speak English as the first fucking language. Can you believe that?

I was kind of taken back by this whole thing here. I was still waiting for the ass-kicking part to start, so I was just agreeing to pretty much everything that he said.

D.E.A. Agent One: You do know that you have a fucking bestseller, right? You have a fucking bestseller, my friend. I'm telling you right now, you have a fucking bestseller. I don't know if you know how high you fucking made it, buddy. You've made it to the fucking pinnacle. You made it to the very top, man. I don't know if you fucking know it. You've got yourself a bestseller. I'm telling you that now.

Well, to my surprise, I didn't know that I had a best-seller. I did know that I made it extremely high, but I didn't think that I understood the level. Of the influence and power that I had developed within the Sinaloa Cartel. I can honestly tell you that I didn't understand exactly what he was saying to me or what I had done. Because it went so fucking fast. The majority of what I learned about the cartel and who I was dealing with, just to be totally honest, I learned watching CNN.

And I was even in denial about that, saying, "Nah, that couldn't be me. I couldn't know these people; I'm just Wayne."

D.E.A. Agent One: You know who you fucking remind me of, right? You know who he fucking reminds me of? What's that guy's name in the movie? You know, the movie they just did with the black guy? You know the movie I'm talking about. Man, you must realize that the film starring the black man is incredibly, incredibly, incredibly massive. That was just in the fucking theater.

He's stating this as he's pointing his finger at me as he's tapping his partner, D.E.A. agent number two, on the side of him. He's really struggling to remember the name of the individual in the movie or the actual movie, and his partner doesn't seem to recall what he's talking about. I have an idea, so I slowly stated what I thought.

Me: Do you mean American gangster Frank Lucas?

D.E.A. Agent One: That's it. That's the fucking movie I'm talking about. Denzel really played that fucking part. That's it, Frank Lucas. That's what the fuck you remind me of right there. You know I couldn't find you, right? You know I had problems finding you. I couldn't find you anywhere. You didn't have a criminal record. There was no type of record. I don't even think you had a fucking parking ticket, man. You would never guess how I found you. Go ahead, show it to him. Show it to him.

Now I had noticed ever since I had sat down and the US Marshall unshackled me that D.E.A. agent two had this folder under his hand with some pictures, which I really didn't focus on, but he was tapping on this one particular picture. But as D.E.A. agent one instructed D.E.A. agent two, he slid what was up under his hand over to me. I grabbed the open folder and focused on my BMW. Pictures that were taken at the raid on Novara Then, right behind the pictures of the BMW that was taken from me back in Detroit, I saw pictures of myself and Mo Green sitting right next to me, handcuffed, on the couch. Of course, why stop there? They handed me the folder because they wanted me to see it. I have also seen pictures. Of me, I AM, and a number of others at the 300-bowling alley down in Atlanta. Some of these pictures also had my very good friends Keith Thomas and Usher in them.

D.E.A. Agent One: This is how I fucking found you. If it were not for that fucking BMW, I would have never found you. And I'm going to tell you how I know about the BMW, one of the fucking drivers from like a long time ago. You probably don't even remember this fucking guy. One of the drivers came to pick up some money from you. The one that was trying to buy your fucking BMW for you. The whole fucking time we were trying to talk to him and find out what the fuck was going on, all he was talking about was your fucking car and how badly he wanted to buy that fucking car.

He just described that car as being completely insane. He's about to be charged with all types of shit, tons of cocaine, and marijuana being imported into the fucking country, and all he wanted to talk about was the fucking BMW you had. I'm telling you again, my friend. I mean, I'm probably beating a dead horse here. You have a fucking bestseller. I fucking swear. You have a fucking bestseller, my friend. You totally have to write a book about this. I mean, there are so many similarities between you and the fucking guy. Frank Lucas. If there's any guy that fucking made it, you fucking made it. I mean, like in the underworld and the whole drug thing.

After D.E.A. agent one finished explaining to me how difficult it was to gather information on me and how he tracked me down, I almost got the sense that it was almost like a victory lap for him. Or something of that sort. He seemed to be venting after a long, arduous investigation, and maybe I was the cherry on top. I don't know. He began to ask me a series of questions. I got the impression these were questions about shit that he already knew. Just like having the US Marshall unshackle my hands. Knowing that my hands would be needed to catch that folder and see all of the pictures and other goodies that they had in it, I got the impression that it was no more than just letting me know their position, where they stood, and pretty much what they already knew.

I'm sure they knew they weren't going to get too much out of me, seeing what I had just done in court and not really being willing to participate without Lorence. And within my mind, for good reason, I had spent over $350,000 on the legal team that he had assembled for me. After maybe 25 or 30 minutes, the US Marshals showed up again, and he cuffed me back up. Shackling me to my waist again In preparation of getting ready to take me back down to the bullpen. D.E.A. Agent Two He never really said anything during the whole process, but at this point he stated that he was going to take a ride down with the US Marshall as he took me to the bullpen.

D.E.A. Agent Two: How are you feeling, Mr. Thompkins?

Me: "I have seen better days."

D.E.A. Agent Two: I'm sure you have, but they can get better.

Me: "Well, I'm sure you are about to tell me how they can get better, but before we get into that, maybe you can help me." Figure out why you look so familiar to me.

D.E.A. Agent Two: We just had lunch together. It was my treat. You don't remember?

Me: Yeah, I remember that part. You could have taken me to a better place. But no, that's the simple one. You are familiar with a number of different places. Like. I94, Buffalo Wild Wings, even decided to visit me in court up in Detroit and, of course, here.

D.E.A. Agent Two: Wow, you remember a lot, Mr. Thompkins. That can really help you make your day better. As I was stating before, I guess the only thing that I can say is that I could neither confirm nor deny. I will tell you something, though. At our little lunch date that we just had. I was fucking nervous. Just based on the whole story of the cartel and the interaction with different U.S. citizens. During this whole investigation and the level that you guys had reached, I was thinking I was about to see some cold-blooded killers, man. Some real tattooed-up bad motherfuckers, man. But once I had that meeting or sat down with you guys, we discussed what we discussed. I'm going to be honest with you about something.

I walked away from that sit-down with a totally different impression of you guys. And I expressed this to my colleagues. I told them that I was basically sitting down with two businessmen. And that's how

I viewed you guys, and I didn't view you like this initially. from that day forward, as two businessmen just trying to do business. However, illegal business is business.

Me: I'm almost confused. Is this the part where I'm supposed to say thank you? And if I decided that I wanted to say thank you for viewing me as something else, who would I thank because you never introduced yourself, sir? I mean, I've seen you in so many capacities. Like the slow driver trying to keep up with the BMW I-94 West, a high-level ambassador from the Sinaloa Cartel, a spectator in the US courtroom up in Detroit, MI, and an agent, slash CIA agent, in an interrogation setting. Can I at least get a name? To put these multiple faces in perspective,

I swear, it was almost like I had said nothing to this guy at all. Like he didn't fucking hear anything that I said to him. It was almost like he was in a totally different frame of mind or in a different world. I don't fucking know. And the clear indication that he was somewhere else, in another dimension, or something else is what he stated to me next.

D.E.A. Agent Two: Mr. Thompkins. Tell me something. Had it ever crossed your mind that maybe you had been set up? I mean, the way this whole process unfolded, had it ever crossed your mind that maybe someone set you up outside of the obvious?

When he asked me that question, that totally took the air out of my body. I leaned back up against the back of the elevator and let my head fall back as it touched it. There was a brief pause as I wondered. I had flashbacks of the past 48 hours and sometime before, but mostly of what Bald Head was saying to me in our last conversation. I sighed. And I made a small little chuckle.

Me: You know. I thought that it may have been the old man. But then it was clear that it was El Chapo. But knowing what I know now, there was no way El Chapo could have done what he did without the old man knowing.

As I had been stating all along. This shit was really weird, and it was getting weirder by the day. The things Bald Head was saying to me, and that very sensitive moment, were just becoming more and more apparent. Everything that I felt was in my wildest dreams and that I was imagining could be possibilities throughout this whole process was actually true. Everything that I was seeing went against what I was totally raised to believe, and we are totally raised to believe in the streets of America. About this whole process. But there were certain words that Bald Head said to me that continued to ring in my mind that I never bothered stating or repeating because I thought they were lies.

D.E.A. Agent Two: Kristal said you would be sharp. Mr. Thompkins, there may be a very interesting backstory for you on this one.

The US Marshall led me off the elevator as D.E.A. AGENT followed close in tow behind me. I heard...

My name is Agent Juan Briano. Listen, I don't give a fuck what anybody has to say. This man moved differently. And when I say he moved differently, he really moved fucking differently. This fucking guy was everywhere; it didn't seem like jurisdiction was a problem that he had to deal with. I'm locked up. I'm indicted. I'm being charged. But somebody please explain to me why this shit continues to keep getting weirder and weirder.

One thing was clear to me so far: Agent Juan Briano couldn't have been D.E.A. And the language that he spoke was similar to the language that the cartel spoke; the cartel never spoke in direct or matter-of-fact statements. It was always riddles. And either you were smart enough to catch on and complete the riddles or finish the sentences that were incomplete, or you didn't belong. This was the language in which he was speaking with me. His statement, " There may be a very interesting backstory for you to this one," That statement was the back story—confirmation of what I already knew; I just wanted to see if my view was myopic or macro. Before he made that statement, he found out that we both spoke the same language.

Lorence Finally arrived down in El Paso on my behalf. He assembled a team of attorneys to help him represent me down there in the Western District of Texas. One of my attorneys went to law school with the US attorney. That would be prosecuting my case. My other attorney actually clerked for the actual judge presiding over my case.

Lorence: Donnie, I spoke with the D.E.A. out of Detroit. I gave them my condolences for their colleague that they lost. That was the agent in charge of your case up there in Detroit. Donnie, I hope you're sitting down for this one. But they made me aware that their colleague lost his life on assignment over in Mexico, not in a car accident on the west side of Detroit, as reported by the media.

Everything Bald Head was saying was appearing to come true, but this was getting More and more strange by the day. This was extremely hard to comprehend and was starting to seem like a movie. Or something. (Hearing Bald Head's final words in my mind.)

Bald Head: My Friend, I'm not telling you anything. That has not already been decided, my friend. Please listen. Do what you need to do for yourself. Because it won't matter. Trust me, my friend. Trust me.

I recall that Bald Head once told me that even dogs will dance, but now I understand:

There would be no dogs dancing, just El Chapo.

Made in the USA
Middletown, DE
08 October 2023

40380300R00347